This book is published with the support of the
Literature Translation Institute of Korea (LTI Korea).

© Copyright 2016 by Bruce and Ju-Chan Fulton

Publisher:

Chin Music Press

1501 Pike Place, Suite 329 Seattle, WA 98101

www.chinmusicpress.com

ISBN: 978-1-63405-910-7

First [1] Edition

Book design by Carla Girard

Printed in Canada by Imprimerie Gauvin

Library of Congress Cataloging-in-Publication Data

Names: Cho, Chŏng-nae, 1943- author. | Fulton, Bruce, translator. | Fulton, Ju-Chan, translator.
Title: The human jungle / Cho Chŏngnae ; translated from the Korean by Bruce and Ju-Chan Fulton.
Other titles: Novels. Sections. English
Description: First edition. | Seattle, WA : Chin Music Press Inc., 2016.
Identifiers: LCCN 2015051422 | ISBN 9781634059107 (paperback)
Subjects: LCSH: Koreans--China--Fiction. | China--Social conditions--Fiction.
 | China--Economic conditions--Fiction. | Political fiction. | BISAC: FICTION / Literary.
 | FICTION / Political. | FICTION / Classics. | LITERARY COLLECTIONS / Asian.
Classification: LCC PL992.17.C38 A2 2016 | DDC 895.73/4--dc23
LC record available at http://lccn.loc.gov/2015051422

정글만리

THE HUMAN JUNGLE

a novel by

CHO CHŎNGNAE
조정래

*Translated from the Korean
by Bruce and Ju–Chan Fulton*

Summer 2016
Chin Music Press/Seattle

Translators' Note

The Human Jungle is our translation of Cho Chŏngnae's novel *Chŏnggŭl malli* (literally, "the Great Wall jungle"), published in three volumes by Hainaim Publishing Co., Ltd., Seoul in 2014. In this translation we utilize the following Romanization systems: McCune-Reischauer for Korean, pinyin for Chinese, and Hepburn for Japanese. We observe the East Asian convention of citing individuals' names with the family name first, followed by the given name: thus, Chŏn (family name) Taegwang (given name).

We acknowledge with gratitude the liaison assistance of Ms. Lee Jin-suk of Hainaim; professors Kate Swatek and Christopher Rea of the University of British Columbia Department of Asian Studies for expert advice on Chinese terminology; and most of all author Cho Chŏngnae for handling with characteristic aplomb the barrage of queries to which we subjected him.

At a time when the translation of Korean literature into English has become an increasingly mercenary enterprise, we wish to emphasize that we were neither asked nor commissioned to translate this work, and have received no foundation or other institutional funding for our translation. Rather, our decision to translate was based solely on the importance to us of the novel and its author.

THE HUMAN
JUNGLE

Cast of Characters

Jacques Cabang: French businessman, a Director of Cartier's Chinese supply chain; business associate of Li Wanxing.

Chen Ke: Chinese official in the Xian foreign ministry handling foreign venture-capital inflow; Kim Hyŏn'gon's guanxi.

Chen Wei: Well-connected member of Shanghai elite; Shang Xinwen's wife as the story begins; later, Chŏn Taegwang's business partner.

Ch'oe Sangho: Chief Prosecutor in Xian, an ethnic Korean; guanxi for POSCO's Xian branch.

Chŏn Taegwang: General trader for POSCO, a South Korean trading company; Yi Chisŏn's husband, Song Chaehyŏng's uncle, and Chŏn Yusuk's brother.

Chŏn Yusuk: Chŏn Taegwang's sister and Song Chaehyŏng's mother.

Chŏng Tongshik: South Korean manufacturer—formerly of tabletop grills, then of baby supplies—in Qingdao; fellow alumnus and business associate of Ha Kyŏngman.

Cooper: President at Gold Groups under Wang Lingling; white American man.

Ha Kyŏngman: Owner and CEO of Guangbao Accessories, a South Korean company based in Qingdao; a business associate of Chŏn Taegwang.

Han Minu: South Korean doctor; Chŏn Taegwang's college friend and Sŏ Hawŏn's South Korean colleague.

Han Mira: South Korean underclassman at Beida, friends with Kim Minji; seeking a tutor through Yi Namgŭn.

Ishihara Shiro: Japanese businessman; friend of Ito Hideo and Toyotomi Araki; patron of Madam Jiang.

Ito Hideo: Japanese business broker; friend of Ishihara Shiro and Toyotomi Araki; patron of Madam Jiang

Madam Jiang: Chinese madam, running a karaoke/brothel catering to Japanese businessmen.

Kang Chŏnggyu: A new employee at POSCO, the trading company where Chŏn Taegwang works; Chŏn Taegwang's protégé.

Kim Minji: South Korean underclassman at Beida, friends with Han Mira; seeking a tutor through Yi Namgŭn.

Kim Hyŏn'gon: South Korean steel salesman with POSCO; later, POSCO Xian branch sales manager; Chŏn Taegwang's friend.

Li Wanxing: Chinese manufacturer; Li Yanling's father; business associate of Jacques Cabang.

Li Yanling: Chinse history student at Beida university; engaged to Song Chaehyŏng; daughter of Li Wanxing.

Andy Park: Architect and President for Gold Groups; US-born, Korean American, Berkeley-educated; married to a South Korean.

Shang Xinwen: Chinese customs official; Chen Wei's husband, Chŏn Taegwang's guanxi, investor in Sŏ Hawŏn's clinic.

Sŏ Chiyŏn: A teenage South Korean girl; Sŏ Hawŏn and Yu Ŭnsŏn's daughter, Sŏ Chunil's older sister.

Sŏ Chunil: A South Korean boy; Sŏ Hawŏn and Yu Ŭnsŏn's son, Sŏ Chiyŏn's younger brother.

Sŏ Hawŏn: South Korean plastic surgeon working in a clinic subsidized by Shang Xinwen; Yu Ŭnsŏn's husband; Sŏ Chiyŏn and Sŏ Chunil's father.

Song Chaehyŏng: South Korean student studying at Beida University in Beijing; originally a business major, now a history major; Chŏn Taegwang's nephew and Chŏn Yusuk's son; Li Yanling's lover.

Sungqing: Chinese migrant worker; Zhang Wanxing's wife; Yi Chisŏn's maid.

Thomas: Head stockbroker at Gold Groups Hong Kong; white American man.

Toyotomi Araki: Japanese steel supplier; friend of Ishihara Shiro and Ito Hideo; patron of Madam Jiang.

Wan Yenchun: Gold Groups president for public relations in China.

Wang Itsan: Chairman of the Gold Groups; Wang Lingling's adoptive stepfather.

Wang Lingling/Sophia: CEO of the Gold Groups; US-born, with a BA from

Harvard and MBA from the University of California, Berkeley; born to a biracial French/Vietnamese mother and a French father, later adopted by her stepfather, the Gold Groups Chairman Wang Itsan.

Yanling's mother: A middle-aged Chinese woman; married to Li Wanxing.

Yi Chisŏn: Chŏn Taegwang's wife; Sungqing's employer.

Yi Namgŭn: A South Korean student in Beijing; Chaehyŏng's friend; Yi Samsu's nephew.

Yi Samsu: South Korean counterfeit apparel-maker working in China; Yi Namgŭn's uncle,

Mr. Yi: Korean manufacturer of car mufflers; business associate of Chŏn Taegwang and Mr. Zhuang.

Mr. Yu: POSCO Xian branch manager; business associate of Kim Hyŏn'gon.

Yu Ŭnsŏn: A middle-aged South Korean woman; Sŏ Hawŏn's wife; Sŏ Chiyŏn and Sŏ Chunil's mother.

Zhang Wanxing: Chinese migrant factory worker; Sungqing's husband.

Mr. Zhuang: Chinese buyer for his brother's company; business associate of Shang Xinwen and Yi.

PART ONE

1. Money—Bright and Shiny, Dull and Dirty

"Welcome, sir! I'm Chŏn Taegwang. It's good to see you."

Like a well-oiled machine Chŏn folded the sign bearing his guest's name and proffered a business card. With his resonant voice and affable smile, he might have been taken for a tour guide.

"Thank you!" Flustered, the other man riffled his pockets. "I'm sorry, I seem to—"

"Please, sir, not to worry. Your reputation precedes you." So saying, Chŏn relieved his guest of the luggage cart with its two bulky suitcases. "Handing out business cards is standard procedure for us, but a physician shouldn't be bothered."

"Still…I'm sure I packed them." The man continued to fumble through his pockets.

"Let's go," said Chŏn, pushing the cart ahead. "This is a madhouse. The people never shut up. I guess it's in their blood," he tutted, scanning the raucous arrival hall.

It was raucous not just because the capacious hall was jam-packed, as you would expect at the airport serving China's economic capital; there was also the energy of the delirious voices. Loud enough were the one-on-one conversations; worse was the cell phone chatter. With state-of-the-art phones and outstanding reception, why did everyone have to shout at the top of his lungs? Chŏn was still trying to figure it out. The faster the economy developed, the more cell-phone users and the more vigorous the seething cauldron of noise. The loud voices were a headache for the PRC government as well. Citizens of a great nation, the people tended to be full of themselves and infatuated with *mianzi*, putting the best face forward. The 2008 Summer Olympics were a heaven-sent opportunity to overindulge these two proclivities. After all, wouldn't two-thirds of the world's six billion people be tuning in? But the proud and noble goal of putting a great nation's best face forward was no easy task. Unless certain bans were enforced, the nation would fall flat on its face, and in the eyes of the world, all the money spent on the Games would add up only to humiliation. And so the government unleashed a time-tested weapon, self-criticism, and solemnly launched the Enhance Our Civilization Campaign, targeting the average Wang and marking ten bad habits for correction. Among the taboos governing public decorum: no slovenliness, no pajamas, no spitting, no bare chests. And make no mistake, "no shouting" was also on the list. Did this stern campaign prove effective? Only until the Olympics were over, at which point the scourge of uncivil manners resumed with a vengeance. The Shanghai airport, which accommodated as many foreign passengers as the Beijing airport, was a cacophony of Chinese dialects.

"Please, allow me," said Chŏn's guest, scurrying up to the cart.

"It's all right," said Chŏn with a grin. "This is your first visit to Shanghai, and as a law-abiding, taxpaying resident of this fair city, I'm at your service. Plus, it's part of my job."

"I'm sorry to trouble you," said the other man with a smile. Then, hands over his ears and head juddering back and forth, "These people are much noisier than the passengers at Incheon Airport." A shadow fell across his face.

"Don't be discouraged, sir. It's annoying, all right, and not a very good first impression, but you'll get used to it. And you'll find things more to your liking."

"Yes, I have some adapting to do," said the other man, his voice and expression brightening. He stole peeks at Chŏn out of the corner of his eye, placed him in his mid-forties, and took inventory of what his host seemed to have learned working for a trading company. Chŏn was quick on the uptake, very smooth, and not just in his manner; he had the voice down too. Very impressive—he wished he had Chŏn's social skills.

Arriving at Chŏn's car, they each loaded a suitcase in the trunk.

"Finally," muttered Sŏ after buckling up. He offered Chŏn his card. "They were in my outer pocket all along," he said ruefully.

Chŏn's face fell. There on the card was the man's name, Sŏ Hawŏn, printed in *hangŭl*, plain as day. What was he thinking? Blessed countryman of Great King Sejong though he might be, he was flying internationally, displaying his passport, and yet carrying business cards printed only in Korean. How obtuse! Chŏn managed to stifle a snort of amazement. Sŏ should have had a set of cards printed in Chinese. All the business owners from back home who were flooding China in search of cheap labor were smart enough to have made this switch, no matter how small their enterprise. Granted there was a problem—the usual titles, president or representative, didn't convert easily. For example, a company president back home was a general manager here. Well, even the sharpest of the company presidents, the ones with an eye for money, had an ignorant, tactless side to them, so why not the good Doctor Sŏ? It was kind of charming, actually. He'd have new cards made for him, thought Chŏn. He saw Sŏ examining the card he had given him. What was he up to? Trying to memorize his given name, Taegwang? No, he was probably making fun of it.

"Poor excuse for a name, isn't it?" Chŏn said as he made a right turn.

"Excuse me?" said Sŏ, looking as if he'd just been awakened.

"It's a hayseed name, the *tae* that means 'big' and the *kwang* that means 'bright.' My father overdid it—either one by itself would have worked, but he had to have both. And here's the result of all his hopes and prayers," *tsk-tsk*ed Chŏn. "A humble department head in a general trading company." He snorted.

"That's not at all what I was thinking," said Sŏ deliberately. "Actually, you make a good impression, Mr. Chŏn. You seem like a good person…in a world that's crawling with sleazy people."

Chŏn glanced at Sŏ. The shadow had reappeared on his face, along with a hint of desolation. He was reminded of the lamb he'd seen years ago on a nature program. It had huddled among rocks and boulders, blood-covered and trembling, no doubt mauled by a predator. A close-up showed what looked like tears gathering in its eyes. *So, even a lamb can cry.* Chŏn had never felt so choked up. And then he'd remembered that cows cry too. When his eyes returned to the television, the scene had changed to a vast grassland. He always wondered what had become of that wounded, panic-stricken creature—had the trembling ended in death?

The image of that wretched creature surfaced at the most unexpected moments. Maybe that lamb reminded him of himself? How many injuries had he borne while working for a general trading company in this foreign land? The lamb had been mauled physically, he himself psychologically. Whenever he had been hurt, scared, or lonely, he had cared for himself, licked his wounds, and refused to be laid low.

Never fear rejection! It's an absolute rule, a fundamental condition, an article of faith in working for a general trading company. If they turn you away at the gate, you go back with a smile on your face. You go back ten times, a hundred times. You keep going back till the gate opens. If you don't have the gumption for that, you might as well pack your bags and go home.

Such were the cold, cruel-sounding words of Chŏn's manager, a seasoned veteran of business dealings all over the globe. A handful of new hires, dispirited by this message, had lasted only a few days. But the manager wasn't exaggerating, nor was he being cruel. And Chŏn was certainly not the only one to experience rejection. Tens of millions of business people were eager to enter the global capitalist economy. They sympathized with one another, for misery loves company, and yet they were competitors. They feared and yet took consolation from one another. Down on his knees, up on his feet, sprawled flat, pulling himself up—such was the route to Chŏn's current position of department head.

And now it was Sŏ who resembled the wounded lamb.

"If I were you, sir," said Chŏn, "I'd try to put the past behind you. You're in a new world with new markets. Take the medical market—is that the term for it? Whatever you want to call it, it's a huge market. If the ROK with its 50 million people is a lake, then China with 1.4 billion is the open sea." Clearing his throat importantly, he swept his arm from left to right. "And it's right before your eyes, from here to eternity. Your new life has just begun, sir."

"I'm not so sure," murmured Sŏ. "We haven't had much in the way of medical tourism from China. Only a handful can afford the surgery."

"Maybe you don't have a feel for the Chinese market yet. Well, that's to be expected. Back home we still assume China has a chokehold on cheap labor, but that's wrong. You won't believe how much, and how fast, this country is changing. It's the number two economy in the world, and that was a surprise—even to the Chinese. The US, Europe, Japan, they all assumed it would take China till 2040 to get its GDP up to four thousand dollars. The Chinese themselves believed that—up until 2010, when they overtook Japan as the number two economy. They cut thirty years from the timetable. For Japan it was a lightning strike, a knockout punch. The US was sent reeling, the EU staggered, and back home all we could do was blink. China the global factory is now China the global market. Did you know China has replaced the US as the number one market for cars and trucks—two hundred million of them, in fact? It also replaced Brazil as the number two market for designer goods for women, and it's only a matter of time until it pushes out the US. And women's buying power is lighting a fire in the plastic surgery industry. Half of China's 1.4 billion people are female, and half of those females are anxious to pretty themselves up. It's a vast market, with unlimited potential—don't you feel it?"

Chŏn fixed Sŏ with a sharp look. The speedometer needle had come to rest at 120 kilometers an hour.

"I see what you mean. But I'm afraid I have a lot to learn," said Sŏ. He realized that Chŏn, department head at a big general trading company, didn't wear that title for nothing; he'd become a China hand and must know what he was talking about. Sŏ began to feel relieved about his future here.

"Don't be too hard on yourself," Chŏn chuckled. "I didn't mean to bog down a physician such as your good self with these details. But I have to show off somehow."

For the first time Sŏ laughed.

"Are you familiar with the name Liu Shaoqi, sir?"

"Liu Shaoqi?" echoed Sŏ.

"No reason you should be. I'd never heard of him myself before I came here. He was the man who, along with Mao Zedong, helped establish the People's Republic. I want to tell you a little story about him. There was a nationwide movement to transform the old society into a Communist regime, and the party members started finger-pointing—cosmetics were a bourgeois waste and the factories making them ought to be shut down. The masses love a good diatribe, but then in stepped Liu, and guess what he said? 'What kind of world do we live in if women can't make themselves up? It's not for us to decide the fate of the cosmetics industry. If the people need it, it will come naturally.' What do you think about that?"

"Well said. So what happened?"

"It was just like he predicted, and remember, he was the number two man after Mao. He knew that deep down women want to be pretty. And now that China's G2, the beautification instinct has exploded. Proof of this—for two or three years now Korean cosmetics firms can't keep up with the demand. And now there's a boom in cosmetic surgery."

Sŏ nodded, resting an assuring hand against his chest. "I think I'm beginning to see the picture."

And Chŏn was beginning to feel gratified about his efforts to allay the concerns of his counterpart. "We're arriving downtown," he said, as much to prepare himself for the traffic as to explain the lay of the land. "By the way, what do the characters for your name mean?"

"They're the 'water' *ha* and the 'distant' *wŏn*."

"A river flowing into the distance. Very poetic." And he meant it.

The next moment Sŏ gasped and bolted forward, his right hand shooting for the handgrip above the door.

"Welcome to Shanghai!" said Chŏn with a grin. But in contrast with his breezy tone, his bulging eyes zeroed in on the road ahead.

The broad highway was mayhem on wheels, a hopeless tangle of every conceivable variety of wheeled vehicle—buses up ahead, bicycles behind them, motorcycles and scooters weaving in and out, pedicabs squeezed up tight against passenger cars, pull-carts dodging the pedicabs, and among them all, pedestrians trying to cross. Never had Sŏ seen such chaos—how could they avoid an accident? All he could do was stammer.

"Try to relax. Just close your eyes. I'm a ten-year veteran of these streets and still accident-free." But the next moment he was jamming on the brakes, and the car lurched to a halt.

"My God, what—where did he come from?" Sŏ stuttered.

"What the fuck's he trying to do!" Chŏn spat.

"He's not moving. Looks like he's hurt bad."

A man and a bicycle lay sprawled on the pavement. Sŏ, blanching, unclipped his seat belt in a fluster and was about to get out when Chŏn grabbed his arm.

"Wait. First see if the son of a bitch is bleeding."

"Bleeding's not the issue. Brain damage could kill him and you wouldn't see a drop of blood. We need to call an ambulance."

Chŏn read the irritation in Sŏ's face—what would a trading company man know about traffic injuries? But when Sŏ reached for the door again, Chŏn snatched him by the sleeve.

"Hold on. I have a feeling about this. Trust me and let's figure out if he's bleeding."

Sŏ released the door handle and focused on the sprawled-out man. Chŏn had been scowling at the man all along, hands clenching the steering wheel.

The pandemonium reached a fever pitch, vehicles honking desperately, the street more snarled with traffic, drivers stopping to gawk at the victim.

"Look!" shouted Chŏn. "Did you see that—the asshole just took a peek at us."

"Well, I can't really tell—"

"Doesn't matter," interrupted Chŏn. "The show's over. He definitely opened his eyes, then closed them again. Son of a bitch is putting on an act." He pounded on the steering wheel. "I wish I had a cigarette!"

Sŏ glared at the figure, wondering why he hadn't seen the man opening his eyes. But then he saw an arm move, and before long one of the man's eyes peeped open.

"He opened an eye!" Sŏ shouted. "I saw it."

"About time," said Chŏn. "He's waiting to see what we do. If we get out and he thinks we're scared shitless, that's when he tries to shake us down. He'll ask for two or three thousand *yuan*. He gets the jackpot, we get the pisspot."

"So it's all an act? He falls down on purpose and pretends he's hurt?"

"You got it. The good news is you're over the first hurdle if you want to live in Shanghai." Chŏn performed a leisurely stretch and yawned.

"How often do you see this?"

"Often enough. Even at one hundred *yuan* a performance, it beats working for a living."

"How long does he figure to lie there, with all this traffic?"

"He's got more time on his hands than the taffyman—an hour, two hours, three—who knows?"

"*Three hours?*"

"Sure. Happened to me a few years back in Nanjing—guy held out that long and I ended up forking over one hundred *yuan*."

"That's hard to believe."

"Sooner you know how to deal with these schemes, sir, the better. You ever heard the word *manmandi*? It means slow and steady—and that's the Chinese for you. We're the opposite, always on the run, hurry hurry hurry. We're like a bunch of fire trucks. But if you're up against *manmandi* and you're in a rush, you'll lose every time. It's our biggest hang-up when we try to do business here. Back when we first arrived, every Yi, Pak, and Kim got the shit end of the stick—they were too antsy. You show your hand in cards, your opponent sees what you have and cleans you out. So if you want to succeed in business here, you have to out-*manmandi* the people—you take things nice and easy. You're in it for the long run. You work on your powers of endurance. That's fundamental. Anyone who wants to live in China, and not just businessmen, has to keep working on his *manmandi*. Hurry-hurry all you want, but you end up shooting yourself in the foot. So, think of this as a good sightseeing opportunity, with our friend there teaching us a good lesson—from now on, relax, build up your endurance, and go with the flow. And you could probably use a nap now that you're here."

Again Chŏn stretched, then rested his head against the back of the seat.

"What's going on?" said Sŏ, gesturing with his chin toward the far sidewalk. "Why are they pointing at us and yakking at each other?"

Chŏn glanced toward the sidewalk and smirked. "Rubberneckers. They like accidents. It's free entertainment."

"But they're really worked up—what are they saying?"

"Could be anything. 'Think he'll survive?' 'Course he will. Do you see any blood?' 'How much you think he'll get?' 'A thousand, maybe?' 'Come on, he'll get two or three hundred, and that's if he's lucky.' 'What if the PSB shows up?' 'It's good for him—they'll ask the driver to step out and say, "Better take him to the hospital.'" 'But if the driver's got insurance, then the guy doesn't get a copper and the show's over.' Something to that effect. Everyone gets to sound off—that's the important thing. Like I said, it's a free show. Might as well enjoy it."

Concluding his oration, Chŏn popped open a can of green tea and took a swallow. He couldn't have cared less that traffic was tied up on his account, or that horns were blasting from every direction.

What a peculiar country, thought Sŏ. How could someone put on an act in the middle of a main road? And what was taking the police so long? Were traffic police big on *manmandi*? And how could traffic be such a mess in a city that ran neck and neck with Beijing? And then once again Sŏ bolted up in his seat. Lo and behold, the man on the pavement had come back to life and was walking in their direction!

"Here comes that man," said Sŏ, swallowing heavily.

Chŏn was impassive.

Arriving at their car, the man knocked on the window. Chŏn reluctantly lowered it the width of a finger.

"Hey you. You run a man over and just hunker down in your car?"

"I'm waiting for the PSB," retorted Chŏn in Chinese. "Why don't you quiet down and do the same."

"Who needs them? Just cough up money for the hospital and we're square."

"Or you can go to the hospital with the PSB and let insurance take care of it."

"Insurance—what insurance!" shouted the man, punching the window.

"Insurance—that's what the Party tells us to do."

"Come off it, you. Fair is fair. My knee's all banged up." The man adopted a servile expression and began pleading. "How about five hundred? And that's a bargain."

"All right, tell you what—if I had my way, I wouldn't give you a copper, but here, take this and let's be done with it."

So saying, Chŏn produced a hundred-*yuan* note and slipped it through the opening. The man snatched it and scurried off toward his bicycle.

"It took forty minutes," said Sŏ, checking his watch.

"Guy sure knows how to treat a guest," said Chŏn with a grin as he started the car.

"Are there others like him?" Sŏ heaved a sigh. "It's going to be tough living here."

"Not really. And remember, we have plenty of that sort back home—it's just a difference in degree. You know, the guys who pick out cars driven by women, stick their foot under the wheel, then extort the driver. Or they wait in a car in a back alley, then come out of nowhere and bang into her car and collect insurance. There are gutless bastards like that all over the world. Here, we might as well think of the money as a contribution to the Chinese government—a handout for our unfortunate neighbors."

"Watch out!" shouted Sŏ.

Chŏn swerved to avoid a car cutting in front of him from the right. The next moment, the car made a U-turn. It was illegal but everybody did it.

Sŏ's nervous eyes flickered back and forth. He was still clutching the handgrip. More incidents: A car went over the curb, landing on the sidewalk. A motorcycle and a pedicab came to a stop in the middle of the street and the two drivers got into a shouting match, gesticulating wildly. A car screeched to a halt in front of a woman leading a little boy across the street.

"Did you see that!" said Sŏ, gaping at the car. "He's going the wrong way."

"Don't worry," said Chŏn nonchalantly. "It's a common occurrence."

"How can that be? This is supposed to be the top city in China."

"Believe it or not, Shanghai drivers are the most law-abiding in the country."

"Really? I would have thought the accident rate was sky-high."

"It is—nationwide. Seventy thousand people a year crossing the river of no return. It's a world record, but not for long, with all the new cars hitting the streets each day."

"Seventy thousand," said Sŏ, slack-jawed. "I can't believe it."

"Well, guess what the figure is for us—4,500 a year. That's 4,500 new souls in heaven. Not so bad, eh? But then China has 1.45 billion people. Do the math and you'll see our fatality rate is much worse."

Dubious, Sŏ tried to run the numbers in his head but kept getting distracted by the traffic.

"Here we are," said Chŏn.

The five-star rating didn't do justice to the New China Hotel and its magnificent marble lobby with the lofty ceiling. Sŏ felt liberated, then found himself wondering about the builder's vision and sense of scale—how many more guest rooms could have been squeezed into the three- or four-story space? Impressions of grandiosity apparently took precedence. But as his anxiety began to dissipate, he realized he was the beneficiary of the vast space.

"You're all checked in," said Chŏn, handing Sŏ his passport and room card. "Think you'll survive here?"

"I guess I'll manage. It's better than any five-star hotel I've ever seen. It's a palace! Is it one of the better hotels here?"

"Actually it's pretty much standard for Shanghai. Which comes as a shock to the Europeans—you know how bad their hotels are."

"Who built it anyway?" said Sŏ. The implication was it couldn't have been the Chinese.

"When the economy started to take off more than twenty years ago, it was the Italians and the French, with a good helping of German technology. But for the last ten years the Chinese have done all the building, which tells you their construction technology has really picked up. This particular hotel went up five years ago, and it's on hundred percent made in China."

"Really? The ceiling's so high ... ." Sŏ took another disbelieving look about the lobby.

"And wait till you see their maglev train. The Germans started it but the Chinese snapped up the technology and finished it. It's much faster than our KTX."

"No, it couldn't be."

"That's a typical Korean response. We think of China in terms of cheap labor, knockoff merchandise, and tainted food. We don't realize that along with their light-speed economic development they're reaching world-class standards of technology in every field. We have preconceptions of the Chinese. We look down on them. It's human nature to dismiss the gains made by others and not give credit where credit is due. But I think you'll find China's an intriguing place—and a lot of fun."

The elevators were state of the art and opened to receive you only when you inserted your room card in the slot. The compartments were draped in red silk embroidered with dragons that seemed poised to leap out at you.

"I'll be back at six to pick you up. Try and get some rest," said Chŏn at the door to Sŏ's room. And with a salute he turned and left.

Quite a guy, thought Sŏ as he watched Chŏn stride down the hall. He couldn't help feeling inadequate in contrast.

The first order of business was to freshen up. The bathroom looked cleaner than dishes fresh out of the dishwasher. Proof positive that China was approaching world-class tourism standards, Sŏ told himself. A few years back, when he'd toured Beijing with some fellow doctors, he'd had the same impression of the hotels there. So it was no surprise that Shanghai, with its economic boom, now boasted such ritzy accommodations. But as Chŏn had implied, Sŏ, like many of his countrymen, harbored reservations about the Chinese—they were filthy, they were lazy, they lied. He couldn't have said when these negative impressions had developed, but they were deep-seated. And wasn't it possible that one or more of these stereotypes held some truth? Ever since the two countries had normalized relations, hadn't Koreans stampeded to buy tour packages for China? The doors to China had opened just in time for full-bellied Koreans swept up in the international travel boom. And China was a cheaper destination than Southeast Asia. But wasn't it a country of Reds, a Communist state in which Koreans wouldn't have dared set foot in the past, a place of horned goblins and bloodsucking vampires? Curiosity gave the tourists an initial charge—that is, until they experienced the ancient and filthy public toilets, which sent them running and screaming. By then Korea had adopted Western-style public toilets, and to tourists accustomed to an unlimited supply of toilet paper, the Chinese facilities were enough to make them faint. It wasn't just that they stank to high heaven and had no partitions; they were also in scarce supply. Sŏ recalled a story about a professor attending a conference here. His intestines were done in by the water and the oily food, and before setting out from his hotel, he'd had to make three trips to the bathroom to clean himself out. By the time he arrived at Tiananmen Square, the urge had hit him again. The professor scurried about, trying desperately to contain himself, but not a public toilet did he see. Plan B was to find a hotel, any hotel. He ran for the first tall building he saw, but hadn't gotten far before a tremor gripped his bowels and he had to squat—sad to say, his sphincter was derelict in its duty. And there in the heart of Beijing this distinguished scholar from the Republic of Korea fell from grace. When the story got around, you can imagine the impression of China it created among the listeners.

But that was then and this was the China of now, single-handedly completing a train faster than the Korean KTX and building state-of-the-art skyscrapers. And all in the space of just over two decades? Sŏ felt a surge of irritation, followed the next moment by a burst of spite—where did the Chinese get off making those advances? And then he was struck by a thought: China had put a man into space and gotten him back safely. Damn, he had to give them credit. He sighed in res-ignation. And hadn't they developed a nuclear device—it was some time ago, but when exactly? Well, it served him right for burying himself in medical texts all this time. Had he read a single volume outside the field in the last ten years? Anyway, hadn't China joined the nuclear club at a time when they still had only a smattering of ancient public toilets? Maybe he should ask Chŏn, the walking encyclopedia on China.

Sure enough, Sŏ thought as he looked at himself in the mirror, people adapt to their environment. He couldn't escape the reality of his situation—he would have to live in China for who knew how long. In the face of this certainty, he felt with a vividness that ran both hot and cold that he was now focused on China. He hadn't felt that way flying out of Incheon Airport.

Exile. Escape.

The words came to him as he turned on the water, still observing himself in the mirror over the sink. The next moment he saw three other faces—his wife and their two children. He squeezed his eyes shut, then opened them. The faces were still there.

I'm sorry, dear.

The silent words welled up from deep inside, moving him to tears. And along with the tears came unstoppable sobs. He turned the tap all the way on and the water gushed out with a roar, drowning out the sobs. But letting it all out only deepened his sadness, which brought a resurgence of sobbing, then a bone-ach-ing grief that transformed into indignation, and finally a last surge of sobbing.

It wasn't fair. The operation had proceeded without a hitch. The patient's vital signs were being monitored. The operation was a success and he knew it—he felt like he was walking on a cloud. His buoyancy was informed not only by medical judgment and the post-op exam, but also by an acute sense of certainty. So sure was he of this instinct that if something didn't feel quite right, he could expect a complication, even if everything had checked out medically.

But that wasn't the case this time. For the first two days, everything was normal. But then the woman developed breathing problems. Emergency measures proved ineffective. Worse, the cause couldn't be identified. She was transferred in critical condition from the clinic to the general hospital, but she didn't last the night.

The moment she passed, he became Doctor Murder. For a physician it was a death sentence. The following day the woman's family arrived and he had to shut down the clinic. He'd expected family intervention—the woman was only twenty-five, not yet married. But then the police launched an investigation.

"You'll have to settle with the family," his attorney advised him. "There's no other way."

"These things happen," said the detective. "People die on the operating table. But for the family it's the end of the world. And the police have to investigate, to rule out the possibility of manslaughter. You heard what your attorney said about settling. He's right. You're in a hole and you have to crawl out. Basically you have two options: the big house or payment. The choice is obvious. Your lawyer's going to save your ass—do what he says."

But reaching an agreement proved difficult. The victim had been a working woman. She had taken three months off from work for the surgery on her cheek. Her family researched the insurance formulas for workers and came up with a demand for a billion *wŏn*—the amount she would have made from a lifetime of employment.

"I know it's difficult," said his attorney. "But try to be patient—I'm negotiating with them." But the attorney seemed more irritated by the day. The family wouldn't budge, and it was wearing him down.

"For a doctor with your reputation," said a friend over drinks, "what a curse. Of all the women in the world, you end up with a working woman instead of a housewife. Thank God she wasn't an actress or her family would've asked for *ten* billion. You need to sweep this under the rug. The longer it drags out, the more *you* get dragged through the mud."

It wasn't just the people with the placards outside the locked door of the clinic—"Doctor Murder, Pay Up" and "Where's Your Conscience? Pay Up." It wasn't even his colleagues gloating from a distance. The worst thing was that they feigned sympathy while fanning the flames of rumor. They loved his failure even more than their own success.

Finally the family launched an invasion. Armed with placards and chanting "Doctor Murder, Sŏ Hawŏn," they held vigil at the entrance to the apartment complex where Sŏ lived. The object of entertainment for all the apartment dwellers, his wife wept, and so did the children. There was no place to hide, no straw to seize. He felt like jumping off the top of their fifteen-story building.

"Those folks could use a grease job—they just won't bend. Nothing I say gets through. And why should they listen? They could end up set for life."

All along the attorney had been trying to lower the settlement to five hundred million. And now he was ready to throw in the towel.

"They're asking too much," yawned the detective, "but what can you do— they've got a knife to your throat. They're like poisonous snakes. No, worse than that. On TV I saw a humongous snake wrap itself around an alligator and squeeze the life out of it. Constrictors, is that what they're called? Anyway, those folks have you in their coils. It's three months now, and you can imagine what they're thinking—they want to eat you alive. If they decide they're wasting their time with us and go to the prosecutor instead, then your wiggle room's gone and you're headed for jail. The lawyer's done all he can. Now it's up to you."

"Don't worry about us, dear," sobbed his wife. Face contorted, shoulders heaving, she bit down on her lip. "We'll get our apartment back, or else we'll get another one. You're still young."

"I'm sorry, honey."

"No, I'm the one who's sorry. I'm so sorry. I wish we could…I just wish I could—"

"Don't say that. I'm so thankful you're not blaming me." He took her, still sobbing, in his arms, and felt her trembling all over.

"I'm sorry, so sorry." She'd said that when they got married, and she'd said it when he opened the clinic—like she was guilty of something. It was expected that if you brought home a doctor, a judge, or a prosecutor for a son-in-law, your parents gave you the keys to a new apartment—and that was just for starters. One such doctor, after a year of marriage, assaulted his wife, accusing her of reneging on the deal, and ended up divorcing her—it made the news. But Sŏ and his wife had been college sweethearts, and she came from a poor family. His father-in-law was a hard-working, law-abiding middle-class citizen.

He'd always bypassed the alumni gatherings, not wanting his wife hurt on account of yapping by the wives who'd benefited from their families' largesse.

Ultimately the settlement came to seven hundred million. To raise that amount he had to sell the apartment and recover his down payment on the clinic. A decade's work as a doctor went up in smoke. No longer could they afford to live in Seoul; they had to rent instead in surrounding Kyŏnggi Province. With heavy hearts they dropped the children off for the first day at their new school, an experience that made him realize the meaning of *heart-rending* for pain and sorrow. It was the little ones for whom he felt sorriest—dozens, no, hundreds of times sorrier than he felt for his wife.

The fact was, cheek augmentation surgery was much riskier than rhinoplasty. A profusion of blood vessels ran through the cheeks, and a delicate touch and advanced medical skill were essential. If in spite of your best efforts you made a mistake, complications could ensue—numbness, asymmetry in appearance, sunken cheeks, malfunction of the jaw joints, pain. In extreme cases the patient lapsed into a vegetative state or died from hemorrhage.

Why then had Sŏ undertaken an operation weighted with such dangers? Well, times had changed. The word had been out for at least a decade: oodles of money were to be made in plastic surgery. It had been a flush time indeed for plastic surgeons. But then the birthrate plummeted—it was now the lowest in the world—and the OB/GYN clinics began closing their doors. What was next, then, for obstetricians and gynecologists who were loath to sit on their butts and starve? Some reinvented themselves as plastic surgeons. The new mega-hospitals, which began luring patients from the independent practitioners, put an additional squeeze on doctors, especially internists with their own clinics. These jilted doctors too re-emerged as plastic surgeons. The flood of new practitioners led to heated competition and a spate of fee slashing— plastic surgeons were in effect cannibal-izing themselves. And then, just in time, cheek-augmentation surgery came to the rescue. Its availability, combined with the omnipresent images of entertainers be-coming ever more beautiful, inspired women nationwide to make themselves pret-tier. Cheek-augmentation surgery cost six times as much as rhinoplasty. Clinics bleeding from cut rates and preparing to shut down couldn't resist the opportunity for a new lease on life. Sŏ hadn't been able to. And now here he was, in China.

"Brace up, honey," his wife had said. "It's not like you're being run out of the country. Instead you're on a search for a new world. You know that Mandarin cram schools are mushrooming here just like the English ones, right? And more and more people are sending their kids to China to study. Why not get yourself established there, and then we'll join you? Then we won't have to send our kids to China to study—they'll already be there! The way I hear it, the US has had its day in the sun, and now it's China's turn. So don't feel bad for the kids. You might actually be giving them a better opportunity. We'll get along fine in the meantime. I'll do what I have to, tutoring or whatever—the kids won't go hungry. Be proud and be tough. Remember, you're our sunshine."

She had hugged him tight as she said this, her breath warm against his face.

And now he silently addressed her image in the mirror. *Thank you, dear, thank you so much. I talked with Chŏn, and I think I've come to the right place. It's a sea of opportunities for plastic surgeons—that's what he told me. There are millions of pa-tients with eyelids and noses to be worked on. We'll live much better here than we ever did back there. It won't be long, dear, before we're back together.*

As he wiped his tears with his fists, he imagined himself shouting these words to her. Just like in the army when the sergeant had beaten him and asked if it hurt, and he'd had to shout, "No sir, it doesn't hurt!" Just like when he was a kid and felt sad and knew he must never be caught crying or he'd get walloped. That was how you became a man. But now, crying himself to exhaustion, he felt relief as the tightness in his chest loosened.

Chŏn returned at the appointed time and handed Sŏ a small plastic box. "Your business cards."

Sŏ fixed him with a dubious look.

"The people you're meeting tomorrow are Chinese," said Chŏn as if gently chiding a child. He displayed Sŏ's Korean-language card and waved it, inviting Sŏ to the obvious conclusion.

"Oh, right … I should have known better. It's been so hectic lately," said Sŏ with a rueful smile. He looked back and forth between Chŏn and the new cards. "How did you manage so quickly?"

"Korea isn't the only place where you can get an order filled in half an hour. Like I said, in terms of technology, China's not much different from us. Any documents you need, whatever the language, you can get copied, forged, counterfeited in the blink of an eye. Business cards are standard procedure."

Chŏn led the way down the hall. "How about Korean tonight?" he said as they entered the elevator. "So your stomach doesn't go into shock first thing."

"I'm fine with anything," said Sŏ halfheartedly, distracted by thoughts of how to repay Chŏn for the new business cards—and that was on top of paying off the guy on the bicycle. Should he offer here and now?

"How about taking in the night lights?" said Chŏn at the restaurant as he worked at his *pibimbap*. "Shanghai at night is famous, what with Kim Jong Il referring to the skyline as the 'Creation of Heaven and Earth.'"

"I'm dragging a bit," said Sŏ carefully. "Maybe next time?"

"Sure, no problem. It's not like we're on a tour with a bus or train to catch first thing in the morning. The Chinese like to show off Shanghai at night because it symbolizes their economic power. But anyone who's seen the world finds it totally prosaic. Big cities are all similar anyway, kind of gaudy and garish. Bottom line, it's a waste of electricity—and think of all the pollutants." Chŏn managed a cynical smile between mouthfuls.

"I was wondering," ventured Sŏ. "I don't know the language, but I understand you're fluent. I'm not aiming that high, but how long will it take me till I can get by?"

"Well," said Chŏn, "it depends on how much work you want to put in, but with your mind, Doctor, I'd say six months until your first plateau, and a year until you're comfortable talking with your patients. The faster you can pick it up, the better. Then it gets easier to make friends and you begin to feel a rapport with the country. And there are plenty of good language programs here."

That night sleep eluded Sŏ until after midnight. How had his life ended up so twisted and tangled? He wished he could go back home. But he had to march on.

At nine the next morning, Sŏ found himself in front of the clinic.

"Look," said Chŏn, pointing up. "Not bad, eh?"

"What—what the …" Sŏ's gaze was arrested by five giant photos hanging from the second story. Each contained a beautiful Korean woman and a smiling man looking on. The smiles were slightly different from one photo to the next, but the man was the same—none other than Sŏ himself.

"Why so shocked?" said Chŏn with a crafty look. "You'll have women beating down your door."

"But why all the women?"

"Well, what do you think? You're the magic doctor who makes Korean pop stars into beauties."

"No," said Sŏ, shaking his head. The blood drained from his face. "I only did one of those women."

"Hey, so you did one, but we'll call it five. Come on, let's go in."

"No, I can't. That would be a misrepresentation." Sŏ shook his head vigorously, not budging. He'd done as Chŏn asked, emailing him a batch of photos of himself in his jade-green gown. Never had he dreamed they'd be made into these five composites.

"Oh do you have a lot to learn," said Chŏn, looking up at the sky with an incredulous smile. "Now listen. This isn't Korea. This is China—TIC. You're going to be hearing this a lot. China, where knockoff iPhone 5s were sold before the real thing appeared in the US. The copycat market of the world, where copies of every name brand you can think of are proudly displayed. China, the Olympic host. You should have seen all the leaders of the advanced countries after the opening ceremony. They swarmed the knockoff market and came out loaded down with full shopping bags. They were convinced. The point is, composite photos aren't some kind of subterfuge. They're standard business procedure. And I find them kind of clever," said Chŏn, checking his watch and reaching for Sŏ's arm. "So why don't you put your Korean scruples to bed, and let's get a move on."

"No way," said Sŏ, deflecting Chŏn's hand. "Not until you do something about those photos."

"Doctor, you're not listening. Who's the one who needs a quick infusion of cash? You don't have time to split hairs. Didn't you say your family is renting a room in the provinces? And you want to bring them back to Seoul ASAP? Money doesn't come in clean or dirty denominations. But it's your choice."

Chŏn turned and started to walk away.

The next moment the image of his children was staring Sŏ in the face. He felt a crumbling sensation and moaned. Yes, it was money he needed. And cash was cash. The bills weren't marked dirty or clean.

He scurried after Chŏn. He had only known him for a day but already felt conflicted—was it fear of the man he felt, or trust?

2. The Architect of My Life Is Me

"Honey, get the phone," said Chisŏn.

Chŏn felt his wife prodding him. "For God's sake!" he grumbled, his tongue thick with sleep. "What fucking idiot…?" Wrapping the quilt around him, he rolled over on his side.

"It's your handsome little darling from Beida!"

Her voice was like thorns in his ear. "Chaehyŏng? What's up with him?"

Kicking off the quilt, Chŏn sprang out of bed.

"Good Lord, you're like Pavlov's dog, and he's not even your son."

Chŏn sensed the resentment but ignored it. By now he realized his wife's antipathy for his nephew was simply an extension of her grievances with his sister. It was a shame that his wife and his older sister carped about each other, but there was no miracle cure. The two of them got along about as well as a dog and a monkey, though maybe not as badly as a mother-in-law and daughter-in-law. Poor Chaehyŏng hadn't done anything wrong, and yet here he was, a punching bag for his aunt. Chŏn had long since decided that the best solution to an insoluble problem was to pretend it wasn't there.

"Chaehyŏng, is that you?" Chŏn's voice was a fountain of pleasure.

"How have you been, Uncle?"

Chŏn felt his spirits lift at the sound of Chaehyŏng's voice. "Are you all right?"

His nephew was as dearer to his heart as his own children. It was Chŏn who had convinced him to enroll at Beijing University, and he considered himself the young man's guardian in China. But being far off in Shanghai was a constant worry.

"Sure." There was a pause. "I just wanted to say hello—I'm here in Shanghai."

Chŏn heard a nervous titter—something wasn't right. "Shanghai? It's not school break already?" He clutched the receiver.

"No. I'm on a field trip with the history club."

"History?" barked Chŏn.

"Yes. If you want to know modern Chinese history, you have to know Shanghai." Chaehyŏng sounded nonchalant, as if he hadn't noticed the edge to his uncle's voice.

"Of course. And it's an important city for Korea too. But your major is business, not history. What your esteemed uncle is asking is how come you have the leisure for a field trip when you need to be concentrating on your major—and you are not in fact on school break." He realized he was sounding like a prosecutor.

"Uncle," sighed Chaehyŏng, "you talk like an old fart. You sound just like Mom. I'm disappointed."

"Hey, kid, have a heart. I'm your guardian here, remember?"

"How could I forget? That's why I want to see you."

"Yeah, right. What you want is a hot time in the old town tonight and for that you need some dough."

"Old town? More like the city of sky towers and toxic air. You think I enjoy choking my lungs out? I wish you'd lose the know-it-all tone and stop treating me like a kid."

That hurt. But Chŏn managed to cover up. "Ha, I can't believe I heard that. I think it's campus air that's the problem—it seems to have swollen your head." He paused to light a cigarette. "So, now that you've said hello, tell me why you're calling."

"Didn't you promise not to smoke inside!" his wife snapped.

"It's not something I can talk about on the phone," said Chaehyŏng. "But it's very important, so—"

Chŏn's guardian instincts took over. "All right, let's meet. You didn't get your-self in trouble…"

"Uncle, I'm not a kid anymore."

"You're right, little guy. You're a grown man. You want to come over?"

"I don't have much time. I'm with a group, you know. Can we meet at the cof-fee shop in your building around twelve thirty?"

"Sure, and then we can have lunch."

"No, I'm eating with the group. All right, I have to go. See you soon."

"Wait." But there was only the dial tone. Chŏn stared at the phone. Where would the kid and his group be eating? Forget about dim sum and all the carts—he'd barely have time for a simple meal if he had to meet Chŏn at twelve thirty. Maybe the kid didn't like eating with his uncle.

"He's here in Shanghai?"

Inwardly Chŏn groaned. "Yeah, on a field trip. Wants to say hello around lunchtime."

"You must be thrilled! You can give him a stash of spending money then stick your chest out."

"Wrong. I thought the same thing, but he shot me down and gave me a scold-ing too."

"What for?"

"He told me not to treat him like a kid."

"Ah-ha. Then what *does* he want?"

"Got me. I thought he was in some kind of trouble, but he said no."

"So you have no clue. Well, I'm in the dark too." She turned away, then sudden-ly her head snapped back toward him. "And *you're* talking in your sleep: 'Don't go, don't, you can't.' Is that supposed to be me you're talking to?"

"I was talking in my sleep?"

Suddenly his dream came back. Sŏ was leaving the hotel, going back home, and Chŏn was pulling for dear life on his suitcase, trying to detain him. The strange thing was that Sŏ was pulling from the opposite side and having no problem drag-ging the heftier Chŏn. No wonder he was pleading, "Don't go."

"Oh yeah." He tried to retrieve the remnants of the dream. "I had a dream about that doctor who just arrived here. He was marching out of the hotel, whining about going back to Seoul, and I ended up in a tug of war with him. It was weird."

"What was the problem—didn't he like it here?"

"No, it wasn't that, although…"

"I think you've got Shang Xinwen on the brain."

"Could be," he tutted, rubbing the sleep from his face.

"How is this doctor, anyway? Does he know what he's doing?"

"Of course! That's why I brought him here."

"He can't be very good if he's crazy enough to come here. What's the matter—is he tired of sitting in his cozy little Kangnam office and processing the line of ladies with all their money to burn?"

"You're ten years behind the times, my dear. There's such a glut of clinics that all they do is twiddle their thumbs and count flies."

"Oh? And where was I when this historic change was taking place?" But her dubious expression was starting to melt. "Are you sure he's the one you were dreaming about?"

"Look—pick a Korean actress who's popular here. He probably took care of her."

"In that case, maybe I should avail myself of the good doctor's services and be beautiful for once in my life."

"God help us! You're over forty and you talk like you're twenty."

"Watch your mouth! A woman's always a woman, even in her eighties."

Good, get your dander up. Now he wouldn't have to mention Sŏ's mishap. Loose lips, especially women's, sank ships. Close to thirty Korean traders and their families lived in this apartment complex. Far from home the weak tended to flock together for mutual protection. The wives in particular needed to dispel their homesickness; they wanted someone to talk to and a shoulder to cry on. He could see it now: If he ever let on to her about Sŏ's predicament, he'd drill her to keep absolutely mum, and after telling the womenfolk she'd drill them to keep absolutely mum, but the initial spark would send smoke through the complex. Once that smoke spread to the next complex, fire would break out, and it would only be a matter of time before the news was the talk of Shanghai. Add the Internet and smartphones to the equation, and what would happen when the bloggers came across the online ad for Sŏ, "Korea's Miracle Doctor," along with the photo montage of his beautiful clients, and began their "Doctor Murder" postings? Sŏ's life would crack like an egg. But why be concerned about Sŏ when he himself would be hit by the waves? No, more than waves—a bullet in the heart.

More important, what about his relationship with Shang Xinwen? The clinic set up for Sŏ was run by Shang's cousin, and it was in response to Shang's tacit request that Chŏn had recruited Sŏ so quickly. The cousin was riding the wave of cosmetic surgery's popularity and had caught the get-rich-quick fever. But he knew Chinese doctors couldn't measure up to Western medical standards. So why not invite a Korean surgeon to join the practice, a move consistent with the Chinese golden rule of partnership enterprise? Here in the most populous nation on earth, the third largest country in the world, women's all-consuming desire to beautify themselves had translated into a booming demand for cosmetic surgery. After twenty years chasing money in a general trading company, Chŏn found the whiff of money as unmistakable as the smell of the salt water—if only he could get that market in his sights! It would be as much of a bonanza as century-old mountain ginseng. And so he had taken Shang's implicit request and run with it. Once the clinic developed into a cash cow, Chŏn would have a good grip on

Shang—hell, he'd have him by the balls.

"The plastic surgery business isn't what it used to be, but who wants to pull up stakes and move to China?" Han, Chŏn's doctor friend from high school, had told him. "You know how we feel about China. But I think I've got the right man for you. He's a top-notch surgeon, but had some shit luck…" Han had repeatedly vouched for Sŏ. "He won't ever do cheek surgery again, but for the nose and eyes, he's super."

And ultimately that was what convinced Chŏn to keep a lid on Sŏ's secret and bring him here.

Shang was a customs supervisor whose domain was cargo clearance for the Port of Shanghai, the economic heart of the country. As such, he wielded the sword of life and death for all the business enterprises in the region, a modern-day General Guan Yu straight out of *Romance of the Three Kingdoms*. His face with its ruddy color of red beans invested him with even greater majesty.

Each and every one of the tens of thousands of businesses from around the globe had to run the gauntlet of import and export inspection if they wished to enter China. Customs was the throat for an astronomical amount of capital, and Shang was one of the pivotal figures who allowed it to swallow.

Any trade agent based in Shanghai yearned for *guanxi* with a figure like Shang, with all the fervor of Christians seeking a personal relationship with Jesus. *Guanxi*—a personal connection with an influential figure—was the be-all and end-all of Chinese society. Without it you were effectively shut out from the government. It was the map to Treasure Island, the magician's wand that made all things possible, the key allowing passage from hell to the gates of heaven.

As customs clearance supervisor for Shanghai, Shang enjoyed executive powers on a par with those of a Korean government bureau head. In China, as in any other country, it was hands-on figures such as Shang who were more effective than even the president. Which explained why foreign firms ran helter-skelter, butting heads to build *guanxi* with a powerful entity like him. But making that happen was like nailing a bird on the wing with a slingshot—the more crucial your position, the more watchful eyes and flying arrows there were to avoid, and the more prudent and unobtrusive you needed to be.

And then there was the Chinese mentality to navigate. You soon learned that at business meetings, instead of getting right down to business, your hosts would settle into their signature laid-back posture, waiting for the paint to dry, and put you under a microscope. They would then scrutinize you every which way, measuring you as a potential business partner in terms of your trustworthiness, your fiber, and your fellowship. To trade agents quick to battle and eager to triumph, the *manmandi* mentality was a steep mountain with stumbling blocks of questions every step of the way. If this was the challenge posed by ordinary businessmen, imagine how much more difficult it was to cultivate *guanxi* with an influential figure such as Shang.

Guanxi had a counterpart in Korea, but it was broader—connections, backing, and a network all in one. The emphasis on bloodline, home region, and school ties had crippled the nation. But in China, it was the foreign firms who found themselves crippled and trying to gain footing. Wandering a human jungle of relationships, losing their direction, stumbling and falling, they scrambled for *guanxi*, which was invisible and elusive but almost palpable.

How fortunate, then, that Chŏn enjoyed bedrock *guanxi* with Shang. Without it Shang would never have reached under the table to Chŏn about his cousin. But he trusted absolutely in Chŏn's confidentiality. And it was in large part through his good graces that Chŏn had climbed the corporate ladder so quickly to department head, his company recognizing Shang's ability to clear their cargo without a hitch.

What, then, if Sŏ decided to go home? What if his checkered past came to light? There would be hell to pay. It would be the end of him, Chŏn thought. If Shang decided to cause trouble, he could pick nits and shuffle documents for six months, a year even, while the company's cargo lay rotting amid the stockpile of containers.

"Uncle!"

"My oh my—how's my Chaehyŏng?" bellowed Chŏn as he hugged his nephew.

No one in the crowded coffee shop looked askance at their unrestrained behavior. On the contrary, the other patrons were just as boisterous. Chŏn recalled a Western reporter writing about how uncivil the Chinese were in public, arguing that they were too disorderly and oblivious for democracy to take root there. Chŏn found the conclusion quite a jump, but for all he knew, maybe there was something to the man's blast.

"You punk! You tick me off, you know that?" blustered Chŏn, giving his nephew a good-natured slap on the shoulder.

"How come, Uncle?"

"My neck hurts looking up at you. You're taller, and I'm getting neck cramps."

"I guess I've grown an inch or so," said Chaehyŏng, grinning from ear to ear and scratching his head in mock embarrassment. He was tall enough to stand out in a crowd, and handsome enough to draw gazes.

"No kidding—so what does that make you?"

"About five eleven."

"I'll be damned—four inches taller than me and you're still growing. Make the most out of it—in the global age, height can give you an edge. Let's find a place to sit."

"I'll order," said Chaehyŏng, gesturing toward the service counter. "What would you like, Uncle?"

"I'd like something other than a damn coffee shop. They take your money, and what do you get in return? You fetch your own order and clean up after yourself, that's what. Who cares about service? We should have gone to a teahouse. They're cheap, they're friendly, and it's full service, right down to pouring the tea. I like a place with class. All right, I'm fine with coffee—black."

"Drip, you mean. Okay, got it."

As Chaehyŏng started for the counter, Chŏn waved a banknote at him. "Hey, take this."

"It's on me." Beaming, Chaehyŏng flashed money of his own.

"Cut it out. If your mom finds out, I'm on her shit list."

"You're guilt-tripping me. All right, you win." With a mock scowl Chaehyŏng snatched his uncle's money.

"Aren't you used to Chinese tea by now?" asked Chŏn when Chaehyŏng returned, drip coffee in hand.

"Well, I guess," mumbled Chaehyŏng. "But I hear there's a lot of fake stuff."

"I told you," said Chŏn, "Asian tea tops the WHO list of the five most beneficial foods. And China is the suzerain of tea. If you're going to live in China, you have to feel Chinese culture in your bones—that's when you'll really understand it. Sorry if I'm nagging."

"Not at all," said Chaehyŏng, shaking his head. "I don't get much opportunity to drink tea—all my friends here drink coffee."

"Kids these days," Chŏn tsk-tsked. "China, Japan, Korea…"

"Uncle, you look different," Chaehyŏng said, making a sad face.

"How so?" Chŏn had his first sip of coffee.

"You look so old. Especially when you're saying, 'Kids this, kids that.'"

"Really? So you're a full-grown man and I'm a stick-in-the-mud establishment type. And I'm talking about kids without realizing it—what do you know." A wistful look flashed across his face.

"I'm not sure I see the connection between coffee and the kids of those three countries," said Chaehyŏng diplomatically. There was a lot of information he stood to gain from his uncle, with his long years of business experience abroad. And his uncle certainly had a way with words.

"All I'm saying is they're coffee-crazy and it's happened in the last couple of years. You can draw your own conclusions."

Chaehyŏng cocked his head inquisitively. "Well…" He had a sip of coffee.

"You said you're with a group." Chŏn checked the time on his cell phone. "And pressed for time."

"I'm good, long as I make it to Lu Xun Park by one thirty."

"That's more like it." Chŏn nodded, stifling an urge to remind his nephew that patriot-martyr Yun Ponggil had taken his life there in protest of Japan's colonization of Korea—the park had been known as Honggu then. He had to be careful not to treat Chaehyŏng like a child.

"You know, I don't think it's simply a matter of which drink best suits your taste. We don't have much of a tea tradition in Korea, so I can understand our fixation on coffee. But the Japanese are hard to figure. They were the first in Asia to open up to the West, but you don't see much Western influence, or much change either—not compared with the rest of Asia. Three things in particular they've kept at arm's length—Christianity has always had a cool reception, coffee doesn't hold up to green tea, and Coca Cola just doesn't sell. All their ad money goes down the drain. The three mysteries of Japan, as they say in the West—they don't tally with all the westernized clothing and buildings you see there. And then a few years ago you start seeing young people marching down the street flaunting sumo-size paper cups of coffee—to me it's weird. Now I worry about China. No one thought coffee would break down four thousand years of tea-drinking tradition. But what do you know, the great wall of Chinese tea culture was helpless—it collapsed. And now Starbucks and the other chains are all over the country—Beijing, Shanghai, Tianjin, Guangdong—and kids mosey down the streets with supersized paper cups of coffee. You have a ten-*yuan* lunch, top it off with a thirty-*yuan* coffee, and you're cool, you're hip. You don't want to be left out, so you develop a copycat mentality. It's all for show, empty vanity." He fixed his nephew with a stare. "Remind you of someone?"

"Well…" Again Chaehyŏng cocked his head.

"You like movies from the West, right?"

"Sure." His nephew snapped his fingers. "All right, now I get it. The people in the movies."

"Not bad, kid. You're pretty quick. And who's the cheerleader for the West? The US, of course. That's who all the little princelings and princesses from our three kingdoms are busy mimicking, and they don't even realize it. It's so stupid."

"Now that you mention it, I can't believe how crazy Chinese students are to study in the US. They're much worse than we are. I know, they think a degree from there is their ticket for getting ahead in the world, but still…"

"All right, I'm done. So what's going on with you?" said Chŏn, cuing Chaehyŏng with his coffee cup.

"Uncle. You have to help me. Please?"

"Are you trying to scare me?" said Chŏn with a dismissive wave. "I don't like it when people try to pin me down."

"Uncle, it's no skin off your back. I'm not asking much."

"Then get to the point. It's not like we're bargaining over a new car or something."

"Fine." Chaehyŏng fidgeted then announced in one breath, "I want to change my major. And I need you to convince Mom."

"What? Did I hear right?" said Chŏn, cupping his ear.

"Yes," said Chaehyŏng forcefully. "I want to change my major."

"To what?"

"History."

"History!" Chŏn's eyes bugged out.

"Yes, history."

"You must be dreaming—no way in hell your mom would agree to that."

"Which is why I'm asking you."

"You might as well drop school instead," said Chŏn. Again he tried the dismissive wave. "How the hell am I supposed to convince her?"

"It's not that you can't. You just don't want to—you don't think much of the idea, do you?"

"What, are you a mind reader now?"

"It's written on your face. Like I said, I'm not a kid anymore."

"Then you know history is a great major for people who want to starve—right?" Chŏn blustered, unable to sit still.

"I may not get rich, but I'm not going to go hungry either."

"What yap—everything I say you can say better. All right, then, be dirt poor the rest of your life. But you think your mom is going to say, 'Be my guest'?"

"*That's* why I need your support."

"So all I do is show my mug and she caves in? Forget it. Not when her boy is bound and determined to suffer. I wouldn't give you the go-ahead either!" As Chŏn's irritation grew, his voice got louder.

"Well, too bad. I'm not underage anymore. I'm not their property. I've got to be me."

"So you're a free agent now? What Chaehyŏng wants, Chaehyŏng gets?"

"That's about the size of it." Chaehyŏng gulped the rest of his coffee like it was water.

"I can't believe this. Where did you get those lines? What's next? 'I'm the architect of my life'? You know, once more with style." Chŏn snorted. "What do you need my help for? You already made up your mind. How do you think that makes me feel?" He grimaced.

"But it's only right that I explain it to my parents and get them to see it my way."

"You're something else. All right, give me some details. What kind of history?"

"When in China, study China, so Chinese history, what else?"

"Excuse me? Chinese history?" said Chŏn with a hollow chuckle.

"Uncle, I wish you'd stop jeering."

"Where did you pick up this idiotic notion anyway?"

"The more I study management, the less I like it."

"Well aren't we fussy. Nothing's perfect. You just have to find something suitable and make it work."

"Uncle, you're an educated man, but you sound like you never went to school. Sure, a person should study something he has an aptitude for. But can't it also be something he likes?" His eyes pressed his uncle for agreement.

Chŏn shook his head helplessly. "You spoiled brat—for God's sake, you're bushwhacking when you could be taking the highway."

"That's what you and Mom always say, but what if I'm not cut out for the highway? Mom hopes I'll turn out like you, and I've put a lot of thought into that, believe me, but I just can't. All the new faces you have to contact, the results you have to produce, it's just not me. It's not in my blood. I feel suffocated just thinking about it," Chaehyŏng said with a shudder.

"Listen, kid, not everyone can be a genius artist or a brilliant scientist. There's no writing on the wall for you and me. Life isn't a make-or-break proposition. It's a matter of adaptation. Take a look at yourself—you're tall, good-looking, the whole package. You won't have any trouble dealing with the big-noses. So cut the crap and hit the highway. No more nonsense," said Chŏn, thumping the table.

Chaehyŏng sighed in exasperation. "Are you sure you and Mom aren't twins? You talk exactly the same. I'm sorry for wasting your time." He turned away, disappointment written on his face.

"Ouch, that's pretty heartless. Well guess what? If it was your mom here, she'd be screaming at you by now. She'd be crying her heart out. Me, I'm being rational, just talking man to man."

"Yes, you're doing a great job telling me 'no, no way'—what's so rational about that? If you took into account my aptitude, my talents, if you were halfway objective, *that* would be rational."

"Wow, listen to you talk—must be something in the water on campus. Your whole life is ahead of you and you're going to spend it on Chinese history? For me, China's the land of milk and honey, and I figure on feeding from that teat another thirty years or so."

"That's not an issue. I'll be getting my dividends. You can count on that. When I get my PhD from Beida, I'll be a shoo-in at the universities back home. Chinese history is booming, unlike other fields, and my adviser said he'd write me a recommendation letter."

"Your adviser?"

"Yes. In the History Department."

"You already transferred!"

"Not yet. But I made up my mind, and I'm starting with the study group."

"Now I get it," said Chŏn, slapping his knee. "A history field trip—it all adds up."

"Uncle. You used to be quick on the uptake, and now you're about as sharp as a slug."

"Lay off, kid. I got distracted by all your charades," said Chŏn, feigning a punch at his nephew. "So, you're not going to be a wheeler-dealer. You do know a Beida degree guarantees you a job at a big firm right here? What about the two and a half years of management you've studied? You going to flush it down the toilet?" He mustered all the care he could in his gaze at Chaehyŏng.

"Please, Uncle, enough. It's thanks to your charm that Mom melted and sent me here. And now I need you to work your magic on her again."

"I can see how you'd find Chinese history intriguing. But it goes back so far and there are so many dynasties—how are you going to keep track of everything? Besides, how's your Chinese?"

"I'm over the hump in talking and in understanding the lectures. Reading was tough at first, but now that I've got the system down it's actually kind of fun."

"Is that a fact. Sounds like you've put in your time. With language it helps if you have a sense of urgency, and then once you're hooked it's full speed ahead. What do you say we have a little chat in Chinese?"

"Uncle, you don't want to give your only nephew a heart attack. Well, I've got to go." Snatching the empty cups, Chaehyŏng sprang up.

"Hey, take this." Chŏn held out an envelope.

"I'm good, thanks. If you can just take care of that business," said Chaehyŏng with a wink.

"You're a sly one," said Chŏn as he folded the envelope in half and shoved it in his nephew's pants pocket. "I go to hell and back on your account." He gave Chaehyŏng a gentle slap on his lean back.

Five days later Shang called.

"Hello, Xiao Ch'wian!"

Chŏn felt his heart warm like a heat lamp. The appellation Xiao Ch'wian, or Little Chŏn, told him Shang was satisfied with Sŏ's expertise, and by extension with Chŏn himself. The *xiao* didn't come easy, especially if you were a foreigner and your counterpart was a high official. It was rooted in trust and fellowship, like back home when you used kinship terms with people you weren't actually related to. There'd been instances of "Little Chŏn" when Shang was drunk, but today was a first—he was sober.

"How about we treat you and the good doctor to dinner tonight?"

From the very first, Shang had referred to Sŏ as Dr. Sŏ. This was a good sign. The Chinese were enamored of titles and crammed every last one onto their tiny business cards. The mother of all titles was a high-ranking position in the Chinese Communist Party, and next came "Doctor." But wasn't "Doctor" a universal favorite anyway? In every country you could count on politicians adding it to their resumes. And think of all the mothers back home who called their dear sons Dr. Kim, Yi, or Pak.

"Sure," said Chŏn, at his informal best. "Long as it's tasty."

"Of course! Food, drink, nothing but the best for us!"

With this jolly promise ringing in Chŏn's ears, the call ended. With the Chinese, if they moved first to treat you to a meal, it promised success in the relationship— especially if "nothing but the best" was added to the invitation.

"Wow, it's been a dog's age since I had a taste of honest-to-goodness *maotai*!" he realized.

Chŏn recalled an anecdote about this best known of Chinese spirits. The owner of a *maotai* distillery kept a stash of it in his car. The only spirit used for official functions, it was forever in short supply. And so the markets overflowed with bogus product made so skillfully that even the inspectors had difficulty sniffing it out. If you were to ask the distillery owners, they would probably tell you that a third of the *maotai* on the market was not genuine, which was why they kept their own supply.

But Shang had access to the real thing, which showed the muscle he could flex in his position. Chǒn could only imagine how Shang would react if he were ever presented with fake *maotai* as a gift.

Chǒn's *guanxi* with Shang dated back exactly nine years and by now it was tough as leather. Chǒn had been a rookie, starting his second year in the country. His job was to prepare a daily business report for headquarters. Once he'd finished, he had the rest of the day to struggle with the language. Fluency offered the best chance of business success in the vast sea that was China.

This was his boss's constant drill. In middle and high school Chǒn had wrestled with English but had virtually no contact with Chinese. How many times had his older relatives given him the knuckle on the head when they learned he'd graduated high school without knowing how to write or read the Chinese characters for his father's name and address? If only he'd known that as soon as he landed his first job—at a company that had launched a full-scale attack on the Chinese market—he'd have to rush off to a Chinese-language cram school.

"Remember, one ramen per person means 1.3 billion in sales!"

The president's shouted slogan caught the fancy of the entire company. Imagine—the ROK's population was 0.045 billion, and China's 1.3 billion. *Off to China we go!* A contingent of fifteen led the way.

That was the beginning of Chǒn's day-and-night struggle with Chinese. And then one day the branch manager in China returned to headquarters in Seoul and called a meeting of the entire work force.

"Do any of you know a really good surgeon? If we can find the right man, we'll have a gold mine—solid *guanxi* with a customs official, and hassle-free clearance. You all know what *guanxi* is, right? So, who's got a name?"

Urgency was obvious in the man's flushed face.

"I do," said Chǒn, his hand shooting into the air as he thought of Han Minu's words: *Let me know if you need anything.* At the time, Han was interning at one of the top hospitals in the land.

"You do? Who?" cried out the head of operations with undisguised joy.

"My brother!" Chǒn had blurted. The next moment he was wondering why he hadn't said, "A high school friend." Was he trying to show off? Then again, *brother* was how he normally addressed Han, and he had every reason to believe Han actually would help him. Put all that together, and out came "My brother."

"Let's go to my office."

And there the head of operations in China was quick to explain. The brother-in-law of a Chinese customs supervisor named Shang was in desperate need of a kidney operation. Shang didn't trust Chinese doctors, but taking his brother-in-law to the US was out of the question, and so he'd decided on Korea. In China, Shanghai women were considered top of the line, and Shang's Shanghai wife was the crème de la crème. Shang cherished her, and she cared the world for her brother. Understandably, Shang was frantic. What's more, he was from the Shanghai area, and Shanghai was the power center of Chinese politics. Shang was a good candidate for director of Shanghai Customs. If the company could help him out, they'd have smooth sailing in China, and Chŏn would reap his share of the rewards.

Chŏn felt the pressure as he called Han.

"Hey, I need your help. It's important." And out poured the story.

"Got it. Get them over here ASAP. I'll set them up with Dr. Nam. He's the best. And I'll be part of the team."

"How can I ever thank you!" Chŏn felt himself choke up at Han's concern.

"Don't mention it. How can I ever forget that time you carried me down the mountain?"

In May some years back, their high school had held a competition—which team could reach Insu Peak on Pukhan Mountain the fastest, starting from Chaha Gate? Han, a senior, was the team leader. Chŏn, two years younger, was the youngest. Jogging along easily, they found themselves among the front-runners. The closer they got to the summit, the steeper and rougher the footing. But they continued without a rest—they were bursting with youthful energy and it was, after all, a competition. But on a downhill stretch they heard a shriek from Han out in front, and down the slope he tumbled. When they reached him he was howling in pain and couldn't put any weight on his foot. He must have broken his ankle. They had to get him to a hospital, said Chŏn, offering Han a piggyback ride. Three of them carried him off the mountain to Chŏngnŭng.

"What a shame! I wanted to leave high school with a bang, not a broken leg," Han whimpered. In fact, he'd torn a ligament, and for a month he needed a crutch. But it didn't stop him from becoming a medical student.

Shang's brother-in-law's surgery, performed by Dr. Nam and assisted by Han, went smoothly. In the recovery room, Chŏn felt all the more grateful to Han as he interpreted for Shang the nurse's remark that Han had made it possible to bypass the usual three-month wait for the services of the highly sought-after Nam. Han really had gone out of his way. Shang's wife couldn't hold back her tears and kept lowering her head in appreciation.

"You're handling it like a pro," said the branch manager to Chŏn before returning to China. "Keep it up—heartfelt service earns heartfelt business."

For the next ten days, until the patient was discharged, Chŏn put everything aside, including his own family, and focused on Shang's brother-in-law and his family around the clock. He arranged for a medical van to shuttle them around. On the eternal battlefield of life you never miss an opportunity to sink your fangs into your prey. And for Chŏn this translated into hovering about Shang's wife and rendering heartfelt service. A smile blossoming on her pretty face was tonic to his fatigue.

After his brother-in-law had regained his health, Shang greeted Chŏn with a bear hug. "You're my *lao pengyou!*" he exclaimed, giving Chŏn's back a hearty pat. Chŏn felt in those strong hands the heart of Shang's wife. *Lao pengyou*, meaning old friend, embodied trust and affection.

Chŏn arrived at Sŏ's clinic to find the doctor washing his hands. He had just completed his last surgery for the day.

"How are things going?" Chŏn asked as casually as he could. Granted, Shang's satisfaction was crucial, but what if Sŏ were dissatisfied? A broker had to be a tightrope walker.

"All right," said Sŏ with a thin smile as he wiped his eyes with the back of his hand. But his face bore a gloomy tinge. Chŏn wondered whether he was a depressed sort by nature or if the blue face was the result of his medical mishap. Either way, he wasn't the most jovial sort Chŏn had ever met.

"How's your interpreter?" said Chŏn, referring to the nurse he'd recruited for Sŏ from among the many ethnic Koreans living in Jilin.

"I'm still getting used to her accent, but no issues in surgery."

"Great. Just wondering," said Chŏn as he settled into the couch in the reception area. "Mr. Shang is tickled pink with you. So now I can lay my nerves down to rest." He chuckled.

"I'll do my best, so no need to worry. There's a lot on my mind, but … I'm very grateful to you. On that first day you said the sky's the limit here, and I think you're right." Sŏ looked down, struggling with his thoughts, then took a tissue and dabbed at his eyes.

"So emotional," said Chŏn, wide-eyed. "Don't tell me you have that many clients already?"

"I do. I'm backed up a week. I feel like I'm back in Seoul ten years ago."

A faint smile replaced the gloom on Sŏ's face. Chŏn chalked it up to thoughts of his family.

"Great. And they'll keep coming, and the more of them there are, the sooner you'll see your family."

"Yes. Deep down inside I didn't know what to expect, but…"

"Well, now you know. Shanghai is where the action is. Plenty of women here who want to fix up their face but can't afford a plastic-surgery vacation in Seoul. After all, twenty million people live here—twenty-three million if you add the part-time residents. That's twice as big as Seoul. Per capita income here is pushing twenty thousand dollars—economically they don't take a back seat to Korea. What's more, the surrounding cities all feed Shanghai, so in time you can't help but get more clients."

"Twenty thousand?" Sŏ was dubious.

"Yes, twenty *thousand* dollars!" Then, remembering Sŏ was a doctor and not a businessman, Chŏn added, "Well, thirty years ago, when Deng Xiaoping launched his economic development program—you know, to open and reform the economy—he couldn't focus on the entire country. Why? It's too big, too many people, and not enough capital. Think about it—China's ninety times larger than we are. So, he started with the special economic zones. The first one was mostly cities in Gwangdong Province, and he had success there, so he followed with the second one, centered in Shanghai and including other coastal cities from north to south. This one was a massive success, and that's when the Chinese miracle really caught the attention of the world. But there was a big problem—the benefits didn't make it all the way through the interior to the west. That left a lot of folks poor and poverty-stricken. So you've got a huge regional gap in development. Dissatisfaction escalates, the people get restless, and the next thing you know, the Party and the government have a threat on their hands. You'd never see something on that scale happening back home, you know. So what the government did was select the interior and the west for the Third Economic Reform. Three or four years ago that's all the government harped about, the Great Western Development. As of last year China was G2, the second largest economy in the world, but when you break down the GDP among 1.4 billion people you get barely five thousand dollars a person. So whenever there's an international economic conference and China's asked to shoulder the responsibilities of its G2 economy, they pull a face and say, 'Hey, we only have a five-thousand-dollar GDP.' They have a point, don't they? So what can other countries say once they've picked their jaws off the floor? It's almost as unexplainable as China's 10 percent annual growth rate over the last thirty years, which is miraculous, and, needless to say, unprecedented. With me so far?"

Chŏn was at his elocutionary best.

"I think so," said Sŏ with a bashful smile. He had been listening intently to the words flowing from Chŏn's lips, but seemed more relaxed. "Though I'm pretty much an ignoramus when it comes to economics."

"All right. Shall we go?" Checking his watch, Chŏn rose.

"Oh, right."

Outside, Sŏ reached for his handkerchief and once again dabbed at his eyes.

"Problem with your eyes?" Chŏn asked, seeing for the first time that they were reddened, the lids puffy.

"No, the problem's over there," Sŏ said, pointing into the distance.

"Excuse me?" Chŏn followed the pointing finger but saw only the disarray of skyscrapers.

"It's the air." Sŏ shook his head with a shudder.

"Ah—sorry to hear that."

"Yes. And my throat," said Sŏ morosely. "Worst they've ever been."

The band of dirty air was like a two-toned curtain beyond the pointy high-rises, the upper stratum dark red and the lower, more turbid layer a charcoal blue.

Maybe a kilometer off? Chŏn wondered as he watched the countless buildings disappearing into the sea of smog.

"I guess I'm immune to it by now. Tell you one thing, though—a decade back it was maybe ten times worse. But then for the Olympics they launched an anti-pollution campaign and got the old, smoky heaps off the streets. That made a huge difference."

"So this is an improvement?" said Sŏ with a frown, shaking his head. "This isn't smog—it's more like poison gas."

"And made in China, with a special blend of three air-pocalypses—vehicle emissions, haze-inducing dust from new construction, and emissions from the coal-burning power plants and the factories in the neighboring cities. You won't find that particular cocktail in New York or Seoul. But first things first," said Chŏn, taking Sŏ by the arm. "Let's find a drugstore and get you some eyedrops."

"It's all right. I asked my wife to send me some." Sŏ pressed down on his eyes with his handkerchief.

"What? You're having eyedrops sent to you from Korea?"

Sŏ nodded.

"Some kind of miracle treatment?"

"Not really…it's just…well…"

"You don't trust anything here."

Sŏ gave a sheepish nod.

"Well, heck—not even eyedrops?"

Regarding Chŏn with his bloodshot eyes, Sŏ shook his head, then blurted, "I even heard there are fake fathers here."

Chŏn laughed in consternation. "Where did you hear *that*?"

"From a tour guide, an ethnic Korean, when I visited Beijing a few years back."

"I can't believe it," Chŏn tutted. "She's giving China a double dose of shit."

"How so?"

"Number one, she's sticking China with the label of Fake Heaven. Number two, *fake fathers* means loose women."

"Oh?"

"You'll see by and by. It's a brave new world here." With a wink to Sŏ, Chŏn led the way to his car.

Climbing out at their destination, Chŏn pointed. "That whole building's a restaurant."

"It is?" Sŏ stared in amazement. "Must be at least eight stories. But how can it—"

"This is nothing. Every big city has them. It's beyond large scale—it's China scale. You've seen the Imperial Palace, right?" said Chŏn, sparing Sŏ the possible unfamiliarity of its Chinese name. "Now that's the scale they love here."

"And the whole building is red," said Sŏ as he climbed the steps to the entrance.

"Ah yes, the three great symbols—the dragon, the color red, and the peony,"

Chŏn explained as he ushered Sŏ through the double glass doors flung open by a pair of receptionists who greeted them with a holler. "The people here believe red expels evil and brings good fortune and prosperity."

They were guided to a private room where Shang Xinwen awaited them. Sŏ's eyes bulged yet again as he entered. It was too big for four, and profusely appointed, containing a spongy carpet patterned in garish colors, a silk wall-covering in dizzying red and gold, and a glittering three-tier crystal chandelier set dead center in the ceiling. All of it smelled of wealth—*guess how expensive I am?* they seemed to be asking. But the decorations were too glitzy and out of harmony, like an overly adorned woman straight from the farm.

As soon as they were seated, Shang offered a toast. "*Ganbei* to our enterprise; may it enjoy the prosperity of the Great Wall."

"*Ganbai!*" echoed the entire party as they clinked their translucent shot glasses of *maotai.*

Chŏn easily interpreted, then offered a quick aside to Sŏ: "It's strong, but you have to do it the Chinese way—one shot."

The spirit burned Sŏ's throat, prompting a cough that he barely stifled. Enduring the potent taste and the keen tingle in his nostrils, he gulped it and felt a sharp current shooting to his toes. He shuddered.

"Now that we've survived the *maotai,* let's get down to business. Director Chŏn, how about finding an officetel for Dr. Sŏ—and please make sure it's up to his standards."

So much for tonight's agenda. Already Sŏ seemed to have passed Shang's physiognomy test.

3. Serving Wine the Korean Way

Sasha's Restaurant occupied a two-story European building. In the tranquility of dusk, it exuded a classic beauty not unlike the elegance of a gracefully aging lady. The walls were crimson, the unadorned rectangular window frames were as white as a wedding dress, and the roof was a silvery mosaic of countless pigeons with outspread wings. The three colors made a striking contrast, transcending the flow of time, making the building breathe with the soul of its architect.

That this pristine European countess dwelled in Shanghai attested to the turbulent history of the Qing dynasty. Ailing and decaying, it was powerless to protect China from encroaching foreign powers. Its incapacitation drew covetous Westerners, and Shanghai was overrun. Defeated in one of the most disgraceful conflicts in world history, the Opium Wars, Qing was forced to cede Hong Kong to Britain.

It all started with Chinese tea. British tea drinkers got hooked, consumption rose, and tea merchants jumped with joy at the easy profits. But a trade imbalance arose—too much of Britain's precious silver was being sucked up by China. Rectifying the loss became an urgent priority for the British government, and a quick fix was devised—the British East India Company would sell its surplus opium to China. But why would Qing, already debilitated and languishing, want to allow the sale of the ruinous substance? It banned the opium trade, and the British took up the sword in response. China was doomed from the start and yielded to Britain rather than fight an unfair battle. And thus did self-proclaimed Gentleman Britain instigate the Opium Wars to fill his pockets.

At first glance you might have thought a mouse was challenging an elephant. But the mouse won handily. No sooner was the elephant down than other mice swarmed in. And why not—you don't turn down a free meal, especially one as economically tasty as this. North went the mice to ravage the coastal cities of Shanghai, Tianjin, and Tsingtao. Shanghai was the main course, situated as it was at the mouth of the greatest river in the land, the Yangtse, the nexus of commercial traffic with foreign nations.

So began the ravishing of Shanghai, all in the name of concessions, and up went the curtain on the history of China as a semi-colonial state. No matter what depredations were visited on the concession lands, the Chinese government remained mute. Given freedom of action, the European nations jockeyed for position to establish their own domains. And in those domains, new buildings sprouted by the day, none of which belonged to China.

Next came the Japanese invasion and the conversion of even more land to colonial status. China bid farewell to its history of dynastic rule, but the new Republic of China was not sturdy enough to block Japanese might. The humiliation great China had to endure until Japan was defeated and the People's Republic of China forged through civil war was so great that the Chinese named this period the Century of Humiliation.

It's a wonder the building survived, thought Kim Hyŏn'gon, loosening his tie while gazing at the venerable structure.

In the past decade there had been no more urgent project in Shanghai than demolishing antiquated buildings and erecting modern structures in their place. Up and up they went, not twenty- or thirty-story buildings but fifty- or sixty-floor towers. These jumbo edifices were proof positive of the great success of Reforming and Opening. With each magnificent new structure, the city trumpeted its accomplishment, and more of its people blindly subscribed to the Party, singing the well-worn verse "Without the Party there is no New China."

With the city encouraging the rabid construction boom, the shouted slogans "Preserve historical buildings," "Limit building height," and "Stop environmental degradation" had as much effect as a Buddhist scripture on a cow. Finally an environmentalist attorney rolled up his sleeves and took up the fight in court, one lawsuit at a time, until he had filed a good five hundred of them. But he was destined to lose, because in China the courts are subservient to the government, and the government to the Party. More to the point, Beijing had announced it would develop Tianjin into an international city five times the size of Shanghai, and perhaps as a consolation prize was planning to develop Shanghai until it supplanted Hong Kong as the Asian financial hub. Even so, Shanghai would be downgraded from the second most important city in the land to number three. This was unacceptable to the city that had borne the brunt of the Century of Humiliation. There was only one solution, and that was to go full speed ahead with construction, till the present four thousand high-rises became forty thousand. And so, not a single lawsuit did the attorney win.

That this two-story building had survived the madness of the construction boom was nothing short of miraculous to Kim. He knew it was a wedding gift to Jiang Kai-shek from the parents of his wife Soong Mei-ling. Was that why it had survived? That fact alone could qualify it for preservation as a historical landmark. The dusk deepened around him, the building soaking up the ambient lighting until it looked positively romantic. Kim slowly shook his head, a bitter taste in his mouth—if it became a landmark, who would want to lease it for a restaurant? If the development plan came to pass, the grand old lady would be gone in half a day, bulldozed into oblivion.

Inside he found a corner table in the bar on the main floor. Half a dozen Caucasians were sitting about. They had a look of refinement and the smell of money. Black people were rarely seen in China. Western enterprises had sensed early on that the Chinese tended to be averse to blacks. So if black people weren't good for business, why send them here? A svelte young woman sashayed among the white men, caressing her long black hair, the swaying of her pliant body proclaiming, *Look at me—I'm a true blue southern China Shanghai girl.*

"Always drooling over the white guys," grumbled Kim. He glanced at his watch and saw that he was early. Might as well check out the girls. The male of the species never got bored eyeing the females. There was always a new flavor to be had. He had another look at this one, and saw her head-on. Not bad. Then again, no woman in a setting like this was wanting in looks—you couldn't sell yourself if your mug didn't whet the male appetite. Maybe the evening was too young, but nary a head was turning in her direction. The moment she exited, another took up the baton. China was overflowing with these women. Kim recalled a clumsy attempt a decade ago to regulate them, but by now "let freedom ring" was the rule.

You want to make an issue, you got one; if you don't, you don't—the operative principle of Chinese society. If you followed this principle and didn't make a fuss, the world spun quietly and the eighty to one hundred million comrades who made up the world's largest female service industry lived comfortably. Kim thought of all the lonely foreign businessmen they had to comfort, relieve, and revitalize, men hard at work in an alien land, their energies flagging. He wondered why Korea hadn't adopted this benevolent principle instead of cracking down on the red-light districts. It was all well and good to clean up the society and make a pitch for women's rights, but if you ignored the inner workings of yin and yang in a complicated social structure, you came off looking rash and stupid. What did we gain, Kim thought, from tearing down the red-light districts? The sex trade went underground, and thanks to the at-your-own-risk service charge, the rates skyrocketed. That was what happened when the government chose to make an issue. And how about the rise in sexual assaults? Why had the most civilized nations of Europe, countries like France and Germany, devised a system of licensed prostitution? And what about eco-friendly, anti–pollution-emitting-factory New Zealand licensing prostitution, albeit late in the game?

"Look at that asshole," Kim snorted as he watched one of the men cozy up to a hostess. "Thinks he runs the country or something?" Again he checked his watch, not noticing the man who had come to a stop in front of him.

"Ah, here you are. Sorry to have kept you waiting." The outstretched hand belonged to Chŏn Taegwang.

"Mr. Chŏn," said Kim, grasping Chŏn's hand. "Good to see you. I just got here myself. Shall we move upstairs? We can talk over dinner."

"I'm not much of a wine drinker," said Chŏn once they were resettled in the French restaurant. "But now that you've got us tucked away up here, how about we splurge? Let's see, what's the priciest bottle?" He began to survey the wine list.

"Agreed, we need wine with a French meal. But the most expensive bottle— are you sure?" asked Kim, the astute businessman.

"You bet!" said Chŏn, summoning their waiter. "The occasion demands it."

Once the bottle arrived, Chŏn was quick to do the honors and hoist his glass. "Cheers!"

Kim followed suit. *Clink.* The glasses came together, the elegant contours reverberating in a sharp crystal ring.

Big-noses, thought Kim in disdain. So many shapes and sizes for a simple glass of wine. Endless variations of the stemmed glass, but all of them making the same silver-bell ring when you toasted. And once the wine is in the glass, you have to savor it first with your eyes, then with your ears as you toast and clink, next with your nose as you tilt the glass and sniff, and then with your taste buds, tongue, and lips. Kim snorted. And *then* you got to drink it! Well, the hell with that.

Kim sipped slowly—not to savor the wine, but in anticipation of what Chŏn had to say. Like Chŏn, he wasn't a wine drinker. The drinks of choice at gatherings with his Chinese clients were the potent domestic spirits. But in China, as in Korea, wine was riding the winds of fashion—another brand-name craze blowing in from the West.

"Well," said Chŏn, draining his glass, "I think we know each other well enough that perhaps I can cut to the chase." Fixing his eyes on Kim, Chŏn spoke forcefully, so Kim would know he was dealing with a veteran. "I landed an order for a hundred thousand tons."

"That's huge—well done!" Kim offered a heartfelt bow, then filled Chŏn's glass. One hundred thousand tons meant eighty billion *wŏn* in sales—more than Kim accounted for in an entire year—and Chŏn wanted *him* to handle the deal. They were yoked, of course, by their common background as sales managers, but more important was the human element—Chŏn was taking care of him. Kim's heart burned with gratitude. He wished he could adequately express his feelings.

"Before I give you the details, I want you to know I didn't go solo on this. My *guanxi* laid the groundwork." Raising his glass, Chŏn signaled Kim to drink up.

"More power to you—*guanxi* is an accomplishment in itself," said Kim, clinking Chŏn's glass in delight. "And tonight's on me."

"How about next time. I'm in the mood for treating. Just promise me you'll deliver. There's a time crunch involved in the construction. And a hundred thousand tons isn't a drop in the bucket."

"Construction?" Kim had assumed the order was from a shipping company or an automaker.

"Yes, construction. Are you familiar with the Gold Groups? They're in real estate development."

Kim shook his head.

"I just found out myself. They're out of Beijing, and this is their first venture in Shanghai."

"Gold," Kim murmured.

"That's right, gold! Pompous, isn't it? I guess it's better to be obvious than mysterious. Everybody wants money, right? And the name's easy to remember."

"It's a bold strategy, aiming point-blank at people's nerve center."

"That's how I see it too," said Chŏn. He slowly tilted his wine glass this way and that. "So here comes another mammoth building, compliments of the Gold Groups."

"Do you happen to know how tall?"

The first consideration for a building wanting inclusion among the ranks of notable Shanghai skyscrapers was the number of stories.

"Eighty-eight floors, what else!"

"Double eight! Ingenious as their name. They'll get a lot of buyers!"

"My thoughts exactly." Chŏn lit a cigarette. "If you're going to succeed in business here, you have to work in the miracle eight somehow. You'd think all the developers would realize that, but they don't."

"So they'll probably name it Double Eight?" said Kim with a sip of wine.

"I'm not sure. But it makes sense."

"Or even better, Gold Double Eight, or Double-Eight Gold. Either way, the public will translate it into 'money money money'—Triple Money. And what a way to advertise the company name."

"Damn, that's terrific. I'll have to pass it along to my *guanxi*." Giving Kim a thumbs-up, Chŏn nodded in satisfaction and lapsed into thoughts about the magic number.

The Chinese affinity for that number was beyond imagination—though *affinity* didn't do justice to their fervor, which bordered on blind faith. The source of the ardor was money. The *fa* of *fachai*, "making money," sounded like the *fa* meaning the number eight. To anyone dreaming of becoming filthy rich, that number was an object of greater worship than the color red. The infatuation with eight permeated their lives. Any date that included an eight was auspicious, making 8 p.m., August 8 ideal for a wedding. And no wedding guest was more welcome than the one bearing a red envelope containing 888 *yuan*. In Chŏn's mind, the opening ceremony of the Beijing Olympics was the clincher, with the torch being lit at 8 p.m. on August 8, 2008. More precisely, at 8 minutes and 8 seconds past the hour, if you believed the media. Far from criticizing the timing as superstition, the 1.35 billion Chinese citizens embraced it with ardor, grateful to be graced with the luck of wealth. It was proof that the government had hopped on the people's money-mania bandwagon to reap their heartfelt support. And where else but in China would unit eight on the eighth floor of an apartment building go for a premium price, and the fee for a quadruple-eight license plate be set at a cool half million *yuan*? Chinese-style capitalism, together with the addiction to the reform policies, had made the eight fetish even more extreme. In contrast, the number four was treated with contempt. Its pronunciation was similar to that of the word for death, the only difference being tonal.

"And now," said Chŏn, his voice an octave lower. He took a long draw on his cigarette and drew closer to Kim.

"All right," said Kim, likewise lowering his voice. "Let's talk."

And just like that a curtain came down over them, invisible yet secure and impenetrable. No one would overhear, no one would learn of the business they were about to discuss. Business was a battlefield involving foot soldiers, and the circumstances of the fighting changed by the minute. There was a sense of urgency to the war—you made quick decisions and you adapted. There were basic strategies but no ironclad rules. Armed only with these fundamental strategies, the infantry had to make split-second judgments to survive. In the process they had to become their own independent commanders, reacting quickly to changing circumstances. Success or failure depended on agility and decisiveness. And secrets were as important in business as in espionage. Once the deal was closed, the entire process was cloaked in secrecy. This rule was the engine of enterprise.

"They'll want samples," said Chŏn.

"How many?" asked Kim.

"Five hundred." Chŏn emptied his glass as if relieving himself of a burden.

"I see." The answer sparked the engine in Kim's mind. *Five hundred tons of steel, compliments of our company? That's some gall—who do they think we are, an African start-up? Our steel is number one on the world market—quality guaranteed. Three hundred makes sense, five hundred is robbery. Then again, the order's for one hundred thousand. A big fat golden egg just rolled into my lap, and I didn't have to lift a finger or schmooze a soul…. Well, hell, the world's in a steep recession. And if I can give three hundred for a fifty-thousand-ton order, then why not five hundred for a hundred-thousand-ton order? Sure, suck up! Keep the stockpile of steel from going rusty and cut the interest on that bank loan. You want a quick return, then selling is the best policy.* It was now or never. "All right." Stifling a sigh, Kim tilted his wine glass back and forth.

"Thank you." With the faintest trace of a smile Chŏn shifted in his chair and lit a fresh cigarette.

Watching the flame from Chŏn's lighter, Kim felt that his belt was slowly constricting him. *Here comes the climax.*

"This time's different—we have a go-between."

"I thought that might be the case," said Kim. But why hadn't Chŏn mentioned this at the outset? Was it a tactic for hijacking the middleman's commission from the manufacturer's profit? This happened from time to time but was tricky to negotiate. When you tied the commission to the standard profit margin, the manufacturer's profit shrank. Chŏn and his general trading company, though, knew all too well the manufacturer's strengths and weaknesses—that it didn't budget for marketing, for example, but that its viability depended on timely marketing—so naturally they would want to keep a tight rein on the terms of the deal.

"You see, he and I have a special relationship."

Kim was beginning to feel like he was in a tennis match—with Chŏn serving.

"And I need to maintain that relationship, because he's high up in the hierarchy."

"I understand. I know how difficult it is to have good *guanxi* here. I'll do right by you, sir. You can count on that."

Not a bad return of serve; Kim opened the door for Chŏn to suggest a figure.

"We know each other too well for me to force terms and let you figure out the rest. We're in this for the long haul." Taking a deep drag and blowing a long stream of smoke, Chŏn continued, "Since we're giving up a dollar at our end, what would your side think about three?" He looked Kim in the eye, his tone perfunctory.

Kim was Chŏn's equal as a negotiator. He met the other man's stare, then retrieved his mental calculator and began tapping away. Three dollars a ton meant 360 million *wŏn*. Quite a juicy profit for opening that one door. But if Mr. Guanxi was high enough on the ladder to be able to open that door in the first place, then maybe he wouldn't turn his nose up at such an offer? High officials here operated on a grand scale, befitting the size of the Chinese domain, and the capacity of their bellies was limitless. Although corruption scandals were subjected to endless criticism by citizen groups, they themselves were endless, revealing both the grand scale and the enormous bellies. So here was Mr. Chŏn's company offering to chip in a dollar per. No different from the sly realtor rushing to close a deal by saying two other parties are interested in the property, so if you want to buy, then shell out now. *It's not as if we can't afford pitching in a dollar, so what are you guys bitching about*—dig beneath the surface, and there you had Chŏn's argument. But if Kim agreed to three dollars per, that wouldn't leave him much wiggle room.

Chŏn was betting he'd go with three, but that meant pushing Kim's company to the edge. Shouldn't he make a counteroffer? Every business involved haggling—where was the fun if you couldn't try to whittle down the price?

What if Kim offered two dollars per? If Chŏn made a face, then Kim could cut back by fifty cents. If Chŏn agreed to that, then Kim's company would pay fifty cents less a ton, meaning savings of fifty thousand dollars for one hundred thousand tons, or sixty million *wŏn*. On the other hand, wouldn't Mr. Guanxi have to have a lot of pull to have made this deal for them? And for Kim's huge company, sixty million *wŏn* was no skin off a flea's hide. And if they took care of Mr. Guanxi, who knew, they might get back their payoff tenfold, a hundredfold, maybe even a thousand or ten thousand times over. Investment in a personal relationship could make the difference between success and failure. Building a sales network was based on human relations, and equally important in human relations was capital investment—especially in this society, where connections meant everything.

"All right, I might be in over my head, but I'll go along with it. Your *guanxi* is our *guanxi*," said Kim, knowing *guanxi* would be their link to future deals.

Chŏn was quick to respond. "Thank you, Mr. Kim. I like a man who's quick on the draw and open-minded. This *guanxi* has political connections that are deep and wide, so there's a lot you and I can do for each other." With a flourish he poured wine for Kim, the bloodred liquid gurgling into the portly vessel until it was half full. "Here's to you." *To hell with the connoisseurs who say to fill it only a fifth of the way*, thought Chŏn, who felt on top of the world. *Let's hear it for Korean style*.

When Kim attempted to return the favor, not realizing the bottle was empty, Chŏn ordered another one. This time it was his glass on the receiving end.

"Let's drink up," said Chŏn, winking at Kim. "It tastes even better now!"

And again they clinked glasses.

Curtained with dense woods, Weiming Lake was a tranquil haven. The Beida campus was larger than most and thickly forested, the mystic lake at its center a divine egg brooded by the trees. Benches were spaced about its shaded verge, each occupied by a couple weaving life stories in their own secret language. The body language varied; some couples were locked in an impenetrable embrace. Here a girl nestled in a boy's arms, there a couple engaged in a passionate kiss, and over there a boy curled up in a girl's lap. Some couples giggled, their fingers intertwined. Others were reading *tête-à-tête*. On another bench a few boys, gesturing nonstop, were having an animated discussion, while closer by, a man sat immobile, looking in silhouette like a lonely heron.

How could this tapestry of human activity be set in a communist state? These young people basked in the freedom of their counterparts in Paris or New York. The changes taking place in China were obvious here, bespeaking not Chinese-style socialism but Chinese-style capitalism.

"Uncle," blurted Chaehyŏng from the bench where he sat, "did you hear

Mom's coming?" He clutched his cell phone more tightly, his frowning face full of annoyance.

"No. What's going on?"

"Darn it all." Why did his uncle have to sound so nonchalant? "What did you tell her that's making her fly over here?"

"When's she arriving?"

"The day after tomorrow. She called me just this morning."

"I was afraid of that."

"What are you saying?" said Chaehyŏng. "This is serious, Uncle! Didn't I explain the situation to you?"

"Hey, kid, watch your mouth. I did my best, but she's your mother. You know how impetuous Korean mothers are—it's do-or-die, and that's where your mom's at. Can you blame her? Her only child gets into a good school, then out of the blue he changes direction and sets out on a hard road—no mother worth her salt would swallow that. You ought to think things over."

"Uncle!" barked Chaehyŏng, bolting to his feet. "Did she send you on a mission to brainwash me?" The girl next to him looked up from her book, startled, and other students shot looks his way.

"Hey, easy on my ears. No, there's no mission. Actually, I came to the same conclusion as your mom. And you can imagine how she feels."

"This is driving me nuts! I told you I'm not cut out for a major in management. Don't you get it?"

"Come on, kid, you're getting hysterical. Quit singing the management blues and be a man. You're lucky to have parents who support you. You're a spoiled brat who grew up trouble-free, but you'd never know it from the way you whine. Go ahead, find out what you're good at and ten years from now—no, make that four or five years—when you can't find a job and your tummy's growling, you'll have plenty of time for regrets. You'll realize you missed the boat by a long shot."

The voice coming through the phone had settled into a rhythm.

"Uncle, I wish you'd stop provoking me. I know how you operate—you're trying to aggravate me, hoping I'll have a change of heart. Don't waste your breath. No one's going to stop me. I've already crossed the bridge. I know who I am and I'm the master of my life—I told you that last time. I'm the one who's pulling on the oars. I have one more thing to say, and then this conversation is over." Chaehyŏng's voice was calm.

"Well aren't we poetic all of a sudden. You drink Chinese water and turn into Li Bo or Du Fu. Why don't you stop posturing. Listen, you've got the rest of your life to soak up your luxuries and your noble hobbies, but first you have to be able to put food on the table. Life isn't a sentimental journey that's all about what you're good at. It's a war, one cold-blooded, stone-hearted battle after another. So wake up."

"Uncle, save your energy. You know, I've always looked up to you. But now you disappoint me. You're supposed to be educated, and yet listen to yourself. You ought to be ashamed of yourself—all I'm trying to do is find my way in life."

"Take off your blinders, kid. Look, it hurts me to hear you talk like you're telling me goodbye. How about me? I'm in the middle—your mom, my sister. Can't you understand how she feels? The moms of the world hold their kids dearer than their own lives, and you know it. A mother and her kid are crossing the street, a car comes out of nowhere, and *boom!* The mother dies on the spot but the kid survives without a scratch. Why? Mom was holding her to her chest. It was on TV, remember? That's motherly love for you, a mother's heart. It's why your mom deals with you the way she does. It's natural. So here I am, sandwiched between my sister and you. She mistreats me, you slander me. What am I supposed to do? I understand how you feel, believe me. But if you look at life in perspective and try to understand your mom, *that's* when you'll know."

"Tell me, Uncle—is motherly love rational or is it instinctual?"

"What are you getting at?"

"The way I see it," said Chaehyŏng coolly, "motherly love is an instinct, and choosing a life path is rational."

"Oh boy. All right, I give up."

"Uncle, one more thing. Do you have any professor friends?"

"A few—why?"

"When you're with them, do you ever get to thinking, 'I'm better off than you guys'?"

"Hell—just spell it out for me, all right?"

"Well, maybe you have more money than they do, but don't you wish you had their status as intellectuals?"

"All right, what's your point?"

"I don't want more money if that means feeling insecure about my intellect."

"Meaning you'd rather be a hungry Socrates than a stuffed pig."

"Exactly. So you *do* know."

"I know enough to get out of the way of you and your mom. I'm going to watch this war from the sidelines."

"Fair enough. But if you could just do this for me—I'm leaving today on another history field trip, so assuming she gets here on schedule, could you tell her I won't be able to see her?"

"What! Where are you off to now?"

"If I tell you, promise you won't come after me?"

"Admit it—you're not leveling with me."

"Then come along and see for yourself."

"Chaehyŏng, I really worry about you."

"Worry about what? We already know who's going to win this war."

"What do you mean?"

"Have you ever seen parents who won over their kid?"

"What the—listen, kid, you're—"

"Got to go—bye."

Chaehyŏng took a seat next to the girl on the bench.

"Wow," said the girl with a grin. "You're always teasing me about talking on the phone forever, but you men can't help it either."

"I guess not," said Chaehyŏng with an affectionate smile as he inched closer to her. "Serious business, you know." He tossed off the phrase in fluent Mandarin.

"Then why were you shouting?"

"Well, I thought my uncle was on my side, but it turns out he's pro-Mom. If you can't shout at someone who betrays you, then who *can* you shout at?" He made a face.

"Well of course he's pro-Mom."

"What! You're on their side too, Yanling?"

"Think about it," she said. "Your uncle and your mom are siblings, and you're telling them you want to change to a major that doesn't necessarily have a future—what do you expect them to say? This war of yours isn't going to end anytime soon."

"It's over as far as I'm concerned." His hand knifelike, he made a cutting motion.

Yanling gave him a dubious look. "Over how?"

"I won," said Chaehyŏng, brandishing his fist. "What else?"

"How could you win? I couldn't catch your conversation, but it didn't sound that way." She cocked her head skeptically.

"I declared victory—unilaterally."

"What? You're not making sense."

"I don't know how it works here, but back home we have this saying: 'Parents can't win.' That's how I got him to surrender. My mom will wave the white flag too."

"I can't believe it," she giggled. "We have the exact same expression. Cool, that's a great strategy. It always works."

Yanling raised her palms, Chaehyŏng did likewise, and their hands clapped together. "So it works here too—amazing."

"Of course. And it's even more effective."

"How so?"

"You've heard of the *faring hau?*"

"Sure—the generation born after the family-planning laws went into effect."

"That's right. And how about the Little Emperor and the Little Princess?"

"That's what they call kids to show how precious they are under the one-child policy."

"Wow, perfect so far. What about 'one mouth, six pockets'?"

"One precious mouth to feed gets lucky money envelopes from six pairs of pockets—two from the paternal grandparents, two from the maternal grandparents, and two from the parents."

"So now you know."

"Yes, and I envy you—no one interferes. Everything's smooth sailing."

"Not necessarily. Maybe with money matters, but decisions involving your future, that's a whole different story. Chinese moms are just as fanatic as Korean moms, probably more so. Look at private education—people make billions running English-language cram schools. And thanks to all the Chinese moms desperate to educate their kids in the US, we'll see plenty more of these billionaires."

"Yeah, that's one thing we have in common—our moms are psychos. They ignore their kids' strong points and their aptitudes. They're always haranguing them, and it's because of their ambition. They call it love, but it's actually confinement—why can't they understand that?"

"You're quite the guy, Chaehyŏng, breaking through barriers and emerging victorious."

"Not quite yet. There is one more hurdle."

"And what's that?"

"My mother is arriving the day after tomorrow."

"Wow," she said, covering her mouth in surprise, the eyes he found so adorable widening even more. "So what's the plan?"

"Sunzi's military strategy—you win by not fighting."

"Win by not fighting?"

"I am going on a history field trip tomorrow."

"To avoid her?"

"Kind of. When victory is at hand, it is best to minimize exposure."

"True. But where are you heading?"

"Before I get to that," he said, his index finger poised like a maestro's baton, "I need you to come along."

"Me?"

"Yes, you." The eyes regarding her held a feverish gleam.

"Just you and me?"

"Yes. Just the two of us."

"But why?"

"I switched majors, remember? And you are my accomplice—admit it."

"All right, but where are we going?"

"Xihu, the West Lake!"

"In Hangzhou?"

"Yes, Hangzhou."

"That's too far."

"That is precisely my point."

She fell silent, her eyes taking on the same feverish gleam as his.

"When do we leave?"

"Tomorrow."

She hesitated a moment longer, then nodded.

Carefully he took the hand resting on her book. Their clasped hands partially obscured the title—*The History of China.*

Early the next morning they met at Beijing Station, dressed casually and exchanging furtive looks and the tight-lipped grins of partners in crime. It had been child's play for Yanling to forestall questions from her parents by whipping up an excuse for her sudden departure. After all, Chinese history, rife with Sunzi stratagems, was her major.

"Ah, *ren tai duo, ren tai duo!*" Too many people. Her pretty face was filled with irritation at the swarm of humanity.

"Yeah, *ren tai duo, ren tai duo!*" Chaehyŏng chimed in, mimicking Yanling's exasperated gesture shooing aside the human tide that was filling the capacious waiting room to the bursting point.

Ren tai duo was an expression always uttered in dissatisfaction. Along with its miniature version, *ren duo*, it jumped out of people's mouths in any bustling locale, and here there was no place that lacked for crowds.

Chaehyŏng recalled a lecture in a course taught by a young professor: "Maybe you can guess what's implied in *ren tai duo*—'Three hundred million of you ought to drop dead.' And there's an implication within the implication—'all of you, except me.' So whenever you hear *ren tai duo*, you have to understand that hidden meaning. Even kids have it on the tip of their tongue—I'd say the whole country has that mentality. If the population shrank by three hundred million, to one billion, life would be a whole lot easier. You could consider this a critical point in understanding China and the Chinese. Along with the fact that they're severely egocentric and selfish...."

From then on, whenever Chaehyŏng heard *ren tai duo*, he thought, *three hundred million of you ought to drop dead—every last one of you, except me.* He felt as if an icy hand had come to rest on his chest.

The super-high-speed Beijing–Shanghai railroad connected the nation's political and financial capitals. The exterior was sleek and modern, the interior elegant and refined. It departed on time, and the digital speedometer displayed above the door to the compartment accelerated giddily. Within ten minutes the indicator had passed 300 kilometers per hour, but you never would have known it—the ride was smooth and comfortable, with no noise and no vibration. The indicator finally stopped at 340.

"This train does wonders for my wounded pride," said Yanling, her eyes fixed on the distant indicator.

Chaehyŏng gave her an inquiring look.

"Did I ever tell you about that China-bashing article in the American press? It said we'll always be a second-rate country no matter how we struggle to improve. But there's nothing second-rate about this train." Yanling was right; the CRH trains on the Hosei line reached speeds of 350 kilometers per hour, compared with 320 for the French TGV and 300 for the Korean KTX.

"Don't let those Yankee pricks get you down. Whites in general think they're so superior. They can't stomach the prospect of China rising to their level."

"Yes, their attitude stinks. They want to dominate everything," she said. "Don't you agree?"

"Of course." And then, with a poker face, "Up with China—my wife's motherland."

"What!" Her face reddening, she pinched his arm.

Chaehyŏng was entranced. West Lake in Hangzhou was so vast that the far end reached to the horizon. If not for the ripple-free surface, the stillness of the surroundings, and the shimmering reflection of the dense forest circling the lake, he might have mistaken it for the ocean.

"Amazing," he said, spreading his arms wide to embrace the scene. "It's huge."

"You've never seen a lake this big?" Yanling asked with a smile. Tall and slender in her formfitting jeans, she still had to look up at Chaehyŏng, who was nearly six feet tall.

"Korea's a shrimp," he said with a regretful look. "You know."

"Then don't be sad. Get your fill of this *huge* lake. Because your wife's country belongs to you too," she giggled.

Miss Demure, he thought as she turned away to cover her mouth. "That's what I want to hear—you, the lake, everything, it's all mine." But when he tried to hug her, she ran off, her laughter jingling in his ears. He gave chase, their shadows skipping along the surface of the water.

"Let's go for a bike ride," she shouted over her shoulder.

"Sure, around the lake."

"We can rent them over there," she called out, and now she was running faster.

Side by side they rode, the sun-soaked sheen of Yanling's fluttering hair and the otherworldly beauty of the lake producing in Chaehyŏng a euphoria more expansive than the lake itself.

"Why West Lake, anyway?" she asked.

"Well…I heard so much about it, how beautiful it is—I always wanted to see it."

"So does it meet your expectations?"

"Yes, and twice over."

"Twice?"

"Yes, because you are here with me."

"Uh-oh."

The next thing he knew, she was pedaling furiously, her tight jeans threatening to come apart at the seams. Chinese girls on their bikes—they really knew how to get a guy worked up.

"Look at the sky!" she said, gesturing across the lake to the west as he pulled up beside her.

"Beautiful, so beautiful," was all he could say.

The sky was a radiant crimson feast, dark flames shooting out from the horizon into a vast sea of fire, the red not the artificial color of paper or dyed fabric but a living, breathing, palpable texture, a natural canvas painted by the sun. This canvas now had an identical twin, its reflection on the surface of the lake. Darker and darker the two canvasses burned, reaching a captivating climax.

"I could die," she murmured in a rapturous voice. Her entire being was infused with the twilight.

Again the flames of desire came over him. *I could die.* He savored the expression, and the ardor of her response to the breathtaking magnificence before them. Coming from her mouth, it was poetry. And then it struck him: *he* wanted to die, right here, right now, with her. Never before had a scene of splendor left him with a death wish.

"This is one of the ten best views of West Lake," she said in a dreamy voice, "and it's all ours." She squeezed his hand.

"Let's go," said Chaehyŏng. "Duanqiao is waiting."

"How do you know about Duanqiao? You've never been here before."

"I saw it in my dreams last night."

"You mean you did some research."

"Of course—we're on a field trip, remember?"

"Aren't you clever!" she said with a grin, flipping her hair back. "Then you probably know the legend of the white snake."

"For sure. It's part of my dissertation."

"Yeah, right," she said, chortling at his nonchalance.

By the time they arrived at the arched bridge of Duanqiao, dusk had extinguished the beautiful sunset. He led her out on the bridge. Yes, it was just right for the fabled love story.

"Yanling, this is for you," he said, taking a small box from his pocket and opening it. Inside were two identical rings.

Gazing into his glowing eyes, she offered her hand, and he slipped the ring on her finger. Then he passed her the box and she reciprocated.

"Yanling, I love you with all my heart." He drew her close.

"And I love you dearly, Chaehyŏng."

Her voice trembling, she clutched him, and then his lips were one with hers. They held each other tighter, and her intoxicating fragrance set him shivering. He smelled the tang of flowers, fresh grass, salt water, and again his manhood came alive. His feverish hands passed down her body.

"Not here, people can see us." She pushed him away, gently but firmly, and they came off the bridge. "You must never give me an umbrella," she said. "You know that, don't you?"

"Yes," he said, "never ever—even in a downpour."

She looked at him with trustful eyes and looped her arm about his waist. He encircled her neck and drew her close.

The legend of Madam White Snake concerned a couple, Bai Suzhen and Xu Xian. On a visit to West Lake, Xu encountered Bai, a snake in human form. It was raining, and when Xu gave Bai an umbrella, they fell in love. Their torrid passion ended in marriage and they lived happily until one day a monk appeared in front of them. He had the power to expel evil, and he saw Bai for what she really was. The couple resisted with all their strength but ultimately had to separate—the monk was too powerful.

Thanks to this legend, Chinese lovers do not give umbrellas as gifts. Indeed, the Chinese word for *umbrella* sounds the same as the word for *separation*.

4. The Rule of the Jungle: The Strong Devour the Weak

As always, the streets were mayhem on wheels, a hodgepodge of bikes, scooters, and every vehicle you could imagine. But there was an order to the chaos— whether you cut someone off, banked a sudden U-turn, or drove the wrong way down a street, you wouldn't be barked at as long as you avoided an accident, even if it was by the skin of your teeth. To Toyotomi Araki it was a mystery why arguments didn't ensue. Maybe it was a collective belief that it was every man for himself, or maybe it was a matter of *manmandi*—or maybe they simply didn't care. Whatever the explanation, the people of Shanghai were masters of defensive driving.

The sidewalks, a disorienting tangle of pedestrians, were no less crowded. The only difference was you needn't fear a vehicular sideswipe or head-on collision. But that didn't guarantee you were safer on foot. Let your mind wander even a moment as you looked for a sign, and a pedestrian crash was imminent. In a metropolis saturated with people, minefields lay everywhere.

A Western tourist couple stooped with age walked along, supporting each other. It wasn't just their clothing that gave them away; no resident of this business hub of Shanghai, not even the elderly, would be seen plodding when everyone else moved along briskly. All the resident *waiguoren*—Asians included—were young people. Like the hundreds of thousands of Baikal teal ducks migrating in search of food, this brassy new generation had flocked to Shanghai in search of money.

Suddenly there was a shadow next to the elderly couple, and just as suddenly the woman's tote bag was gone. The woman staggered, and the man caught her. She reached for the thief, shouting, "Help—help me!"

The man shouted too, his voice weaker, and took off after the purse snatcher.

"Police!" the woman screamed, running after her husband. "Police, help!"

But no police, no member of the Public Security Bureau, was to be seen.

The pursuit unfolded in slow motion. Instead of running for dear life, the purse snatcher was enjoying a power walk. *Catch me if you can!*

Finally the woman spotted her bag swaying in leisurely fashion from the man's shoulder. "Help! Get the police!" she screeched. But except for a few bored spectators who spared her a glance, all continued on their way, heedless and impassive.

"Should we help them?" said Toyotomi. "Looks like he's operating solo."

"Are you nuts?" snapped his companion, Ito Hideo. "Those guys carry weapons."

"Then let's just watch the show."

"That's more like it. Did you hear what happened to that Chosenjin?"

"A *Chosenjin*? No, what?"

Chosenjin. A pejorative straight from colonial Korea a hundred years ago. The word literally meant "Chosŏn person," but to the Japanese it meant "Korean bastard." Just like "Japs" or "runts" reflected not just Korean anger and hatred toward the Japanese but also a bitter combination of grudge, condemnation, and revenge, "Chosenjin" harbored longstanding contempt, disregard, and disrespect toward Koreans.

"There was a long line of people for a sale at a shopping center, and a Chinese guy kept trying to cut in. The Chosenjin must have told him to stop. Well, you know the Chinese—they want to save face as bad as money, and this one got pissed off. So he pulls out a box cutter and *whick*!"

"Those things are razor-sharp! What happened to him?"

"Who knows—not that I really care."

"Maybe the guy just landed here and thinks he's more civilized than the locals."

Punctuating their conversation with sips from venti coffees, the two men took in the street theater to their hearts' content. In the meantime the purse snatcher disappeared into the human tide, leaving the elderly couple bent over in despair.

"Guy's heartless, even for a crook!"

"Heartless, how?"

"Targeting Westerners—he must be desperate. Won't help China's reputation."

"Hideo, where have you been? TIC—this is China, remember? The land of knockoffs, burned software, and stolen industrial know-how. The laughingstock of the world. And does the government blink an eye? Who the hell's going to care about a purse snatcher?"

"You're right, Araki. I guess I'm too Japanese. So how long will it take to civilize them?"

As if in response to the rhetorical question, a man cleared his throat loudly and spat, then brushed past them, leaving a yellowish glob clinging to the sidewalk. "Pig!" Ito muttered, scowling at the man's back.

"Come on. It's Saturday afternoon and we've got time on our hands. Let's get a foot massage." And with that, Toyotomi set off.

"*Koshitsu*," said Toyotomi to the woman at the foot massage parlor, asking for private rooms.

"*Hai!*" said the woman with a practiced smile. She guided the two men down a narrow hallway.

"How's it looking?" asked Toyotomi.

"So far so good," said Ito.

"By Monday?"

"Wednesday at the latest."

"Damn, why so long?"

"Don't get yourself worked up."

"It's all about pride, you know."

"And not just pride. Yes, I know."

The woman stopped at the end of the hallway.

"Get a good rest."

"You too."

The men were ushered into separate rooms.

In the cramped room Toyotomi stripped down to his undershorts and sprawled out on the bed. He reached for the pack of cigarettes. Japanese, of course—Mairudo Sebun, Mild Seven.

In came a woman with a wooden bucket containing a bath towel. She looked girlish and pretty in her simple uniform. She put down the bucket and turned off the light. At the head of the bed a night-light announced its existence, barely strong enough to illuminate the room.

She undid her top, flaunting youthful, bouncy breasts. Down went her pants, revealing a scanty thong as red as the Chinese flag. Toyotomi felt a hot charge in his chest and wondered if the thong served as a good luck charm. As if on cue, she unrolled the steaming towel and placed it over his body.

Again Toyotomi checked his watch. Another day at the office was drawing to an end. His thumb was curled over his cell phone display, the umpteenth time he'd felt the urge that day, but there it stayed. He hadn't wanted to pester Ito on Monday, the start of a new week. But by Tuesday afternoon, his cell phone was beckoning him. He held fast, knowing it was Ito who would want to call as soon as possible—as the broker, Ito was the one in the hot seat, after all. And so Tuesday had passed.

Today, Wednesday, Toyotomi's thumb had been poised for action, but nothing had happened. Another flop? As the hours went by, this ominous thought coiled itself about him. Had they been outmaneuvered…? No, no way. Once again his thumb stopped short of its destination. He clenched his teeth in frustration. They shouldn't even have to compete with Chosenjin, but to be shouldered aside by them? That would be worse than losing to them in soccer or baseball. With sports the hurt was emotional, but with business there was monetary loss as well as damaged pride.

Stop it. He had to calm himself. Especially now. This was China, not Japan. It was the land of *manmandi*—he should be used to it by now. They couldn't work Nippondo-style, waving the big sword. No, they'd have to be more *manmandi* than the Chinks. And manage not to eat themselves up in the process.

He tried to light a cigarette, jabbing the lighter in vexation. Finally the flame flared up in his face. He flinched, the cigarette dropping from his mouth.

"*Baka*! Can't the idiots make anything right?" He gaped at the lighter. Chinese-made for sure.

Japan had stopped making disposable lighters twenty years ago, unable to compete with the cheap Korean versions flooding its markets. Korea underwent the same process, the rise in domestic labor costs weakening its competitive edge while China quickly mastered the simple know-how. It was a natural business cycle, like water flowing downhill, eventually to evaporate.

Toyotomi took a new cigarette and lit up. His square face, normally amiable, was masked with irritation. He had just taken a deep drag when his cell phone jingled.

"*Moshi moshi*!" Ito's voice was urgent, but something about the curt tone brightened Toyotomi's mood.

"It's you."

"*Totsugeki*!" The Japanese battle cry. "We're all set!" Sure enough, Ito sounded like a soldier ready to charge.

"All right, all right. Great job, Hideo. *Totsugeki* for sure." Toyotomi felt the triumphant flush of an officer just assured of victory.

"We need to celebrate," said Ito.

"Sure, it's the perfect occasion."

"Nothing like booze to boost our spirits."

"How about we add a well-wisher to the party?"

"Good thinking. But we need to keep the lid on for the moment, so…"

"How about Ishihara?"

"Great choice. His mouth is a steel trap, and he plays hard."

"All right—I'll give him a ring. I can't wait."

"Me neither. See you soon."

Ending the call, Toyotomi buried himself in his sofa and heaved a sigh. The snowbank of pressure began to melt, releasing the stress he'd borne from this latest deal, a delivery they absolutely couldn't afford to lose. They were supposed to supply the entire order, but along the way a spoiler had emerged, a Korean firm prepared to supply ten tons of the order. Here was a battle Toyotomi had to win, even if it yielded a smaller profit margin, even if there was no profit. Pride was at stake. A Korean firm! The only one who could compete with Japan as a supplier of steel was Germany.

"Toyotomi san, welcome! I knew you were coming!"

The woman greeting him like a long-lost brother wore thick makeup. Her flowing speech and theatrical gestures were those of a Japanese woman, but she was Chinese to the bone, earthy and cloying.

"Perceptive as ever, Madame Jiang, especially when the smell of money's in the air. And your Nihongo is vastly improved, is it not?"

"That is the least I can do for my dear clients, you know. I must work extra hard on my Nihongo, so you will feel right at home with us." She laid on the charm, playing to perfection the role of bawdy madam.

"Of course! That earns you our love and our money besides."

"Yes, money is my emperor, my god in heaven. Oh, shame on me. I'm talking too much about myself. How silly of me."

"Not at all. You're candid. Is there anyone in this world who doesn't like money? Church ministers, Buddhist monks, they're full of platitudes, but they like to rake in our contributions. With you, Madame, what we see is what we get—honest and with a heart, straightforward and pretty. You're the same inside and out, not like those lofty souls. That's why I've always liked you."

"Goodness gracious. How can I ever thank you? You really do understand me. That's why I like you, Toyotomi san." Overhearing her, you might have thought she was in bed with him.

"Hey, Araki, you started without me. Stop hitting on her and order some booze," said Ishihara Shiro as he entered the room.

"Shiro. Here you are." The two kindred spirits shook hands. "I was just shooting the breeze till you got here."

"So what's the occasion?" said Ishihara as he pulled out a pack of cigarettes and offered them to his friend.

"Let's wait till Hideo gets here," said Toyotomi, taking a cigarette. "I'm still not clear on all the details."

Just then Ito rushed in as if he'd been waiting in the wings. "Last one here—my apologies for being late. I had to send up a detailed report."

With Ito's arrival the madam took over, her bright smile looking like it was fresh from a plastic mold. "The pretty girls are at your service. Enjoy!" Opening the door to their private room, she bowed from the waist, like a Japanese hostess.

The room was much more than the three men needed just for drinking. It was larger than a private room in a restaurant and the decorations were gaudy. One corner was occupied by a pair of plush sofas, with a large glass-top coffee table between them. On the wall opposite one of the sofas was a supersize flat-screen TV, and in front of it a large space designated by a sign reading Karaoke.

The door opened and a young man in uniform entered, his head mechanically bobbing in greeting. In his wake came a train of young women—one and then two, now half a dozen, soon ten, and finally a full dozen. They stood attentively before the three men. Still with a virginal tinge, they were pretty by any standards. They posed in anticipation, all alike wearing short skirts exposing sleek and slender legs.

From their plush sofa the three men scanned the offering, pointed index fingers passing back and forth among the array. The tense faces of the women followed the passage of the fingertips. A dozen women from which the three men could select, a four-to-one ratio. Another TIC moment.

The three index fingers pointed back and forth. Out went one woman, and then a second. The third finger pointed to the door. "Wansu agein!" shouted Toyotomi in English. He wouldn't be caught dead speaking Chinese.

"Hai!" answered the uniformed man, and he herded the women out. Their impassive expressions suggested this wasn't the first time they'd gotten a thumbs-down.

"This place must have seen better days," muttered Ito. "But no worries—with five hundred girls there have got to be some to our liking. Let's not spend all night picking them out—another couple of rounds should do it. What if we take turns? That's part of the fun, and only in China."

A second array of women was ushered in, and again the index fingers began their scan.

"You!" Ishihara made a selection.

"You." As did Ito.

Toyotomi, though, drew a line in the air from right to left, ending at the door. Out went the remaining ten women. Another dozen arrived. Puffing on a cigarette, Toyotomi registered the girls with his eyes only, and finally his finger rose. "You!"

Groping the thigh of his selection as she poured him a drink, Ito said, "I always wonder about three things here."

"Oh? And all along I thought you were the expert," smirked Toyotomi.

"Bear with me. First, how many girls do you suppose end up in places like this?" Ito asked with all the gravity of a professor presenting a research paper.

"Are you serious?" said Toyotomi. "We all know it's eighty to a hundred million."

"Not true," said Ishihara. "Nobody knows for sure."

"That's the perfect answer to any question in China," said Toyotomi, nodding.

"One hundred million?" Ito shook his head. "No way, it's got to be more."

"And the number goes up by the day," Toyotomi declared. "It's the women who are flocking to the cities from the farms. It'll be a hundred and twenty million before long."

"A hundred and twenty million?" Ishihara's mouth fell open. "That's the entire population of Japan!"

"The second thing I'm curious about," said Ito, serious as before, "is all the money these women pocket. It's got to be a hell of a lot."

"Nobody knows for sure," Ishihara said again.

"And question number three," said Ito. "Does all that money get factored into China's GDP?"

"Who knows?"

"I do," said Toyotomi with supreme assurance. "Of course it's included. They count everything they can in their GDP. Remember the story about eating dog shit."

"What!" said Ishihara.

"You haven't heard about those two zillionaire idiots?" asked Ito.

"Oh, yeah," said Ishihara, bursting into laughter. "For a hundred million dollars, right?"

There were two billionaires, Big Nose and Big Ear. Day and night they bickered about who was wealthier. One day they met for a stroll in the park. They had talked themselves blue in the face bragging about their newly gained wealth, leaving each other with a sting of jealousy, when they saw what appeared to be a lump of gold. A closer look revealed it to be a pile of dog shit. Freshly discharged and still steaming, it looked velvet soft in texture and had an inviting color. Big Nose eyed the deposit. What if I got the arrogant bastard to chow it down? Put that mean son of a bitch in his place? There has to be a way. He put his mind to work and then it hit him. Why not make a bet? Big Ear was the kind of guy who would bet his daughter, even his wife, if the stakes were right. How much should he try? He couldn't simply whet the guy's appetite. He'd need to stake enough dough to blow his mind. So, one hundred million dollars. Wait, that was too much. Then again, why not? What he really wanted was to set him up and screw him over. Let the world know that Big Ear was a shit eater, and he'd live forever after in shame—that would be worth a hundred million, easy. So it was decided.

"I've got a deal for you," said Big Nose to Big Ear. "You eat that pile of dog shit and I'll give you one hundred million dollars on the spot."

It took a moment for Big Ear to process the offer. "Did I hear you right—a hundred million dollars?"

"That's right."

"How can I trust you?"

"Let's be honest," Big Nose scoffed. "If you don't have the guts to do it, just say so."

"I didn't say that. You show me the money, I'll eat the whole thing."

"You sure—you can eat shit?"

"A man's word is good as gold, right? Like I said, show me the money."

"You got it—right here." Taking a blank check from his pocket, Big Nose filled it out for a hundred million dollars, thinking You've got to be kidding. You're just bluffing. But what do you know? Without a moment's hesitation Big Ear cupped the pile of shit in his palms and tucked into it. Oh hell! Imagine Big Nose's shock when Big Ear finished his repast and stuck out his hand. Bye-bye went the check— what else could Big Nose do? But as they continued their stroll, Big Ear grew embarrassed and then enraged—he'd been teased and ridiculed by Big Nose. He deserved more respect than that.

Big Nose too felt vexed and victimized. Who would have thought the asshole would actually do it? He ate it like a dumpling. There goes 100 million. Bitter, he felt his heart pound and his legs tremble. But then another pile of dog shit came into sight.

Well met! thought Big Ear. Now I'll get even with that son of a bitch! Stifling the urge to slap his knee in delight, Big Ear said, "My friend, if you eat that I'll give you 100 million here and now."

Big Nose perked up. "Are you sure?"

"Sure I'm sure. Trust me. The question is, can you or can't you?"

"Why not?"

"Then show me, and the hundred million is yours."

"Fair enough. Here goes!"

Big Nose scampered to the pile of shit. Just like Big Ear, he scarfed it down and stuck out his hand.

What a spiteful bastard! Big Ear tutted and handed back the check. The two of them walked on in silence, lost in thought. What had they gained? For an answer they sought out a distinguished economics professor. He listened and managed to deliver his verdict politely: "You two gentlemen are indeed patriots. Thanks to you, our GDP rose by 200 million dollars."

The three ladies swiftly poured beer, and the three men clinked glasses.

Ito tutted, frowning. "We crushed the *Chosenjin* all right, but there are still two unknowns."

Toyotomi shot Ito a look. "Namely?"

"Mystery number one, we haven't figured out who their *guanxi* is, and number two, we know nothing about the chairman of the Gold Groups."

"Who cares who they are?" Toyotomi reached for his beer, then decided he needed a cigarette.

"Maybe it's not so important for you and your steel company, but for us and our trading companies it's crucial we know. This deal should have gone through easier, and I bet their *guanxi* continues to go to bat for them."

"That makes sense. But it's a cinch to study up on the Gold Groups chairman."

"How so?"

"One click on the Internet."

"Good thing you work for a steel company," said Ito with a smirk and a here's-to-you gesture with his beer. "Nothing ever gets complicated there."

"What else do you need? All the info's right there on your screen."

"Sure—and it's garbage, all of it. Every site I visit, a couple dozen questions come up."

"What do you mean?"

"For example—the chairman is actually a woman, Wang Lingling, or Sophia Wang, take your pick, born in 1977. MBA from UC Berkeley. The company expanded to China in 2004. Real estate, construction, chemicals, securities…You're good at solving mysteries," said Ito, giving Toyotomi an expectant look. "Smell anything?"

"Well now," said Toyotomi, a hand playing pensively about his mouth. "Born in '77? Which makes her…"

"Thirty-three, of course," said Ishihara, silent until then.

"Yeah," said Toyotomi. "A thirty-three-year-old woman who graduates from two of America's top schools, Harvard and Berkeley, coast to coast. She's got a Chinese name and an American name, she pops up in China in 2004, and now here she is at the head of all these mega-enterprises. Who's her granddaddy? That's what I want to know. She didn't get there all on her own."

"You're right. That's a lot of question marks," said Ito, regarding his glass of beer pensively. "So what do we have for clues?"

"Let's see," said Toyotomi. "The English name makes her an overseas Chinese, maybe LA or San Fran—there are a lot of Japanese in those areas too. Maybe one of those well-heeled overseas families shipped their brainy daughter back home with a solid start-up fund. And then…"

"And then?" Ito prompted him.

"And then… well… then," said Toyotomi, sounding like a broken record.

"Yeah, me too," said Ito. "That's where things get hazy. It's a black hole. Damn! Hey, come here, cutie." Drawing one of the women close, he slipped a hand down her blouse.

"Oh," she bleated, barely managing to suppress a scream. Rational young hostess that she was, she had to control the way she defended herself. If she allowed her instincts to get the better of her and got herself dismissed—well, she'd be lucky to escape with a hair-pulling dressing-down from Madame Leopard Jiang. The alternative was getting handed over to her thugs, who would beat her to a bloody pulp and send her packing. And heaven help her if she tried to find work elsewhere—in this booze-and-body business she'd instantly be tagged as damaged goods, a bad-for-business broad, and off she'd go down the road to poverty and begging. There was a proverb you learned early on—*xiao pin fu xiaoso jiang,* or "People scoff at you if you're poor, but not if you're a prostitute." With no wherewithal of her own, this young hostess was well aware that her present job was the easiest and fastest way to make money.

And so her stifled protestations segued into randy humming in time with Ito's hand roaming over her bosom. *Wow,* she imagined him thinking, *look at me turn this girl on.*

"Back to Wang Lingling," said Toyotomi. "Or Sophia. We need to check her out. Less than a decade here and she's already successful. Ten years younger than we are and she's got every sector covered. It doesn't figure. We're men, damn it, and she's the one with the balls." He heaved an exaggerated sigh.

"How many women get rich overnight here?" said Ishihara, making a face. "Or anywhere else in the world?"

"Best show I ever saw here was the young chairwoman who dished out 1.6 billion *yuan* in alimony to her ex," said Ito, an alcohol flush blooming on his face. "Remember her? What a lucky bastard!"

"So we're all agreed—Wang and the *guanxi* guy are important. Then what's our plan?" said Toyotomi, trying to put on a sober face.

"We'll figure it out," said Ito with a dismissive gesture. "We're as well connected as the average country's CIA. Come on, down the hatch."

They drank, and Ishihara winked at Ito, bouncing a hostess on his lap. "So how's your wife? Still suspicious?"

"Yes—still. We've been apart too long. Her doctor thinks she's neurotic out of loneliness. But deep down she knows I won't trade her in for a Chinese girl—I guess I should be thankful." Ito smiled bitterly.

"Suppose she knows you have a mistress?" asked Toyotomi.

"Who me, Mr. Innocent? Only if you rat me out."

"Bringing the whole family, like the Koreans do, causes problems," said Ishihara. "But going it alone like us isn't any easier. Life's a bitch! Hey, kittens, aren't you drinking?" He offered his glass to his hostess. Accepting it with no hesitation, she looked at him with bedroom eyes that Ishihara could have sworn contained dollar signs.

"Still, it's less of a headache without the family, and it's fun to choose a local," said Toyotomi.

"And it's better for the kids," said Ishihara. "No one likes moving to a new school."

"And what would they learn here anyway? It's so screwed up," declared Toyotomi. "Unless it's the US or Europe, best to leave the kids back home."

"For sure," said Ito. "Why drag your kids to a place where there's zero etiquette, fake food, and bad air? Here's for you, doll." He poured for his hostess.

"You too," said Toyotomi, presenting his hostess with a glass full of beer. Obligingly she gulped it.

"How about some music?" Toyotomi pointed to the TV. His hostess jumped to the task.

"Good girls. Come here." He rose and beckoned the three hostesses, and they fell in line before him. Taking a roll of hundred-*yuan* bills from his pocket, he counted briskly, then with a flourish stopped at ten and thrust the money at his hostess. Her face blossomed in a smile, and she received the gratuity with two hands, bowing ninety degrees at the waist. A thousand *yuan* was half a month's salary for a factory worker. He repeated the ritual with the other two.

"All right, girls. Time to take off your clothes and show us what you got," said Toyotomi, mimicking a striptease and pointing to the big glass table. "Let's go, shake it!"

The hostesses exchanged glances, then tucked their money beneath a sofa cushion and stripped naked.

5. A Mother Waves the White Flag

Chŏn Yusuk chewed on her lower lip, an unconscious habit that left her lip more blistered and visibly swollen by the day. *You stinker, let's see who wins. Trying to avoid me? I'll rot and die before I let you study Chinese history. You might as well beg for a living. I sacrificed for you, I economized, got you tutors, sent you to cram school, and this is what I get—rotten, unfilial behavior? Have a heart.*

She'd been here several days now, keeping a vigil, blubbering and lamenting to herself, chewing on her lip. Her son wasn't in his Beida dormitory, and her brother, the boy's uncle, who spoke Chinese like a native, had come here to make inquiries only to find that no group had left on a history field trip.

By now her face was beyond wretched. She wasn't bothering with makeup, except for a dab of facial cream and a back-and-forth with her lipstick. She'd sat out in the sun these last several days. To hell with her face. She was armed to the teeth back home—mask, ultra-sunblock, and wide-brimmed hat for her late-afternoon walk. But here, with her son gone, she couldn't care less if her skin were damaged or unsightly spots sprouted. The boy's change of heart was cataclysmic—her heaven had turned to hell. There could be no worse disaster, no deeper shock and disappointment. Her one and only son, the apple of her eye.

"Mom, why the fuss? You're such an embarrassment," her daughter had said, her tone icy and scathing. "You're all emotion, no rationality. Try to compose yourself, like Dad. Things could be a lot worse—what if Dad suddenly walked in with a ten-year-old kid? Chaehyŏng made it clear he wanted to go his own way. Mom, you're overdoing it. I *hate* people who are totally sentimental."

"What!" she had snapped. "You know nothing about how I feel. You're not even married, and listen to you yapping like a know-it-all. How can you not be concerned—he's your only sibling! You heartless bitch!"

She wanted to show she could be rational and escape her daughter's contempt. But what exploded from her dragon mouth was a stew of emotions. Chalk it up to a mother's heart.

"Aren't you concerned, dear?" she'd asked her husband after Chaehyŏng declared himself a Chinese history major.

He'd taken the news silently, his face impassive. Which only added to her frustration and anxiety. Finally he'd said, "Yes, I'm concerned, but I'm proud of him too." He'd even sounded a bit choked up.

"Proud?" she snapped.

"Well," he said evasively, "I feel like he slipped out of the nest, like he's all grown up and I sent him out on his own."

She felt like cursing him for his nonchalance. Just then she remembered a television program about a study on parenting among mammals. A male chimpanzee and his offspring were placed on a metal platform, which was then slowly heated. At a certain temperature father and son began scurrying about the platform in search of a cooler spot, and when the platform got too toasty, the father jumped onto the back of the son. But when the mother and son were placed on the platform, it was the mother who whisked the son off his feet to her bosom.

"I'm going there to see him."

Her husband had merely nodded, looking at her intently. No use, his silence was telling her. Which only made her more determined to leave.

And now, as she waited for her brother, she drank what was left of her bottle of water. Her stomach was growling, but she'd only picked at her breakfast—eating wasn't on her mind now that she was in China. Water was all she cared for.

"Be sure to get it from the hotel shop," her brother had instructed her. "And just Evian—don't trust what's bottled here."

Fake eggs, bottled water you shouldn't drink—what a demented place. And her own son wanted to study the history of this weird country—*haigo*! It was blasphemy!

"You don't know the whole picture," her brother had said when she'd voiced these concerns. "Forget about Chaehyŏng for the moment and you'll see this is a country worth studying. There's so much that's intriguing. The more layers you sort through, the deeper you dig, the more you get hooked. Consider this—except for the last two centuries, China was the richest country in the world. It's a miracle—"

"No wonder!" she'd interrupted. "You've been getting him all worked up."

"No no no." Her brother had waved her off. "I'm just telling you the facts."

Taking her last swallow of water, she looked vacantly at the sky through the hotel lobby windows, tears pooling in her eyes. *In the nest the child is yours—on the wing he's gone.* These words, murmured by her own mother, echoed in her mind. Had her mother meant to soothe herself with this reflection as she brooded over her own children's departure? This brought another sigh.

"Sister, sorry I'm late," said Chŏn Taegwang, steadying his breath as he rushed in. "Our meeting with the boss dragged on forever. You must be starving—let's go eat."

"No," she said, shaking her head listlessly. "I don't feel like eating."

"You're going to get sick. Look at you—I think you're sick already. And that's a problem here—you can't even tell if the medicine's for real." His tone was firm.

"I wish. Now that I'm betrayed by the boy I held more precious than my own life, I'd rather be dead." A dual stream of tears flowed down her haggard face.

"Come on, Sister. Parents and children don't betray each other—that's ridiculous. Now get up—you need to eat and get your strength back. *Then* you can track him down."

"All right, then how about dim sum—something simple." She allowed her brother to help her to her feet.

"You need more than a few dumplings. By the way, Brother-in-Law called."

"My heartless husband—what does he want?"

"He wants me to take care of you. I'll have to answer to him if I don't."

"Did he mention Chaehyŏng?"

"No, and I didn't either. But I'm sure he's concerned."

"He doesn't care. And you're no better. Men are callous idiots. No compassion. They only care about themselves."

"Allow me to express my regrets. We do try to think rationally, you know."

"Shut up!" she barked, quivering with emotion. "And damn your rationality!"

Chŏn picked out a Korean restaurant and ordered *kalbi* for them.

"Sister, you've been here ten days now. I keep thinking," he said, "as long as you're here, Chaehyŏng won't show up."

"What?" she faltered. "What do you mean?"

"What I mean is field trips usually run two nights, three days, or four and five at the most. But it's been a week and a half and he hasn't shown up. He's hiding out, waiting for you to give up and go back home. I'm sure of it."

"Are you out of your mind?" she said. "My son is not that mean."

"Sister, listen to me. Chaehyŏng wants to change his major. We all know that, and so the longer you're here, the worse it is for him—if he won't come back here to face you, then how can he return to his studies? So it's up to you."

"What are you saying?" she said in a tearful voice, her lips trembling.

"The battle's over. It's like Chaehyŏng himself said—parents can't win over their children. He's a determined kid and he's not going to yield. When men need to decide what's right for them, they don't listen to anybody—that's the way we are. So you need to accept that it's over, Sister."

"Good heavens," she said, tears spilling from her eyes. "I'm supposed to accept that he goes off on a tangent and pays for it the rest of his life?"

"That's premature. What you need to realize is that a person's life can lead him in countless directions."

"Look, I know what I'm talking about," she said, her voice unsteady. "I've done my research. Do you have any idea how difficult it is to find a job? Chaehyŏng may think it's easy getting a teaching job, but look at all the PhDs who can't find a permanent position even ten or fifteen years later—what kind of a life is that? The way you talk, you must think I'm stupid."

"Fine," said her brother. "I'll tell you what—if he can't make it in academia, I'll find him a job. All he needs is proficiency in Chinese, and he'll find plenty of ways to make a living here. So leave him to me. And don't write off your husband. Remember—a husband and wife are an entity, but a parent and child are separate. You need to understand he's growing into a man and practice letting go. This is a good opportunity. Don't make things hard on yourself—you're educated enough to know better."

"I just don't know—my heart feels one way, and my mind thinks another. I never thought this day would come," she said, shoulders heaving.

"I have to go back to work the day after tomorrow," he said.

"I know. I've put you to a lot of trouble. All right, then, back home I go." She forced a smile.

"I'll keep you posted."

"Chaehyŏng—you're free, free at last," cried an ecstatic Yanling as she darted inside.

"Really—she left?" shouted Chaehyŏng, putting down his book.

"She must have. I haven't seen her all day." She smiled mischievously.

"She is one stubborn woman," he said, stretching his arms high in triumph. "I thought she'd give up after a few days, but she lasted a week and a half. Thank God—sleeping on this hard floor is killing me." He pounded the small of his back in relief.

"You should be thankful—a Chinese mom would have hung in there a month or two, easy," she said, unstrapping her backpack. "Mothers are mothers, no matter where they're from."

"*Aigo.* Mother's love—to me it's protective custody. They treat us like babies forever. It's so stifling—and I've had enough."

"Chinese moms are maybe even worse. You can almost see the mad gleam in their eyes. Think about it—what if you were allowed only one child?"

"Yes, but Korean moms are so extreme. I'm disgusted with them—they ignore their kids' opinions, set their goals for them, and drive them into a corner. The poor kids are driven to cram schools, and back home they're stuck at their desk till way after midnight. I used to nod off at school from first period on. The teacher's voice was like a lullaby. Kids aren't superhuman—they can't fight off sleep. So practically the whole class is conked out, heads on their desks. The teacher throws up her hands. *All right, I give up—you kids can catch up at your cram school.* And the kids think, *Fine, now we can sleep.* It's weird—what's happening to public education? People are calling on the government to regulate the private tutoring industry. But what can the minister of education do when these nutcase mothers keep pushing their kids into cram schools? The best he could do was announce they'll only certify public educators, not private instructors. In other words, don't entrust your kids to uncertified instructors. You think any of those mothers got the message? No—so the cram school industry is booming, and the cost keeps going up. We had a six-day TV special about students in different countries preparing for university entrance exams. Half a dozen advanced countries were featured, a different one each day. It turned out that none of those countries had private cram schools, and high school seniors slept an average of seven or eight hours a night. They interviewed a doctor who said the human body is programmed for seven to eight hours of sleep a night, and if you come up short you have to make it up the next night. Well, that didn't convince our moms either. The cram schools just kept increasing. The only way to get rid of those schools is to shut them down. But in a democracy that's not going to happen." Chaehyŏng sighed deeply, his shoulders slumping.

Yanling gave him a sympathetic look. "I feel the same."

"But why all the cram schools *here*?" said Chaehyŏng.

"Don't you see? Mothers' madness creates endless competition. Like Chinese moms say, the competition starts from baby's first step."

"In a way," said Chaehyŏng solemnly, "I am sorry my mother did not get to see me."

"I can understand. A meal together would have been nice," Yanling said glumly. "You wouldn't be her son if you didn't feel that way."

"When I leave here it will be sweet and sour," said Chaehyŏng, stretching.

"So what's sweet and what's sour?"

"So sweet saying goodbye to your tiny room and your itsy-bitsy bed and hard floor; so sour I will not be with you." He made a face.

"Yes, I was just thinking how nice a full-size bed would be." Her sensuous gaze coiled itself about him.

"That would be paradise!" He pulled her magnet-close, and her delicate fragrance coursed through his nostrils and deep into his lungs. Waves of heat charged his blood, rushing over and through him. Trembling, she clung to him. It was now his body that spoke to hers, and its language was potent.

Their lips came together. Hers, firm yet tender, had a narcotic scent. He pulled at her pants.

"No... not now." But her voice was faltering.

"Why not—we can do it now, and then again later." Inflamed with desire, he inched her tight-fitting pants down over the curve of her buttocks. Whimpering, she removed his pants and they collapsed onto the bed, a naked, heated tangle, two pliant bodies supple with youth. He regarded the gentle outline of her face, the deep eyes, her vernal bosom full to bursting. Her pinched waist left the mounds of her buttocks all the more voluptuous. The torrent of his desire carried him atop her and he felt the gates of heaven come open. Their two bodies coiled like a pair of serpents, came apart, and coiled again and again, a heaven-sent vessel navigating a cosmos of ecstasy, united body and spirit in pure white flame.

And then they were still as ash, the ticking of Yanling's Big Ben alarm clock registering the depth of the silence.

"You're getting heavy," she said with an effort. "Come next to me."

He slid down beside her. Their bodies glinted with perspiration.

"Oh, I love this." Caressing his naked body, she pulled the sheet over them. Then, hugging her still silent partner, she said, "I want to live with you. I'll never go back to the dorm."

He noticed a new, voluptuous scent coming from her. "Same with me, but this bed will not work," he said, eyes still shut. "Not for sleeping anyway." A conclusion he'd reached after the elbows of his long arms kept banging against the shower stall.

"I know. We can't very well sleep on top of each other," she giggled.

He cupped her breasts and murmured, "And we cannot take turns sleeping on the floor, either."

"For a double bed we'd need a room half a size bigger. But the rent would be so steep. And I can't ask my dad to pay for a bigger room just so you and I can live together. So we'll have to be patient for the time being," she said, drawing a succession of imaginary hearts on his chest.

"I am sorry not to be of much help," said Chaehyŏng, pulling her close.

"Don't feel burdened. I just want to be with you day and night. But we'll see each other during the day. And school is so close." With a bright smile she rose.

The moment he'd first entered Yanling's officetel room he'd felt like staying forever. A perpetual wellspring for his lust, she had already captivated him, and he couldn't bear being separated. But the room was too small. In Beijing with its sky-high rent, an officetel for a single person barely accommodated that person. Most of the floor space was occupied by a twin bed. The remainder was filled with an impressive spectrum of the necessaries of independent living—a desk big enough for one opened book but not two, a dresser, a counter and sink, a fridge, a shower and toilet, and even a shoe cubby. The space was the epitome of modern practical living and a model for how to extract money from covetous renters.

Chaehyŏng knew these state-of-the-art officetels were found only in Beijing, so of course the rent was exorbitant. Initially, officetel buildings were built for the employees of global businesses, but by now most of the units were occupied by university students. Yanling's father must have been very wealthy, thought Chaehyŏng. He must adore her.

As she combed her long hair back, her ample bosom swung like a pendulum, spawning new waves of desire. He kept his ardor at bay by considering what had surprised him the most about China—the acceptance of premarital cohabitation. It was considered natural for a young couple to try out living together and either advance to marriage or go their separate ways. It was a practical means of boosting the chances of a successful marriage, as well as an antidote to the sexual chaos of early adulthood. Most young people might try living together once or twice, but for some women it could be as many as half a dozen times. Feminine virtue wasn't an issue. It had puzzled Chaehyŏng—what had happened to the land of the eminent Master Gong? In contrast, kids back home were more sensitive to traditional standards of behavior, at least on the surface. Not so long ago some had started trying out cohabitation, but always on the sly—because if you ended up marrying a man different from the one you were shacking up with and the news leaked out, the revelation could be grounds for divorce.

China had overtaken France as the country with the highest rate of premarital sex. When had this happened? Chaehyŏng had heard it dated back to Chairman Mao's proclamation of the New China. And it was Mao, after all, who had killed off the legacy of Confucianism, targeting Master Gong as public enemy number one in order to eradicate backward, feudal China and erect the new socialist China in its place. Included in the anti-Confucian rhetoric was Mao's slogan "Women hold up half the sky"—the perfect foundation for women's liberation. Made popular by the fervent support of the female comrades, this quote became Mao's second most famous proclamation.

And now, through shimmers of drowsiness, he flashed back to the first time he'd ever seen her. Escaping the tedium of his business management studies, he had come across a campus exhibit of artifacts from old China. Everywhere in the spacious hall, guided tours were under way. Straggling disinterestedly among the artifacts, he froze at the sight of a woman. Her eyes met his, and suddenly his chest was on fire, he felt dizzy, and his extremities were numb and trembling. Never before had he felt such a shock to his system. She turned back to her tour group, her face flushed and her voice faltering.

It takes two tenths of a second to fall in love, he had read in a study. *You better believe it,* he told himself now.

"Sweet dreams," said Yanling. With a peck on the forehead she tucked the sheet over him.

The silence lengthened. The senior director took occasional sips of coffee. Kim Hyŏn'gon was suffocating. Why didn't the director get on with it? More than once he had to stifle an urge to loosen his tie. The director's silence was like a noose around his neck, the implied threat of discipline hanging heavy in the office. He could imagine what the director was thinking: *Are you aware of the damage to the company? You need to shoulder the blame. We have a mess on our hands. The least you could do is speak up so I don't have to.* These tacit grievances made his head pound, and his neck begged for release from the constricting tie.

What if he was forced to resign? The faces of his wife and two children flickered in his mind's eye. He could almost hear his wife's tearful pleas, her anxious, raspy voice. *Honey, no way. You shouldn't do that. Never willingly quit. Remind them how much you've contributed to the company. And think about the kids.* Kim quivered, trying to contain the moan that was about to escape through his clenched teeth.

The image of his wife sobbing and pleading mirrored his own despair as a forty-five-year-old father of two. Submitting a resignation notice would push him to the brink. He would stand up to the rousting and the pressure. He would accept the censure. No way would he resign. Then again, how could they ask him to resign? They had been doomed from the start, for God's sake—the other side had been too powerful. But this thread of hope to which he clung grew more tenuous as the director remained silent.

"Well, Mr. Kim."

Kim shot to his feet. "Yes, sir." The director looked as high and mighty as the two-star general who reviewed young Kim's first military parade march.

"You know..." Another sip of coffee.

"Yes, sir." The words were out of his mouth before he realized he was repeating himself. He noticed he was clasping his hands together like a penitent.

"I tell you, this damned business …" Another sentence left hanging. The director made a face, wiping his mouth as if he'd eaten something bitter—was it the word *resignation*?

"Yes, sir …." Kim was mad at himself for groveling, but his tongue kept betraying him. He was a puppet in the hands of a ventriloquist wife.

"As if things weren't screwed up enough already," said the director with an effort.

"Yes, sir …." Kim was coming apart at the seams. In his time here he had come up against countless masters of *manmandi* who scanned and examined him, weighing and measuring, but never had he felt so frustrated, so choked up that he wanted to scream. Before, when making a deal, he would counter the challenger's *manmandi* with his own. But not now. The director had a noose around his neck and was tightening it.

"It's a damn fiasco." But instead of elaborating, back to his coffee he went.

"Yes, sir …." But inwardly Kim was crying out, *Quit the coffee taster act and get on with it! Fiasco? Meaning it's worse than asking me to resign? You're firing me instead?* By now he was rubbing his clasped hands together.

"So what I'm saying …." Yet again the director broke off.

Kim was struck with a ludicrous thought—his boss had constipation of the mouth.

"Yes, sir …." He had an impulse to resign on the spot and get it over with. Again his wife came to the rescue. *Honey, you're out of your mind—you can't do that. Please, stay calm. Think about the kids.*

"The au-auditors are coming."

"Sir? The auditors?" If the manager's voice was wavering, then Kim's was shaking. The audit team was from his own company. If you weren't in the spotlight, then no worries. But if the heat was on you, then the auditors were as dangerous as the secret inspectors of Chosŏn, raising the hair of the populace and shaking up the land, or the black-robed, bloody-eyed, blue-faced messenger from Hades. No one emerged unscathed from the audit team, any more than a man was released intact from the royal interrogation yard or the magistrate's chambers.

Now Kim understood the director's reluctance. Before long the team would be flying over the Yellow Sea, bound for Beijing. Heavy indeed would be the shoe that dropped on them, the censure extending even to the director and the president, who oversaw the dozens of branch offices here. Kim had no idea the deal was that important—and now important had turned into critical. His head drooped helplessly.

"We could spend all day talking about competitive markets, capitalism, and all that swell stuff, but to put it bluntly, money makes money and the strong devour the weak. Believe me, I understand exactly what happened. The deal got out of hand, and then it snowballed."

"Sir. If I had ten mouths, I couldn't find the words to justify my actions," said Kim, bobbing his lowered head again and again. "There's no one to blame but myself. Please forgive me." He was genuinely sorry. He was devoted to the company and worked his fingers to the bone trying to spin gold.

"There's nothing I can do to exonerate you, not when they're flying the audit team over."

All Kim could do was swallow. His neck was stiff, his mouth dry.

"I just wish we'd known a few days earlier," the director tutted. "At least then we could have pulled the plug before production went into high gear." Every word was charged with fretfulness and pent-up anger.

"I'm sorry, sir." Another round of head bobbing. The director, poor guy, looked like he'd been hit by a bolt from the blue. Headquarters allowed each branch to succeed on its own, but had to take on responsibility for deals that turned sour. Kim had been chewing on the very same sentiment until it was grist in his belly—if only he'd been quicker to realize the deal was dead in the water.

"I just wish we'd known before the steel was loaded—we're talking *tons* of steel—or at least before the damn freighter left port. What a fucked-up mess! We've got a freighter coming across the West Sea—what do we do with the tonnage? How long do we dock the ship? Who pays the dockage fees? We're screwed, two, three, four times over—no wonder the dirty-diaper brigade's on the way." The dam had burst and out spilled naked frustration and anger.

"I'm so sorry, sir." The scale of the potential capital loss eluded Kim, but he knew the director wasn't exaggerating. So, the auditors were on the way—he'd catch flak for sure. He heaved a sigh. He could almost feel the dark, hairy hand of the messenger from hell clutching his neck, and he made a decision: he would plead to save himself. He would pledge anything to avoid being canned.

"I need your honest answer," said the director. "I see two possible quick fixes. First, can you find a place to dump all that steel inside a month?"

Kim shook his head.

"In that case, can you get the dockage fee waived for a month? That means getting Chŏn and his company involved."

"Well…" The first thing that came to Kim's mind was Chŏn's *guanxi*. He moistened his lips. "I'll do my best, sir."

"I need more than that. I need a definite yes. If you can't give me that—"

"Sir, I'll accept any consequences, but please…" Again he could almost hear his wife speaking through him.

"Do you really mean that?"

"Yes, sir. I understand the extent and gravity of the damage."

"Do you really?"

"Yes, sir."

"Then I want from you a detailed explanation of the circumstances *and* of how you feel about what happened. I'm expecting a truthful report. Do I make myself clear?" The manager rose.

"Yes, sir. Thank you. I'll do that, sir, truthfully." *Truthfully*—now it was the manager he was parroting.

Kim wrote the incident report. During three hours of squirming and fidgeting, he tore up a dozen sheets of innocent A4 paper before he had a first sentence to his liking. He wished he were writing a feasibility study instead, which required a transparent, well-organized business plan. An incident report was lengthier, almost like a work of fiction. You described what happened, how it happened, and how you felt about it. The more paper he destroyed, the more he lamented his rudimentary Korean composition and rued his neglect of pleasure reading.

As he tried to link the sentences together, he was careful to focus on two things. One, he needed to avoid excuses. Two, he had to stress his awareness of the gravity of the incident and his desire to redeem himself. Both objectives resulted in more wasted paper and cold sweat. He looked back to the past and saw, along with the flickering faces of his wife and children, his own youthful face reflecting his dream to be a branch manager someday.

"You can relax now," the director told him the following day, after his report had made it up to the president and back down. He clasped Kim's hands and patted them. "You can go back to Shanghai. The president is pleased with the report; he sees the whole picture now and feels hopeful."

"Thank you, sir," said Kim, choked up. It was like being extended the legendary rope from heaven after being pushed to the brink of a fall.

He went outside and looked up. The sky was less murky today, hazy and leaden as usual, but not as inky as yesterday when he'd arrived from Shanghai. *Honey, I escaped the chopping block. It's going to be all right.*

He checked his watch—there was time for a walk before he had to return to Shanghai. Looking about the streets and noticing yet more majestic buildings that seemed to lose themselves in the sky, he realized that Beijing, like Shanghai, was different from a year ago—the aspiration for skyscrapers had reached the manic stage now.

But Beijing was different in another way as well—where had all the bicycles gone? For Kim, the current of wheels flowing through the vastness of Tiananmen Square was the most memorable image here. Not so many years ago the same beautiful scene could be had in all the cities of China. But a decade of hyper-development had sounded the death knell for bicycles and ushered in the automobile craze. Kim spotted only a few bicyclers now, and they'd been banished to the sidewalks, where they looked wretched and intimidated.

"*Ren tai duo!*" said a man crossing the street. He cleared his throat and spat.

The next morning Kim awoke feeling pain up and down his back; he could barely open his eyes. He suspected it was the flu but mentioned nothing to his wife. Meeting Chŏn was the only thing on his mind. He made the call from his office.

"Yes, how did it go?" was the first thing Chŏn asked.

"I have to see you—it's urgent," said Kim, pounding out a tattoo on his sore back.

"So," said Kim when they met. "Here's the problem: our audit team is going to come down on us hard, and I need a month's worth of dockage fees to disappear." He sighed. "Would it be possible for you to talk with your *guanxi*? Maybe a 100 percent waiver is asking too much, but just half? We're all in this together, remember?" A jittery Kim tried to read his counterpart's reaction.

"Just a month, you said?" Chŏn raised an index finger to confirm.

"Yes. My boss thinks a month will do it."

"What if it turns out you need more than a month?" asked Chŏn with his incisive gaze. "Does he think you can unload it in a month?"

"He thinks it's possible"—Kim made a spreading motion with his hands—"but our top man in Beijing needs to get the word out to all the branch offices."

"You've got a hundred thousand tons; find fifty buyers, that's two thousand per. Well, it's feasible. And you say your president's on board?"

"Yes, according to the boss. He doesn't think it's the end of the world, but he wants it wrapped up fast."

"You're lucky to have a president like that," Chŏn said as he lit a cigarette. "He's been here twenty years and he knows the ins and outs. So if all goes well, you won't be on the hot seat, right?"

"I hope not."

"Let's hope it's more than just hope."

"I think I'll be safe." Kim had yet to convince himself of this, but phrasing his answer thus would encourage Chŏn.

"All right, then, I'll approach Shang. It's up his alley, so it shouldn't be too difficult."

"Thank you, sir." Kim felt a surge of emotion. When a business deal went sour, people usually weaseled out. But not Chŏn.

"Not at all. We're all in the same boat."

"I hope you'll excuse me—I'm a bit under the weather," said Kim with a sheepish smile.

"I thought so. I'm not surprised. The pressures on a nine-to-fiver are bad enough, and when you add rogue business deals, it can be the death of you. Me, I'd love to kiss office work goodbye. Here we are in a world market, China the ex–world factory, and get-rich-quick opportunities sometimes come your way, but you don't have the capital to make them work. Doesn't it drive you crazy?"

"Yes, it makes a man drool, but it's only pie in the sky." Kim smiled bitterly as he hoisted himself to his feet.

That same day Chŏn visited Shang, who gave his usual noncommittal response to requests for favors that involved money. Chŏn moped, considered his options, and decided to check in with Shang's wife. This was the perfect time to cash in on the offer she'd made after her brother's surgery—to look her up if he was in a fix.

And so it was that Shang decided to waive 30 percent of the dockage fee. Chŏn successfully pleaded with his boss to pay another 20 percent.

"Mr. Chŏn, I owe you so much," said Kim when he visited a week later. His voice trembled and his eyes were bloodshot. "Thank you. And I wanted to say goodbye."

"Goodbye?" Chŏn's mouth opened in surprise, his cigarette dropping to the floor.

"Yes. I'm being transferred to Xian."

"That's out in the middle of nowhere. Sounds like exile."

"I'll survive. We're on the Western China Development bandwagon, and I'm one of the pioneers."

"Coming from your company, that's bullshit," snapped Chŏn. "From urban gentility in Shanghai to provincial mediocrity in Xian. It's too much!"

"Maybe not. Beijing is putting as much money into the western region as they did for the east. Maybe we'll have more opportunities now. And an opportunity for the company is an opportunity for me. I don't want to be in sales forever. Maybe my misfortune will turn into fortune. What do you think?" Kim eased into a smile.

"You're serious?"

Still smiling, Kim nodded.

"All right, why not?" said Chŏn. "Life's a gamble, that's my philosophy. Once you make branch manager, let me know, and I'll go see you there."

6. Defeat Is Not an Option

"Hey, Ito—any progress?" Hunched over his desk, the *oyabong* looked up and fixed Ito with a mean scowl. Rage simmered behind that scowl.

"I'm still waiting, sir." Ito tried to fight off the chilling gaze.

"You're waiting? No, you're sounding like a broken record, that's what," said the man, his bushy eyebrows twitching.

"I'm sorry, sir. I'm doing my best…." Ito brought his knees together and tried again to brace up.

"Sorry? Doing your best? You've got a full menu of excuses, don't you."

"Not at all, sir. It's just that—"

"It's just that you like to take your sweet time—is that it? Or perhaps you're incapable?" The *oyabong* tapped the desk once with his middle finger.

Ito felt a stabbing sensation, and in spite of himself he gasped. "No—no, sir. What I'm trying to…" But he could only rub his hands together, distracted by the implication that he was lazy.

"Or you're getting tired of your job. You're complacent, is that it?"

Ito imagined the man brandishing a sword, working him toward the edge of a cliff. "No, sir." There was an acid taste in his throat. He wanted to cry out. But the *oyabong* was the opposite: as he became angrier, his voice grew more subdued, and his words frostier and more terrifying.

"I'm sorry, sir. If you could give me just a few more days…" Ito had an urge to relieve himself; he crossed his legs at the ankles and squeezed.

"How many days is 'a few more'?"

"Two to three days, that's all, sir."

"Do you understand how much a single day costs us? We breach our contract, and that costs money. What's worse, we lose credibility with our customers."

"I'm very sorry, sir."

"Headquarters wants answers—we can't just sit on our butts. The merchant ships and freighters are stacked up waiting for clearance, and the shipping lanes are jammed. It's like our company's arteries are clogged. We're slitting our own throat. Remember, you've only got one neck, and me too." This time it was his three middle fingers tapping his desk three times.

"Yes, sir. I'll keep that in mind and take care of the matter." Bowing at a ninety-degree angle, Ito withdrew.

And now he was the one seething in anger. He was in charge of customs clearance for the company, but what had happened was not his fault. A general trading company had a triple mission: carving out new markets, arranging for the goods to supply those markets, and securing shipping and distribution. No glitches with shipping and distribution had occurred until recently, when customs clearance had come to a standstill. Which was peculiar, considering he'd oiled the various officials at every stage with the customary gift-giving. It was thanks to his attentiveness that business had been running like a conveyer belt.

Something had gone wrong. There had to be a snag—but where? Freight clearance, both incoming and outgoing, had frozen, and Ito needed to find the cause. He mobilized his frontline Chinese subordinates, but all he got were reports such as:

"My counterpart has no clue."

"My guy thinks something's fishy."

"They think the documents are just getting shuffled around at the upper levels."

"They suggested we need to work with the higher-ups."

"They asked me whether we rubbed the right man the wrong way."

"These answers are useless," barked Ito, more cantankerous as the delay wore on. "I need solid information."

But what could his Chinese underlings do, dealing as they did only with lower-level government officials, at best section or subsection chiefs? They weren't privy to decisions made above—that was how organizations here worked, and if you wanted to survive, you didn't stick your neck out. And then there was the Chinese Communist tradition of aligning command and discipline. All of this contributed to a lack of ready communication up and down the various rungs of the ladder and among the ladders themselves.

Ito didn't believe everything he was hearing from his subordinates. Accustomed to a socialist work ethic, they were quick to seek out the safe way, tried to minimize complications, and had a stunted sense of personal responsibility. So why would they roll up their sleeves to find out what Ito wanted now? Their proclivity for time-killing had him cornered, and he wanted to slap them around. *Didn't these idiots learn anything besides the language when they studied in Japan?* The answer was no—instead they stuck proudly to the disposition and routines that Ito found so distasteful here.

"Section Chief Wu," said Ito, approaching the man's desk.

"Yes, sir." Wu looked up. A Japanese subordinate would have jumped to his feet if he noticed his boss was out of sorts. But Wu was Chinese, and the Chinese rarely acted on the expressions they read.

"What have you been doing!" Glowering, Ito made a stabbing gesture at him.

"Excuse me?" asked Wu innocently.

"Stop the charade—you're planted on your duff and you've given me nothing."

"Pardon me, sir? I've reported all my findings to you. Are they nothing?" Woo looked dumbfounded.

"You haven't reported shit, and all you can say is 'Pardon me'? What a joke!" Ito erupted, kicking the leg of Wu's desk. That brought four of the other men jumping to their feet. But not Wu, who glared at Ito with an ashen face, hatred shooting from his eyes.

"You've embarrassed me in front of all my coworkers. I'm done here. Please prepare my severance pay." Lips trembling, he sprang up and walked out the door.

"What the … ?" Ito was baffled. Should he follow after him, or let him go? Then he realized his mistake. To the Chinese, *mianzi*, or face, was second in importance only to money, and in front of Wu's subordinates, Ito had obliterated his face. Face, reputation, and dignity were cardinal virtues of Confucianism. Master Gong's emphasis on the way a man carried himself still held a tenacious grip on the Chinese psyche—in spite of Chairman Mao's "Down with Confucius" campaign during the decade-long Cultural Revolution.

Ito sucked on his cigarette, trying to calm himself. He had tried to quit, but no luck, precisely because of aggravations such as this one. According to the doctors, smoking to ease stress could double the harm to an already stressed body. To Ito, this prescription of the noble doctors' was stupid—what the hell did they know about stressed businessmen? He took several long draws, each an *up yours!* to the doctors.

Another wave of disgust swept over him. Nothing about this country suited him, except the plentiful supply of cheap women. Correction: the variety of teacups was a drawing point, but there was always the question of quality. The cups were genuine, all right, but the paint and glazing were an issue. At least one researcher from the West had warned of the potential harm to tea drinkers from chemicals seeping out of the cups in reaction to boiling water. This was regrettable, but he would not indulge his tea-sipping propensities if carcinogens were involved.

Well, not much good would come from harassing his underlings about their concern for *mianzi*, but why the hell did they have to connect face-saving with work? Back home, it was standard practice for mid-level managers to push their subordinates around. You had to set an appropriate tone for the office and maintain momentum for the task at hand. Yet another oddity of the work environment here.

Overseeing his Chinese charges was quite a feat. Sure, there were the cultural differences, but the real problem was that he and his Japanese colleagues, unlike the super-competitive Koreans, had never mastered Chinese. Regardless of their position in the business hierarchy, the Koreans took an all-or-nothing approach to studying Chinese —they were like soldiers going through shooting drills before being shipped off to the front line. It wasn't just that their companies pushed the language lessons and paid for them; the employees themselves regarded fluency in Chinese as a trophy—they were like infantrymen coveting machine guns. Ito had never understood the Korean mentality. He appreciated the necessity of mastering English, French, or German—but Chinese? *If we're expanding our markets in Southeast Asia—to Indonesia, Malaysia, Vietnam, Cambodia—do we have to learn the languages of every last one of those countries? Fuck that! Not with our superior products prompting them to fall all over themselves learning Japanese.* His company had never rewarded the employees for studying Chinese, and what good would it have done, with the employees looking down their noses at the people here to begin with? They could hire an interpreter or two—thanks to Deng Xiaoping's having sent students to study in the US and Japan, plenty of Chinese were fluent in Japanese. Those same students now worked for foreign companies. A job with a Japanese or Western company offered a higher salary; it was a badge of honor, good *mianzi*.

Ito lit another cigarette. What to do with Wu? He was a senior employee with solid *guanxi*. Sacking him would be an immediate problem—he wanted to visit Customs tomorrow and would need an interpreter if he was meeting with any official at the level of director or above. No one but Wu would dare accompany him, for Chinese public officials dealt only with those at their own rank. *Son of a bitch Wu, leaving me stuck, but damned if I'll go after him. Japanese don't do that— we have our* mianzi *too.* It was too bad he himself had such a quick temper—and being dressed down by his *oyabong* was no excuse. He realized this was a problem with Japanese in general. To Japan and the rest of the world, *nippondo* and *seppuku* were admirable displays of loyalty and determination, but to the Chinese they added up to rashness.

What a fucked-up country. Let me out of here! Ito sighed deeply, longing for the times he'd spent in the US and Europe.

No second chances for insubordination. A principle he'd learned in officer training for the Self-Defense Corps. It had been followed by two managerial golden rules. The first: *Once betrayed, twice betrayed.* And number two: *Forgive the remorseful, but eliminate the cheats and the liars.*

Wu had been insubordinate, no question about it. *Fucking moron! You take care of your* mianzi *just fine, but you're working for a Japanese company, remember? You're no good—you tried to shit all over me, your boss, and when I called you on it, you stomped out and quit. You scum! I can see why you did it—you'll have no problem finding another job now that your economy's up and running. In your fat head you're thinking only of yourself.*

Ever since China had ascended to the G2 throne, 95 percent of the Fortune 500 companies had been hunting the Chinese market for prey. To climb out of the domestic recession, Japanese companies, large and mid-sized, were feverishly trying to expand in China. Needless to say, Chinese with a good command of Japanese were a sought-after commodity. And anyone who worked at a foreign company expected a premium salary. Ito could understand Wu's acting up. But that didn't lessen his vexation that China had usurped Japan's status as the number two world economy, and he was furious with the side effects he had just witnessed. Again his anger flared. *Fine. You son of a bitch. I'll never forget your betrayal!*

Back to business. Ito called Toyotomi. "Hey, I have an urgent matter to discuss—can we meet?" He was ready to leave, regardless of the answer.

"What's up? You sound like you're having a panic attack. 'Urgent' doesn't sound like good news…. All right, I'll be here." Toyotomi was always quick on the uptake.

"Well," said Toyotomi in his office after he had heard Ito out. "You definitely have 'urgent' written all over you. Damned if I can unravel it."

"Yeah, I've got a mystery to solve," said Ito, frowning. "And I'm flying blind, especially now that damn Wu quit. I'm thinking I need to hire one of your guys—it's the only way to get up to director level."

"That shouldn't be difficult. But what about me—how can I help? How about you and I barge into their office?"

"Sure—and get sent right back out the door," said Ito, shaking his head. "Remember our company's make-or-break rule?"

"Call first!" said Toyotomi like a machine.

"Right. And arrange to meet their man at a neutral place."

Toyotomi nodded. "Good thinking—he won't release in-house info in house." But then his face clouded over. "But meeting him's no guarantee."

"So, we need a punch."

"A punch?"

"Yes, I have an idea."

"Which is?"

"A magic bullet."

"Great, that explains everything! So when do we start punching?"

"Now. I need to get off my butt."

"Wow, running for dear life. Looks like a tsunami is on the way."

"Your words, not mine. But yes, that's how I feel. Like my time in Shanghai is up if I flunk this deal. And then, of course, I would no longer have the pleasure of your company."

"That's life for us nine-to-fivers—we're like dayflies. All right, I'll contact him."

"Please. And then call me—I'm going back to the office." And Ito scurried out.

The best way to treat your guest here was at an exquisite restaurant serving sumptuous food and the finest spirits. Public officials' love of a free meal was second only to the clergy's. This was especially true in China, with all the emphasis on dignity and the big face. The Party officials in this single-party, dictatorial state loved to exercise their power, and you couldn't hope to benefit from their largesse if you didn't treat them in the fine manner to which they were accustomed. Knowing this, Ito arranged a dinner, starting with shark fin soup, at a glitzy restaurant.

"This Wuliang-ye is one hundred percent pure and genuine. You have my guarantee—our chairman personally ordered it from the distillery. It's for our eminent guests. Please relax and enjoy." Smooth as silk, Toyotomi displayed the bottle as if to the emperor. His Chinese sales department chief was quick to interpret for the Chinese customs director.

"Is that so?" said the director self-importantly as he examined the bottle. "Do you mean to tell me your boss knows the owner of the distillery?"

"Oh yes," said Toyotomi. "They're very close. They invite each other on trips. They're golf buddies—I even think they have the same handicap—they're like brothers." As the old Chinese proverb went, lies didn't cost money.

"They play *golf* together?" Having established the relationship, the director smiled in satisfaction as he accepted the bottle from Toyotomi.

"We thank you, sir, for making time for us in your busy schedule. Well, to everyone here, *kanpei*." Toyotomi lifted his shot glass.

"And thank *you* for this rare treat, a bottle of genuine Wuliang-ye. *Ganbei!*"

Toyotomi and Ito gulped their shots Chinese-style and exchanged glances of assurance—well begun is half done, to judge from the director's pleased expression.

"How is your golf game, sir?"

"Well, it could be better. I don't seem to see much progress." Spoken with the helplessness of one who was hooked on golf. The director scratched his head in regret. His public-official haughtiness had dissipated.

"To me golf is like playing go. And I imagine you handle yourself well at the go table too. Director, are you aware that we make excellent golf clubs?" Toyotomi sent the director a meaningful look.

"Of course. But with my paycheck, I'm lucky if I can buy a new putter."

"That is unfortunate—we can't have a golf aficionado lacking the proper equipment. Let me think…" And then Toyotomi made his move. "What if I had a set delivered to you?"

"Oh, no, I couldn't do that." The director waved off the offer, his surprise bringing him out of his seat.

"Please," said Toyotomi, "allow me to be of service." He sealed the offer by bowing once, twice, and then a third time.

Toyotomi and then Ito offered the director a drink, exchanging glances all the while.

Bam! How's that for a magic bullet, went the first glance from Ito.

Not bad. He's softer than I thought. Already sinking his teeth in, Toyotomi glanced back.

Coveted Chinese spirits packed a potent punch. Thanks to the generous offerings of Toyotomi and Ito, in no time the director's eyes were weepy, his speech slurred.

"It's such a pleasure to be able to meet with you, sir," ventured Toyotomi, offering the director a Zhonghua cigarette from Yuxi—where the finest tobacco in the land was grown—and not a Mairudo Sebun, which were too mild for Chinese smokers. "Actually there's this matter…"

"Oh?" The director straightened, trying to salvage the majesty of his official position. "What seems to be the problem?"

"Well, sir. It's nothing really serious. But you know, Mr. Ito's company has been experiencing a holdup with a shipment, and we're wondering if there's a problem." Toyotomi kept bowing, ever the humble supplicant.

"Holdup?" The director seemed surprised. He blew a stream of smoke. "Since when, may I ask?"

Ito was quick to answer. "It's been about a month, sir."

"And were you notified of any problems with your paperwork?"

"No, sir. Nothing."

"Nothing?" The director cocked his head and pointed up with his thumb. "Did you happen to rub someone the wrong way? Or maybe give one of the officials the wrong impression? Anything like that?"

"We've searched for any possible answer but don't have a clue. Which is why we're so frustrated," pleaded Ito, attempting to be as polite and deferential as a Japanese man could be.

"Do you know the saying 'The geese only come when the north wind blows, and the ripples only happen when a stone is thrown'?" The director gazed at Ito.

"Yes, sir," he fibbed, recalling a similar Japanese saying.

"That should give you the answer," said the director, picking up his shot glass with an air of finality.

"Yes?" said Ito in confusion.

Toyotomi came to the rescue. "Ah, yes, sir. Right you are. I'm afraid we didn't catch on right away. And so we thought to inquire of you, Director—"

"Listen," interrupted the director. "As you are aware, our port is constantly flooded with traffic. The quicker we clear cargo, the better for us. You're talking of a month-long delay. That's impossible, unless a critical mistake's been made. The fact that I'm in the dark means someone above me made a decision. Let's make it simple," he said. "What exactly do you need?"

"As we mentioned, sir, all we want is to find the source of the matter. We can take it from there," Ito assured him.

"All right, I can do that. Give me a couple of days."

"Thank you, sir," said Toyotomi. "And please keep a lookout for your new golf clubs—they should be at your front door by tomorrow morning."

The director merely played with his glass.

Chŏn was having dim sum with Shang. There were so many choices when you dined out here—and such a price range, from one to a couple hundred *yuan*. It was the same at dim sum restaurants, with their host of steamer baskets and plates. Expensive restaurants were often as crowded as small eateries—there were countless mouths to feed in this mega-population, and also a public mistrust of food quality, the rampant bogus food items prompting well-to-do diners to flock to pricy restaurants in the belief that, as with consumption in general, you bought high when you weren't sure about the quality.

"The clinic is rolling in dough," reported Chŏn as he savored a dumpling. "The demand is insane, and Sŏ is being run ragged."

"All thanks to you, Mr. Chŏn. We are fortunate to have the good doctor!" A smile spread across Shang's fleshy face.

"But your cash flow makes me feel like a beggar. Look at all the clients, and the profit! I bet the profit margin for an operation is 99 percent. But for us salesmen roaming the streets like mangy dogs, looking for a buyer? Less than 10 percent, I would say." Chŏn released a sigh.

"Well, foolish me, I thought I was talking with a businessman, but you don't sound very clever with numbers," Shang said bluntly as he popped another morsel into his mouth.

"Excuse me?"

"Your calculations are off. What about the rent, the medical staff, and all the rest?"

"Oh, right," said Chŏn, slapping his forehead and nodding. "I get indigestion when I think about how well Dr. Sŏ is doing—I guess those expenses slipped my mind."

"Actually I'm as envious as you are. Speaking of Dr. Sŏ, we don't want him living like a monk." Shang frowned.

"I beg your pardon?" The dumpling pincered by Chŏn was frozen in midair.

"You know what I mean. Doesn't he go in for this?" said Shang, displaying a pinkie.

For Chŏn the little finger was as obvious a symbol for a woman as flour was for bread. "Of course he does—he's no saint, and as far as I know he's not sterile either. He's a healthy buck of a man."

"Just my point. He needs a duck bath at least once a week. That will keep him charged up for work and he won't get homesick."

"Duck baths are expensive, you know."

"Of course I know. And the good doctor deserves that much."

"But what if he wants to keep his nose clean?" Chŏn murmured.

"The more duck baths he sticks his nose—and his male equipment—into, the better. Make him feel right at home here."

"Still, shouldn't there be a limit … ?"

"You don't have them in Korea?"

"Not the hard-core places you are talking about."

"Poor saps! Then what do you do for skirt-chasing? And how's a girl supposed to make money? That's a weird country you're from."

"Can't help it. Our government clamped down on the sex industry—you couldn't run a duck bath even if you tried to hide it. It just wouldn't work."

"You mean your government actually enforces prostitution laws? Unbelievable. You make fun of us because we're a dictatorship and you're a democracy. But to me that policy is just plain dictatorial. Here we have women's bodies on sale and you pay for the ones you like—now that's democratic. What do you say about that?" said Shang, deliberately setting down his chopsticks.

"You're right, sir. That's why I love China. It's why I've spent a decade here, keeping my salary in circulation."

"Anyway, take care of that poor doctor. Make sure he gets his bath!"

"Your wish is my command." Chŏn performed a deep bow.

But he found Shang's adamant request distasteful. The mandarin duck bath had arrived from Taiwan, along with an infusion of Taiwanese capital, around the time Deng had opened the country's economic gates. The alleys of Shanghai were strewn with business cards featuring girls in erotic and obscene poses. The nude girls, eye-catching in their voluptuous beauty and provocative poses, were one thing, but the descriptions beneath the contact information—each touting the girl as the most sensual, the most erotic, the raciest—embarrassed him. The words were unspeakable. The girls would perform any act to please the client so that he could justify the whopping charges. Lured by the array of services, some men consumed a month's salary in one night. Others divorced wives who proved in comparison to be duds in bed. Chŏn had heard that about half of all Chinese girls capable of drawing a man's eye became *ernai,* mistresses of powerful officials, or ended up in the sex trade. The term *mandarin duck bath* was supposed to have originated in the image of a curvaceous woman lathered in bath foam washing her client.

"By the way, sir, I have a question." Chŏn spoke in an undertone as he picked out a steamy tidbit from a newly delivered plate.

Shang looked up with an inquisitive gaze.

"It's about Diaoyu—those islands are Chinese, right?"

"What kind of a question is that!" Shang scowled, banging the table for emphasis.

Chŏn looked about but no one was paying attention. "I'm sorry. I know it's a sensitive topic. The runts are getting out of hand with their claims, and it doesn't seem they'll back down from their bullshit nationalization of the islands. It has me worried—that's why." Chŏn looked concerned on the outside, but inwardly he was gleeful at the brilliant way he'd irked Shang. It was a typical reaction from Party members who liked to show others who the boss was. Chŏn appreciated the irony. After *ren tai duo*, the most common expression he heard here was *tudi tai da*, "the land is too big." Everybody was ready, willing, and able to answer "Too big" to questions such as "Why isn't the census accurate?" or "How come that's not a real police station?" or "Why can't they do anything about fake food?" "Too big" was too often simply an excuse.

For all their problems with their "too big" land, the Chinese coveted land almost as much as they coveted money. There were few issues on which the Chinese were more united; Chŏn could almost picture the Party and citizenry high-fiving each other and saying, "We're in this together." Shang's explosion testified to the craving for land.

"What's there to question? It's as clear as daylight—those islands are a rock-solid gift from heaven. Not a shadow of a doubt." Shang's voice was oratorical, his gestures pretentious. In this role he reminded Chŏn of a country bumpkin, so earnest and so ready to fly off the handle. "Clear as daylight" was presumably insufficient, requiring Shang to buttress it with "gift from heaven." Here, *heaven* meant the absolute. The emperor was "the son of heaven," and the land was "all under heaven." Pledges of loyalty, blood oaths, and protestations of love—all were made under the aegis of heaven.

"Now tell me what *you* think, my *lao pengyou*." So saying, Shang leveled two fingers, rifle-like, at Chŏn's chest. A chill swept over Chŏn. If he blundered, Shang's mortal *qi* would spear him. He was all too aware that a man here would sever a long-standing relationship in one stroke if his counterpart turned disloyal.

"Of course there's no doubt," said Chŏn solemnly, fixing his gaze on Shang. "Just like Tokto is heaven's gift to Korea, Diaoyu is heaven's gift to China."

"Tokto and Diaoyu, our two nations' gifts from heaven. That's what I like to hear! You're a straight shooter. I think I'm getting to like you." Shang finished his cup of tea and heaved a sigh of satisfaction. "Since we're on the subject, what about Taiwan?"

Chŏn smirked inwardly. The man was so puerile! But then he remembered it was he himself who'd started this piddling game.

"It's a Chinese province, of course. Taiwanese independence is a political show—everybody knows that."

"You are sure?"

"Sure I'm sure."

"Then how about Tibet?"

"Belongs to China. Tibetans should be thankful for all the backbreaking work you put into getting Tibet up to standard—they've reaped a lot of benefits."

The answers rolled off Chŏn's tongue. Only they weren't his answers; they were propaganda from the Chinese government.

"Do you really mean that?"

"Yes, I do."

"And Xinjiang?"

"Xinjiang Uigur—it's part of China. Once they get a taste of modernization, they'll assimilate. It's only a matter of time."

"Great. Sounds like you have your head screwed on right." With a satisfied look, Shang took his glass of beer and tapped it against Chŏn's.

Trusting someone can be dangerous, Chŏn thought. How far could it go, each man pretending to go along with the other man's pretending?

"One thing I want to be clear about. Considering their past with us, what's your feeling on how the Japs are acting toward our two countries?" Shang, like most Chinese, was relentless on this subject.

"It makes me wish them an early death. They killed thirty-five million of your people, and four million of ours, and we're still waiting for a genuine apology. They string along all their former prime ministers and go to that shrine and worship their bloody murderers as patriots. And then there's the malarkey about no proof the comfort women were forced into slavery—and some of those women are still alive! And they still want us to believe the Nanjing Massacre was fabricated—as if the Massacre Memorial Hall isn't evidence enough. And now add Diaoyu, and our Tokto. It makes me boil." Chŏn tsk-tsked, then wiped his lips in distaste.

"Hey, I know! We'll fix their obnoxious behavior once and for all!" In his excitement Shang almost shot to his feet. "What a terrific idea!"

"Terrific? How?" Chŏn was half surprised, half dubious.

"Yes. I've got it!"

"I'm all ears."

"All right, listen. As you know, I have quite a few friends in the PSB. I'll get them riled up and unload them on the Japs. Everybody knows the karaoke bars where all the Jap tourists flash their money and have orgies."

"That's right."

"I'll get the police to raid them—a crackdown on prostitution. How about that?"

"You're talking hundreds of men—can the police handle that many?"

"Why not? We round them up and bring them all in."

"Wow. Think of the shock waves."

"That's the idea. The larger the scale, the better the effect."

"And the timing couldn't be better. Once the press get their hands on it, the news will be all over the world." Chŏn could visualize the scene.

"You are a *laoshang*, all right—you're knowledgeable, you're quick on your feet, and your judgment is sound." Shang nodded in confirmation and gave Chŏn a thumbs-up. *Laoshang* designated a Korean trader who was considered trustworthy.

A few days later, a headline in the evening newspaper brought Chŏn to his feet, gasping in shock: "Three Hundred Japanese in Custody for Patronizing Prostitutes." Thoughts hit him like lightning bolts: Shang's stunningly swift action. An orgy involving three hundred men. Headline news. What would the ripple effect of such a scandal be? His heart pounded, trembled, jumped—as it had when he'd first been infatuated with a woman, when a big lie he'd launched struck a fatal blow to a competitor, when he'd clutched the signed contract to his first multimillion-*wŏn* consultation. The characters of the headline were the size of melons. The photo of the police raid was palm-sized.

When was the last time they ran a full front-page article? Chairman Mao's death? No, it was when Deng Xiaoping died. How could a sex party involving three hundred Japs and three hundred Chinese prostitutes rate equal coverage with the passing of the great hero who had rescued four hundred million comrades from poverty?

Only then did it come to Chŏn. It was the Diaoyu dispute—they were targeting the islands.

Giddy, Chŏn flung open the door of his office and pranced out.

"Sir?" said one of his staff. "We have a meeting, you know."

"Yes, I know. I'll be right back."

Chŏn hustled out to the street and bought a copy of every newspaper he could find. The orgy had made the front page of each. Presumably it was the same story written from various angles. So why buy all of them? Because each newspaper headline brought a new surge of adrenaline in response to this knockout blow to the Japs, who were always snatching business from him. He was thrilled and yet fearful of Shang, who, not content with holding up the Japanese freight shipment, had undertaken this public retaliation. The Chinese were so tenacious. Once victimized, they exacted full revenge.

"What a day," said the news vendor, stretching his arms wide in joy. "They're selling like *bing* cakes."

Nearby, several men, newspapers in hand, were holding an impromptu debate.

"It's unthinkable!"

"Those Japs are animals—how dare they, here in front of our eyes!"

"What do you do with the sons of bitches?"

"I say convict them and let them rot in jail."

"Jail? So the taxes on our hard-earned money go to feed those bastards?"

"Then what?"

"Chop their heads off. That's what we do with drug dealers. They humiliated us. They shamed our nation. That's an unforgivable crime, a betrayal."

"Chopping three hundred heads is one thing. But three hundred Japanese heads? Think of the uproar."

"Then how about a cross-country tour? Parade them around like we did during the Cultural Revolution. Make them wear dunce caps with big characters, 'Lechers With No Respect.' That'll teach 'em a lesson. What do you think?"

"It's not enough. We need to cut their balls off—like Emperor Zhu did," broke in Chŏn, referring to the Ming dynasty founder. He turned back toward his office.

"That's a great idea!"

"Yeah—no have, no can do. That's the best punishment for sure."

"*Wei*, what's the rush?" one of the men called after Chŏn, his hand beckoning him. Little did he know that this man who spoke fluent Chinese was a *waiguoren*.

Scanning the newspapers, Chŏn gloated. *See what happens when you bite people? They bite you right back. Act like hyenas, and they turn into hyenas too.*

The stories were similar in content but different in presentation and style, offering Chŏn's voracious palate a banquet of tastes. He tried to grasp the ultimate goal of the news release. The articles were uniformly strident—Japan's behavior was audacious, supercilious, and obnoxious. All of this was leadup to the Japanese provocations toward Diaoyu. What fun to read! And about time someone held them accountable instead of moping in indignation.

Next Chŏn turned to television. The Olympics had brought cable TV to every foot of Chinese terrain, even the mountainous backwaters, and television was more influential than other media. After all, the provincial dailies were only copycats of the Shanghai press, and the cameras captured scenes that were beyond the reach of the newspapers. Justice would be served in showing three hundred men packed in jail cells. Who were these men? *They were no-good Japanese, that's who,* thought Chŏn. *They slaughtered fifty million people throughout Southeast Asia, and have they ever offered a sincere apology?*

And there they were, not so long afterward, canvassing Southeast Asia for markets. Their audacity had worked as long as the nations of Southeast Asia remained underdeveloped. But then a challenger emerged, Korea, and the Japanese stronghold developed cracks. And when the second contender, China, turned up, the quality of their goods improving by the year, the Japanese monopolies crumbled. Japan, unlike other advanced countries, had never been at ease in the vast Chinese market. *If they had stanched the wounds of history as Germany had done…,* Chŏn thought. But they neglected those hurts, so Chinese sentiment toward Japan remained as acute and heated as that of Koreans.

The television coverage was equally satisfying, the footage more provocative than Chŏn had expected. The anchors relayed the critique with controlled expressions. The reports included scenes of Diaoyu and gruesome images from the Nanjing Massacre Memorial Hall.

Finally Chŏn logged onto Weibo, and was met with an inferno of public opinion. Feeding on the flames of two thousand radio and television stations, the blaze engulfing the world's largest netizen audience, some six hundred million people, was incendiary. In any nation, an international land dispute was a sensitive subject, involving both populism and jingoism. What Chŏn now saw in the mass of nameless citizens was anti-Japanese populism amplified into hate-spewing xenophobia, a brutal jungle of bloodthirsty words and blazing rage.

Choking on the savage language and horrific sentiments, Chŏn expelled a gush of air in spite of himself. *You want to make an issue, you got one; if you don't, you don't.*

7. The Blight of Xian

The platform was red, its carpet matched by the curtains draping the towering back wall. The groundbreaking ceremony for the Gold 88 Building in Shanghai was as garish as an outdoor concert. Two lifelike dragons, each coiled in the shape of an eight, guarded the sides of the platform, the *cintāmaṇi* in their mouths shining an even brighter gold against the red background. The harmony was splendid, the double-eight dragons symbolizing the new Gold 88 edifice, and the wish-fulfilling beads in their mouths, the Gold Groups itself. The dragons and the color red reflected traditional Chinese aspirations for success and deliverance from bad luck and evil spirits.

Arrayed in the open area below the platform were two hundred tables, each set with white linen and a triangular placard identifying the ten guests. As the sun set, the seats slowly began to fill, the guests ushered in for the gala that would follow the ceremony.

Toyotomi Araki and Ito Hideo presented their invitations and were guided to a table on the periphery.

"Damn," Ito grumbled, "we're out on the margins."

"Easy," whispered Toyotomi. "We're just extras here, remember?"

Ito nodded as they sat. "I feel like I went to hell and back just for this tiny perch!" He pulled his chair close to the table.

Toyotomi did likewise. "So much for being the steel supplier for this project," he said with a sardonic expression.

"Is that platform glitzy enough for you?" snorted Ito. "Looks like the wall was papered with hundred-*yuan* notes."

"What do you expect?" said Toyotomi. "It's the Gold Groups debut in Shanghai. You've got to primp. Looks like their Mulan chairwoman knows how to spread money around."

"In any event," said Ito, "we're going to run up against obstacles…."

Toyotomi sent him an inquiring look.

"We need binoculars to see her fair face."

"Relax. She'll have a spotlight on her. You'll get to see her face and then some."

"But why eight o'clock? Who eats dinner that late?"

"Where have you been?" said Toyotomi. "Today's the eighteenth, and the ceremony starts at eight. Don't you get it?"

"Yes, I get it. So why not August 18 instead of September 18?"

"August 18 was the original date, remember? But something got fouled up."

"That's what I figured. But wasn't their Communist Revolution supposed to get rid of superstition? What a waste of effort."

"Yeah, a skin-deep revolution. In their hearts the people haven't changed."

As the tables filled, the platform grew less opulent in the deepening dusk. Suddenly the air reverberated with a high-pitched male voice: "Ladies and gentlemen, distinguished guests, thank you all for taking time from your busy schedules to attend this evening's ceremony. Our Gold Groups chairwoman has just arrived, and we will soon begin."

Ito noted the sound system was good. "Right on time," he said, checking his watch. "Five to eight."

A fanfare sounded and a bank of lights came on, washing over the platform and beyond, illuminating the stately arrival of a white Cadillac stretch limousine flanked by two sedans. The limousine stopped in front of the platform and two men in black suits hopped out of the escort vehicles to open the door for the star of the show. In her white evening dress, with the two bodyguards at her side, she progressed toward the head table, where she gracefully shook hands with each of the guests. She then made her stately way up to the platform, a spotlight following her every step.

She came to the center of the platform. She was a tall woman on whom a low-cut dress was sheer audacity. A red peony, flower of flowers, adorned the left side of her bosom. The picture was complete—the platform with its red bunting, the statuesque woman in her white dress, and the peony vivid as a blood drop on snow.

She eased up to the microphone. "*Nimen hao*. I thank you all for coming. My name is Wang Lingling and I am head of the Gold Groups." She eased back to her position on the platform.

"Wow," murmured Ito. "She's a queen."

"Impressive. And sexy too."

"In a few moments," announced the master of ceremonies, "we will proceed to the ribbon-cutting for the Gold 88 Building. I ask our honored guests to take their places here on the stage."

As their names were called, the nine men from the head table rose one by one and were ushered onto the platform.

"Quite the lineup," crowed Ito. "All heavy hitters—political and financial honchos."

Toyotomi made a shushing gesture at him. "That's a high-powered woman." He shook his head in admiration just as the next announcement came over the speakers.

"At eight minutes, eight seconds past the hour of eight on this day, September 18, we commence the ribbon cutting. On the count of three, our illustrious guests will cut the ribbon."

At the center of the array of luminaries holding the colorful ribbon was CEO Wang, stately and dazzling.

"How's your eyesight?" Toyotomi asked Ito.

"Not bad."

"Can you see her?"

"I sure can."

"What does she look like?"

"Beautiful enough to make a man's pecker come to attention."

"Come on, no potty talk," said Toyotomi. "Just look at her and tell me what you see."

"She's definitely sexy. Not sure that's good for a businesswoman."

"That's not what I mean. Does she look Chinese to you? I can't decide."

"Maybe, maybe not," said Ito. "You think she's too good-looking to be all Chinese?"

"You tell me. Doesn't she have some Western features?"

"What, you think she's a mongrel? Come on, her hair is black."

"And as we all know except you, black is the dominant hair color."

"Oh yeah—genetics! All right, now that you mention it, her eyes are larger, her nose is higher, and I can see she's taller."

"Ladies and gentlemen. The count begins for the Gold 88 Building. One, two, *three!*"

A roar burst from the assembly, and strings of firecrackers popped in all directions, flashes of light embroidering the night sky. The festivities drew a heated crescendo of applause.

"All the bells and whistles," muttered Ito as he clapped mechanically.

"They have to have their firecrackers," Toyotomi responded, eyes fixed on the stage. "Otherwise it's like *manju* without the filling."

"It's ridiculous. They invented gunpowder, but all they used it for was to scare off goblins. Hell, the Westerners and then us, we used it against them. But did they ever make the connection? No, they still go nuts over firecrackers." Fortunately, no one could have heard him over the deafening applause.

"What do you care? If they want to set off firecrackers to ward off evil and bring good luck to their descendants, let them. We have our superstitions too."

The applause died down, but the crackle of firecrackers continued. The politicos and tycoons returned to their table.

"Ladies and gentlemen," came the voice over the speakers. "This ends the groundbreaking ceremony for the Gold 88 Building. Please allow us now to wine and dine you to the accompaniment of sweet music. We are grateful to our honored guests for gracing us with their presence. Thank you again."

As soon as the speakers fell silent, a grand melody commenced from the orchestra, which had finished setting up during the concluding remarks.

"Impressive. It would have been a long night if they had called up everyone who has a pedigree. But they kept it short. Surprise, surprise." Toyotomi pondered. "But that woman is a mystery."

"Yeah, she's different. Get the people here up on a stage and they don't know when to shut up. But she's no motormouth. Do you suppose it's her American education?" Ito had a drink of water.

"After I googled her, I had a hunch she'd look different in person. And I was right—she's definitely half and half."

"Sure, why not? Chinese have been in the US as long as we have. Somebody in her family might have married a white guy."

The dinner menu was Western. Women in black uniforms delivered the plates like revolving machines.

"Aha!" said Toyotomi, pausing in the act of slicing his meat. "I thought she was perfect, but there's a crack in the armor."

"What's wrong?" said Ito, looking up from his plate.

"The Western dinner. Not your typical good service from the Chinese."

"I'm sure she's aware of that. Serving a Chinese meal outdoors takes a lot of preparation. So she opts for Western."

"Makes sense, I guess. In any event, it's good to be able to see her in person."

"You sound like you're onto something?"

"Nothing specific. It just seems she has all the ingredients to build a business empire at light speed."

"See?" Ito teased. "And the main ingredient is her good looks—which, by the way, seem to be working on you."

"Doesn't hurt to be a good-looker. Especially here, where the more power you have, the more women you keep as window dressing."

"It's the same in the US, France, even Africa," said Ito. "It's a global phenomenon."

"Good looks, deep pockets…"

"Is that all you got out of this evening? Let's focus on what *we* need to do. She's out of our league, remember? We common folk need to stick with our own kind and go digging for new delivery outlets."

"Agreed—deliveries," said Toyotomi. "Eventually her past will leak out—like every other secret in human history. Suppose we learned all about Eve—what would it gain us?"

"You've got it," snickered Ito. "Let's change the channel. But damn, I wish I could hold her tight just once. She's hot."

Toyotomi tutted. "You're like a dog in heat! You've been a good boy the last few days, and now you're getting itchy again."

"When the well's full," said Ito, tilting his glass, "you have to pump it out. What do you say we have a nightcap then clean the pipes?"

"No way," said Toyotomi in a hushed tone, shaking his head. "Too risky. Log onto Weibo and see for yourself. The going rate for beating the shit out of one of us is fifty *yuan*. Going around at night speaking Japanese…God knows what would happen. Best to keep a low profile."

Ito frowned and the chunk of meat poised at his mouth returned to his plate. "It's getting out of hand, the violence and all."

"What do you expect?" said Toyotomi. "If you're going to occupy the G2 throne, might as well act like royalty."

"Fuck yeah!" said Ito, his voice swelling. "That's understandable. But the roundup doesn't make sense. They open up all those flashy bars, pack them with working girls, then clamp down? And it's Japanese men they targeted! I'd like to know whose idea this was."

"Yeah, it's damned unfair," said Toyotomi, gesturing again for his friend to quiet down. "But what can we do? We don't know who we're dealing with, and prostitution is, after all, illegal." He wiped his mouth with his napkin. "Let's change the subject."

The guests at the head table rose, and with choreographed precision Wang Lingling saw them off, clasping hands with each man and offering him a "Thank you for coming, and see you again soon."

When all the dignitaries were gone, she settled into the white Cadillac limousine, which glided off, escorted front and back by the two sedans.

The two dozen men at the sky lounge bar broke into applause as Wang made her appearance.

"Thank you!" With a radiant smile she gestured to them to sit, then took her place at the head of the oval table. They were the presidents of the Gold Groups companies, all of them handpicked by her, most of them Caucasian, and among them no women.

"How was it?" She looked around the table.

An Asian man broke the silence. "The Chinese guests seemed to find it a bit unusual…no congratulatory remarks, too short, not very exciting. One man said he'd never seen such an odd groundbreaking ceremony. Things like that."

"We expected as much. It was my way of suggesting they scale down these ceremonies. But do they want to change? Are they even aware of what they're doing? To waste food is to waste money and environmental resources, and hogging the microphone is so provincial. The authorities are quick to clamp down on the Internet, yet so obtuse when it comes to correcting bad habits. It's a mystery to me." With a wry smile she surveyed the men. "We left them with a lot of questions—which was the basic idea, agreed?"

"Yes," said another man. "You definitely piqued their interest!"

"Flattery will get you everything," said Wang, "except president for life."

"Such wisdom in a chairwoman," said still another man.

"Now that's *real* sucking up," came a quick response, which drew an outburst of laughter.

"I'll do you all one better," said the Asian man. "Here's to our Madam Chair for making our debut in Shanghai an absolute success." He ended his toast by clapping; others hurrahed.

"Cognac all around, please!" called Wang to the bartender. Cognac, because it was without equal in status and rarely counterfeited.

Sipping her drink, she regarded the Asian man. "PR is up to speed by tomorrow, correct?"

"Yes. Actually all the networks are running our ads starting tonight."

Which told Wang she had been right to put a Chinese in charge of local PR.

"And you're checking the Internet and the daily newspapers and the weekly magazines. And by tomorrow we'll have fliers plastered over the whole city."

"Yes, Madam."

"Also, we need to get the most out of Weibo. Especially now that we have their attention. Do you see?"

"Yes, Madam."

"What's your scenario for them?"

"Well…" Momentarily fazed, the man quickly straightened in his chair. "How about a posting: 'Gold 88, what a fantastic name. We'll be rich for sure if we live there. And all the eights at the groundbreaking—just like the opening ceremony at the Beijing Olympics. And the CEO in the white gown with the red peony— who is that goddess anyway?' Something like that."

"Bravo! I love your insight, President Wan. It's all about Weibo now—they have a longer reach than newspapers, maybe even television. Let's keep up the good work."

"Yes, Madam."

"Where's Andy Park? Andy," she said, addressing another Asian man, "it's time to move ahead with the interiors."

"I'm on it," said the man.

"So, to reiterate," said Wang, "we *must* succeed here in Shanghai just like we did in Beijing, Tianjin, and Jingdao."

"Yes, Madam, of course."

"We also have to realize that success can breed complacency, which can ultimately lead to failure. So far we've had one success after another. But what if it's too good to be true? Andy, what's your reading?"

"We forget the past and reinvent ourselves—we need a fresh start."

"I agree," said Wang. "So, a familiar design but a different effect. Space that's sophisticated and beautiful, yet practical and convenient. Are you up to it?"

"All the way."

"That's what I want to hear. You have my trust, Andy. So we'll keep our focus on the best building materials—from France and Italy. Shanghai is different—there's a lot of money here. The important thing is that Shanghai people *love* Western refinement. But for all my ambition, I brought us into this market late. Why? I wasn't ready. Actually I was scared. And now that we've done our apprenticeship in the other three cities and had success—stardom, even—I'm afraid that same success might pose a stumbling block.

"Andy, I'll say it again—I trust in you. So find the best materials, create the best product, and sell it at the best price. We all know we get top dollar for a high-end product, especially in Shanghai, with all its multinational corporations and well-heeled Chinese. Those are our two markets, and our luxury suites will suit anyone's exhibitionist pride. So, when are you leaving for France and Italy?"

"I'm putting together the itinerary."

"Great. The sooner the better." Her face softened. "How's your new baby, your number two?"

"Doing just fine, thank you."

"Is your wife still hesitant about coming over?"

"She said she'll join me when the air quality improves."

"I feel for her. Mothers want clean air for their little ones."

"I guess. At the expense of the husband."

"How so? You're living oceans apart and you've already produced two babies. I'd say you're managing pretty well." This brought Andy a razzing from the others. "I have another appointment, so I need to say goodnight. Enjoy yourselves, and tomorrow we're back at work! And now if you'll excuse me." With a wave to all she rose.

The window of Kim Hyŏn'gon's office in Xian looked out onto a dark curtain. Visibility was two hundred yards in the murk and dusk; beyond, all was opaque. The daily smog cover showed no sign of lifting. Kim gazed at the sullen cloud, glad he wasn't outside breathing it in. Since the day he had arrived in the country he'd heard people harp ad nauseam about the polluted air, but he'd never seen it as bad as this. Beijing and Shanghai had been polluted, the loathsome air making him appreciate the quality of the air in Seoul, which seemed heavenly in comparison, but the dense smog in Xian was positively vile. In Xian, a 2,500-year-old city with a living history, the foul air hung heavy day and night, a by-product of the building boom that was part of China's Western Development strategy, a manifestation of the central government's desire for a balanced economy nationwide. And so it was that development fervor translated into polluting this rare treasure of a city.

Ironically, Kim was indebted to the process that had unleashed the toxic air.

With the local government buying into the development hoopla, he'd been able to process all the permits at lightning speed, receiving everything he needed to register and incorporate the steel plant in which foreign investors would sink their money. Yoked to the building-first mentality, local officials were quick to welcome any and all investment, trying to catch up to the eastern region, which enjoyed a standard of living three times better than that of the wretched west. How vexing and dispiriting that their eastern cousins gorged themselves on meat, their faces glistening with animal fat, and had dumped their bicycles to splurge on cars. Xunzi, the Confucian thinker, had said that water floats a vessel but can also swallow it. Many were the dynasties that had been submerged in a human tide, bearing out Mengzi's declaration that when the state miscarries its duty, the subjects are entitled to rebel. And so it was that the officials in Beijing, students of history that they were, had wisely decided to tackle the west. The bureaucrats here in Xian pounced on the golden opportunity to deflect local carping, and welcomed with fanfare any outside venture that smelled of investment. These ventures had the effect of shrouding in dust and smoke this city of treasured artifacts and historic sites. For their part, the people of Xian tacitly acknowledged that a better life came at the expense of polluted air and its by-products—itchy, burning, watery eyes and the black gunk coughed up from stinging throats. The human body certainly was impressive, thought Kim. It was so adaptable, able to lower its sensitivity threshold, inuring itself to pain and suffering.

"You'll get used to it," he'd been told by Chen Ke, his contact at the local ministry that handled foreign venture-capital inflow. "Give yourself a couple of months." The manager's cartoonish smile revealed teeth yellowed either by poor dental hygiene or the notoriously potent Chinese cigarettes. Kim couldn't decide which.

"I hope so," Kim had said as he dabbed at his smarting eyes with a handkerchief. He tried to sound amiable, but inside he wasn't smiling. *Are you stupid, or what? You're being suckered into a venture-capital crapshoot. You're ruining a jewel of a city and it's a damned shame. Is getting rich the priority? Why not keep the focus on tourism and get your city back to where you can breathe again? More people travel abroad every year, and every year more of them come to China. Xian is their next stop after Beijing. Wake up before it's too late—preserving your heritage is the only way you'll survive.*

But Kim was daydreaming and he knew it. The truth was, these civil servant clowns could be counted on only to safeguard their positions or develop ever more artful schemes to embezzle the tax money that came in like clockwork, compliments of the citizenry. They managed to cover their behinds by pitching the idea of development for the nation and a rise in living standards. The rule of thumb was that you were more or less honest if your gentle hand skimmed no more than 5 percent of the project budget; there were no worries if you helped yourself to 10 percent; but you were asking for trouble if you raked off 15 percent.

Kim had learned about Xian by reading up on Chinese history, one of the job requirements, along with a command of Chinese. His company preached that you mustn't just focus on selling. You were here for the long haul, not on a brief sojourn, and you had to understand your customers and their society and culture. Studying Chinese history would prompt you to learn more about China, and the more you learned, the more you would admire the people. This gave you a huge advantage over a salesman concerned only about his bottom line. It was well worth investing your time and effort in understanding the culture and history of China. At 1.3 billion souls, it was now the world's largest market and growing fast. If you wanted to compete in the global market in the twenty-first century, you had to succeed in China. All of this had been drilled into Kim and his coworkers.

A few days earlier, a visit with Chen having concluded more expeditiously than anticipated, he had experienced Xian firsthand. How different from reading about it in a book. He felt the spirit of the city suffuse him. It was a museum of two millennia of history and not just a stuffed display. For someone today, with a life expectancy of 70 years or longer, how unfathomable was the world into which the Buddha was born 2,500 years ago, or the world of his near contemporary, Confucius—or the world of Jesus, some 500 years more recent? But here in Xian the royal family and their subjects from that remote period welcomed you in the present in living color, with a material culture coursing with energy—thanks in large part to the commoners who throughout the numerous dynasties had diligently crafted household items of exceptional aesthetic quality.

The daring forms and the harmony of these 1,500-year-old treasures, based in the brilliantly intermingled Tang *Sancai*, created a sublime beauty that appealed to contemporary sensibilities. They jumped out at Kim as if from a time machine. Their creators were artisans, the lowest social class in the dynasty; they were treated like animals, the subject of scorn and contempt from the powerful ruling class. *What had those powerful men contributed to the culture?* Kim wondered. There would be so many places to visit when he needed an escape from work. He might like it here after all. Xian was definitely a gift to him.

And now, thanks to the scientific layout of the city, Kim had no difficulty finding the teahouse suggested by yellow-toothed Chen Ke, even though it was in a back alley. The Tang network of city streets had been laid out for maximum efficiency. The grid resembled a go table with rectangles in addition to squares, the size of the space corresponding to its functions. Kim was amazed—a blind man could find his way among these squares. Practical street design, an object of pride in the West, had existed here more than a millennium earlier. How prodigiously farsighted the planners.

Feudalism here, as elsewhere in the world, was based on an impregnable class structure consisting of scholars, farmers, artisans, and tradesmen, in that order. There were also the lowborn, the slaves, the butchers, and other pariahs. The city planners—engineers in modern parlance—belonged to the artisan class. How were the artisans treated in comparison with the scholars? Ironically, about the same as the soldiers. But the soldiers were regarded as inferior. Kim recalled the old Chinese saying that good metal is not used for nails, nor talented individuals for soldiers. He could imagine the scorn and mistreatment borne by the lower-class city planners, regardless of their brilliance and creativity.

He reviewed what he knew about the history of the city. It was called Changan during the Tang dynasty, when it was the eastern terminus of the Silk Road, and as such a magnet for artisans from throughout the empire. The constellation of superb artifacts in Xian was their legacy. Most prized among them were jade ornaments, porcelain, and tea, as well as silk products, their preciousness indicated by the gold radical in the Chinese character for *silk*. To obtain these treasures, merchants from India and points west thronged the Silk Road to Changan. From the Korean Peninsula and points east, merchants, scholars, and Buddhist monks willingly undertook the long journey for the countless sights, learning opportunities, and products. Farther east, Japan was so thirsty for the new goods and the culture coming via the Korean Peninsula that it developed water routes to Tang. As a result, Changan became the beating heart of the Tang dynasty, which itself was the epitome of China's thirty-six dynasties. Not until Chairman Mao founded the People's Republic did China again enjoy the expanse of territory, the abundance of life, and the cultural splendor of the Tang period. No wonder Chinese today considered the Tang dynasty their proudest and identified their culture with it to such an extent that overseas Chinese referred to themselves as *Tangren*, people of Tang, and to their communities, known to outsiders as Chinatowns, as *Tangren jiye*, avenue of the Tang people.

Out of habit Kim checked his watch before entering the teahouse. He was twenty minutes early for his meeting with Chen. The importance of being on time or even early had been drilled into him ever since he had gone into business. Many were the golden rules he had adopted: never take no for an answer; don't talk business over the phone; arrive twenty to thirty minutes early for an appointment; never let go of an old customer; keep your appointment book on you at all times; remember the birthdays and anniversaries of your clients and their good wives; and never forget to thank a person for any tidbit of a favor.

Arriving a minute late could doom a deal—after all, he was the hungry one. Even in a more casual meeting, being late created cracks in a relationship based on trust. One too many "I was held up by traffic" excuses would ultimately be revealed as "I don't care much about you" or "I've got better things to do."

Why the devil does he want to see me? The question had nagged at Kim since yesterday, when the official dealings had concluded without a hitch and with a smile on everyone's face. In China, a request for a meeting by a government official never failed to leave him with a splitting headache. You were powerless because they were brandishing the sword, no matter its size. Officials back home and here differed in terms of power—the former were little more than working stiffs whose prerogative was limited by the laws of the land, but the Chinese were Communist Party members before they were government officials, and as such were above the law. Party members currently totaled eighty-five million. Kim never ceased to be amazed that China was number one in so many respects—one hundred million women in the pleasure industry, and before long, about that many Party members.

These almost one hundred million Party members, twice as numerous as the population of the ROK, were no ragtag flock but rather top students, and they joined the Party only after a stringent selection process. But Party membership brought no salary; on the contrary, members paid dues. They were armed with a sense of duty to the Party, the pyramid atop which sat a single autocratic chairman. The Party selected the government officials, who exercised power and influence to a much greater extent than career civil servants in other countries.

Abandoning these thoughts, Kim entered the teahouse.

"*Wei*, Mr. Kim!"

Kim started at the joyful voice, then saw Chen, wearing a toothy, cheek-to-cheek smile, rushing toward him.

"You beat me here!" said Kim as he clasped Chen's hand. He sensed urgency— why in heaven's name would a person wielding the authority of a Party member and a government official come to a meeting twenty minutes early and wait for him? Kim was used to dealing with Party members with Himalaya-high noses.

"Of course," said Chen in an amiable voice. There was no trace of haughtiness to his expression. "I was the one who suggested this meeting, wasn't I? Please, have a seat."

"Thank you. Yes, I do remember." Kim strained to read his counterpart's intentions.

"I hope this little teahouse is all right with you," ventured Chen. "I know you would rather have coffee."

"Actually, sir, I prefer tea. When I arrived ten years ago I was a coffee drinker, but I've long since converted and now I absolutely love tea." This was no sweet talk. Kim was genuinely fond of all the redolent teas and their health benefits.

He took a quick look about the interior. There were no other patrons. The tranquility and old-world charm of the teahouse were all theirs.

"That and your fluent Chinese make me feel like you're a *lao pengyou*."

"Oh my," said Kim, his smile broadening. "I would very much like to be your *lao pengyou*."

A woman in a stylish *qipao* arrived with a tray containing teapot and cups and placed it on the table, then stood at attention. Chen waved her off. "I'll take it from here."

"Sir, as someone who has just arrived and knows no one here, I'm grateful to hear you say I'm like a *lao pengyou* to you. Please treat me that way and feel free to tell me what's on your mind." And just like that the groundwork was set.

Chen blinked and wiped his mouth nervously. "I'm so glad to hear you say that.

Well then, here goes. Since you'll be hiring for your new plant, well, I was wondering if you might consider my nephew for your sales department. I'm speaking of my older brother's son. Since university he's been working in sales for an electronics firm—this is his third year. He's been after me ever since I mentioned your company established a branch here. And my brother is all worked up as well. They know your company is the best in Korea, and known all over the globe. I'm sure you're aware that for young people in China, the top priority is to work for a foreign company."

The blue streak left Kim momentarily speechless. He was amazed at how the usual *manmandi* approach changed to blitz warfare as soon as self-interest entered the equation.

"I see. Well," he said, adopting a gentle tone, "as a matter of fact, I'm always looking for the right person, and I welcome your recommendation." He made a bow of acknowledgment.

"Excuse me?" faltered Chen. "Are you…decided? But you haven't seen my nephew…."

"Please consider him hired," said Kim, the epitome of geniality. "You have vouched for him and that's good enough for me." Nothing imprudent about that—he was laying the foundation for an emotional bond. And how could he refuse Chen's nephew with his two-plus years' experience in sales?

"I'm speechless," said Chen, clutching Kim's hand in both of his. "I've never seen such a debonair gentleman from Korea. We are *lao pengyou* for sure. You can be certain I'll repay you."

"Thank you, sir," said Kim, tightening his own grip. "I look forward to a long friendship with you."

To Kim, Xian was both wasteland and jungle. With nary a local acquaintance, he was burdened with building a steel plant and producing 100 to 150 thousand tons of steel a year. The branch manager and the admin head were responsible for constructing the plant and setting up the machinery, but Kim the sales manager was in charge of distributing the product. Who could understand the despair, the helplessness, the dismal loneliness of a sales rep thrown into a new market? And in a nation where *guanxi* was absolute power and your physiognomy weighed heavier than your experience, the credentials of your manufacturer, and the quality of its goods, those feelings were all the more intense. How enthralled Kim was, then, when *guanxi* presented itself out of the blue in the person of Chen. Who would have thought it possible? *I should be the one thanking* him. Chen wasn't some low-level official—he was a manager in a large city!

Kim knew his good fortune had nothing to do with him; it resulted instead from the public trust in his company, POSCO, and its products. The POSCO branches in Beijing and Shanghai had to contend with a high turnover rate, given that three years with the company guaranteed a Chinese a job at a domestic firm that came with a 50 to 100 percent increase in salary. Kim now saw firsthand in this jungle called Xian the estimable result of public trust.

Such trust had had to be earned. Outside Beijing and Shanghai, POSCO was shunned. The land was huge and salesmen ran up against various obstacles—experiences they called nosedives. Many were the nosedives survived by the sales force, thanks to which a Chinese manager in this back of beyond had come to recognize the POSCO brand. Kim was ready for another nosedive upon learning of his transfer to Xian, but now he could breathe easy in the hallelujah moment of *guanxi* descending.

"I must share this wonderful news with my nephew! I will contact you soon." Chen rose, ready to sprint out the door.

"By all means, sir." Kim rose as well.

A government official's request on behalf of a job prospect carried enormous weight. If you said no, you could expect retaliation someday. But if you went along, you stood to acquire good *guanxi*. Staffing a key position with an acquaintance or relative of an official was potentially an excellent business decision.

Kim recalled the story of a Korean bank that established a branch in China and was approached by a government official with a request that they hire a young woman. The woman had no work experience whatsoever, but under the circumstances, they hired her. One day a man deposited five hundred million *yuan* in the bank, an amount close to a billion *wŏn*, or not quite a million dollars. He also opened up two hundred accounts in which to direct-deposit his employees' pay. It turned out he was a successful businessman and the father of the new hire. He was stupendously wealthy and she didn't have to work, but he knew a position for her in a foreign company would make her a future trophy wife. Not every man could marry a woman working for a reputable foreign company.

Three days later Chen called Kim. "How about a drink tonight?"

Chen arrived at the bar with a companion. "This is Ch'oe Sangho, the chief prosecutor in Xian, but more importantly my *lao pengyou*. He is Chinese-Korean, and he will be very helpful to you."

Considering the man's trunk-like neck and the vigor he radiated, Kim was dazed. *Chief prosecutor? What a jackpot!*

"Pleased to meet you," said Kim as he rose to greet the man. "I am Kim Hyŏn'gon."

"And I am glad to meet you, sir," said the other man as he offered his hand.

When they were once again seated, Chen called out, "To the friendship of three *lao pengyou*!" He then poured each of them a glass of *baijiu*.

Kim was taken aback by the sight of the potent spirit gushing into water glasses and not shot glasses. But the next moment he was thinking, *Well, hell.* He sucked in his belly and reminded himself of the time a prospective buyer had promised an order if Kim downed five water glasses of *baijiu*. The deal had gone through. A capacity for alcohol could be a plus in the business world.

"*Ganbei!*" cried Chen. The other two followed suit.

8. Student Grit

"Did you hear about the event this afternoon?" said Yanling to Chaehyŏng as they left the lecture hall. "It sounds like fun."

Chaehyŏng shook his head. "No—tell me."

"An American magazine is doing an open interview with our students."

"An open interview—what's that?"

"Just like it says. They ask the questions and anybody can answer."

"Questions about what?"

"A variety of subjects."

"So, two big countries, Number One and Number Two, wanting to show off?" Chaehyŏng grumbled. "Sounds kind of vague to me."

"Aren't you man enough to let go of your tiny-country inferiority complex?" she teased, linking her arm with his. "With both sides talking, maybe we'll find some commonalities."

He placed his hand over hers where it rested on his arm and smiled. "You're tempted, aren't you."

"You're not? You're a history student now. And we're living in a history that keeps unfolding. An interview with a foreign journal by us Beida students could be a historical moment."

Chaehyŏng had other ideas—he'd recently checked out a sex therapy manual, which confirmed, thank God, that his sex drive was not an anomaly—but managed to suppress the familiar itch and stay on topic. "What time does it start?"

"At two."

"We have class then."

"I told you—instead of a dead, boring history class, how about a live one?"

"Listen to you."

"What do you mean? I'm wise and smart."

"Of course you are. But guys don't like a smart girl, you know."

She snorted. "I don't care what any man in the world thinks—except one." She tightened her lock on his arm.

The five-hundred-seat auditorium was packed with students, some spilling onto the steps. Chaehyŏng scanned the crowd. Another epidemic of America frenzy. How many people would be here if it weren't an American magazine? Maybe a similar crowd for a French one, but if it were British or German, barely half. For a Korean magazine, maybe a fourth, and for a Japanese one, forget it. China's rabid idolatry for things American was surpassed only by its lust for money. Sure, it was a trend among the young people, who could be excused for their immaturity and for buying into the cultural paradigm of preferential treatment for members of the been-there-and-done-that-in-the-US club. But why did the old ones also fawn over the US?

"Did you eat something bitter?" she whispered.

"What?"

"Why the frown?"

"Too many kids."

"So what?"

"Why do they drool over everything American?"

"You should know," she scoffed.

"What do you mean?"

"Koreans are worse."

"How so?"

"You depend on the US to defend you. But *we're* independent."

"And lucky—you don't have North Korea to worry about."

"That's a sore subject for us. You send home all the money you make here, and yet you leave it to the Americans to defend you. And you know how the US and China keep an eye on each other. So how does Korea figure in? The view here is that Korea's a *kungfu* fighter in a china shop. In other words, our relationship with Korea will come apart if Korea keeps relying on the US."

"I read that too, and it bothers me. Our biggest trade partner is China—25 percent of our trade is with you; with the US, it's 17 percent. A few years ago it was the opposite. But North Korea is still our biggest challenge." Sadness clouded his face.

"It's not as if there's no solution," she said, combing her hair with her fingers. He shot her a look. "Meaning?"

"Meaning why not declare yourself a neutral state, forever!" Her eyes sparkled.

"That's insane coming from a history student. Our situation's more complicated than that. Tell you what—let's come back to this. Fair enough?" He took her hands, trying to ease his tangled feelings.

"Hello, and welcome," came a voice in English, drawing their eyes to the stage. At the podium stood an Asian man.

"Thank you all for coming. We are hoping in this interview to showcase China for the rest of the world in an open and fair forum. The format is somewhat unusual. First, you, the subjects of our interview, are from the top university in the land. Second, it's open to any of you who wish to take part. We want to hear as many voices as possible, and we want you to be yourselves. That way our readers around the globe can understand China better. We ask you to keep these objectives in mind and jump right in."

A successful overseas Chinese, thought Chaehyŏng. Chosen by the magazine to highlight yet another American success story, just as the present American ambassador to China was chosen for his ethnicity. There was no interpreter either— non-English speakers need not participate.

"I'll share presiding duties with my colleague. Shall we begin?" And with that he handed the microphone to a Caucasian woman with red hair and blue eyes. The hair looked out of place among all the heads with black hair.

"Our first question," said the woman. "This is an era of globalization, in which intellectual property rights are protected. Last year China astounded the world, and especially the economic superpowers, by achieving G2 status. You are to be congratulated on this happy occasion. But in contrast with its lofty status, China continues to manufacture knockoffs of brand-name goods, and it illegally copies patented designs. China's failure to pay royalties in accordance with international regulations has been condemned as uncivil and unethical. We would like to hear what you young intellectuals, as representatives of your country, think about this matter."

The woman had come out swinging. A chilly silence came over the auditorium. The only movement was Red Hair's rolled-up sheet of paper tapping against her left palm like a metronome. The rhythmic movement looked all the more relaxed in contrast with the frozen stillness of the students.

Halfway toward the stage, a student slowly rose. All eyes turned in his direction, sending him tense, piercing looks.

"I first ask a question and then I answer." He cleared his throat but remained calm. "Do you know we make three inventions—gunpowder, compass, and paper?"

"Of course. We're aware of that."

"We invented gunpowder and compass one thousand years ago. We made paper one thousand nine hundred years ago. They spread the world. Do you know if those Western countries give us royalties?" The young man sat down.

"Well, I have to confess, it never occurred to me." Red Hair looked about the audience as if for an answer.

There was a smattering of applause, and then a buzz, and then the auditorium rocked with a crescendo of cheering.

"Please," said the Asian man as he took the microphone from Red Hair. "Let's keep some order here. That was a brilliant answer." The man was fluent not only in his spoken language but in his body language and gestures. "But I see a possible problem. At the time of those inventions, we did not have international laws protecting intellectual property rights."

Again a curtain of silence fell over the auditorium. Chaehyŏng watched the same student rise sluggishly. Was he trying to save face? Was he ready with a counterpunch?

"Yes, you mentioned correctly. International law is the product of the geopolitical superpowers who own the properties. They are arbitrary developers. They promote their interests. They impose their developments and the third-world countries must implement. So Chinese people should suggest the government make a law to protect our inventions. The government will accept our proposal because it involves public interests and billions of *yuan*. So I ask if all the superpowers will pay China the back royalties." More applause.

"Interesting," said the Asian host. "But an ex post facto law is a bad law, and not in common use."

"But is the superpowers' arbitrary law different from ex post facto law? With our G2 status we can make a law too and ask the world to implement. Maybe it gets rejected. But there is one clear message. World people will know how much China gave to world culture and civilization last thousand years."

This time cheering and shouting accompanied the applause. Cocking his head in frustration, the man returned the microphone to Red Hair.

"I thank you for this energetic exchange. Let's proceed now to the next question. It also concerns several other countries besides China. Some of you may not be aware of this, but since 2008, Apple has been trying to clamp down on iPhones made with pirated technology. The Chinese government has not been cooperative, and recently Apple had to give up. But now that China is G2, what do you think about this?"

A student shot to his feet. "First of all, there is a problem of confusion between G2 and GDP. G2 is an indicator of economic power; it depends on foreign currency reserves. It has nothing to do with GDP, and in GDP we are *not* number two in the world. Our GDP is officially recognized as $4,500—that is the level of a developing country. Has Apple 'clamped down' on fakes in other developing countries? I don't think so. What they tried to do here is against the principles of the Chinese government, which are based on parity. That is why our government is not cooperating."

"That makes sense," said Red Hair. "However, there seems to be a contradiction here. Other developing countries either do not manufacture knockoffs, or if they do, not in mass quantities."

A hand shot high and another student rose. "That is not because those countries are morally opposed—they simply lack the technology. And speaking of contradictions, what about the connection between small quantity and no clampdown—does that make sense? You say you are a democratic country, but you do not show equality—I never understand that."

"Your reasoning is interesting. But how can your government justify its lack of cooperation on illegal manufacturing?"

The next student to answer spoke the best English so far. "As in any country, our government has a duty and a responsibility to protect its citizens' assets. The manufacture of knockoffs is a legitimate business in China. In fact many of our citizens are employed in the factories that make those products. If the government accepts Apple's demand and shuts down those factories, countless people lose their jobs. Do you expect our government to accept Apple's demand without a fight? Besides, an Apple iPhone is four times as expensive as a counterfeit, and yet the quality does not differ. The government must protect its less fortunate citizens and help them afford a modern life. Furthermore, manufacturing counterfeits is the perfect way to practice technology. The manufacturers are mastering advanced technology with no support from the government—isn't that a great way to serve the national interest? Therefore, why should our government cooperate with Apple? If Apple had known of these factors, they would not have had to waste their efforts here. There is one more thing that Apple must know. I do not have statistics, but I am sure that as many authentic Apple products are sold here as in all other developing countries combined. As Chinese citizens seek a higher standard of living, they will want the real thing, which means they will buy more and more Apple products. There is no need for Apple to feel victimized here."

"Right!" someone shouted.

"You're the best!" a woman called out.

"Great English," said a third student.

"Yes, a clear answer in perfect English," said Red Hair with an awkward smile. "But somehow I feel you're representing the government rather than your university."

"I am a citizen first in our People's Republic," said the student in a solemn tone. "Soon I will join the Party. And I am a doctoral student second."

"This has been a good learning experience. Thank you for your lengthy answer." Shaking her head in exasperation, she handed the microphone to the Asian man.

"This interview has been superb, better than we expected—all of you are really engaged, and we appreciate that. Our next question involves the lawsuit over Apple's iPad patent. As you may know, a Chinese citizen predicted Apple would come to China, and he copyrighted the word 'iPAD'—small 'i,' capital 'PAD.' Apple was unaware of this when it introduced its iPad. The Chinese man sued Apple, and the sale of iPads was suspended. The Chinese court ordered Apple to pay the man sixty million dollars. And Apple agreed. What is your opinion on this?"

The auditorium broke into a wave of murmuring.

"Sixty million dollars? How much is that in *yuan*?"

"I can't do it in my head. Where's your calculator?"

"That guy's going to be a gazillionaire—his descendants will love him."

"For sure. He's a genius."

"No, he's not. He's a con man who put China to shame."

"Lighten up, will you? You're so boring."

"Those Americans...always fussing about copyrights...serves them right!"

"Yeah. They were asking for it."

"Sure. An opportunity like that, you're an idiot if you don't take advantage."

"Why didn't I think of that—I'd have cleaned them out."

"Sure, why not? It's a megabucks company. They have money to burn. Con man or not, you have to go for it."

"Zhuge Liang has nothing on him—he's a master tactician."

"Please," said the Asian man, trying to talk over the voices. "We understand this is a surprising development, but if you could save the chatting, we would like to hear your thoughts."

"Excuse me," said a student, "your question is...?"

"What do you think of the decision by the Chinese court?"

A different student rose to field the question. "As one of us mentioned, to fulfill its duty and responsibility, our government is committed to protecting the citizens."

"Even in cases of fraud?" said the Asian man.

The student recoiled, and another one rose to answer. "If that is fraudulent, the plaintiff is also half responsible. You do know that." He stuck out his chin toward the podium.

"I'm sorry," said the Asian man with a puzzled expression. "Apple is half responsible for what?"

"If Apple wanted to protect its products, it should have done its homework before register the patent and market in China. What is the reason they neglect this? Do they perceive we are good people and do not cheat? Or perhaps they look down on us. If Apple neglect to defend itself, then why our court would want to take their side? And, when in Rome, do like Romans—isn't that how you say? Our law means to protect our citizens, and the court followed the law in making its verdict."

With a rueful smile the Asian man returned the microphone to Red Hair.

"We believe this exciting interview will be of great benefit to the people of the world as they attempt to understand you and your country. We have a little more time, so let's continue. The next question is, how can Chairman Mao be a god?"

Shouts broke out.

"Chairman Mao *is* our god!"

Wary of the possibility of coming across as blasphemous, Red Hair spoke slowly and deliberately: "Yes, we understand. We just want to know why. As does the world."

Silence descended, until finally a student rose. "You yourself, how do you define the existence or nonexistence of a god?"

Red Hair nervously repositioned the mic, knowing she was venturing farther out onto thin ice. "Well, there's no clear answer to that…it's up to the individual, and how he or she would define freedom of belief and choice."

"That's right. If you believe in a god, then he exists. If not, he does not." And with an arrogant sneer the student sat down.

Red Hair picked again at the mic. "We're almost at the end. My last question is, how do you regard the US?"

More silence, and then a student rose. "Can be a friend, can be an enemy." Typical Chinese sentence structure, with no subject. The audience responded with hurrahs and applause.

"What's wrong?" Yanling asked as she and Chaehyŏng were leaving. "You look down."

"Oh, it's nothing," said Chaehyŏng, passing his fingers through his hair. "Except my head is swimming."

"A lot on your mind?"

"More like a jumble of thoughts."

"Why? I don't think that interview was anything special. Maybe you react differently because you're Korean?"

"You little devil, I can't hide anything from you."

"Let's go for coffee," she said, linking her arm in his. "I need to hear this."

He nodded, and off they went. "Yanling," he said after they'd walked awhile. "Do you believe Chairman Mao is a god?"

"Is that why you look so miserable?"

"Not just that."

"I knew you might think it's strange. Well…what can I say? The more time passes, the more godlike he feels…. Well, that's not exactly accurate—but what's wrong with deifying him? Don't you sometimes pray to someone when you have problems? He's the one who comes up when I need to pray." She spoke calmly and deliberately, trying to organize her deepest thoughts.

"Why him? I know Jesus isn't a presence here, but you have the Buddha, Confucius, the Bodhi-Dharma, General Guan Yu—so many gods."

"True, but they're so far away in time it's difficult to feel any effect. The Chairman is much closer—we can still feel his power."

"Even though he's only human," said Chaehyŏng with an anxious look.

"I think that's the difference between us and *waiguoren*. Of course the Chairman was human, but we all know that what he accomplished was colossal. As time goes by, we live better and we keep feeling it all started with him. And his accomplishments get larger as his political mistakes get smaller. Can you understand that?" Her piercing gaze harbored a shadow of doubt.

"What about Deng Xiaoping's accomplishments?"

"That's the question we always hear from *waiguoren*. If not for the Chairman's superhuman achievements, Deng would get no credit."

"Superhuman?"

"You know what I mean—you've read all his books."

"Well, of course I know the three achievements. First, in five thousand years of Chinese history, China was never larger than it is today. Number two, he instituted land reform and distributed land to the 85 percent of the farmers who were sharecroppers, to give them a livelihood. And third, he uprooted the five-thousand-year class system and established an egalitarian society." Spoken like a grade-school student reciting a history lesson.

"Good memory. But it's too much to accept him as superhuman, right?"

"Actually it's not, but to worship him like a god still seems a bit—"

"Chaehyŏng," she interrupted, drawing from him an awkward smile, "did you ever wonder why our Communist Revolution is one of the world's big three, along with the French and Bolshevik revolutions? Think about that."

"But I just can't feel it—is it because I'm not Chinese?"

"Maybe. But the more you understand China, the more you'll feel it. One thing is very clear—Chairman Mao is the epicenter of our modern history."

"Yes, I know that."

"Look at that line!" she said peevishly as they came near a Starbucks shop.

Chaehyŏng snorted. "They're cashing in just like Coca-Cola and McDonalds. Why the craze for Starbucks?"

"It's only natural. Our tea has a delicate fragrance, like mums, and coffee has a rich, sexy aroma, like jasmine. How can you resist? So, what should we do?"

"Might as well wait."

And so they fell in line.

"Something else on your mind?"

"The students." He smacked his lips as if he'd eaten something distasteful.

"What about them?" She fixed him with a pointed gaze.

"It's good I went there. It was a shock, but it got me thinking," he said glumly.

"Oh? I don't remember anything particularly shocking about it."

"Well, you're Chinese."

"Come on, out with it. You're making me crazy."

"Wait—who's the one who told me to practice *manmandi*? Can't you see I'm trying?"

"That's a pretty flimsy excuse. Didn't I tell you Chinese turn from *manmandi* to *quaiquai* when self-interest is involved?"

"Oh, you're so thoughtful, my princess."

"Stop teasing me and get to the point."

"All right. Well, I was shocked at how fearless they are. Their English was so-so, yet they weren't afraid to speak up to the Americans. Where do they get that audacity? It's amazing. I like it."

"Really." She frowned in bewilderment, then shot Chaehyŏng an apprehensive glance. "Koreans don't do that?"

"Not unless they're 100 percent confident."

"But why? Prudence is good, but not to the point of being timid. You just have to say what you can. If you're a little clumsy, so what? If you want to get better, you have to keep trying. Right?"

"Exactly. We know that. But we can't do it. The Chinese can. I wish I knew why."

"Hmm…is it a matter of temperament?" she asked gingerly. "A small-country inferiority complex?"

"Maybe. But what surprised me even more was how up-front and honest they were answering embarrassing questions about China. In situations like that we lose our tongues. The Korean government could never refuse to cooperate in something like the Apple investigation. But your government and students are all on the same wavelength. Maybe it comes from big-country nerve?"

"We're almost there. Americano?"

"Sure."

They found seats.

"Anything else swimming through my lover's mind?"

"I was impressed with how well informed the students are. And *very* impressed with how they express themselves and how well they think on their feet."

Down went her coffee and up went her hand to cover her mouth as she giggled. "Gabbing is a by-product of a socialist society. All those students you saw, they're among the top English speakers at Beida, and it's for sure they'll join the Party. Can you guess the basic qualifications for Party membership? You have to be someone, you have to be competent, and you have to be able to bluff. So they're good talkers. Next issue?"

"I just realized how hard I have to study. The universities here graduate six and a half million a year, tops in the world, and if the ones at the interview are any indication...I need to hyper-focus—I'm scared witless here."

"And I am so proud. My honey knows just how to tickle my ears—all the right words, with a nice coating of sugar." She smiled mischievously.

"Seriously. I need to go to a cram school and get back to work on my English. I've been concentrating on Chinese since I got here, and now I need to do the same with English. I have to be as good as those guys at the interview. I don't want to spend the rest of my life intimidated by other people's English."

"Me either. I don't want people thinking I'm a loser. So I'm going to that cram school with you."

"Super. Togetherness is everything. Let's go. I need to talk to my uncle."

"What, your family's on call whenever you need money?"

"Sure. Korean moms will sell their blood for their kid's education, and especially for English lessons."

"Chinese moms too. They're haunted by America—they turn into gullible idiots. Call it motheritis. Are you ready?" Sweeping back her long hair, she rose.

After they had parted, Chaehyŏng returned to the issue that had jolted him hardest, a matter he hadn't mentioned to Yanling. *Can be a friend, can be an enemy.* How could they say that to American journalists! And not just to the journalists, but to the country they represented, America. Korean students would never have spoken up like that. So many differences between Korea and China. He felt defeated and didn't want Yanling to see that side of him.

When Chaehyŏng was sure his uncle was done with work for the day, he called.

"How come you work such long days?"

"Did I hear right? Are you attending to my calendar? My nephew sounds all grown up. What's happening?"

"Uncle, I have a favor to ask."

"If it's like the last one, forget it."

"Are you busy?"

"No. That's why you waited for me to finish work. Right?"

"I just wanted to make sure. You're always rushing me…. I know you trading company guys are always trying to look busy."

"Careful how you talk. It's a damn good thing we *are* busy, and by the way, you can thank us for the economic boom we're having back home."

"Ah yes, the benevolent purveyor of things Korean. Dynamo of the national economy."

"Save the compliments till you tell me what pain-in-the-ass favor you're asking."

"Nothing painful about this one."

"Then out with it!"

"I've been thinking…I need to take an English class. Would you please ask Mom to send me money?"

"English? I thought you were good enough already."

"Not quite. I had a serious reality check today."

"What do you mean?"

"It's a long story."

"If you can tell it in an hour, I'm all ears."

"All right, here's what happened." And Chaehyŏng spun the story of the interview. Everyone needed a sympathetic ear, and for Chaehyŏng that ear belonged to his uncle. Chŏn would listen to his pleading, and was the perfect counselor and problem solver.

"So…my dear nephew had a shock and decided he needs to learn English. Do I have that right? Well, my hat's off to you. You can hit me up for a favor like that anytime. And this will help thaw out your esteemed mother. Why not call and ask her yourself? Then you can mend fences."

"No. It gets complicated if I talk with her. Like they say, what parents call interest children call interference. And revisiting old business means new stress for me."

"Listen to this crook! He asks for more money, and yet—"

"Meaning yes, you'll ask her. Thank you, Uncle. And next, I've got a question—how do the Chinese get off acting the way they do? They've got balls and don't give a shit."

"Aha, you're beginning to see the light! Maybe you'll understand when you reach my advanced age."

"Meaning you've figured it out?"

"Sure. It's as plain as the Great Wall and the flowing Yangzi."

"Uncle, I wish you'd lose the corny sayings. You sound like a Chinese politician showing off by reciting ancient poems."

Chŏn snorted. "And you've picked up enough schooling to sass me. Tell me, what are the three most common adjectives describing Chinese culture?"

"Let's see…large, expansive, and excessive."

"Not bad. And—"

"Excuse me, Uncle. Could you dispense with the questions? We were talking about the Chinese and their nerve."

"What's wrong with me asking questions?"

"They make my heart drop and my brain seize up. I have to make sure I give you the right answer. Too much stress isn't good for me."

"Stress? I think it's fun."

"Not me. It feels like a panic attack. I almost answered 'Food, architecture, and manners,' until I remembered you said adjectives—that was the hint. What if I gave you the wrong answer? You'd call me an idiot and tell me to give up my studies and go home—I know you would. I feel like such a lame brain."

"Yap yap yap. Stop wetting your pants over a little quiz and grow up, will you."

"Listen, Uncle, I..." He managed to swallow the words—*I may look like a kid to you, but I've got a woman and I'm living with her.*

"You're what? What were you going to say?"

"Never mind. So—large, expansive, and excessive."

"Hey, where's your sense of humor? All right, the point is, the answer to your question is in those three words. Put them together and you can see why the Chinese characters for *China* are *chungguo*, "middle kingdom"—the Chinese think they're the center of the world. And that fuels their self-esteem and their pride in everything about China that's large, expansive, and excessive. That mentality has been with them since God knows when. It's part of their DNA. To the rest of us it comes off as arrogance. You might say it doesn't make sense, but that doesn't make it go away. I'll give you an example. In the late 1980s China opens the floodgates to foreigners. The previous decade they were focusing inward; they had to establish an orthodox doctrine and a solid foundation. So, China lifts the Bamboo Curtain, just like the Soviets lifted the Iron Curtain. Tourists flood in, and global hot spots like Paris and Rome are all left high and dry. It's boom time. So, Beijing charges all these foreigners three times as much as the locals to see the Forbidden City and the other sights. 'You want to see? Then you have to pay.' Now that's nerve. And that's how Mr. Wang does business. You spend all that money to fly to China, so how can you not see the Forbidden City? What do *we* do back home? We give *discounts* to foreign tourists—hell, we practically give away the store. You see the difference in mentality? Did you ever hear about the woman in the tour group from back home? It was a bunch of government officials, and she was charged the rate for the locals to get into the Forbidden City. Was she thankful? Hell no, she was so pissed off at being mistaken for a Chinese that it ruined the rest of her trip."

The two of them burst into laughter.

"Get the idea? The tourists put up with it. There are more of them every year, so up goes the Chinese nerve quotient. Those entrance fees are still the same, but what a shot in the arm they must have given to the GDP back then. But in terms of obnoxiousness, the best is yet to come. Before the Apple fuss, French and Italian name-brand companies were already calling for investigations into Chinese knockoffs. The government played dumb—'Hey, our counterfeits are good advertisements for your products.' And they were right—twenty years later those same French and Italian brands—the real thing and not the knockoffs—took over the market here. It's only a matter of time before China takes over from the US as the number-one world market for brand-name goods. Why shouldn't they be riding a high horse? Maybe you don't remember, but several years ago Chinese consumers staged a boycott of the Carrefour supermarkets. It was fallout from the sale of French armaments to Taiwan. China warned them, but the French were clueless. And when the Chinese went in for the high-speed rail, who did they go to for technology? Germany. France went nuts, but did they learn a lesson?

"Let's flash back to the Seoul Olympics. There was a French actress who made a huge stink about eating dog meat. She even urged people to boycott the games. Said dog eaters didn't deserve to host the Olympics. She was one of the biggest sex symbols ever; guys around the world drooled over her. So she sends a letter of protest to President No T'aeu—how can we eat dogs? They're man's best friend. I guess the ex-glamor girl was full in the body but empty in the head. There are lots of creatures that are people-friendly—cows, horses, pigs, sheep, chickens, ducks—and we eat them all. Well guess what—our government treated her letter like a missive from the queen, and boy did we hustle to hide the dog-meat restaurants in the back alleys. We didn't call it tonic stew anymore; now it was four-season stew. What do you think she did in 2008 when the Beijing Olympics came around? Zilch. The French must have been scared stiff of more retaliation if she ran off at the mouth. She was over the hill by then, but not so demented she didn't get the point.

"And look what China did when Japan took custody of that Chinese fishing boat captain during the islands vendetta. As you like to say, they threw a knockout punch—they boycotted Japanese products, they boycotted tourist travel to Japan, they banned exports of their stash of rare-earth materials. And Japan caved in. That's the power of China. But don't forget where their *real* power lies. For the past two decades, China and its cheap labor have been the world factory for household goods. Who do you think benefits the most? It's consumers in the advanced countries. Global economists have *praised* China for helping stabilize the world economy. And *that*, I believe, is the real power of China. It's their belief in that power that gives the Beida students the audacity to stand up to American reporters. Remember what Napoleon said? 'Let China sleep, for when she wakes, she will shake the world.'"

"Wow, he got that right!"

"Though it took two hundred years. All right, your hour's up."

"I know. Who did you say that French actress was?"

"Brigitte Bardot."

9. Ephemeral Is the Migrant Worker

"Are you all right, *ayi?*" said Chŏn Taegwang's wife, Chisŏn. "Have you been crying?"

"It's nothing," said Sungqing, not looking up from her dishwashing.

Chisŏn gently rested her hands on the maid's shoulders and searched her face. "Your eyes are so red. What happened? Is it your apartment-mates?" Sungqing had once told Chisŏn, weeping, that she often quarreled with them.

The maid shook her head, covering her mouth to suppress the sob that was about to erupt. "No, it's not that."

"Then what?" Like the other wives of the trading-company men, Chisŏn was loath to lose her Chinese maid, whose service made it possible for her to enjoy a comfortable life here. Oh, the faces the wives would make if their maid had to miss a day of work. None of them wanted to return to the drudgery of household chores they had long since given up. The longer Chisŏn lived here, the more she detested housework.

"Well, what happened was—" And then the tears gushed forth.

"What is it?" Chisŏn said, her voice louder than she'd intended. "It must be serious."

The maid nodded, the sobs continuing to escape.

"Please, tell me."

"My husband…" Finally, she managed to spit it out. "He fell."

"What! At work?"

Biting her lip, the maid nodded.

"Was he hurt?"

"He's hurt bad, still unconscious." Large teardrops spilled onto her cheeks.

"Oh my god, was he working on a high-rise?" said Chisŏn. "What did the doctor say? Will he be all right?" And then she was crying too. She wiped away the tears with the back of her hand.

"It's too early to tell. The doctor said he will know more after my husband wakes up." Sungqing shuddered as she tried in vain to stanch her tears.

"That's terrible. The company will pay his hospital bill, won't they?"

Chisŏn had never understood the pay-first policy of the hospitals here. Or why the people in this *mianzi*-loving culture abandoned all thoughts of face when it came to paying for treatment. Even emergency patients went untended unless the cost of service was paid up front. Treatment was subject in large part to how much was paid, and how fast. If patients ended up dying, it was their own fault. Yet more ammunition for the foreign journalists who were wont to point out that China was more capitalistic than the capitalists. What was worse, a surgery patient was expected to pay the medical staff a hefty gratuity based on the difficulty of the procedure. Chisŏn remembered a story about a vengeful nurse who, receiving no tip after a Caesarian section, had left a pair of scissors inside the new mother before stitching her back together. Such happenings were so plentiful a saying had emerged—China, land of 1.3 billion anomalies.

"I'm not sure. They paid something…but they blame him for the accident."

"What!" said Chisŏn, her voice trembling. "Those weasels—they want to dump him, don't they?"

"I'm so scared. About his injury, and then the company blaming him. I was with him all last night."

"But you need to take care of yourself, too. You have to play smart, so they will not try to take advantage. Those companies are like meat grinders—too many workers are victimized."

"Yes, I know. Especially people like us when we're hurt or sick. I'm so worried." Again Sungqing tried to compose herself.

Migrant workers like Sungqing and her husband had washed into the cities from the poverty-ridden farm villages. They formed the lowest economic class— the urban poor—performing the grimy work that made possible the economic miracle that had stupefied the world. There were an estimated quarter billion of them—the largest pool of migrant workers in the world. *Estimated* because statisticians tended to blow up a figure as much as tenfold if it reflected well on the government, or shrink it by like measure if it made the government look bad.

"Do not let them see you hanging your head. Look smart, show them you can be nasty," said Chisŏn, displaying a tightened fist. "Remember your dream, *ayi*— you want to save up so you can open a shop back home and send your only son to college. Stay focused on what's important."

"I will do that," said the maid with a deep bow. "Thank you."

Chisŏn restrained herself from saying, *Maybe my husband could help; he knows people who are high up.* Chŏn was a *waiguoren*, and in any event no official would condescend to a wretched migrant worker. Among all the shocks Chisŏn had weathered here, two were especially stunning—women's disdain for chastity and the severe discrimination between party members and average citizens. Party members and officials were divine figures who lived on high; in comparison the average Wang was a cave-dweller. The Party captains and high officials were notorious for their black Audis with the quadri-circular icon, and if there was a Guinness record for audacity and wantonness, these types would hold it, hands down. Weren't there speed limits? you might ask. Sure, toothless ones. And nowhere was this kleptocracy as brazen as when a crowd of pedestrians and vehicles had to be cleared so half a dozen black Audis could parade off from the poshest restaurant. Witnessing such abuses, Chisŏn boiled over at how easily the principles of the communist revolution were flouted, especially the principle of human equality. Weren't the comrades the masters of their nation? And the citizenry— instead of protesting such nauseating behavior they soaked it up. What if it had happened back home? Well, it depended for one thing on who was involved— was it a lowly party rep or the chairman of the National Assembly? The higher the position, the more flak he or she would catch. She should be thankful for living here, Chisŏn would remind herself in the midst of her outrage—it made her appreciate how democratic and humane was the society from which she came.

If only she could help poor Sungqing—she must have hated coming here today with her husband still in a coma! But what if she lost her half-day job, which provided 1500 *yuan* per month, or about 250 dollars—a dream job for a migrant worker and one that was highly sought after. And no wonder—you worked in a clean and comfortable setting rather than on a road crew or at an apartment construction site. Not to mention getting freebies such as a satisfying lunch and the occasional item of clothing or food.

No, she couldn't ask her to stay the entire shift. "*Ayi*, why not work just two hours—you should be with your husband."

Embarrassed, the maid was quick to respond. "No, no. I'm all right."

"The work can wait. You should check on him."

"No, really. It's all right. But thank you anyway," she said firmly with a shake of her head.

But to Chisŏn she seemed nervous rather than thankful. And then Chisŏn understood. "*Ayi*, are you afraid I will not pay you for the hours you miss?"

The maid looked down at her feet. "Yes, ma'am. I can't afford—"

"Oh no, *ayi*. I wouldn't do that. You know I feel for you, and that's why I suggested," said Chisŏn, pounding her chest in frustration that the situation boiled down to money. "You understand, yes?"

Tears once again pooled in the maid's eyes. "I am so sorry. I was not sure. Thank you, thank you." And with each thank-you came a bow.

At the hospital Sungqing found her husband, Zhang Wanxing, conscious, grimacing in pain.

"Oh, *airen...*"

"I'm sorry...." Even these words were an effort for him.

"He's lucky to be alive," said the doctor. "The hard hat saved him. I see no injuries other than three crackled ribs and a fractured femur. Even so, I suggest a good long rehabilitation."

Sungqing's heart throbbed with concern. "How long?" Lengthy treatment would exhaust their savings.

"A month or two."

"So, it could be two whole months." She closed her eyes tight and did some figuring. How much would the hospital bill be? And would the company take care of it, or would they just walk away? Her worries mushroomed.

After the doctor had left, Zhang looked about the room nervously. "Is anyone here from the company?" he asked, unaware that the company representative had disappeared as soon as he regained consciousness.

She kneaded his arms and the uninjured leg. "I'm sure someone will be here.

You just worry about getting better. Like the doctor said, good thoughts lead to good health." But deep down inside she was less optimistic. Her mind was filling with crushing what-ifs—what if no one from the company came? No, they wouldn't be that heartless. He'd been injured on the job. And they were a big company. But migrant workers were suckers for the big companies, weren't they? If you were hospitalized you could kiss your hard-earned savings goodbye—every last *yuan* would go toward the bill. But the real danger was being crippled. For an unskilled, uneducated farmer, your body was your sole asset, you had to be capable of manual labor.

The deeper her thoughts, the more her worry-balloon puffed up. No, nothing of the sort would happen. As she was kneading his limbs, she dozed off. This pattern repeated itself throughout the night, her depleted body increasingly ponderous and her anxiety building to a flash point. *No, I'm getting carried away. They'll have a heart. Bad as he's injured they'll help him somehow... I just have to be patient.*

The next morning, before she left, she said to him, "Honey, when the company man comes, you can't let him walk all over you. You need a cool head. You have to look nasty, and..." She racked her brain. "And don't let them slight you...you have to be very strong; you can't be a softie, all right? Focus—really focus." For reinforcement she displayed a clenched fist. Her hand was gnarled and raw, not a young woman's hand. Her hand was the result of years of rough work on the farm and in the kitchen.

The niggling thoughts continued to assail her while she worked. She would stand in place, lost in thought, the vacuum cleaner running. The wash cycle would finish but she would forget to transfer the laundry to the dryer. The dishes she was washing clanked together dangerously. Working four hours apiece for two families had never felt so long and tedious.

Finally, she returned to the hospital. "Any visitors, honey?"

Her husband turned toward the wall, his lips tightening.

"I was afraid of that."

More silence. She couldn't even hear him breathe.

"Talk to me, please. Tell me what we should do."

No response.

Rage shot up, tears flowed, but she managed to say, "I'll go see them tomorrow. I can't let them treat you like this, I'll kill myself first."

Finally, he spoke. "That's enough, woman. Help me get ready to leave."

"What? The doctor said you needed a couple more months here."

"Well, guess what?" Zhang sighed. "They told me the company paid for five days—one, two, three, four, five."

"And they're kicking you out?" she screamed through clenched teeth, quivering in rage.

Zhang heaved a deeper sigh. "What did you expect? If I want to stay longer, I pay now—otherwise it's pack up and get out."

"Bastards deserve to die!" she half-screamed, half-sobbed, her face streaked with tears. "You can hardly move. I thought hospitals were supposed to help people."

Zhang gazed blankly at the ceiling. "Stinking-rich sons of bitches," he muttered. "To them we're peasants, dirty helping hands, we're not even human. *Ren tai duo, ren tai duo.*"

Stifling her sobs, she went to find a doctor. A nurse intercepted her. "The doctor has completed his examination of your husband," she said in a frigid tone. "Is there something you would like me to pass on to him?"

"He told us my husband needs two months of treatment," Sungqing quavered. "But you're asking him to leave when he's hurt so bad he can't even walk—"

"That's been discussed. If you want two months' treatment, you'll have to arrange it in advance. Don't worry about his lack of mobility. We can provide a wheelchair so he gets home safely—of course you'll need to pay for it in advance."

Sungqing could only gape at the woman. The venomous bitch—was she born heartless?

Back to her husband's ward she rushed. "I'm going to your company," she said, breathless with anger.

Zhang shook his head. "You're wasting your time. The security guy won't let you in. He probably wouldn't let *me* in."

She made a face. "What are we going to do? Look at you, how can they ditch you like this?"

"I know, it's damn vexing. Let's think it over. We'll go home, and I'll work on getting better. *Then* I go see them."

"How is going home supposed to help you get better?"

"The doctor said I'm over the hump. I'll be all right if I keep checking in with an outpatient clinic."

"The company, this hospital, they're blood-suckers. They have all the money they need and still they're hungry for more. What do they care about people like us?"

"Save your energy. Sure they're after money—that's why they're loaded. There are too many of us migrant workers. We're like weeds. A government job is out of our reach, so we're treated like pigs. But I'll manage. Don't you get worked up, please." He clutched his left side, where the ribs were cracked.

"Try not to talk, honey. You need to rest." What was best for him? She made a decision. "You're not going home. First we need to fix you up. We'll use our savings."

"What! No way do we touch that money," he said, shaking his head obstinately. "That's for our little emperor. So he can go to college." Poor, worthless peasant he might be, but his only son was a little emperor.

Her retort was stronger. "That's silly. He needs his parents before he goes off to school. Once you're taken care of, *then* we worry about our little emperor!"

Zhang shook his head, which brought a painful frown. "No. I will not use that money."

Unflinching, she regarded him. "Think—what happens if you neglect yourself on account of money? You'll be crippled the rest of your life. Then what? You can't earn money and I'm the only one working. We live like beggars and our dream is shattered—we can't send our little emperor off to college. Look, I know how you feel. But we have to put out your fire first. Our savings we'll get back from the company."

Zhang avoided her gaze. "I can't," he murmured. "It means too much. ...."

Sungqing was undeterred. "We *are* using that money. It won't go to waste, I'm telling you. We'll get it all back."

"It sounds good, but..." Doubt clouded his face.

"Don't worry, we'll get that money back. We're not crooks—we'll show them the receipts."

"Honey, I'm sorry." And his wretchedly haggard face said as much. "Why did I have to get hurt?"

The hard work of persuasion was over, but starting the next day Sungqing was on pins and needles. The hospital bill was exorbitant, but she couldn't haggle, which to her was a way of life. It was half the fun of buying something. Why couldn't she try to bargain down the cost of treatment?

Two months of hospital costs—it was a nightmare to calculate. It would wipe out their savings and then some. Three years of savings, every nerve tuned to the ultimate goal that had brought them here from the ancestral village.

Keeping house for two families brought home 3,000 *yuan* a month, about 500 dollars; his earnings were 2,000 *yuan*. After paying 1,000 in rent and 1,500 for food and other expenses, they sent the remaining 2,500 back to the village, where her in-laws cared for the little emperor, 1,200 going for the boy's school fees and general upkeep. Even for a grade school boy the expenses were endless. Gone were the days when textbooks were a pupil's only need. Their little emperor and his classmates now needed children's books, the World Heroes set, the *History Illustrated* books, the science series, and more.

Letters arrived from her in-laws, composed with the help of a neighbor. *We can't ignore the little rascal; he wants those books so he can grow up to be big and famous. Can you believe he tries to teach us what he learns from those books? He is so smart, smarter than we are, and it's because of what he is reading. We know how difficult it is for you to save money, but we just couldn't be stingy with him.*

Reading this letter, Zhang felt he was walking on air. He wanted to kick up his heels and dance. He promptly wrote back. *So our little emperor is going to be a big emperor. By all means, please go ahead. It is not a problem. Studying hard to be a big emperor! All successful people read lots and lots of books—isn't that what they say? Knowing that he likes to read makes all of our hard work worth it, here so far from home.*

Sungqing had planted the idea of migrant work in Zhang's mind. Riding the whirlwind of money promised in the cities, the young were fleeing the farming villages once they came of working age. Work awaited them the day they arrived, whereas back on the farm all they could look forward to was breaking their backs in the fields, with little to show for it. What would you do if you heard the factories would hire you as soon as you landed in the city, pay you a thousand *yuan* a month, and give you a raise once you picked up some skills? Sungqing's heart fluttered whenever the neighbor kids sent money home and when they came back for Chunjie, the lunar new year, proud as could be, stylish in the latest fashions, and armed with bundles of gifts. She could see it right in front of her—the new world had arrived! Chairman Deng, affectionately short and stout, had made it possible for comrades to live well. He was the sun in this new world, second in brilliance only to Chairman Mao.

"Honey," she had said. "Let's go to the city like everyone else. We'll work and get rich, you and me. Then we can send our little emperor to college."

"I know," said Zhang, "but—"

"But what? Why all the moaning and groaning? Are you afraid? Every other man takes off without looking back."

"Aren't you forgetting something? We don't live just by ourselves."

It was then that she had realized how thoughtful he was. Fortunately, his parents made it easy for them to decide. And don't fathers-in-law tend to dote on their daughter-in-law? "Go, you two, we'll be fine. The sooner you start earning, the better. You're not getting any younger. The baby will grow up right here," said Zhang's father, pointing to his bosom. "Your filial duty is to show us you are living well. So pack up and be on your way." And so it was that with her in-laws' blessing Sungqing and her husband had joined the migration to the city.

The next morning Sungqing stopped buying street food for breakfast. The meals were cheap, one or two *yuan* at most, and tasty—beef soup with rice noodles, congee with black egg, bean soup and a bun—each sufficient to fill a laborer's stomach. Working four hours in the morning on an empty stomach would suck up her strength, but she had to endure if they were to extend her husband's treatment.

The next challenge was to find work she could do after the two back-to-back housekeeping shifts, anything to bring in a few extra *yuan*. In desperation she thought of working as a hostess at a karaoke bar or a room salon. The next moment she smiled bitterly. At age twenty-five she was over the hill by industry standards, and she had a plain face—no way could she light a fire in a guy's mind while she lightened his wallet.

Like most migrant workers, she had spent her youth working in the fields. If you came straight to the city in your late teens, you'd find work in the factories and the room salons. But if you were over twenty-five, you were treated like you were on death's doorstep. Factory rejects couldn't be choosy; they had to plunge into any opportunity that came their way. For all the glitter and shine, the cities offered no shelter to the migrants. You had to find any work you could just to eat and earn.

They were like migrating birds, only it was work sites that drew them instead of warmer climes. And it was thanks to this migrant work force that the urban skyline now offered a sweeping panorama of skyscrapers. No matter how advanced your weaponry, you compelled surrender only when your infantry deployed it in their grunt work. The same was true of construction work—however high-quality the materials, the gigantic buildings were not completed until the laborers did the detail work. It was they who built the transportation arteries of the land, the highways and tunnels that had honeycombed China in record time. The manned satellites, the high-speed rail, everything that boosted a third-world economy based on cheap labor to a proud, first-rate technological nation—it all owed to the feats of the migrant workers. Without them, rail lines would never have stretched through the mountainous terrain to Tibet in such a short time.

Afraid Chisŏn and her other mistress would second-guess the quality of her work if they knew of her money concerns, Sungqing withheld her ill-fated saga from them, simply reporting that her husband's company would pay for his treatment.

It was their housemates to whom she confided, and her story brought a shower of indignation. "Sons of bitches. It's unbelievable," said one, quickly chorused with, "May Heaven strike them with lightning, and their generations to follow. They neglect worker safety, then blame the poor guy for falling. How can they do that?" Or, "Yes, the ones with money are the worst. How much is a hospital bill compared to the boss's paycheck?" It was a familiar topic of conversation, with familiar lines. "I'd say blood from a bird's foot, a drop in the bucket." "So what's your next step? Must be damn annoying. Can't you report it to the PSB?" "Are you out of your mind—who at the PSB would take our side?" "He's right, those officials are as crooked as the rich. And we're outcasts, we're on our own." "Yes, in their eyes we're scum." "Fuck yes! And we're treated worse and worse." "But why? The haves get more, the have-nots get less, and soon we'll have nothing. Something's terribly wrong. Someone has to be responsible." "You wish. Goddamn world without a soul, it can go to hell for all I care."

They were no less angry than Sungqing. In this emotional wasteland of a city, with no arm to lean on or shoulder to cry on, she drew comfort from them. They were the only ones who would empathize. Their gripes ultimately dissipated within the confines of the apartment, and yet she was grateful for their vehement words, the same ones she wanted to scream to the world. But still she felt lonely.

For three years she and her husband had known them only as housemates. They had flocked to Shanghai from every corner of the land, and here they were living fifteen to an apartment in a city of sky-high rents. The different accents and regional dialects created difficulties. She sometimes wished one of them could interpret, so that the man from Szechuan to the west could communicate with the man from Heilongjiang to the northeast. How did all these people manage to live in the same country? Not just the dialects but the customs, manners, even the thought patterns were different. The teeming residents divided the sixty-six-plus-square-meter space into four sections. There were daily outbreaks of squawking. *Quaiquai* was the word on everyone's lips when it came to sharing the kitchen, the laundry room, and the bathroom, leading to more squabbles. The fifteen of them were forever contending over the utility bills.

To Sungqing it had never felt like home. New apartments in China were marketed without the finishing touches, on the belief that the new owners would furnish and decorate to their liking. How considerate of the builders—we wouldn't want a nefarious owner tearing down their creation to remake it in his own image, would we? Rental apartments likewise came unfinished. Why would the owners waste money on the renters, who if it was up to them probably couldn't have afforded the accoutrements? What did they care if their new apartment looked raw and ugly, as long as it had the basic necessities of heat, water, and electricity?

Month-to-month rentals were clustered in the satellite cities, where land was cheaper. Blocks of these units were owned by the fabulously rich, who had no qualms about hiring hulking thugs to drive out tenants if the rent was late, dumping the stragglers' belongings onto the street.

In any metropolis there were also cheap rentals catering to young salaried workers, the living space—there as with the migrants—divvied up as small as possible and layered with bunk beds. Colonies of these impoverished young workers were also to be found in the slums, where they were called ant tribes by the migrant workers.

In addition to skipping breakfast, Sungqing now walked to her housekeeping jobs instead of taking the bus. Still, by the end of Zhang's first month of treatment their savings were exhausted. When they were unable to make the next payment, the hospital discharged him that very day.

One last time the doctor reminded Zhang, "You can seek outpatient treatment, but we can't be responsible for what happens if you leave now."

Sungqing's earnings as a housekeeper were inadequate for the purpose, so once again she looked into night-time work, dishwashing at a restaurant or doing the laundry at a foot-massage parlor. But there were no openings. By day she smiled to others; at night she cried herself to sleep. If only she could take time off from her housekeeping duties and seek out her husband's employer. But by now the two mistresses were so used to their cozy lives that they would sooner touch a poisonous snake than dirty dishes. The more comfortable you became, the more comfort you wanted; it was human nature. For Sungqing, pleading her sad-sack case again to either of them would be to cut her own throat.

She found herself praying to the spirits in heaven, hands clasped together. She understood now why people visited Taoist or Buddhist temples, and why along with offering prayers they burned precious incense as if it were money. If only she prayed with all her heart, if only she had the money to burn incense, then she could hope for her husband's recovery.

But her ardent prayers had no visible effect. When first he began walking again, a month after he left the hospital, he had to push off against the wall just to stand up, and could take only one tottering step at a time.

"What the hell is wrong with me?" he shouted.

"Honey, be careful!" said Sungqing in alarm. "Try to stand up straight!"

Back to the hospital they went.

"What did I tell you?" the doctor scolded. "You need proper treatment. Your fracture seems to have healed, but the bones are out of alignment—there's nothing to be done." And with a dismissive wave he terminated the consultation.

Sungqing felt weak in the knees. "You mean for the rest of his life he ..."

Steadying her, Zhang said in a sinking voice, "Honey, let's go."

Every day he attempted a few desperate steps with the aid of his walking stick. But whenever the left leg took his weight, pain shot to his brain and he broke out in a cold sweat.

She tried to be patient. "Take your time, honey. Try not to overdo it."

"No, I need to keep working at it," he said through clenched teeth, mopping his sweaty face. "I'm going to see those bastards. The longer I wait, the worse it'll turn out."

What good will that do? Why waste your time and energy when you're still weak? These words were on the tip of her tongue, and there they stayed. He already felt helpless—how could she add to his despair?

No longer did she expect anything from the company. She knew of many migrant workers injured on the job, and never had there been a satisfying outcome or sufficient comp package. Instead, she focused on finding work that was within his means. But it was all in vain. And she was well aware of all the able-bodied men who went with their pull-cart to the market first thing in the morning, to push and shove for a load to haul, only to come home empty-handed at the end of the day.

Her husband wasn't even forty, an age when a man was full of life. How could he be crippled the rest of his days? There had to be work he could do sitting. But what—and where? Maybe not manual labor, maybe something that involved a skill? But old dogs couldn't learn new tricks, and even if he'd been young enough to learn a trade, who would want to teach him out of the goodness of his heart? She grew ever more flustered, her despairing mind going obstinately in circles.

After a week and a half of learning to walk again, Zhang left for the construction company, determined to see the supervisor.

He gazed up at the building he'd been working on; it was much taller now. What if he'd fallen from the tenth floor instead of the fourth? He thought back to the horror he'd felt when the veneer floor of the scaffolding had given away, the fear of death washing over him. He tried to remember the color of that death. Was it red? Pitch black? He wasn't sure. What he *had* been sure of—it was so vivid— was that he was about to die. And then he had felt only nothingness. Leaning on his walking stick, he wondered if it was his good luck, or a curse, to still be alive.

Give me back my life! Arming himself with these words, Zhang gritted his teeth and took one last look up at the great building. In his mind he was making a life-or-death decision. He was staking his life on compensation for what he had lost.

He took a deep breath and released it. He took a step toward the massive gate. His left leg wobbled. He took another step.

A security guard in uniform and hard hat blocked him. "Hey, where are you going?"

Zhang peered at him. "You don't remember me? I'm Zhang Wanxing. And you want to know what I'm doing here. It's been a while since I stopped coming to work, hasn't it?"

The guard backed off.

"Look, my friend—not very pretty, am I? You need to be careful. Someday you might get hit by one of those trucks and end up like me. They didn't pay to fix me up. They ignored me, and now I can barely walk. So where am I going? To see the foreman."

"Well, he's, uh—"

"Relax," said Zhang with a reassuring tap on the guard's shoulder. "I'll tell him I shoved you out of the way and marched in." He set out for the side door, where the workers entered.

"What a mess," the guard tutted as he watched the limping Zhang. "How could a healthy man…"

"What are you doing here?" snapped the foreman the moment he saw Zhang.

Listing to the left and then managing to straighten himself, Zhang hobbled up to him. "See for yourself—look at me!"

The foreman sneered at him. "We're done with you."

"Watch your mouth," Zhang snarled, brandishing his walking stick. "Say that again and you're a dead man. I may be crippled but I have enough strength left to kill a piece of shit like you." He drew closer and fixed the foreman with a murderous glare, the point of his stick leveled at the man's eyes.

The foreman cringed and backpedaled. "What are you doing? I'll call the police," he muttered. But his desk cut off his retreat.

Again Zhang narrowed the distance between them, walking stick still poised for attack. "Go ahead. And when they get here they'll find both of us dead."

"Why are you doing this?" whimpered the foreman. "What do you want?"

"I want my life back. The life you took away from me. And I'll get it, or else die trying."

"All right, I understand. I know it's unfair. But you have to talk with management, I only do what they tell me."

Zhang raised the walking stick high. "You idiot! Was I injured in the board-room? No, it happened there! Right outside—there! And you're the one who was on duty. Don't you get it?"

"Yes, I get it," said the trembling foreman. "All right, I'll report to them. Give me a few days."

"I'll give you *two* days. And then I'll be back."

Zhang decided to say nothing to his wife just yet, for fear of disappointing her if something went wrong. And what a nice surprise if the outcome were successful.

Anxiety gnawed at him the next two days. How would it turn out? He wasn't one to dream big. All he'd ever wanted was to be able to open a shop back home. It was his childhood dream—freedom from having to till the soil, and a guarantee of an easier life.

Two tension-filled days later he returned to the construction site and hobbled up to the gate. Three men were waiting for him. A chill went up his spine.

"What the fuck is this?"

The men lunged and took hold of him. "Shut up, you son of a bitch."

"Let me go!" he screamed. "Let me go!" He writhed and squirmed until they managed to pin his arms and legs and gag him. Then he was shoved into a car and blindfolded. He felt like he was in a cave. It had all been so sudden.

He was driven somewhere, then hauled out and pushed down a flight of stairs. He counted the steps—thirty-four. Two floors down from ground level? He heard a clunk and what sounded like a heavy metal door wheezed open. He was shoved inside, and the blindfold was removed. The door thunked shut. He rubbed his eyes and blinked, but saw nothing in the pitch dark.

He was a prisoner! He had heard of underworld gangs with their own jails--did this one belong to the company? What would the company need a jail for? And why had they brought him here? Who were they, anyway, hired thugs? Anything was possible.

He was sucked into a vortex of fear. No one knew he was here. They could kill him and leave no trace. Why hadn't he told his wife? He shuddered, then told himself he'd done the right thing. If she had known, who knows what she might have done—and then she might have been vulnerable too.

Long hours passed. He wet his pants twice, though he hadn't taken a drop of water.

The door clunked open. Again he was blindfolded, then stuffed into a car and taken away. When the car stopped and he was pulled out he smelled salt air, and the next thing he knew, he was aboard a rocking vessel. They were taking him out to sea! That was where the thugs got rid of you, weighing you down with rocks or metal.

There was a bang, followed by the roar of an engine, and the boat lurched into motion. He was placed flat on the deck, his arms were tied behind his back, and for good measure his ankles were secured.

He felt a blustery wind, and then the boat stopped. Off came the blindfold. Blinded by a light, he clamped his eyes shut. That earned him a punch to the chin.

"Open your eyes, asshole."

Head spinning, he forced open his eyes. He needed to see the faces of these scum. But all that registered was the intense ray of light. It was a flashlight beam.

"Listen carefully, shithead. You see this knife? I could slit your throat and throw you to the sharks and by morning there'd be nothing left of you. But we're taking pity on your wife and kid, so we'll give you one more chance. What do you say, want to call it quits? Or are you going to act up again?"

"No, no, sir. Never."

"Never again. Right?"

"Yes, sir. Never again."

"All right, beggar. It's your lucky day. And you work for one sweet company, otherwise we wouldn't be stopping here."

He was taken off the boat, loaded back into the car blindfolded, and dumped in the middle of nowhere. The car sped off. He removed the blindfold, but it was night and he had no clue where he was. He took a deep breath, painful after the day's beating. Home couldn't be too far.

He found his way back that night. The entire saga had taken place in the course of a day. He collapsed in bed, telling Sungqing he had been out looking for work. For two days he was sick.

When finally he rose, it was all he could do to speak. "I'm so sorry, honey, but I really want to go back home for a visit. If I can just see our little emperor's face it would do wonders for me."

Sungqing was overjoyed. "That's a wonderful idea—I'll have some money for you tomorrow."

The man standing in front of the skyscraper scattered leaflets in the air.

"Give me back my life!" he shouted as the leaflets flew off on the wind. "Give me back my life!" He hefted a large plastic container and doused himself with an orange liquid. For the third time he cried out, "Give me back my life!" Then he took out a lighter. There was a tiny flame, and the next moment an explosion, followed by a flame a hundred times larger.

Passersby cringed while security guards rushed out from the building.

The flames engulfed the man and he burned furiously. And then his writhing slowed and weakened.

From inside the building a man looked down on the scene. "Clean it up before the reporters swarm in," he barked. "Leave no trace! And call the PSB and make sure they secure the area. Move!"

"Yes sir!" cried half a dozen men to the company chairman before scurrying out.

The self-immolation merited not a line in the papers or a mention in the broadcasts. Business continued as normal in this extravagant, bustling city—you never would have known a man had set himself on fire. The death of a migrant worker was like a tiny bubble of foam disintegrating on the vast ocean.

10. Forgiveness Is a Gift of Reflection

"Honey, look." Chisŏn held a fifty-*yuan* bill against the light, examining it from various angles.

No response from Chŏn.

Impatiently thrumming the bill, she called out to him, "I want you to look at this—I think it's counterfeit!"

"What?" came his voice from a distance. "I can't hear you, I'm shaving."

She scurried to the bathroom door. "Look, Mr. Peace-Under-Heaven, you've been living here so long you're way beyond *manmandi*. You've turned into a slug." Peevishly she fanned the bill so he could see it in the mirror. "It was in with the money you gave me yesterday. Where did you get it?"

"What's the big deal? How much is it anyway?" said Chŏn to the image of his wife in the mirror as he worked the razor down his cheek.

"It's a fifty."

"Hell, maybe if it was a hundred," he said, looking away from the mirror.

Barging into the bathroom, she stuck the bill in his face. "Listen to the big shot. You've been hanging around the overnight millionaires too long. Check this out."

"Yup, it's fake all right."

She scowled. "You know it's fake but you take it anyway? That's stupid. Where did you get it?"

"What does it matter?"

"I'm going to exchange it."

"Oh come on—how long have you lived here?"

"What do you mean?" she said, looking as irritated as she sounded.

"They'll just play innocent—unless you have CCTV evidence."

"I'm so mad—on your miserable salary how can you laugh off a fake fifty-*yuan* bill?"

"You need to take better care of yourself," he said philosophically. "You do know that stress and anxiety are the main causes of cancer, right?" By now the razor was making leisurely strokes up and down his other cheek. "I bet it was that cab driver a couple of nights ago when I was out drinking. It's one of their favorite tricks when they pick up someone who's drunk."

"Don't you know by now?" she said, stamping her feet in frustration. "You need to be careful with your money, even if you're blind drunk—we're living in copycat heaven, remember?"

"So what's new? And why are you being so bitchy?"

"It's happened too often. I can name you half a dozen times."

"That's not as bad as a dozen."

"You want me to drop dead of indignation? Huh? So you can get yourself a new wife?"

"Your favorite line. Well, why not? I'm dying for a new wife."

She held up the bill in both hands as if to rip it in half. "How can people live here? You can't trust anything, it's all bogus."

"Whoa, no so fast."

She gaped at him. "Why not? Oh, so now you remember the taxi driver?"

He gently pulled the bill free. "No. I want it for a souvenir."

"What"

With an amiable smile he waved the bill triumphantly. "I thought I told you. Last year I gave a fake fifty to one of the top guys from headquarters—he wanted a souvenir. Boy was he excited! You can never find this stuff when you need it most."

"The hell with souvenirs!" she snorted. "Fake cooking oil, fake dumplings, ginger, soybean sprouts, pork, cucumbers, baby powder, ice cream, peanuts, even fake eggs—how many souvenirs do you need? You're right, I'm getting neurotic. How can they counterfeit *food items*? These people are beyond saving!" With one last burst of tutting she fled the bathroom.

If tsk-tsking were an Olympic event, Chŏn said to himself. "*Aigu*, my dear lady," he said in a singsong tone, "dost thou deem thy homeland, the Republic of Korea, the purest of the pure, the freest of fakes? Might thee deign to guess the reigning champion, ever since Liberation in 1945, of counterfeit chili pepper, fake sesame oil, bogus honey? What sayest thou? I pray thee venture an opinion on intermingling our rice, black pepper, and salt with their Chinese counterparts and purveying said items as Korean? And dost thou recall the falsification of the origin and circulation dates for beef, pork, and chicken? I beg thee, fair lady, speak."

From the far corner of the apartment came a shriek. "Stop hamming it up. We're a class above the people here. You get so defensive whenever I talk about China. Since when do the Chinese need you as an apologist?"

"Me, defensive? Can't we be a little more forgiving and indulgent toward our number-one market? China's not the only country with problems. Speaking of counterfeit money, can you guess which form of payment is most welcome in the West—cash, travelers check, or credit card? It's the card of course. You get a ten percent discount on a card purchase and a big smile for a bonus. But try a hundred-dollar bill and you get a hard look. They flip it over front and back— they make you feel like a criminal. And forget the discount. Wouldn't you feel like someone's country cousin, carrying such big bills? What that tells me is they have enough counterfeiting problems of their own. And Korea's the same—fake money and now fake bank checks."

"Here you go again, edifying the masses! Get it in your head that back home we have nowhere near the problems they have here."

"Where's your proof? How can you compare a country with 1.4 billion people to a country with 50 million? Back home we compare today's China with us in the seventies or eighties. Remember what Korea was like then? As good as China today? No way, not even close. You want examples? How about number of electronic goods per capita, number of televisions, automobiles? How about the highway system, the number of universities, the number of books published? No comparison with China now. I don't get it—why do Westerners and Koreans still think China's so backward?"

"Enough—my ears are hurting. Stop talking to me like I'm your student."

"Honey, this is basic. Sure China has problems with air quality, public etiquette, corruption, freedom of speech, and all. But what's our frame of reference? We brag about we accomplished back home—it took us thirty or forty years to get where the West did in two centuries. Here, I'd say twenty to thirty years—from stinking outhouses to flush toilets, from the abacus to the computer. But can't you see where unchecked growth and concentrated development might come with a certain amount of chaos? Think about that the next time you see a Chinese guy naked to the waist screaming into his cellphone on a main street. This kind of transition happens everywhere, and eventually the problems get fixed. But Westerners don't see it that way; they're always finding fault with China, and that's why they're still shaking their head at the country exploding into the world's number two economy. That's what happens when you don't want to get off your high horse. I hope someday you can change your outlook on China. Then maybe you won't get heartburn over a stupid fifty-*yuan* bill."

She rolled her eyes. "What a shame that such a distinguished gentleman is going to seed here. I wish I could ask the government to provide a sedan chair for its supreme mouthpiece. I'm terribly sorry I lack the *guanxi*."

"So catty." Chŏn smiled bitterly as he applied aftershave. "Well, I've done my part—the rest is up to you."

"Yes, and what's up to me is different from your holy mission. First, I don't care for the new maid, and second, that fifty *yuan* could have bought a few days' worth of groceries."

"What's wrong with the new maid?"

"She's different from the old one. I have to keep nagging—it's going to take a while to break her in."

"Have you heard from Sungqing?"

"You are so naïve, Mr. Been-There-Done-That," she fumed. "Tell me, have *you* ever heard from someone who left for a better-paying job? She must have found a place offering a few more *yuan*—so much for loyalty. The people here would go through fire and water for money—it's disgusting. I bet if we ran into each other she'd pretend she never saw me before."

Chŏn imagined a pair of skewers emerging from her sharp gaze. "Honey, it's over," he said with a pat on the shoulder. "Where money is concerned there's no father and no son, right? And it's worse if siblings or strangers are involved."

"I know, but I can't help it!" And then, after a pause, "About that wedding you're going to—whatever possessed your co-worker to have it on a Sunday? That's the only day people have off."

"So what? They'll get more guests."

"Hmm. Meaning more red envelopes."

"Of course."

"And that's my point. They don't care if it's a day off. It's the money they're focusing on. Oh, how I hate the people here."

"He's a loyal subject, you know."

"What are you talking about?"

"If he gets married on a weekday no work gets done, right?"

"Oh my god. And your CEO still doesn't know you're stud material for one of the presidencies?"

"I wait patiently for the day my luminous qualities are revealed to the world."

"And I'm not holding my breath, my lord." Chisŏn leaned against the bathroom doorway. "By the way, did I tell you our ladies' club held a vote? It was unanimous."

"Excuse me?"

"You forgot, didn't you?" With her finger she drew a line around her eye.

"What? Double-eyelid surgery?"

"Why so surprised? The hubbies are all opposed, we're all in favor. Something wrong with that?" She snorted.

"You're all doing it?"

"Yes. The whole gang, all sixteen of us, we even got ten percent off. Some of the guys made noises about divorce, so guess what—we hired a lawyer and decided we'll file for divorce as a group if we have to. Who wants a stick-in-the-mud husband who doesn't understand his wife's needs? No thank you. And you're welcome— we're not thinking about nose surgery." So saying, she spun away from him.

"God help us," he moaned, wrapping his head in his hands.

Well, what did he expect with all the trading-company wives living in the same apartment complex. He pictured the sixteen women standing in line at the door to Sŏ's clinic—it was ludicrous. But he couldn't very well ask Sŏ to turn them away. It wasn't as if Sŏ had put them up to it. Still, this was the last thing he expected when he had invited Sŏ to China.

He wrestled with the issue but soon gave in. Hell, it wasn't his eyelids getting slit. But then he got to wondering about Sŏ—how good was he, really?

The wedding was being held in the grand ballroom of a hotel. Chŏn arrived to find dozens of huge wreaths in place at the ballroom doors, and a double line of guests waiting to register and to offer the congratulatory envelopes. The length of the two lines bespoke the economic clout and extensive network of the bride's father.

Taking his place in the sluggish line on the groom's side, Chŏn killed time checking out the other guests. As meaningful as the ceremony would be for the couple themselves, for guests like him it was a tedious play with a predictable ending—no twist and no hidden, symbolic meaning.

Bored with examining the guests, he thought about the groom, Li Changchun. Li was the envy of his co-workers. The son of a high Party official in Shenyang, he was marrying a Shanghai princess whose father was a wealthy businessman. Li had all the qualifications for a son-in-law—a high-ranking Party member for a father, ancestral home in the North, graduate of a well-known Shanghai university, and last but not least, employment with a foreign firm. Such qualifications endowed a potential son-in-law with as much *mianzi* as a Cadillac or a diamond-studded Rolex.

The preference for northern men—those born north of the Yellow River—was rooted in solid historical and scientific evidence. Compared with southerners— those born south of the Yangzi—they were sturdy-boned, physically strong, unyielding, and resilient—perfect qualifications for a man. Their physical strength was a crucial factor in China's long and majestic history. Many were the southern dynasties that surrendered to the northerners and suffered the humiliation of having to pay them tribute. The Northern and Southern Song dynasties from a millennium ago paid tribute to the Liao and Jin dynasties. Southern Song fell to Genghis Khan, and thus was the Yuan dynasty born. Zhu Yuanzhang rebuilt the strength of the Han Chinese and drove out the Mongols, but his Ming dynasty in its turn was subjugated by the Manchurian Qing.

Thanks to his grasp of Chinese history, Chŏn was aware of the qualities attributed to northern men. The people here liked to say that if you had a mortal grudge to satisfy, the fists of northeastern Manchuria were the men for the job. The pepper-loving men of Sichuan were well known for their stud power, but took second place to the men of the Northeast, where the groom was from.

And compared with northern women, those of the South had petite faces and willowy, slender bodies with tiny waists and taut skin. Playboys liked to call them soft-boned southern ladies.

The marriage, as it turned out, was the best of both worlds, the union of a northern man with all the essential qualifications and a southern woman.

Chŏn drew near the registration table and took from his inner pocket the red envelope that was de rigeur for any and all occasions for rejoicing, whether New Year, a birthday, or the launching of a new business. Bowing politely, he offered the envelope, then signed the guest book.

One of the three men on duty shamelessly opened the envelope and counted. "Eight hundred and eighty-eight *yuan!*" He thrust the money to the man in the middle, who ran it through a counterfeit money detector.

Chŏn closed his eyes and tutted. He'd seen these devices all through his ten years here but had never gotten used to them. He was abashed—was it really him, the source of the money, that they were checking? Granted, counterfeit tender was a serious concern, but the alacrity with which they attempted to ferret it out doomed them, in Chŏn's eyes, to implanting the negative image of a people who knew nothing but money.

The money detector was a must for banks, of course, but also for large, thriving restaurants, which preferred cash payments to credit cards. The credit card was like a withering tree. Some huge cash handlers even carried a personal money detector.

It wasn't just the machines that did the detecting. Anywhere you wanted to spend a hundred-*yuan* bill you could expect the receiving party to check on the geniality of Chairman Mao's benevolent, Buddha-like face. A bookshop owner would examine the Chairman's face against a strong light, an antique shop keeper would flick a fingertip against the taut bill, and a fruitmonger auntie would crumple the great Chairman's face and then uncrumple it to see if she still recognized it. A large denomination, the hundred-*yuan* bill was an object of suspicion.

Chŏn's gift having passed inspection, the man in the middle transferred the cash to the man on his left, who fed it into to a massive briefcase. In lieu of a receipt Chŏn had to settle for a handwritten "Thank you for the 888 yuan."

Triple eights symbolized the most prosperous, the wealthiest, and the happiest life. They were perfect for expressing the depth of Chŏn's attention to his underling.

Otherwise Chŏn found Chinese weddings peculiar. He was used to the uproar but found the happy-go-lucky nattering excessive. And when you added the the big beat of a band, you could practically feel the earth rumble beneath your feet.

In the raucous banquet hall Chŏn kept checking his watch. It was twenty minutes past the appointed hour but the ceremony hadn't started. He asked one of his Chinese staffers to look into the holdup. It was the Korean in him. He always reminded himself to practice *manmandi* but in situations such as this he couldn't help getting annoyed. The Chinese were like rocks—they didn't inquire, they didn't complain, they simply waited. Such patience was beyond Chŏn.

The staffer rose from their table. "I'll find out."

Chŏn smiled in spite of himself. In a culture where you didn't bow to superiors or offer a seat to a senior citizen or a woman on the subway, the man had managed to pick up some Korean etiquette since coming aboard Chŏn's company. Chŏn was still trying to figure out how women in skirts or dresses could sit with their crotch open and their panties in view and not think twice about it.

The staffer returned and reported to Chŏn: the man with the fattest red envelope of all had yet to arrive, and thus the delay.

Chŏn snorted. Among the 1.3 billion unusual happenings, this was a new one. How fat did an envelope have to be to keep hundreds of guests waiting? Especially considering the affluence of the wedding party. But the guests, basking in the joyous occasion, cackling, chattering, and toasting, didn't seem to care. Would he ever understand this inscrutable jungle of a society?

"Sir?" said the staffer in an attempt to mollify Chŏn. "Did you know he's getting married twice?"

"Why twice?"

"They're having another ceremony in Shenyang."

"Why Shenyang?"

"It's too far for the groom's guests to come here. The ceremony today is mainly for the bride's side," he said matter-of-factly.

"Is that the only reason?" Chŏn wondered if lucky money was also a factor.

"Well, of course there's the collection," explained the man. "You can imagine how much the groom's father has spent in that area."

It made sense, thought Chŏn. The groom's father was a high Party official. And back home such officials, especially national assemblymen, could reap hundreds of millions of *wŏn* by staging a razzle-dazzle wedding. Here where the money god was worshiped, why miss out on a legitimate golden opportunity?

Fanciness, extravagance, indulgence. But at what cost to one's health? Chŏn wondered. You didn't read about Coca-Cola damaging your teeth or other bone structures—the comrades had been loyally consuming the beverage for at least three decades. McDonald's hamburgers? You never knew what kind of beef went into them, or that their fat content might be unhealthy. The public was not educated in the evils of fat—who would want consumers to know it contributed to high blood pressure, diabetes, and heart ailments? People around the world tended to eat more meat when their living standard improved, as if in revenge against the poverty they had suffered. And here people savored their improved standard of living by eating meat. A fatty hamburger and a thirst-quenching cola was a match made in heaven, leaving a satisfied smile and an oily gleam on one's face. A decade ago Chŏn would never have seen a fat person, but now they were all overweight. And cigarettes? Anti-smoking campaigns were making the rounds of the globe. But thus far Chinese society was immune to them. The local cigarettes were notoriously potent. Mao and Deng, the two national heroes, were chain smokers, free from the yoke of nicotine only when they slept. And yet Mao had lived to eighty, and Deng to ninety. So why be bothered? This blithe attitude was manifest in the ever more lavish wedding ceremonies. Chŏn knew of no social campaign for taming their extravagance.

"I'll be back," said Chŏn. "I'm going to the men's room."

His staffer half-rose and bowed. "Yes sir."

Just like a Korean, thought Chŏn. But he wasn't coming back. He'd done his triple-8 duty. They wouldn't miss him. Hell, maybe they'd be happy he'd saved them the cost of a meal. *Bon appetit!* With these thoughts he slipped out a side door.

Outside the hotel he practically jumped at the sight of the long train of red vehicles. They were stretch limousines, Cadillacs. One of the latest emblems of the nouvelle society.

In spite of himself he began counting. There were twelve of them! Compliments of the bride's father. Chŏn had seen equal numbers of Mercedes, BMWs, and Audis, as well as the occasional red stretch limo, but never a dozen glitzy Cadillacs in one place. Imagine the father's bloated pride and the spectators' ballooning envy when the red procession paraded down the avenues of Shanghai after the ceremony.

And then it hit him—everything about the wedding was show business, the trappings as fuel for the flame of exhibitionism. Another embodiment of Mr. Wang's ingenuity, an expression of his inimitable DNA. The red color? Why not? No more difficult than making fake eggs. They could do the painting overnight. How much would one of those limousines cost? Wouldn't matter as long as you could buy on credit and make monthly payments—that's how clinics could afford the most advanced medical equipment.

Not for the first time Chŏn licked his chops at his prospects in this city of millionaires. The government had changed its focus from exports to domestic consumption. The thought of it made his heart throb—there were a hundred and twenty million potential consumers with annual incomes of ten thousand dollars or more, and another sixty million for whom the figure was twenty thousand dollars or more. Domestic consumables was not an empty slogan, but a golden market. It took the spectacle of the red Cadillacs for the reality of this market to hit home. What brilliant ideas could he come up with to fetch his share of this continent of consumers? All he had to do was bait his fishing rod.

Keep your eyes open, he reminded himself with an imaginary lash. *Don't skip a beat.*

Ito was apoplectic. "He shirked his responsibilities and then he quit because his pride was injured. He received his severance pay, so there was nothing for him and me to discuss." His face was a mask of bruises, scratches, and indignation.

"*Tai guo fen!*" snapped the PBS man.

"What's he saying?" Ito asked his interpreter.

"Well." The interpreter hesitated. "The PSB always talk like that. It means something like 'arrogant.'"

"What?" Ito tutted. "That doesn't make sense."

The PSB man scowled at the interpreter. "Is he bad-mouthing me? Tell me."

"Oh no, sir, nothing about you," said the interpreter, trying to smooth over the situation. "He was just saying it's unfair."

"Why is this guy here anyway?" said the PBS man in exasperation.

"Two guys assaulted me," said the outraged Ito. "And Wu was looking on—he was *smiling*. You need to arrest that guy."

Once this had been interpreted, the PSB man said coldly, "That's your side of the story. Do you have evidence—a witness, photographs?"

"It was at night. I was by myself. No witnesses. But I saw him clear as day, with these eyes." Indignant, he articulated each word, stabbing at his eyes for emphasis.

Turning away from Ito, the PSB man muttered, "If we processed all these reports we'd never get anything done. There's never enough of us."

"Don't you see my face?" Ito protested. "There's your proof."

"Were you disabled as a result?"

"Of course not," said Ito, frowning in confusion at the question.

"Did you sustain a life-threatening injury?"

"No."

The PSB man rose. "Then consider yourself lucky. I suggest you learn a lesson from this experience." And with a dismissive wave to the interpreter he ended the interview.

"I can't believe this," grumbled Ito.

"Let us go," muttered the interpreter as he rose heavily to his feet. "This is how it goes here."

"Learn a lesson?" said Ito as he stood. "What's that supposed to mean?"

Toyotomi, when he heard the story, *tsk-tsk*ed nonstop. "I'll be damned. A wasted trip all right—you end up with your feelings hurt more than your face."

"You think I should try to get even?"

"Get even? How?"

"We can play that game too. We've got something they don't—the Samurai spirit. One stroke of the sword…"

Toyotomi saw the blood wrath in Ito's eyes. "I can understand how you feel."

"Did you know you can bring guys in from Vietnam or Myanmar? They do their job, get back on the boat, and disappear. And nobody's the wiser, see?"

"What?" Toyotomi's eyes grew wide. "How can people not know? There's always loose lips, right? And loose lips sink ships—the guys themselves know, even if they're the only ones. Eventually it gets back to you, no matter how indirectly you're connected. So come on, get a hold of your feelings. I know it's maddening. But remember, there's no such thing as a perfect crime."

"Uh-uh. I give the order, and then *I* disappear."

"What? You abandon your wife and kids, you quit a top-notch company when there's a decade-long slump back home, and you throw away your life like it's dirt?"

Ito frowned at Toyotomi. "How can you say that? What if you were me?"

Measuring his words, Toyotomi said, "It's natural you feel that way. But if it were me I'd take this as a learning opportunity and bide my time for payback."

"Well, so transcendental all of a sudden."

"Come on, don't be nasty. If you were me would you be saying, 'Sure, go ahead and do something stupid'?"

Ito dropped his gaze.

"Well?"

Ito remained silent.

"You know the old saying," said Toyotomi. "'Three measures of patience avoids one murder.' The Chinese character for 'patience' combines the knife radical and the heart radical, right? In other words, being patient means enduring the touch of a knife blade against your chest. So suck it up. Not once but three times. For you and your family too." He placed his hand on Ito's. "How about I buy you a drink? I know how mad you were with that idiot's lecture, believe me—I had the same experience five or six years ago. Our company chartered a bus and we went to a temple where a famous Tang monk practiced. We were stopping in a village when a mob attacked us. There must have been two dozen of them, young guys, with axes, sticks, you name it. They were breaking windows, smashing in the side of the bus, and the driver yelled at us to duck down and stay still, otherwise we'd be dead, and then he took off like hell. Later when we stopped he said we could have been robbed and beaten—no particulars, just mob mentality. Even the emperor's *guanxi* wouldn't have helped. Instead you have to be smart like Zhuge Liang and run like hell. It's the best tactic. The driver asked if any of us had read *Water Margin*. He said that mob was like the bandits in the book. Even after the revolution, there were traces of the bandit mentality everywhere. And that for me was a learning opportunity. A policy mandate from Beijing takes five years to filter down to the local level. Another way of putting it, a hundred-page document from Beijing ends up one page long by the time it reaches the village. That's just the way it is. When we filed a complaint we got a lecture from the PSB—they told us not to ever waste their time like that again."

"Are you serious?"

"Don't be surprised. That's when I started learning what works and what doesn't work here. We just have to play along." Toyotomi smiled bitterly. "Do you remember Kato Yoshikazu, the writer? He said we should respect *mianzi*—it's a more valuable currency than money."

Ito smiled ruefully. "I guess so."

Toyotomi tugged at Ito's sleeve. "Let's have a drink."

Off they went to a Japanese restaurant, a favorite of their fellow expatriates. They found a private room; after the big raid, the karaoke bars were no longer an option. The aftershock was like a magnitude seven earthquake, making all the local Japanese feel vulnerable. The madam of Toyotomi and Ito's preferred karaoke lounge swore she would guarantee their safety, what with her connections to the PSB, and begged for their continued patronage so she wouldn't go out of business and starve, but the allure of the karaoke bars had long since soured. They could have reminded her that the madam of the bar where the three hundred Japanese had been rounded up also had links—up to the PSB and down to the triad bosses. These women were a cogwheel that meshed with the police and the gangs and were a popular subject of movies and television dramas. The madams tickled you with honeyed words, but they were only puppets, and always within reach of the PSB. Toyotomi and Ito were not so naïve as to be seduced by the woman's coquetry into venturing back into the karaoke-bar minefield.

Toyotomi hoisted his tiny plum-blossom sake cup. "Here's to you."

Ito silently clinked his own against it. The bruises and cuts on his face were more prominent.

Downing his sake, Toyotomi pincered a chunk of sea-cucumber sashimi and asked about the project Ito's company was bidding on.

"You mean the hospital?"

"Yes."

"It's well under way."

"So far so good?"

"Yes. I'm breathing easy now."

"Great. I know it's a huge project."

"Two hundred billion dollars' worth!"

"And everybody wants a piece of the action."

"For sure—Germany, the US, even Holland."

"Are you comfortable competing with Germany and the US?"

"Yes. We're in a much better position in the pricing war. And then there's our *guanxi*."

"We definitely have an advantage there—the Western countries don't invest in their *guanxi* like we do. A cultural difference, I guess. And we fit in better."

"Let's hear it for thousands of years of DNA working its magic inside us."

"Ah yes, the mysterious DNA. Part of us forever, and yet we can't see it." He tilted his glass towards Ito. "You know, this project might be your big opportunity for a promotion."

"Maybe."

"Then forget about that PSB *baka* and go for the gold. Drink up."

"Thanks," said Ito, and the two men toasted.

After a sip, Toyotomi narrowed his eyes. "Correct me if I'm wrong, but isn't Beijing focusing on three areas for improving public welfare–health, education, and housing? Which would make medical equipment the next big market, wouldn't you say?"

"You must have noticed all the mega-hospitals going up."

"It's going to be a sweet time for your company. But still, China seems so behind in terms of Western medical science."

"Yeah, just like Russia. And Russia's even bigger than China."

"Suppose there's a commonality between socialism and backward medicine?"

"Hard to say. On the other hand, why are Koreans so advanced in Western medicine? Did you know Korea's a destination for medical tourism from Russia and China?"

"Yeah. But there are also too many things I don't understand about Korea. All that Hallyu fever, that new Finex steelmaking technology they developed after *we* helped them with the groundwork, and now Samsung has overtaken Sony; they rose like a phoenix from the IMF bailout. And just look at the Red Devils— they've got a rabid global fandom. Damned if I can understand it. The only thing I know for sure is why they keep beating us."

"In soccer?"

"Can you imagine them going home after losing to us? They'd be treated like criminals—they let the people down. Their national identity is still tied into the humiliation of being occupied by us. They all agree that payback is the answer."

Ten days later as Toyotomi was flipping through the newspaper he was stunned to see that Germany, and not Ito's company, would be supplying medical equipment to the new general hospital going up in Shanghai. How could it be?

When he managed to reach Ito, his friend heaved a thunderous sigh. "It was a last-minute knockout—Ziment got the contract."

"What happened?"

"It's a long story." Ito sounded as if he wanted to die. "If you want to meet me this afternoon, I'll tell you." He paused, and Toyotomi could hear paper rustling in the background. "No, let's make it lunch instead."

Toyotomi couldn't get down to work. A 170-million-dollar deal—a gigantic sum. And poof—up in smoke. He had thought it was in the bag. Ito must feel like killing himself. Forget about promotion, he'd probably get canned. Had his friend been caught off guard? Or had the German company had its sights on this prize all along and launched a blitzkrieg attack to capture it?

"What a fiasco," explained Ito at lunch. "Everything got screwed up. Our Hitachi products came up short. Ziment came up with a product comparison chart, and beat us in the price war. Believe it or not, these people chose quality over quantity, and they have the currency reserves to pay for it. Isn't it funny— we thought we always had cutting-edge technology; I guess we got complacent. Anyhow, that wasn't all. Ziment had *guanxi*—a German company with *guanxi*, damn it all! They hired the son of a high-level party official who'd studied in Germany. But the big blow was that the grandfather of the Party secretary who runs the hospital was a victim of the Nanjing Massacre."

Toyotomi practically jumped out of his seat. "No."

The Massacre remained an intensely sensitive issue in Shanghai, which was virtually a neighbor to Nanjing.

Ito heaved a sigh. "I expected rough seas but not a damned tsunami."

Toyotomi sighed as deeply as his friend and said bitterly, "It was meant to be. You couldn't help it."

Ito shook his head violently. "I feel so hopeless as a trader here. China, Korea, Indonesia, all the Asian countries are demanding an apology from us, and what do our shithead politicians do? They keep aggravating them—they claim the Massacre was fabricated when for god's sake you can see all the evidence at the

Nanjing Memorial Hall. Hell, Germany apologized, but do you see us doing it? Every day we create more enemies, and it's us traders who are on the frontlines. How are we supposed to survive?"

"You're right," said Toyotomi. "Why can't our Prime Minister learn from Willy Brandt? Kneel down like the German chancellor did in Warsaw and apologize to the world?"

"We've got a real crisis on our hands."

The two men exchanged groans.

PART TWO

1. Friendship and Business

Never in his life had he seen such a landscape, thought Chŏn Taegwang as he looked down from the airplane. Valleys branched off from countless other valleys, hills and mountains rising among them, the ridge tops truncated into ovals. The ovals were manicured and he could only assume they were farmed. And then he knew—the loess plateaus! The unusual geology brought to mind the Grand Canyon, but the formations and usage were totally different. The Grand Canyon inspired awe with its rocky, precipitous cliffs and plunging basins, but the oval plateaus he saw beneath him fell away less steeply and had a mysterious grandeur—and people actually farmed them. He remembered now that they'd been formed by erosion, the work of millennial rain- and snowfall. The precipitation, continually washing away the softer surface layers of earth, gathered in rivulets and streams and rivers and bigger rivers. Where did all that water flow to?

Of course—the Huang He, the Yellow River! He was flying over the headwaters of the mighty river that spilled into the Yellow Sea, west of the Korean Peninsula. The plateaus seemed boundless even as the plane passed over them at 450 miles an hour. Enchanted by the wondrous landscape wrought by nature and its exhaustive cultivation by human hands, Chŏn gazed down until his neck grew stiff.

How high were those plateaus? And for how many centuries had people been working that land, climbing up and down, bearing the harvest on their backs? He could only imagine how exhausting a life it must have been. Then again, was there such a thing as an easy life? A solemn mood came over him, lifting only when the plateaus passed out of sight. How fortunate to see them firsthand.

Thoughts of the hardships of farmers inevitably led Chŏn, bound now for Xian, to wonder about the meaning of his life as a businessman in a foreign land. Farmers aided by nature reaped the bounty of the land, but salesmen were like moths drawn by the flickers of commerce emanating from the artificial and absolute Titan called money. In its worship of the money god, capitalism is clear-cut and straightforward, cruel and merciless. Lured by the awful power of that god, salesmen were infantry fighting a silent battle on the frontlines of enterprise. But to what end? What was the gain? These questions inevitably yielded more regret, along with a sense of futility. You can't kill money in revenge, and after years of chasing it helter-skelter, all the salesman is left with is wretched old age and dependence on a pension. When Chŏn observed the drooping shoulders of his fifty-something seniors slipping down the icy slope of their career-end, he began to feel his story would turn out like theirs.

Kim Hyŏn'gon was there to greet him at the Xian airport.

"*Aigu*," said Chŏn, almost hugging Kim in his delight. "It's been a long time. Great to see you, Mr. Kim!"

"Thank you for coming all the way out here," said Kim as he led the way to his car.

"My pleasure," said Chŏn, surveying the airport. "It was a quick trip, and comfortable too, not like ten years ago. All the planes look new, and that takes a lot of the trouble out of traveling. Times have changed here!"

"Air travel must have been a challenge a decade ago."

"That it was. I'm told by the Yanbian Koreans that fifteen years ago if you wanted to fly from Yanji to Beijing, you took a Russian-made turboprop for four hours, and it was so noisy you couldn't hear yourself speak."

"And now it's all jets. One measure of a stronger economy."

"Of course. Did you like how Hu Jintao flexed his muscles in France last year? You know how depressed the US and EU economies were, but he throws a purchase order for a hundred airplanes—not ten but a hundred! The French swooned and the Germans drooled with envy—I guess they finally realized how China managed to build the Great Wall and the Forbidden City." Chŏn's cheerful voice buzzed with excitement.

Kim nodded. "What do you think of their public image? They stick out their chest as a self-proclaimed Great Power, and it's not out of conceit or exaggeration. I guess you can get away with that if you have a huge country with a billion and a half people."

"That's China for you. And the US across the far Atlantic, imagine how they felt when Hu placed that order. Obama's all hot and bothered about his gloomy second-term prospects while playboy Sarkozy is humming a love song—his victories in foreign politics have almost sealed his bid for a second term. And *then*, guess who shows up on US shores and orders *twice* the number of airplanes. Bang! That's Cool Hand Hu for you. And that's the scale they play on—you want to be a world kingpin, you come here."

"Yes, I remember those orders." Kim was still nodding but he sounded peeved. "I had mixed feelings, though."

"I know. For us it's envy, from beginning to end. The more we think about China, the more complicated and annoying it feels. So, how's life in Xian?"

"It's good. I'm glad I'm here."

Chŏn fixed his eyes on Kim. "For sure? You're just saying that to make me feel better."

"Not at all. I've grown fond of the city with all its history. And the work is going smoother than I anticipated."

"That's a relief. Now I can tell you how depressed I was when you left. I blamed myself that a good man was sent to hell. Your face kept popping up in my mind. It was torture."

"Oh no!" blurted Kim. He felt himself choke up. It was rare in his experience for a business partner to be so considerate involving a deal. "I should have given you an update. I had no clue you were worried."

"I was going to come here anyway. Even if you hadn't invited me."

"But how were you able to get away? You're a busy man."

"You know, the business we're in, we can't do everything over the phone. And besides, my boss feels responsible about that fouled-up deal too."

Kim lowered his head in gratitude. "That's very thoughtful, I appreciate it." And then he looked up. "It's hard to believe this is your first trip here—how did you manage to avoid this two-thousand-year-old treasure chest for so long?"

"I wonder about that myself. What with smelling out money and chasing down deals I guess I never had a chance to take in all the history. So what else is new." Chŏn sighed.

Kim responded with a dreary grin. "It's the same back home—the tourists in Seoul go up Namsan Tower and take a boat ride on the Han, but not the busy Seoulites. The tourists here pick out package deals, and we working stiffs spin around after our deals like hamsters on a cartwheel."

Downtown, Kim found a Chinese restaurant. "We don't have many Koreans here, so there isn't much in the way of Korean restaurants."

"Not many Koreans means … ?"

"About two hundred, according to the local Korean Residents Association."

"That few? Well, it is undeveloped out here in the Western interior, after all."

"Two hundred pioneers riding the bandwagon of opportunity. I'm sure they've experienced more adversity than we have, but probably more success too."

"That makes sense."

"Care for a drink?" asked Kim as he flipped through the menu.

"No, it's too early. Let's have a light meal, and then get down to business. We can have our fun tonight."

"Good idea."

As Kim was ordering, Chŏn lit a cigarette. Putting away the menu, Kim took his cup of tea and eyed Chŏn. As if on cue, Chŏn opened up.

"There's a huge Western-style hospital in the planning stages in Shanghai, and the government has pledged to support the entire project out of their public welfare budget. Guess who got the contract to supply the steel—and it's the same amount as last time. Which should help us recover from that fiasco."

"Really? You mean a hundred thousand tons?"

"Yes," said Chŏn, "One hundred thousand tons!"

"It must be a gigantic hospital."

"You bet—Western style, Chinese scale, two thousand beds. Considering Shanghai has twice the population of Seoul, or three times if you count the floating population, it actually seems small to me—why not ten thousand beds? Their medical facilities are so out of proportion to their population."

"Still, a hundred thousand tons—"

"Actually, that's only half the amount of steel going into the project. Our *guanxi* was dead set on revenge for what happened last time, and set out for the whole two hundred thousand tons, but we ended up with half. You know how many Chinese steel companies there are, so there were lots of power plays. Anyway, we agreed it's only fair to include you on the team."

No sooner had Chŏn finished than Kim brought the teacup he was holding to his mouth. His heart churned with emotion and his eyes welled up with tears. It was either cry or sip tea and he managed to take a mouthful and let it trickle down. But then he felt a spasm in his throat, followed by a searing pain, and he had to force himself to swallow. The choking sensation wouldn't go away, and he felt himself succumbing to his emotions. As his heart trembled and his tears threatened to burst forth, he realized that never in his life had he felt so grateful. He had long since grown used to saying goodbye without looking back. The more distant the event, the more distant his memories and feelings about it—especially with business deals, which to Kim amounted to cold-hearted slicing and cutting. In the business world you let bygones be bygones and focused on the next deal and the next partner, without qualms or soul searching.

He came all this way to repay me? Head down, Kim felt himself quivering from the waist up, his shoulders shaking and the hands holding his teacup trembling. He could almost imagine his ears and the strands of his hair vibrating.

Chŏn silently observed Kim through the thin veil of cigarette smoke, giving him time to compose himself. He noticed Kim's eyelids, nose, and mouth twitching and felt a wave of emotion in his own chest. Kim's reaction was like a thousand-fold thank-you. It told Chŏn how lonely and painful his working life must have been.

"Here we are," said Chŏn as soon as their meal arrived. "Let's dig in, Mr. Kim."

"Excuse me," said Kim in a choked voice, "I'll be right back...."

"Take your time."

It was then that Chŏn knew he'd done the right thing coming here. He'd assumed Kim would feel obliged, but he couldn't have anticipated the extent of the man's reaction. He now saw Kim in a new light—the man didn't muzzle or hide his emotions. Most businessmen Chŏn knew kept their naked feelings to themselves. They would be gracious, of course, but their emotions remained hidden behind a mask of pride and face-saving. Chŏn was used to relationships based on business, but with Kim the veneer of formality had dissipated. Chŏn trusted the man all the more for his genuineness.

"I'm so sorry," Kim said sheepishly when he returned. "I didn't expect to hear—"

"You sure you should be so on board?" Chŏn joked in an effort to alleviate Kim's discomfort. "What if history repeats itself?"

"If you thought there was reason to chicken out," said Kim with a ready grin, "you wouldn't be here."

"What a compliment!" said Chŏn. Then with thumb and forefinger he made an A-OK sign. "No, this time it's for sure. My *guanxi* is high up in the bureaucracy. You know how ambitious high officials are."

Kim shook his head. "Everyone likes money, but public officials *salivate* over it—I've never understood that."

"You've heard the saying 'familiar but unknowable'? It's perfect in this situation. We're familiar with it but we don't quite understand it. I guess from their perspective, any profit from their position is a bonus, and there's no feeling of guilt."

"Exactly. An official I know said they all do it, otherwise they're considered incompetent. 'Conditional co-existence'—that's how an American reporter put it. Or you could call them bedfellows in crime—spreading the guilt around. Do you suppose there's any other country in the world where public officials put the public interest so far behind their own well-being?"

"What I don't get is the competition for *ernai*. How can the government ignore their officials keeping mistresses? Makes me pray to God I'll be reborn as a Party official here." Shoulders shaking in mirth, Chŏn managed a mouthful of food.

"Does your *guanxi* have an *ernai*, too?"

"Do bears shit in the woods?"

"But didn't you say his wife is the beauty of all beauties?"

Chŏn chuckled. "You know how it goes—the ones with brains can't compare with the beauties, and the beauties can't compete with the sweet young things. She's a beauty all right, but unless she's Yang Guifei the formula applies to her, too. I play dumb around him but I sense he has quite a stable. And it costs money to keep all the young chicks in line. Thanks to them he needs to keep working, and thanks to his work, our business goes smoothly—it's a wondrous world we live in."

Kim shook his head. "Whether it's cars for their *ernai* or dinner parties for friends, they know how to throw money around. They need to feed from more than one money trough to support all the pretty girls. Who knows how long your man will last, but one thing's for sure—he must be enjoying life."

"I don't think we'll see changes any time soon, what with the public turning a blind eye to all the shenanigans. And there's no shame for girls who sell their body. It's the easiest way they can make money."

"Speaking of the public, it's like they're there but they're not there. I feel like I know them, but only on the surface. Can you explain to me why a billion citizens act surprised when scandals involving officials go public?"

"It's complicated—enough material for a dozen dissertations." Chŏn lit another cigarette.

"You're heading back tomorrow morning for sure?" said Kim as he put down his chopsticks.

"Yes. I have a few matters I need to chase down quick."

"Then this afternoon is the only time to show you around." Kim spread out a map. "Anyplace in particular you'd like to see?"

"My very own tour guide," said Chŏn with a broad grin as he pocketed his cigarettes. "I wouldn't know where to start. This is your territory, so you choose."

"All right, let's try the city walls, the museum, and the Terracotta Warriors. That should get us thirsty enough for a few drinks tonight."

"Great. I've only seen photos of the warriors—now I can see them up close."

Kim eased the car back from its slot and they were on their way.

"I was thinking," said Chŏn. "This project might get you back to Shanghai."

"I'm not so sure," said Kim with a glance at Chŏn. "It all depends on personnel movement within the company, and I hate asking favors. I'm settling in better than I thought. I'm even getting to like the city—there's so much history." With a relaxed smile he looked Chŏn full in the face.

"I know, Shanghai is the toughest city to do business in," tutted Chŏn. "Too many weasels. But in terms of economy they're like heaven and earth, Shanghai and here. It's a damn shame to have worked there and then end up here...."

"Please. It's not as bad as you think, really. There are reams of money in circulation here, what with the push for western development."

"Plenty of haze too," said Chŏn. "Is that where it comes from?" he asked, pointing to the thick dust.

"That's it—and it's getting worse. I was talking with a visitor from back home about the air pollution here..."

Chŏn perked up.

"...and he's old enough to remember back to the 1970s and 80s when we sent people to the Middle East. They worked in an oven, and here we are forty years later working in a toxic-gas environment. That got him going a tale of woe about what a tough life Koreans have. I had mixed feelings listening to him."

"He got that right!" said Chŏn, who had been nodding in time with Kim's account. "The story of our life...."

"You know, the local government is going after foreign investment big time. They're competing with Chongqing nearby. And I'm one of the beneficiaries. As is one of our conglomerates—they worked a special deal to build a supersize electronics factory, and they'll need ten thousand workers."

"Ten thousand?" said Chŏn, wide-eyed.

"Most of them from here, of course. They'll bring managers and top-of-the-line skilled workers from home, but the great majority of the work force will be local. The expectation is, the workers' wages will grease the wheels of development here."

Chŏn's brain was aswirl with figures. "An operation that size, electronics manufacturing, an influx of skilled workers along with management and their families, plus all the suppliers—we're talking maybe three thousand Koreans coming here. And you'll get tourists from home too...."

"And a few days ago I heard the local government is talking with a university hospital back home to have a branch built here. Which would mean even more people coming over."

Chŏn's eyes were twinkling. "A massive migration of skilled labor. The local officials must be pretty sharp. How many Korean tourists do you figure?"

"Well, I run into them almost every day—there are quite a few of them and the numbers are growing."

"Overseas travel does top most Koreans' wish list." And then, talking almost to himself, Chŏn murmured, "The Korean community will expand so fast here…."

"Here we are," said Kim.

Outside the car Chŏn craned his neck to look straight up at a massive stone wall, its majesty enhanced by its ash color. No gaps were to be seen in the mortar—even a brave man would have found it unnerving to attempt scaling.

"My god, how tall is it?" Chŏn wondered out loud.

"Twelve meters."

"Damned if I could climb three. And it looks too smooth to hold a rope ladder."

"That's Chinese scale for you."

"Yes," said Chŏn. "Huge country, grand scale, thousands of years of pride."

"No way can we compare," said Kim as they made their way up a flight of steps to the top of the wall. "The size of their palaces, the pagodas, the temples…."

"The Great Wall, the Great Canal, the Summer Palace, the tomb of the Qin Emperor—they still intimidate me, they're so massive. Here's one more mystery in the land of many mysteries—how did they ever build them?" Chŏn scoffed at himself, "Coming here, I've had this thought working its way inside me, and not for the first time—while I'm in China I'd like to see all the famous sites. But why does that make me feel so sad and pathetic? I guess because it's out of reach for a salary man like me."

"Don't be discouraged. Dreamers make their dreams come true, right? More than non-dreamers, anyway. That's my dream too—especially after I came to Xian."

Chŏn sighed in resignation. "People here say there are three 'too's—too big to go all the way around, too many people to see, and too many dishes to sample. Can people like us ever—"

"Look," Kim interrupted. They were at the top of the wall.

Chŏn's jaw dropped. "Oh…"

"It's wider across the top than the Great Wall, isn't it?"

Eyes agape, Chŏn followed the wall as it stretched out into the distance, then shook his head. "Twice as wide, I'd say. Wider than a two-lane highway—hell, two dump trucks could fit side by side."

"And it goes all the way around the city, about fourteen kilometers. How many soldiers would you need to man it? Take a guess."

"Fourteen kilometers," Chŏn murmured. "That's about thirty *ri*?" He grimaced as he made the calculations. "If it's this wide, maybe five thousand men? Or seven thousand? But if it's more than thirty *ri*, then ten thousand, I bet."

Kim erupted in laughter, "The answer is, 'Nobody knows.'"

"You got me." He paused. "That's right, who would know?"

"I figure people come up here with two goals in mind—admiring the wall or taking in the 360-degree view. But I've got another reason. I like bicycling around it. I feel like I'm riding a time capsule two thousand years into the past, and my worries melt away. Whenever something's nagging at me, I come up here and hop on my bike."

"You come up here to ride a *bicycle*?"

"Sure. You get twice the benefit—exercise and scenery. I wish we had time for that today."

"Why would you want to bicycle on top of a national heritage site? It's a sacrilege!"

"Why not? Remember, this is China." Kim grinned, then tapped his foot against the bricks of the surface. "Check these out. They're specially made, ninety percent red clay and ten percent jade, fired at fifteen hundred degrees Celsius. Notice the ash color—it's a result of the chemical reaction between the clay and the jade when they're baked. They're stronger than rock, strong enough that you could drive a tank over them. So who cares about a flimsy bike?"

Chŏn cocked his head. "They use precious jade for *this*?"

"Jade doesn't get precious until it goes through a long process that ends with delicate carving. And did you know that the Qinling range, the one that stretches out eighteen hundred kilometers from Tibet, is full of jade?"

"You should open up a tour company," said Chŏn admiringly, "especially with more tourists coming from back home." He scanned the surroundings. "How long does it take to go all the way around? A couple of hours?"

"Oh no. Half an hour or forty minutes at the most."

"Then let's do it. I'd like a ride in that time capsule myself—it'll make for a great memory."

"Terrific! Some things you just have to make time for. There's a bike-rental place over there."

"These guys," said Chŏn. "Business really does run in their blood...."

Setting out on their rentals, they saw an exuberant couple pedaling toward them. "I should have packed a pretty girl for this trip," Chŏn grumbled.

Kim bowed. "Excellency, please forgive your humble host for his negligent reception."

Chŏn worked the pedals in unison with Kim. The air was fouled with a reddish, smoky fog, but as Chŏn rode through it he felt caressed by the originality of the ancient city. They were passing a file of modern buildings, each of them seven or eight stories. Chŏn noticed the rooftop balconies and the traditional tiles and wondered if they were unique to Xian. In any event, the buildings were a harmonious fusion of modern Western functionality and traditional Chinese beauty.

"I feel like a new man," Chŏn exulted after they had returned the bicycles. He stretched leisurely. "I'm so glad we did that. What a memory!"

"Next time I'll have a couple of beautiful maidens stashed away."

Chŏn produced a sly chuckle. "When you're far from home you miss a warm body," he lamented. "That's an eternal truth. Why do I keep thinking about the Qin Emperor, instead of stately Xuanzong of Tang fooling around with Yang Guifei?"

"It's a logical connection, Xian and the first Qin emperor. He's the one who gave Xian a wakeup call twenty-two hundred years later and made it famous the world over."

"As if it was asleep all that time?"

"I'm talking about the discovery of the Terracotta Warriors—the Eighth Wonder of the World, the main reason tourists flock here from all over."

"Ah, right," said Chŏn as they went down the steps. He frowned. "Isn't the emperor's legacy supposed to be pretty complicated?"

"That's what I've heard. He did some good things and some bad things—plenty for the historians to chew on."

"I can't say I have a very good impression of him. This may sound stupid, but do you think of him as a sage or a tyrant?"

"I've been wondering about that ever since I got here. I could go either way, and I guess the historians go back and forth too."

"Sending his loyal subjects all over the land to find the elixir plant…." Chŏn made a face. "He was so childish and yet he managed to unite the country."

"That he did." Kim darted ahead and led Chŏn across the street. "Watch your step." The traffic was no less chaotic than on the streets of Shanghai.

Kim went up to a vendor. Pointing to the dozens of pieces of jade on display in different shapes, sizes, and colors, he said to Chŏn, "I told you this is jade country, right? Carry a piece of jade around and it gives you energy and brings good luck. I don't think it's superstition so much as a matter of its mineral effects. So, I'd like to give you a jade seal. This guy is a street vendor, but he's as good as anyone you'll find in a shop. He does excellent carving. Please, pick out a piece and he'll make a seal for you."

"It's all right." Chŏn retreated and tried to wave Kim off. "I'm not sure when I'd ever use it."

"Then I'll pick one for you—my gift." Kim selected a red cube.

"Please." Chŏn tried unsuccessfully to snatch it away from Kim.

"You're not going to be a section chief forever," said Kim, poker-faced. "You can use it once you make company president."

As they waited they heard only a screechy, grinding noise. Chŏn was skeptical. But less than ten minutes later he was presented with a piece of paper bearing a clear vermilion imprint of the Chinese characters of his name.

"I never expected *this*!" he said in a voice choked with emotion. "Thank you. It's something I'll cherish forever." He examined the jade seal cradled in his palm. How had Kim known he wanted to be a company president someday? Maybe it was like they said, you project into another's mind what you yourself are hoping for. Businessmen wanted to be their own boss, just like politicians wished to be president.

Next on the tour was the museum. To reach the entrance visitors had to make their way through a souvenir shop.

"Why put the knickknacks *here*?" said Chŏn. "It's so commercial. Only in China!"

"Most places have the shop at the exit. You know what they say—it's for the tourists. They don't care about the congestion."

"The later in life you learn something the more it possesses you. I guess that applies to countries learning capitalism."

"Like a suppressed craving that leads to addiction?"

"I wonder what Chairman Mao in the heavens above would say."

"He'd probably blame Deng."

"Humpty Dumpty Deng wouldn't put up for that. He'd stand up to the Chairman, ask who deserves credit for China's G2 status, and for enabling China to challenge US supremacy. He'd say that if it were Mao, then China could have collapsed like the USSR, its tarnished empire gone *poof*. He'd tear him to pieces."

Chuckling, Kim covered his mouth conspiratorially. "I can see that."

They saw quite a few Westerners, studious-looking and silent. Were they American? If so, with their two hundred years of history they must have felt the weight of the three thousand years of Chinese history made tangible in this museum.

Kim retreated a few steps so that each man could better appreciate the exhibits. Each visit brought the excitement of something new. He was always discovering a display he'd overlooked, was always charged with new thoughts about what he was seeing.

A few exhibition halls later, Kim rejoined Chŏn. Pointing to a display case with a magnifying glass for the item inside, he whispered, "I want you to see this. It came from the tomb of the Qin Emperor's grandfather."

"His grandfather?" echoed Chŏn as he bent down to look. "That makes whatever it is more than two thousand years old."

"Yes. The unification was two-twenty-one BC, so his grandfather would have lived about twenty-three hundred years ago."

"Is it a bird? It's hard to make out, even with the magnifier."

"Yes, a woodpecker, made of gold."

Chŏn gawked at the object. "A woodpecker?"

"It's considered a good omen here."

"It looks like a grain of rice."

"Smaller, more like a sesame seed."

"No! How could they carve something so tiny? Well, now I can see a bird shape. Did they have magnifiers back then?"

"Hard to see how could they make something like this without them."

"My god," said Chŏn. "All right, I give up."

Kim couldn't tell whether this was an expression of admiration or a lament. For its part, the woodpecker beneath the magnifying glass kept its millennial silence.

"Exquisite," said Chŏn as they left the museum. "It's a more distinctive display than you'll find in Beijing or Shanghai."

"I would think so, seeing as how Xian was the capital of seventeen kingdoms over a period of twelve hundred years. And there are three or four other museums besides this one."

"Now I can see why—the craftsmanship back then, it's wonderful."

"But the craftsmen themselves were a despised class—mongers, they were called. They lived lives of drudgery so the royal family and the nobles could live lives of luxury. It's thanks to those mongers that these museums exist, drawing crowds and feeding the locals generation after generation. They must have had a devil of a life!" So saying, Kim started the car.

Chŏn sighed. "Just like the migrant workers now!"

Soon they were outside the city proper. A wall of roadside stands appeared.

"What are they selling?" Chŏn exclaimed. "They look like apples but—"

"Pomegranates. I didn't know what they were either, first time I saw them. They're in season now."

"Why so many stands?"

"They're one of the favorite fruits here. See all those pomegranate orchards?" said Kim, gesturing left and right.

"So that's what they are. Pomegranates aren't very popular back home."

"They should be. They're rich in vitamins, good for your health."

Chŏn rolled down his window. "Let's try one—something else to remember Xian by."

"Sure. They're pretty good, quite sweet actually. The sour ones go to the pharmaceutical companies. They're made into some kind of medicine."

Kim pulled over, bought a pomegranate, and cracked it in half.

Chŏn gave a jubilant thumbs-up as he munched on the kernels. "Tasty! It's sweet all right, just like you said, and refreshing."

"Then eat up. It's the best stamina-booster for guys," said Kim.

"Look out, ladies, here we come. Two studs out on the town with a belly full of pomegranate juice!"

"Right on. And in case you forgot, we're in Yang Guifei country."

And with a horselaugh they set off to see the Terracotta Warriors.

The site was swarming with jabbering tourists. Seeing all the Western faces,

Chŏn began to understand why this archeological find had been dubbed the Eighth Wonder of the World.

"There are three pits," said Kim with Chŏn in tow. "The first is the largest and best preserved."

The pit measured some 60 by 230 meters and had a skeleton of steel pipes that gave it the stark look of a makeshift building. The tourists bunched up at the entrance before breaking into disorderly streams down passages left and right. To safeguard this UNESCO World Heritage Site, the tourists were kept at a distance from the horses and soldiers, making it impossible for them to appreciate the detail of the sculptures and their life-size scale.

Chŏn lapsed into thought at the sight of all the warriors in military formation, as ashen as the color of the city wall. The warriors and their horses had been fired and baked in the same way as the bricks of the wall, for burial with the emperor—a form of funerary art. Born in a harmony of red clay, jade powder, and heat, after two thousand years underground they were unearthed and reborn under the bright sun. Who had created these six thousand soldiers, four hundred horses, and one hundred chariots, all of them life-size? Not ordinary potters but rather supreme artists who re-created the intricacies of individual facial expressions, postures, hairstyles, and uniforms of this army of men. Despised and scorned in a cruel class system, they labored for an idiotic emperor, one who ultimately resigned himself to death after a futile search for the elixir of eternal life but remained so fearful he arranged to be accompanied by a host of soldiers. No speck of dust was left of this man. He had been outlived for millennia by the artwork of the obscure and enslaved craftsmen to whom he had thundered his orders.

Chŏn was struck by the foolishness of this emperor's final endeavor. To think that what he saw before him was only an estimated 10 percent of the emperor's tomb. He couldn't begin to visualize the massive scale of the construction that had taken place 2,200 years ago. *The mania of the man!*

"What are you thinking?" asked Kim.

Chŏn passed a hand down his face then grimaced, as if trying to dispel the awe he felt. "The emperor, what else?"

"Are you interested in seeing his tomb?" said Kim as they left the pit.

"Isn't it off-limits now? You can only walk through the woods outside it, right? I'll pass, thanks."

"Good decision. No fun being a check-list tourist."

Back outside, Chŏn lit a cigarette. "I never thought much of the man behind the construction of the Great Wall, and this only confirms it. On the other hand, I finally solved my great mystery." He took a long draw on his cigarette.

Kim sent him an inquisitive look.

"Here we have the first emperor to unify the country—he defeated six kingdoms. But he lasted only fifteen years, the shortest of the dynasties. Other dynasties were tyrannical too, but why did this one fall so quickly? Now I know why."

"Good for you. That's why we need to see historic sites. It's depressing to think about that period. As soon as he united the land, he set out on his two massive projects—three million laborers working on the Great Wall, seven hundred thousand on his tomb. Guess what the population was back then? twenty million. Every male, unless he was very young or very old, was mobilized! In the meantime, who did the farming to feed those millions of laborers, who made it possible for the elite to be well fed and clothed? The women, of course. Qin must have been hell," sighed Kim.

"Yes," said Chŏn, "a reign of terror. And then there's that pleasure palace he had built. But for such a selfish guy he was pretty smart. Didn't he come up with the law that killed off three generations to discourage rebellious minds? But in the end, terror didn't work anymore, did it? The people had enough. They must have loved seeing fifteen years of suffering brought to an end!"

"History has its gratifying moments," said Kim. "You know he also standardized writing and measurement. But I think his greatest 'accomplishment' was to show that the power of the people is strong enough to topple a dynasty."

Chŏn shook his head in grudging admiration. "A perceptive theory expressed with a biting tongue—you're full of surprises, Mr. Kim…. But how many dynasties after that repeated the same mistakes?"

"'We learn from history' sounds nice but does anyone actually do it? Unsolicited advice tends to be useless."

"Good point. Look at Emperors Yang of Su and Xuanzong of Tang—tyrants, both of them. And politicians past and present are the same sort."

"Those two and the Qin Emperor, the three notorious despots of China. A combination of unlimited power and limited humanity."

"I guess you'd have to be an emperor to understand," said Chŏn, "but how could Yang build the Great Canal, this great accomplishment, then let the dynasty sink while he was boozing and womanizing in the pleasure boats? And how was it possible for a famous couple like Xuanzong and Yang Guifei to be overthrown by farmers?"

"They had to work at it. Notoriety doesn't come easy, you know."

Chŏn laughed. "Bull's-eye." He pulled out a cigarette.

A little girl ran toward them. "Persimmons!" she hollered. "Do you want some, mister? They're very sweet." Displaying a small plastic basket filled with the fruit, she stared up at the men.

"Well?" said Kim to Chŏn. But his eyes showed he had already decided, and he produced some money. "How much?"

With a shy smile the girl said, "Fifteen *yuan*."

Basket in hand, Kim looked around. "Where do we eat? In the car?"

"How about that bench? Then we can take in the view," said Chŏn. As they headed in that direction he examined the persimmons. They were reddish-orange and the tops were white and powdery. "They're tiny as ping pong balls," he complained.

"They don't look like much, but doesn't that fuzzy top get your mouth watering?"

Picking one each, they peeled the fruit.

"Oooh!" said Chŏn the instant he tasted it.

Kim took a large bite and grinned. "What did I tell you?"

"Looks are deceiving. I've never had persimmons this sweet; they're like candy. So long to Qin and all our lousy feelings."

"Help yourself."

The two men gorged themselves.

Counting the calyxes in his lap, Chŏn said, "I've had seven already."

"Same here," said Kim as he collected the calyxes and peels.

"How many did she give us anyway?" Chŏn murmured as he checked the flimsy basket. "We stuffed ourselves and there's so many left."

"Thirty, maybe—three layers of ten each?"

Chŏn stretched and yawned. "For which we paid the equivalent of two dollars US. We can bitch all we want about inflation, but compared with back home, this is a land of milk and honey."

"Back home this basket of persimmons would go for ten thousand *wŏn*, easy."

"You sound like a North Korean spy," said Chŏn. "Your figures are out of date—more like twenty thousand." Both men chuckled.

"What do we do with the leftovers?" said Kim as he rose.

"Have them for dessert," Chŏn said, snatching the basket from him.

"Great idea. Especially since we don't get dessert in the restaurants here."

As they walked to the car, they noticed vendors of miniature warriors roaming in search of tourists. The persimmon vendors were scurrying about as well.

"Were there persimmon trees back when those warriors were created?" said Chŏn.

"Probably. Though maybe not cultivated like now."

Looking off into the sky, Chŏn mumbled to himself, "All those craftsmen, they must have been damn tired and hungry. I wonder how many they could put away on a fine autumn evening."

Kim glanced at Chŏn, knowing the other man's compassionate imagination had taken him two thousand years back in time. He once again felt the warmth of spirit of this man who had come such a distance to visit him.

"On our way back," said Kim as he started the car, "should we check out Daean Pagoda? It was built by the monk Xuanzang to store the sutras he brought from India."

"Fine by me," said Chŏn. "The more I can see, the better. I like the way Nanjing's being preserved, but it's nothing compared to Xian." He made a face. "There are so many treasures here, let's hope they're not ruined by the development boom."

"You're catching on. The local people like to say they have treasures everywhere; you just have to dig and three thousand years of history open up. But when the subject changes to development you can see the blood in their eyes. The public officials see only in front of their noses, the morons!"

"Sixty-seven meters," Chŏn murmured as he read the sign and looked up at the pagoda.

"And it dates back fifteen hundred years," said Kim. "It's more than just a pagoda."

"Such a giant pagoda, such a wee woodpecker. The grandest to the tiniest. And all the more precious for coming from the blood and sweat of the obscure and deprived, rather than the privilege of the elite."

"Pretty much my thoughts ever since I've been here."

After dinner, they had more persimmons and gave the remaining half dozen to their waitress. She didn't appear to regard the gift as unusual.

"Last stop is karaoke," said Kim, ever the tour guide.

"What about the three no-nos?" The rules of the pleasure quarters had been standardized a decade earlier—no sitting close to the guest, no drinking with him, and no singing with him. Fair enough in a temple or church. But in the private rooms of a bar? Come on. In practice, the three proscriptions amounted to throwing meat to a tiger and expecting it not to eat, or placing a naked couple together in a room and asking them not to touch each other. The operative principle, as always, was, *If you don't make an issue, no problem.* And so there was incessant traffic to the countless bars—business was booming.

"Don't underestimate us. The hotspots are the same everwhere, hip city or sleepy countryside. I won't disappoint you!"

"We're off to meet the girls of Xian!" Chŏn proclaimed as he marched gallantly toward the car.

2. A Stepfather's Love

"The report came in—we're good to go in the interior." Hands on hips, Andy Park leaned back, stretched, and then smoothed his hair.

"Bravo!" said Wang Lingling, laughing. "I can breather easier now."

"Huh," he grunted, his soft smile giving away his good nature. "I'm still nervous."

"You?" she said. "I'm the one on the high wire. Can you imagine what it's like to have to finish a project before Chunjie and keep all your frustrations to yourself?"

"I can imagine that thanks to your infinite patience it won't be an issue."

"You're not just reliable, Andy. You're quick to catch on." She set about tidying her desk. "So, you're going home for Chunjie?"

"That's right. But there's still another matter to discuss with the interior." He tapped the tip of his pen on her desk.

She straightened and eyed him inquiringly.

"The rebate," he said matter-of-factly.

"Yes," she said in the same dry tone. "The rebate...."

"You know it's four percent."

"Four? Isn't it usually three?"

"Yes. And that's what they offered."

"What then?"

"I said three percent wouldn't cut it."

"Andy, you said that?"

"Yes. These are austere times. Under the circumstances, our purchase is a lifesaver for them. We can't miss this opportunity, right?"

Her eyes opened wide. "Our architectural artist has a talent for negotiation!"

"So, we got an extra one percent." He grinned. "It's a piece of rice cake making money—I never realized that."

She looked him square in the face. "I want to hear what you said to them."

"Oh, that's in bad taste." In a faux blunt tone he added, "I may have to report the extra one percent since it's part of my job, but I don't have to report the details."

"All right," she said with a smile. "But you didn't have to report that one percent, you know—you could have just kept it."

"Madam CEO, we've talked about that. I don't want to cheat. I couldn't take the guilt—there are no secrets in this world. Besides, I'm paid generously, so why be greedy? I do receive a performance bonus."

"Andy Park, you're a breath of fresh air in this conniving world of ours. You remind me again why I trust and respect you." Briskly she rose and offered her hand.

He took it. "Why thank you."

"Shall we go? It's time for dinner," she said, slinging her bag over her shoulder.

Park folded his jacket over his arm. "How's the housing bubble here?" he asked as they set out for the elevator.

"Still hot, as we would expect in China now. The fallout from the financial meltdown back home won't shake the steady growth here, and neither will the economic doldrums in the EU. All that speculation about the bubble bursting missed the mark. But believe me, that didn't stop me from wasting a lot of nervous energy." She pressed her hand to her chest for emphasis.

"I don't really follow economic developments, but I knew the negative forecast was off."

"Really?" she said, eyeing him. "Then you must know more than you let on. You're an architect, and architecture is a science, I suppose; not a guessing game."

"You're right. No research, but I wasn't guessing. I was thinking that if you're going to judge someone you have to take their circumstances into account. But when Westerners assess China they get hung up on circumstances. Which is probably why they're biased in their judgment. And why their economic forecasts are inaccurate."

"Bingo, Andy. Circumstances. But what's the real issue here?"

"Here we go, another riddle."

"All right, let me spell it out for you. As Asians don't we tend to catch on to circumstances through intuition?" She arched her eyebrows.

"Asian? Meaning race?"

Her gaze softened. "I'm glad you get it. You can count on white people to have a superiority complex toward Asians. Which leads to repulsive notions about China—it's primitive, and so they despise it, scorn it, don't recognize it for what it is."

The elevator doors opened to reveal a pair of hefty men in black suits and one of Wang's secretaries with her briefcase. Andy tensed. The trio were ubiquitous, standard procedure for the CEO when she was in China. Three other bodyguards stood by with the three limousines, making a total of five, protecting her front and back. If any of the presidents beneath her considered it excessive, they kept their thoughts to themselves. Not that they had to rein in their tongues when talking about their omnipotent female CEO; rather, the flourishing company could afford an outlandish security budget for their chief executive in the precarious environment here.

In the restaurant, clinking her wine glass to his, Wang asked, "Did you get enough wine when you were in France?"

"It would have been nice to enjoy it with someone," he said after sniffing the bouquet. "As you know, I don't drink when I'm on the job."

"That's right, I forgot. You're scary when you focus. No drinking or sleeping; you're like a soldier on the frontline. American-born, but Korean through and through. The tenacity is built-in, isn't it? From your people getting jerked around all these centuries by the great powers."

"Well, there's that," he said, frowning. "Remind me, what was your major—anthropology? cultural history?"

They laughed.

Andy continued, "I know you studied management, but I'm amazed at the way you devour books. Are you aware how much that intimidation factor adds to your CEO position?"

"How so?"

"Are you really not aware of that? The presidents are absolutely on edge when they're sitting across from you."

"What, are they afraid I'll test them? If they're worried about general knowledge, maybe they ought to try some reading themselves—they have plenty of time for drinking and foot massages."

"I hope this doesn't sound rude, but I think for them there's something about a woman with your looks who's always got her nose in a book. That was my first impression of you in college, too, you know."

"Yes, I know, some people still think books and looks don't go together. But my stepfather taught me that books are lifelong mentors. He kept me reading. Though I guess Steve Jobs is part of the story too."

"Jobs?"

"Yes. He said his creative imagination came from reading humanities books, not so much science books."

"More power to you. The older I am, the more I drink and the less I read."

"So humble. Say, O counsellor of mine, I've been meaning to ask—what do you think about targeting Chongqing and Xian, the core cities for western development?"

He swirled the wine in tiny circles in his glass. "I'm not sure. I'll need to do some research—I'm not very familiar with those cities."

She gave him an affectionate grin as she poured him more wine. "This isn't an exam, so tell me. We've worked together long enough that we know what to look for."

Here she goes again. It was only a matter of time before she would cast her gaze toward the region. But where would her ambition end? How much money would be enough? When would her cupidity be satisfied? Everybody said you did business for the fun of it and the money came naturally. They had worked together for a decade, but she remained mostly a mystery.

"All I know is where those two cities are on the map. They're so far from Beijing. The region itself stretches all the way west to the desert in Xinjiang and the mountains in Tibet. I think I can understand why the central government decided to launch the project there. The economic disparity between east and west has left a deep gap between the rich and the poor, which leads to social unrest, which becomes a political threat."

"See? I knew it. You dug beneath the surface and look what you found." Her mouth sipped wine, but her eyes hastened him to continue.

"I think the government's aim is true, but it's difficult to predict the outcome."

"Because the goal's too murky, right?"

Andy felt her gaze pulling him like wires. Her beautiful face now wore the mask of a charismatic but unfeeling businesswoman.

"Nothing new there, as everyone can see. The two cities are deep inland and shut out from the marine advantages enjoyed by the eastern cities. We could rely on high-speed rail and the highways, but that wouldn't be enough. We need to be aware of what's involved when you unload containers from a ship, and then transport them on trucks for days. You use up time, fuel, and labor—that's a triple loss. Not the conditions to draw international business. As it happens we have a precedent in the US. Capitalism there has a hundred-and-fifty-year head start on capitalism here. And look what happened to the American Midwest—it got scrawny while the East and West coasts beefed up, and a hundred and fifty years later the gap still hasn't closed. So even if Beijing pushes full-scale development, sharp-eyed foreign businesses will probably stay away, and then…" He emptied the glass.

"What did I tell you? You're one up on all the specialists. Don't you want to switch to management?"

"What you really mean is, you want to fire me."

"Ha ha. No, what I mean is, the central government's investment in the region is astronomical. And it'll stay that way for years. ..." Her face could not conceal the elation she felt at the opportunity to sit down at an economic feast.

"I see only one way," he said. "Initially we don't invest; we simply bid on government projects. The profits might be limited but the deal is one hundred percent secure. We can't dive into a direct investment for big profits here, like we're doing in Shanghai. If foreign companies don't come to those two cities, our luxury apartments won't sell."

"Now you're talking." She snapped her fingers.

"Don't believe everything I tell you."

"It's all right, I've already decided."

"But can we compete?"

"Let me worry about that." She offered a toast.

Suppressing further questions, he touched his glass to hers.

Let me worry about that. But what was her plan? The question nagged at Park as he drove back to his villa. It was a good thing he hadn't pressed her on it. Back home, keeping boundaries was a matter of professional courtesy; being intrusive could doom a relationship and in some cases was unlawful. Why, then, was he so tantalized by her as to feel he ought to warn her? It bothered him that he had to bite his tongue. Let me worry about that—she was fearless, resolute, defiantly confident. And charismatic enough to have lined up men from Berkeley and Harvard for the Gold Groups presidencies. He wondered if her brains were a function of her mixed blood, or her stepfather's discipline. She had all the right attributes. Why, then, did he feel so unnerved about her assurances?

Her cockiness had always bothered him. So far she had found smooth sailing here. Backed by her tycoon stepfather in San Francisco, she had spread her wings in the updrafts of China's economic miracle.

Every new project that began with a Let me worry about that led to a splendid accomplishment. She grew into a queen with a jewel-studded crown, and her presidents became ever more loyal subjects dedicated to good management and progress. It didn't hurt their pride that they earned a hundred times more than the rank and file.

So how was it that he was swept by anxiety while she maintained her amazon-like confidence in the glitch-free completion of a project? Please be careful! You've heard that the PSB knows everything. You should act as if they planted a bug inside you. Why did he want to tell her that? And what would her reaction have been? Would she tell him to kiss his future goodbye? Would she interpret his warning as, You're doing something illegal?

None of the presidents questioned how she was able to manage numerous mega-projects with no apparent difficulty. They tacitly agreed she was working on behalf of the company and themselves, and responded with fanfare to her marvelous capability. They were always on guard to complete their assignments quickly and efficiently. Esteemed gentlemen that they were, they were careful to respect her ferocious privacy.

Park couldn't help fretting that her every movement was captured on the PSB radar. The PSB had no more qualms about spying on citizens or infringing on their civil liberties—or snooping on foreigners round the clock—than about turning a blind eye to the manufacturing of fake designer goods, which was illegal but, more important, proof positive that the country was advanced. The safest way to live here was to keep a low profile. Unless, that is, you were one of the Three Fools: he who believes the PSB won't know, he who believes he can deceive the PSB, or he who believes he won't be caught. Even Master Kung, whose sayings were out of date, had it right when he said, Do as you're told if you want to stay out of trouble.

Why the hell should he stay in a country where the authorities could be watching him twenty-four hours a day? When he thought about how the PSB had summoned his secretary to ask about his comings and goings the previous day and why he'd turned off his cell phone, whether they'd done it out of menace or clumsiness, he shuddered in disgust and wanted to pack up and leave.

If they could train their binoculars on a company president and focus in on him, couldn't they do the same with his CEO? But why should he worry himself silly while she paraded like a peacock, had the charisma of a lioness, a wolf's smarts, a deer's agility, and a fox's cunning? Wouldn't she know if she was on their radar? Was it possible she'd tenderized a top PSB enforcer with the silky application of her nectar? If that were the case, then his worries were definitely uncalled for. Besides, as much as it kept him on edge, what could he do about her sky's-the-limit ambition?

"Have some spring water, darling," said Wang in nasal, singsong Mandarin to the naked man lying on the bed. "Nothing like cold water to recharge you from the fatigue of our rain and clouds." She offered him the glass. But what actually made him feel like a bull was her entwining voice and the firm, bouncy breasts visible through her loose gown. Realizing this, she made only a token effort to tie the garment.

"You and me and the rain and clouds!" He sprang up to a sitting position and tugged on the arm holding the glass of water.

"Easy, darling," she squealed. "You'll spill it." She let him draw her near.

"I haven't heard that expression for ages," said the man, referring to the stock phrase for lovemaking. "You lived in the US so long, yet you know all the right expressions. Lucky me to have you—so beautiful and yet so smart!" Placing an arm around her, he toyed with her breasts.

"Don't overdo it, darling. I can't have you burning out. We want to enjoy a long and steady relationship, don't we?" She handed him the glass.

"Right you are." The fiftyish man drank the water, set down the glass, and pulled her close again.

She hugged him and whispered, "Plus, tonight is special. You can't go home late, remember?"

"I know. Just a little longer." He drew the sheet over them. "You are so pretty, and sweet, and full of charm," he said, pulling her tight. "I'm so happy you're mine, my ernai."

In her most mellifluous tones she responded, "At your service, my dear. It's my pleasure."

What a sap! Ernai? Have you ever seen an ernai who spends money like me? You're the ernai, my mister ernai! We like men like you like women. The more different the faces, the pleasure, the excitement, the better. You can have your uses. Especially if you're powerful, educated, and handsome. Lucky you—out of the billions of men in this world, you just happen to suit me all right.

"But you're right, tonight is special and I should be going."

Reluctantly he rose and got back into his clothes, while she quickly changed into a dress.

"I have something for you." She held out a small box.

"What's that?" He pretended not to see as he knotted his tie, but his downcast eyes spotted the box.

"Just a little something." Which proved to be a gold watch, its face studded with diamonds that glittered with the movement of her hand. His face blossomed into a grin.

Flipping over the finger-long tag to display the purchase price, she whispered in the softest of tones, one that no high-tech recording device could pick up, "If it's not to your liking, you can return it for cash minus ten percent. I set it up that way." The price was 620,000 yuan.

"Oh, you shouldn't have…." He cleared his throat importantly and feigned a nonchalant look.

Placing the watch about his left wrist, she said, "Just tuck it in your pocket. No one will know." The next moment she had stuck his left hand in the outer pocket of his overcoat, and the box under his armpit. Finally, she buttoned the coat. "Presto—out of sight."

"You shouldn't have," he murmured again.

"It's nothing," she whispered. "Just remember what we talked about. Ten percent. Ten."

Again he cleared his throat. "Isn't it too out-of-the-way for business?"

She shook her head no. "Not for me. Once I set my heart on a project I'll fly to the moon for it."

"Listen to you. I like your gumption."

"Now you know why I have twenty men under me."

"Yes, indeed. You're a Mulan all right."

"Why not a queen?"

"Yes, why not," he chuckled. "Except you're more than a queen."

She opened the door for him. "As soon as you get off the elevator, my men will take care of you."

"Thank you, Lingling. It was such an enjoyable evening." He lifted a hand in farewell and was gone.

A gold, diamond-studded Rolex was the most coveted watch in China, a preferred bribe for hundreds of high-official Party members. A dozen such watches were to be found in Beijing. How, you might wonder, could a dozen Rolex watches be used to bribe several hundred officials? Wang had whispered the answer to her paramour: the recipient takes the watch back to the store for a cash refund, minus a 10 percent restocking fee; the next recipient does the same, and the watches keep circulating.

Sipping coffee, Wang gazed out the window of the room behind her office. The sky had darkened before she noticed, and was embroidered by the magnificent fireworks, and by the firecrackers Beijingians had lit as soon as night set in. It was Chunjie eve, the biggest holiday of the year. Except for the bedridden and nursing infants, everybody was eager to set off firecrackers to chase away evil spirits and ensure prosperity in the new year. Even toddlers were everywhere to be seen, clapping and jumping for joy.

The more affluent you were, the more firecrackers you popped. And the more mianzi you cultivated and the more you liked to show off, the more you displayed your economic clout. Some might spend a month's paycheck on firecrackers; the less patient took out a loan before payday. Some companies shot them off in strings of thousands to display their prowess.

Any day of the year, the fireworks and firecrackers grew louder and more frequent as the night deepened, climaxing at midnight. But the beautiful, enchantingly colorful lights were accompanied by chemical fumes. As the night wore on, the pollution index shot up. By eleven, it was often sixty times higher than the average daily reading, and around one in the morning it was off the charts of the US embassy. In some cases it was days before the stagnant, toxic air was once again fit for human intake.

The penchant for setting off firecrackers was a pious ritual observed not just on Chunjie but also on Harvest Day, at business openings, even when people moved or purchased a car. It was little different from Koreans incorporating a grotesque pig head in an offering ceremony. China's fireworks tradition intensified with the open economy policy as the market picked up and people became richer and wanted to be richer still.

How much money did they waste on firecrackers? Wang grumbled to herself. Everyone was curious, but the answer, as was often the case, was, Who knows?

They generated so much waste and pollution! Why couldn't the government do something? The answer was, the Party and the government were reluctant to cause ripples, wanted to avoid being the target of the residents' ill will, didn't want to constipate this lucrative sector of the economy.

She tutted as she watched the mesmerizing dance of fire. Savages, she thought. Why hadn't the centuries-old firecracker been upgraded to useful weaponry by now—guns, artillery, tanks? Instead it was used to expel evil. Didn't anyone remember the humiliating history of this land? It was stupid—positively stupid. Her vexation bubbled over. Toxic air had discouraged her from venturing outside to return to her fifth-story villa, and she had locked herself in her seventieth-floor office the past five days. Air pollution tended to sink, and now during the New Year's celebrations her villa was for sure enveloped by it. Why risk shortening your life span? And so she took refuge in her high-rise office and the secret bedroom tucked behind it.

It took three days for the smoke shrouding the Beijing skies to lift and the sun's rays to filter through. Heaps of firecracker husks crowded the shadowy alleys. Like rain coming with a dark sky, a rash of fires and injuries were reported throughout the country, some from the thousands of defective sparklers that had competed for sale. Wang recalled that two years earlier here in Beijing, and three months before its scheduled opening, the new China Central Television network complex had caught fire because of an unauthorized fireworks display by local residents fêting the end of Chunjie. But on the following Chunjie, comrades set off fireworks as usual. The country never flinched! Where had that attitude come from? Was it because China was now number one in foreign-reserve holdings?

The intercom buzzed. "Madam," said her secretary, "it's your mother, from the States."

In English came a voice: "Sophie, it's Mom."

"Hi, Mom. How are you? Is everything all right?"

"Honey, you need to come home right away. Your dad is ill."

"What! What is it?" She jumped to her feet.

"I'm not sure. He just collapsed. The doctors said we need to prepare for the worst."

"Is he conscious?"

"He comes and goes. He's been asking for you."

"All right. Tell him I'll be there. I'm leaving right now."

She put down the phone and burst into tears. Not so much from sadness as from the heartfelt shock of the prospect of losing her stepfather, the absolute power in her life, the person who had made her what she was today, the mapper and planner of her life who had bestowed on her a love more effusive than Niagara Falls.

Dabbing at the tears with her handkerchief, she buzzed her secretary. "Get me on the next flight to San Francisco. And get Mr. Cooper to prepare five envelopes with a thousand yuan each." This being the amount of the fine she would have to pay if any of her limos was stopped by the PSB for speeding. "I'm leaving in ten minutes." She went to the safe and retrieved her passport.

A Caucasian man scurried into the office, his face ashen. "You're going to San Francisco? What happened?"

"I'll explain on the way to the airport," she said as she put her desktop in order. "My father is very ill. Be ready to leave in five minutes."

"The Chairman? Oh no." He put his hands to his head.

"Cooper!" Her crisp voice slashed at him. "I said we're leaving."

He came to attention. "Yes, ma'am, I'm ready."

The trio of limousines sped off, the one in front sounding its horn breathlessly, hazard lights flickering, practically inviting a stop from the PSB officers who blanketed the downtown area. And sure enough, three times they were stopped, each for less than a minute as the driver offered a quick explanation, an envelope, and a driver's license, and was met with the return of the license and a salute. They soon reached the airport way.

"I'll be back as soon as I can. But it might be as long as ten days if he passes on. I'm leaving everything to you. Check the construction progress like a hawk. I don't want any surprises." Her instructions were perfunctory.

"Yes, ma'am," said Cooper.

She fixed him with a gaze. "I'd like to have called each of the presidents. But I can't."

"I understand. I'll pass on the message. We're all behind you."

The limousines kept on, and after one final PSB nab they were at the airport. An hour later she was bound for San Francisco. Joining her in first class were the secretary and two bodyguards, the other cabins being fully occupied. For five times the economy fare, they had the luxury of flat sleeper beds.

As the aircraft climbed, her stepfather Wang Itsan's face floated before her eyes, his appearance changing with the passage of her memories of him. Tears streamed down her cheeks, drawn by the prospect of his impending death. His love for her was so warm, so deep and ardent, exceeding even the love he felt for his own son, Yungli. The bestowal of that immense love had begun when he noticed that little Sophie was able to add the bill for his restaurant customers in her head at the age of five, only a month after she learned to add and subtract. The epitome of that love was to back her with his funds and dispatch her to China. And yet she was not his biological daughter, but only a smart, twenty-six-year-young stepdaughter with an MBA from Berkeley. Along with the funding he had supplied a few powerful guanxi out of concern for her gender.

"Remember, boy or girl, these days you can do anything. You're twenty-six, but that's not young. History shows us generals who controlled the world at twenty. Women have babies at sixteen. You can do it. Go to the big lake and swim for your life. I trust you." She could still hear his ringing voice. That warm, lovely voice wrung more tears from her eyes.

He was only seventy-five, at the height of his senior years in the US, where a male's life expectancy was eighty-five. He enjoyed golfing and minded his health, his only medication being pills for high blood pressure.

He was the one who had enticed her to take up golf in high school. "You're old enough to have a boyfriend, you know," he said to her while they were shopping for a set of golf clubs in honor of her beginning high school.

"Not me," she protested. "And I hope never."

"Why not? You're such a pretty girl, and smart as a whip."

"I'll never find a man like you, Dad."

"That's right, and there's no girl as sweet and pretty as you, either!" And with that he hugged her tight.

Golf didn't just offer health benefits; it was also the best way to build a social network. She realized how considerate he was, in this and other ways, when she plunged into business in China. He embraced her with his steadfast love, filled in what she lacked, righted her wrongs, and guided her step by step along the path of life. The startup funds he had provided her at no interest were to be repaid as she became profitable. In fact, she had wanted to repay him as soon as possible, and as much as double the amount. It was the least she could do in return for his love. How jubilant he would be! The prospect made her heart throb. She had driven herself at work, she was so close to paying him back ... but now he was ill. She felt another surge of tears.

Her pretty, biracial mother, whose father was French, was intelligent enough to have finished college, a rarity at that time for a woman in Vietnam. Thanks to her degree, she found work at an American company in Saigon and fell in love with one of her American co-workers. Then came one of the greatest shocks of the twentieth century: the greatest superpower in the world lost to the Viet Cong. Saigon, expecting any moment to be overrun by the enemy, became a lawless, every-man-for-himself hell. Imagine a throng of people fighting and screaming to board a large vessel, with only limited space for people with connections and money; everyone undertaking an exodus for survival, frantic to squeeze into a boat, refusing to give up, climbing aboard any craft that would take them out to sea—a boat of any size would make it to America, or so they believed. But soon the boats were out of fuel and food. Neighboring countries refused to accept them. They were the Boat People and they floated over the vast sea. For a brief time the world showed interest, but soon they were forgotten. A generation of refugees died at sea, and no one knew how many.

Thanks to her American husband, Sophie's mother was able to cross the Pacific without becoming one of the Boat People. But love proved to be a dangerous gamble, and her happiness lasted only until he abandoned her when their daughter was six months old. It occurred to Lingling now that her mother, the beauty in Vietnam, became the ugly duckling in America. She was neither white nor Asian, and her husband fell for a white-skinned, blue-eyed, blonde-haired woman.

She had no memories of her biological father, and her mother kept not a single photo of him. She kept only his surname—Johnson. The substance was gone; only the husk remained. A mean-spirited man, he left them penniless. That must have been why white men were anathema to Sophie's mother, and blonde women almost as bad.

But hatred was not a place she could dwell; the refugee had to make living for the baby. More than once she was tempted to plunge into the sea, but her baby's blinking eyes killed the urge. She was lucky to be in America, the land of opportunity, and she found work as a hotel housekeeper.

Before the end of her first year of work, she hit the jackpot. The hotel owner, Wang Itsan, a San Francisco tycoon, fell in love with the pretty twenty-four-year-old housekeeper and moved her and the baby girl to a grocery store he owned in Chinatown. The store had been in the Wang family for four generations. His great-grandfather was one of the coolies who'd built the Golden Gate Bridge, a man who had doggedly saved up money and bought a tiny neighborhood grocery store—a safe bet, he reasoned, since everybody had to eat. As a Chinese businessman he believed in three principles: skipping a meal if you miss a goal; no giving on credit—or, if you did, being prepared to take a loss; and no lending money, even to your wife. The Wang family adhered to these principles, and as the shop flourished they diversified into other businesses. Success arrived in due course, and in Itsan's case the business was hotels. But he still kept the store.

Itsan moved Sophie and her mother into living quarters attached to the store and gave her mother the job of managing the shop. She found dealing with customers much easier than her cleaning chores at the hotel. The bright smile on her pretty face was perfect for the job.

Itsan did not add Lingling to his family genealogy until she was five. Until then, she was merely Sophie, the fatherless daughter of the woman middle-aged Wang was fond enough of to put in charge of the store. He made a daily stop there and one day discovered the girl was interested in numbers. He taught her to add and subtract, and to use an abacus and before long noticed she could do the calculations in her head.

"Look at you! I thought your mama was the smart one, but you're already a step ahead of her. You'll be something special when you grow up." And that's when he added her to the family register as his daughter. That night, Lingling's mother had wept as she thanked him for opening up a halcyon future for the girl. A decade later, Lingling realized his love for her mother was another big reason he had registered Lingling. A mistress could not be registered as his wife.

Not long after he became her stepfather, he stopped by the store with a book. He sat the girl on his lap and taught her how to read. Marvel of marvels, she turned out to be a speedy reader as well. "You're a smart cookie. I've never seen a girl like you."

She was over the moon with his praise but wondered if she really deserved it for such an effortless activity. It was fun to read, an easy-does-it pastime.

He emphasized the importance of learning Chinese. He was always saying, "You're my daughter, which makes you Chinese. Wherever you are, and however long you live outside China won't change that. So you need to speak like we do at home." Chinese conversed in Chinese and wherever possible did business with one another, perhaps out of a wish for mutual prosperity, and to keep wealth in Chinese hands. Whites came to Chinese restaurants, but the Chinese rarely went to White-owned eateries. Chinatown with its Chinese speakers was a Chinese enclave in the US. Their solidarity was a mystery and a source of tension to others.

From her studies Lingling remembered President Grover Cleveland once proclaiming that the Chinese, "as an element ignorant of our constitution and laws, impossible of assimilation with our people, and dangerous to our peace and welfare, constituted a danger to the peace."

Until she graduated from high school he continually urged her to read. "There's only so much to be learned from even the best teachers, the rest you get from reading. Books are the best teachers. The more you read, the more you learn about the world."

Whenever he bought a book, another stitch in the embroidery of her education, he reminded her that books came in different levels of depth and density and to read accordingly. By the time she arrived at UC Berkeley as a graduate student, she was the envy of her peers.

When she decided on the MBA program there, he had said, "A businessman's job is to bring in money, a general's job is to win battles. There's nothing more powerful and long-lasting than money."

She noticed a glass of wine and realized she hadn't seen the flight attendant deliver it. She found her wallet, inserted her index and middle fingers in the coin pocket, felt the familiar sensation of worn, creased paper, and carefully pincered the hundred-dollar bill. She looked at it intently as the memory came back. She was nine and had just left the store with her stepfather.

"Oh, no." She watched the dime she had dropped roll into a storm drain.

"Aren't you going to try and find it? Stick your hand in."

She wanted to cry as she looked up at him. "But Dad, it's yucky."

Stern and loud came his voice. "You can always wash your hands. Go on, try to find it."

Her mother rushed out, wondering what had happened. Why not ask her for help, Lingling had thought. But then she noticed an expression she had never seen before on her mother's face. She was glowering, her eyes livid and her lips clamped shut. Hurry up and do it! the girl imagined her screaming. The next thing she knew, she had fallen to her knees and stuck her hand down the drain. Whenever she touched something nasty, she cringed and shuddered and shut her eyes. Just for a crappy dime…I can't believe he's making me do this! But finally she found the errant coin.

"Good girl. Come here, sweetie!" He took her grimy hand and led her back inside to the sink and carefully washed her hands. Then he took out his wallet. "Here's your reward!" He handed her a hundred-dollar bill and pocketed the dime. This was the bill she had stored in her wallet all these years. His face overlapped the face on the bill and fresh tears dripped onto her cheeks.

Another limousine awaited her at San Francisco International Airport. En route to the hospital, she felt as if her heart was turbocharged—she kept wishing they could pay with an envelope for the privilege of speeding, like in Beijing.

He was on his last legs. His voice was so strangulated she had to put her ear to his mouth to understand him.

"You're here…. Thank you. I have three wishes. Please help your brother Yungli, he needs you. Don't worry about paying me back…. And China…"

Nodding, she put her ear closer to his mouth, but that was the last she heard.

3. A Heaven Fit for a Man

"I'm just not sure," said Chaehyŏng's mother, her gaze returning to her son. They were on their way to the airport.

"Mom, please. I've been hearing that from you all summer." His tone betrayed his irritation.

"And you know I have every reason to be repeating myself. I know it's spilled water and I should move on—you're a grown man and you know what you're doing—but still it's difficult. Maybe I'd feel different if we were rich, but knowing you have a bumpy ride ahead of you—"

"Mom, come on!" he barked. "You're coming out to the airport just to bitch at me."

"You heartless thing," she murmured, her eyes filling with tears. "You have no clue how I feel." She bit down on her lip and looked back out the window of the taxi.

"Mom, I wish you'd stop worrying. I'm working hard so I can be a professor someday. I don't have it all planned out yet, but I'm predicting China will be America's biggest rival and will become much more important to us. Like you said, there's no guarantee I'll be a professor. But I'll be all right. I could run a Chinese language cram school here in Korea and make a good living—you know the money's good. And—" Just in time, he swallowed the words. He'd come within a whisker of mentioning Yanling. Cooler head that she was, if Yanling decided to teach language, their cram school would be a hit for sure.

"Well, I'm not going to live forever. It's your life and I hope you know what you're doing with it."

Her sigh was like thread spooling from a bobbin. That sigh spoke to him with warmth and a tenacious love.

Bags checked and boarding pass in hand, he wondered what to do. If he scooted for the gate, his mother would feel left out.

"Mom, let's have some coffee."

She looked up at him in confusion.

"My treat. Come on." He took her gently by the arm.

And then she understood. How sweet of him. And she melted like a cube of sugar in hot water, feeling sorry for herself and at the same time proud of him. And then it hit her—she had never sat down over coffee with her son. Feeling his hand on her arm, she scolded herself for her outpouring of emotion. How could she ever hope to persuade him if she turned into a jellyfish at the suggestion of a cup of coffee?

He returned with the coffee and several packets of sugar. "Is it true your generation takes one spoon of sugar, and grandma's generation two?"

"Where did you get *that* idea!" she said, flicking away the packets. "I'm the same as you, no sugar."

"That's cool—too much sugar and salt are bad for you." Grinning, he sat down across from her.

Surely she could have a decent conversation with her son before he returned to Beijing. But what to talk about? Savory words, spoken with grace and refinement, were beyond her reach. It was as if her brain were bleached out. Until he left for college she had talked and he had listened, and the most frequent thing she said was *Study hard,* along with a laundry list of *Don'ts.* There had been no rapport, no sharing, no mutual respect but only unilateral commands coming from her. Had she ever had a genuine conversation with him?

She heard her daughter scolding her. *Mom, how can a woman who went to college be so ignorant? Look at all the money you wasted to educate yourself. What is it with Korean women—as soon as they get married and have kids they turn into snobs. They don't let their kids go and they run themselves crazy—it's kidmania and they have no clue what they're doing to themselves. It makes me want to gag.*

Silently they sipped their coffee. If only she could dispel the awkwardness. But the more pressure she felt to launch a conversation, the more helpless she felt. Chaehyŏng must have felt the same, and he rescued her.

"Mom, you want to hear something funny? A bunch of rich Chinese guys go to Japan and after they've seen the sights they hit the shops. First stop is a world-famous electronics store that Japan is so proud of—this was back when Japan was number one in electronics. They're practically peeing their pants, they're so excited. And then one of them says, 'Hey, look—they copied our Sona!' The others come running and they all start shouting; you know how they are. 'He's right, they copied our Sona.' 'Lousy Japs! They can't hide their true colors.' 'They invade innocent countries and never apologize.' 'They're arrogant, all of them!' Finally their guide says, 'What are you guys talking about? Sona is *our* fake. Sony's been around for years.' Pretty good, eh?"

"I can't believe it." She giggled, covering her mouth in a ladylike gesture. "That *is* funny."

"The Chinese do some funny things. I've got a few more—want to hear them?" It was so good to see his mom laughing and to feel the awkwardness between them soften.

"Sure." Her son, in his efforts to mollify her, brought to mind her husband when they were courting.

"You know, there's one thing North Korean defectors just don't understand about us in the south."

"Mm-hmm?"

"Not all the high-rises and the cars, but the rolls of toilet paper hanging nicely in the public toilets—we must be really rich down here since nobody takes them home."

"Ha."

"Next, what are the two things the Chinese who come here can't understand?"

"Tell me."

"Number one, the public toilets are as clean as their homes. Number two is all the doves together with people in the parks along the Han River."

"The toilets I can understand, but why the doves?"

"They're edible—why not make them into a tasty dinner?"

"Oh my god. That's disgusting." She frowned and laughed at the same time.

"Well, they eat anything and everything."

"So I've heard. Anything with four legs except a chair." What fun it was to actually *talk* with her son.

"And anything with wings except an airplane. And anything that swims except a submarine."

"That's terrific," she giggled, then clapped her hands together. "I have to remember that one for the next time I get together with the girls."

"Sure, we're all into recycling now. And did you know, one belly laugh zaps all cancer cells for eight hours."

"Really?" she said with a contented smile. "You little know-it-all." And then, with a doubtful look, she frowned. "You've eaten dove?"

"Mom, you have to be rich to afford dove meat and such. You can only find it at really fancy restaurants. But yes, I've tried it."

"How, if it's so expensive?"

"Some of our officials were invited over by the Chinese government, and me and some other students did the interpreting."

"Really?" she said, her voice rising an octave. "You were one of the interpreters?"

He made a face. "Mom, it was no big deal. And there wasn't really a selection process."

Show some class! she told herself as she saw the shadow fall across her son's cheerful face. She hastened to follow up. "All right, so how was it?"

"My stomach thought it was great. They grilled it, nice and chewy and savory."

"Yuck! How could you?"

"I've tried snake too, the poisonous one we call *salmosa*."

"What!" Her eyes grew large. "You're living dangerously all of a sudden."

Chaehyŏng checked the time on his cell phone and rose. "Mom, I have to go."

They walked silently to the departure gate, but in that silence she felt warm and thankful, unlike before their coffee. Her little boy had grown into a man who could loosen his mother's knotty heart; he was now a full-grown adult.

Showing his boarding pass and passport to security, he turned back to her. "Take care, Mom. And don't worry about me."

"All right. You have a safe trip," she said, suppressing an urge to run and hug him. "And remember, no skipping meals. And watch your health!" Short though her sendoff was, she choked up at the end, her voice trailing into weeping.

The door to the security area slid shut across his back. *He's gone.* She stood where she was, unable to move. The door reopened and she peered in vain at the meandering line of people for a glimpse of him.

Some of her friends had lost a son to marriage, and without exception they had lamented that there came a day when they were no longer 'mom' to their son but instead 'mother.' Every last one had complained of loneliness and a hurt they never before experienced; their hearts had dropped; the blood had drained from their brains. If now she was to see a girl walking alongside her son, those hurtful feelings would be hers.

There's nothing I can do about it. And off she trudged, wearing a lonesome smile. She tried to memorize the jokes he had told her. How thankful that she could brag to her friends now. At the same time, she readied herself for the lectures that inevitably came from jealousy: *Don't get your hopes too high. They're sweet when they're single, sour when they're married. Start to get used to it, or you'll end up a sad sack.*

Inside the Beijing airport Chaehyŏng scanned the vast arrival hall. Where was Yanling? Had she had a change of heart? It was one thing to trust Yanling, but quite another to buy into the culture of promiscuity among Chinese women. It wasn't unusual for a girl to live with one guy and have casual sex with another. No problem as long as she kept the two of them in the dark about each other. If others happened to find out, they wouldn't think her unethical or immoral, would not in fact think much of it at all. Problems arose only if the two men found out about each other. But the disgruntled party would simply walk away and that was that. Back home, though, the boyfriend gets into a scuffle with the girl or a fistfight with the contender and someone ends up with a bloody nose or fractured ribs. In the worst cases, knives are produced. There the cheated-on seeks to harm the girl for revenge, but here, thanks to the tenet "Respect the woman and serve the wife," he is able to let go. Hell, thought Chaehyŏng, the guys even do housework here—they clean, they cook, they wash clothes.

Businessmen from back home always got irked at first. "So what the fuck *do* they do?"

"You just said it—the most important job."

"What do you mean?"

"Do I have to spell it out for you? Think about what you just said."

Chaehyŏng understood how in a society where the majority of the women worked outside the home, able-bodied husbands would want to help with the housework. And the law punished men if they battered women, but not women who roughed up their men. There were plenty of battered husbands who lived under the little woman's thumb. It was heaven on earth for women here, and you could find no trace of Master Gong's teaching, "A wife should follow her husband." Wanting to show the world that the power of its people lay in the Master's teachings, the central government decided to build a Confucius Institute in every country. To its astonishment, Koreans proved the most exemplary adherents. Which might explain why the very first institute had been built back home. Three hundred more institutes, built at light-speed, then appeared across the globe. At the same time, China pumped new life into the relic that was Master Gong, erecting a gigantic statue of the sage in Tiananmen Square—a cameo appearance, as it turned out, for the likeness was spirited away not quite a hundred days later—and reviving his legacy throughout the land. But there was one notable omission from this campaign—"A woman should follow her husband." You might as well try to find ginseng in the sea or fresh vegetables in the desert. Poor guys, thought Chaehyŏng—they were *chiquan yan*, henpecked husbands, and they knew and accepted it.

Yes, China had become heaven for women and hell for men. Just as tree leaves shake in the wind and drums sound when beaten, turning the status of men and women upside down was a natural outcome of Chairman Mao's New China and his dictum, "Women hold up half the sky." Unleashed, women grew rabid, and their frenzy built to anarchy when Mao extended executive power to his wife, Jiang Qing, during the decade-long Cultural Revolution. Along with Red Guard mayhem toward cultural assets, the red flag was raised high to demote Master Gong and shred men's millennia-long predominance over women.

Chaehyŏng considered the Chinese character for 'male:' it consists of two elements meaning 'field' and 'labor,' suggesting a man working in the fields. So, you make dust fly in the fields and come home to rest, which was the law of the land back home—"Labor must come with a break"—leaving the housework to your good wife. That was the traditional division of labor, and Mao turned it upside down. Why not make a new character for 'male,' thought Chaehyŏng. It wouldn't be the first occasion of changing times resulting in the creation of a new character. Take the character for *ka*, for example, created with the increasing use of various sorts of playing cards: it consists of two elements meaning 'above' and 'below' to describe the top-to-bottom action of card-shuffling. With an agrarian society changing to an industrial one, men's workplace, the fields, changes to the factory or the office. Add housework to the mix, and we need a new character. Because Chinese characters are ideographs, the various meanings should all be reflected in the character. If we take the example of the top-to-bottom structure of *ka*, why not add, on top of the character for 'male,' the character for 'female,' since the one now suffers under the other. Or, instead of the character for 'female,' add the character for 'house,' to indicate that the man shares in the housework. If the central government wanted characters to precisely convey meaning, Chaehyŏng thought, it should get on the ball and change the character for 'male.'

Such thoughts brought memories of good-natured joshing by his Korean friends here.

"A brave warrior like you, are you primed to take on all the housework?"

"Just remember, a pretty face lasts only ten years, but slavery is forever."

"Did you sign up for cooking classes? Appliances can help with housecleaning and laundry, but with cooking it's all up you and your tender hands!"

"What's so special about Chinese girls? Do they have a gold or a silver ring hidden up you-know-where?"

He could handle their ridicule with a shrug, but understood they were only half joking. For a Korean guy, these issues were not to be taken lightly. Housework would be a problem. Would she expect him to do *all* of it? Cooking, scrubbing the toilets, making the bed? Who would want to live like *that*? Would Yanling do it instead? Hell no. But he couldn't give her up on account of that, no way. Not necessarily crucial issues, but worth considering. There was only one solution: make enough money to hire a maid. Could he do that by studying history? Now *that* was a serious issue.

From the airport he rushed to her officetel and sounded the buzzer; no one home. Maybe she wasn't back from Gwangdong? *What the hell?* He pulled out his phone to text her, but caught himself. They'd promised not to communicate during the break.

The following day she still hadn't arrived. Was she sick? Nothing obviously wrong with her when he'd left. He kept fidgeting with his phone. No news the following day either. Something bad must have happened—a car accident? As the what- ifs and she-must-haves accumulated, the pins and needles grew sharper. He lost his appetite. When he tried to read, he couldn't finish a line. He grew more fretful and depressed, kept reaching for his water bottle.

Then one day there was a furious knocking on his door. "Namgŭn!" he barked as he opened the door. But he couldn't help bursting into laughter as he said his friend's name.

"Shithead!" said Namgŭn with a playful attempt to punch him. "Don't get going on my name."

"Hey, you're no fun. And it's not like I'm the one who named you."

His friend's name never failed to get Chaehyŏng laughing. It all went back to a kid from home, newly arrived here. Introduced to Namgŭn, the kid had said, *Yi Namgŭn… what a name! Yi the Pecker. Or, assuming you have hair in all the right places, maybe we should upgrade you to Yi the Penis. Steer clear of admin work, you need to be a politician, a statesman, you'll have the entire female vote under your belt. What a great name! You're set for life.*

Namgŭn had flown into a rage. "Son of a bitch!" He had lashed out with his fist, breaking the kid's nose. He had had to send a letter home asking for money to pay the doctor bills.

His father's quick response impressed everybody. It started with "To my pride and joy," expressed a father's profound love, and ended by encouraging his son to keep up the good fight and defend his name. Namgŭn had circulated the letter among his Korean friends here and the effect was instantaneous—they stopped teasing him. For sure Namgŭn's father had fulfilled his fatherly duty, Chaehyŏng told himself.

And then one day Namgŭn had blurted to Chaehyŏng, "It's ridiculous how the guys laugh at my name. What about all the Yi Sŏnggis in the world—do they get called 'Yi the Genitalia'? And Han Sŏnggyo—'Han the Intercourse Man.' Im Shinhaeng—'Im Go-and-Knock-Her-Up.' Chin Segyun—'Chin Goes Viral.' Ku Ch'ungje—'Ku the Insect Killer.' O Set'ak—'O the Laundry Man.' Kong Muwŏn—'Kong the Public Servant.' Chin Chungdok —'Chin the Addict.' Yi Pyŏngwŏn—'Yi the Hospital Man.' And don't accuse me of being sexist. For the girls we have Yi Kyomi—'Yi Get-it-On,' and Kim Nanja—'Kim the Little-Miss-Egg.' Assholes! What do they know about a name?"

Right now Yi Namgŭn and he was breathing hard. "Chaehyŏng, I need your help!"

"What is it?"

His friend's triangular face with its sharp chin pleaded with him. "You know my uncle. The PSB pulled him in again. He's been calling me all day; damn cell phone feels like it's on fire. Help me, and you'll drink free the rest of the week."

"When are you going to get serious about learning Chinese? You can't go on like this."

Now his friend was holding his head and shuddering. "I'm sick of learning Chinese! All those damn characters turn my head numb."

This was serious—his friend wasn't exaggerating. Namgŭn hated Chinese like other kids hated math or English. He and all the other Chinese-language haters wanted to go back home, but didn't want to disappoint their parents—who needs parents being hysterical? And so they went through the motions here, wasting time and money—no different from kids studying in the US for ten years and coming home empty-handed.

So off to the jail they went, Chaehyŏng requesting they be allowed to visit Namgŭn's uncle. At the same time, Namgŭn deftly slipped cash into the hand of the PSB duty officer. That was Namgŭn, quick to act. He had probably had to perform this service before.

"Kid, what took you so long?" barked the uncle as soon as the two friends walked into the meeting area. He liked to show off to the PSB.

"Long to you, Uncle," Namgŭn shot back, "but light-speed for us." He and his uncle interacted more like squabbling pals than relatives.

"Hello, sir," said Chaehyŏng, introducing himself with a bow.

"Hello," responded the man half-heartedly before shouting again to Namgŭn, "You little shit, don't tell me you still need your friends to talk for you—what the hell have you been up to all this time?"

"You got that right," Namgŭn shouted back. "Ten years or a hundred, no fucking way I'll learn Chinese. What do you want, anyway?"

"Son of a bitch. What a waste of money," said his uncle, jaw set, glaring at him. "Here," he said, giving Namgŭn his personal seal and bankbook. "I need twenty thousand, now."

"That's twice as much as last time!"

"Of course it is, you dumbass. Just like everything else. I guess I'm wearing out my welcome here. So what are you waiting for? Take this stuff and go. Twenty thousand is nothing compared to what I make here."

"Oh yeah, I forgot how smart you are!" said Namgŭn as he took the seal and bankbook. "Chaehyŏng, ask that guy if they'll release him as soon as we pay the fine."

"It's good you're concerned about him," said Chaehyŏng outside the meeting area, "but aren't coming on a little too strong?"

"Are you kidding? Can't you see why I'm so pissed? He comes all the way here to sell fake handbags, and by now he's a regular customer for the PSB. It's embarrassing as hell. He's the one who dragged me to this shithole, you know." He cleared his throat noisily and spat.

Instead of good Chinese it was bad habits his friend had learned here, Chaehyŏng said to himself. "Sir, will he be released as soon as he pays the fine?" he asked the duty officer.

"Sure. The faster he pays, the faster he's out. We're full up here, we can always use more room," said the officer, euphoric over Namgŭn's gratuity.

Chaehyŏng interpreted for his friend. "The faster the better."

"Of course. Money's the great cure-all here. Sons of bitches." Again Namgŭn spat.

"Why not? Everybody loves free cash—you can forfeit your ticket to hell and buy a maiden's balls. I love money too, don't you?" said Chaehyŏng with a provocative stare.

"Yeah, I know, your shit smells better than mine, but you don't need to show off just to shut me up." Namgŭn gave Chaehyŏng the finger, then hailed a taxi.

Inside the taxi Namgŭn crouched over his uncle's bankbook. "What the hell?" he exclaimed, eyes bulging, "Look at this."

"Damn," said Chaehyŏng, goggling at the figures, "he's got almost three hundred and sixty thousand!"

"How much is that in *wŏn*?"

"A hundred and eighty for one *yuan*, so about sixty-five million. Wow," he said, smacking his lips in envy.

"No wonder it was me he called," said Namgŭn. "He has a Korean-Chinese girl who helps him but…"

"Right, you don't want to show your gold to a thief," said Chaehyŏng, calm and deliberate. "Seeing is believing, but then you want what you're seeing. He shouldn't trust her with that much money in the bank."

"Yeah, that's a fortune she could make off with. Remember all those small businessmen who got swindled that way?"

Namgŭn nodded, but he kept staring at the figures in the bankbook.

Chaehyŏng cocked his head. "All from fake handbags—amazing!"

"I'm thinking that's not his only account," Namgŭn murmured. "I bet he has larger ones."

"You sure?" said Chaehyŏng, his head swaying ponderously in disbelief. "He has that much cash?"

"You have no idea," said Namgŭn bitterly as he pocketed the bankbook. "He's stinking rich—no one knows *how* rich, not even my aunt—and he's a sly bastard."

Chaehyŏng smirked. "Well, good thing you're here."

"The one thing he has going for him is he's good with his hands—I just wish he'd put his skill to better use," said Namgŭn dolefully.

"He'd have to be talented to make a bundle over here!"

"Damn right he's talented," said Namgŭn, straightening in his seat. "I bet he's number one back home, and maybe the whole world. He's like a human sewing machine –looks at a bag and in no time comes up with one that's better than the original. He's a wizard. He gets a kick out of telling me the quality control inspectors for the French and Italian luxury brands can't tell them apart. You should see the embroidery and lettering he turns out on his sewing machines. And he's wasting all that talent on counterfeits!" Namgŭn was practically frothing at the mouth.

The nephew could be a good publicist for the uncle, thought Chaehyŏng.

With the twenty thousand *yuan* in hand they returned to the jail, and Uncle was once again a free man.

"It's too much," Namgŭn grumbled as the three of them left. "Twice as much as last time."

"You dunce!" barked Uncle, loud as the local men. "Everything's gone up!"

"Wow. Nolbu the miser speaks! You just wasted twenty thousand *yuan*, and it's easy come, easy go."

"Kid, you've got shit for brains. The fine is only fifteen thousand, the rest is *bunppai* for that guy. That's why I got out so quick. You guys have a lot to learn."

Namgŭn kept glancing in embarrassment at Chaehyŏng. "My dear little uncle," he blurted, "would you please stop showing off your fucking Japanese. There's a Korean word for it, remember? *Punbae*."

Reading Namgŭn's expression, Uncle grumbled to Chaehyŏng, "Listen to that little shit. Jap lingo is what you learn when you start working at a *mising* at age eighteen. What am I supposed to do? Little bastard."

Chaehyŏng was quick to answer. "Please, Uncle, it's not an issue for me."

Uncle brought his fist so close to Namgŭn that it poked his nose, "See, punk. Why should I be ashamed of anything?" Then he murmured to himself, "Not bad. This one's from a well-bred family," and kept nodding in approval, seemingly pleased that his nephew's friend had referred him as "Uncle."

"Don't be a nag. I look at you sideways and you get your dander up. What's he supposed to say when you get in his face like that? He just wants to be polite. Whereas you're full of it."

"Stop yapping—you could learn some manners from this one!" Scanning the vicinity, he said to no one in particular, "See any *bao* shops? I'm starving. "

"They're all over. Right there, for example! You're in China, remember?" Namgŭn led them into the nearby shop. As soon as they were seated, he said, "Uncle. I'm going to ask you something, and I'll be up front about it."

"What now?" said his uncle as he pulled out a cigarette.

Namgŭn shot him a look. "*Baozi* isn't enough for what we did for you."

"Don't I deserve some respect?" thundered his uncle, glaring at him. "I've got my pride, you know, and heart too."

"Please, Uncle. How can you talk about pride and heart? For decades you made knockoffs back home, and now you're doing it here. Tell me, how many times have they locked you up here? It's embarrassing!"

Uncle brandished his fist, "You punk! What am I going to do with you?"

Chaehyŏng watched them with a grin. *What a weird family*. And yet he found nothing negative about their relationship. On the contrary, it was somehow affecting.

"I promised him he'd drink free for a week," said Namgŭn, sticking out his palm to his uncle.

"Stop it," said Chaehyŏng, slapping his friend's thigh.

"Why? I told you, he's a penny-pincher. If I don't ask, I'll never get any money out of him," said Namgŭn nonchalantly.

"I'm supposed to give money to a piddly thief? You're a disgrace to your uncle."

"I'm a disgrace to you? If I am, it all starts with you, the knockoff king—you and the PSB. Anything more I need to say?"

"Can you shut up long enough to tell me how much you want to extort me for?"

"What does your conscience tell you?"

"A hundred?"

"I knew it, " Namgŭn snorted. "Mr. Generosity himself!"

"Hey," said Chaehyŏng with another slap on the thigh.

"Rotten twerp. All right, two hundred." With a grand gesture, he deposited two hundred *yuan* in his nephew's palm.

"Come on, Uncle, run the numbers. First, the taxis. Then the bribe. And the time we wasted. And this is all? I deserve at least a thousand, even two thousand, but considering you get shaken down by the PSB, I'll be generous and call it five hundred—not one *yuan* less." Namgŭn sealed his mouth. Chaehyŏng cringed.

"Here." Uncle practically threw the money at him. "Might as well pull a gun on me!"

"Why not call it quits, Uncle. Draw the curtain on the knockoff business, go back home, and have yourself a good life with Auntie," said Namgŭn before taking a mouthful of *baozi*.

Swallowing his half-chewed food, Uncle bawled at him, "I told you to drop it!" Chaehyŏng looked about in panic, but to his surprise no one paid attention. It was then he decided Uncle was a perfect fit for life in China.

"I only mention it because you've been at it so long," said Namgŭn, suddenly serious. "You must be fed up by now."

"Kid, you don't know squat about life. You have to tell yourself it's only a job—you don't worry about whether you like it. I'm not in my twenties anymore, but I can still work. If your grandpa had given the rest of us a hand like he did for your father and sent me to college, I wouldn't be peddling fakes for a living. He sent his eldest son to college, and the other six of us, the girls through middle school, the boys through high school. I think he kind of pitied me because I was the last one, but by then he was too old to scrounge up money for college tuition. If only I'd gone to college I would have turned out way better than your father—"

"*Aigo*, Uncle," Namgŭn interrupted. "I've heard that story a thousand times."

"I know. But when something's unfair, the feeling doesn't go away no matter how much you bitch about it. Anyway, making fakes is a dirty business back home but here it's heaven—really." To punctuate the statement, he popped an entire *baozi* into his mouth.

"Heaven?" Namgŭn stopped chewing and regarded his uncle.

"Sure. Back home it's ridiculous, the government has a fit, they must figure they're a nation of luxury goods and they have to lock you up for spoiling their image. Here it's the opposite—why bother, aren't we all in the same boat? That's their attitude. Here there's a crackdown maybe once in several months, and only if one of the name-brand companies raises hell. They take photos when they burn the fake shop down, but it's only window dressing. They keep the fines and the gratuities, and all's well that ends well. Compared with what we make here on fakes, it's blood from a mosquito. The fake-market economy here is ten times the size of the one back home, maybe hundreds, hell, maybe even thousands. I tell you—heaven."

Far from feeling fed up with his work, thought Chaehyŏng, Uncle seemed to enjoy it.

"Don't you have a lot of competition?" said Namgŭn.

"Sure, but not all fakes are the same. Mine, of course, are five-star, but it's downhill for everybody else."

He ought to be in show business, Chaehyŏng found himself thinking.

"How could there be so much difference?" said Namgŭn. "Aren't you the one who taught the folks here how to make fake handbags? Sounds to me like a half-assed job of technology transfer."

"Watch your yap. And stop talking about fakes. I can teach them the basics, but from then on it's up to them. You keep the core skills to yourself. Like the man says, show no one your wallet, not even your father. Miracle formulas, family recipes, you don't give away the crucial details till you're on your deathbed."

"I still don't understand the differences in quality. Those fakes all look the same."

"That's because you're a dimwit. Gangsters don't fight to decide who's top dog—one glance at the contenders and you know. It's the same with counterfeits, especially if you're selling them—you know through intuition what's five-star and what's not. It's scary how much the vendors know, and they've never touched a sewing machine in their life."

"All right, I get the point. So how much longer are you going to stick around?"

"Hell, I'm just getting started on—what's it called?" He made a face. "Not exporting, but what you do with products you want to buy and sell…what's the expression?"

"You mean domestic market activation?" said Chaehyŏng.

"That's it! Hey, you're a smart one." Slapping his knee, Uncle shot a look at Namgŭn as if to say, *Wake up, boy*. "So if I can get my bags activated domestically, I got myself a sweet deal. And *that's* the heaven I'm talking about. I can't leave now. Plus, I have five ladies depending on me. Back home they'd be old and no good, but here I trained them and I pay them good a salary. I'm a proud patriot. I'm creating jobs overseas, just like our government tells us to do. Yeah, I'm a patriot all right."

"Hats off to the patriot. What a pile of shit—patriots don't put their country to shame."

"Listen, you little prick, you're in over your head here; you've got better things to do than study, right? Your grandpa was a master bamboo craftsman, and you have to have some of his DNA. So why not forget about the books and go in with me? I'll teach you every trick and secret I've got up my sleeve, promise. Then you'll be good for thirty more years here. And you can expand—back to Korea, and then there's the Philippines, Indonesia, Vietnam, Thailand, all over Asia. Women here are mad about my top-notch bags; you'll see for yourself."

"Hello, Uncle, you can come back to earth now. And then you can take my phone number and stick it you-know-where. And don't take it out the next time you're in jail. Come on," he said to Chaehyŏng, "let's get out of here." And he sprang to his feet.

"Nice meeting you, sir. Until next time…" Chaehyŏng rose uncertainly, reluctant to offend Uncle with an overly hasty departure.

Two days later Chaehyŏng found Yanling back in her officetel. Answering the door, she threw herself into his arms and burst into tears. "I want to kill myself."

He hugged her with relief. "What happened?"

"Something bad—back home." Now she was sobbing.

Feeling her tremble, he embraced her more closely. "Can you tell me?" He wondered if something had happened to her father.

"No, I can't. I'm so ashamed." Her head swayed back and forth, and then she buried herself in his chest.

"Ashamed of what?" he said, searching for a clue.

"It's so embarrassing. You'll never understand. It would never happen in Korea."

"Yanling, I wish you wouldn't say that. What matters is I love you, there's no need to feel you shouldn't talk to me about family matters. So tell me, please." With one arm he drew her close and with the other he patted her back.

She nudged him just enough to give herself some breathing room, then in between sobs told him the story.

"My mom's not doing well—I worry about her."

A chill came over him. "Why?"

She ushered him to her chair and then, tears easing, sat on the edge of her bed. "I just found out I have two brothers."

"What!" He took her hand and patted it. "Take a deep breath and tell me about it."

"You know, ever since the reforms, all the powerful high officials and nouveaux riches have taken *ernai*."

"And?"

"My father got a whiff of the winds blowing out of the Special Economic Reform Zone in Shenzhen and got into the action, and he became super-rich. Maybe he thought he had too much money, and why not spend some of it on an *ernai*? He wasn't blatant about it, and Mom decided to look the other way and say nothing. She liked spending money, and I guess she assumed other rich wives had to put up with it, too. I was too young to know better. Having an *ernai*, showing off your money and power, it's sick Chinese exhibitionism, all of it. And it's gotten worse—men like him whose child is a daughter got greedy and jumped onto the produce-a-son bandwagon. Of course that's a violation of the one-child policy, but if you're rich and powerful you pay a fine and get away with it. All along my mom was living in the dark, and just recently she discovered that two sons, ages five and ten, were added to our family register."

"She must have been stunned!" said Chaehyŏng, all in a fluster.

"In fact, she fainted. But guess what my dad said. He said he couldn't help it,

Mom had had her tubes tied—again, the one-child policy. Anyway, it was a poor excuse and it made Mom absolutely furious. Then it got worse—he said he could afford to have two more sons. But the worst thing was, he threatened her, said he'd divorce her unless she kept her mouth shut. Can you imagine that? If she wasn't so angry I think she'd kill herself. Disgusting, isn't it? And now you'll want to leave me."

"Never!"

"It's all so incongruous. What do you think will happen to your mom?" He wished he had a suggestion to offer.

"I don't know. I can't ask her to divorce him, and I don't want to tell her to put up with it. If I were her, I'd probably kill myself."

"Wow, you are scary." Tongue lolling, he tried to make a face to lighten her mood.

"It's not just her problem, it's mine too."

"How so?"

"I'm so disgusted with my dad, I don't want to depend on him for tuition or anything else. I just don't know what to do."

"Yeah, really. That fine you were talking about: how much is it anyway?"

"It differs from one city and province to the next. I think he paid eighty-four thousand."

He made the conversion—more than fifteen million *wŏn*. "That's a hefty amount."

"It's nothing for a rich businessman. The sad thing is, some of them actually compete to see who can produce the most sons. All the more reason to alienate the poor."

"I can understand the growing resentment. But what if the babies are girls?"

"It's not an issue. They end up *heihaizi*—bastards who never get registered. It's as if officially they don't exist."

"Ghost kids. Thirteen million last year, according to government reports, but I doubt that. From what I hear the actual figure is somewhere between one hundred and four hundred million."

"What are the chances the government would accept those figures?" she sneered.

"Well, maybe they slash it to ten percent of the actual, so thirteen million?"

"Who knows! I guess it's better we don't know for sure."

"The more I know, the less I feel I know here. Just look at the statistics. How can there be thirteen million ghost kids? That's five times the population of Mongolia, twice as many people as in all of Tibet, it has to be a world record!"

"What can we do? There's government pressure to have one child only, there's a deep-rooted preference for sons, and girls get neglected while everybody waits for a son. I'm in a bad position now."

"Why?"

"Isn't it obvious? I was supposed to inherit everything, and now it's only one third. Two more sons and it's one fifth. Who knows, maybe it will be one tenth."

"Let's save that for later. How about some dim sum? It's already one o'clock."

4. Shang of the Jungle

"What's wrong with it?" asked Shang Xinwen with a disapproving smile.

Sŏ Hawŏn noticed the disapproval. "It's quite risky," he said matter-of-factly.

Chŏn Taegwang interpreted in the same tone. Sŏ's Mandarin had improved, but he still needed help in conversation.

"Aren't all operations risky to some extent?" said Shang, knitting his eyebrows and draining his glass of beer to show his displeasure.

"Side effects have been documented for this procedure, even loss of life." Sŏ's face was tinged with gravity.

"And yet it remains popular in Korea."

His *guanxi* was beginning to sound like an interrogator, thought Chŏn.

"The truth is, too many accidents reflect poorly on the clinic, and doctors tend to avoid it."

"But it all comes down to skill. And I know you're the best at what you do." Shang looked at Chŏn as he said this.

Chŏn's beer was beginning to lose its taste. He wasn't comfortable with the call for help Shang was signaling with his eyes, but he had to remain neutral.

"I realize the surgery would be tremendously profitable, but from a medical point of view I have my doubts. It's not simply cosmetic, like eyelid or nose augmentation. It involves the grinding and reconstruction of bone, and there lies the risk. And ethically I don't agree with surgery on major body structures unless they are no longer functioning." Sŏ was firm and objective.

In his interpretation Chŏn focused on accuracy. This turned out the next moment to be a crucial blow to Sŏ.

"Or is it a matter of getting shaky knees when you do a procedure like that?"

Chŏn moaned inwardly. It was a mean thing to say to a professional. And it wasn't as if Shang ran the clinic. How to interpret? Shang was already drooling over the profits to be made from chin augmentation surgery.

Hearing Chŏn's interpretation, Sŏ closed his eyes. The next moment all the images from that nightmare operation back home replayed themselves at high speed.

"You may think of me as you wish. But I would remind you I will not engage in any unethical medical practice, and what's more I can't afford to be held liable in a foreign country if an accident should happen in the course of surgery. If you're having doubts about me, perhaps it's time for a new doctor."

Chŏn cheered inwardly. What a surprise coming from this meek-looking man.

The magic doctor most definitely had nerve to spare. The interpretation reeled off his tongue.

"Excuse me? A new doctor?" Shang paused. "There is some misunderstanding. What I meant was that you could make ten times more performing that operation. Well … if we are talking about a procedure dangerous enough to put a doctor in jail, then of course you shouldn't do it." Frantic to recover from his slip, he motioned nonstop while looking to Chŏn for help.

"Dr. Sŏ, please disregard what he said. He's been blinded by money. You know such people will do anything to get their hands on it. And now he's scared of losing you. He will never say it again, so just forget about it," said Chŏn, holding Sŏ's arm in supplication.

"Please let him know I'm serious and I don't want to hear it again." Sŏ had found himself in a dilemma when the subject of chin augmentation surgery had first come up at his clinic back home. Now the issue was finally behind him and he could breathe easy.

Turning to Shang, Chŏn switched back to Mandarin. "Dr. Sŏ said he will forget what happened provided the subject does not resurface."

Shang nodded. "I guarantee you that will not happen."

Chŏn interpreted and Sŏ nodded in acknowledgment.

"We are *lao pengyo. Ganbei.*" Shang raised his glass.

"*Ganbei!*" Chŏn and Sŏ brought their glasses together with his.

"Coffee?" asked Sŏ in the taxi bound for his officetel.

"Good idea," said Chŏn, guessing Sŏ needed to clear the air about the conversation with Shang.

Deposited near Sŏ's officetel, they located the Starbucks on the cross street. The coffee chain was spreading like weeds in the rainy season, the fourth largest US purveyor of food and drink in the land after Coca-Cola, McDonald's, and KFC. Not just coffee but the craze for it was addictive.

"I find Shang odd, how about you?" said Sŏ after his first sip.

"I'm not sure, "said Chŏn. "But don't take what he said the wrong way. His cousin inquired about that particular operation, and he felt obligated to ask you." Chŏn felt sorry for Sŏ, living apart from his family back home, and wanted to ease the doctor's mind.

"I understand you want to give him the benefit of the doubt, but as a businessman don't you sense he's more involved in the clinic than we were initially led to believe?" The eyes gazing at Chŏn were filled with suspicion.

"I can see where you might come to that conclusion, but I tend to think not. He has too many fish to fry at work, and money's not an issue—he's certainly rich enough not to need being involved in the clinic." Chŏn realized that in spite of his efforts to remain neutral he must have sounded like he was siding with Shang.

Sŏ was quick to respond. "If you think so. Maybe I'm being overly sensitive." He nodded.

"I could be wrong," said Chŏn. "I'm only a third party. Anyway, just keep an eye on him—probably no harm done if he's involved in running the clinic." But Chŏn felt less sure-footed than he sounded.

"Maybe I'm the one who's odd and he just wants to help his family, which is a good thing. Perhaps I'm guilty of a preconception," Sŏ said, the suspicion clearing from his face.

"Not necessarily. If you think he's overstepping and pressuring you, that can be stressful. And that's the impression I got just now. But I think you handled it very well, doctor."

"Well, thank you. I guess it's all about money…" A forlorn smile flickered on his face.

Chŏn saw a weary, lonely man far from home. Here it was again, another wave of melancholy; it washed in at every corner they turned. Wasn't there anything more to life? In Sŏ, Chŏn began to see himself.

"How is your Chinese partner? Is he getting better?"

"I can't tell, maybe because our specialties are different. So-so, I guess."

"He's not very skilled?"

"Well, skill depends a lot on interest. I'm not sure how interested he is…."

"Then, that's a relief. There's no problem until he gets hawk-eyed about upgrading himself. I was curious about that." Chŏn sipped his coffee. "Mmm."

"What do you mean?" Sŏ, bleary-eyed from the beer, gazed at Chŏn.

"It's an issue of knowhow. What I'm saying is, you have plenty of time until he walks. Once he picks up everything you have to offer, he's gone, so take your sweet time with him. That's why I'm relieved."

"Is it very common?" Sŏ blinked innocently.

"It happens all the time in business, especially in technical fields, It can get cruel and merciless. They worship you when they need your skill, then ditch you when they've sucked all the juice out of you. Take the software field. Two or three years ago China was still tenuous with software but pretty up-to-date with hardware. For example, their hotels were five-star, but they weren't generating maximum profits. Why? Because the local managers weren't that good with software. Which is why most of the good hotels hire a foreigner to manage operations. You'll see a few Koreans doing that here in Shanghai. The local insurance industry is also behind, and the companies have been scouting Japanese and Koreans. Guess who got the nod? We did, of course. There's the unsettled history between the two countries, but the Japanese are angling for a big signing bonus and tend to look down their noses at the locals."

"Are you saying China never had an insurance industry?"

"That's right. It's a weakness in socialist countries. That's why they need to learn from the capitalist countries."

"So they recruited a lot of people from back home."

"Yes, mostly retirees from the insurance industry—paid them high salaries too. But the Koreans didn't mind the store."

"How so?"

"They didn't pace themselves."

"You mean they transferred their expertise too quickly."

"Right. And then they were dumped."

"They didn't see it coming?"

"They must have. So they lived it up while they could."

"I'm confused."

"It's simple—you need three years, five at most, to train someone in the software used in the insurance industry. So the guys recruited from back home realize they're living on borrowed time, so why not live the good life along with pulling in a big paycheck. So as soon as they started working here, they got hooked on girls and booze. At the end of the day you bust ass to a drinking party with all the exotic girls you can dangle your you-know-what at. Before long they'd lost their advantage. You've heard that female beauty is the oldest spy trick in the book, and it's still the most effective. That's what they did with these guys, got them drunk and listened to them spill all their knowhow. Less than two years later they had to pack up and leave. They probably wasted a year's salary on booze and girls—they got caught in a net. And the Chinese insurance industry went on a roll—they finally got to stand on their own two feet!"

"It's scary here," said Sŏ, shuddering in disgust.

"That's nothing," said Chŏn. "It can get mean depending on how bad you want core technology. No gun battles yet, but it's an industrial spy war for sure."

"Makes my head spin. We should get going," said Sŏ, checking his watch and rising.

A week later Chŏn took a call at work.

"*Wei*, this is Chen Wei." It was a woman's voice, calm and mature.

"*Wei*." Chŏn's brain reeled. Who the hell was this?

"I guess you don't remember me." Punctuated with a faint laugh.

"I'm very sorry. You're…" Chŏn kept bowing as if the woman was right there in front of him.

"I understand. It's been a while. I'm Shang Xinwen's—"

"Oh my," Chŏn interrupted. "I'm so sorry. How could I be so dense? A decade shouldn't matter… I should have remembered." And now he was bowing nonstop as her face came vividly to mind. Had it really been that long? Her name hadn't surfaced in his conversations with Shang, which always concerned business.

"I understand. You have too many things to remember." She laughed brightly, then, more gingerly, said, "I would like to see you."

"By all means. What time is good for you?"

"The sooner the better. Even today."

"Today is fine, I'm available anytime." His mind had already shifted to service mode; he was the private and Shang and his good wife the generalissimos.

"Thank you so much. Could we make it an hour from now?"

Why did she want to see him? Chŏn wondered after the call had ended. Was her brother ill again? Why had she called instead of Shang? Whatever it was, he feared the worst.

An hour later they were sitting across from each other, paper-thin teacups in hand.

"Did Shang tell you about us?" said Chen.

"About the two of you?" said Chŏn with a cautious glance at her face, poised over the rim of the cup. "News?"

She snorted. "He's being cagey. We're divorced."

"Excuse me? But why?" He realized in spite of his shock that the question might be improper.

"That's not why I wanted to see you. Well, actually it's related. I shall be brief. Did you know he had a train of *ernai*?" She gazed at him with a knowing smile.

He could only murmur, "Well, I guessed...."

"And did you guess how many?"

"Well..." In fact, he had guessed three or four.

"Don't be shocked when I tell you this—seven!"

"Seven..." No, he wasn't shocked. Comparatively speaking, and for a high official, seven could be considered exemplary. A few months ago Chŏn had read of a rural official who had set a new world record—146 mistresses. The man must have had the stamina of the grandfather of all seals. To support a harem of that size the man must have been equally diligent at embezzlement and collecting bribes.

"Those officials are putrid, all of them. I know what they're up to, and I know I'm not getting any younger, so I just ignored him. But a month ago he asked for a divorce. Some girl sucked his heart out. So I signed the papers." All spoken matter-of-factly.

And it was accepted here, Chŏn realized yet again. Men and women had affairs, the affairs played out, and they moved on with their lives.

"I see...." He could only nod. He noticed the fine wrinkles on the middle-aged woman's face, but she still retained her youthful beauty.

Her face took on a spunky look as she sipped her tea. "The main reason I wanted to see you is to ask what your company specializes in."

Chŏn was taken aback. "You mean our lines of business?"

"Yes. The items you deal in."

"The answer is in our company motto—no matter what, no matter where, no matter how far. We deal with anything and everything profitable: buying, selling, and transporting."

"That's fine, then." She brought her hands together in silent applause. "I have received a favorable alimony, and I do not see myself remaining idle at an age when I can continue to be productive. Otherwise I would be bored. So I thought about going into business, and you came to mind. I can be your *guanxi*, you know. I believe you know of my family background, yes? You and me, *win win*. But I do not wish to affect your obligation to Shang Xinwen. He and I are no longer involved; you can work with me and continue to do business with him. What do you think? Are you interested?"

Chŏn tried to focus. She wanted an answer right now, and he did not want to blunder. Would joining her bring opportunity or calamity? Would he gain another *guanxi* or lose the strong one he already had?

"Thank you for thinking of me, madam. If the two of you were to independently consider me as a business partner, it would a great honor. I hope that is the case." He wanted to follow with *Please give me some time*, but that would sound as if he were worried about Shang's reaction. His palms felt clammy.

"I think I understand. You are concerned that Shang would be opposed. Please do not worry. I have spoken with him. Can you guess what he said? He said you are reliable, and he wishes me luck in my venture with you. The only reason he lost interest in me is that I am getting old. Basically he is not a mean person, you know." Her voice was sincere and calm—business-like, in fact.

"Wonderful!" he declared in relief. "If the two of you have settled the matter, fine. Rain or shine, I'm ready to jump in if you are."

"Rain or shine?"

"Why not! The more business I do, and the bigger it is, the better. When it comes to business, I'm as greedy as crafty Cao Cao."

"Well, I like a man with a hard edge. I knew I could bank on you. Do you like Cao Cao?"

"Well, everyone seems to think Liu Bi is the most important character in the Three Kingdoms story. But I like Cao Cao—he is greedy, smart, cunning, very good at handling people, and capable of evil when the situation requires it. He seems like a real person, my kind of man."

"I agree; Cao Cao is the best. Manly, prone to a few lapses, but always debonair. I see that you and I talk the same language. I have a feeling we will be good partners." Her face radiated vigor.

"What could be better," said Chŏn, feeling like a bear with wide-open jaws, perfectly positioned to lunge at the big salmon jumping upstream.

"Shall we talk business?" she said, finishing her tea and straightening. "What I have in mind is to secure an accessory corner at Walmart China. Chinese women are starting to acquire a taste for personal style, and that includes accessories. You must know a reliable accessory manufacturer, yes?"

Chŏn was impressed. "I believe that is an accurate analysis. Yes, I do have a client whose quality is guaranteed and who does innovative designs. One telephone call and we have a deal."

"Excellent. Can you contact him immediately?"

"Yes, I can. His factory is in Qingdao. I can be there tomorrow. May I provide the name and background information of our contact on the Walmart side, for example, whether he is American or—"

"Ah yes. He's Chinese. The sales director, and one of my relatives."

"Excellent. I will leave tomorrow for Qingdao." Nothing like blitz tactics— food tasted better served hot.

"How refreshing," she said, her face blossoming in joy. "You have the charm of Cao Cao after all."

After they had parted, Chŏn remained skeptical about the divorce. After all, it was thanks to Shang's doting love for his wife that she had accompanied her brother to Korea for surgery, where Chŏn had first met her. How could he ditch her? And he felt it strange that Shang had not mentioned the split. Of course it was a private matter, nothing Shang would want to broadcast, but still there lingered a disagreeable taste. As recently as a few days ago, Shang had given no inkling, the picture of equanimity. It was unnerving how many layers of secrets were buried beneath the surface of the people here.

But another part of Chŏn accepted Shang's divorce. It had become a fad, like golfing for men and cosmetic surgery for women. He recalled reading that in the past year there had been 760,000 more divorces than marriages. Every day 5,000 couples untied the matrimonial knots. Another world record?

Again he thought back to the swift currents of change since the opening and reforms, the rage for mammonism, a society saturated with sexual freedom. A decade earlier the central government had enacted a law whose effect was to fan the flames of the divorce craze. If the two parties agreed to the divorce, they had only to submit a notice bearing the personal seal of each, and it was official. Chŏn could visualize the scene, complete with emotions overflowing: *That's it, I'm getting a divorce. Fine, no skin off my back.* Stamp, stamp! And away they went.

However many social trends or systems Chŏn encountered here, the one he would never understand was divorce. To him it was natural for a husband and wife to become weary of each other, to hunger for a side dish, a different source of sustenance, squabbling their way through thick and thin until they arrived at their graves. Chŏn remembered a classy saying: the wayfarer remembers not the shade he enjoys on his journey. Shang, however, seemed to have had a good memory for his rest areas and had made a U-turn back to one of them. The divorce was only a loss if Shang's new lover wasn't something like a beautiful twentysomething college girl fluent in English—in which case Chen, for all her grace and power, her beauty and heart, was no match. It was commonly rumored that high officials had developed heightened tastes for their *ernai*, their acquisition a kind of graceful pastime, and they tended to fancy college girls. Indeed, at Beida there was supposedly an *ernai* club. And reports had leaked out of rows of black sedans with the four-ring Audi emblem parked at university entrances as early as eight or nine a.m. to pick up *ernai* for a picnic.

What exultant campers these public officials must be, thought Chŏn. They'd been handed the baton of a cultural tradition passed down over thousands of years among the emperors and the elite.

How pathetic the public servants back home were! If their counterparts here were to learn that in Korea having a mistress is considered a malfeasance more flagrant than bribery, their sympathy would be astronomical. Here, citizens had come up with a term for their *ernai*-loving bureaucrats—*seguan*, 'horny officials.'

Chŏn thought of Shang's son—wasn't he studying in the US? The boy must have been in shock. Had Shang considered the effect of the divorce on his son?

Asking himself these questions gave Chŏn occasion to question his own character. On the scale of small- to broad-minded, where did he rank? He smirked at the thought of Chisŏn and her band of sisters marching into Sŏ's office for double-eyelid surgery. In spite of such extravagances she was the sky to their two children and his own safe harbor. No matter which woman might emerge from the shade, he would remain in her restful nest. Her new eyelids, rather than making her distinctly prettier, put him in awe of Sŏ's skill. But a flicker of doubt remained.

Chŏn's next task was to consult with his branch manager.

"Securing exclusive sales with Walmart China throughout the country?" the man was quick to ask. "If we succeed in that, we're guaranteed steady returns on our investment, don't you think?"

"As long as we get it down in writing." Chŏn had already drafted a contract.

"As long as fashion's in vogue and the women here want to be hip, we could make a killing on this. Have a good trip." Veteran and optimist that he was, the branch manager knew a good opportunity when he saw one. Carrefour and Walmart offered direct distribution networks within China's vast consumer market, and his company was about to cast its net.

Next came a consultation with his good wife.

"What?" Chisŏn pooh-poohed. "It sounds like a yawner to me. Designer goods are one thing, but you're talking about cheap accessories. Don't you remember how exciting it was when you used to sell rice cookers?" she asked sarcastically.

"Fancy-pants designer goods and cheap accessories—it sounds like my dear lady is turning into a fashionista. May I clue you in to the way the business world works? The golden rule for making money here is *boli duomai*—small profits and quick returns. More than half the seven hundred million ladies in the land want to look like Yang Guifei, and half of them actually have the means to do it. So you buy one of something. Then you buy another to match it—you don't want the first one feeling lonesome. Then another for your next trip. And each purchase adds up. You know how women's minds work. Regardless how cheap the jewelry is, can't you see the profits coming in?"

"It makes sense, I guess." But she kept shaking her head dubiously. "But it's not like those items sell for tens of thousands of *wŏn*."

"Well, thanks to your good husband who brings home big money, you keep looking higher and don't see what's happening at ground level. I have a story for you. There was a man who made straw shoes. One day a wholesaler came up to him and offered to pay ten times the going price if the man made his shoes specifically for the elite. Imagine his excitement—the rich guys would go around in *his* straw shoes, and he'd get ten times as much money for every pair he made. So off he runs to one of his straw-shoe friends, and you should have heard him brag. His friend put on a sad face—what could he say? Ten years go by and guess what? Who was the big money maker? His friend. Why? He sold his straw shoes to the commoners. And that, my dear, is the magic of *boli duomai*—less profit but more sales." Chŏn relished talking business.

"I get the point. You know best, and I'm just an ignorant girl."

So much for the spousal consultation.

The flight to Qingdao was barely long enough for a leisurely cup of coffee. Like the short hop from Seoul to Cheju Island, thought Chŏn. Deplaning, he tried to recall Ha Kyŏngman's face. The outlines were hazy—he hadn't seen him in four or five years. So close by plane, but so far in terms of business opportunities. Where had all the time gone? he lamented as he buttoned up his coat.

"Hello, Mr. Chŏn!"

"*Aigu*, Mr. Ha. Nice to see you. You're looking good." Exuberant, Chŏn offered his hand.

"How many years has it been? I'm embarrassed to say I had to think for a moment when you called yesterday. That's what a time lapse does to an old man."

Chŏn was impressed with Ha's charisma and ebullience. He was a tall man and looked to be in good shape—he must have been a longtime fitness buff.

"You, getting old? I'd say you're younger, and you look pretty fit. I can tell from a businessman's face how well he's getting along, and yours tells me you're rock-solid and plugging along, am I right?" Recognizing the upbeat energy projected by Ha's handsome face, a glow he didn't remember seeing before, Chŏn dispensed with his customary sugarcoated greeting.

"Well, no fooling you. Yes, I have a good setup here—can't complain."

"Wonderful—really wonderful! I've heard too many stories about Korean companies here filing for bankruptcy, closing down, and vanishing overnight—doesn't leave a good impression with the Chinese. So it's great news you're doing well, I'm happy for you."

The two *wonderful*s were expressions of relief from deep inside. Every hiccup in the Chinese economy tended to pose challenges for the Korean enterprises in Qingdao.

"Everybody's wailing about how bad off they are, so I try to put on a gloomy face. But I can't hide from a mind reader like you," said Ha as he led Chŏn through the terminal and to his car.

Chŏn stopped before a huge frame attached to a wall. "Still there," he sighed as he gazed up at the calligraphy of Chairman Mao.

"It'll be here forever, just like his portrait in Tiananmen Square."

Arms folded at his back in gentlemanly fashion, Chŏn read the poem to himself word by word and felt himself being sucked into it. He was forever curious about Mao—the man was so complex and cryptic, an intellectual jungle.

Snow: To the tune of Qinyuanchun, February 1936

North country scene:
A hundred leagues locked in ice,
A thousand leagues of whirling snow.
Both sides of the Great Wall
One single white immensity.
The Yellow River's swift current
Is stilled from end to end.
The mountains dance like silver snakes
And the highlands˙ charge like wax-hued elephants,
Vying with heaven in stature.
On a fine day, the land,
Clad in white, adorned in red,
Grows more enchanting.
This land so rich in beauty
Has made countless heroes bow in homage.
But alas! Qin Shihuang and Han Wudi
Were lacking in literary grace;
And Tang Taizong and Song Taizu
Had little poetry in their souls;
And Genghis Khan,
Proud Son of Heaven for a day,
Knew only shooting eagles, bow outstretched.
All are past and gone!
For truly great men,
Look to this age alone.

"What do you think of the calligraphy?" Ha asked. "Is it any good?"

"I would have to say so," said Chŏn, his gaze remaining on the poem. "Because it's Mao's."

"That sounds funny."

---

*Author's Note: The highlands are those of Shensi and Shansi.

"Not necessarily my opinion, but that's what everyone says."

"That makes things easy. I'm no expert, but the fullness of the writing, it somehow feels finicky rather than stable."

"I think that's absolutely right. It shows the spirit of Mao the soldier, a man of the sword. 'Political power grows out of the barrel of a gun.' You remember that one, don't you? I feel the same kind of chill from this poem."

"Mao the soldier?" said Ha, cocking his head in puzzlement. "Sounds strange."

"That's because we've always seen him as the Chairman. But remember how he used to say, 'From my experience on the battlefield...' or 'I know because I was a soldier...'? He was very proud of being a soldier. During the Long March, he fought Chiang Kai-shek's forces, and then the Japanese, and then Chiang's army again. He was always a soldier, but afterward he was the Chairman, not the generalissimo."

"But would a soldier write a poem like this one? It just doesn't seem very soldier-like."

"True. He was a complicated man. He probably wanted the world to know he was a man of letters as well as a man of the sword."

"I can see that in the poem. With the Chinese I might praise the poem, but between you and me I don't care for it much. Listen to this—'Qin Shihuang and Han Wudi lack literary grace, the emperors Tang Taizong and Song Taizu lack poetic talent, all Genghis Khan knows is archery. So there must be a real hero on the way. Who could that hero be? Well, none other than *me*.' His face must have been burning when he wrote *that*. Before I came to China I thought of him as a great man. But when I learned enough written Chinese to be able to read this poem, I lost interest in him."

"Hmm, your ideology is questionable, comrade! Remember, the PSB knows all about you," Chŏn joked. Laughing, they moved on. "I had exactly the same reaction. At the Great Wall a few years back, before I ever got to read this poem, I saw another poem by the Chairman. It began something like, 'He who has never climbed the Great Wall cannot be deemed a Man.' I got to wondering how a man of the revolution could say such a thing. Had he forgotten all the lives wasted on the construction of the Wall over the two thousand years from Qin to Qing? Why show off his manly spirit when he could have expressed rage against the tyrannical dynasties and lamented the sacrifice of his comrades? That's what the Later Han poet Chen Lin did nineteen hundred years ago: 'How can you fail to see the skulls that support the base of the Great Wall?' The Chairman showed off his poetic talent, but he was a soldier with a mountain-high spirit, not a poet-revolutionary whose heart went out to his comrades. A true poet should have said something like, 'He who has never climbed the Great Wall and heard the moaning and wailing of the people cannot be deemed a Man.'"

Ha regarded Chŏn in amazement as he located his car keys. "You're so erudite for a businessman. I saw the same poem but never thought twice about it."

"Knowledgeable—ha! I just like to read in my spare time—makes my life here more enjoyable." Chŏn looked in all directions as he crossed the street. "I came across 'Qinyuanchun' a few years after I arrived here and I figured out right away why he wrote it. The answer was right there in the poem. All the legendary emperors he mentioned were flawed. The only flawless one was he himself, the emperor of emperors. How could a man with such a mentality hope to hear the moans of the people who built the Great Wall? How could he feel their pain?"

"Aha! You're the one who needs to watch his tongue!" Winking at Chŏn, Ha motioned him into his car.

Fastening his seat belt, Chŏn said, "There's a historian whose research bears out my belief that Mao wasn't so much a socialist revolutionary as an emperor of a newly united China."

"Who?" Ha asked as he set the car in motion.

"It's Wang…Wang something. It's on the tip of my tongue. Damn it, I'm getting old," said Chŏn as he pounded his forehead in mock frustration.

"Yes, I can see you're on your last legs." Ha chuckled, then turned serious. "Actually, I envy you. Turning fifty, a man feels old and pressured."

"Anyway, this Wang guy wrote that Mao was after all an emperor. So if he was an emperor, then what would that make the party members? That's the issue."

"Isn't it obvious? They become the elite."

"That was too easy. Let's see if I can come up with something more exciting."

"All right, I'll take longer to answer next time. But what you say makes sense. People became powerless in the face of sword-waving party and government officials. I feel really sorry for them."

"And yet China is now G2. Surprise, surprise. What a mysterious mishmash of a country." It was then that Chŏn remembered the historian—Wang Gungwu. Wang had argued that the new Communist state was a kind of surrogate for the old empire-state and that Mao revived the concept of a charismatic founding-father emperor and was a latter-day benevolent despot.

Ha's Hyundai Equus glided into downtown Qingdao.

"You're a countrified patriot," said Chŏn. "If you were Chinese, you'd have changed to a Mercedes or an Audi a long time ago."

"Instead of this?" Ha gently tapped the steering wheel. "Too many times I've heard the same thing from my Chinese pals, and I still can't tell whether they're praising or mocking me. Actually I've already traded in one Korean car, and here I am with another. I bet you'll do the same."

"I guess it's in your blood. But you won't get a loyalty plaque, you know." Chŏn enjoyed a belly laugh at his own jest.

"Old habits die hard. We get 'buy Korean' drilled into us and feel guilty if we don't." Ha smirked, recalling that Korean company presidents here drove Equuses, and their managers Sonatas.

"I guess that's one of our virtues. The weaker and smaller we are, the more solidarity we need. You've heard people here mention the 'triple shock,' right? They're amazed by our phoenix-like recovery from the ashes of the Korean War, our rebound from the IMF crisis—thanks in part to the gold-donation campaign, which generated twenty tons of gold—and the spread of Hallyu and the progress we've made in international sports. You can accomplish a lot if you work together."

"Agreed. People here love our television dramas and never stop saying how taken they are with the acting and the beautiful faces. I actually approached our consulate about trying to capitalize on Hallyu here." Ha's voice had a touch of anger.

"And?"

"They told me not to waste my time. Focus on business instead."

"It figures. Public officials everywhere have the same mindset."

Ha made a quick turn. "What would you like for lunch?"

"Seeing as how Qingdao has the best Korean food in the country, I can't pass it up."

"You know everything. I'll take you to a place with the best kimchi"

"Let's do it." Chŏn's mouth was watering already.

The city center was more orderly than that of Shanghai—there were fewer cars, and the distinctive red-roofed brick buildings enhanced the grandeur and dignity of the city. The four-to-five-story century-old buildings were a combination of solid architecture and noble elegance, the heritage of the German territorial concession.

In several respects Qingdao was a twin sister of Shanghai: it was a major eastern seaport; the site of Western-leased territories during the ailing Qing's century of humiliation; the heart of the nation's industrial center ever since the capitalist reforms; a jumping-off point to cities throughout the land; a traffic hub for Korea, Japan, and the Pacific; and in this Pacific Age a foothold to Northeast Asia.

As Chŏn replayed this historical background in his mind he marveled at the surge of Korean business influence in this picturesque Germanic port, part of the nation's second leap after the Korean War—from home turf into the international business arena. Back in the day, there had been as many as twenty thousand business enterprises from home, some seven thousand of which had survived the ebbs and flows. Add a hundred thousand Korean expat residents, and you had plenty of eateries for the foodies.

"How about the traditional set menu?" said Ha once they were settled.

"Sure. With mustard-leaf kimchi, Chŏlla style."

"Of course. And for a thirst-quencher?"

"When in Qingdao it's got to be Qingdao," said Chŏn as if chanting an advertising jingle.

Ironically Qingdao beer was among the top ten Chinese brands—not Maotai or Wuliangye, but a beer of German-British origin produced in China and marketed to the West. Originally it was marketed in Hong Kong and other territories along the eastern cost. The beer retained its original taste from those times.

"Here's to you!" Ha lifted his glass, Chŏn clinked it with his, and they drank thirstily.

"Wow!" Chŏn wiped foam from his lips.

Ha followed suit. "Terrific, isn't it? Makes me a happy man."

"How about I go over the details before the food arrives?" said Chŏn.

"Actually I made my decision when we were on the phone. With you involved I don't need to think twice, I'll just do as you say. One of the reasons I'm where I'm at is because you helped me secure German machinery for making the accessories. If I'd chosen the cheaper Japanese ones, it might have been a different story. It's a sick feeling when your machines break down and you have after-service problems—several people I know here had to close up shop as a result. But the German machines are workhorses, day in and out, never a headache. I keep thinking about you telling me I absolutely had to invest in German machinery back then, and I'm grateful for the harangue." He smiled. "All right, let's dig in, I want to show you the factory." Ha gave Chŏn a refill of Qingdao.

"I can't wait," said Chŏn.

And again they toasted.

.

5. Artisans, the Soul of China

To Jacques Cabang the shimmering sound of the *erhu* playing the evocative tune was a plaintive falsetto. It sounded odd in the crimson light of the posh lounge.

Sitting sideways against the table, he smoked a cigar twice as thick as an index finger. Between puffs he sipped wine from a glass with a big fat bowl. He'd never really thought about it, but his pensive, downcast look tended to charm women into thinking he was a wealthy banker.

Smokers would tell you he wasn't working seriously on the cigar. You tend to drag hard the more you smoke, and inhale more deeply when something's on your mind. Cabang, though, was puffing for show.

As he had another taste of his wine a woman in gaudy makeup glided in. All eyes were on her. Cabang was impressed by the shapely body in the clinging black *qipao*. The floor-length dress was embroidered with a shower of tiny red flowers that tried in vain to defuse the thigh-high slit. Barely visible were the high heels that made her look so tall. Every step she took seemed to expose more of her thigh. Cabang's downward gaze darted between her long legs, the wine rendering his view of her *qipao* more piquant.

She greeted him with a subtle gesture, her hand seeming to blossom like a flower, and her silent lips froze in a *Hi*.

Delectable, Cabang thought. His blue eyes, the only part of his body that moved, darted to her face. Having failed to draw a response from him, the woman moved on to the next table. Cabang sat back and took in the solicitation. A few more soubrettes, each clad in a different *qipao*, put on the same show. He could pick one of them or search elsewhere. What a wondrous nation! A fountain of maidenhood to choose from, so much cheap labor to produce the items that would ultimately be shipped back to his boss in France. For Cabang, it was *la belle vie*. Even in Paris you wouldn't find a man on a salesman's salary living like this.

He could complain about the flood of bogus food items and about the pollution. And he wasn't alone—the super-rich among the Chinese were equally disgruntled and every year, it seemed, more of them left for the US, which brought the additional bonus of an American education for their children. He figured half the would-be immigrants to the US were Chinese.

Eating at a fancy hotel solved the fake food problem, but there was no escape from the pollution. His company made up for the latter with an overseas allowance and performance bonuses, but to Cabang the boundless supply of girls was a hidden benefit.

And voila, the *qipao*! Another marvelous discovery in this land of marvels. The haute couture houses in France and Italy could not have come up with this come-on dress, which intensified the mystique of the female body wrapped inside it and, *mais-certainment*, boosted his sexual appetite! *Les Chines*, he thought, puffing on his cigar, his eyes following the outlines of a leggy new girl—those little devils really knew how to enjoy themselves, body and soul.

The *qipao* was Manchu in origin, baggy and loose with side slits convenient for horse riding and chores. The style traveled south and caught the eye of the foreigners in the concessions, where it evolved into the slinky dress of today, the slits rising to the knee or higher. The glimpse of thigh when the body moved drew shouts of joy from the menfolk, and the new style was an instant hit among the high-class women of Shanghai, from whence it spread nationwide, in various patterns and colors, in the 1930s. In the revue industry the slit is as high as it gets, and today the dress is considered traditional Chinese attire.

Cabang was pouring himself more wine when two Chinese men approached.

"You're all alone—no luck?" said the older man, Li Wanxing, who was fiftyish and portly and looked bullheaded. The younger man interpreted in English.

Cabang replied in English, "I suppose all the pretty ones went north."

English was the medium of communication for French and German businessmen, it being easier to find English-language interpreters.

"I don't think so, it's still early. The beauties will be crawling in once they smell the money—like moths tempted by light. You know Guangzhou has lots of cash, and where there's lots of money there's lots of pretty girls. So you're fine. This beats Shanghai and Beijing!" In spite of the older man's rush of words the interpreter didn't have to take notes.

"I am not disappointed. And *manmandi*? That is me, *manmandi*." Cabang winked.

"Ah yes, patience is a virtue. If you don't find a girl to your liking here, we can always go somewhere else. How goes the expansion of your shop?"

"I should not complain except I wish the construction work to proceed more quickly. My connections at Cartier are impatient. Every day there are more customers for designer goods, and every day we lose more business."

"I know. Too many lazy sacks of shit, too many feeble excuses—weddings, family matters, *deng deng deng*. That's the socialist mentality. It's been thirty years since the reforms, but we still have to wrestle with those slugs—their mentality is a headache. Anyway, even my daughter at Beida has a keen interest in designer items. They are wildly popular. It's a bonanza for your company."

"Mr. Li. I did not know your esteemed daughter attends Beida. Could you tell me her name?"

"Yanling."

"What a pretty name!" Cabang straightened in his seat. "Perhaps we should discuss our business?"

Li leaned toward Cabang. "Do you have a new order for me?"

"Let us discuss that." Cabang placed his 007 briefcase on the table, opened it gingerly as if handling an explosive, and extracted a small package. Layer by layer he unwrapped it, his hairy, chubby hands moving clumsily, the fingers shaky.

Li frowned as he gazed at Cabang. He considered the Frenchman pathetic and wondered if the man's hands had suffered nerve damage. His mouth half-opened, as if he was about to bark, *Give me that, you idiot!* His stubborn, unyielding face was more unforgiving than ever.

The third wrap came undone to reveal a crucifix.

No wonder, thought Li with a smirk.

"This is the very crucifix you would see on the pontiff's cane," Cabang solemnly declared, meeting Li's gaze. "Can you carve it exactly like this?"

"In jade?"

"Yes, jade."

"You definitely want jade, correct?"

"Why do you ask? Is it difficult?" Cabang was flustered.

"It's not that. There's nothing our workers can't do."

"Then what is the problem, if I may ask?"

"I'm afraid a jade carving of this size would be expensive, you know."

"Please—that is the last thing on my mind." Said like a man sitting on a million euros.

"You know, jade is not just some colored stone. It's a gemstone."

"Silly me," said Cabang sarcastically. "That shows you how much I know. But I am proud to say we sell only to select buyers, those with deep faith and deeper pockets."

"Their pockets could be ocean-deep, but it's complicated to make something like this. We're talking a lot of money here." Frowning, Li shook his head dubiously.

"Mr. Li, please do not underestimate the Christians. Your ninety-thousand-dollar jade Taoist wizards are selling most excellently, why have doubts about the crucifixes? There are approximately 2.35 billion Christians in this world, you know." Here the interpreter had to take pen and notebook and make calculations. "Let us consider a mere one percent of those Catholics, or even one tenth of one percent. I can guarantee you that one percent of them will buy. How many would that be? Let us say two hundred and thirty million. Or to be safe, if it is only one tenth of one percent, then we still have a grand total of more than twenty-three million. Believe me, the fanatics will pay, however expensive..." Here Cabang stepped on the brakes before he got too far ahead of the interpreter.

Listening to the interpreter, Li looked bored and lit a cigarette.

"This is very important," the interpreter reminded him.

Don't make me laugh, thought Li. *If you mean the more expensive, the more demand there is, then cut the crap and say it. You and I are businessmen...*

"So, what do you think?" Cabang asked as he re-lit his cigar.

"I can see it's a terrific idea," said Li, grinning from ear to ear and nodding vigorously, as if trying to work a kink out of his neck.

"But there is one concern," said Cabang, fixing Li with his gaze and displaying a cautioning index finger.

"A concern about what?" said Li, wondering if a request for a favor were on the way.

"Whether you can produce two hundred and thirty thousand crucifixes."

"You don't need them all at once."

"True. But if they are *very* popular..."

"Don't worry. You give me a good price and I'll round up every jade carver in the country," Li said before releasing a long trail of smoke.

"You sound so confident."

"You should know by now what we're capable of—you've been coming here ten years now, you're a veteran. Let me tell you a story: About fifteen years ago a Japanese buyer told me he wanted five million bed covers in two weeks. Each cover was hand-embroidered with fifty different flowers and yet the price was dirt cheap. The Japanese raved about them—labor costs in Japan were so expensive they couldn't home-grow hand-made items. So what did I do? Did I say, 'Oh dear, I'm not sure I can deliver you that many in two weeks'? Hell no, I went out and found young ladies all over the country—this was before they flooded the cities. Now do you understand? This is China!"

"*Incroyable!*" said Cabang, shaking his head in disbelief.

"Hell, I could have delivered him ten million."

"And you concluded that deal all by yourself?"

"No. Sewing, embroidery, that stuff is chicken feed. I let a friend take care of it."

"He must have realized a huge profit."

"Yes, he did. But there's something I should tell you—a few years ago he was stabbed to death."

"What—in a robbery?"

"No. He started a new business with that money but stepped on someone else's turf—that's what you get for trespassing."

"Silly me—I thought you enjoyed a free market," said Cabang. "And now you tell me the top dogs urinate on lampposts to mark their territory?"

"This is China, don't ever forget that," Li snapped.

"China—here we go again."

"Are we finished?"

"No, not yet." Meticulously Cabang rewrapped the crucifix. "How long will you require to make the sample?"

"Three, four days."

"And I would like to have red."

"You Westerners like red too?"

"To be sure. We are not as crazy about that color as you, but after all, the sun is red and Jesus our savior is as precious to us as the sun."

"I like that. I can see you Christians fighting over our crucifixes."

"Now you are a believer."

"Whatever. I hope all goes well. And the bigger the order, the more we like it—odds and ends are a nuisance. But why this particular Jesus on the cross?"

"There are so many different crucifixes with so many different faces, but I believe this one is the best. It is the finest artistic representation I have seen of Jesus's suffering on the cross. When I view it, I feel his pain all through my body; I feel I am being saved. And I am confident all believers will feel the same. Mr. Li, I genuinely hope you can prepare for us an exact replica."

"Relax. Our people don't screw up, remember? You don't like, you don't pay."

"I have always trusted in you. We will talk about the price when you are ready with the sample."

"Fine. What's next?"

"Ah yes, this one." Cabang produced a bracelet of wooden beads from his pocket.

"I'll be damned," said Li as he examined it. "Carved prayer beads. For Buddhist disciples."

"I was in total shock when I came across this. *Voici*, on this tiny bead, two face carvings, a Westerner on one side, an Asian on the other, so delicate and real. Could I find such a specimen in Japan or Korea? Impossible. Only in China. I should stop here for the interpreter." Cabang finished his wine and once more re-lit his cigar.

The interpreter silently snorted. *You mean stop and guzzle more wine.* And sure enough, while he interpreted, Cabang poured himself not one but two more servings.

"In this twenty-first century," Cabang continued, "when everything is done on demand by machine, China is the only country capable of carving this delicate and detailed. Maybe India and a few of the African nations can do the carving, but in quality they would not come close. What you do with jade and other materials, it is a miracle. It is so charming it is alchemy. It is inevitable I am a Sinophile. I am fascinated by your living arts and crafts." Returning to his wine, he motioned to the interpreter. "Please."

Idiot, the interpreter silently grumbled. *Stop your damn running off at the mouth and get down to business. All your fancy big words. Who doesn't know you're a French art fanatic. Art, fart, it's all you talk about.*

"I wish this bracelet made of jade, two-thirds the size of the wood beads, and the faces changed into Jesus's face. Can you do it?" Cabang leveled another piercing gaze at Li.

"Well…" Drawing out the word, Li stretched like an elastic band, his mouth pouting and his face sullen.

"No?" Cabang said nervously.

"Well…" Li's expression remained ambiguous.

"What is the problem?" In spite of himself Cabang had tipped off Li to how urgent he felt.

"I already told you there's nothing our people can't do," said the pokerfaced Li.

"Then, there is no issue."

"Well, you forgot something. We businessmen often say time is what?"

"Money!" said Cabang, feeling like a quiz show contestant.

"That's right. And carving in a small space is more—"

"Difficult. Of course." So far so good.

"Then, you have your answer to whether we do the bracelets. We agree that the bracelets will take longer but cost you less than those jade crosses. But I can't be losing money on a job. There is one solution. You pay me double for the bracelets. Then I'll take on both jobs."

"Hmm. The bracelets are unique, but will my customers pay twice as much for them as for the crosses? I think not. *C'est dommage!* My jade bracelets could be a grand success. Jade is soaring in popularity—its mineral effects are known to be beneficial for circulation and helpful for people with arthritis. People in the West adore things Asian, and jade makes such an elegant accessory—it comes in such beautiful colors. Think of the Eastern mystique that Westerners can enjoy."

"I have an idea. Let's use wood. It's much cheaper than jade. You can sell to all those Christians. Small profits but quick returns—*boli duomai,* you know?" The smoke from Li's potent Chinese cigarette chimneyed out of his mouth as he gazed expectantly at Cabang.

"Oh, I am not sure. Bracelets are accessories; they should be elegant and beautiful. How can wood compare to jade? Westerners will not go *oulala* over a wood bracelet." Cabang kept shaking his head.

"I understand. So let's push the idea that the red wood brings good luck. It lasts forever, it's beautiful, it's lucky wood that's been used for ornaments for thousands of years, and now we carve Jesus on it. Pray with this bracelet and Jesus will bring you good fortune, along with money and protection. Your sales people pitch it that way, they push all the right buttons, see?" Li gazed at Cabang like a cat regarding a tiny mouse.

"*Fantastique!* The power of words, they hypnotize the buyer. Words, the sustaining power of all religions—who said that?" But then a shadow of uncertainty crossed Cabang's face. "But if they are so cheap, how do we make a profit?"

"Monsieur Cabang. You've heard about the fake eggs."

Cabang grimaced. "*Mais oui*, but I have never eaten them."

"You haven't? How do you know?"

"Because I always eat at the hotel."

"Really. Do you realize that thirty to forty percent of the five-star hotels use fake eggs?"

"You cannot be serious?" Cabang half rose from his chair in alarm.

"What's so shocking about that? I guess you haven't been here long enough," said Li with a gleeful expression.

"Those hotels, they should be ashamed of themselves," Cabang huffed. "Were they deceived? Or perhaps they knew but they did not care."

"Who knows? Say both and you'll be a hundred percent right."

"What do you mean? Is there nothing your government can do?" Cabang growled, all semblance of French gentility having vanished. The possibility that he'd consumed fake eggs did not settle well.

"They did do something. Scientists tested them and found no substance that is harmful to humans. It's no longer an issue."

"I cannot believe it. Regardless, they should take harsh measures with the fakes. If the government is soft, the fake manufacturers will take over."

"You can't afford to think like that. No harm done to humans, and the government wants to protect people's livelihoods. It's a wonderful country we live in, isn't it?" Li snickered—what fun it was watching Cabang's temper boil over.

"I am so mad at such things I just want to go home." Cabang tightened his fists.

"Sorry. I didn't mean to lead you in that direction." Li straightened himself. "I was going to talk about *boli duomai*. People always fuss about whether it's worth the trouble to make fake eggs for a chicken-feed profit. Instead, why not use your brains to develop worthy projects that will bring in a pile of money. The problem is, they don't know shit about business. See? If you get one *mao* profit for an egg, think about a hundred million eggs, a billion eggs, five billion. I heard of a guy who became a billionaire off of fake eggs. That's the magic of *boli duomai*. Do you get it? And so?" Feeling like he'd hooked a trophy fish, Li reeled in Cabang.

"All right. Let us do it. We are businessmen, we will cross the Sahara and climb Everest if we smell a profit. But the size of the beads, you must shrink them by one third. The ladies do not want big clunky ones." Cabang released a long sigh.

"Not a problem. These are the size of cherries, and you would like them shrunk to beans. Our people can do six faces per bead, three front and three back, along with a couple of pines. Compared with that, two Jesus faces, one front and one back, will be easier than popping a dumpling into your mouth."

"You can squeeze six monks and two pines onto a prayer bead?"

"So much you don't know, Monsieur Cabang. I tell you what. Come to our shop tomorrow and I will make you a present of one of our bracelets."

"I am beside myself at the finesse of your artisans. My hat is off to them, nameless workers enduring thousands of years of contempt and scorn while sustaining a tradition of highest workmanship! Without them, would there be a Chinese civilization and culture? They are your soul and driving force. How extraordinary and everlasting! This is why I adore La Chine. They create art so undefiled, so immaculate—I cannot believe they would ever make fakes." French artmonger that he was, Cabang unraveled this creed like a rubber-faced actor.

"You're so paranoid about fakes. They're not all bad. Some are good, believe it or not. At least one fake proved to be a life-saver."

"What! Save how?"

"There was a guy whose business failed and he went bankrupt. He couldn't find a way out, so he took rat poison with his wife. And guess what? They didn't die!"

"The poison was fake? I don't believe it! *C'est fou*, your country!"

"Are we done?" Li asked as he fondled the beads of the bracelet.

"Just one more thing—a reorder." Cabang pulled out his memo pad, as did Li, and then they both leaned forward.

"I need one thousand more of the horn hairpin."

"That many?" Li haltingly jotted the order, and then looked to Cabang for confirmation.

"It is quite the popular item. The ladies fall for the exquisite carving of the rose, as well as the natural grain. There is nothing more graceful and chic for a woman wearing her hair in a bun, especially if you look from the back. Thanks to you, Mr. Li."

"Thank *you*. Western ladies like roses, don't they?"

"Yes. Lucky roses for them, lucky peonies for your ladies. But did you know there is a flower that has totally opposite meanings for us and for you? I mean the chrysanthemum. To us they mean death, but to you they are one of the four gracious plants symbolizing a man of breeding and learning."

"Then should I make a chrysanthemum for you?" Li winked.

"Meaning you and I take rat poison? But let us make it the fake one." The two of them had a good laugh, and Cabang concluded his order: "And finally, five hundred rose brooches and one thousand heart necklaces. That will do it."

"I thank you. And you can count on speedy delivery as always."

"And I trust you as always. The word *manmandi* is not in your dictionary."

You said that before, thought Li, grinning in satisfaction as he tucked away his memo pad. He recalled Cabang quoting Napoleon—no *impossible* in the great man's dictionary. *Well, no need to thank me. There's no* manmandi *when it comes to making money. Instead we go for* quaiquai.

The following day Cabang met the interpreter and off they went to the antiques market. In Asia, shopping was his pastime as well as his business. Addicted to the thrill of bargaining for unique, incredibly rare items at dirt-cheap prices, he also picked up practical business ideas as he rummaged among the items. The antique markets of Asia were all different, the expression of distinct cultures. But, thought Cabang, the Chinese markets were the best, hands down, whether it was variety you sought, quality, ingeniousness, artistry, or price. The vendors had no concept of displaying and packaging the ancient items mummified in caked layers of dust, but they did have a knack for haggling. For their part buyers like Cabang had a gift for unearthing gems among the disordered piles, an almost psychic propensity for discovery and a talent for thinking on one's feet. At the basis of it all was a kind of X-ray vision. Cabang could always find something even after others had combed through the inventory. He lived for the excitement and joy, the sense of accomplishment and satisfaction at the moment of discovery. China had never disappointed him.

As with every antiques market Cabang had ever visited, this one was a dizzying chaos. Vendors lined both sides of the alley, their clothing saturated with destitution, sitting impassively behind spread-out wrapping cloths displaying as few as half a dozen items. Their looks were deceiving, Cabang had learned. In fact, most were hard-core dealers with rolls of money. Their dream was to own a shop of their own, and to this end they would skip meals to save. They were encouraged by the stories of rags-to-riches shop owners with plush establishments who took their sweet time over tea, who had meat for lunch and used toothpicks afterwards. If for once in their life they could latch onto a thousand-year-old item, it would be like winning a lottery. That clandestine wish for a windfall might bring an antique vendor affluence or grief.

Cabang's blue eyes darted down the alley and he came to a halt at a display guarded by a woman. The interpreter gave him a dubious look. On a grimy cloth lay three items. Cabang braved a squat, an act he hated as much as kneeling or sitting cross-legged. Surprised, the interpreter quickly followed suit.

Pointing to a small box, Cabang signaled the interpreter with his eyes per their routine.

"*Duo shao?*" said the interpreter. How much?

"Five hundred," said the woman, spreading wide the fingers of her hand as she sized up her customer.

What a grubby woman! the interpreter silently tutted, thinking she had inflated the price. The woman looked as grimy and needy as the display cloth.

"One-fifty," said Cabang, trying to stick to the principle of starting at one fifth the asking price and settling for one fourth. The extra fifty *yuan* was because he liked the item.

"No. Four hundred." She shook her head and spread four fingers.

"One-sixty!"

"Nooo." She frowned and again shook her head. "Three fifty."

"One-seventy!"

"Three hundred."

"One-eighty!"

"Two-eighty."

"Let's go!" Placing his hands on his knees, Cabang laboriously rose.

Snatching up the item and placing her finger on the lid, she croaked, "Here, look! Don't you see the butterflies fluttering?" The interpreter conveyed this to Cabang.

Cabang bent down in disbelief to examine the article. "What are you saying? Butterflies fluttering?"

The round tortoise-shell box was about ten centimeters in diameter with a delicately carved lid. The carving was of a tangle of leaves and branches, but on closer inspection Cabang discovered five double-winged tiger butterflies amid the foliage. The woman touched them again.

Cabang sucked in his breath. They were in fact fluttering, weren't they? Again he investigated the box resting on her palm. Then he placed it on his own palm and gingerly touched the butterflies. And wonder of wonders, there they came, fluttering out of the bushes! He kept touching the butterflies, kept observing their movement.

Finally he figured it out. The pair of curved feelers were securely intertwined with a curved branch while the main body of the insect was unattached except for the bottom tips of the hind wings, which slid under another branch, secured from detachment. *Merveilleux!*

How was it possible? Cabang's discovery left him tingling in excitement. He carefully raised the lid just enough to better appreciate the three-dimensional effect achieved by the intertwined layers of the tiny branches and leaves that secured the butterflies. He then flipped the lid all the way open to see that the carving had penetrated the bare three-millimeter thickness of the lid to produce five dainty, fluttering butterflies in all. He was spellbound by the magic of it—a berry-laden plant from which a butterfly fluttered, with four others dancing around it. When had this protean artisan lived? Would Cabang ever understand a land where such a miraculous item could be bought on the streets?

"Twenty more!" barked the woman as she stuck out two soiled hands to the interpreter.

The euro equivalent of two thousand dollars for sure in Paris. Muttering silently to himself, in a burst of bravado Cabang produced two hundred-*yuan* notes. In a flash the money disappeared into the woman's pocket. She wrapped the box in a dusty sheet of newspaper as Cabang watched with a self-indulgent grin.

Finishing his rounds of the street vendors, Cabang moved on to the shops. In one of them he caught sight of a large bamboo brush holder. Measuring some ten by twenty centimeters, it had a chocolate color and a carving of what seemed to be a flock of birds. But a closer look at the abstract pattern revealed a swarm of bats. He flinched—to him bats meant evil and witchcraft—but then turned the holder about and inspected it. He could make out perhaps a hundred bats detailed in various ways, with different wing spans, pairs that appeared to be kissing, pairs that seemed to be arguing. And were those clouds in the background?

Should I? It was a marvelous item, bats being a talisman of good fortune here even though ominous and satanic to him.

"Should I ask how much he wants?" the interpreter asked, more out of boredom than anything else.

Until then Cabang had paid no attention to the interpreter. "Not yet. I need to think more. By the way, why do bats symbolize happiness and good luck?"

"Well, you see, the characters for 'bat' and 'good luck' are similar," said the interpreter, writing them on his memo pad for Cabang to see. "So they symbolize many sons and many happy occasions."

"How fascinating."

A man who looked to be in his sixties approached them and spread four fingers.

"What?" The interpreter looked puzzled.

This time the man made his display to the interpreter and said, "Four thousand." Stunned, the interpreter said to Cabang, "He wants four thousand."

"He must think I am a rich foreigner snob."

"Well, he has to make a living." The interpreter's tone was blunt.

The man flashed a notebook to the interpreter and pointed to an entry. "Look! It's from Tang. The real thing. A nobleman's fine item. I need the money so tell him I'm giving a discount. He should act quickly. It's his good fortune to have come across such a rare item." He kept his finger on the notebook entry as he continued his glib spiel.

Listening to the interpreter, Cabang made up his mind. *Real thing, my ass! You're a thief and a liar. If you were smart you would have said Qing or Ming instead of Tang. If it was really from Tang, four million, or even forty million, would be a bargain. It's a fine piece, regardless. If not for the bats, I'd try to work you down to fifteen hundred.*

Cabang motioned to the interpreter. "Let us be off."

"Wait!" hollered the man as he followed them outside. "How about two thousand? All right, you can have it for one thousand."

The interpreter smirked. "How did you know it was a fake?"

Cabang snorted. "He is worse than the scum that make fake rat poison. He might as well try to convince me it belonged to Qin Shi Huangdi."

"You know your history!" said the interpreter.

"It is basic, straight out of China 101."

Four days later Cabang visited Li's jade processing plant. Emerging from the taxi, he had to block his ears to keep out the shriek of the grinding.

"Well look here, a brand-new building," he said in greeting to Li.

"You noticed. You're a quick-witted fellow all right." Proudly, Li gave a sweeping glance across the complex.

Cabang followed Li's gaze and nodded. "An up-and-coming business."

"Thanks to our booming economy," said Li with a beaming smile. "See, jade is a coveted gemstone that everyone wants for an accessory. But back in the old days the commoners couldn't afford it, and even if they could they were prevented by class discrimination. But now there are more rich people, and everybody's equal, so my business is going well."

Of course it was, thought Cabang. The Chinese were jade fanatics. Women couldn't be satisfied with just with one jade bracelet, they would want several, or even half a dozen, each in a different hue to enhance their beauty and femininity. Besides, jade did wonders in making them look wealthy.

The gemstone was marketed in an endless array of colors and prices. Quality was equally variable, two bracelets of white jade perhaps appearing the same but one costing as much as thirty times the other. Supplying a beautiful girlfriend with such a bracelet could suck a man dry. Jade was desired by grandmothers and tweens as well. Its market, in fact, was the seven hundred million women in the land.

Cabang had seen briefcase-size jade displays with delicate carvings of Taoist wizards or the ten symbols of longevity. Such pieces went for half a million *yuan* and were a token of status, position, and wealth. With the ban on tiger hunting, the tiger-pelt bribe of times past had been replaced with a block of meaningfully-carved jade.

The studio was distant from the factory and the whine of the grinding.

"Ah." At the sight of the jade crucifix Cabang sank to his knees and crossed himself. "Wonderful! It is very, very good!" Raising his thumb high, he gave Li a jubilant smile and followed with a vigorous handshake. "Thank you so much."

Gazing at the crucified Jesus resurrected in red jade, Cabang once again marveled at the talent of the artisans who had created silk four thousand years ago and baked modern pottery two thousand years ago. Their DNA had worked its way down the generations. G2 stardom was the result not so much of good governance by the Party as the efforts of 100 million laborers exerting their talents in every manufacturing sector, as well as the 250 million migrant workers in all their sordid plight laboring virtually for free.

Cabang's company had rocketed to the next stage thanks to this cheap but astonishingly talented labor pool. Just as drug dealers would risk their lives for huge profits, Cabang had staked his economic life on transforming Chinese goods into French designer items in hopes of generating a fat profit margin. His hairpins sported a huge markup in Cartier's French boutiques and were popular among well-heeled Chinese expats who liked designer goods and preferred roses to peonies.

It would be nice if there were more Christians here. But with China Westernizing at full steam it was only a matter of time. *Renminfu*, the gray Mao suit, was extinct, having vanished faster than the bicycles pushed out by cars.

And now Cabang was singing a victory anthem for designer goods here. Even if China hadn't yet unseated the US as G1, its frenzy for such items had surpassed Japan's consumption and would soon overtake the number-one consumer, the US. Spearheaded by nouveau riches such as Li and their stables of *ernai*, China had filled its shopping basket and was now devouring the designer-goods market like locusts.

Overwhelmed with gratitude, Cabang pumped Li's hand like a jackhammer.

6. Motherland and Homeland

"What else, Cooper?"

From her desk Wang Lingling shot the handsome man in his thirties a look that left no doubt who was in charge. Her tone was frosty.

Cooper handed her a report. "This is where we're at. I know we need to speed up, but we ran into a deadlock with the steel supply."

"A deadlock? Can't we do anything about it?" Frowning, she scanned the report.

"We have two bidders competing to deliver the steel. We always work with the locals when we go into a new territory, but the power plays involved with steel are getting bloody. Frankly, I don't see a solution."

"Because each side's *guanxi* wants a monopoly, you mean."

"Yes. The city government and the prosecutor's office."

"And both the suppliers are local?"

"No. The former is Chinese, and the latter Korean."

"Korean? You mean POSCO."

"That's correct."

"They lost their last project to the Japanese."

"Yes, the Japanese had a more powerful *guanxi*—a Party member."

"The safe bet for us would be to buy half and half from each supplier. That way we have an ally in the administration and an ally in the judiciary."

"I agree, but I don't see how," said Cooper, who was beginning to look like a cornered rat.

"If POSCO is involved," she said, "then there has to be a Korean *guanxi* in the prosecutor's office."

"Yes, but…" He looked even more crestfallen in the presence of his CEO.

"I see. Call Andy Park."

"Why Andy?"

"Korean to Korean—blood ties, you know. Call him in," she ordered brusquely, pushing Cooper's report to the side of her desk.

"Andy," she said as soon as he rushed in. "I need you to fly to Xian. We've run into a problem and it's holding up construction. I want you to sort it out."

But that's not my area, he almost said. Seeing her flustered, he could almost feel her loneliness as a businesswoman. And realized she trusted him enough to send him as an envoy even though he was out of his element.

"Cooper. Get hold of Xian POSCO and then arrange a flight for Andy. Andy, I need to explain what's going on." Rapid-fire orders given with decisive gestures.

"I feel like I'm watching Genghis Khan on the battlefield."

"I'm embarrassed to have to ask this of you, and I know it's not your area, but we're in a fix."

"What happened to your *manmandi*? You're rushing. China will keep moving forward in the next twenty to thirty years, and remember, we're not even forty yet."

She leaned over her desk and beckoned him closer. "You're right. But it all depends on the nature of the project. Especially when that project is government-funded. We have to nail it, get it done quickly. So, please listen, Andy."

What are you saying? Instead of speeding up you should be slowing down. You're not the rash, brash type, so this must be really urgent. But where's the fire? Is capital reinvestment the issue?

But Park knew better than to voice these thoughts. There was an old saying that if you counsel the throne three times you lose your head. Nero was merciless in this respect, and the same fate befell the subjects of honest tongue who criticized the riotous lifestyle of Emperor Yang of Sui. The head of a company was not subject to counseling, advice, and discussion, but rather held power no less absolute than that of an emperor. Add to this equation the power of money, and the obvious solution, Park told himself, was that you had to hold it in.

"What I'm about to say…" And she proceeded to explain the situation.

"That was some wake-up call," said Kim Hyŏn'gon at the Xian airport as he offered his business card to Park.

Reciprocating, Park asked with a smile, "Really? Why is that?" In Kim's smile he felt a warmth different from the usual plastic smile of business associates.

"I never imagined a Korean president as part of the Gold Groups. So I went online, but you're not listed on their home page." Kim said this very cordially.

"Well, I'm in charge of construction, that's why. Our home page shows the management side—it's the best way to advertise what we do."

"I understand—management is the core of the operation. You've been here before, right?" Courtesies exchanged, Kim had a question to ask: Wasn't Park too young be a company president? He had to be in his thirties, maybe ten years younger than he himself. But he decided to be patient.

"That's right," said Park as they wound their way through the teeming crowd. "I was here before to check on the construction site, so this is my second visit. It's very impressive, the city is better preserved than Nanjing."

"Yes, I fell in love with it myself. Thanks to us, though, I have no clue what the future will bring."

"Thanks to us?"

"Actually, thanks to the economic boom out here in the west. But you and I are part of that boom. We're here to make money. We know construction and development will ruin much of what's left of old Xian, and yet it's that long history we love. What a paradox!"

"I see your point. I haven't been able to size up the area as much as I'd like, but I have to admit I'm skeptical about whether industrialization at any cost is the way to go. In fact, we could say that about China as a whole."

"You're right," said Kim as he ushered Park into his car. "But the politicians don't like hearing that. From where they stand the economic gap among the different regions needs shrinking, and that goes for the gap between the haves and have-nots too—they have a lot of populace-appeasing to do. In any event, like the Chinese say, idealism is one thing but the present is now. The government associates development with a better life—the push-and-propel kind of message gets absolute support from the people. So the wise thing for us is to ride the tide."

Park nodded. "There's something to what you're saying."

"The manager has an appointment," Kim announced as he started the car, "but he'll join us later at the office, if that's all right with you."

Kim was ambivalent about Park's visit. Memories of the role of the invincible Gold Groups in his relocation from Shanghai to Xian remained fresh in his mind. And here he receives a call from that same conglomerate requesting an immediate meeting for an urgent matter. So now he's a fixer for the Gold Groups, accommodating an enterprise that used to be unapproachable. Well, hell, Park's agenda would reveal itself in due course.

Should he ask Park about that steel delivery? Neither he nor Chŏn Taegwang had ever learned all the details, especially the behind-the-scenes work of the two *guanxi*. They knew only the result—a bitter defeat at the hands of the Japanese. He felt the memories of that deal gone bad riling him up all over again. Oh well, it was water over the dam, he should suck it up.

In any event, he managed to retain his composure. With a company president arriving in person to discuss a grave matter, he couldn't waste energy moping over the past. For business people the eternal present lay in the hardheaded pursuit of a profit margin. What was right for business was maximum profit, and you were judged by how well you carried out that objective. Why poison yourself with sappy sentiment at a time when you need to put your best foot forward? With this in mind, he forced himself to focus on his visitor.

Park lurched forward and pointed outside. "What the … This is a busy street …"

Kim looked to where Park was pointing but saw nothing to arouse his attention. "Excuse me? Ah, those men—they are not wearing shirts."

"How can they do that in the middle of the street?" said Park. "It's not even that hot."

"Is this the first time you've seen a man in public without a shirt?"

The shirtless men were repairing bicycles, by now a rare sight in the big cities, where the my-car wave was surging.

"No. It's rude but not unheard of in the US. But it's not allowed in Beijing or Shanghai—I guess I assumed it was the same here."

"It's a long way from Beijing to Xian. Remember," said Kim, "it takes five years for a central-government directive to reach us out here."

To Park, the comment sounded like a variation on the question of how long he had been in China.

"It's been three years since the etiquette campaigns in Beijing around the time of the Olympics, so it's another two years for the campaigns to reach Xian? You sound like a wizard China-watcher. I'm afraid I'm not quite as forgiving. I rant at bad civic manners—they embarrass me. Five years is absurd. Look at the US. It's a bit larger than China but policy gets implemented almost instantly, all the way to Alaska and Hawaii. Without a mechanism for speedy consensus, fat chance China has to be a modern society—it's a basic prerequisite. You know why the mammoth became extinct, right? It got so big it lost function in its peripheral nervous system. It took two whole seconds for its brain to register an injury to its foot. Plus, over time its immune system was compromised. To me, China with its huge, unbridled population is like a mammoth. I see only one solution—give the provinces autonomy." It spilled out as though Park had rehearsed it.

"Mr. Park. Do you understand what you are saying?"

Park looked perplexed.

"What if I went to the PSB and reported our conversation?"

"Excuse me?"

"We'd be lucky just to get kicked out of the country. More likely we'd serve jail time."

Park nodded. "I'm aware of that. To a government that hates talk about Taiwanese independence, provincial autonomy must sound just as bad."

"It's not just the government—it gets the people worked up too. And not for love of country. Rather, they believe many different states in the same country means terrible wars with huge casualties. Whereas one country united means peace under heaven. Long history taught them that lesson—the country splits, it takes war and casualties to unite it, it splits again, more war and casualties, and on it goes."

"Well, of course they're worked up. They've been fighting to the death since the Warring States period two thousand years ago. They probably split and united a few dozen times before Mao and the PRC. The fear of division must be in their DNA by now. History is all about killing and being killed—doesn't the human race have any more to show for itself?" Shoulders drooping, Park released a deep sigh.

Kim glanced at Park, surprised by his acumen in Chinese history. The business-man was having a difficult time reading his counterpart. Kim had gotten nowhere with the Chinese-style physiognomy he'd tried upon first meeting Park, and now he was trying to size up the man's character. First of all there was his age—mid thirties?—and his job title—Gold Groups Company President. But his Chinese history spiel was the climax. Andy Park—what the hell kind of name was that, anyway?—background in architecture, in charge of Gold Groups construction, and the attitude of a two-bit philosopher. How much reading had he done? Hell, anyone could peruse a dozen books and show off like Park. Kim had done so himself, and his major was business. But all of this still left Park as hazy and mys-terious as ever. Kim told himself to keep his guard up—the man shouldn't be taken lightly.

"The Chinese mindset makes me anxious, it leaves me with a sense of crisis. Tribes in the Amazon may be uncivilized, but they have an inborn genuineness. The Chinese have tried burying their traditional culture in modernity but it keeps colliding with modern civilization. The IMF predicts that in 2016 China will catch up with the US and become G1—is that what it will take for those guys to put their shirts on?" Earnest and enthusiastic, Park sounded to Kim like the leadoff man on a debate team.

"I'm thinking along the same lines. Their economy is expanding to a global level, and their culture should do likewise. Government and media tend to take the initiative in this area, so I think we'll see change before long." Kim spoke in a neutral, diplomatic tone, reining in his view of Park: *You sound as American as your name. Anything below your standards is uncivilized and barbaric.* He recalled a story by an American correspondent for National Public Radio. The meat of rats captured during a government campaign to eradicate the plague virus had been dumped by profiteers on city restaurants, where they were transformed Cinderella-like, barbecued and skewered, into tasty "mutton." The Chinese had protested the implied accusation in the story—there had been no outbreak of plague in the countryside and therefore no tainted meat, and the meat was prop-erly cleaned, deboned and cooked like any other. Why criticize a people as unciv-ilized and barbaric just for living a different lifestyle, with different expectations and values? Wasn't such disapproval itself uncivilized, a form of cultural slander and violence? It was time to put a damper on narcissistic, self-righteous notions of superiority. This was no longer the 20th century; it was the 21st century, an Asian century.

"You're Korean, but the name..." Exchanging business cards with Park, the branch manager threw him a curve.

"Yes." Park smiled, unfazed. "My parents immigrated and I was born in the US."

"I see; you're an American citizen, that explains the name. But your Korean is perfect, no accent...."

"My parents used both languages until I was in kindergarten, but Korean only from grade school on. That's the way Chinese families educate their children, so even seventh- and eighth-generation Chinese Americans still speak the language. But Korean American kids tend to lose ground in the second generation and by the third generation the language is gone. My parents didn't want that to happen with me, and I didn't either."

"That reflects well on your parents! It's good to meet you, Mr. Park." The manager offered a handshake.

"Thank you, sir." Grinning, Park shook his hand. The handshake and the manager's rapt delight told Park he'd been accepted. It was as Madam CEO had predicted: the alchemy of close ties began with blood if not school or home region.

In deference to their guest Kim brewed tea in the local manner and the manager presented Park with the first cup.

"Thank you." But Park was dubious. Was the tea genuine? Where did it come from? Was it loaded with pesticides? He knew China was suzerain of tea as well as silk, pottery, and jade, and was aware that China's tea was as varied as its cuisine. But he foreswore it in favor of coffee, which was less likely to be bogus and adulterated.

What to do? He'd been told "Dump the first brewing and drink the second," but he suspected two brewings were not enough to flush out all the toxic fertilizer. And so he feigned composure, took a sip, and pretended to savor it. The sooner he finished here, the less tea he'd have to drink.

"You may have realized from my card that I'm not usually involved in closing deals. Today I'm here as a trusty messenger for my CEO." Park was nervous and thirsty, which made him sip more tea than he'd intended. "As you know, a research and development complex will be built here, and bidding and lobbying for supplies is ongoing. The nature of the contract is such that the identity of the construction company has yet to be made public. What I'm about to say is confidential, and I hope you will keep it that way. The Gold Groups are in charge of construction."

Kim and his manager eyed each other with a shrewd gleam, letting the information sink in. The stiffness of their expressions masked their impression that this was a powerful young man.

"Ms. Wang, our CEO, wishes a speedy outcome that is workable for both contenders for the steel supply. She suggests that each side be allowed to supply half." Park looked to the manager for a response.

Again Kim and his manager regarded each other silently, mindful of the influence of their *guanxi*—an ethnic Korean and a Chief Prosecutor with twenty years' experience, known to the local Korean community by his Korean name, Ch'oe Sangho. With his eyes the manager signaled Kim to respond.

Finally Kim broke the silence. "We understand your CEO's wishes, but our competitor might not agree with her suggestion, even if we did." He spoke deliberately, word by weighty word, like a child who has just learned how to read.

"That should not be a concern. Ms. Wang will handle that issue personally."

"She will?"

"Yes. I believe in her absolutely. She is ambitious and very skillful. Believe it or not, from faraway Beijing she managed to outbid the Xian city government for this project. In comparison, she can maneuver a steel company with her little finger. Even so, she wanted me to deliver you this message—as of now it's a two-way competition, but due to the logistics, it could soon be three-way if Japan gets word of the project. And if Japan gets involved it could be another déjà-vu for POSCO, since the Japanese don't work just with a *guanxi* but with a political strategy involving a top CCP official, someone out of the reach of our CEO. She believes in POSCO and would rather not see a repeat of the previous mishap." Park released a long sigh and picked up his teacup.

The manager hastened to replenish Park's cup, and gave Kim another eye cue. Kim took a deep breath. It was a grim prospect indeed, losing out on even half the hundred thousand tons of steel. "If she is willing to be responsible for the other party, we will attempt to persuade our *guanxi*." His tightened fist was shaking.

"We appreciate your prompt decision," said Park with a satisfied smile. "We will notify you of the outcome in a few days." He offered Kim his hand.

Kim cupped it in both of his. "I'm placing my trust in *you*."

Park added his other hand to Kim's. "Thank you. I will do my best to repay your trust. Today, for the first time, I experienced Korean *ch'emyŏn*, or as they say here, *mianzi*. In English, there is no such word."

"Are you staying the night?" asked the manager, more relaxed now.

Park checked his watch. "No sir. I need to get back on the last flight. The sooner we get to work on this issue, the faster we resolve it."

The manager rose briskly. "Let's check you in on your flight first. And then I think we'll have time for dinner—what do you say?"

"Once the construction starts," said Kim to Park as they left the office, we should have more opportunities to see each other."

"Of course. I'll likely be on site till it's completed. Perhaps you can show me around then."

The manager answered for Kim. "No worries there. Mr. Kim is like a professional tour guide. What's first on your sightseeing list?"

Park flashed a mischievous smile. "I'm more interested in Emperor Xuanzong and Yang Guifei than the tomb of Qin Shi Huangdi and the terracotta warriors."

"Of course. Any man would be curious about her beauty."

"I am indeed curious. How pretty could she be to topple a dynasty, how madly infatuated could a man be to let the splendid empire collapse? I must visit Huaqing Hot Spring, the fountainhead of pleasure for the two lovers."

It was not just his name that was different, thought Kim. "What is your favorite food?" he asked as they approached the street.

Park hesitated before saying, "Whatever is safe rather than fancy."

Kim nodded. "You really are paranoid about your food. I know a hotel restaurant we can trust."

Park lurched to a halt. Kim and his manager stopped beside him.

"How can they promenade around in a full set of pajamas?" An elderly couple in flowery red pajamas was walking toward them. Each held a white puppy wearing a red ribbon.

"Perhaps you haven't seen pajamas in public in Beijing or Shanghai," Kim whispered. "And dogs are a new fashion trend here. If it bothers you so much, just look the other way."

How to explain? thought Kim. The couple was out for an evening stroll, showing off their nouveau wealth. In recent years fancy pajamas from the West had become a status symbol. Like men going topless, pajama wearing in public was especially prevalent in the hinterlands.

Keeping a pet was a byproduct of the one-child policy. The global trend toward nuclear families had hit China, prompting the elderly to fill their empty nest with a pet. The fervor for the four-legged creatures had elevated their status from pet to companion, and there were now two hundred million of them. Who knew how many more there might be if the economy continued to expand? The pet shop was an up-and-coming enterprise.

Three days later Park notified Xian POSCO of his CEO's decision, and Kim signed a contract to deliver 120,000 tons of steel, worth 93 million dollars, to the Gold Groups.

The manager hugged Kim. "Well done. I couldn't have hoped for a better retirement present." He would be retiring in a year.

For the next several days Kim was in constant motion arranging delivery. Being busy, running on the adrenaline rush—this was the excitement that fueled a businessman. A ninety-three-million-dollar sale was practically a year's quota, and in one meeting Kim had hit a home run! In his euphoria Kim kept thinking about Park's last stab: "Thank you, Xian—I can look up at the sun without sunglasses!"

Early one morning as Kim was checking his schedule for the day, the admin head told him he had a visitor.

Kim waited for an explanation.

"She's been pestering me the last three days."

"Why me?" said Kim by way of reminding his junior that an admin head was in charge of administration and personnel matters.

"Well, she's an ethnic Korean and I don't…"

"Ethnic Korean?" Kim raised his eyebrows.

"Yes, so I can't just ignore her."

"Who is she anyway?"

"She's young, twenty-six years old."

"Qualifications?"

"Business major, from Yanbian University."

"Then she's probably from the Yanji area." Kim shook his head doubtfully.

"Yes, she said she came all the way just for us."

"She did?"

"I got the impression she's checked up on us."

"All right, bring her in."

Kim thought about what Ch'oe, the Chief Prosecutor, had said in a tipsy yet pressing tone during one of their drinking sessions:

Of course we're concerned about our future, but we have a different problem now— the population of ethnic Koreans is shrinking. We're about two million now, which puts us number thirteen out of the fifteen minorities. We're scattered all over China as well as South Korea, trying to make a living ever since the reforms. Look at me, I'm thousands of ri away from Yanbian, and even though it's autonomous I'm worried about the future of our prefecture. The bigger problem is that the women who have left are angling to marry the Hans. We don't want to be discriminated against as a minority, and if you ask the next generation they'll say the same thing—hell no! Remember in Tang, the minorities had the same complex, they wanted to be Tang. What will happen if this trend continues? We have to preserve our heritage; we have to help each other.

His words had resonated in Kim's mind ever since. And it wasn't just during the Tang Dynasty. In the Roman Empire, the minorities were proud to be Roman. What an opportunistic mentality—the strong will prevail and offer safety and comfort. This thought left Kim bitter.

At a subsequent get-together—maybe number five, Kim reckoned—Ch'oe had told him, "You're all right—you're polite, you know when to keep your mouth shut, you're knowledgeable but you don't advertise it, you work hard, and you're a true sinologist. That's good, I really like you. How about being my little brother?" And in fact he had done brotherly duty—or perhaps it was more a manifestation of "help each other"—by sticking his neck out for Kim in the Gold Groups deal.

Chen Ke, he of the gold tooth, had subsequently roasted Kim. "I'm so jealous. I brought you two together and you never invited me to your brotherly ceremony. I should follow my own advice and never trust anyone. If I fix you up with a woman you're supposed to treat me five times. But brotherhood is *really* special—what do say ten times? All right, maybe that's extortion, so let's say six—you and the other guy each treat me three times."

The woman ushered into Kim's office wasn't much to look at—short, thin as a stick, and sporting a mug Kim might have rated a three on a scale of one to ten. Her dress was unadorned and worn, giving her a slovenly appearance. In an age of image-says-all, with prospective employers increasingly emphasizing one's outer appearance, even men went in for plastic surgery and cosmetics to survive in the job-market jungle. And yet this woman wore no makeup whatsoever, and her cheap, mucky clothing left a sordid impression.

An interview would be a waste of his time, Kim thought. Still, she was an ethnic Korean. Ch'oe's voice was ringing in his ear: *We have to help each other.*

And then Kim noticed a peculiar sparkle in her eyes with their peaked corners. In her gaunt face those searching eyes were translucent, deep, eager to say something. And that's when he remembered the admin head saying she'd traveled a long distance to get here. No wonder she looked so tawdry. Not for her the frill of a short plane ride.

Taken by the clarity of her eyes, Kim asked, "There are so many companies to choose from—why us?"

"Because I'm Korean." Her quivering voice was as clear as her gaze.

"I know, but that by itself does not guarantee employment with a Korean company."

"Please do not misunderstand. I did not mean that. But not only am I Korean, my grandfather was in the Northeast Anti-Japanese United Army. I know that POSCO was the one and only company founded with funding from property claims against Japan, and I have always dreamed of working for you."

"Ah yes, the Northeast Anti-Japanese United Army!" Kim straightened, recalling that the history of Korean resistance fighters combining with the CCP army against the Japanese imperial army in Manchuria had led to the Yanji area being designated the first Autonomous Prefecture of the fifty-five minorities in the land.

Kim regarded this radiant-eyed granddaughter of a resistance fighter in a new light.

"How did you learn the history of our company?"

"It's basic knowledge among the Yanji people. They have a huge interest in the motherland."

Her words, articulate and unflinching, reflected intelligence and intellectual maturity. She referred to Korea as the motherland; like all other ethnic Koreans she probably called China the homeland. How perplexed, disappointed, and betrayed those back home on the peninsula felt toward their ethnic brothers and sisters on that day in the 1980s when the ROK signed the diplomatic treaty with the PRC and the everlasting forbidden country opened its gates to ROK citizens to mingle with their motherland counterparts in Manchuria. Sentimental from blood ties and the unforgettable history of sorrow, forced relocation, and resistant fighters drenched in blood, those from back home were eager to embrace their ethnic cousins in their hardship in Manchuria. But when they heard the offspring of those resistance fighters saying, "The ROK is our motherland and China our homeland," what were they to think? It took years for them to digest their boiling emotions, their sense of betrayal, and consider the situation more objectively.

"You studied business at Yanji University?"

"Yes." She quickly opened her bag and offered Kim a pair of documents. "Here is my diploma and this is my transcript."

Scanning the grade report, Kim realized he had been right to recognize the intelligence in her eyes.

"We have many branches here, but why did you choose this one? It's the farthest from your home."

"I did an Internet search and decided you are more likely to hire people because your branch is the newest. I also believed this is the best place for me."

"Best in terms of your assets?"

"As a business major I can do accounting, sales—whatever you need."

"Are you saying you're capable of sales work?"

"Yes, I am."

"I hope you understand what's involved in sales."

"I understand sales as selling our products to those who have no prior knowledge or experience with our country."

"And it's a process of merciless, endless rejections. Can you accept that?"

"Yes, I can. There is a perfect Korean saying for that—little strokes fell great oaks."

"It may be a perfect saying, but it's only a proverb. Two dozen little strokes might still yield no results."

"Yes. It's possible. But I believe a POSCO salesperson can knock down any tree in less than five tries."

"Can you please explain?"

"POSCO has an iron-fisted reputation the world over for quality, therefore it shouldn't take that many tries."

"Aha!" Bells were ringing in Kim's head. "Is there anything else I should know?"

"I'm in urgent need of money. My father was ill for a long time and passed away two years ago. I worked to support myself during college. I have a younger brother whose tuition I want to pay—as you may know, the government allows the minorities to have up to two children. My mother can only do chores that don't pay well."

"I see. I'll talk with my manager and get back to you tomorrow."

"Thank you for your time, sir." She bowed deeply, almost banging her head on the coffee table, then exited.

Watching her depart, Kim imagined her sordid apparel transforming into the most splendid gown.

7. An Outing in Beijing

The traffic in downtown Beijing was building. Not quite rush hour, but drivers wanting to avoid standstills—it might take an hour by car to cover a distance walkable in ten minutes—had gotten a head start. Vehicles on the streets were more numerous by the day. To curb the explosive surge, the city had devised a lottery-style quota system for new vehicle registrations. But the my-car fest was unstoppable and you could no more limit growth in the number of vehicles, registered or unregistered, than you could the waxing and waning of the moon or the blossoming and withering of flowers.

Yanling checked her watch. "Can't you find a short-cut? I'm in a rush."

"Don't get irritated," growled the young cab driver. "I don't like being stuck in traffic anymore than you do. You can always get out and run."

"I'm sorry, it's nothing personal. Just do the best you can." But her tone was frosty—gone was the sweetness she used with Chaehyŏng.

She pulled out her cell phone and entered a number. "Mom, it's me."

"Are you almost here?"

"Not quite. The traffic's not moving."

"Already? It will take time, then."

"Mom, where are you anyway? Are you waiting outside?"

"No. I was just about to go out."

"Good. Then please be patient, I'll be about ten minutes late."

"All right. My heart sank when I heard the phone."

"That heart of yours—keep fixating on it and you'll be sick for sure."

"I know. But the damage is done. That sorry excuse for a husband—it's galling!" And then came a *thump!*

Yanling startled. "Mom, will you *stop* pounding your chest? You'll have a heart attack if you hit it wrong. And just remember who'll be dancing on your grave when *that* happens."

"Don't worry. He'll have to get his exercise some other way. I plan to be around for a while, till I see him dead and rotting in his own damned coffin."

"That's right, Mom. Be tough. I'll call you when I'm almost there."

Ending the call, she leaned back against the seat. Her cell phone had proved its worth and the traffic was no longer a concern. She smirked, well aware of the Jekyll-and-Hyde nature of the small device. It could be a blessing or a curse, a loyal, ubiquitous secretary or a hideous Satan. How similar it was to money, the elixir of human desire and yet the wellspring of myriad tragedies! She shuddered whenever she upgraded to a new phone with more functions, knowing that the poison of selfishness was coiled cunningly within it. Companies constantly devised new models, disguising their thirst for profits beneath the sales pitch of cutting-edge technology. To Yanling it was commercialism at its worst.

What happened when consumers addicted to the juju of their cell phone were presented with a new addition to the market, with new functions? Well, they tossed their perfectly fine gadget in the trash and rushed to the store to camp out all night for the upgrade. Steve Jobs was praised unsparingly as a 21st-century tech-savvy mind, but to Yanling he was just as much a crude materialist imbued with the money god.

And what about Bill Gates? Precursor of Jobs in the IT industry, he had to wait in the wings while Stevie-Come-Lately took center stage. Only when the hapless Jobs was claimed by cancer did Gates return to the limelight. It was because of their lifestyle and legacy more than their inventions that the two were compared by columnists.

Gates, who had become the wealthiest person on the globe two decades earlier, had long since been returning his wealth to society and had created a foundation promoting health worldwide. When the younger Bush, branded by some as the worst president in American history, had proposed tax cuts that would benefit the superrich, Gates had joined his lawyer father in opposing them, arguing that the rich must pay more, not less, taxes. As did Warren Buffet, a contributor to the Gates Foundation.

In interviews Gates had said his children would inherit only a tiny portion of his wealth. When China became G2, he invited Chinese tycoons to donate to his foundation, but not a single one obliged. Nor did Jobs. Ravaged by cancer, walking like a zombie, knowing he faced a death sentence, to the end he devoted himself to developing Apple products. Columnists continued to remind their readers which of the two technocrats would leave a weightier legacy.

Yanling was reminded of these columns whenever she faced a decision to upgrade. The arrival of a new model meant that domestically, one hundred million cell phones would be dumped in the garbage. What about the rest of the world? What a waste of the earth's resources, not to mention the possible damage to the brain.

"We're here!" the driver called back to Yanling, waking her from her reveries. She spotted her mother. "Mom, why are you here, anyway?"

"Are you sick of me already?" said her mother, eyebrows arched.

"No, it's the opposite—I wish I could drop out of school and stay with you. That's the problem." Sad-eyed, she regarded her mother.

"Don't you ever. Not even in your dreams. Do you understand why I ended up this way? It's because I didn't go to college."

"What are you talking about?" said Yanling as she linked her arm with her mother's. In they went to the hotel coffee shop.

"All those stupid *ernai* are college girls." She snorted. "It figures, the dumb-ass, he only went to high school!"

Settled at a table, Yanling looked across at her mother. "Don't waste your time moping about those girls. It's a new trend—you can blame it on the reforms. And it's not just you who's affected. In the old days, every powerful rich guy had a herd of concubines. It's a vice that's always been around. So don't be hard on yourself."

Yanling knew her father was a victim of the Cultural Revolution. She still didn't understand the causes of that decade-long purge resulting in anywhere from five to twenty million casualties—no one knew the exact figure. Nor did anyone realize the extent of the damage to the country's cultural heritage. Yanling remembered only that Premier Zhou was able to dampen the frenzy by suggesting that cultural relics be preserved because they were the product of the people's blood and sweat. Unfortunately, the universities had shut down, and the teenagers who lived through the Cultural Revolution became the Lost and Uneducated Generation.

Her father's wounds had grown into an inferiority complex, which he relieved by using the money he'd amassed in the wake of the reforms to stock his stable of college-girl *ernai*. She felt sorry for her father even as her heart went out to her mother.

"You'll never understand how I feel—even when you're married."

"I do understand. A husband taking an *ernai* can turn the saintliest wife bad. Mom, I know how you feel. You've lost all your interest in life." She grasped her mother's hand and held it tight.

"I've thought it over," her mother said deliberately, "and I'm filing for divorce."

"Mom, no."

Her heart sank. What could she say? There'd been no warning. She'd presumed her mother was here to unload money on designer goods, one of her stress relievers after she argued with her husband. Her mother was right—she had a lot to learn before she could genuinely empathize in her mother's time of sorrow. Her mother was here to talk about splitting with her father, not to splurge in the boutiques.

"Mom, is that what he's thinking too?"

"No."

"Then it's your idea?"

"Yes. I'm so vexed."

"I know that. But think—who would love to see you divorced?"

No answer.

"When you're removed from the family register who will replace you?"

Silence.

"Mom, listen. You're not doing charity work—why make things easy for those girls?"

No response.

"And have you thought about me? What will happen to me after the divorce?"

Her mother merely looked at her.

"If you give up at home and *ernai* number one moves in with her boys, what happens to me? How do you think Dad will treat me?"

Her mother kept her silence.

Yanling was jolted by a thought—her inheritance! She couldn't dare hope to get even a third. It would be much less. Yes, she had to block the divorce.

"I hadn't thought about that," her mother said with a sheepish smile, more composed now. "But you'll be fine, you're all grown up now."

"Then do it," hissed Yanling. "And I'll kill myself the same day, I swear."

"What? You can't do that."

"Sure I can. Plenty of skyscrapers to jump off of."

"You're crazy," her mother said with teary eyes, pulling her daughter close. "Don't say that again. All right, I give in. I'm sorry. I'm putting it out of my mind. And you promise me you'll do likewise."

"Mom," said Yanling in a choking voice, "you have to brace yourself, I know it's hard."

"Yes, I know. I have to for your sake. But what do I do now for fun—?"

"Mom," Yanling interrupted, "do like the others. You're not the only victim. Latch on to some of his money and go shopping, travel overseas with your friends, find a boyfriend…the possibilities are endless. These days sixty-year-old women are going after forty-years-young men. And you're forty-nine, just a spring chick with soft feathers." She reminded her mother that some couples had no qualms about each of them having an affair, that there were mothers who took their teenage son to trysts with their lover, that high officials liked to sit with their arm around their *ernai,* displaying the trophy for all the world to see. All of this and more she had seen for herself.

Stroking her daughter's hand, Yanling's mother was reminded of her own hands when she was that age. "What a big girl you are. Already a senior!"

Rejuvenated, Yanling sprang up. "Mom, let's have our own revolution—we'll go hunting for designer goods."

"I don't need—"

"Mom, please. I know you've always wanted something nice, but the best you could do was buy fakes, because you wanted to save. But now that Dad's splashed his money on *ernai* and betrayed you, it's your turn. A buying spree's not going to dent his bank account. Don't be a sad sack—that's one of the reasons he gets away with treating you like he does. By the way, do you have any idea what his assets are?"

"Assets?" She looked agape at her daughter, frowned, and shook her head. "No clue."

"You should pay more attention."

"How about you?"

"I don't know either, but I'm going to find out."

"Great. We don't want *ernai* number one's kids going on a joyride."

Yanling thought about her father, who had always treated her with love and affection. But what if that changed? Anxiety ballooned inside her. Why the blind preference for sons over daughters? Forever inscribed in tradition was the love of the color red, the dragon, and the male offspring. Chairman Mao, crusader against millennia-old bad habits, could not slash through the shield of the son-worshipers. Upon founding the PRC, the Chairman had eliminated the predominance of man over woman, the submission to man by woman, and the practice of female foot-binding—he had achieved genuine woman's liberation and gender equality. And yet the preference remained a blemish on the jade of Mao's legacy. Had the Chairman erred, or perhaps overlooked the issue? Or had he intentionally disregarded it, male that he was?

This noxious preference was said to have resulted in anywhere from one to two hundred million unregistered girls—in effect, living ghosts. Estimates in the Western media ranged as high as four hundred million.

The unregistered girls were often sold or kidnapped for a measly one or two thousand *yuan*, depending on their age, looks, and perceived caliber. People generally downplayed the mushrooming rumblings about the ghost girls, guided by tried-and-true principles of keeping one's nose out of others' affairs and not meddling in unprofitable business. If pressed, they might hum a breezy rendition of *ren tai duo*.

Yanling knew the boy preference was more pronounced in the farm villages. Otherwise why would the government consider it necessary to wave the omnipresent banners emblazoned with the eight red characters *From Birth Let Us Always Love Our Girls*?

At marriage a woman entered her husband's family register, a red X having been placed beside her name in her own family register, the same X that signified a deceased family member. To her family the newlywed had symbolically died. If your priority was to preserve the family line, wouldn't you expect heaven to smile at the arrival of a male heir?

Once again Yanling sank into anxiety about her murky future, and finally her thoughts about her father's *ernai*—how many of them were there, anyway?— served to release her foot from the brake that until now had stayed her from pursuing high-end designer goods. She would revenge herself on the father who betrayed her mother! She would get even with the *ernai* upon whom he had showered his money. Vengeance in an expedition for fancy items.

She recalled what her sweet Chaehyŏng had said about his family. They weren't rich, just middle class. If he was lucky they might have barely enough money to buy him an apartment. Well, she now rationalized, since she couldn't expect much from his family, she had better do her own procuring, and the sooner the better. What a smart girl she was! And with her mother here the timing couldn't be better!

Arms linked, they left the hotel.

"Mom, you have some knockoff handbags, right?"

"Of course, a couple. Just like everybody else—why not."

"Today we're going to get the real thing. Then you can dump the fakes."

"But why? They're really good-quality fakes. Japanese and Korean women go all the way to Hong Kong to get them."

"Remember, Mom, you're not a knockoff."

"Of course I'm not."

"You're *real*," said Yanling, fixing her with a stare. "And from now on you're going to buy real things. If the *ernai* get real things in Hong Kong, then why do you get stuck with the fakes? Do you understand what I'm saying?"

"You're right," she said, nodding.

For the first time Yanling saw enlightened gaiety in her eyes. "Good. Your new life starts today. Let the payback to Dad begin! We can beat him, you know. And chew him up too. Our revenge is to spend his money." She locked her mother's arm even tighter in hers.

"I'm not sure what I'll do without you. I understand now why your daughter becomes your friend when she grows up. I'll go a step further—you're my treasure." Choked up, she stroked Yanling's hand.

"You know, Mom, starting a new life is more than just lavishing designer goods on yourself and being friends with your daughter. Those aren't the main things. Like I said before, you need a lover. You've lost confidence in yourself as a woman—you think of yourself as a jilted wife who's lost her charm. Before long you'll have no appetite for life, no hope. You'll feel bored, everything's tedious, you don't want to see anyone…in the end, you're dangerously depressed. That's why a lover would be a godsend for you. What do you think?"

"Amazing! You're a miracle doctor—you found my sore spot. My perceptive daughter, I'm so proud of you." Eyes still teary, she caressed her daughter's hand harder and faster.

But it wasn't only for her mother's sake that Yanling was campaigning. She was worried about her mother latching onto her. If the woman lingered in Beijing more as a friend than a mother, then what would happen with Yanling's relationship with Chaehyŏng? Should she tell her mother about him? Maybe not. Her mother was not mentally stable at the moment and might fly off the handle. What if her mother tried to unload herself on her fiancé? Or perhaps she would reject him, thinking he had snatched her sole source of support.

Yanling's senior year at Beida had come with a pond of worry in her heart. That Chaehyŏng was Korean was an ever more pressing issue as the time drew near for her to make the announcement to her parents. But as the days passed and their love deepened, along with her desire to complete the relationship through marriage, the pond of deepened too. Yanling anguished over the possibility that her father would not welcome him with open arms. Was it because the Chinese felt superior to other Asians? To Westerners they might feel inferior, but to the minorities within China they acted like the macho of all machos. For this 2,400-year-old mindset the country could thank Master Meng, who had treated all the surrounding tribes as barbarians.

Was it any wonder, thought Yanling, that the Chinese had mixed feelings about Koreans? It was no secret that China at the time of the reforms looked up to the ROK and Singapore as economic models. The ROK had resurrected itself after the Korean War and performed the miracle on the Han in record time in spite of the most adversarial and confrontational situation imaginable—its neighbor to the north, the Democratic People's Republic of Korea. That tiny cut-in-half country had staged a successful Olympics—and at a time, in the ninth year of the reforms, when China was struggling to provide its populace with three meals a day. But once relations between the PRC and the ROK were normalized, Korean companies hit the coastal cities of Qingdao and thereabouts like a tsunami. Chinese young men and women scrambled for jobs with these companies, learning a new line of work, earning a salary, and experiencing firsthand the little tiger that was the ROK.

More startling to Yanling was the popularity of Korean television dramas. Hallyu had swept China, and men and women, young and old, kept their eyes glued to the screen. Newspapers kept their readers updated on the programs, fiction writers constantly drew inspiration from them. But the people still had skewed notions—why did Koreans have to be such arrogant little bastards?

In time, of course, her country had become G2, the second largest economy in the world. And now her fellow Chinese were doubting what Korea could offer them—it was after all a shrimp of a country! Thank heavens they still liked Korean dramas and envied the handsome actors and winsome actresses. These mixed sentiments were especially strong among parvenu like her father.

Venturing into the Guomao mall, Yanling affectionately asked her mother which boutique they should raid first.

"Louis Vuitton!" she announced.

"There it is, and all the others. And after that?"

"How about Gucci?"

"And then?"

"Cartier."

"And after that?"

"I think those three will do for now."

"But why stop there?"

"They'll have all the big-ticket items. After that there won't be much to see."

"Good thinking, Mom. I agree. Nothing like good-quality, high-end products to catch the eye."

"How about you? Where to?"

"I vote for LV too!"

"Let's go. I've always wanted something from there."

"Me too. I'm dying to get a shoulder bag."

"Why not? We get our revenge and look chic doing it. Go head, you prick, shack up with as many of those airheads as you want. The first one hurt, I'll admit it, but after that it doesn't matter, you can have a hundred of them for all I care. I'll get even, spending all that money I saved you over the years."

Her loud voice fit right in with all the other Chinese voices around them as they sashayed toward the Vuitton emporium.

Tiananmen Square is vast, the gate itself high, and the Chinese would have it no other way. The square is ruled from the center by the portrait of Chairman Mao Zedong, who can be seen from every angle. His face with its gentle, benevolent smile looks down on the people, who come to see him during the four seasons, all year round.

It was midday and the square was crowded when Chaehyŏng and his mother's family arrived. As boorish as the throngs on the Champs-Élysées in Paris and the flocks jammed into the Namsan cable cars and onto the Han River pleasure boats in Seoul, the crowds here were country folk or foreign tourists. Just as Christians might hope for a once-in-a-lifetime visit to the Holy Land, and Muslims to Mecca, the Chinese wish to pay their respects, if only with a brief nod, to the Chairman resting in his mausoleum. For those few moments there come tottering visitors from the westernmost reaches of Sichuan and from villages far north in Heilongjiang. Mao is not merely the embalmed figure reposing in his crystal coffin for over three decades; he lives on in the hearts of his people as a holy figure. One of the mysteries of modern China is the great number of those who independently and voluntarily worship the Chairman.

Chaehyŏng's grandfather squinted in the direction of the great gate. "My little Chaehyŏng, I see that banner on the left reading 'Hurrah for the PRC,' but what does that banner on the right mean, 'Hurrah for the World Comrades United'?"

Scowling like a little boy, Chaehyŏng said, "Grandpa, you're testing me, aren't you? You know what it means." He wasn't sure what his grandfather's intentions were, and was trying to play safe.

With a cynical smile his grandfather said, "Kid, I don't get it. Does it mean the citizens of the world should unite and create a socialist state?"

"Yes, that's how I understand it," said Chaehyŏng with a wry smile. The warning light of his grandfather's anti-communism had come on.

"Crazy bastards!" shouted the old man, not caring who might hear him. To Chaehyŏng it was like a blast from a steam engine. "What a crock of shit. They went first for communism and starved to death, so they try capitalism next and guess what—now they have enough to eat."

Chaehyŏng covered his ears and turned to his mother. "Mom, help!"

Grimacing, she took hold of her father. "Dad, please, this is China. And of all the places in China, you're right in the middle of Tiananmen."

"Everything I said is the truth," he protested.

Chaehyŏng's Big Auntie, the eldest of his mother's three sisters, chimed in, "Dad, yesterday you were amazed at how China has developed, so why the fuss now? These days the socialist countries are withering on the vine. They're all turning capitalist. It's about time you let go of your anti-communist mindset."

And then it was Chaehyŏng's grandmother's turn. "*Aigu*, my idiotic, shriveled-up old man." Affectionately she worked a fist into her husband's forearm. "Why can't you forget the war? Yesterday is history, today is now. Remember, your son has been working here and your grandson is a student. Wake up, for heaven's sake. If you make the young ones uncomfortable, they'll ignore you."

Chaehyŏng came to his grandfather's defense. "I think Grandpa's right about that slogan. Foreigners tend to laugh at it once they understand what it means. But the people can't take it down—Party decree, you know? It's a dilemma for the Chinese. We should understand that, and enjoy our sightseeing. How about it?" He searched the faces of his family for approval.

His grandfather guffawed. "That's my boy. Great idea. I can see you're putting in valuable time on your studies." He patted Chaehyŏng on the back.

Little Auntie gestured with her chin toward the Chinese flag. "What do those five stars mean? I know the stars in the American flag mean the states."

"Right," said Chaehyŏng. "From the top down, the stars represent the Chinese people—the working class, the peasantry, the urban petite bourgeois, and the national bourgeoisie. The single big star means the Chinese Communist Party."

"Does that mean the CCP is supposed to be the best?"

"I would say so. They founded the New China."

"I don't agree. They put themselves higher than the people."

"See—I told you communism is evil," the old man grumbled.

Grandma scowled. "Hush, dear."

"Here it's very different from back home," said Chaehyŏng. "You might as well accept it. Every country works in its own way." He winked at his grandfather.

"Listen to the little ingrate. I remember when you took your first steps, and look how big you got. I guess we're getting old. Where does the time go?" The old man rubbed Chaehyŏng's back.

"Grandpa, stop. If you were one of the great Chinese poets, you'd probably feel that the meaninglessness of time can be meaningful in its own way, you know?"

His grandfather blinked quizzically. "What?"

"Grandfather's meaningless time has transpired meaningfully for his grandson, see?"

"Excellent! Well put, my boy." The old man beat gleefully on his thigh, the picture of contentment.

Little Auntie was overjoyed. "What a marvelous grandson. I haven't seen Dad so happy and smiling for years."

Big Auntie scowled at Chaehyŏng's mother. "No more regrets about him changing his major, he's doing just fine."

"Chaehyŏng," asked his grandfather, "was the square always this big? This is where the envoys from Chosŏn used to come."

"No. They expanded it after the PRC came to power, to celebrate the New China. They modeled it after Red Square. From here it's about an hour's walk to the Forbidden City."

"That long?"

"Yes. All our envoys made that walk, and by the time they went through the outer gates and then the inner gates, they were intimidated—totally submissive. As we just saw at the Forbidden City, you had to pass through many buildings before you got to see the emperor. Have you heard of the three-times-nine bows?"

"Three what?"

"It's how they had to greet the emperor—they knelt three separate times, and each time they bowed all the way to the ground nine times."

This revelation brought a chorus of ridicule from the three aunties:

"Good grief!"

"What for?"

"It's ridiculous!"

"I guess that's how you humiliate a small, powerless country," the old man tutted before deliberately turning his back on the thoroughfare to the Forbidden City.

Little Auntie nudged Chaehyŏng. "We're done with the photos—let's move on."

"Where to?"

"You know where—the place your sweet aunties have always wanted to venture to."

"Do you really have to?"

Little Auntie feigned surprise. "Don't tell me you're getting cold feet."

Baby Auntie, the youngest of his mother's three sisters, took his arm and gently shook it. "We personally asked you for a special favor from your friend's uncle. Yesterday, remember?"

Chaehyŏng frowned. "I will never be able to understand women," he grumbled. "What's so special about counterfeits?"

His grandfather cheered him on. "That's why they don't have hair on their faces."

"Can't you shut up?" said Chaehyŏng's grandmother. "It's none of your business."

His mother looked at him with concern. "Is something wrong? Did your friend's uncle back out?"

"It's not that. I've already arranged it with him."

Little Auntie threw a fake punch at him. "Then what? You little devil, are you trying to give us a heart attack?"

Baby Auntie pretended to pinch him. "You like to tease the stupid aunties, admit it."

Xiushuijie, Silk Street, was bustling with traffic, foot and vehicle, all in pursuit of counterfeit designer brands. Drivers didn't hesitate to honk and the noise was deafening. Where had all the *manmandi* gone? Instead *quaiquai* ruled the day whenever you stood to profit, wherever you could benefit—why wait patiently for an elevator when you could keep jabbing at the buttons?

Chaehyŏng pointed up at a stylish modern building. "All six floor are markets for fakes."

"Looks more like a department store to me."

"Yes, it does. A huge building with fake merchandise, right in the middle of the city—amazing."

"I can't believe it. It's such a nice building."

"I heard that during the Olympics, all the heads of state came here to shop."

"The Chinese are spunky all right! Where does it come from?"

"Wow, I wish I had their nerve."

"Yes, why don't we?"

While the aunties were marveling at the building, Chaehyŏng's grandfather was admiring the huge characters for Xiushuijie that had been written on one of its walls. "That calligraphy is wonderful!"

"You are now entering Counterfeit Designer Goods Heaven," Chaehyŏng intoned. "One thing I should remind you of: It's swarming with people. Imagine a department store sale back home. Who do you have to watch out for in the crowd? Yes—pickpockets! Too many shoppers lose their presence of mind, and then their money and their passports. You don't want the hassle of having to get a temporary passport just to get home. All right? So we act as a unit—no stragglers, that's dangerous."

"Are you a part-time guide?"

"Listen to the boy talk!"

"All that Beijing water got to his brain."

Ignoring the aunties' bantering, he led them inside. They were hit with a blast of body heat and an avalanche of gruff voices. The stuffy air heavy with the odor of human bodies clung to them.

The arcade shops were divided by a narrow corridor that could accommodate barely three abreast. The shops themselves were two hundred square feet at best, and uniformly adorned with a pair of twentysomething women hawking the wares. Chaehyŏng wondered if they were the daughters of migrant farmers.

One of the women called out to them in Japanese.

Bu shi Riben guizi, shi Hanguoren!" Chaehyŏng yelled back. Not me, I'm Korean.

The woman immediately switched to Korean. "I am so sorry. You look alike. We like Koreans more than Japanese." She put on a bright smile fit for an actress. "Come in. Everything is a good price."

Chaehyŏng understood her dilemma. It did require an effort to distinguish among Japanese, Koreans, and Chinese. He usually sensed the difference, but could not have explained precisely why.

They passed by the shop. Another woman called out in Korean, "Come in. All cheap here." To make money they focused all their faculties on determining a group's ethnicity. This wireless detection would continue until the end of the corridor, still some distance off.

"Ours are the best," hollered another vendor in Korean. "Come in!"

"Her Korean is perfect!" gushed Little Auntie, securing her handbag more tightly in her armpit.

"They all speak at least five languages other than Chinese."

"No kidding!"

"Yes. English, French, German, Japanese, and Korean."

"But they don't seem to have much education."

"High school, maybe. They just learn the basic phrases."

"They're no good," Chaehyŏng's grandfather muttered. "They don't learn the proper way. They all talk like farmers, no manners."

"Dad, don't be silly," said Big Auntie, trying to cut off the fractious old man. "They're only worrying about selling stuff, not about proper learning or etiquette. Taiwan and Turkey are the same." Big Auntie the globe-trotter.

"You should know by now not to take him seriously," Chaehyŏng's grandmother tutted. "You know as well as I do his heart isn't in this. He's just out of sorts and acting cross."

"Dad, you said you'd go along with us," said Baby Auntie in a singsong tone as she linked arms with him. "Don't break your promise."

"Don't mind me, just enjoy yourself," he said nonchalantly, waving his daughters off. "Your mom has done a good job domesticating me."

Chaehyŏng felt sorry for his grandfather on the one hand and worried on the other. His aunts were cavorting like fish, but the old man looked sleepy as a moviegoer who can't wait for the film to end.

He wished he could take the women straight to Namgŭn's uncle's shop on the second floor, where each could buy a handbag, and then they could call it quits. But how would he survive the ensuing barrage of complaints? Women would trade a two-day city tour for a fake bag that left them with empty pockets and a maxed-out credit card. You see and you desire! The high-quality counterfeit designer goods lured them with whispers: *Get me now. I'm the best counterfeit you'll ever see. And no one knows the difference. I look great on you. Buy me now, you won't regret it. You'll never have another chance.*

The shops in the long, narrow corridors were stuffed with goods piled to the ceiling. The rents were exorbitant, Chaehyŏng assumed, and the vendors were making best use of the space.

His grandfather made a face and said in an undertone, "So many big-noses."

"Always," said Chaehyŏng. "They can't afford the real thing but they want to show off."

"You mean they pretend it's genuine?"

"Sure. The bumpkins back home won't know the difference."

"Well," the old man tutted, "I guess even the West has its idiots."

How to entertain his grandfather? Men were so different from women. Tagging along to the market was no fun for his grandfather, or for him or his father either. Today he had volunteered as tour guide to give his mother a boost in the eyes of her family, and as apology for the pain he had caused her with his change of major.

His grandfather came to a halt. "What's that?"

"What are you looking at?"

"There, right in front of us, those four characters in red, don't they mean 'quality guaranteed'?"

Chaehyŏng followed the old man's pointed finger. "That's right!" But what was a 'quality guaranteed' sign doing in a market for counterfeits?

His grandfather was equally mystified. "Didn't you say everything is counterfeit here?"

Chaehyŏng broke into a laugh. "Now I get it. I've been here a dozen times but I've never seen that sign. It says all the products here are genuine counterfeits! Oh my god."

"That's a good one!" the old man brayed. "These folks are different, they have *balls*!"

The women caught up with them. "What's so funny?" said Chaehyŏng's grandmother.

Chaehyŏng pointed. "We're getting a kick out of that sign."

"'Quality guaranteed'?" said Big Auntie.

"The quality of the counterfeits?" said Baby Auntie, bug-eyed.

Little Auntie gaped at the sign. "How can you guarantee a fake?"

Chaehyŏng's mother shook her head. "These people are something else."

"Hey, kid," said his grandfather. "Where's the bathroom?"

"I'll show you," said Chaehyŏng. Along the way he asked, "Grandpa, what do you remember from the war?"

With a gentle look at his grandson the old man said, "What do I remember?" He paused. "You wouldn't know. It's been sixty years, but I can almost see it happening right in front of me." He shuddered. "It was absolutely freezing, and all winter long the Chinese came at us, one human wave of soldiers after another, and we and the UN soldiers kept getting pushed back. A human tide; that's frightening. Just soldiers, only a few of them armed, coming at us. We mow them down and here comes the next wave, and the next, and the next. How many of them were there? God only knows. I don't know how I survived. I've had nightmares ever since. An enemy country sends waves of soldiers at us … I never dreamed I'd be back here." He heaved a long sigh.

Chaehyŏng tightened the arm that was circling his grandfather's shoulder. "You're right, I can't imagine it."

"Probably better you didn't, it's a lot to live with. But it couldn't be helped, and it's all in the past now."

"Grandpa. We also have amity and diplomatic ties with Vietnam now, just like with China. Maybe this trip will help wash away the horrible memories. In the future we'll have to be close friends with China."

"I know, I've sensed that. We should forgive and forget. So, can you make a living from studying Chinese history?"

"Yes. No worries there."

"All right, I'll hope for the best."

They arrived at the toilets, and Chaehyŏng released his grandfather. The old man rubbed his back affectionately.

As he waited for his grandfather Chaehyŏng recalled a news report from a couple of years back. Heavy rains were flooding the rivers, and the damage, casualties, and number who had lost their homes were mounting by the day. An embankment was about to collapse, the old dykes breached by the force of the water, threatening more casualties and damage to nearby cities. The government dispatched three hundred thousand Liberation Army soldiers, who ran sandbags on their shoulder to the riversides. Dumping the bags onto the flooding dykes and jumping into the swirling water, they had built sand dams. It was a crude and risky strategy but it saved the dykes. Chaehyŏng had been awed then, and he was awed now to learn that China had implemented this human tide strategy six decades earlier.

8. Money Brings Money

Chŏn Taegwang felt for Ha Kyŏngman. If Ha had been able to supply Walmart China with his accessories, it would have been his great leap forward as a businessman. The good ship Domestic Market was enjoying favorable winds and calm seas. Those who sailed that ship were primarily women, and lately women in China were spending half of what men made in the new capitalist society. Women dominated the market, and if you were in business you had to reach them.

Ha's Guangbao accessories—the name meant "shining jewels"—were perfect for stimulating women's appetite to adorn themselves. Imagine their potential. Without market outlets, a commodity is about as marketable as a white elephant. As they say, a pearl has no worth till it's strung. It was a match made in heaven, Chŏn thought—the omnipresent Walmart and Ha with his inventory of 150,000 varied accessories.

The conditions were ideal, except for one problem—both parties were headstrong. The Walmart China sales director, Chen Wei's cousin, flaunted the superior WMC sales network and demanded the moon from Ha. But Ha refused to give away the store, which already had good footing and tried-and-true products.

Chŏn the general trader had two nicknames. The first was Nomad. He would herd his products anywhere with green grass. The second was Give It to Me One

More Time: he would walk himself footsore and talk himself dry-mouthed and sink his teeth into a potential deal and not let go. But sometimes even the most tenacious mind cannot win.

"Mr. Chŏn, think about Walmart China. Suppose we sell fifty of an item in one day in one of our stores—how many would we sell in a month? In a year? Next, multiply that second figure by the number of our stores in the entire country. We're talking about a golden fishery. You still have a hard time visualizing this, and I won't cry if you don't want to go ahead—I have a line of suppliers waiting to get a foot in the door. To be honest, I wasn't inclined in the first place, but I thought I would give it a try since it's my cousin Chen Wei who asked me." Chen Wei's cousin wanted a 3 percent commission on every accessory he sold for Ha.

"He's crazy," said Ha. "I'm aware of the Chinese fixation on money, but what he's demanding is preposterous. I'm not giving him a three percent commission on what I supply him, so why should I give him three percent on what he sells, when Walmart China would already have a profit margin of twenty-five to thirty percent on sales of my accessories? Do I dig dirt for business? I'm not going to do all the work and let Mr. Wang get all the profit. I know my products are not name-brand items, but on the other hand I don't offer them to street vendors or counterfeiters. They are designed by hard-working designers. I guess it was meant to be." Ha was as proud as his upright appearance.

Meanwhile, Chen Wei was getting anxious. "Mr. Chŏn. What if they met in the middle? That's your job, right? I can't just approach your supplier when I don't know him. But I'll talk with my cousin, and you please try the supplier again. It's not about money. I want my maiden voyage to be smooth and pleasant. It has to be successful."

Chŏn could not have felt worse. Even a monkey could fall from a tree, and even Chŏn could fail in a deal. When that happened, he felt like a hunter who had zeroed in on his target and taken a deep breath but missed the mark and had to watch the prey escape. It was an empty feeling that wouldn't go away soon. And to rub salt in his wound, he felt unable to adequately express his regrets at wasting Ha's time and energy. He couldn't entice Ha with good prospects for the domestic market when the man was already producing at full tilt and even exporting.

"I think he's sick. He's a moneymonger," said Ha during their phone conversation, by way of prefacing his decision not to go ahead with the deal. "If he wants a kickback on every item that goes through his hands, he'll be sitting on a pile of money in no time. I wouldn't lose on this deal, but I'm not about to do a crash landing—it's not as if I'm desperate and about to file for bankruptcy. Hell, let's change the subject. How long are you going to be a salaryman anyway? Don't you want to have a career of your own? Especially when the market is so strong here?" And that was Ha's parting shot.

Don't you want to have a career…Wise words that settled deep in Chŏn's heart. How true!

Ha was someone to envy. Back when he had switched to German machines for making his accessories, he was ready to take the next step. And did he ever—within a few years he had gained the summit, solid and steady. His triumph was all the more dazzling at a time when numerous companies in and around Qingdao were restructuring.

During Chŏn's visit to Qingdao, Ha had playfully boasted, "I have fifteen presidents under me. Every company that makes the news seems to have a CEO, and heck, don't I qualify?" Chŏn knew Ha's management style was innovative, but also risky—would it work in the long run? Ha believed that the only way to stabilize his company, increase production, and efficiently manage his human resources was to appoint a president for each production line, who in turn would choose a group of forty to fifty workers and manage that group independently. Ha decided to stay on as CEO to oversee overall production and sales. The new management style accelerated the company's growth. Employee pay was set by each president. Competition among production lines grew, spurring production, which in turn made the company work force more stable because fewer workers were leaving for better compensation elsewhere.

"It doesn't bother me that less money goes into my pocket. You don't have to be greedy to be profitable. If you make poor decisions, you screw yourself and end up having to close shop. Having a vocation means you enjoy working till you die, I guess." Ha grinned. "In the last four or five years a lot of small and medium-size Korean companies here have had to shut down. They all complained about the four-insurance policy the government made all businesses enact last year—they want to screw up Korean enterprises and kick them out of the country. Our media back home jumped on the bandwagon, but they were wrong, wrong, wrong. Companies from other countries are affected too, not just ours. Can you imagine how the Chinese government must feel? Betrayed, of course. For twenty years they gave us cheap leases, they gave us tax breaks, they went easy on companies trying to weasel out of their tax obligations, they extended special benefits, and what do they get in return—bitching and moaning. Raising the minimum wage, forming labor unions, providing a basic insurance package—these are all growing pains. We went through the same process. We can't expect China to remain like it was twenty years ago. That's a miserly, small-minded attitude on our part. Remember back in the 1960s when we worked fourteen hours a day for a rat-tail salary, waiting our turn to get better pay as our economy grew—we were grateful just to have a job. Well, China's the same. These last two decades they've worked hard to be a global leader in highway construction, high-speed trains, appliances, automobile manufacturing—all of them high-tech industries. So what happens with the simple technology from our companies? Well, they've mastered it the last two or three years and now they're challenging us. And for that we say they're betraying us? That's silly. For me, China is the best place to do business. And believe me, business is going to be good here for the next three decades." Ha punctuated his sermon with a beaming smile.

As Chŏn bid Ha farewell, he wondered if he would be smiling like Ha at that age. He had to admit he wasn't sure, a thought that left him dejected on his plane ride back to Shanghai.

His phone rang.

"Wei, it's me, Shang."

Chŏn's face brightened. He'd been waiting for this call.

"Can we meet at seven tonight at the usual place? We can talk about that matter."

This was how Shang talked on the phone, not so much because of his stupendous I-am-your-guanxi attitude, but more for the benefit of the PSB, in case it was listening in. People liked to joke that the PSB knew when you farted and burped, and Chŏn wondered what would happen now that Internet real-name sign-ins had been mandated by Beijing.

Chŏn was buoyed by the prospect of another deal with Shang—big money was involved, and the counterpart was a big shot. Energized, he rechecked the files he had put together in preparation. When he realized he was prancing uncontrollably about his office, he decided it was time for a foot massage.

The foot massage—a Chinese institution. According to traditional Chinese medicine, the pressure points in the foot were directly connected with the internal organs. To the uninitiated, this might come across as persiflage bordering on superstition or, worse, quackery. There were plenty of diagrams of the qi points in the foot, and the corresponding organs, their purpose seemingly to allay the suspicions of potential consumers.

For Chŏn it wasn't a matter of credibility but rather stress relief, not just in his feet but all over. And the sweet nap that came with the massage didn't hurt. The price of this perfect interlude for killing time and lifting one spirits? Twenty-five yuan, about four dollars. In Korea it would cost ten times as much. Chŏn wondered if this was why some of his countrymen still believed China offered the best values under heaven.

Off to his usual place he went. Foot-massage venues ranged from small parlors with several rooms to huge buildings, the latter as common as restaurants with eight floors. Cheap and sought-after, the parlors were big moneymakers. Huge though they might be, they were flooded at lunchtime by stressed-out office workers and no empty chair was to be found. This newly commercialized, cash-only business, a product of the rapid urbanization that accompanied industrialization, could not help but be inviting.

And not just to the local people. Exploding foreign tourist traffic brought even more popularity for the massage, which was now included in package tours. Westerners who might laugh at what they considered a bogus and outlandish theory of foot qi spots and their connections to the inner organs woke up from their session yelping "Wonderful!" with a double thumbs-up.

At the entrance Chŏn looked up, marveling at the size of this building used entirely for foot massage. He wondered how profitable it was. Boli duomai. Waving to the receptionist, he called out, "Zhang Tangtang!"—the name of his masseuse.

"Perfect timing!" said the receptionist. "She is free now." She guided him to a chair.

As soon as he had changed into his gown, a woman appeared with a bucket and greeted him, "Hello, Chŏn xiansheng," using a title of utmost respect. She set the bucket on the floor.

"How is Shang?" It was his standard greeting, Shang being Zhang's daughter.

"Thanks to you, she's doing well," she said with a bow.

Zhang was an immigrant from the countryside, one of millions in cities throughout the land working for puny pay. With her broad, homely face and needy, countrified look, she was deemed suitable for bottom-of-the-wage-scale foot-massage work. Some of the anecdotes she told him had grabbed his attention.

"When I had my daughter we were both kicked out." This could happen in rural Sichuan, where the preference for boys amounted to a religion. Having a baby girl was a curse. She might have stayed to try for another baby, but no way would her husband's family pay the exorbitant penalty. And so mother and daughter ended up on the street.

"I must work for two reasons," she had said, continuing her story. "I have to send my daughter to college, and I need to register her. That costs a lot of money."

Chŏn was confused.

Scanning the surroundings, she had whispered, "See, she can get a dead person's identity and register that way if we pay a big kickback to an official."

What a country! Yet another new entry in Chŏn's encyclopedia of China. The country was an eternal spring of novelty, and at the same time ambiguity. No wonder people said that by the end of a six-month stay in China you acted like you know all, after a year you resigned yourself to talking only about your field, and after ten years you kept your mouth shut.

Getting the daughter registered seemed to be the priority, so Chŏn took her as his masseur and added five yuan per session as a gratuity. There being no tradition of packaging and customer service, tipping was a welcome surprise. As a measure of the family's gratitude, Chŏn became xiansheng.

As Zhang started working on his foot, Chŏn thought about Shang Xinwen. How rapacious was the man, really? He was a good guanxi in a perfect position. Education, position, and money—together they opened all doors. How rich was he? Chŏn had no clue, but one thing was for sure—Shang had many other clients besides him. He had to be as greedy as the fallen star Bo Xilai. Bo was a classic combination of smarts and poor judgment, a tall, handsome, innovative party princeling who under the banner of Western Regional Development had made Chongqing into direct-controlled municipality number four. From Chongqing Party Secretary, he had advanced to Politburo membership and everyone predicted he would soon head the country. But his ostentatious corruption and extravagantly depraved life style had led to his downfall. He was arrested, tried and convicted, and jailed. This was the man who had cast himself as a revivalist of Chairman Mao's legacy, challenging the staid and corrupted ways of Chinese politics, waging a campaign against organized crime, and building affordable housing for the poor. For this he had earned the love of the people. How could a person be so different on the inside and the outside? Chǒn wondered about the other higher-ups—maybe they were even more corrupt. A foreign source estimated Prime Minister Wen Jiabao's personal assets at twenty-seven billion dollars. Only five years earlier he would appear in public clad in a shabby jacket, the "people's Prime Minister." As the people back home liked to say, "You might know how deep the well is, but not a person's mind." Amid such thoughts Chǒn slipped into somnolence, to be woken eventually by his masseuse.

After returning to his office for the files, he set out for the restaurant.

"This is the product certification." Nervously Chǒn held out two documents to Shang.

"Why two of them?" said Shang, leaving the papers suspended in midair.

"This one is from the US and this one is from the EU," said Chǒn, bringing the documents into closer view.

"Hmm. The Korean product is rated as high as the German one—interesting."

"Yes. International certification."

Shang ran a finger down both pages. "That's good but…" And sent Chǒn a piercing look.

"Please—this product passed the Korean government's stringent inspection and then that of the US and the EU. In Korea, document forgery is unthinkable," said Chǒn, knowing Chinese document counterfeiting was superlative, such that fake passports passed airport inspection.

Only then did Shang accept and pocket the papers. "Good. Not one, but two certificates. We can consider our challenger defeated. Mr. Zhuang will be very pleased when he sees these—he'll be comfortable making the switch to your client."

"After which he will want to go to Korea to survey the site?" Chǒn said, to keep the momentum going.

"Of course. Hopefully soon."

"In person, the company president?" To Zhuang's whale of an automobile manufacturing company, the Korean muffler supplier was like plankton.

"That's part of his passion for the job. It's his biggest asset in the eyes of his older brother, the CEO. And it's one of the reasons he handles the purchasing."

"We will make sure he is treated like royalty," said Chǒn, knowing all too well this responsibility would fall on his shoulders. "It is the best way to do business."

"Don't sweat it. In Korea you don't have problems with fake whiskey and you have plenty of pretty girls. Just make sure to put together a nice package for him."

"By all means."

"As an old-timer you know a business deal involves more than just a quality product. Especially if the offers are the same, it's the extras that sweeten the deal, right?"

"I understand, sir. I will put on a show the gentleman will never forget and make sure the deal is sealed as swiftly as possible."

"Thank you. I have complete trust in you. You've never failed or disappointed me."

"That is very generous of you, sir." Chŏn lowered his head. Everybody liked to feel superior and respected, and especially the Chinese with their love of mianzi. Shang's praise was a sugarcoated business gesture, but Chŏn didn't mind. Why turn down a free compliment?

"So much for that—how about some dinner?" And as he invariably did, Shang ordered the most expensive course on the menu, starting with shark's-fin soup. He wasn't paying the bill, but he acted in stately fashion, with no hesitation—he was after all the guanxi. The meal was a thousand yuan per person, a thousand times more expensive than breakfast for your average Wang but the standard set-menu price if you were treating a high official.

Wealth was number one on everyone's wish list, followed by a sumptuous meal. After money, the priorities were food, housing, and clothing, in that order; back home it was clothing, food, and housing. Chŏn still wasn't used to the idea of people splurging on food and when they still looked needy.

High officials had their favorite restaurants, and you didn't want to fling egg on a man's big face by deciding on your own where to meet. The officials liked a restaurant that was off the PSB radar and where they could soak up gratitude from the owner. It was customary for the restaurant to compensate the big man with a 10 percent kickback on the cost of the mal. If you were hosting a party of ten with a thousand-yuan meal each, you could count on getting a thousand yuan back. It wasn't so much an issue of money as of proper treatment. Withholding a kickback meant disrespect and humiliation. That the Chinese were number whizzes was no surprise. Chŏn never ceased being amazed that his Chinese hosts were more capitalist than the capitalists in the West.

As tipsy as Shang got on the baijiu with which they washed down their fancy meal, he let slip nothing about his former wife. Chŏn remembered Chen Wei telling him she was trying to save the marriage. What a cold-hearted guy Shang was, Chŏn realized yet again.

"You'd better prepare for your trip. It could happen any day—I'll let you know." Shang was also eager to land the big fish on their line.

"What's bothering you, honey?" said Chisŏn as they awoke the next morning.

"Nothing, why?" Behind the casual reply Chŏn was touched by her concern.

"You were tossing and turning all night."

"Trust me, I'll be fine."

"I'm sure you have a lot on your mind, but you shouldn't be so hard on yourself that your sleep suffers. I get nervous watching you."

"All right, I get the message. Everything will be all right." With a silent nod of thanks for his wife's thoughtfulness, he eased himself out of bed. His head felt dull and heavy, and it had nothing to do with drinking. For the first time he was acting as a free agent—he had to keep it a secret, and he felt helpless.

He reported to work, then left for a long walk, his destination a teahouse where he could make a call in private.

He affected a deliberate and weighty tone with just the right tinge of arrogance: "Ah, Mr. Yi. We're almost ready to strike. I have a few last details to discuss. Would it be possible for you to make a quick trip over here?"

Yi's voice, unlike Chŏn's, was willing and urgent. "Sure. It's only a two-hour flight—I'll check the schedule and call you right back."

Chŏn pictured a man so antsy he couldn't sit still. "Good idea. The sooner the better. All right, then..." Trailing off in the gravest tone he could manage, Chŏn ended the call.

At the other end of the line Yi could scarcely contain himself. The recession had lasted too long and there were too many competitors. The domestic market for car mufflers was saturated; he had to go international. And now a golden opportunity was emerging. He felt like he'd come across a hidden grove of precious wild ginseng.

Chŏn regarded his cell phone. "What a wonderful world," he murmured. "This little baby is magic!" Its basic function, not to mention round-the-clock capability, felt even more incredible, appealed to him even more dearly, at times like this. And speaking of magic, it was only two hours by air from Seoul to Shanghai. Yi could catch the first flight of the day, have a leisurely dim sum, conclude his business, and take the last flight home. China is so close, he thought, and not just geographically.

Closing his eyes and taking a deep breath, he sipped his tea. It was his favorite brand—Dragon Well of West Lake. He savored the refreshing aroma, grassy yet rich, could almost feel it in his heart. It was very close to Korean green tea, but had a taste of its own. Green tea was grown in so many places, but West Lake had held him captive for a decade now. A lovely gift. Taking another sip, he felt the deep, mysterious aroma soothe his mind and lead his thoughts. Coffee might have surface chic, but it was no match for tea.

As he lingered over the tea, his thoughts crystallized. Yi was scheduled to arrive at four p.m. Chŏn would give him time to check into his hotel before he called. He held the upper hand, and he knew Yi's travel agent would handle the flights, hotel, and ground transportation, and if enough money was involved the service would be silky and pliant. For Chŏn's part, a posture of cool indifference would render his counterpart more receptive.

When finally he called, Yi panted out a reply, as if in his anxiety he had sprinted all the way to the hotel: "Ah yes, I just arrived."

Instead of saying, Yes, sir. I'll be right there Chŏn responded in a matter-of-fact tone, "Excellent. I'm in a meeting right now—it's related to what you and I have been talking about. How about if I come by around six-thirty. You might want to take a shower and have a nap. Even short flights can be tiring, you know. All right, then …" In fact, he was having a foot massage.

Chŏn took his sweet time getting to the hotel and at six-thirty on the dot he knocked on Yi's door. After they had exchanged greetings Chŏn said dryly, "I made a reservation at the restaurant downstairs. Best to keep a low profile, right?"

"Yes, I agree. Just the two of us. Good." Yi was a hefty fellow whom Chŏn made for maybe five years older than himself, but you wouldn't have known it the way the man kept his head bowed. To Chŏn it was unbecoming, even though the hierarchy was manifest: he had the power and Yi did not. As a department head of a general trading company who could open a supply route to a foreign buyer, Chŏn had the power of life and death over a midsize manufacturer.

"Let's take care of our business before the meal arrives," said Chŏn as he served his guest tea in the restaurant.

"Yes, everything out on the table," said Yi, head bobbing ever more frequently.

Chŏn shot Yi a look. "Are you aware that when you do business in China the function of a guanxi is critical?"

Yi kept his head lowered, as if in obeisance to a king. "Yes, I am. I'm told the guanxi is absolute."

"The guanxi involved here is someone I've been associated with for a long time."

"I see." If Yi had bent any lower his head would have been under the table.

"I've worked with him the last ten years on some big projects, and we've had stellar results. On this deal he's done ninety-five percent of the work—the rest is up to me."

"I see."

"The fact is, we have three companies, including yours, in the running, and the choice will depend most crucially on product certification, which in your case we've secured. So it remains only for me to interview you."

"Ah, yes sir. You will have my unconditional best offer. I'll treaty you royally, so your guanxi knows how special you are."

Chŏn doubted his ears. Yi was saying all the right things, almost too easily. Considering the modest size of his company, he seemed very skillful.

"First of all, I must know your scale of production. What are you anticipating?"

"May I say this, sir? The more the better, I believe."

"That, of course, is every businessman's desire. What I mean is, what do you have in mind for your first shipment?"

For the first time Yi looked Chŏn squarely in the eye. "At least a hundred thousand …"

Chŏn produced a condescending smile. "Sir, I expected better of you. How about five times that amount?"

"Excuse me? F—F—Five hundred thousand?"

"Is there a problem? Either you can or you can't."

"Well of course we can, we could supply a million. I was just trying to catch my breath—it is after all the first order." Yi's face was peach pink.

"That's the scale my guanxi operates on."

Yi lunged toward Chŏn and took his hands. "Mr. Chŏn. Trust me, please. Help me." His hands were trembling and his voice as well. "I'll offer you one percent of all our sales, separate from the rebate, of course. Please help me. You'll forever be my benefactor."

"If we succeed, how long do you expect the partnership to last?"

"Well…" This time Yi refrained from saying, The longer the better.

"The German company enjoyed a ten-year monopoly, and now they've been scaled back to fifty percent. Our guanxi now decides who supplies the other fifty percent."

"Oh my. Mr. Chŏn. Please put in a good word for me. And just remember, one percent profit sharing."

"Well…a hundred and twenty dollars per, and one percent of that…then—l"

"Yes, that's right."

Chŏn put his index finger to his lips. Sipping his tea deliberately, he said in an undertone, shaking his head ponderously, "You know words, like clouds and the wind—"

"Yes, to be sure. Everything's above board, I promise. I'll write you a promissory note. I'm not a small-minded guy, you know. I never forget my savior. Let's ask our server for something to write on." So saying, he produced a pen.

"Really—you don't have to do that," said Chŏn. But he was quick to press the service button on their table. He felt his tangled thoughts rearrange themselves in orderly fashion. Engulfed by the emotion of his arrival at the summit, taking a deep, triumphant breath, he celebrated with a cigarette.

Yi finished his note before Chŏn finished his cigarette. "I'm sorry, I don't have my seal with me. How about just my signature?"

"I have a better idea. Write your name—the Chinese characters, that is—on the note and give me three hundred yuan. I'll send out one of the errand boys to have a seal made, a nice jade one. He'll be back with it by the time we finish our meal. Half the money will go for the seal, and half for the boy."

Again Chŏn pressed the service bell. He had read of a wealthy man back home who had written a note pledging half his assets to a certain university. But after his death, when the university attempted to collect on the pledge, the dead man's children filed suit to block the transfer, claiming they hadn't been informed of it. As for the note, who was to say their father hadn't been distracted and/or manipulated into writing it, or that it hadn't been forged? The judge denied the university's claim on the basis that the note bore no cachet of the deceased's seal. To Chŏn, then, a promissory note was toothless without the imprint of a seal.

A week later Chŏn was bound for Korea with Zhuang, the Chinese buyer.

"May I see the factory?" said Zhuang as soon as greetings were exchanged.

Yi was perplexed. "Sir, you must be tired—I was thinking you might want to rest today and we could visit the factory tomorrow?"

After interpreting, Chŏn whispered to Yi in a scathing tone, "What's the problem? You're not ready for him?"

Yi made a no-no-no gesture with his hands. "It's not that—"

"Good. He just wants to swoop in and see the factory as it is. You don't need to fuss over prettying it up for him. But let them know we're coming."

The factory was in Hwasŏng, Kyŏnggi Province. Zhuang was silent along the way, as were Yi and Chŏn.

Zhuang's silence was a smart move, thought Chŏn. He knew Zhuang was a follower of Sunzi's Bingfa. Silence was effective, because it made you seem important and tended to intimidate others. Zhuang was no fool...With such musings Chŏn tried to fight the drowsiness settling over him.

At the end of the factory tour Zhuang extended his hand to Yi. Judging from his smile he couldn't have been more satisfied. "I am very impressed. I believe that a ship-shape factory produces a quality product, and I'm sure you do as well. I am greatly pleased."

Surprise, surprise. The factories Chŏn was accustomed to were cluttered, especially if they involved metalworking. But Yi's muffler factory was more like a living room that had just received its spring-cleaning.

Chŏn knew that back in China messiness was not necessarily a flaw. Perched on stools on sidewalks smeared with dog poop and strewn with garbage, people relished their meal while watching passersby clear their throats and spit. Western reporters in their outrage wrote that China was hopeless. Although the unsightly scenes were inching into oblivion in the wake of China's new G2 status, the deeper you ventured to the countryside, the more in evidence they remained. With so much filth in public view, one could only imagine how dirty an unseen factory might be. No wonder Zhuang was so satisfied as they left. "I'm good with the factory," he announced. "No need to talk further. We'll close the deal tonight."

Yi bowed to his Chinese buyer with the alacrity of a performer of a three-times-nine bow. Zhuang was his emperor, his money god.

Having shown Zhuang to his room at the hotel, Chŏn felt his edginess yielding to fatigue. If only he could have a foot massage! It was just the thing for all the ailments that came with living in China. Yi was so close to achieving the dream that Chŏn had long held for himself.

There was a knock on his door. He opened it to see a flustered Yi.

"If you have time before dinner, would you mind if we had coffee?"

"Is there something you need to tell me?" Chŏn said in an unwelcoming tone, wanting instead to shower and rest.

"I'm sorry… It's not urgent, but this is my first time dealing with the Chinese, and I would be grateful for any advice. I know you must be tired…" The more Yi said, the more he emphasized his words.

"First time, eh?" Remembering the promissory note tucked away in his pocket, Chŏn tried to suppress his fatigue. "All right. Let's go."

Over coffee Yi said with eager eyes, "I think I just cleared the first hurdle… But I'm sure there are many more ahead, so please…"

"Well, the Chinese like to say that you let your life go, but not your money. The deal that's ahead of us is about that money. We tend to think of the Chinese as slow, wily, and two-faced, and I would say that's half right. When it's none of their concern they're all manmandi; when it's about business they're all quaiquai. Look at Zhuang today, super-quaiquai—you wouldn't see a Korean business owner that spry. He could have sent an underling here to look for mufflers, but he wanted to see for himself. I say 'wily' and 'two-faced,' but he's really no different from us—we don't let on how we're feeling, we use gamesmanship when we're trying to make a deal. One thing you want to remember—money makes money. Pay less, make more, push and pull, tip the scales a little bit this way, a little more that way, it all depends on the situation. He might surprise you with an aggressive offer or a deep discount. He's a master, sly and calculating. But to me you're a veteran, an old soldier. You'll do just fine with him." And with that Chŏn finally removed his businessman's mask and smiled an unfettered smile.

"I guess you should know—sales is more challenging than manufacturing," said Yi. "One last thing—I've heard the Chinese are expert negotiators and I'm just worried he wants the whole store dirt cheap. Where do I hold the line? That's my biggest concern."

"Naturally. Just don't rush into anything. And remember. The German mufflers sold for two hundred dollars, and no discount. You're asking a hundred and twenty, and a discount is negotiable. Yet the quality and performance are the same. You're the dealer, not him. He has to choose you even if he doesn't get a discount. He's saving eighty dollars apiece on half a million mufflers! Think about that, stick your chest out, and charge."

"Thank you, that's what I needed to hear." Yi had to restrain himself from clapping in triumph.

Dinner was in a private room at the Chinese restaurant in the hotel.

Staring at Chŏn and Yi, Zhuang spoke word by careful word. "As you both know, I want our negotiations kept secret, regardless of the outcome. That is basic business etiquette."

After Chŏn had interpreted, Yi politely responded. "To be sure. Our dealings will remain between us. With my partners in business I see nothing and hear nothing. I have never departed from that policy."

Chŏn was both relieved and optimistic. Yi had a firm grip on the reins.

Zhuang smiled as he fixed Yi with his gaze. "I like that." And then he came out swinging. "You and I both come from a culture of bargaining. We've agreed on a hundred and twenty dollars a unit—what else can you come up with? And let's not get bogged down in haggling, that can get tiring."

"We have a saying," said Yi. "Haggling is better than buying. But Korea has been enforcing a fixed-price policy for forty years. Now that you have brought it up, I would like to offer a five percent discount as a courtesy." He punctuated the offer with a bow. The ball was in Zhuang's court.

"I didn't come all the way here expecting a measly five percent. How about ten?" Zhuang's face was as stern as his tone—take it or leave it.

Suddenly Chŏn's neck felt stiff and his heart was thumping. Would the promissory note end up in the recycling bin? Who would have thought Zhuang would come on that strong? How would Yi respond? It was all Chŏn could do to interpret.

Yi gave Zhuang a piercing gaze, sizing him up. "Ten percent? Well. Why don't we give you twice that—twenty percent. But, under one condition. We get the entire order—one million mufflers." Yi took a deep breath and released it.

Inwardly Chŏn moaned. How could he be so brash? The deal was over. With a bitter feeling he interpreted.

"Hmm. Twenty percent?"

"Yes. Twenty percent."

"And that's in addition to the rebate."

"Yes, I believe the standard rebate is two to three percent on average."

"Are you sure you can supply a million?"

"A man's word is as good as his bond."

"What if you fall short?"

"I'll pay a penalty of ten times the purchase price, and make sure it's specified in the contract."

"You're a very confident man. All right, then. On one final condition—you give us a five percent rebate." Zhuang paused to let his words sink in. "And I would like you to deposit two percent of that rebate with our company, and the other three percent, plus the twenty percent discount, in my account in Hong Kong. Mr. Chŏn, make sure he understands."

It was highway robbery! Chŏn fumed inwardly as he interpreted. Zhuang was bilking his brother, the CEO, out of big money! How much was he pocketing from this auto-part caper? How rich was Zhuang anyway? Well, as long as he didn't damage his brother's company…Otherwise there would be hell to pay.

"As you wish." Springing to his feet, Yi bent ninety degrees at the waist and bowed to Zhuang.

"Good heavens," said Zhuang with a hearty laugh as he took Yi's hands in his and pumped them up and down. "It's been a long time since I've met as fine a fellow as Guan Yu, and even longer since I've seen a man as spirited as Zhang Fei. Excellent—we'll sign tomorrow."

Chŏn had to agree—Yi was a man of great caliber! As the saying went, you never knew a man until you'd dealt with him ten or twenty times, but this Yi really had nerve. What a coup. He thought again about the promissory note. Now that the order had doubled, would the terms of the note follow suit? What if whizbang Yi tried to play innocent and said, No way, I earned that double order all by myself? In that case, thought Chŏn, it would be a matter of brash and abashed—he hadn't been brash enough when he'd drafted the note, and would end up abashed if he tried to alter it now. As he watched the outpouring of joy from the two men, he could almost see bundles of cash whirling before his eyes.

9. Here Comes Daddy

Embracing his two children in the lobby of the New China Hotel, Sŏ Hawŏn realized he could no longer reach around their backs and link his fingers—how they had grown! Like plants in a drought, children somehow manage to grow even when conditions aren't ideal. Holding them tighter, Sŏ kept apologizing. He choked up and his heart ached.

His good wife one thing different story—he sensed her support, understanding, and consolation. But with the kids he felt oppressed. Would they ever respect him as a father? Would they hold a grudge against him? Having to transfer to a different school must have been even more painful than moving to the countryside. He felt all the more guilty that he had never explained to them why. He himself had experienced the same hurt in high school and even now the thought of it practically made him moan. Would they ever forgive him? Or would he have to live with guilt the rest of his life?

For a child, changing schools can be tantamount to rebirth. Sŏ had come across this statement, by the Swiss pedagogue Johann Pestalozzi, in medical school. It was true, he realized, at least with his own experience in high school. And thus one of the conditions of the marriage vows he concluded with his wife was that they would not transfer their children.

In his weekly letters to the children Sŏ had made sure to ask how they were adjusting. In recent years bullying at school was frequently reported on television; there were even episodes of violence by groups of girl students. New students were easy targets.

It was surely thanks to his wife's caring nature that daughter and son, who alternated writing, assured him they were not being bullied or assaulted, they were doing fine, and instead they worried about their father's health. They couldn't wait for the day they would once again live together with Daddy. That line always brought tears to his eyes. No words could express his gratitude to them that they had survived the transfer, and that unexpressed gratitude transformed into guilt. To repay them, he had brought them to Shanghai for a short visit.

His daughter scowled. "Daddy, why weren't you waiting at the airport?"

"I wanted to. But I had so many patients, I'm sorry—"

"Are you an idiot or what?" his son challenged her. "Daddy has to take care of his patients so he can have time with us."

She transferred her scowl to her brother, her eyes bulging. "My smartass little brother, Master Sŏ Chunil. You're the idiot!"

"Got you!" The boy stuck out his tongue at her.

She waved a fist at him. "You're such a brown-noser. I'm ashamed to have you as a brother."

"And you have zero sense. Sŏ Chiyŏn my sister? Forget it!" And out came the tongue again.

And that's when Sŏ's wife, Yu Ŭnsŏn, stepped in. "Come on, kids, let's not be squaring off."

In the meantime Sŏ was beaming at his twofold pride and joy—his daughter, already taller than her mother and brother and beginning to fill into a woman, and his son, a sixth grader whose voice was beginning to change and whose teasing of his big sister was developing into a fine art.

"Kids, let's get a cold drink," said Sŏ in full Daddy mode.

"Ice cream for me, Daddy," his daughter cooed.

"I want Coke with ice," said his son.

"No," said Ŭnsŏn with a look of horror. "Not in the hotel, it's too expensive."

Sŏ gently took her hand. "Honey, you promised."

"Mom, you're such a party pooper," her daughter pouted.

"That's right," said her son with a frown. "She always has to be Mom."

Sŏ's wife glared at them. "Watch your mouth, you two."

With a forgiving smile Sŏ led his family into the hotel lounge.

Sŏ ordered in Chinese, but his wife heard the word *Coke* and said, "No, not for him."

"Mom," said their daughter. "You can't do that."

"Then how about ice cream."

"Mom, we're on vacation," lamented their son. "I'll give up Coke when we're back home, I promise. But now I'm free to choose what I want."

"You're right," Sŏ declared. "When you're on vacation."

"My dear doctor," his wife pleaded. "We talked about not drinking Coke. Tooth decay, harm to internal organs, bone damage…"

Son gave Father a thumb's-up and wagged the digit. "Daddy's the best."

Daughter said, "Daddy is something else in addition."

"Something else what?" said her brother.

"Listen to his Chinese. Dad, it's only been a year and you sound like a Chinese person. You're a genius, Dad."

"An Einstein. Right, Dad?" said Sŏ's son. "I already knew that."

Sŏ waved his hand in embarrassment. "Hey, I'm not used to all these compliments. I barely know a few easy phrases, only enough to communicate with my patients."

He was being humble; the fact was, he seized every free moment to study the language; his survival depended on it.

Watching the children enjoy their treat, Sŏ's wife asked in an undertone, "Do you have many patients in the summer?"

"Yes. During Chunjie, everybody has fifteen days off—time for people to rest up and have fun. That's when I get hammered. The visible effects of the surgery are gone by the time they go back to work. It's the same during summer vacation."

"That's great. Though it must be hard on you."

"I knew it would be like this—an ocean of cosmetic surgery. I think coming here was a good decision." He held her hand under the table so the kids wouldn't see.

"Daddy, where do you like it better, here or Beijing?" asked his daughter, more calm now that she was halfway through her ice cream.

"Well…everybody asks me the same question. It's hard to say. The two cities are so different. Beijing is the political capital, Shanghai is the economic center. Or you could say Beijing is the powerhouse for the nation, and Shanghai is the moneyhouse for the economy. Beijing people always say Shanghai people only know money, and Shanghaians say Beijingers only wear power hats. Beijingers complain that Shanghaians treat everyone else like hicks, and Shanghai people complain that Beijing people treat everyone else like servants. So, which side do I choose? Especially as an outsider. After we arrive in Beijing you guys can decide for yourselves. Think of it as a good learning experience to go along with your vacation trip." He couldn't help smiling—it was so long since he'd been Daddy.

The reunion of husband and children drew a blissful smile from Ŭnsŏn.

Their daughter turned serious. "Daddy, are you saying they fight between regions too?"

"You know the meaning of regional fighting?"

"Yes, Daddy, we learned it in social studies." Her eyes asked why he was surprised.

Sŏ edged closer to her. "What did your teacher say?"

"He said…we have the tragedy of north-south division, and we also have division by region, which is a curse. He said we shouldn't let that happen." Her eyes gleamed proudly.

Sŏ nodded. "What a nice teacher."

"The teacher is great," chimed in his wife, "but you're a great student because you remember what the teacher said."

Their daughter waved no. "Please, Mom, let's not show off. It makes me uncomfortable."

"Your mother's right," said Sŏ. "We know you're a smart girl."

"You guys. You don't know jack," their son snapped. The couple burst into laughter.

How wonderful to have this family vacation! Sŏ told himself yet again. It was so much fun, so easy, he felt like he was melting. Gazing at them, he recalled the dark days when it seemed he was about to be swallowed by the nightmare of having to flee. Thinking there was no hope of climbing out of the deep abyss of despair to reunite with them. And now this miraculous day had come!

One day Chŏn had posed the question: "Dr. Sŏ. Don't you miss being the man of the house?"

Sŏ had merely looked at him.

"Why not bring your family over for a visit? Don't say you're not ready. Money doesn't make the opportunity, *you* do. You've worked like a dog the whole year, including holidays, when everyone else has time off. But even dogs deserve a rest. And you can afford to take a break. A family vacation will do you wonders—you strengthen your role as head of the family, you make your good wife feel better, your kids get to experience China, you can show your family you're doing well.... What's life for if not to create nice memories and have fun time with your family? If Master Gong will forgive me, I'd like to make a suggestion—your family needs a round of therapy, and a China trip to see Daddy would be just the thing."

Chŏn the wise therapist. Sŏ felt deeply grateful.

And speak of the devil, in rushed Chŏn. "I'm so sorry to keep you all waiting. Hello, I'm Chŏn Taegwang."

Sŏ sprang to his feet. "Honey, this is Mr. Chŏn."

Hands folded together politely, Sŏ's wife bowed. "How do you do, sir? I'm Yu Ŭnsŏn. I've heard so much about you I feel I've known you for a long time. Thank you for all the help you've given us."

Chŏn returned the bow. "I'm the one who should be grateful. Dr. Sŏ never stops working. He puts me to shame—I've learned so much from him."

Sŏ introduced his daughter and son.

Chŏn produced a *hongbao* and offered it to Sŏ's wife. "May I give this to the children? I was thinking of treating you to dinner, but I don't want to take away from your time together—you only have three days. Besides, your children might find me boring. So this is for them."

She regarded the red gift envelope—"Oh my, how wonderful!"—then looked to her husband.

"It's all right, honey," Sŏ said to her as he smiled at Chŏn.

"I hope you'll forgive me, it's not much," said Chŏn. And finally she accepted it.

"Hey, kids," said Sŏ, "I want you to know that Mr. Chŏn planned out this trip for us. There are so many places to see, but we'll focus on Shanghai and Beijing, which is like seeing half of China. Or Paris and Rome, only we'll stay in the same country. This could be a really memorable trip!"

After shaking hands with the children, Chŏn disappeared out the door.

"Wow, he looks dandy." Sŏ's son gave their departed visitor a thumbs-up.

"Huh, you're smelling money and brown-nosing already," his sister snorted.

"He's a nice guy," said Sŏ. "Thanks to men like him, our economy is improving. Let's hear it for people who are working hard, far from home! All right, let's get started. We have three days, but today is almost half gone and we're leaving early in the afternoon, so strictly speaking we only have two days left. We have to make good use of our time. I talked with a guide and got some ideas, but why don't you check these and let me know where you might want to go." Sŏ produced pamphlets from the inner pocket of his jacket and handed one each to his son and daughter.

Sŏ's wife picked up her coffee mug. "Honey, let's not waste their time—what do they know about China? Why don't you plan our route?"

"Mom," their daughter snapped. "Why do you always have to be like this? It's no fun."

"That's right," said their son. "You're acting like Hitler."

"You guys," said Sŏ. "What your mom's saying makes sense. I'll work out a plan where we see the best of Shanghai. What time is it now? Five already? We should move; the traffic here is five times worse than in Seoul."

Sŏ rose and beckoned the others to their feet.

His son drew next to him. "Daddy, where are we going first?"

Smoothing his son's hair, Sŏ said, "To Waitan. It's a must-see. I'll tell you about it on the way."

As they neared the main entrance, a man rushed to meet them. "Are you ready?"

"Yes. We're going to Waitan first." And then, fixing his children with a broad smile, Sŏ said, "Remember this man?"

"Yes, he's Korean too." The boy recognized the guide who had picked them up at the airport.

"That's right," said Sŏ, taking the boy's hand. "He's from way up north in Manchuria." His daughter took his other hand, and outside they went. The sky was murky with smog as usual, but to Sŏ it was as spiffy blue as could be.

"All right," said the guide as he started the van. "We're off to Waitan."

As Sŏ had expected, the sun was setting by the time they arrived. The afternoon heat had eased and it was perfect for a stroll.

"This is the heart of Shanghai," said Sŏ. "Look at the streets to the left and the streets to the right, with the river in the middle, and you can see the city's modern history—do you see what I mean?"

Putting her index finger to her lips thoughtfully, Sŏ's daughter stared at him as if to say, *Daddy, stop beating around the bush and just ask a straight-out question.*

"The buildings look different," his son ventured.

"That's right. They're different in shape, height, and size. The ones on the left side of the river are older, but on the right side they're modern, most of them built after the reforms. A hundred and seventy years ago, China was forced to establish diplomatic ties and open their ports to Western powers like England, France, and Germany. Shanghai was one of those ports. The left side was leased to foreigners, and the foreigners went on a building spree. A little out-of-the-way fishing port suddenly looked like a European city. Look how grand and handsome and sturdy those buildings are. Can you guess why they were built like that?" Sǒ looked expectantly at the children, and their mother gave them a bright smile.

"Obviously," said their daughter, "they expected to stay forever."

"Of course," chimed in their son.

"You're both right," said Sǒ. "That was their mentality. But after World War Two, they had to give up their benefits. Those buildings must be over a hundred years old. That river is the Huangpu, and across it to the east is the Pudong area of the city."

His wife frowned. "Why are the new buildings so tall—they're kind of intimidating. I thought we had overdevelopment, but this seems way worse."

"They consider it development, not overdevelopment. And like Mr. Chǒn said, other cities are copying Shanghai. The Chinese love anything huge, you know." Sǒ smiled sardonically.

"Is their infatuation with the US is as sick as ours? They must want to copy New York City. Who knows, maybe it will be worse here. Aren't people afraid the ground's going to cave in?"

"That's a sharp observation," said Sǒ. "According to the newspapers, some areas of the city are in fact settling. The bedrock can't support all the mega-buildings. But do they care? No, they keep right on building. I don't know whether they're being clueless or daring. They respond with their favorite saying, *mei guanxi, mei guanxi*—'none of their concern.' They sound so relaxed and worry-free, not like us."

The son wedged himself between his parents. "Daddy, why is the water so dark? And it smells like poop."

"Good question," said Sǒ. "Did you know China has two very long rivers, starting way up north and coming down to the south? The one farther north is the Huanghe, and the one to the south is the Yangzi. The river here is the end of the Yangzi. Want to hear a funny story? There's been a huge movement of farmers to the cities, especially here, the economic capital—they're looking for a better life. But because they're unskilled, they do manual labor. They're hired by the day. And *they're* the ones who built all those high-rises in the last twenty years. But because they're unskilled and poor, the city people call them hillbillies. The migrant workers, meanwhile, say the Shanghai people are living off *their* sewage and bath water. Do you get it? All those migrant workers followed the river here from the Sichuan countryside. So you have the right idea, son. All the Sichuan poop and bath water are in that river."

"*Waaa*, your gags are getting better, Dad," said Sǒ's daughter, covering her mouth in ladylike fashion and giggling.

"Can I pee in the river?" His son pretended to pull down his zipper.

"Sure—as long as you don't mind being locked up for two weeks." Sŏ laughed with the children, while his wife, through teary eyes, kept her blissful smile.

"Two weeks?" said their son, pouting. "Back home we just pay a little fine or the nice policeman lets you go."

"Just kidding, I made it up. Two weeks is the penalty for drinking and driving. I used to think that if you peed in the middle of this big city they'd treat it just as seriously. But actually nobody does anything about peeing and pooping in public here."

"What!" the two children screamed in unison. "Pooping too?"

"Yes. And not just in the megacities like Shanghai, but next to the highway, or in the truck parks—you can see a truck driver doing his business in between a couple of trucks. The police just look the other away."

"Pooping, not peeing?" their son exclaimed, while their daughter shuddered in disgust.

"They're long-distance drivers," said Sŏ. "What if they have a stomach problem—are they going to care who's watching?"

His wife nodded. "Actually, it makes sense."

"Yes. If you don't have an issue, then there's no issue—that's the way things work here."

"What's that supposed to mean?"

"It's an interesting concept, and one of the keys to understanding this society. Think about it. It's a matter of convenience: You want to make an issue out of something, you've got an issue; if you don't, then you don't."

Reciting what he had said, she smirked. "That *is* interesting. It's like a koan. There seem to be a lot of layers to this society—but it has its appeal."

"I'm finding it more fascinating the longer I'm here and the more I get the hang of the culture. I wasn't like that before, you know."

Their son drew near and looked up at his father with an innocent smile. "Dad, you're not just a medical doctor, you're a China doctor too. You know so much about everything here."

Sŏ gave the boy's ear a playful tug. "Oh, no. The China doctor is Mr. Chŏn. He knows a hundred times more than I do. This is all I know," he said, indicating the tip of his little finger.

"A hundred times more?" said his daughter. "Is there that much to know about China?"

"Sure. Maybe what Mr. Chŏn knows is a hundredth, or a thousandth, or a ten thousandth. You know how big this land is, and how many people live here?"

"Yes, we do," his son proudly announced. "We checked the Internet."

"Great—you did your homework. Now, how about Pudong next? It has a world-famous restaurant where we can see the city."

Again Sŏ linked hands with his children. His wife took their son's other hand

and four abreast they set off down the boulevard toward the bridge and the waiting van. Before he knew it Sŏ was humming the folksong "My home town in the mountains with the flowers blossoming." He was accompanied by his daughter's nasal voice, and when his son and wife joined in, they had a family chorus. The sunlight was retreating, and a thin mist rose, curtaining the riverfront area known as the Bund. Lights glinted on in the sweep of skyscrapers, heralding the famous night-light show. Through the Bund they walked, humming, the sky colored with the sunset. At the end of the boulevard they saw the van.

"Are you hungry?" Sŏ asked his family as the van drove off. "We're eating on the other side of the bridge." He was tempted to ask their impressions of Waitan, but thought better of it, recalling his daughter's pointed response earlier.

"That's the place." As they climbed out of the van Sŏ pointed out a tall structure. His son gaped at it. "That's weird."

"Isn't it? It looks like two ladders connecting two balls, and it's so high—is it a building, a tower, an alien ship? It's strange-looking all right. And way up at the top is where we're going to have dinner!"

Head craned back, his daughter said, "Daddy, I see it. Look, there's something sticking out. That's the tower, right?"

You tell me, you little smartie," said Sŏ, overjoyed at her perceptiveness.

"It's like the Namsan Tower in Seoul, maybe it's a TV tower," she said confidently.

"That is correct, miss!" he shouted, as uninhibited as the local people.

Sŏ's wife flinched in embarrassment. "Oh, *honey*."

"It's the landmark of Shanghai, the Dongfang Mingzhu."

"What does that mean?" his son asked.

"It means Pearl of Asia. Westerners built this area and that was their nickname for it. Do you know why it's a landmark? It was built with one hundred percent Chinese technology, and according to *The Guinness Book of World Records*, the elevators are the fastest in the world."

"How fast?" said his son eagerly.

"Forty seconds to the rooftop restaurant, and that's two hundred and sixty-three meters up."

"All that way in forty seconds?" the boy said, transfixed.

Sŏ's wife clutched her head. "I can't do it—I'm already feeling woozy."

Taking her arm, Sŏ said, "Honey, you'll be all right. I tried it and I was fine."

"Daddy," ventured their daughter, "did you say this cool building was all built by them?"

"That's right. Remember how long it took us to get where we are today? Forty years—starting in the 1970s. Well, China started ten years later, in the 1980s, and it only took them thirty years to catch up with us. Do you know why? Well, there are six and a half million Chinese students studying science, and another half million graduate students—the most in the world. Are you following me?"

"Not really. My brain's getting overloaded."

He patted her shoulder. "I'm sorry."

"So you did your homework for us," his wife chimed in.

"I tried, anyway. It's not easy being a daddy. I have to keep up with the kids, you know." He winked at her.

The elevator took off with the son keeping an eye on his father's watch. *Amazing!* Forty seconds was too long to hold his breath under water, but here in the elevator it passed in the blink of an eye.

"Wow!" he shouted as soon as the elevator came to a stop. "Forty seconds exactly. What do you think, sis?"

"So what?" said the girl. "This is nothing compared with launching a spaceship, right?" Only two years separated them but already she talked like a young adult.

How different their thought patterns, Sŏ told himself. Chalk it up to their age difference but also the different learning environment in grade school and middle school.

Through the windows of the revolving restaurant, the colorful fireworks brightened the deepening night sky. On all sides were high-rises galore, a sea of distinctive shapes and unusual colors competing for attention. The revolving restaurant, its motion almost indiscernible, was a large playground filled to capacity, a theater for the iridescent light show performed by the high-rises. It was all so enchanting.

Sŏ's son and daughter were entranced by the festive collage outside. As he watched them he felt his physical and mental ordeal of the past year melting away. Now he could enjoy the fruit of the hard work he had put in every day.

"Hey kids, the food is here. It comes in courses, so we can take our time and catch the view."

The children turned back to the table. His son took hold of his chopsticks. "I'm starving. Hey, it's awesome—look at the view."

"China's so different from what I thought," Sŏ's daughter murmured as she sampled the tea. "All the negative comments I've read aren't true. That forty-second elevator ride was actually awesome. And I *love* the view."

"Hey, kids, slow down," said Sŏ, "take your time chewing. That's important, especially when you're traveling."

"Here we go again," said Sŏ's son. "I haven't heard that one in a while."

His daughter flashed a smile. "I forgot, that's your table reminder number one."

"Isn't this restaurant too expensive?" whispered his wife.

Making sure the children weren't listening, Sŏ said with a frown, "Nothing is too good for our family, your highness."

"I'm sorry." Eyes reddening, she lowered her head.

It was almost ten when they returned to their hotel. "No squabbling in bed, all right?" Sŏ reminded the children.

"Dad," said his daughter. "He's not worth squabbling with, he's only a grade-school kid. Besides, I could knock him flat with one punch. But don't worry, we have separate beds."

His sleepy-eyed son didn't take the bait and simply waved good night.

"Honey, have you been getting the interest?" said his wife as she lay down beside him.

"Yes," he said, his arm around her. "Every month. Are you concerned?"

"No, just hoping everything goes well."

"We're seeing steady growth in the business. I think the investment is secure, so please don't lose any sleep over it."

"What a thoughtful man to give it to you, especially considering you're a foreigner."

"Don't be too grateful. He's doing it for his own benefit, first and foremost."

"Why is that?"

"They want to make sure I don't leave. There are plastic surgery clinics popping up everywhere, but they're not doing well—the skill level of the doctors isn't up to par. I've been approached by several other clinics. My partner knows that, so he has to take good care of me."

"I've never doubted your capability, but it makes me feel good you're in demand."

"Thanks, dear. Just be patient and soon we'll be over the hump."

"I know it's difficult being here, but I think you made a good decision."

"I agree."

They held each other close. It had been six months since they'd last seen each other, during the three-day Chunjie break.

"Daddy, I had a weird dream last night," said Sŏ's son, a plate heaped with food from the breakfast buffet sitting before him.

Sŏ hefted his coffee mug. "Want to let me in on it?"

"I was swimming in that poopy Huangpu River."

"Yuck!" said his sister. "You have such awful dreams." She pretended to pinch him.

Thank heaven he was sitting between them, Sŏ thought.

"Good for you," he chuckled. "It's your lucky day—a poop dream means you'll get some money!"

"A poop dream is as good as a dragon dream," said his wife. "We're going to have a great day." Yesterday's fatigue had disappeared from her cheery face and she looked rested.

"Mom, you too! You're pathetic, all of you. Do you hear anyone else talking about yucky dreams over their food? I can't eat anymore." So saying, she covered her mouth and gagged.

Sŏ winked at his son then said to his daughter, "I'm sorry. You know Koreans always like to interpret dreams. Anyway, let's talk about something that's clean and smells nice."

"You're so finicky," said his wife to the girl, a sour look on her face. "What's wrong with a good dream?"

"Dad, where are we going today?" said his son as he crawled into the van.

"You'll find out when we get there."

The van snaked through the back streets and, after pulling off a few death-defying stunts, arrived at Lu Xun Park.

"You know who Yun Ponggil is, right?" Sŏ asked as they emerged from the van. "The martyr?"

"Sure," said his son. "And Kim Ku too."

"Is this Hongkou Park?" asked the girl, already one step ahead of her father.

"That's my girl. Right you are. This is where Mr. Yun threw his bento-box bomb toward the Japanese." Buoyed by the children's interest, he spoke in an energetic voice, relieved he didn't have to explain the historical significance of the site.

Deep inside he had been anxious—what if they hadn't known? A few days earlier he'd tuned into an education special on a Korean network. A reporter was asking a student the meaning of the Samil holiday. Not knowing it referred to the March 1, 1919, Independence Movement, the student simply said Samil meant "three point one." Next an older student was asked the meaning of 8.15. With no hesitation he answered "eight point one five" rather than the August 15, 1945, Liberation Day. The reporter was flabbergasted and repeated the question. "I don't understand," said the student. "Is it some kind of sports event?" The reporter then asked, "Don't you take history at your school?" "Sure," said the boy, "but we're getting less history and more English." The reporter turned to a female student. "Japan refers to Tokto as Takeshima and claims it's theirs—what are your views on that?" The student backpedaled in embarrassment, saying, "I kind of forgot—I'm studying for the college entrance exam, and history is an elective now. Sorry." The program concluded with students from the US, France, Germany, and Japan saying they studied history three hours a week.

Sŏ was left with a lump in his throat. He felt like he'd just discovered his heart had a leaky valve. Because of his medical training, he himself had spent minimal time studying history. Still, he worried about the pathetic level of history knowledge displayed by the younger generation. He was prompted to revisit some of the fundamental questions of life. *We Koreans, who are we anyway?*

Curtailing history classes to accommodate more English classes and changing history to an elective meant stunting the souls of their children. How many other countries did that? His lingering despair had prompted him to bring his son and daughter to this park.

"So how did you learn about Yun Ponggil? At school?"

"No," said his daughter. "He's in the Biography of Great People series—Mom bought it for us."

"I'm reading them too," reported his son. "If I don't, Mom gives me a knuckle."

"Thank you, honey," said Sŏ. "Don't go easy on him."

"Hey, Dad!" shouted his son, making a what-gives gesture. "I thought you were my pal."

Sŏ pointed to the sign. "You know, the name of this park was changed from Hongkou to Lu Xun when the new China was established."

"What does Lu Xun mean?" asked his daughter.

"It's the name of Chairman Mao's favorite writer."

"He must be pretty cool if they named this park after him. Have you read anything by him?"

"Yes, something called *The True Story of Ah Q.*"

"Was it fun?"

"No, it's kind of heavy. But it made me think."

"What do you mean, heavy?"

"Maybe you can read it some day in college when you're thinking back on today. It might be more fun then."

"Fair enough."

"Let's go inside. We can see Lu Xun's tomb and a statue of him."

"So that's why they changed the name of the park."

"There's also a memorial hall. This big park is devoted to him."

"Wow, he *must* be a great writer. I'm definitely going to read him."

"Good for you," he said, smoothing her hair. How gratifying to have a conversation like this with a daughter he still regarded as a little girl. Once again he felt proud of her. And—surprise—of himself for planting Lu Xun in her mind.

The immediate vicinity of the statue was well maintained, different from other public places Sŏ had seen here. The writer evidently commanded great respect from his people.

Gazing thoughtfully at the statue, his daughter said, "Oooh, scary."

"Maybe stern rather than scary." As soon as the words were out of his mouth he felt himself blush. It was time he stopped correcting her.

They walked down a path, stopping at a sign reading Plum Garden.

"This is the martyr's memorial. Right here is where he threw the bomb. How about a photo?" Standing in front of a near-derelict two-story Korean-style structure, they were photographed by an obliging passerby.

The display at the memorial was crude and the items in the gift shop little more than trinkets. The city was obviously more interested in collecting entry fees and peddling souvenirs than keeping up the site. For each of the children Sŏ bought a plastic paperweight bearing an image of the martyr and the building. "Here. You can set it on your books or your notebooks."

"Dad, it's kind of messed up," said his son.

His daughter scowled. "Yeah, what's our government doing?"

"Hey, this is China, remember? There's only so much we can do to change things. Our government had to ask several times just to get this little place set up, back in 1994. Before that there was nothing here to remember Mr. Yun by. So we should feel thankful."

Paperweights in hand, the children moved on, pouting. Even their sullenness looked proud and cute to Sŏ.

Their next destination was the site of the Korean Provisional Government during the period of Japanese colonial rule. The children greeted it in silence. Sŏ interpreted their reaction as shock and let it sink in, pleased that he had fulfilled another educational duty.

"That sucks," said Sŏ's son as the family emerged from their tour of the building. "It's worse off than the other place."

"Hard to believe it used to be our government building," the daughter muttered.

"Well, we didn't have a country back then. At least this place gave Mr. Yun a base to carry out his heroic act. Right? Anyways, this is the end of our tour. What do you say we get a cold drink?" Sŏ scurried around and found a place for them to sit.

In the afternoon, he guided them to the Shanghai Museum and the Jade Buddha Temple. At the temple the children were fascinated by the foot-and-a-half-long, finger-thick sticks of incense lit by worshipers, the pungent blue smoke spreading all over. The jade Buddhas were less impressive.

The following morning it was off to the Ocean Aquarium, the last stop on the tour. The children delighted in Asia's largest aquarium. The scale and variety of ocean life seemed to win over both domestic and foreign tourists.

Sŏ bade them farewell at the hotel, where he had welcomed them just two days earlier. He had to get back to his patients. His wife and children would fly to Beijing and join a tour group.

"Goodbye, Daddy!"

"Dad, take care!"

The van was out of sight, but the voices kept whirling in Sŏ's ear. *That's right, I'm your daddy!* He moved on leaden feet, mouth clamped shut to suppress his grief.

10. Tenacious Temperament

The train spewed its passengers at Taishan Station after a three-and-a-half-hour trip from Beijing. Buses were tortoises in comparison, taking up to twelve hours even though the highway was now 95 percent paved. Despite condemnation of the red ink dripping from the colossal construction budget, the high-speed rail project had gone full steam ahead, the government touting the people's thunderous welcome of this new transportation link and guaranteeing the public huge long-term benefits.

Beijing's investment in the project came with another, ubiquitous benefit. Civil engineering projects had as much one-hand-washes-the-other potential as apartment projects. And with the new rail system, once you accounted for the 10 percent of the budget that ended up greasing the wheels, you had a safe fishery whose stocks were easily harvested. Passengers didn't have to know the inside story of this public works project to appreciate the cataclysmic speed of the new rail line. They were grateful to their government—even if the fares were exorbitant.

The passengers scrambled to get off. Boarding and leaving public transportation was always a shoving match. Lining up meekly would only get you pushed to the back. The operative principle was instant, showy gratification for oneself and cruel indifference to others.

"Ultramodern technology and chaos," grumbled Yu, the branch manager of Xian POSCO. "What a mix!" Watching the frantic exodus toward the rear exit, he prudently decided to wait before retrieving his overnight bag.

Kim Hyŏn'gon smiled uneasily. "A familiar scene—and it's not going away anytime soon."

Yu shook his head. "Not in our lifetime, anyway. It's been like this the fifteen years I've been in country."

Fifteen years? thought Kim. Which meant Yu had spent half his working life here. By now he knew all the ins and outs of the local business culture. And at the end of the year he was retiring.

"That's us thirty years ago," he said. "We're a bit more civilized now."

"Yes, I remember what a mess it used to be. The difference is, our government and the media campaigned for fixes—how much of that do you see here?"

"Right, it's all about development."

"And so the Western press drops the hammer on them—'uncivilized country,' 'hopeless society'..."

"And 'it's a minor miracle they're G2, and a major miracle if they make G1.'"

"But China's G2 because it has a bottomless pool of cheap labor—cultural level has nothing to do with it."

"They're looking through a peephole: if you aren't democratic you're barbaric."

"These tourists are well-to-to, but look at them—no public etiquette," said Yu. "Let's make our move." With that, he fetched his bag.

"At least now we know how famous Taishan is," sighed Kim.

"Getting to the top of this mountain is number one on their wish list. And number two is paying tribute to Chairman Mao, right? This crowd is about to spill over the edge, and we're adding to it." Yu smiled ruefully.

"People hate emperors and kings but swarm to the mountain where those same rulers paid tribute to heaven—go figure."

"There's another reason," said Yu with an impish grin.

Kim looked quizzical, then snapped his fingers. "You live an extra ten years if you climb to the top."

"You saw right through me," Yu let out a burst of laughter.

But Kim sensed despair in that laugh. "What's so funny?"

"Wanting to live another ten years without earning it," said Yu forlornly.

"You're too humble..." Leaving on this trip, Kim had never imagined confronting the despondency of a man facing retirement—was Yu suggesting his life had been meaningless?

"This is a special bonus," the president of China operations had announced at headquarters in Beijing. "In recognition of your extraordinary achievements in Xian." The "special bonus" turned out to be a six-month paid vacation for Yu, a personal gift from the president. "You'll have plenty of time to unwind—enjoy yourself."

Company men tended to think of retirement as a death sentence—a severed relationship with an organization, alienation from society, removal from the labor force and consignment to the trash heap of humanity. It was like being castrated. Kim knew of retirees who had sunk deep into depression.

Yu was about to cross that watershed. What could Kim say? He empathized with Yu's mixed feelings—he himself would face that same threshold in ten years. Was there any company man who wouldn't feel remorseful receiving this death sentence? How many could resist the emptiness facing Yu?

"I've always looked at you as a winner." Kim murmured.

"I'm just being facetious," said Yu with forced cheer. "We're all greedy—we might be a hundred years old but we don't want to die. And even if the retirement age went up to seventy or eighty we might still want to work. So never mind me and let's have some fun, our first and last trip—deal?"

At the mention of 'last trip' Kim felt a lump in his throat.

"Mr. Yu. Speaking of last trips, how about I take you on another trip *after* you retire? There are so many places to see here. We've been to many of them but it was always on business."

"I'd have to say thanks but no thanks. Though the offer itself means as much to me as that second trip."

"Excuse me?"

"I'm very grateful to you, but my policy is, once a man's gone from the company, you don't want him hovering around your desk. I'll tell you a story. The president of the China office of one of the *chaebŏl* retires. One day he decides to go back and pay a visit. He marches in like a king, expecting a royal fanfare, and guess what? He gets the cold shoulder! One guy yells at him, 'What are you doing here?' Turns out this guy had been on the receiving end of a very public scolding from him. So our former president scurries out with his tail between his legs. All he wanted was to re-connect with the guys as he set up a new business. The lesson is, once you leave, don't look back—you're already history."

"Sir..." was all Kim could manage. Yu's stark post-retirement policy, the loneliness he'd experienced as top man, was a wake-up call.

"You already helped me out in a big way," said Yu. "When I was transferred to Xian so near my retirement, I was so upset I didn't want to talk with anyone. Xian?

I was boiling mad and depressed, all at the same time. Then you came along and all of a sudden admin was a breeze—you got the ball rolling and brought in results beyond our imagination. The word got back to headquarters, and now they're calling me home. I can't thank you enough. Plus, I have you as a travel companion!" Yu took Kim's hands in his own.

Kim could only mumble an inarticulate reply as he closed his hands about Yu's.

And here they were now at Dai Temple, where the emperors had worshiped the gods of heaven and earth, the temple for which Taishan was best known. The first emperor to let heaven know of his deeds was Qin Shi Huangdi and he was succeeded by seventy-five emperors of thirty-six dynasties.

Did people dream of climbing the mountain itself, or was their goal to bow and pray and light incense for the gods of heaven and earth at this sacred place, hoping for prosperity as had the emperors? Kim wasn't sure. Why not both?

"Incredible." Yu marveled at the temple's gigantic stone gate, which performed double duty, fending off evil spirits and calamities as well as proclaiming the splendor of the site.

"According to the brochure," said Kim, "it's the most majestic and beautiful gate ever built."

"They might be right. Look how delicate the carvings are, and that stone looks so hard. The people who did that work..." Looking up, Yu craned his head back until Kim thought he would fall over.

"Their talent, the execution, it's marvelous." Kim too had bent so far back it strained his voice.

Before the gate stood four stone lions so lifelike they seemed poised to leap up roaring. The columns and crosspieces, rising ten times the height of a person, were a profusion of elegant carvings. The two men marveled at the roof. Reinforced with a second layer, it was majestic and opulent but deftly fashioned—there was nothing crude or stodgy about it. The artisans had incised the stone with as much life and precision as if they were working with wood.

"This alone is worth the trip!" A smile spread across Yu's face as he squinted at the structure.

"I think I agree with the brochure about 'the most beautiful' part," said Kim.

"Can you guess what I was planning to do after retirement?"

Kim waited silently for the announcement.

"Instead of going off to Europe I was thinking of sticking around—plenty to see here. There's just one minor problem." He grinned wryly.

"Problem?"

"I'm too healthy. What if I live past eighty? If I spend all my savings on travel—even though it's cheaper here—I'll be spending myself out of house and home. I'll be out on the streets by the time I die."

"I see..." Again Kim fell silent. He'd never really considered the savings part of the equation.

"I've worked in the US and it's a big country too but you won't see such treasures there. It took years of polluted air and fake food, but finally my eyes are opening to the real China. I feel like the schoolyard dog learning to read the primer! This country is a treasure chest."

"Like they say, the past lives on in Xian, the present in Beijing, and the future in Shanghai, right? I'm thankful I ended up in Xian. It gave me a new appreciation for Chinese culture and the artisans who never get credit for it."

"Well aren't you a deep one. We just keep to our cubicles, don't we—never get to know one another, or even talk much. It's sad." Yu produced a hollow chuckle.

"True enough," said Kim. No wonder you couldn't always stay friends with your co-workers once you quit. Working for a company was like taking a train toward a common destination, but each person got off at a different stop.

But now that they were out of their cubicles, Yu was positively chirpy. "Qin Shi Huangdi came all the way here from Xian. Imagine his poor, suffering retainers."

"The dynamo of tyranny. He got to rattle along in a carriage on dirt roads, but his courtesans were on foot—ouch! That's despotic."

"Why would the people in a socialist country continue to blindly worship the emperors who oppressed their ancestors? You wouldn't catch us doing that."

"Maybe then it was the awe that people felt, and now it's power and authority."

"After fifteen years here I say it's stupid to try to know, and even more frivolous to *say* you know."

Kim mulled over this last statement, thinking he should get to know Yu better after the man retired.

They came next to the majestic wall of hand-molded gray brick that surrounded the Hall of Heaven, the twenty-four-acre enclosure where the emperors had worshiped the gods. Passing through several small buildings, they arrived at Tiankuang Hall, the main structure, where the son of heaven had knelt to pray to the gods. Outside was a small structure roofed in bronze in which an urn sent puffs of blue from dozens of large red incense sticks.

The incense gave off the acrid smell of smoke—no delicate fragrance here. Kim pointed to the urn. "Look at those sticks—they're huge!"

He drew close to the urn.

"Ten times larger than usual. How odd."

"They look like upside-down baseball bats."

Yu frowned at the smoke.

"The manufacturer must be a happy man. I'll bet ten times thicker means ten times pricier."

"You've got a quick brain," Yu chuckled.

Two women lit thick sticks as gold as the stars on the PRC flag and placed them in the urn.

Guessing the color was associated with the dragon, and in turn the emperor, Kim asked them if there was something special about gold-colored sticks.

"Special as in ten times more expensive," one of the women boasted. Her fleshy skin and jaunty dress smelled of money.

"Which means it costs—"

"I got them from that monk over there, he said they come with a sure-fire blessing. He wanted eight hundred but I got him down to five hundred." Then she considered Kim. "What's it to you?"

"Just that you worked a good price," said Kim. He beckoned Yu. "Are you in the market for a sure-fire heavenly blessing?"

"That's pretty sly."

"Salesmen have to sell. And to sell we have to use our yap."

"My hat's off to Chinese salesmanship—little leaguer baseball bats for incense, gold wrapping for a higher price, esteemed monks doing the sales. Welcome to the land of the money craze."

"Five hundred *yuan* would buy five hundred meals for a migrant worker, but it's a penny for a parvenu. There are always people who can air out the soft deep pockets of the rich."

"Capitalism in action. What do you say we call it an evening?" Yu yawned loudly as he stretched.

Kim smiled. He couldn't imagine his companion acting so carefree in the middle of Seoul.

The next morning they got off to an early start, hoping to hike up the mountain and return by afternoon.

"Do you remember how many steps it is?" asked Yu as they set out from their hotel.

Kim checked their brochure. "Seven thousand, four hundred and twelve."

"No way can I do that—knees are too creaky."

"And who wants to walk up a mountain on manmade steps?"

So they settled on an option mentioned in the brochure—a taxi to the next village, and then a bus and a cable car, leaving only a two-hour hike to the top, as opposed to six hours entirely on foot.

From the bus Kim looked out onto a landscape of rock interspersed with scraggly-looking trees. Why weren't there more of them, considering people had been coming here for 2,200 years? And look how they held onto life, roots extending into the tiniest of cracks in the rock. He could almost hear the hardy trees screaming, *How weak and fragile you humans are!*

The bus climbed a precarious hillside. Boulders were everywhere, the road an obstacle course. Higher up, considering the expansive view, Kim said, "You'd have to be incredibly determined to carve out a road like this—and a daredevil temperament wouldn't hurt."

"For sure there's nothing the Chinese can't do. But in terms of engineering Taishan can't really compare with the Great Wall and the Grand Canal." Yu shook his head in awe.

For the passengers it was harum-scarum time as the bus huffed and puffed its way over a succession of steep passes. For the driver, humming along with the ear-numbing tunes blasting from the radio, it was show time.

The cable car departed from the Midway Gate of Heaven. Having survived the hair-rising bus ride, Kim and Yu were seized with a new fear as, airborne in the cable car, they climbed steeply past the boulder outcrops: *What if it's not safe?* In a society where food could be both fake and unhealthy, was a cable car reliable?

As the car lurched higher, the view opened to the far horizon. For Kim it was incredibly beautiful. The great temple with the exquisite gate they had visited the day before shrank to a mere dot, then disappeared. He was reminded of astronauts reporting that from outer space they could see the great rivers of Earth, but only one man-made structure—the Great Wall. The rowdy media coverage of this discovery was a shot in the arm for the Chinese; the world viewed China in a new light, and Qin Shi Huangdi was promoted from tyrant to holy emperor. Alas, the claim was shaken by a Chinese astronaut, a scientist no less, who said that the Great Wall was *not* visible, at least to him. He must have looked long and hard, thought Kim. In the presence of nature, enclosed in the Taishan cable car, Kim realized anew how trivial human civilization was.

"That *shijo*, how does it start?" Yu asked fretfully, tapping his forehead with the knuckle of his index finger. "Long time no sing."

"A *shijo* about Taishan?"

"Yes, it starts with Taishan."

"The one that goes, 'Tall as Taishan may be, it is still beneath heaven'?" Kim sang softly.

'That's the one!" Yu looked about sheepishly to see if anyone had noticed.

"And the next line is ..."

"Come on," Yu said to himself, frowning, and the next moment his face brightened. "Got it—'Climb and climb, the summit remains distant, all one can do is look up and lament how tall it is.'" Kim joined in at the end.

"Here we are on Taishan reciting this *shijo*!" Yu laughed in jubilation.

"Let's hear it for two cultured businessmen. This is something to remember."

The car arrived at a platform swarming with people. Some had overnighted at one of the nearby inns and were waiting to go down. Did they believe the God of Heaven would bless them more if they slept closer to Heaven and the summit of Taishan? Kim wondered.

From here the Heavenly Path led to the summit. Looking up at the unobstructed 1,500-meter-high peak, Kim savored the beauty of this realm of the gods.

To the left of the path was a dense cluster of eateries, shops, and inns. Wherever you went there were always people looking to grab you, thought Kim. Touts crowded in front of the shops and eateries, their shouts echoing from the mountainside:

"Rest here. Cold drinks."

"Rest here. Blessings from the God of Heaven."

"Please come in! May the goddess Bixia bless you!" Bixia was the goddess of the mountain, the daughter of the God of Heaven.

"How about a cold drink?" said Kim. "It's still early for a meal."

"Sounds good. We have plenty of time."

"Any suggestions?" said Kim, scanning the surroundings.

"They're all pretty much the same...."

Kim smirked. "Then we might as well get a blessing from the God of Heaven."

Yu nodded with a chuckle. "You know what they say about a good sales pitch."

"What would you care for?" said Kim as he flipped through a grimy menu.

"It's kind of muggy. How about Tsingtao—that's about as genuine as we're going to find here."

"The price sure is genuine—it's robbery," said Kim, gaping at the figure. "I know we're high up, but still..."

"It's a golden opportunity for price gouging," said Yu, motioning to Kim to order.

They drank the cold, smooth-tasting beer straight from the bottle. For the moment all was forgotten.

"Our blessing from heaven," said Yu.

"Best beer I've had in China," said Kim, wiping his mouth with a grand gesture.

Just then one of the touts, a man with a potbelly, came inside and shouted, "There you are! You're late, and that's bad for our business."

"Damn—it—all—what—are—you—bitching—about—what—did—I—do—wrong?" The target of the scolding—a man with a shoulder pole—was still panting from his exertions. Dripping with sweat, he looked like he'd just climbed out of a river.

"One of the guys who brings up supplies," said Yu.

Kim's eyes darted toward the man. "How much do you think they pay him?"

"A laborer?" Yu shook his head.

"He toted stuff all the way up here. I guess that's why the beer's so expensive." Kim considered his empty bottle.

"I want you here earlier tomorrow," said the man with the big belly. "The later you get here, the worse the food tastes. Here." He stuck out a twenty-*yuan* note.

The sweat-soaked laborer snatched the bill. "Thank you!" And then he disappeared.

"Twenty *yuan*!" Yu stared saucer-eyed at Kim.

Kim repeated the amount.

"I don't believe it."

"Ripping off a laborer. That's too much," Kim tutted.

Beer finished, they left. They had just started up the path when they discovered the man curled up to the side, eyes closed and listless. Worried, Kim drew near and nudged him. The man's eyelids opened reluctantly.

"Hello, sir. I am a Hanguoren. We saw you back there. Could we buy you something to drink? And I would like to ask you a question."

"Korean, you say?" Wiping his sweaty face, the man looked at Kim. "Your Chinese is very good."

"Well, I have lived here for ten years. Can we go somewhere and get beer?"

"But the way I look …" The man's eyes dropped and he shook his head.

"Just give him beer money, that's what he means." Without Kim noticing, Yu had joined him.

"I see. Then I will give you money for beer and you can have it later. But first may we talk?" Kim tried gently to help the man up.

"Talk about what?" said the man, still wary.

"Did you actually pack that load from all the way down there?"

"I sure did. One step at a time." The man spoke as deliberately as he had to the tout, but was no longer as cautious.

"That is more than seven thousand steps," said Kim, aghast.

"Yes. I'm not a bird, so I have to touch down one step at a time." A typical Chinese description.

"And he pays you only twenty *yuan*."

"Only? No, it's much better."

"Much better? What do you mean?"

"Four or five years ago it was ten *yuan*."

"Would you not be better off doing something else for work?"

"No. A farmer like me? Can't read or write? No skill? This is best. There is work every day. You go to a big city, everything is expensive, maybe no work for several days—I might starve to death."

"How many trips a day do you make?"

"Just one. Half a day coming up, half a day going down, and the day's gone."

"What do you think about, usually?"

"Hmm … well, I'm not sure," he said, tilting his head in puzzlement. "Nothing, I guess." He smiled innocently.

"I'm sure it's like he says, a step at a time," said Yu. "In a kind of trance. Like a marathoner—once you get through the pain, you kind of blank out and just run."

The questions kept coming to Kim. "Can you make a living?"

"Yes. One day's earnings takes care of the three of us for two days. My wife also works a little."

"But it's demanding work, isn't it?"

"It's better than dying. And there's this beautiful view." He smiled broadly, revealing yellowed teeth.

"Are there many of you doing this work?"

"Hundreds, I'd say."

"You come all the way up and go all the way down for twenty *yuan*? That seems too little. What if all of you together asked for better pay?"

"I know. But even a little is better than nothing. My grandpa had to work and he never got paid at all." Another idiotic grin. He was so Chinese, thought Kim. He endured his hardship and pain in silence, and his patience was tenacious. There you had it, the Chinese temperament.

"Thank you for your time, sir. Here's some money for your beer." Kim offered him forty *yuan*.

"Oh no, that's too much!" Startled, the man pulled back.

"Not really. That is what the restaurant bilked us for one bottle." Kim managed to place the money in his palm.

"No. Even ten is too much." The man kept shaking his head and retreating.

"Do you know how we were able to meet you? It is thanks to the God of Heaven. This money is from him, and I am the messenger. So you can thank the God of Heaven." Kim stared at the man, wondering if his words had sunk in.

But the man was at a loss.

"You have a long way to go, so please take it." Kim closed the man's hand over the money.

"Oh, *hen ganxie*." How grateful he was. His eyes had filled with tears.

"I'm impressed," said Yu, making a wry face as they resumed their climb. "It's not too late to change your job, you know."

"To what?" Kim stared at Yu.

"You brought the God of Heaven down. That's more than even a writer could do. Have you ever thought of writing?"

"A writer? Oh, I see what you mean. Well, being a salesman," said Kim, scratching his head sheepishly, "I've done plenty of improv."

"What an eye-opener. For a lousy thirty-six hundred *wŏn* they climb seven thousand steps up and seven thousand steps down, every single day! These people are rubber tough…Where else in the world could you find someone like that?" With a shudder Yu shook his head.

"I couldn't believe it myself—that's why I wanted to talk with him. And what he said about hard labor being better than dying, and low pay being better than no pay at all—that really hit me. How can he be so optimistic and adaptable? It's probably something they're born with—and the reason China can handle its problems."

"I like your outlook. Calm and serious. You should stay in-country till you've solved these riddles. All right, up we go."

It was three p.m. when they arrived back at Taishan Station.

"I really enjoyed that," said Yu. "You're in charge now, and I'm sure you'll make the most of it. So until next time…" He extended his hand.

"Please take care, sir," said Kim in a choked voice.

He felt tears well up as he watched Yu turn and disappear into the crowd. Yu must have been feeling the same way. He would soon leave Beijing for the home office back in Seoul. Kim wondered what Yu would do in retirement. Well, he had plenty of time left to figure that out. Did retirement really mean rejection, alienation, and separation? Or was it a second life, a creative rest, self-cultivation? *I guess that's up to me.* Soon enough he would confront what Yu was facing. Would he be ready? The prospect demoralized him—where was the long-term plan for his well-being? Well, retirement was still distant—best to focus on the here and now. And with this boost to his spirits he made his way toward the platform for Shanghai.

Once on the train he took out his cell phone. "I'm about to leave Taishan."

"All right," said Chŏn at the other end. "I'll be waiting."

Steeped in fatigue, Kim slumped down into his seat and closed his eyes. Gentle ripples of sleep washed over him.

There was Yu, a tattered beggar, kicking and screaming, trying to get into the office. A gaggle of smartly dressed men shoved him out the door and down onto the hall floor. Yu rose and yelled himself hoarse. "Where's the branch manager! I want to see Mr. Kim!" Kim pretended not to hear him and devoted himself to his drink, snickering along with the pretty woman across from him. *What are you doing here?* he was thinking. *You said you wouldn't be coming around anymore. Look at you, you ought to be ashamed of yourself. Is this your idea of retirement?*

His eyes snapped open. *What the…* Had that been him in the dream? Rubbing his face, he looked outside. Fast and powerful, the train sped toward Shanghai. But the dream stayed with Kim, leaving a bad taste. Suddenly he wondered if Yu could afford to retire. He hoped so. *They give you a retirement seminar, don't they?* Kim tried to erase Yu from his mind. He had a nagging feeling that as a result of his own promotion, Yu was being pushed out early. He'd wanted that branch manager's position, but now it was coming back to haunt him.

"So you're branch manager—congratulations!" said Chŏn.

Kim had barely finished breaking the news. "Actually I'm acting branch manager—it doesn't become official until he retires."

"Come on, Mr. Modest—if the tiger's gone that makes you the king. Remember what I told you about misfortune turning into a blessing? Anyway, I'm excited for you." Chŏn gave him series of double thumbs-up.

"And it wouldn't have happened if not for you. The managers in Beijing, at headquarters back home, they were all sure I'd screw up again. I can't tell you how…" *Thankful* was coming next, but it didn't do justice to the scale of his gratitude, so he left it unspoken.

"It was the least I could do to make amends for my part in that fiasco. It really bothered me when they dumped you out in the country. Remember how happy I was to catch up with you in Xian? I can still taste those sweet persimmons we had at the emperor's tomb."

"Actually I'm not here to brag about my promotion." Kim shifted in his seat.

"Excuse me?" said Chŏn, suddenly on guard. Is there something—"

"No no, nothing like that. I can't remember if I've updated you, but the university back home gave us the go-ahead on the branch hospital in Xian. And I'm supplying half the medical equipment with the help of my *guanxi*—he's been with me ever since we hired his nephew. And the university wanted a strong public presence there. So it all worked out. I wish we'd snagged the entire order, but we can't complain about half. So I'm wondering if you can handle the supply for me?"

"Pardon? Me?" was all Chŏn could manage. Kim would draw no personal benefit from Chŏn's involvement, which meant he was doing it for Chŏn's sake. Supplying half the medical equipment for a general hospital…. Chŏn did the math—he was speechless.

"I'm off to meet the reps." Kim brushed off his hands in a that's-that gesture and rose. But that was as far as he got.

"Mr. Kim!" Chŏn grabbed him in a bear hug.

PART THREE

1. The Triad

"One hundred million a year," declared Li Wanxing, stabbing the air with his index finger. Li was holding forth at a bar in Guangzhou, his audience Jacques Cabang, Cabang's interpreter, and a hostess for each of the two principals.

Cabang frowned. "A hundred million?" He glared at the interpreter. "Did you get that correct?"

"Sir, I interpreted correctly," said the man, miffed.

"All right," said Cabang. He gestured the interpreter closer. "Can we ask him again to make sure?" He turned back to Li. "Are you saying we can sell a hundred million a year?"

Li leaned back, glass of wine in hand. "I guarantee it—trust me."

"Within a year! Not five years. That is a very large number." Cabang kept shaking his head.

"I'm saying a hundred million at the bare minimum. If we're lucky, two or three hundred million." Li's tone bordered on arrogance.

"You must be intoxicated. I cannot believe it. Twenty million maybe, but two to three hundred million?"

"Cabang," said Li with raised eyebrows, "have I ever misled you?"

"No, not once." Cabang tensed up.

"Did I ever make a bad business decision?"

"Not with me."

"So, will you trust me or not?"

"I know I should," Cabang faltered, "but it is such a huge number…"

"What do I have to do to convince you? Don't you get the figures?"

"Mr. Li. Do you know how big France is? The population is only fifty million. That is a very large market, but two to three hundred million in sales? I cannot fathom it. I hope you understand what I am trying to say."

"Fifty million—that's all? Then how can France…" Li swallowed *act like a stuck-up superpower*. "All right, let's see if we can get *you* to understand. In your country you don't have—well, do you know the term *shousheng*?" To the interpreter he said, "Hey, explain to him."

"The Chinese zodiac, twelve animals," said the interpreter with a nervous gesture, "one of which is tied to the year of a person's birth—"

"Oh, I know," Cabang interrupted. "Dragon, dog, rooster, cow, pig…right?" he said, ticking them off on his fingers.

"Hmm," Li murmured, "impressive. And he starts with the dragon…" And then out loud, "1.4 billion of us were born under that *shousheng*. So, how many babies were born under each animal?" He looked into Cabang's blue eyes.

"1.4 billion divided by twelve, that makes 120 million…no, that is not quite right…let me start over, 110 million—"

"Is he brain-dead or what!" Li barked at the interpreter. "Oh fuck, just tell him a hundred million, period!" Li was not one to get hung up on details. After a sip of wine he was back on the offensive. "May I ask one more thing?" The interpreter made a sour face and fought back the urge to suggest that Li not be condescending. "At Chunjie we like to give people born in that animal year a set of red underwear, for repelling evil spirits and blessing them with prosperity. Are you aware of that?"

"Yes, of course."

"Excellent. One more question." The interpreter silently cried out, *Quit while you're ahead, before he pulls the plug on you*, but duly interpreted. "Can you guess how many pairs of those red underwear we sell?" It was then that the interpreter realized why Li was circling the issue.

Cabang came to the same conclusion. "I see; you want to explain the reasoning behind your belief in sales figures of two to three hundred million. But I would still say one hundred million." Cabang celebrated his alacrity with a mouthful of wine.

"Aha! You got it. Which definitely qualifies you to be my partner."

The interpreter phrased it as follows: "That is correct. I am happy my partner has such a quick mind." Why risk offending Cabang with *qualifies you to be my partner*?

"But…"

"But what? Anything you want to know…" Satisfied that Cabang was coming around to his way of thinking, Li had a sip of wine. As he reached for a snack, his hostess deftly popped a morsel into his mouth.

"What I am trying to say," said Cabang, "is that selling a hundred million pairs of red underwear is not the same as selling two or three hundred million, is it?"

"You still don't get it. Let me ask you this." Li straightened as the interpreter inwardly moaned, *Please don't.*

"Mr. Cabang, can you guess what every Chinese lady wants most to hear?"

"Obviously, that she is pretty or beautiful. Even if she is ugly."

"Wrong."

"Excuse me?"

"I said you're wrong!" Li barked.

Cabang bristled. "I think not. That is the universal wish of women. From Alaska to Africa."

"Cabang, you think you know about China because you've been in and out of here for a few years, but you don't know shit. You're wasting your time here."

"Pardon me? Did you say 'wasting'?" The Frenchman's ill humor showed on his face.

"What they want to hear most is, 'I hope you make a lot of money,' or, 'You look like you're rich.' Then they can look pretty, beautiful, sexy—whatever. Your 'universal wish' does not work in China. Remember that."

"No. How could that be ..." Cabang's eyes darted to the fetching maiden beside him and then to the one next to Li.

"Why don't you ask your companion, then?" said Li, gesturing with his chin toward the woman.

"All right. What would you rather hear," said Cabang to the young woman, "'I hope you make a lot of money' or 'You're pretty'?"

"Make a lot of money, of course!" She sounded like an answering machine.

Cabang turned to Li's companion. "How about you, honey?"

She replied instantly. "Money, of course."

"So, now you understand why we have the potential to sell two to three hundred million?" Li's gaze told Cabang he thought he was helpless.

"It still does not add up. I cannot imagine we would sell that many in *ten* years, much less one." He shook his head more forcefully.

"Cabang. Stop thinking about the population of France—this is China. Can you guess how many of the 1.4 billion of us wish to be rich?"

"All of you, I am sure. No one dislikes money, and everyone in the world wants it." Cabang realized he was starting to sound like a grade schooler.

"That's it. We won't count the little kids, but the rest want to get their hands on money till the day they die. It's the best gift. Now you understand."

"Well, it makes sense now that I think about it." But Cabang was reluctant to commit himself.

"Then how about this—we ditch the two-to-three-hundred-million deal and go with twenty to thirty million. Are you interested?"

"Definitely!" came Cabang's voice, as if springing out unbidden.

"Then we're agreed. And if we can't sell them all, I'll buy them back, with cash."

"Wh—what?" said Cabang, stuttering in surprise. "Are you se—serious?"

"Do you want to watch while the lawyer writes up the contract?"

"If you are so confident your plan will work, why do you want to do business with *us*?"

"You really don't know? It's your *brand*. You're known all over the world. Remember, when I tag our product with your name, even if it's *ten* times more expensive, everyone will covet it. It's the dark side of the human mind—why not take advantage? *That's* why I want a partnership with you."

"I finally see what you mean. That is a stupendous venture indeed," said Cabang. "But how did you develop the idea?"

"I have to confess it's not all mine. I learned some time ago that Koreans here like to give gifts to their business connections. The gift doesn't have to be all that much, but the person on the receiving end always looks delighted. Goal achieved. For example, a Cartier coin purse with a hundred *yuan* in it. The purse means you're going to be rich, and the money is like a good-luck charm—I heard that's a Korean custom. Can you imagine—we Chinese get the gift, plus we know what the money's for. Everybody's wearing a huge grin. Besides, it's not any old Cartier coin purse, it's a *red* one. Chinese love Cartier as much as Louis Vuitton and Gucci—they're all so visible. And you know we're in love with the color red. Ingenious, isn't it?"

"To be sure. But would you not say we are off to a late start?"

"That's what I thought you'd say. Look, I'm not an idiot. I wouldn't be suggesting it if I didn't think it were possible. There's one little detail that decides everything—the color of the purse." Li paused for wine.

"What about the color?"

"Hey—give me those," Li ordered the interpreter, who produced two gaudy, palm-sized items, a coin purse and a booklet with a plastic cover.

"Can you guess which color we go for?" said Li, his eyes interrogating Cabang.

"This one, of course," said Cabang, pointing to the small book.

"That's correct. And you know this person, right?"

"Yes, the Chairman."

"And this book?"

"I'm not sure."

"Don't worry about it. Many of our young people have no clue either. But you *do* know about the Cultural Revolution?"

"Yes, I have heard much about it."

"This *Little Red Book* was distributed during the revolution. You do know why it's red, the color of the Party, our favorite color?"

"Is it not the color of your flag?" said Cabang.

"Bravo," said Li. "Now compare the two colors. We wanted a red coin purse, but this isn't really red, is it?"

"No, it is not. More like purple."

"Precisely my point. You and I know these two colors are different. This purple is the closest to red among the designer goods. Now do you understand?" said Li, his eyes boring into Cabang again.

"We make a coin purse with the Chairman's red and put our tag on it, and you guarantee we can sell that many?"

"Absolutely. What do you think?" Li's beady eyes shone with anticipation—he was back on the money trail.

Cabang swallowed heavily and gave Li a deliberate nod. "I still am not sure about two to three hundred million, but I see the possibility of twenty to thirty million."

"We have another issue." Li signaled the change of subject by slurping the remainder of his wine. His lady-in-waiting unobtrusively provided a refill.

Cabang caught the young interpreter stealing a glance at the cleavage revealed by her low-cut dress. Poor guy—no glass and no girl.

"For a couple of years now our country has been focusing on local production. Are you aware of that?"

"Yes."

"And not just automobiles and appliances. If we want to capture the hearts of our consumers, we have to make the purses domestically. 'A French designer purse manufactured locally for Chinese consumers'—that's the kind of pitch that will boost Chinese pride. We love *mianzi*, and that purse will make a wonderful gift."

"Domestic production— a stupendous idea! We might sell a billion!" Cabang, business mind rebooted, clapped his hands together.

"I guess that's enough for today," Li announced, picking up the *Little Red Book* and nonchalantly eyeing the Chairman's face beneath the plastic cover. "Not a bad-looking man...." Below, imprinted in gold, was *Quotations from Chairman Mao*.

"Mr. Li. I will contact our home office immediately." Cabang was off and running in pursuit of profit.

"Hey, what's the rush? There's still a crucial matter to settle."

"Which is?"

"The motive—something that drives people to buy. When we have that, we hold all the cards. And then we're talking one to two, maybe even three billion in sales."

"What?" With a lost expression, Cabang regarded Li and the interpreter in turn.

"Look, there's more than one type of Cartier purse—some are long and some are short, some you can fold once and some you can fold twice, some used by men and some only by women. You don't just have one tie and one belt, do you?"

"Then what is the X-factor for the Chinese buyer, if I may ask?"

"I'm not yet at liberty to reveal that. You Westerners love your intellectual property rights, and I do too—so I'm registering copyrights. If you want to continue our talks, then report to your company about our progress. When your company is ready to work with me, my lawyer and I will announce my intellectual property."

"Intellectual property... I see." But he didn't, really. What a transformation— Li the outsourcing contractor into Li the preacher for intellectual property rights. What was the X-factor? Something Li knew but he didn't—it probably had deep roots in the culture. Did the concept of fate enter in somehow? He thought he'd been here long enough to become knowledgeable about the country, but now he wasn't so sure.

One thing he did know—local production was one of the new marketing strategies created in response to China's strong domestic market, a market consisting of the most coveted consumers on the planet. That school of fish might ultimately number two to three billion—where would he find a more lucrative fishery?

"I'm not a patient man," said Li, banal and yet brutal with hegemony tightly in his grasp. "If your company isn't interested, I'll look for another one."

"I understand. I will act expeditiously," said Cabang. "Please give us a few days."

"Very well. That's all for now." Gesturing to Cabang's hostess, Li rose and said to Cabang, "Have a nice time with your lady friend tonight."

As soon as Li's eyes met hers, the young woman took Cabang's arm and her face lit up in a smile that said to Li, *No worries, sir*. The next moment she was the doting hostess, her smile and manner different from those of the other hostesses, who were sick of being browbeaten by drunken customers.

"Yes, Mr. Li," said Cabang. "And I will have a decision for you immediately." He shook hands with his counterpart.

"I hope so."

Cabang imagined a jockey whipping his horse toward the finish line. With a resplendent smile he said, "The French also are hungry beasts in the presence of money, you know."

Off went Li in his chauffeured car. Cabang bowed toward the limousine as it pulled away. His hostess drew near and locked her arm around his.

"Lucky you," mock-pouted Li's hostess.

Cabang's hostess, indicating him with her eyes and tightening her hold on his arm, said "Isn't he handsome?"

"All white guys are," said Li's hostess.

"Please tell this lady I can't take her to the hotel," said Cabang to the interpreter. "Business calls." So saying, he detached his from the hostess's.

"You work this late at night?" asked the interpreter.

"It's daytime there," snapped Cabang. The embarrassed interpreter conveyed the message.

Shaking her shoulders no like a disappointed little girl, the young woman whimpered, "Oh, no. I don't like—"

The interpreter broke in. "When they say no they mean no. Maybe we'll meet again. I'm sorry."

"I was so excited, and now…" grumbled the sad-faced hostess, looking at Cabang. "Will there ever be a next time?"

Ignoring her, Cabang stalked off to his car.

"What time shall I come for you?" said the interpreter when they arrived at Cabang's hotel.

"I'll call you," said Cabang, preoccupied.

In his room he took off his jacket, threw it on the bed, and immediately called France. "*Bonjour, mademoiselle*. This is Director Cabang calling from China. I must talk with the president."

The secretary said, "I'm sorry, he's not here at the moment."

"Is he out of town?"

"No."

"Then, please tell him I'm flying home to see him about an urgent matter."

"May I brief him?"

"Simply tell him I have exciting news."

"All right. We'll be waiting for you."

Cabang found the secretary's voice was gentle and alluring. Next he called the airline and requested a first-class seat on the eight-thirty departure to Beijing the following morning. On hold, he lit a cigar and waited.

"Yes, sir. I have that seat for you," came the reservationist's artificial voice, delicate as a desiccated petal.

"Thank you. I want to continue on to Paris, in business class."

"I'll check that for you, sir."

Cabang smirked, envisioning the woman's calculating smile. He was sure business class would be half empty.

"I'm sorry, sir, business class is sold out."

Cabang paused for a moment. "Then first class, please."

"One moment, please, I'll check that for you."

Cabang loosened his tie and wondered how his boss would react to the first-class reservation—directors were allowed business class but no higher. To his boss the issue wasn't so much money but hierarchy. The onus would be on Cabang to justify his choice.

"Sir, yes, first class is available."

"Then book it for me, please." He hung up.

So much for that. Removing his shirt, he heaved a sigh at the thought of the four a.m. wake-up call. He contacted the front desk, made the request, and reserved a taxi pickup at four-thirty. Slouching in his chair, he checked his watch—eleven p.m. Thank god he hadn't brought the hostess. Futzing around followed by a four a.m. wakeup? No way. Too bad, she was kind of sexy. So many girls, all over the country, all too eager to cozy up to him. But this was no time to chase minnows—he had a shark to catch, and time was short.

Washing up, he crawled into bed. How the country had changed! Close to midnight he could book a flight the following morning, all by himself. Twenty years ago it would have been impossible. That's what G2 status could do for a country. Back then it was a socialist mentality and everything was paralyzed after five p.m. Customer service was practically nonexistent, the nation a convenience hell. As part of its super-speed economic growth, China now met global standards in the service industry, exemplified by the airline twenty-four-hour reservation line he had just used. The powers-that-be were now aware that meticulous, polished service reflected economic power and would heighten the nation's global status. How fast China was rushing pass him! He was tantalized by the two-to-three-hundred-million figure—how best to package it for his boss?

His flight to Paris departed with perhaps a dozen unoccupied business class seats. Well, chalk it up to capitalist commercialism, thought Cabang—the lawful pursuit of profit, open competition for pricing. *I'm sorry sir, business class is sold out*—rather than subterfuge or a lie, call it a legitimate business tactic. Sell high to satisfy an urgent demand, and once the demand is met, everyone's happy—sort of.

As soon as the plane reached cruising altitude Cabang stretched out in his seat—might as well get his money's worth. As he always did in first class, he thought about the economy section. Many were the sites of money-ordained class segregation in a capitalist society—ferries, trains, hotels, concert halls—but none was as blatant as a three-cabin international flight. Money talks and customer service listens—it's a straightforward arrangement, yet vulgar and cruel. *Hey, don't get mad. Did we stop you from making it to the cushy seats? Make money, come on!* This is what capitalism preaches. Which was why Cabang had purchased a first class seat, five times as expensive as one in coach—he stood to make a heap of money. This in mind, he beckoned the flight attendant with his fingertip.

"Wine." Five hours left to enjoy the perquisites.

Displaying the wine list, she asked in English, "Which would you like, sir?"

After naming his pick, Cabang switched to French: "How is the weather in Paris?"

"*Pardonnez-mois, monsieur.*" Blushing, she bowed, and when once again they made eye contact she was no longer the flight attendant but a charming Chinese lady. Standard wisdom was that the Chinese tended to favor Americans most and then the French, but Cabang knew the women, at least, preferred the French and their designer goods. The US had built itself into the strongest player, but France dominated the designer goods market and its most loyal consumers were the Americans and the Japanese. That is, until China rose to G2 status and elbowed the Japanese aside. And by 2016 it would overtake the US, according to IMF forecasts. Cabang had already decided China would capture the gold medal for designer goods consumption.

"That's quite all right," he said, looking into her eyes. "I myself can't tell who's who in this part of the world. But tell me, do you like Paris?"

"Yes, I love Paris," she said in fluent French. "Every season is beautiful and Paris is the best city in the world. I will never be bored there, even after a hundred trips."

"How beautiful your French is!" He pondered a moment. "I don't mean to offend you, but I must ask—did you memorize that?" He squinted at her in amusement.

"Not at all," she said, dead serious. "That is how I think of Paris. And I wrote about Paris in an essay contest for our airline."

"I see. That's the best description of Paris I've heard. And how long have you studied French?"

"About ten years, beginning at my university."

"Very impressive, very elegant."

"*Merci bien, monsieur.*" She turned her flushed face aside, delicately concealing her smiling lips. Her shyness reminded Cabang of a water lily, a mysterious

Asian flower that was about to open, a demeanor he would never see in Western women. She was the new face of globalized China, speaking English and French with equal ease.

Letting the wine linger on his tongue, he brainstormed the pitch he would throw his boss. The man had supremely keen instincts, and he would be interested in the new opportunity, but he hated drawn-out explanations. If Cabang did his homework, five minutes at most would be sufficient to convince him of this lucrative opportunity.

His boss was sensible enough to know that Asia had emerged as the new fast lane to market, overtaking Europe. He was already enthralled by China, Japan, and Korea. The three countries were difficult to distinguish in terms of their people, indeed could be viewed as twins or triplets. First of all, the women much preferred Caucasians.

He thought back to his first overseas assignment, in Japan. His boss there warned him that Japan was a paradise for white men, especially Americans and French, who received the utmost in treatment and respect. Barmaids competed to sit next to them—not that they tipped more. And young Cabang had to be careful as well about the college girls, who were flirtatious go-getters. Cabang soon learned the wisdom of his boss's words.

Early stereotypes portrayed Japanese as bowing, doll-like figures with springy waists—a courteous people who would bend over backwards for Caucasians. But, Cabang felt, over time the excessive deference had engendered among Westerners an attitude of superiority, arrogance, and then disdain. In the 1800s, Meiji Japan had begun importing technology from Europe. Japan's sense of inferiority to the West spurred developments in science and technology that, ironically, led to over-confidence and—eventually—the outbreak of the Pacific War. But defeated in the world war and under governance by the West, which channeled even more technology its way, Japan rose from the ashes. It achieved jaw-dropping development and entered the ranks of the advanced nations.

The newly powerful Japanese economy enabled tourists to swan about overseas and incited a voracious appetite for designer goods. To meet the demand, foreign manufacturers flooded in. What fun for Cabang, poring over photos of the Japanese immersing themselves in the riptide of Western culture.

The most striking photo was of the emperor in top hat and tails signing the Imperial Rescript of Surrender on board the USS *Missouri*. There, among the uniformed military of the Allies, was this Asian man dressed in garb that had gone out of fashion a century earlier in the West. To Cabang he looked like a ghost.

Worshiped as a living god, the emperor occasionally appeared in public so attired. The empress for her part sported a new floral hat at each spectacle, something you might see in an old film of the nobility on a country outing. The new parliamentary members were carbon copies of the emperor in their swallow-tail coats and hats. While the leading government figures looked like dedicated followers of antiquated fashion, everyday citizens sank deeper into the inferiority complex of being yellow and Oriental at a time when supremacy meant being Western and white. For the West, they were the most eager of cultural importers, adopting Western books, fashions, food, and architecture.

If they can't beat you they can join you. Cabang remembered hearing the Japanese baseball announcers shout *homuran, homuran,* and on the streets *t'ak'ushi, t'ak'ushi.* And then there was the joke about Japan being annexed as the 51st US state.

Japan was the West of the East. It preferred and admired the West, fantasized it was the West, and despised its Asian neighbors. And it had never formally apologized for its war crimes, had it? But one country's delusion is another country's real-world benefit, Cabang mused. The US was the most popular destination for Japanese tourists, and next came France. And in consumption of designer goods the US had the largest appetite, and Japan had come next—that is, until China had caught up.

What about Korea? Cabang knew the country had been humiliated as a colony of Japan, and cut in half by a civil war. The ROK favored the West and Westerners as zealously as the Japanese. Their Westernization had begun with clothing—you rarely found Koreans in traditional attire—and housing.

What distinguished Korea, then? Well, it was the land of cosmetic surgery, a field in which it was ahead of Japan and China. Cabang knew Koreans were number one in the world in cosmetic surgery per capita, and that Chinese and Japanese rushed to their neighbor across the water on medical tours to enlarge their eyes and heighten their noses. All three countries longed to look like Westerners. But it was Korea's educational system that really boggled Cabang's mind. How in the name of King Louis XIV could they send twenty trillion *wŏn* down the drain every year studying English at cram schools, when the ROK GDP was barely twenty thousand dollars?

In any event, the Koreans were as good for France as the Japanese and the Chinese. They were besotted with Paris and avid for designer goods—in fact, for their population they were the top consumers of such products in the world. What a wonderful country!

That left China for Cabang to consider. Did they too favor whites? He recalled a doggerel making the rounds in China recently: *Beauty number one crosses the ocean, beauty number two becomes an* ernai *for a foreign businessman, number three becomes a business woman, number four goes to Shenzhen and Zhuhai, number five becomes a karaoke hostess, and beauty number six goes to Guangzhou and Shanghai. Crossing the ocean* meant marrying a white man and moving overseas. Chinese men for their part liked putting in a few years with a foreign company, after which they'd be scouted by a Chinese company and hired for triple the salary. English cram schools constituted one of the ten most lucrative businesses in the country, since a degree from a US school was a guarantee for success. In this respect China was cut from the same mold as Japan and Korea.

Blue jeans were the most coveted post-reform item. And then there was the premium placed on skyscrapers, proud symbol of China's development and perfect for casting the mirage that its cities were the equal of Western metropolises. Beautiful centuries-old buildings were bulldozed to make way for edifices shored up by kilometers of reinforcing rods and tons of concrete slab. Too bad for that, and for the infernal pollution and the fake food. Otherwise China could be a global tourist mecca—forget about France! As a Frenchman Cabang was grateful for the cultural self-destruction he witnessed in China. Would it ever realize that tourism offered a dustless, smokeless gold mine?

And in China as in Korea—for Chinese bodies as for their cities—Westerner-wannabes' appetite for Western aesthetics was voracious. Chinese consumers frenzied for cosmetic surgery and designer goods. It was worth the pain of the incisions, the extractions, and the augmentations to look like a beautiful Westerner. But was it really? Cabang had to wonder.

In some cases, the dark side of idolizing whiteness was clear. After the visit by US Secretary of State Condoleezza Rice, media analyst and human rights activist Liu Xiaobo brought to light a barrage of netizen postings attacking her: she was ugly, she was a black ghost, how could the Americans have selected a black chimpanzee as secretary of state? Was it any wonder Cabang rarely saw dark-skinned people in China? Such must have been the ambivalence the Chinese felt for the US.

Cabang opened his eyes to find the flight attendant gently shaking him. After a lavatory visit he had coffee and collected his thoughts in preparation for the five-minute briefing for his boss. And then his mind was off and running, scribbling on his mental notepad.

Ah, Paris—still beautiful and lovable. Cabang's pride soared and he felt a surge of energy.

"What did you say, Cabang? Two to three hundred million?" The president's eyes transfixed him.

"Correct," he said like a soldier answering roll call.

"Let me ask you … how do you feel about the chances of success?"

"One hundred percent, sir. Absolutely."

"You mean you would bet your life on it?"

"Yes, sir."

"I feel I can trust you, but what I want to know is, what did Li copyright?"

"I've thought about the possibilities, but I'm coming up blank. He knows things about Chinese culture that I can't fathom."

"In that case, either we swallow him or we include him. Do you know if he wants a flat payout? Or does he want profit sharing?"

"We haven't gone that far, sir. We just talked about the product."

"I see. I want you to bring him here."

"Excuse me?"

"Bring him here, to Paris." Cabang saw in his eyes all the details this instruction implied.

"I see, sir. I'll leave immediately."

"Please do. I never would have imagined China becoming such a strong market. Thanks to you, the company is flourishing. I honestly had doubts when the media predicted our economy would continue to grow because of the explosive sales of designer goods. But your predictions were right—two of ten Japanese buying designer goods, five out of ten Koreans, and nine out of ten Chinese. But with China you missed something."

"Excuse me, sir?"

"What I mean is, those nine or ten Chinese buy not one item but fifteen or twenty."

2. Thou, My Love

Chaehyŏng, shorts-clad and shirtless on a sweltering day, was tapping away on his keyboard. The summer heat—as notorious in Beijing as its winter cold—had arrived. Recent desertification in northern China was being associated with severe changes in the weather. And there was always the air pollution.

Knock, knock.

"Yes?" he barked. An interruption was the last thing he needed when he was struggling to produce an essay for class.

"What the fuck?" yelled Yi Namgŭn as he barged in. "You're working on a paper in this oven?"

Chaehyŏng scowled and swiveled his chair around—his friend's voice set him on edge as much as the knock on the door. "I knew it was you."

Namgŭn snorted as he flopped down on Chaehyŏng's bed. "So now you can see through walls."

"Every sound has a face."

"My ass," said Namgŭn as he produced a cigarette. "Arrogant bastard, next thing you're going to tell me is every fart has a face."

"Of course. You're a blaster and your dad's a squeaker, right?"

"And can you tell when it's your loving little Yanling knocking at the door?"

Chaehyŏng closed his eyes as if at that very moment he could hear the awaited sound. "Of course. It's so nice and soft..."

Namgŭn lit his cigarette. "Oh, is our little Chaehyŏng in the mood? So what are you up to besides sweating over a paper?"

Chaehyŏng frowned. "Hey, put it out. Second-hand smoke, remember?"

"Stop being such a fussy prick," said Namgŭn, blowing a cloud of smoke in his friend's face. "No way my smoke is going to kill you."

"Shit." Chaehyŏng tried to fan the smoke back in Namgŭn's direction. "How did I end up with a barbarian like you for a friend? Don't you have any term papers?"

"Relax, pal." Namgŭn made an A-OK, money-solves-everything circle with thumb and forefinger and smiled jauntily. "Who wants to write a fucking term paper in this heat?"

Chaehyŏng started at the implication that his friend had bought off his exams. "What if you get caught?"

"No worries—it won't happen, not at my school."

"But still…you won't graduate if they nail you."

Namgŭn took a drag on his cigarette and laughed impishly. "Chaehyŏng—alias Goody Two-Shoes. Look, I won't get caught, and even if I did I wouldn't give a shit—I'm not fixing to be a big-ass professor like you. I don't need to wear a blue ribbon to graduate."

'What do you mean? You have to show your parents you earned a diploma."

Namgŭn wagged an index finger and gave Chaehyŏng a you're-pathetic look. "What's the use? I tell you what—you learn how the world works and I stop calling you a moron, how's that? Anyway, my paper didn't even cost a hundred *yuan.*"

"You might as well have stolen it—and I suppose your parents will never get wind of this?"

"Well, if you think I'm deceiving them you're wrong. In fact their little hearts will rest easy. Look, I put a lot of thought into this. Why do I need a diploma if I'm inheriting my father's business? I've put in four good years here and got to see things. That's good enough, don't you think?"

"You have a lot of balls. That's why you don't study Chinese very much."

"Maybe. Hell, you can study for both of us. You're like a machine. *You* think studying is fun. Don't get sore—there are plenty others like me. This is life, and we all end up in the same place. Doesn't much matter how we get there."

"Garbage philosophy!"

"You don't agree? You go to cram school or you go abroad to study, you work for a big conglomerate, and so what? You get a little more pay than others, you work maybe twenty years, and you get dumped like *you're* the garbage. Is that better than me? Who knows, maybe I'll end up richer running my own business. I'll have some fun doing it, and I won't have to work myself to death. Are you listening, my head-in-the-clouds scholar pal? You and I will die in the end and turn to dust. So don't get heat stroke over that paper."

"It's your life. But nobody's handing *me* a business. Which is why I have to bust my ass over this." He fetched his shirt. "Anyway, what are you doing here?"

"I need you to go somewhere with me."

On went the shirt. "Your uncle's in trouble again?"

"I wish. Then I could weasel more money out of him."

Chaehyŏng brandished his fist halfheartedly in Namgŭn's face. "You're such an ass."

"Let's go. You're going to like this."

"First I need to know what I'm going to like. Unless it's more important than this," he said, pointing to the monitor, "I'm not going anywhere."

Namgŭn tapped his friend on the shoulder. "Hey—have I ever gotten you in trouble? I know I'm not as smart as you, but I have a better network and I know my way around, see?"

"Now that's reassuring," said Chaehyŏng. "It's comforting to know you're so far ahead of me." He offered his friend a deep bow.

"Then trust me and let's go. There's something nice waiting for you. You'll thank me for it." He rose from the bed. "We're out of here."

"Pops in out of the blue, frisky as hell—hopeless," Chaehyŏng grumbled as he changed into pants. But truth be told, he could use a short break.

He smirked as he followed his friend out. How would Namgŭn's parents react? Well, Namgŭn was a big boy, he'd manage to graduate somehow. There were a thousand universities in China, perhaps the most of any country in the world, their purpose to turn out high-caliber talent after the reforms. But there was a vast difference in quality among them. What was worse, the overinvestment in universities led to an oversupply of human capital, and the glut of unemployed graduates had become a new social problem. As in Korea, college graduates wanted a posh position with a high salary. But such jobs were filled in a split-second and new positions were slow to appear. It made for a badly tangled skein of yarn.

Chaehyŏng was led to a familiar place, the Starbucks in front of his university. As always it was thronged with young people, money flowing out of their pockets and east across the Pacific where rich America grew wealthier by the second.

"Chaehyŏng, here." Namgŭn pointed to a seat across the table from two girls. "Ladies," said Namgŭn, "meet your tutor, Song Chaehyŏng."

"Hello, I'm Han Mira."

"Nice to meet you, I'm Kim Minji."

Both girls looked up at Chaehyŏng and nodded, and then their gazes darted toward each other—he was so tall and handsome!

"What do you mean, tutor?" said Chaehyŏng, ignoring the girls' greeting.

Namgŭn yanked him down. "Sit. It's all good. They're little sisters of a couple friends of mine, see? They're freshmen, spring chicks. You know how language is for freshman. So they're staying here this summer, studying Chinese. And you're not going home either, you're preparing for grad school, right? So why not tutor them and save up a few *yuan*? The pay is good." Namgŭn was more polite in the presence of the girls.

"What do you mean? There are cram schools all over. And I'm not even a native. Koreans should learn Chinese from the Chinese. You have to jump right in. Besides, I don't have the time."

"We know," pleaded Mira. "But the cram schools are too crowded, and too advanced for us—we wouldn't be able to catch up. Won't you please help us?" She crossed her hands over her chest in supplication.

"Yes, it's urgent," said Minji. "If we can't find a good tutor, we might have to go back home." Her tone was tearful. "We're missing a lot of what people say. *Please* help us."

"See, we're serious about studying Chinese, not like him," said Mira, indicating Namgŭn. "We're in big trouble if we can't communicate, right, Namgŭn?"

"Hey hey hey," said Namgŭn, arching his eyebrows, "this is what I get for coming outside in this heat and trying to do you girls a favor?" Good-naturedly he raised a fist.

Minji scowled at him. "Don't try to scare us. And just for the record, you're not really a student, you're an overstayed tourist, right? We're not going to be like you; we have to fulfill our dream."

Namgŭn produced his habitual snort. "Cut the overstayed-tourist crap. All right, I'll admit it, Chinese characters give me brain cramps, so I said screw it. Who needs Chinese to get rich? So what's your girls' dream anyway—why are you so google-eyed about learning the language?"

"So a big company hires us," said Mira.

Minji replied coolly, "Self-realization as a professional woman."

"Are you kidding? Self-realization as a professional woman—where have I heard that before? You make two or three million *wŏn* a month, four or five at best, schmooze around for a while, and when you're past your prime you get a pink slip—then what? Self-realization, your silky butt!" He pretended to gag.

"What's wrong with that?" snapped Minji, eyebrows raised. "If you're going to be so negative, how's he ever going to tutor us?"

"Yeah yeah. What I'm saying is, you're here for studying, not yapping. So turn off the hot air and lose the sassy attitude. You two are nothing to look at, and it makes me want to puke seeing you show off…damn."

"Now you're showing your true colors," clucked Mira. "You pretend you're open-minded, you go on about men and women being equal, but inside you're a male chauvinist, a typical two-faced Korean guy."

"What do you expect from him?" said Minji. "A guy who's nothing but has to show he's something. More women are passing the bar exam, more women are becoming prosecutors, and guess what—the top graduate of the Military Academy is also a woman. So what's left for guys?"

"Wow, a seminar on women's rights—that's impressive, girls. I guess we're done here. Have fun. Hey, Chaehyŏng, let's go grab a cold beer."

Flustered, Mira motioned them back to their seats. "I'm sorry, *oppa*. We take it all back. Like you say, we were just yapping."

"You don't scare us, *oppa*," said Minji. "I think he's already decided to take us."

Namgŭn sank back down in his chair. "That one's got nerve, watch out for her,

Chaehyŏng. All right, girls, no more guff, got it?" He slapped Chaehyŏng on the thigh. "Take good care of them, all right?"

"I'm sorry, I just can't. I changed my major, you know, and I've got a lot of catching up to do. And I need to get ready for grad school." Chaehyŏng was talking to Namgŭn, but looking decisively toward the girls.

Another slap to Chaehyŏng's thigh, this one harder. "I can't believe you. Lighten up and help the young ladies with their studies—do your patriotic duty. Besides, you don't want me to lose face."

Finishing his coffee, Chaehyŏng started to rise. "Yeah, you're in a tough position, but look at me. I'm at a crossroads and I don't have any time to lose. All right?"

"All right. *But*, you have to take a break. Nobody can study twenty-four hours a day. And the girls aren't asking for all-day lessons. Have a heart. Look how pretty they are! They'll be a nice change of pace for you—plus, you get some money out of it."

While Chaehyŏng attempted to digest this, Namgŭn turned to the girls looking uncertainly at his friend. He switched to entertainer mode.

"Hey, anyone interested in a story? Great, I thought so! All right, imagine yourself in the future when anyone can travel in space. There's a problem, though—the fares are astronomical. Now imagine the wife of an obscenely rich guy. She says to him, 'Honey, I want to visit outer space. It's my dying wish.' He tells her hell no. 'What?' his wife says. 'You promised—you said you'd give me anything I want. You lied! You miser, you tightwad.' 'All right, go ahead,' he yells back. 'As long as it's one way!' What do you think about *that*?"

"One way?" said Mira. "How could he?"

Chaehyŏng burst into laughter.

"I can't believe it!" said Minji, drumming on her friend's shoulder. She looked half indignant and half amused.

"Some husband!" said Mira. Both girls giggled.

"Well," said Namgŭn with a poker face, "where are your manners, young ladies? You expect to be entertained for free? And where's the encore request?"

Minji clapped gently and called out, "Yes, encore, encore!"

Mira added her applause.

"All right, I must oblige my dear fans. Here we go. A man on his deathbed says to his wife, 'Honey, when I'm dead and gone, I want you to marry that Kim guy, the company president.' His wife was shocked. 'What are you saying, dear? He's the one who screwed you over. Don't you want revenge?'" Namgŭn paused dramatically. "And her husband says, 'Yes—and I'll get it if he's married to you.' Those were his last words."

The girls responded with a chorus of *ohmygod*s and giggles.

Chaehyŏng erupted in laughter. "The overstayed tourist is a half-assed comedian."

"How about one more?" said Mira.

"If you insist," said Namgŭn. "But the audience has to choose."

"Is your repertoire that big?" said Minji.

Namgŭn pretended to straighten a nonexistent necktie. "Young lady, I could encore you all night."

The girls urged him on with rapid-fire clapping.

"What are you waiting for?"

"Yeah, come on."

Namgŭn cleared his throat, adopting a pretentious air. "How about something with a moral for all you great young minds? And see if you can ramp up the laughter. Here we go. One day God stacks up wads of money until he's got a nice little trillion-*wŏn* hill. Then he picks three guys—a businessman, a beggar, and a clergyman—and says to them, 'See that flag over there? Move as much money there as you can with your bare hands in twenty-four hours, and you get to keep it.' The three of them scoot off toward the hill and get down to work." Namgŭn eyed his audience. "Who do you think moved the most money?"

"The beggar," said Minji.

"Wrong."

"The businessman," said Mira.

"Wrong."

Chaehyŏng was lost in thought, eyes downcast.

"The clergyman, right?" Namgŭn pressed him.

"No," Chaehyŏng said solemnly. "All three of them died."

"*Dingdong*. Right you are."

As Minji blinked in confusion, Mira asked for an explanation.

"Now you see the difference between freshmen and seniors? Like they say, the bamboo gets taller every day. You want to know what happened? The three guys were so anxious to move that money they didn't eat, drink, or sleep. They were knocked dead by money."

When the girls remained silent Namgŭn announced in a theatrical voice, "The moral of the story is, 'No one gets revenge on money.'"

Chaehyŏng rose. "Thanks to all of you for a good time. I've got to go."

"Hmm," Minji murmured as he walked away, "I think I like him."

"Don't waste your time, he's taken. The proud owner is a southern Chinese beauty. Tall and slender and a fantastic body."

"Really?" Mira murmured. "Why Chinese? Where's his patriotic spirit?"

"Forget patriotism—he's a big believer in love without borders. He's water over the dam, ladies. Forget about him and let's go eat."

"Just because there's a goalie doesn't mean you can't shoot," said Minji.

The monitor was as indifferent as when Chaehyŏng had left. It put on a solemn, steely face when he had a report or a term paper to write, but was happy and bright when he watched a movie or played a video game. Just now he was reluctant to face it. Writing, especially writing that was crisp and original, seemed ever more difficult. How did the professors do it? Some mysterious talent seemed to flow for them like spring water, nurturing new shoots that blossomed into distinctive flowers. He both envied and was awed by their accomplishments.

Academic writing was a constant concern for Chaehyŏng and his classmates. He'd come to realize that the scholar's obligation to churn out one fresh piece of writing after another was a rough road that lacked signposts—the complete opposite of the curiosity and fun of field trips. Sad to say, the stiff-faced monitor seemed unimpressed with such thoughts.

"It's not because of your Chinese," Yanling had once told him. "I'm the same when I have to write. I get scared and begin to doubt myself. Professors too, I've heard." She punctuated the comforting words with a kiss.

Her words were like a cold, refreshing drink, but he knew his cunning mind would eventually play more tricks on him.

His cell phone sounded. The display told him it was Yanling. He could almost see the monitor grinning at him.

"Are you sick of me already?" Her voice was unexpectedly hostile.

"What do you mean?"

"You had a change of heart, didn't you?"

"What are you talking about?"

"Is that the Korean style?"

"What happened? Is something wrong?"

"If you're sick of me and you changed your mind, then be open about it, Chinese style, and go your way."

"Yanling, you're talking nonsense."

"Nonsense? You act cheap and pretend you don't?"

"What am I pretending?"

"Don't play dumb. I saw it with my own eyes."

"Saw what? This is driving me nuts!"

"Your big date at Starbucks. What a wonderful time you were having."

"Oh, that! Well, you're wrong. It was nothing."

"I'm wrong? I see. Then as of right now, we're breaking up."

"Yanling, what the hell are you talking about?"

The phone went dead. All in a fluster he called her back. A recorded message told him her phone was turned off. Again he got dressed, and rushed to her officetel.

"Yanling, come on. Open the door. I can explain." Gasping for breath, he banged on the door. No sign of life from inside. "Yanling, open up. It was nothing, honest. You have to hear me out." He banged more loudly. Still no response. He wondered if she was out, then shook his head—studious as she was, she wouldn't have gone anywhere unless it was urgent. "Yanling, open the door. You'll regret it if we don't talk." He yelled till his throat hurt and pounded till his fist grew numb.

"I'll never, ever regret it," came her shrill voice from inside. "And if you don't stop that racket I'm calling the PSB."

"You know Namgŭn—those girls are his friends' sisters and they want to learn Chinese. His Chinese is no good, so he asked me to teach them." Out spilled his explanation onto the innocent metal door.

"Don't lie to me. You just met those girls and you're all having the time of your life and laughing yourselves to death?"

Shit! So she had seen him when he was laughing. That explained everything.

"Yanling. I told them I didn't have time for tutoring, and Namgŭn wanted to lighten the mood, so he started telling jokes. If I tell you the jokes, I bet you'll laugh too."

"What if I don't?"

"Then we break up."

"All right. Remember that." She opened the door.

Pulling her into his arms, he said, "What's wrong?"

She pushed him away. "No," she said, her tone frosty. "Tell your jokes first. And they'd better be funny."

He dutifully stepped back.

She glowered at him, fuming. "Are you sure you aren't tutoring them?"

He glared back at her. "Absolutely not. I don't even have time to write my term paper."

"You're sure? I want to check with him."

"Go ahead, you can call him now." He offered his cell phone.

She pushed the phone away. "Sit down and tell me the jokes and we'll see how funny they are."

He sat in the chair as directed. She was opposite him, perched on her bed.

Joke number one. He wedged the small of his back into the chair, rewinding the story. It all came back, but could he regale her as Namgŭn had his audience?

He told the joke, finishing, "…'As long as it's one way!'"

Yanling turned her head away and covered her mouth.

"You're free to laugh, so be my guest." He spoke louder than necessary but inwardly heaved a long sigh of relief.

Joke number two. When Yanling started laughing, his confidence soared. He made a mental note to remember these stories for future use. "…and I'll get it if he's married to you."

"Oh my!" She burst out in gleeful laughter and back came the gentle girl he knew.

He pondered over the third story. Would she find it too serious? He wanted to show her that Namgŭn had meant this story to carry some weight, that he wasn't a sleazy buddy trying to fix Chaehyŏng up with some girls.

"All right. One day God stacks up wads of money…" He felt the story flowing free and easy. She nodded gently, a smile filling her face. "Who do you think moved the most money?" He leaned forward with his eyebrows up.

"The beggar!"

"I'm sorry, miss, incorrect."

"Then, the businessman?"

"No."

"Oh no, then the clergyman."

"Wrong again. They all worked themselves to death moving that money…"

"Oh no. And that's the answer?" She nodded, mulling it over.

"Do you believe me now?"

"I'm sorry. I misunderstood." She smiled sheepishly.

"It's all right. I can see why."

"I don't like seeing you with other girls; not even *looking* at other girls."

"I won't. I only have one girl and that's you, Yanling."

"Sure?"

"Sure."

"Promise?"

"Promise." He pulled her into his arms.

Again she pushed him away. "First there's something I need to know. We're going to graduate soon. When are we getting married?" She stared at him.

"Married?"

"Yes. Why—you don't want to?"

"Not that I don't want to. But I have a long way to go. Master's degree, doctorate…"

"What does that have to do with marriage? You can still study. I read a report in the American press that married couples study harder and achieve more."

"I know that, but my parents have to pay—"

"Don't worry, I can take care of that. So?"

His mother's face popped into his mind's eye. The timing wasn't right, and a Chinese girl as a wife? Here it was right in front of him, the issue he'd tucked away on the far back burner. Yanling's expectations wouldn't allow a let-me-think-it-over answer. Nor could he let her go. She was the only one, the true one, and he loved her and wanted to marry and live with her forever. There was only one strategy, a tug-of-war with his parents, and it had worked when he changed his major.

"All right. We'll do it." And with equal resolution he embraced her.

"Chaehyŏng, I love you." Finally she allowed him to pull her close.

"And I love you, Yanling." He searched for her lips as he eased her pants down and she unlooped his belt. As their lips tightened and their breathing warmed, they rushed to peel off each other's clothing.

Wang Lingling scanned the room. "I hope you checked everything."

"Yes, madam," said Thomas, head stockbroker at the Gold Groups Hong Kong affiliate. "We started this morning—the security team have been in place all day. It's all set. Please rest assured." He was deferential in the extreme.

Wang swept her gaze over Thomas and then Cooper. "I can't trust Taiwan, and Hong Kong is worse. There it's like we're sitting in the living room of the PSB."

"We understand," said Thomas. Cooper contributed a knowing nod.

The three of them went outside. Wang fixed her gaze on the two men. "There are just the three of us, you know." A reminder of why they were at this secluded home.

Cooper seemed dispirited by her gaze. "Yes. We have tight security here."

"As always," said Thomas in a reassuring tone. "There's only yourself, me, and him, and," he looked up into the night sky, "heaven."

"That's what I like to hear," said Wang. "When do we start?"

Cooper glanced at Thomas before answering. "The sooner the better. Year-end always comes fast."

"Agreed," said Thomas. "It's a huge project and we need to get our algorithms up and running. The longer we delay, the more risk of security lapses, and the more we have to rush. So I vote for starting immediately."

"All right," said Wang with a decisive tap on the patio table, "we start tomorrow." To the men's ears that tap was like the rap of a gavel. Silence fell over them.

"Thomas," murmured Wang. "Bring out the drinks."

"Sure."

Out came a bottle of red wine and three glasses. Thomas did the honors. The silence deepened.

Finally Wang lifted her glass and the men followed. She motioned for a toast and they brought their glasses together. The crystal produced a clear, lovely ring. "We're in this together. I'll make sure you both get a handsome reward."

Cooper bowed. "And I'll make sure it works out perfectly."

Thomas's bow was less perceptible. "There's nothing to worry about."

And with that, like the Oath of the Peach Garden in the *History of the Three Kingdoms*, the Oath of Hong Kong was sealed.

Wang picked up her handbag. "All right, Cooper, back to Beijing you go. I'll follow tomorrow. We can have lunch when I get there."

Cooper rose. "All right, I'll see you then."

The three of them left separately. Back at her hotel, Wang felt unusually fatigued as the psychological weight of the massive project fell onto her. Sinking into an armchair, she covered her face with her hands and the image of Wang Itsan on his deathbed rose before her.

Daddy, I did it like you suggested. I'm not rushing and I'm in control, so everything will be fine. But you have to stand by me. You're my fortitude. As she prayed to him she felt her leaden heart lighten.

The secret to acquiring money is not to use your own.

If profits are certain, then don't hesitate to invest an immense sum. If not, don't spend a dime.

The president has a term of office, but not the wealthy.
When you spend money you get everyone's attention.
The wealthy are the envy of the emperor and the president.

These axioms, all from her father, guided her in her daily business, providing constant food for thought.

She took her time undressing, then climbed into the shower and set the water as hot as she could bear it—her favorite remedy for fatigue. Before she knew it she was humming "I Left My Heart in San Francisco" and the familiar, homey scenes were unfolding before her. The reel stopped at the image of her poor, unfortunate mother. Wang Itsan gone, she seemed lonelier and more piteous. As Lingling hummed, the hot water washed away her tears. Thinking about her mother always brought her to tears.

I won't let you follow in my steps. You have to study hard and educate yourself. The words were engraved in her brain like an inscription in marble. Words repeated umpteen thousands of times. Especially when her mother read for little Lingling a book her father had brought home for her. Reading was always fun, but more meaningful when the little girl was reminded by her tearful mother that they both had to escape the cycle of their lives.

She repeated the song until thoughts of San Francisco were gone, then shut off the water. Wrapping herself in the oversize bath towel, she left the bathroom with a much lighter heart. She loved a hot shower; it was like a whole-body massage.

She applied her makeup a dab at a time. Not that she was meeting anyone; she was just loath to vegetate in front of her television like some aging spinster.

The sky lounge at the Four Seasons Hotel felt soft and elegant, different from the ambience at mainland hotels. She looked out at the twilight and the colors reflected onto the thin strip of water between Kowloon and Hong Kong islands. Miniature boats plied the waters. The Hong Kong skyscrapers seemed wisdom incarnate compared with the frenetic jostling for position of the high-rises under construction in the mainland metropolises. The myriad high-rises, and the people they beckoned, and the money those people attracted from all over the world, had lifted these tiny islands to the status of a world-class city—there would be no Hong Kong without them. The combination of water and high-rises livened the view, and now the grand array of buildings was lighting up like women decorating themselves for the night. The world-famous nighttime panorama of Hong Kong was a capitalist battlefield on which glitzy ads for global companies vied to enchant tourists during their brief sojourn.

Whenever she was here she thought of Deng Xiaoping and Britain. A century and a half after the Opium War, with the principals long since dead and gone, Britain assumed that concession would translate into ownership. Little did it expect humpty-dumpty Deng to push a musty, century-old treaty in its face. Rather than involve himself in a war of words, Deng simply pointed to the treaty. To the tall, haughty British he might have looked like a tubby yellow midget, but they failed to notice that this particular pygmy came with a huge brain. Like a self-righting doll he rose from the knockdowns of political turmoil and grasped power. If only the British had known his tenacity, they would have not let it be known that they coveted Hong Kong. Eventually, his perseverance won the day and Britain retreated.

And then, miracle of miracles, when Hong Kong was returned to China in accordance with the treaty, the PRC had declared a policy of "one country, two systems" and pledged not to interfere. The wealthy were skeptical, and many took flight overseas to Chinese enclaves such as the greater Vancouver area in Canada.

But the Chinese government kept its promise, and as a testament to the birth of Chinese-style capitalism it allowed Hong Kong plutocrats into the Party. This eye-popping change brought back the renegade wealthy, and Hong Kong flourished. Its financial market ran neck and neck with Wall Street.

As she watched the glittery expanse outside the plate-glass windows, Wang thought of Andy Park. What would he say when he found out? Ever since her visit to Xian, he'd been popping up in her mind. .

Shaking hands with her at the airport in Xian he had said, "You don't have to come back to this polluted place. I'll take care of everything." He had insisted on coming out to see her off.

"I'm sorry we're having to speed up construction," she had hastened to mention. What would he think about that statement now?

"Quite all right. We have to be flexible." The smile on his tanned face was so innocent and benign.

That was the last time she had seen him. He had not questioned her on-the-scene-commander presence, her sunburned cheeks ample evidence of the length of her stay. Andy Park never doubted anyone, even himself. The extra rebate he had given to the company. The secret she had kept from him had bothered her on the flight here from Beijing. The Gold Groups division of labor sometimes held important information from circulating even among the presidents. She should not be bothered, but why then did Andy keep surfacing in her thoughts?

She felt sorry for herself harboring these feelings. But she was afraid of the harm he might come to through this plot of hers. This worry did not extend to the twenty-plus other men who were beneath her.

Choose your people half on their capability and half on their makeup. Drink together, gamble together, hike together, and travel together. Weed out the guys who are selfish, who don't get along; guys who are frivolous, impatient; the guys who bellyache, the lone wolves, the backbiters, the ones who renege on their promises. Then you'll know who's left. This too was her father's teaching.

The ones who were left became the Gold Groups presidents. Early on she'd noticed a different scent coming out of Andy—or was it a scent coming into her? A whiff of compassion? Either way, their rapport had a quality that others lacked.

She ordered a bottle of the most expensive wine in the lounge, along with two glasses. She sampled the uncorked bottle, signaled her approval, and waited for her glass to be filled. When the waiter was about to pour the second glass she waved him off. "I'll take care of it."

Andy, I'm sorry. I hope one day you'll understand me. I know you will—you're a thoughtful, caring artist. And she filled his glass.

When out of the blue Andy got married in Korea, she felt a crumbling sensation deep in her heart, in a place she had kept just for him. Disguising her feelings, she presented him with a job-well-done pep talk: "I believe in you and respect you—you're a man worth loving." Only later did she realize you could love and believe in someone without really respecting him. She still couldn't decide if her profession of respect had been a smart move or a pathetic attempt at sweet talk.

Hey, Andy, drink up. I'm going to finish this bottle and go to sleep.

"Excuse me, miss, may I join you?" A tall white man was standing next to her.

"What for?"

"You look lonely." He had a revolting male smell.

"Do I look like a high-class call girl?"

"Not at all …"

"What floor are you on?"

"Nine."

"Nine? That's a long way down. I'm on forty-five. My men can take you there, they're waiting outside that door. I'll let them know you're coming."

"Oh no, miss. I'm sorry." And off he scurried.

Owing perhaps to her mother's suffering, she had never been attracted to white men. Nor had she been able to excise her feelings about the faceless man with the blond hair who had abandoned them. She had met countless Caucasian men who were smart and handsome. A few had approached her, but her first reaction was always fear—fear that she would one day live out her mother's misfortune for herself.

Quite a few found her attractive. She didn't take them seriously. She looked neither white nor Asian. She knew she wasn't so much attractive as distinctive. And where she came from, distinctiveness wasn't an issue—there were so many different people. For her, the issue was meant being abandoned by the white father she would never look just like. She sometimes wondered if there was a psychiatrist who could explain that to her. Watching this white man disappear, she muttered, "If only you were Andy…"

3. To Win the World

Ha Kyŏngman set out from his office with his secretary, who toted a red bundle. No words exchanged, they moved like clockwork to his car. The Hyundai Equus glided into an alley of crummy dwellings, a traditional neighborhood that still retained a sense of history. Ha's secretary led him to one of the homes, where she put her best voice forward and called out softly, "*Wei*, we're from Guangbao."

An old woman came right out. She broke into a bright smile and the wrinkles filling her face disappeared. "Look who's here! Ha *xiansheng*. Please come in."

Ha grinned in delight. "Hello, grandmother!" he said in fluent Mandarin.

"You look more handsome than ever," she said. "Come in, please."

"Grandmother, my business is going well and I have peace of mind, and it is all thanks to your constant concern."

Patting Ha's hand, the old woman led him inside. "Concern? I guess, for what that's worth. You do all the work and leave nothing to chance, just like a man should."

In the living room stood an old man smiling like a peony in full blossom. "How nice to see you. You haven't forgotten us and you visit bright and early."

Ha responded with an equally blooming grin. "Happy birthday, grandfather."

The man motioned Ha to sit. "How is business? Plenty of orders, I hope?"

"Yes, thanks to you, it is going very well."

"I'm so happy for you. Other Korean factories continue to close, but heaven takes care of you because you take care of everyone else."

"How nice of you to say that. But it is I who should thank you for helping me. Please allow me to greet you properly on your birthday." Ha prepared to prostrate himself in a bow.

"That's really not necessary. Please, have a seat…"

The old man bypassed the sofa he had indicated for Ha and sat squarely on the floor. And thus began the ritual. Ha had been visiting this couple for ten years.

When the old man was settled Ha performed his bow. And as always he thought of his late father, who upon hearing that Ha was venturing to China had preached to him the importance of respecting the elderly. Being polite didn't cost you anything, his father had said. Human nature was the same wherever you went. His father's reminder had been more accurate than Genghis Khan's arrows. By the time Ha had established himself here and was ready to perform his filial duties, his father had passed on. How Ha had wanted to show his weary father the Great Wall, even if it meant transporting him piggyback. But he could only weep at his grave. His father had sold off the family home and lands and given Ha the proceeds for his business. Ha's guilty conscience could not be washed away by wailing, and ever since, he had bowed to his Chinese elders as if to his father, and always with his father's voice in mind.

Rising from the floor, Ha gathered his hands together and intoned, "May you enjoy long life and the blessings of heaven!"

Teary-eyed, the old man said in a trembling voice, "*Ganxie, hun ganxie*. Over a decade… and all the time you have treated me better than my own child has. I wish for your business to grow like wildfire and prosper." A big bow could indeed stir a man's heart.

"Thank you, sir." Ha collected the red bundle from his secretary and presented it. "Please accept this humble gift, grandfather."

"Oh my. How can I deserve..."

Ha next produced a *hongbao* from his pocket, "And I wish to offer you this tiny sum." The red envelope bore two characters written vertically with ink and brush—the top one, *shou*, meaning "long life," and the bottom one, *fu*, meaning "blessing." The *fu* character was written upside down, reflecting the belief that blessings cascade down from heaven.

"I should retire from this world," said the man, as custom demanded. "Every year I prove more of an annoyance to you." Eyes still misty, the old man regarded the envelope—how much was inside? But he must have known—a red envelope always contained an amount appropriate to the occasion.

Eyes brimming with affection, the old lady offered tea to the guests. "Ha *xiansheng*, drink. May your business prosper and may your years with us be long!"

"*Ganxie, hen ganxie.*" As Ha accepted the tea he kept bowing, not out of duty but straight from the heart. The neighborhood elders and their collective wisdom were like a guardian angel. Some years back, during the Chunjie holiday, several Korean businesses had been looted, but Ha's was spared, thanks to the elders watching over his factory. And while they harped about other foreign bosses and ran down their companies, to the young women who made up the vast majority of Ha's work force, they gave an encouraging pat on the back.

Rising, the old man motioned to Ha. "You are a busy man, you should be on your way."

"Until we meet again, grandfather."

Back at the office, Ha checked his watch—door to door the visit had taken thirty minutes. Hanging his suit jacket and removing his tie, he changed into his windbreaker with the company logo. His visit to the old man was one of several service activities scorned by his Korean colleagues. They thought it was a waste of time, an annoyance, and a bad example to the workers, who would think he was putting on airs and would ultimately lose respect for him. Ha turned a deaf ear to them. Along with the home visits he had launched a daily sweeping of the street to his factory, a crew of five spending thirty minutes on the task and Ha joining them except when he was away on business. Soon he had added a weekly village cleanup. All of Ha's workers took part—Ha had persuaded them it was good exercise considering their sedentary jobs. The workers broke up into groups and listened to music as they swept. The neighbors welcomed the tidying up because they were short-handed, the young ones having left for better-paying jobs in big cities elsewhere.

These volunteer activities drew more sniping from his colleagues, but he continued to ignore them—some horses are never tamed. Instead he extended his cleanup campaign to a monthly scouring of the beach. Qingdao was a city of beaches before it became home to the famous beer, and keeping the beautiful shores clean meant keeping Qingdao alive. Ha's critics could yammer all they wanted, but Ha and his phalanx of volunteers could be counted on every month to pick up the cigarette butts and collect the garbage. The beach-cleaning eventually involved pickup games of volleyball, tugs-of-war, foot races, and high jumping, all of it in good fun. The participants were rewarded with snacks and drinks and—above all—prizes, for a sporting event without an award was like flat beer and plain pork. The prizes consisted of the most sought-after accessories produced by the factory. These were a big hit with the women, who made up 90 percent of Ha's work force—they could decorate themselves with the accessories then and there—and especially the men, who now had a ready supply of gifts.

The beach cleanups brought an unexpected outcome—a good citizen award presented by the city to Ha's company. Well, you don't look a gift horse in the mouth. Ha became friends with the mayor and met now and then for drinks with the head of the local environmental protection bureau. He now enjoyed the powerful backing of the city government in a country monopolized by the Party, though he didn't really need to exploit this newfound *guanxi* since his company produced for export rather than domestic consumption.

And surprise. The backbiters traded in their sneers for smiles and, desperate for *guanxi* of their own, lined up at the tidy entrance to the factory to pay Ha a courtesy call.

Next came the scholarship program. The first awards went to five recipients and by now fifty students per year were being funded. That figure had remained constant for years, ever since the tsunami unleashed by the US-induced global recession had swept over the accessories market. The ballooning fantasy of neoliberalism that money would generate more money had driven the US economy to the verge of collapse. Ha knew that capitalism could not exist without manufacturing. Manufacturing was the foundation of capitalism, and capitalism its offspring. The neoliberalists in all their frivolity flouted this principle, and businesses like Ha's that depended on relatively unskilled labor were the casualties. It was all Ha could do to maintain the current number of scholarships. For Korean businesses in China the recession brought numerous collapses, followed by bankruptcy and in some cases absconding executives. Worse, China imposed new labor laws that in turn increased the burden on businesses.

Offering scholarships not only benefited students from poor families, but also promoted closer ties with Korea. Another unexpected bonus.

Ha's policy of respecting the elders was a boon to the migrant workers as well. When they saw him treating the neighborhood elders, they felt as if he were treating their own parents. Ha for his part was grateful to the elders for providing a homey environment for his workers. He created yet another neighborhood civic event, a senior citizen festival taking place spring and fall. The elders danced and sang with abandon, tipsy on joy and libations. The workers couldn't let the elders have all the fun, and so they let down their hair and launched a talent show as part of the festival.

"Guangbao is our treasure," the elders proclaimed time and again. "May it prosper a thousand years, and we along with it."

The city officials advised Ha they wished to confer upon him honorary citizenship in Qingdao. Cold water would have satisfied Ha for an award, but what really pleased him was the recognition he was receiving while numerous other Korean businessmen were closing up shop and fleeing practically overnight.

"Sir, the shipment to the US is ready," announced Ha's production manager.

"Thank you." Out he went to the loading dock, where the truck was waiting, rear doors open and ready to receive the boxes coming down from the ramp. Right arm raised high, he shouted, "Ready? Go!" Down slid the first box. Ha took it in hand, made sure the packaging was up to standard, and passed it to the man doing the loading, the two of them working like a relay team. Ha wasn't one to loiter in his office, and personal inspection of an outgoing shipment had long since become a ritual. He wanted to have personally seen to each and every shipment across the Pacific, to feel the satisfaction of handling the fruits of his workers, and to encourage them to take pride in their hard work and professionalism.

Instead of instructing his workers from the sidelines he took part in grunt work like stocking; he put in overtime with everyone else to meet the holiday rush— just like he was an active participant in the post-workday pickup games. The women in particular were beside themselves with delight at his dexterity when he occasionally lent a hand to the making of the brooches and the necklaces, and they were grateful knowing that if they had to work through the night he would be right there alongside them. Unlike elsewhere, there were no troublemakers at the Guangbao factory.

Ha felt his back stiffening as the last of the boxes was loaded, but what a sight it was, the truck full of brooches and necklaces that would soon transform to bundles of money. He banged the side of the truck. "Good to go!"

Goodbye, he silently prayed as he watched the truck depart for the harbor. *I hope each of you meets a nice owner.* Every such departure reminded him that he and his wife had arrived in Qingdao to invest thirty thousand dollars in a second lease on his business life. This time they advantage of cheap labor, but still it was like trying to catch an eagle with a slingshot or subdue a tiger with a kitchen knife. What else could he draw on besides his time with an American accessory company and a failed attempt at running a Korean factory? More than once his helplessness at the start of his venture here had left him wet-eyed. But then came the magic decade of opportunities and success. As the saying went, winning the hearts of the people meant winning the world. And now that his business had grown a thousand-fold, he asked himself rhetorically, *Didn't I win the world?*

At the same time, he realized this gift from China would pale in comparison to the opportunities that would soon become available. The nation would transition from a world factory into a world market and the women, who accounted for 98 percent of the nation's consumer spending, would begin adorning themselves with designer goods and accessories. How big would his gift from China grow in twenty or thirty years' time? He felt his heart palpitating at the prospect.

"Sir, you have a visitor—a man sent by Mr. Chŏng."

"What is it?" Ha said disinterestedly as he paged through some documents.

"He said it's urgent, sir."

"Urgent?"

"Yes, he said the boss has been taken into custody by the PSB."

Ha's head jerked up. "What? The PSB!"

"That's all he told me, sir."

He closed the file. "Send him in."

"What's going on?" Ha asked as soon as his visitor was admitted.

"He's locked up."

Ha frowned. "So I heard. But why?"

"Apparently it became known that he supports independence for Taiwan."

"Did he actually say that?" Ha felt a wilting sensation.

"Yes—he was there on business recently."

"Of all the damn headaches," muttered Ha.

"He asked if you could visit him."

"Do you know how it happened?"

His visitor's hands were trembling as well as his voice. "I have no...no idea, sir."

"All right, I'll go see him. Is that it?"

"I can drive you there."

"Look, you're trembling," Ha tutted. "You need to calm down before you get behind the wheel. Forget it, please, I'll take my car."

With a sheepish smile the man scratched his head and said, "I'm sorry, sir. Thank you, sir," before scuttling out.

Ha moved to his sofa. His heart told him to steer clear of Chŏng and not get involved. The man had gotten himself in hot water, and a visit to him by Ha, if misconstrued, could be disastrous.

Ha reviewed the three big taboos—mentioning Taiwanese independence, defaming Chairman Mao, and criticizing the Party. Of these Chŏng had apparently committed the most egregious. What would be the harm in disparaging the dead Mao, and what use would it be to complain about the invincible Party, like an ant protesting about an elephant? In contrast, asserting or supporting Taiwan's independence could inspire treason and conspiracy—it was a potential calamity.

You might as well stick your hand in boiling water or douse yourself in gasoline and light a match. It was monumental stupidity, and if Chŏng had assumed the PSB would never know, then he was as naïve as a man who assumed his *ernai* would love only him. PSB surveillance was like a home-security system—if China was the living room, then Taiwan, Hong Kong, and Macao were the bedrooms.

Ha canvassed his memory for anyone who might help Chŏng. He wished he'd exercised more savvy and cultivated his *guanxi*—something he hadn't really needed to do as an exporter. What about the head of the environmental protection bureau? By himself Ha the humble accessory maker couldn't hope to wrangle a visit to Chŏng in jail. But what if he was backed by a city bureau head? He was keenly aware that Chinese society potentially had more connectivity than the newest smartphones.

"So, Mr. Ha, what is your plan?" asked the environmental bureau head in a somber tone.

"First, I will visit him and listen to what he has to say and then—"

"Why would a businessman make waves over a political matter?" the director broke in. "You know our duty is to cull out such people, regardless of their business. This is not something we can simply sweep under the rug."

Ha lowered his head. "Yes, I understand the magnitude of the problem. I am not here to ask favors, and I would not want you to be compromised on my account. I ask only for a special visiting session to see how he is doing."

"A special visit." The bureau head considered. "All right, I'll arrange it in light of all the good work you've done for us. But please understand we dislike most those elements that encroach on our national interest. Why do they meddle in our internal affairs? I don't know your relationship with him, but I advise you not to become involved—it could be risky."

Ha flinched—*risky* to Guangbao?—but managed a "Thank you, sir."

"If you can wait about two hours I will have your visit arranged."

"Thank you very much, sir." As Ha left City Hall, he looked up at the sky. Why was he so nervous and tense? Had he done something wrong? For Ha, asking any sort of favor was dispiriting, especially when it involved a politically sensitive matter. If the PSB in fact viewed Chŏng's behavior as a national security issue, what would happen to Chŏng? The thought drew a gloomy, helpless sigh.

Chŏng Tongshik was a manufacturer of table-top grills and, like Ha, had been drawn to Qingdao by the prospect of cheap labor. Unique when introduced by Chŏng a decade ago, the grill had been nicknamed the Golden Goose—it was almost as popular as monosodium glutamate in Southeast Asia. His business had flourished, and the buzz of excitement had kept him working many a late night to satisfy demand. His labor costs were one fifth what they would have been back home, it was difficult to keep the sales outlets stocked, and Chŏng's pockets were bursting with the proceeds. He doubled the size of his factory and became the envy of the other Korean businessmen here.

But after a few years the bubble popped. Chŏng's workers soon mastered the uncomplicated technique and left to start up their own factories. Popular as it was, the grill was a long-term possession, not something you traded in every year for a new model. And so it was that Chŏng's business fell into the double-whammy slump of a limited market and dog-eat-dog competition. Chŏng's ship was sinking, and try as he might, he found no way to bail himself out.

"Scumbags! I put food on the table for the sons of bitches and they stab me in the back. Damn them." This had become Chŏng's rant, in moments tipsy or sober, ever since his plant manager and sales manager had opened their own factories. He wanted to do them in, but it was a free and open market. He had no ears to borrow, no one to hear his moans. Then again there wasn't much sympathy to go around. Other Korean businesses were suffering the same fate, especially if the technology they used was as simple as making cotton gloves, chopsticks, toothpicks, or cigarette lighters. It wasn't long until Chinese-owned factories sprang up to manufacture these items. It was only a matter of time, Ha realized. Such technology transfer was not unique to China but had taken place decades earlier back home, where bonded factories contracted by Japanese companies had quickly mastered manufacturing techniques and counter-attacked Japan by unloading their products in Southeast Asia at rock-bottom prices.

The practice was not a violation of business ethics or a matter of shameless ingratitude, but an economic phenomenon as natural as high pressure filling a trough of low pressure. As long as the exploiters of cheap labor had to bring their technology out in the open to make easy money in a poor economy, why shouldn't the exploited find a way to acquire the necessary skills and make the product themselves? If the exploiter had not expected this outcome, he was the one to blame—skills easily learned could not be protected by international patent law.

The damage experienced by Korean companies was the tip of an iceberg that had also threatened to sink Japanese companies. The biggest Japanese victim of the imitation movement was Honda. Honda motorcycles initially proved a sensation in China—they were inexpensive, convenient, and a means of fast transportation for those fed up with bicycles but unable to afford a car. Chinese companies were up in arms to copy them. Rallying their know-how and skill, they dissected the Honda motorcycle and stitched it back together into a crude machine that made a racket like a motorcycle and had a low-displacement engine but was faster than a bicycle. Though a dowdy imitation of the Honda, it was incomparably cheaper and consumers gobbled it up like sweet dumplings. It was a winner! the ads proclaimed. The Chinese manufacturers jumped for joy at the massive sales and promptly served notice to the vast Southeast Asia market, until then monopolized by Japan.

Riders in the Philippines, Indonesia, Vietnam, and Thailand already favored motorcycles, which beneath the steamy sun beat sweat-inducing bicycles and expensive cars. Dumped at bargain prices but boasting larger engines, the Chinese makes were a big hit. Poor Japan could only watch helplessly as its markets bled to death, only to be given a new infusion of life by the upstart Chinese companies asserting their *boli duomai* strategy. Some of the first tycoons in the PRC made their fortunes through these companies.

With China taking control of new, advanced technology in every walk of life, those who were quick to extract technology from the Korean companies could be considered patriots. Why not, thought Ha—companies back home had done the exact same thing.

But Chŏng was enraged at the slowdown in his sales, and how could he keep his factory running when his workers were being lured in massive numbers by his Chinese competitors? He had gone to Ha for advice. "I'll be out on the street if I have to keep digging into my savings," he had said. It was then that Ha learned they had gone to the same university, which drew them closer. To close down his factory Chŏng would have to pay off the employees and put up with harassment from his lenders. And the accounts due? Chŏng would have to kiss them goodbye during the liquidation proceedings. The Chinese government granted special benefits to foreign companies, such as long-term leases of factory sites at practically zero interest, and a tax exemption for any factory that actively manufactured for at least ten consecutive years. But Chŏng's business had begun to fall apart in his sixth year, so if he were to close down he would have to repay all the benefits according to the government formula. What would stop Chŏng with his empty pockets from doing a runner in the middle of the night like so many of his brothers in business?

"You can't bankrupt yourself—you have a family. You should catch the next flight out. You did well while it lasted, and now it's time to move on." Ha was telling Chŏng what he wanted to hear, knowing this was why Chŏng had sought him out. *A politician must have ambition; a merchant must have no conscience.* It was a common saying here, in a society where a business could end in bankruptcy and success could be attended closely by failure.

"I wish I were you," said Chŏng. "No one's going to highjack your business. You're an innovator—you have to keep coming up with new designs." Ha realized how fortunate he was. Unlike Chŏng, who produced only one model of grill, Ha had to keep up with the latest fads, and had come up with as many new designs as a cat had lives.

And so it was no surprise when Chŏng vanished one night, shedding his factory like a snake its skin. The Chinese government took over the factory and didn't bother pestering the Korean authorities about Chŏng. Why go after the absconders—they were small fry in comparison to all the Korean factories on the east coast that were still up and running.

Ha thought back to the good old days, when China was host to more than ten thousand Korean factories. Those factories were instrumental in transforming the socialist mindset of killing time on the job. Through firsthand experience of capitalist labor practices the work force gained the manufacturing expertise that made it the core engine of the reforms and the corresponding economic development. And all this training came free—it cost Beijing nothing.

Ha forgot about Chŏng—out of sight, out of mind. And so it came as a shock when Chŏng popped up three years later. After trying out various products he had settled on baby needs—bottles, pacifiers, bibs, clothing, pillows, and to a lesser extent formula and food. The timing was right: Chinese mothers valued Korean baby products for their safety, quality, and design. And even with the one-child policy there were twenty to thirty million babies in the land. Perhaps most influential in Chŏng's choice was public outrage at fake baby-milk formula that was revealed to contain a toxic additive, melamine, that had sickened thousands of babies and proved fatal to dozens.

Chŏng's new business thrived owing to public confidence in his made-in-Korea brand. Before long he had expanded to Taiwan with dreams of becoming an import-export man and not just a dealer.

And here he was in jail now.

"How are you feeling?" asked Ha, alarmed at Chŏng's appearance. His friend looked awful.

"I'm fine. Thank God for that," said Chŏng, his parched lips trembling. "What do you think should I do?"

"I'm not sure." Ha spoke warily, not wanting to demoralize Chŏng. "I just got the news and my head's spinning…. I need to think the situation over."

"I'm wondering if this might be best," said Chŏng, making a circle with thumb and index finger.

"Ah yes, money. That's always an option."

"Especially here. Can you ask my wife to put together what she can and bring it?"

"Sure."

"Is it possible for you to contact the embassy or the consulate?"

"I think that's a good idea."

"Please. I'd appreciate it."

"Will do."

"And if there's anything else that comes to mind…"

"Of course." And finally Ha brought himself to ask what had happened.

"I have no clue. I feel like I got tricked by a goblin. I took a couple of my contacts to a bar. We had drinks, hostesses; it was a good time. And when the booze hit, we started talking politics. Well, the guys popped the question. And I figured, when in Taiwan you tell the folks there what they want to hear. So I said I agreed with them. And that's it. They were calling me *lao pengyou* all over the place, we were a happy bunch all right. And I was feeling no pain. And then what do you know… I get stopped at the airport here. I'm still trying to figure it out. I'm thinking maybe one of the girls ratted on me." He shook his head morosely.

"Who knows…" Certain that their conversation was being monitored, Ha refrained from speculating about Chŏng's two contacts.

"How many times have they questioned you?"

"None. And that's what's driving me up the wall."

"Well, when they get around to it tell them exactly what you told me—you wanted to keep the guys happy, it's good for business. See?"

"Got it."

"And keep telling them you made a mistake and you want to ask forgiveness. There's always a way to soften a steely heart."

"Right. I'll say I know I did wrong. And I'll wear the skin off my palms begging."

Ha felt hopeless as he left—was there someone else he could consult? Back in his office he dialed Chŏng's wife. In contrast with his own wife, who had a keen interest in the China-Taiwan relationship, she was slow on the uptake.

"How much should I bring?" she asked.

"Whatever you can put together was what he said."

"I see. Is he going to prison?"

"It's too early to tell. But the sooner you get some money to him the better."

Conversation concluded, Ha had a cup of *pu-erh* tea. The hot beverage worked its magic, and up came Chŏn Taegwang on his mental screen. Ha decided to call him.

"Too bad," tutted Chŏn after he'd heard the tale. "That's a topic you want to avoid even muttering in your sleep—and for all we know, there's more PRC sympathizers than police in Taiwan."

"My thoughts too. What would you say if I went to the consulate?"

"To ask for help?" Ha imagined Chŏn shaking in silent laughter as he asked the question.

"Well, that's what he wants."

"I gather you're not crazy about the idea. Have you ever known our holy grail consulates to help out expats? All they're interested in is making themselves look good. Well, if that's what he wants, I guess you have to give it a try. He's probably grabbing at straws. And you know what they're going to say. 'Did someone put you up to this?' Or, 'we don't have the manpower.'"

"You're right. So, any bright ideas?"

"It's a sensitive matter, so we need to be careful. If the government wants to send a message to foreign companies, they could give him a stiff sentence. Think about it—if Taiwan gets independence, then what about Tibet and Xinjiang— that's two thirds of the land in the whole country. And here the guy gets loaded and starts blabbering and figures he's out of reach. The thing is, China doesn't mess around. Look at all the drug kingpins they execute—my intuition tells me the same thing happens back home, but it's just not written up in the newspapers. They probably wouldn't execute him but they could lock him up twenty or thirty years. You know they have the balls." Chŏn was voluble and in his own way eloquent.

"So what can we do?"

"Off the top of my head? Well, first, don't waste your time with the consulate;

keep in touch with your environmental director pal. With your service record, I'm sure he'll go out of his way for you. See if he'll deliver the money from the wife to the PSB. Have him talk with the mayor too—the mayor's name is on those plaques they gave you, right? A second idea—and maybe more workable—is you file a petition with the signatures of all the expats in Qingdao. They're a powerful clique in the city's business circles and they can ratchet up pressure on the authorities by letting them know everyone's watching."

"That's a terrific idea. I'll get going on that tomorrow."

"Too bad you got caught in the exhaust—it's not going to help your business."

"Can't very well turn my back on him—fellow alumnus and all."

"Right. Especially when we're far from home. Don't be afraid to call me."

And so Ha ditched the idea of pleading for help at the consulate. He lacked patience with haughty attitudes and toxic remarks and didn't like to be disappointed. Instead he launched the petition drive. The responses weren't encouraging:

"The guy's crazy. Don't you think we should steer clear of him?"

"What if I get in trouble too?"

"I'm not interested . . . ."

"I'll wait and see what everybody else . . ."

"You really think it'll work?"

"If he's already on the PSB shit list . . ."

"You pay your money and you take your chances, no?"

"Sorry, I'm too busy . . . ."

The excuses and refusals threw him into despair. Scarcely half the expats had signed. How could he have been so naïve as to assume they would all be sympathetic? There were of course the acquaintances who were willing to sign, but he soon grew numb having to state Chŏng's case to each and every one. The refusals were sucking out too much of his energy, and the results didn't justify the time he'd put in. What if he'd had to deal with a group of strangers? Canvassing didn't make him an arbiter. And so he gave up.

Time to call Chŏn again.

"You know how it is, people covering their asses. Don't feel bad. You did right throwing in the towel. So it's back to your director pal."

"Isn't there some other way?"

"Nothing that comes to mind at the moment . . . ."

Ha ended the call and considered. He still felt perturbed by the bureau head's "meddling in our internal affairs" comment. It was an understandable reaction, coming from a civil servant, but the prospect of a second abject plea for help was disconcerting. Chŏng and his damn mess!

Ha recalled two recent snafus that reflected how seriously Beijing took the Taiwan question. The reticent expats would surely have known of them. There was a live television interview with a prominent Western political figure, whose overly positive outlook on China's economy must have been scripted for her. She even called for the *yuan* to be adopted as a key currency by the global economic system. And then came the question on Taiwan. Maintaining the status quo would promote international stability and peace, she said. Television screens around the world promptly went blank.

And there was the international conference that began with a buzz of excitement as the participants spoke of China's economic growth. But the preliminary optimism gave way to hushed murmurs when the conference papers were distributed along with a map of China—a map from which Taiwan had been erased. Was it an oversight? Was it intentional? The murmurs gave way to agitated hisses. The costly conference was immediately cut short.

Ha practiced his script and paid another call to the bureau head. "He was intoxicated. His businessman mentality got the better of him and clouded his judgment. He knows he made a mistake and wishes he could apologize a hundred times over. If he were to receive a prison sentence and the Korean media reported it, I am not sure how Korean citizens might react. Might I suggest that the government consider deporting him instead? That would be a death sentence for a foreign businessman, but perhaps no feathers would be ruffled. Deportation might be preferable to igniting a fire that could burn both of our countries." Ha concluded by asking if the bureau head could arrange for him to meet with the mayor.

"Honey, you've been neglecting the business, you seem distracted." It was the first time his wife and work partner had spoken out, and Ha had the rare feeling of being in the doghouse.

Part of him wanted to say, *Dammit, I've done what I can and I'm not going to worry about him anymore.* But what if Chŏng were sentenced and locked up? Once again Ha's guilty conscience won the day.

"I know and I'm sorry. I hope you can be patient—it'll be over soon."

Three weeks later the PSB loaded Chŏng onto an airplane and he was deported under the condition that he never again set foot in China. Ha hadn't been able to see him, indeed did not learn of this outcome until later. The day he heard the news he looked up at the easterly sky from one of the Qingdao beaches he had adopted. The same tiny white blossoms of foam that washed onto shore back home lapped close to his feet, making landfall where Chŏng had come visiting so many years ago.

4. The Dreams of a *Baofahu*

Red banners hung above the luxury shop on the busy street in downtown Guangzhou. From its closed door a line snaked around the corner and out of sight. Across the street Li Wanxing gloated and nodded—not so much from satisfaction but as a memory aid, one nod for every five customers. He was up to three hundred and trying to follow the line around the corner.

Jacques Cabang was his usual boisterous self, prancing and exclaiming with boyish glee. "*Sacrebleu*. I never dreamed there would be so many customers."

Li's eyebrows went up. "What are you talking about—you didn't believe me?" He glanced back and forth between the interpreter and Cabang.

The interpreter quickly put this in English and added, "You must explain. What you just said hurt his feelings."

"Oh, dear heavens. Of course I believed you. If I did not, we would not be working together. See? We even invited you to Paris. It is just that I am amazed at the crowd. You are an excellent planner with sharp insight, and a superior businessman."

He's a quick one, the interpreter had to admit as he hurriedly jotted down a summary of Cabang's remarks. *Of course our boss is "excellent," "sharp," and "superior."* He had always known Li could throw his weight around, but this newest venture was amazing—all those people going after a little coin purse! Just to make sure Li took it the right way, he dressed up Cabang's words.

Staring at Cabang, Li cleared his throat. "Is that really what you think of me?"

Cabang jabbed a finger at the line. "But of course. I have known your superior capability, but this time you have taken my breath away. Look at that line—it is longer and longer."

A man rushed up to them. "Boss," he panted, "it's more than we expected. Should we open thirty minutes early, and tell the hundred we hired that they can go home?"

"What the fuck you are talking about?"

Cabang jumped at the thunderous tone, even though he didn't understand the words.

"I'm just saying…they've been waiting for a while."

"Are you stupid or what? You should know by now we can stand still all night long once we set our heart on it. Besides, the longer you have to wait for designer goods, the more you're willing to pay—don't you know that? Scram, you idiot!" His foot snapped out and made contact.

The blow sent the man staggering backward. Gasping, he managed to straighten, then, face contorted in fear, whimpered, "I'm sorry, sir."

"I said get lost!"

Stunned, Cabang removed himself from the line of fire, afraid Li would kick the man again.

"Yes, sir." The man scrambled off down the street.

Watching the man disappear, the interpreter pondered what he had just seen and gave Li an admiring glance. The old crime boss couldn't hide his true colors. A hundred extras! Zhuge Liang had nothing on him.

Cabang inched up behind the interpreter. "What is the matter?"

"Boss, he's asking what's going on?" said the interpreter.

"Tell him. Except for the hundred extras."

"Sure." The interpreter did as instructed.

Cabang said, "No wonder. Well, it serves him right." He signaled a thumbs-up and nodded.

The line kept growing. Passersby asked around and reversed direction, hurrying toward the end of the line. Orderly lines were the rule in Guangzhou, part of the Special Economic Zone under the first banner of reform and development.

Pulling out his cell phone, Cabang said "I thought your idea of launching a new product was impressive, but I never imagined such an explosive response. I would like our president to see this, he will absolutely love it. Allow me to take a photograph, and I will send it to him."

Photo opportunity concluded, Li turned about, gesturing to Cabang to follow. "Now that we've seen the turnout with our own eyes, shall we head over? It's show time."

Cabang pocketed his phone, a beam creasing his face. "Thanks to you, I see my value index climbing already—and my year-end bonus too." He cast a contented eye across the street at the red banners with their gold lettering.

"'Designer purses, custom-made for China,'" read the interpreter. "And that one says, 'Lucky coin purse for wealth and happiness.' And that one there reads, 'Special gift for new product launch.'"

"Five at a time, got it?" Li growled to the two men standing guard at the entrance.

The men came to attention. "Yes, sir!"

Cabang enjoyed the éclat of Li climbing onto his high horse to display his partnership with the French designer firm.

The doors opened at noon, right on schedule. Li and Cabang entered through the back door and sheltered themselves behind the cashiers.

The first five customers, as soon as they were admitted, dashed to the display of red purses, arrayed in various shapes and sizes. Two of them, a man and a woman, each picked out a purse. The woman opened hers, pulled out what lay inside, and jumped for joy. "Oh my! It's there, it's there!" The man did likewise and shouted in elation, "*Dui ya, shi shi shi!* Me too." In the hand of each was a hundred-*yuan* note. Fresh off the press, paper-edge sharp, the highest denomination in the land featured the god of prosperity himself, the handsome Chairman Mao.

The woman put the bill to her lips and kissed the Chairman, then repeated the ritual three times.

The man observed the love of his life indulgently.

"Honey," said the woman, grabbing his arm and shaking him out of his reverie, "look here."

"What?"

"The name of the purse—*Lihua*. Isn't that lovely?"

"It's lovely all right. And what's that above it?"

"Blossoms."

"So many?"

"Let me see…how many…"

"Looks like eight of them."

"Of course—for money."

"Yes. Eight flowers arranged like the number 8. Like the circles of an Audi."

"I hadn't thought of that—you're so sharp, dear!"

"*Lihua* means money, eight flowers means money, the way they position the flowers means money—"

"Meaning we're going to be rich!" the woman interrupted in her pearly voice.

"That's what I say."

"Those French people read our minds."

"That's why the banner says, 'Custom-made for China.'"

"They did their research—great, isn't it?"

"I'm surprised. It's a very nice touch."

She touched the precious purse to her cheek, "The color and the shape, I'm so happy. I'm going to be rich for sure."

The man gave his purse a squeeze. "Me too."

"But, what should we do?"

"What do you mean?"

"I want one of every style."

His eyes widened. "What?"

"Can't I?" She looked as if she was about to cry.

"Maybe tomorrow. I only have enough for one each today."

"That's too bad. Today is the only day we get the gift money."

"What if we place the others on hold—why don't you go ask?"

The woman scurried to the nearest attendant.

"I'm sorry, ma'am. The special is today only."

The woman returned with a pout.

"I thought so." Then, seeing his sweetheart on the verge of tears, the man said, "All right, pick out what you want and I'll go get more money." And out he rushed.

Li and Cabang looked at each other.

"Amazing!" said Cabang. And then, seeing that Li seemed not to understand, "*Lihua.*" He had practiced the pronunciation over and over. He stuck his thumb up high. "Your purse and their response. The name works like magic—who could resist buying it? Your idea is so ingenious! The best."

Li gave Cabang an arrogant glance. "Now do you believe those figures I predicted?"

Cabang chuckled, but with none of the haughtiness Li had come to associate with Westerners. "Yes, indeed. I really do." He was already intimidated by the power Li would radiate as soon as the first proceeds were in hand.

The Lihua purse was a sensation with the other three early birds. After they had opened the purse to make sure the gift money was there, they returned to the gilded emblem, captivated. Each corner of the emblem bore a pair of blossoms, and each pair was connected to the pair on each side by a slender branch. The resulting square contained the two characters for "pear blossom." Among all the pretty blossoms, that of the pear symbolized wealth and prosperity, and no pear blossoms were lovelier than gold ones on a red background. In thrall to the brand name and the crisp hundred-*yuan* note inside, the five customers headed in turn for the cashiers.

The purses were priced at thirty-five hundred *yuan*, a thousand more than the cost of other designer purses. Cabang remembered that Li in Paris had made a pitch for this higher price—"The more expensive it is, the better it looks and the more it sells"—and his boss was only too happy to agree. The gift money was blood from a sparrow's foot—barely a drop.

Li's product was a hit with the other customers in line, and sales took off. His idea for the purse came from the gift-giving custom of Korean businessmen, and the eight blossoms making a lively connection with money came compliments of his designer. As for *lihua*, Yanling had reported during a weekend visit, "Daddy, there's a place in Seoul that all the Chinese tourists visit. Can you guess what it is? It's Lihua Women's University—they call it Ewha. They all take photos with the *lihua* blossoms in the background. Do you get the connection?" She was hinting that *lihua*, botanical symbol of wealth and prosperity, was similar in pronunciation to *lifa*, "money blossoms." Thus the connection between *lihua* and money.

Gazing at every customer leaving the store with a purchase in hand, Li was confident he could surpass Shanghai's Sanqiang men's underwear, a brand that had subjugated the land. *Sanqiang* meant "three guns," which a populace accustomed to catchy brand names was quick to understand as three shots—*bang bang bang*. In other words, the wearer could fire his weapon three times a night. Women hurried to buy them and outfit their men. From Shanghai the word spread all over the country. Women loved buying the *bang bang bang* underwear and the company hit a bonanza. You could never downplay the weight of a brand name.

What was to stop Li from overtaking Sanqiang? Sanqiang made men's briefs. The Lihua coin purse was made for anyone, male or female, who dreamed of being rich. What was more, the purse was outlandishly expensive in comparison with the underwear, and as Li had long since learned, "expensive" translated into "highly sought after."

Li noticed with pleasure that customers left without having their purses gift-wrapped. They were in seventh heaven as they fondled the lovely logo for all the world to see.

Cabang was all smiles and yet one concern remained: "What if we run out?"

"I had the same thought. We need to boost production." And with that, Li left the store.

What a bonanza! pondered Cabang as he trailed behind. *Good luck catching up, America. But how can a country that went through a socialist revolution still be so superstitious? The GDP is only five thousand and yet everyone can afford an expensive coin purse? What if the GDP shoots up to twice or four times what it is now? Imagine the sales figures! France will have a perpetual designer goods boom. The superstition here, I must take it seriously. Li, the ignorant bâtard, isn't the only one who's going to make a killing. I can do it too. I'll find an old wives' tale connected to money.*

Cabang felt his stomach churn with envy. Catching up to Li, he studied the man's face.

"We need to launch in the other big cities, yes?"

Li slowly shook his head. "We should wait a few days."

"Is there a reason?"

"Yes." But instead of elaborating, Li looked off in the other direction.

Cabang sensed Li putting on airs. The coin purse project had brought a change in Li's attitude with every corner they turned. Despite his foul mood, Cabang reminded himself the wisest course now was to accept the power that money had over Li—not to mention his partner's sniffiness now that he'd had a taste of real capitalist success.

"And?"

"We need to advertise our conquest."

Cabang smiled brightly as he let this sink in. "Ah yes, ads, the media. We need time, right?"

"Wrong. Getting the media involved is expensive. But there's another way— we can get a better outcome for a lot less money."

Cabang was lost. "Well, if newspaper ads are expensive, TV is probably prohibitive…. But if you have a cheaper option…"

The interpreter wanted to whisper *Internet*, but figured Cabang would eventually come around.

"My my. Whatever has happened to my shrewd French businessman? Do you remember your phone camera and the photos you took to show your boss in Paris?"

"Phone…photos…" Cabang snapped his fingers. "*Mais oui*, the Internet!"

"Took you long enough. Do you happen to know approximately how many Internet users we have?"

Here was Cabang's big chance to redeem himself. "The last I recall, you have about six hundred million netizens and nine hundred million cell phone users. I am sure those numbers have grown—tops in the world, I would bet."

"That is correct, more or less. So, do you think the news of our opening might be posted today?"

"Now I see," said Cabang, nodding. "The netizens will go berserk posting the news of their prized purse. That is good thinking!"

"And I don't think we need the hundred-*yuan* gift any more."

"And why not?"

"Didn't you see today? We don't need a carrot for our customers any more. At this point it's just an annoying waste, don't you think?"

"I agree, but…" Cabang cocked his head dubiously.

"What's the problem?"

"I'm afraid the netizens might plaster the websites with complaints about unequal treatment. Money madness, you know?"

"They can post all they want. Why should we drain our hard-earned money? You don't need to worry, I'll handle it."

"No, the bonus must stay," said Cabang. "We cannot besmirch our image and reputation; our president will not allow it. May I contact him about this?"

The interpreter added a cautious suggestion to Li. "I think you should go along with his opinion."

Li decided he had bigger fish to fry. "Fine. We'll do as you say. Who needs to save money? Instead we'll throw it at them, one hundred *yuan* for every buyer!"

Already, compliments from Li's hundred extras, the posting "Designer purses, custom-made for China! Special hundred-*yuan* gift for new product launch" had begun popping up on various websites.

The following day Cabang hit the road to launch the coin purse in the other big cities. From each city he contacted Li with the same news: "Hurrah—shining victory." And each time the image grew more vivid in Li's mind of his Lihua cresting the waves of popularity to douse the Sanqiang briefs. Damn it all, he wasn't just going to be rich, he'd be filthy rich. He was already a rich man with half a dozen companies in the black, and to attain his two dreams would make him a bona fide tycoon.

My lucky Lihua. A touch of red dye on cowhide, a little tinkering with the design, the gold imprint, and some zigzag machine stitches, and there you go—that'll be 3,450 yuan, please. Of which 20 percent goes for labor, ads, and whatnot. Without the logo it would go for a hundred yuan on the local market. A designer item is magic!

Forty percent of the profit margin was his. His lawyer had advised him to apply for an international trademark—he wouldn't regret it when the item became popular and the money started washing in. One hundred million coin purses were as good as sold. What if they sold a billion, or three billion, or even only five hundred million? He couldn't calculate all the zeroes.

A week later Cabang was back. "You should have seen the response—the customers went ballistic! I have never seen anything like it. You are a psychic—you know what the people dream of. I am now a true believer in the domestic market—we will definitely sell a billion purses—one billion!"

Li's mean spirit uncoiled itself. *The power of money gets to white guys too! So now I have myself a little white valet. Let's have some fun with him.*

"Monsieur Cabang, did I hear you say that the best way you people treat your guests is to invite them to your home?"

"Yes, I believe I did."

"Well, we treat *our* guests a bit differently. We like to take them to the most expensive restaurant with the best food. Even so, how about I invite you to my house?"

"How wonderful!" said Cabang with a deep bow. "It will be my honor." Cabang had benefited from such largesse in several other Asian countries.

"Can we make it the day after tomorrow?"

Cabang bowed even deeper. "By all means. I thank you."

Two days later a Rolls-Royce appeared at Cabang's door. Along the way to Li's home in a suburb of the city, he eyed the interior incredulously and took stock of his partner anew, wondering how much money Li had stashed away. The man was a typical parvenu, a *baofahu*. A Rolls-Royce! He snorted. He'd heard of Rolls-Royces in China, but a common businessman like Li—heaven help us! Leave it to the Chinese market to bail out the fancy gas-guzzlers. Well, who cared? If La France could frolic in the China market, why not L'Angleterre? What a country this was!

And then Cabang's philistine curiosity got the better of him: "How long ago did he purchase this?" he blurted to the interpreter.

"Maybe a month? He bought it when he moved into the new house."

"He had a new house built?"

"Yes. You'll see. It's in a very nice Western style. And located in a new neighborhood for our comrades who are better off."

Cabang's curiosity kept gnawing at him. How could Li afford a car that cost as much as half a million dollars, as well as a glitzy Western-style house? Rolls-Royce sales grew 170 percent a year worldwide, but 800 percent in China, thanks to guys like Li.

But Li's business didn't involve modern factories and cutting-edge technology. Instead his work rooms turned out primitive hand-crafted items such as jade and trinkets, firecrackers and incense, and plastics, relying on workers laboring for the lowest of low wages. He also leased real estate—a line of business that at least sounded better. How could a man who ran sweatshops afford a Rolls-Royce and a new house?

Finally Cabang's snobbish proclivities got the best of him. "I still do not understand," he said to the interpreter.

"What is it you do not understand?"

"Your boss. How can he be so rich with the factories and business he runs?"

"You are a Frenchman, and of course you would never understand."

"What does that mean?"

"Do you know how much we love to pop firecrackers and burn incense?"

"I believe so. You are serious enough to put up with the escalating pollution."

"It is good you know that. Since the reforms, we are even more passionate about such activities, and it is because we all wish to become rich. In our province those businesses are monopolized by a select few individuals, and recessions are unknown."

"A few? Is it not free competition?"

"Remember, we do not have your kind of capitalism. Think of it as our brand of socialism—socialist market competition, you might call it. That is all I will say for now. Please do not ask me so many questions, it makes me uncomfortable." He frowned.

"I still have difficulty understanding. Then why does he have a plastic factory? That is not much of a business, is it?"

"You are a French businessman all right. You have been coming and going for years, but you have no clue about us. Can you guess how many plastic bags we use a day?"

"Well…maybe a hundred million? Two hundred?"

"Are you serious?"

"All right, two hundred million!"

"You have no idea, Monsieur Cabang. One billion a day!"

"A billion!" said Cabang, goggle-eyed.

"Amazing, is it not? Our population in Guangdong Province is one hundred million and we use ninety million bags a day. But only a couple of factories make them. Is it not possible a man could grow rich with that one factory?" The interpreter gazed at Cabang.

"Amazing indeed. An outsider could live here his entire life and never understand much. So many *questions*…"

Cabang couldn't stop shaking his head. He wanted to question the interpreter further—how could monopolies exist here? But he resisted the urge—he didn't want to alienate his lifeline. He would be a blind man without a cane, a performer without his music. There were many good interpreters, but it wasn't easy finding one with whom you were in sync.

The Rolls-Royce glided to a stop. Cabang was overwhelmed by an expanse of verdant landscape and beyond it two buildings guarded by a small phalanx of topiary ornamentation. The green lawn was as large as a plaza, and contained a swimming pool whose clear water left him feeling refreshed and lent elegance to the buildings. Beyond the pool a gracefully arching bridge connected the two buildings, its railings clad in blooming green flourishes and fairy lights that seemed to wink and dance.

But what captivated Cabang were the twin reddish marble mansions. They were the ultimate in luxury, a queen in a red gown and a king in a matching cape standing ready to receive him. He was reminded of the coffin of Napoleon, his hero and the man he identified with history itself. He would forever cherish the Russian red porphyry coffin in its open crypt—how could that same red stone exist here in the form of two houses?

"Oh my," said Cabang, stiff with awe. "Mr. Li must have a huge family."

"Actually," the interpreter smirked, "the one on the left is empty. No one lives there."

"What? Then why bother to make it so big?"

"Monsieur Cabang. You are stunned by my boss's fancy houses, correct? That is precisely the effect he wishes to produce."

"You mean he wishes to show off his"—Cabang made a flamboyant gesture—"his *mianzi*."

The interpreter nodded.

"Here you are," said Li the gallant host, emerging from the house on the right. "I've been waiting for you. Come in!"

With a bow Cabang shook hands. "Thank you for inviting me. You have such a beautiful home. It reminds me of an Italian museum." What the heck, brown-nosing didn't cost you anything.

"What?" said Li, rejoicing in Cabang's praise. "You mean to tell me you knew at a glance it is made of the most expensive Italian marble?"

"Yes. In France we use red marble for that which is most precious and valuable." Cabang was about to mention Napoleon's coffin but caught himself in time. How could he compare a living person's house and the dead hero's coffin? The superstition-loving Chinese would box-and-saw him, a chilling thought.

"You're our first Western guest. The proper etiquette is to show one about, is it not? Please allow me to lead the tour." Li was smiling ear to ear, which was not how Cabang usually imagined him.

The interior was Western-style as well. The furnishings were busy and colorful, Italian items, maybe expensive but poorly matched. This did not stop Cabang, as he moved through the different rooms, from repeating himself silly: "Beautiful! Wonderful! *Très belle!*"

Outside, Li pointed to the trees. "Those five Japanese pines, look how straight they are. I paid half a million *yuan* for each one."

"Really? They are so elegant. Like beautiful women."

Li guffawed. "Monsieur Cabang, the suave French gentleman, you are most impressive." As he moved to the bridge he grumbled, "I've showed my Chinese friends around, but they're ignorant barbarians. None of them can appreciate it like you."

Beneath the bridge was a pond with several dozen carp the size of massive arms wending their way through the water.

"Also Japanese. Each one cost five hundred *yuan*."

Cabang shifted his sugar-coating into a higher gear. "Wonderful! This is the abode of the gods. Now I have seen everything."

Li was the picture of contentment. "Monsieur Cabang, I knew you were knowledgeable, but not that you have such perception and good taste. I'm quite taken with you. Let's go inside. We should start dinner."

The dining room looked out onto the garden, where lamps were turning on as evening set in.

"It is a lovely house." And then Cabang popped the question he knew Li was waiting to hear. "I wonder how much it would cost to build one like it."

"A should explain that a friend of mine modeled his house after the White House. *I* wanted the White House, but he beat me to it. That made me angry. It cost him about ten million, so I spent the exact same amount for this house, but I used Italian marble."

"I see. I would say your house is better—his is only a copy but yours is unique." Now Cabang was in overdrive.

Li burst into laughter. "Monsieur Cabang, you are a most excellent judge of quality. I knew you were different." In a rush of pleasure, he clapped loudly toward the kitchen. "All right, let's get the girls out here."

A few minutes later two women in short-sleeved *qipao* appeared, lipsticked smiles pasted on their faces. Cabang looked at the interpreter in puzzlement. Where was Li's wife? The interpreter blinked meaningfully but Cabang remained oblivious.

"Hey, Cabang, this is my number six, and that's number seven. University graduates, both of them."

The two women performed delicate bows that reminded Cabang of butterflies.

The interpreter instantly added, "Not for bed. Please do not touch them. They will help you drink."

Cabang was eager to know more. Did the brazen presence of these *ernai* mean that Li's wife was elsewhere? He wished he could ask the interpreter.

They settled at the table, the pretty women sitting next to the men and pouring *baijiu* for them into little ceramic cups, their manner as lovely as their looks. Gazing at the *ernai* serving him, Cabang thought how nice it must be to have *ernai*. With money and power, you could have as many as you could afford. In the 21st century, when equal rights for men and women were becoming a global trend, this might be the only country that openly recognized concubines. What a peculiar teaser! The Chairman had announced that "women hold up half the sky" and yet these college girls were ending up as *ernai*. With each mountain of mystery Cabang climbed, he encountered yet another. Well, *ce qui sera sera…* In any event, it was heaven for men. Correction: it was heaven for the haves and hell for the have-nots. No wonder people said that half the pretty girls in the land become *ernai* for the rich and powerful and the other half were barmaids. *How many* ernai *do you want sitting in your lap,* mon ami?

So many questions in the short time his cup was being filled.

"You must like swimming, sir," said Cabang. "What a nice big pool." Under the lamps and the perfect summer evening, the gently lapping water in the Olympic-size pool tempted him to plunge in.

"Not really," said Li. "You saw the big tub, didn't you? I love a hot bath with the girls massaging me. See, the guy in the white house had a pool, so I built a bigger one." Emptying his *baijiu*, he told his *ernai*, "I forgot about the dogs, it's time for their dunk. It's so hot out. Can you tell the guys?"

Merde! Cabang wasn't sure he'd heard the interpreter correctly. Dogs in that nice pool?

But sure enough, big as calves, they were brought in on leashes by the security guards, who shouted orders as they released the furry, restive beasts poolside. The dogs jumped right in. A dog's life wasn't so bad, thought Cabang as he watched the animals paddle to their heart's content—especially with a master as benevolent as Li.

Li's woozy, drink-reddened eyes came to rest on Cabang. "*Monsieur,* did I say I have two dreams?"

"Yes, I believe you did."

"Would you like to know what they are?"

"I would *love* to know what they are."

"If we sell a billion of those coin purses, I can achieve them both. First, I will be officially invited to join the Party." In 2002, the Party had begun inviting the wealthiest comrades in the land to join its central committee. "Second, I will have my own private jet."

"I definitely believe you will achieve your dreams. With more diversity in design, size, and materials, we will have even better sales. For example, we could try calfskin, goat, alligator, and ostrich. I bet we could sell the alligator and ostrich purses to our VIP customers for ten times the price of the others."

"Now that would be hot! As we like to say, the more dough you have, the more you want. Alligator and ostrich—I could use them as gifts for the high officials." Li edged closer to the table. "How long will it take?"

"Not long, once I contact the design team. We have every kind of leather, you know."

"Excellent. I knew we'd come up with some bang-up ideas. *Ganbei!*"

"*Ganbei!*" Cabang met Li's outstretched glass with his own.

"I just don't understand it," said Cabang as the Rolls-Royce pulled away from Li's estate.

The interpreter was hit with the smell of alcohol on Cabang's breath, "What is it you do not understand?"

"I know how much he wants to show off, but why in Hades would he build a house in which no one lives?"

"Do you think my boss is the only one who does that?"

"You mean there are others?"

"Of course. That is how he learned."

"What are you saying?"

"Monsieur Cabang, it is natural you do not understand. You have seen only the big cities, never the countryside."

"Why do you say that?"

"It is like this. We have many *huaqiao*—you know, the overseas Chinese—and sixty to seventy percent of them are from this province. For years they have worked like dogs and now they have returned home in glory and they want everyone to know it. To show off, one of them constructed a six-story building in a flash—but just the frame. Others copied him, including Li. That is why you can see so many ghost buildings in Guangdong."

"Aha. But I still do not understand why it is necessary to show off so much. Why is *mianzi* so important?"

"I am Chinese myself but I could not tell you. Even Freud would not know. There are so many things with no obvious reason."

"It is too much here, it makes me dizzy." Cabang wrapped his head in his hands.

The next morning Cabang went to Li's factory to order more jade items. A man holding a sign was protesting outside.

"Another protester—what does the sign say?" Cabang asked the interpreter.

"Let me see…it says, 'I too am human. After five years making gemstones I am suffering from silicosis. Compensate me!'"

"Another industrial illness."

"As long as jewelry processing continues…"

"Has Mr. Li changed his policy on workplace safety?"

"I am not sure, but I think not."

"He is more rich every day—should not his attitude change as well?"

"It all depends on the worth of the worker. It is all about *ren tai duo, ren tai duo!* And no way will *that* change."

"That is ridiculous. What about human rights?"

"I suggest you kill that notion. You are about to see my boss, and he absolutely hates hearing that kind of talk."

Cabang swore inwardly. It wasn't as if he was a UN Commission for Human Rights inspector. But he couldn't help being reminded of the awful scene he had witnessed five years ago inside this very factory.

Back then the factory was much smaller, more like a workroom, and filled with powdery dust and the screech of cutting and grinding. How could people work in such conditions? There must have been a hundred workers, mostly young men from the countryside, all busy with the precious stones. Clouds of floury dust rose from the shrilling machines. Cabang saw no fans. No one wore masks. All day they breathed that dust, and if they happened to work overtime, then sometimes all night as well. Cabang had lasted barely ten minutes, and by then he was having difficulty breathing, his eyes were burning, and his mind felt hazy. He thought he was going to die.

Cabang remembered his interpreter at the time saying, "The workers tell me their spit is blue, red, or yellow, depending on the color of the stones they work with." Cabang was afraid that anyone who worked there even a couple of years would come down with lung disease, even if the workshop had proper ventilation along with masks and eye protection for the workers.

"Please, not a word," the interpreter had told him. "It is no use. Everywhere you go, China is the same. If you want to have a good business, just keep mum." That interpreter too had repeated the *ren tai duo* mantra.

When Cabang emerged from the factory the man with the sign was gone. Cabang decided not to pester the interpreter. It would only elicit another round of *ren tai duo*.

Cabang made a tour of his outlets and a week later contacted the interpreter to let him know the new purse designs had arrived by email.

"The president had to go to Seoul; he will be back in a few days."

"What happened?"

"He left on a medical tour."

"I do not understand—is he sick?"

"No, he and number seven are having cosmetic surgery. He wants all his wrinkles removed, and for her to have bigger eyes and a higher nose. It is a new trend among the *baofahu*."

What could Cabang say to that?

5. Forgiveness Remains a Gift of Reflection

It was summer vacation but students, male and female alike, were still digging into their books at the Beida library. Most were seniors, and they were braving the summer heat to prepare for the fierce job competition they would face upon graduation early the following year. In recent years unemployment among university graduates had become a major social problem.

The cities on the east coast had the opposite problem: for two years running the factories were short twenty million hands, despite urgently enacted wage hikes. Now that inland economic development was in full swing, the influx of migrant workers to the coastal cities had reversed. Elated by the modernization of their home region, the workers had rushed back home, where employers awaited them with open arms and paid them no less than what they'd earned in their homes-away-from-home. And the jobs came with benefits. Most important, the workers could live with their parents—no more exorbitant rents in the coastal cities, no more landlord tension. Instead of bland, overpriced meals, they could savor home cooking. Gone too the lost and lonely life of strangers in a strange land.

But the surplus of university grads remained a headache. The highly educated sector of the work force had plateaued and openings were scarce for the new graduates spewing onto the job market. The need for these workers, most intense during the reforms, had diminished; before anyone realized it the economy was saturated with degree holders. It was unavoidable—other countries with healthy economies were bogged down in the same way.

And so it was that each of the new graduates was left to fend for himself or, increasingly, herself. This "individual problem" translated into "free competition":

no one telling you what to do or interfering with your possibilities for infinite growth. Intriguing on the surface but in actuality it was a law of the jungle—the strong would survive while the weak were devoured. To survive in that jungle, these Beida seniors were giving up their summer.

But a small percentage of the library denizens were studying for the pleasure of learning or in anticipation of graduate study. Among them was Chaehyŏng, who was browsing the stacks in preparation for a field trip to Nanjing.

He heard a stifled whisper. "Hello, Chaehyŏng."

He scanned the stacks and there was Yanling beckoning him.

Tiptoeing quickly toward her, his lips silently formed the word *shenma.* What?

She put her mouth to his ear. "Everyone to the lecture room." Her warm, ticklish breath gave off a leafy scent intensely strong and fresh, as if she had wrung all the green juice out of summer.

He held her hand and whispered back, "What's up?"

"Not now—let's go."

"Is it worth interrupting our study time?" he muttered as he followed her down the hallway to the library exit.

"Some Korean reporters are here."

He came to a stop. "Reporters?"

She looked up at him. "Why so surprised?"

"Not surprised, I just don't want to deal with them—I always have to watch my mouth. You remember how crazy the last interview got."

"Why worry? Compared with us, they're amateurs."

Chaehyŏng snorted. "As if not quite four years makes us professionals?"

"It does as far as history is concerned."

"So this is about history?"

"Yes. For a special report."

"A special report on what? Has anyone told them how big and complicated this country is?"

"That's why they'll only scratch the surface." Mischievously she prodded his shoulder. "So relax. Aren't you glad the Korean media is showing interest in us? That means Koreans in general are getting more interested in China." She locked her arm in his.

"Do you like it that China and Korea are getting closer?"

She smiled and her arm tightened about his. "It depends on what you mean by 'closer.'"

At the office of one of their history professors they found, gathered around the scholar, seven other Nanjing field trip students as well as a news team from a Seoul daily—the Beijing correspondent, a photographer, and two reporters, a man and a woman.

"From the distant past our two nations have maintained a deep relationship," said the professor. "We are bound by a common destiny to remain cordial friends united by mutual interests." From the gravity of his tone, you might have thought he was addressing an audience of hundreds. "To solidify this strong foundation, the two countries must have a profound understanding of each other, and the most effective catalyst to that end is the press. We are fortunate to have with us today reporters from a leading daily in Seoul. They are preparing a special report on China and they ask our cooperation. My wish is that all of you participate actively in this interview, knowing you have a crucial opportunity to contribute to the advancement of relations between our two countries." Like most intellectuals, the professor had been admitted to the Party only after a long apprenticeship in debate and discussion, and this left him sounding dry and rigid.

The Beijing correspondent then introduced himself. "I have been here four years and still have much to learn about China, but I will attempt to serve as guide and interpreter, so please bear with me. We are planning ten installments for our special report, focusing mainly on the economy, but also on political, social, and cultural issues. Today we would like to discuss politics and culture in conjunction with a visit to the grave of Edgar Snow." The correspondent spoke with native fluency. In contrast with the professor he was comfortable with his student audience. How different a similar message could sound coming from a socialist intellectual and a capitalist reporter, thought Chaehyŏng.

"This site visit will be a good experience for our students," said the professor as he led the group outside.

"Excuse me," asked the male reporter in Korean. "How often would you say your students visit Mr. Snow's grave?" The Beijing correspondent interpreted.

The professor was crestfallen. "Well...not often...maybe never...our department never has, so I assume other departments as well...only those interested, perhaps."

What happened to the spirited oratory? thought Chaehyŏng. He drew Yanling aside. "I just realized—there's going to be a problem."

"What problem?"

"The site looks like shit."

"Yeah...kind of..."

"So what do we do?" tutted Chaehyŏng, shooting a look at the professor's back. "We don't have time to do a cleanup before they get there...we should have known."

"Not much we can do now. It's embarrassing, but maybe the reporters should see the truth."

Yanling held him tight, as if fearing he would rush off to the site anyway. Would her Chinese classmates have done the same? Silently she thanked him for his concern about the garbage-strewn site, and for the unadulterated passion he felt for her and her country.

The path to the grave skirted Weiming Lake and led through a dark-green canopy of trees. The lakeside benches were unoccupied, and in the summer heat the still water had a desolate, defeated look. The clamor of cicadas was all about.

Arriving at the humble memorial, the professor gestured sheepishly. "It's not much to look at—I'm afraid no one tends it."

Resting on a rough-hewn granite slab was a rectangular marble gravestone inscribed in Chinese and English with "In Memory of Edgar Snow, American Friend of the Chinese People." The site was flanked by two squares of ground that might once have borne grass but were now weed-straggled and bare, littered with cigarette butts. The foot traffic, sporadic and haphazard, had compromised what was left of the natural setting. Chaehyŏng noticed, hugging the corner of the granite slab, a single wildflower with several desiccated blossoms.

The news team fell silent, faces hardening. What a perfect spot for a grave, thought Chaehyŏng, all by itself and offering a beautiful view of the placid lake in any season. It lacked only frequent visitors with tender hands.

The female reporter broke the awkward silence. "Shall we bow?" From her bucket bag she produced a small bouquet wrapped in tissue. Gently removing the dried-up wildflower from the foundation slab, she replaced it with the bouquet. Then she and her three colleagues bowed silently while the professor and the students looked on.

The party then descended toward the lake, except for the photographer. "May we ask a few questions?" said the male reporter. "Edgar Snow's *Red Star Over China* was translated into Korean in…1985, I think it was. It was through this book that we learned about Mao Zedong, the Chinese Communist Party, the Red Army, and the Long March. I understand it was published decades earlier in the West and that Snow is credited with introducing the Chairman and the Party to the rest of the world. Mao was so pleased, he is supposed to have said the book could serve as his biography. So why did the honorable Chairman decided to situate Snow's memorial site on the Beida campus?"

After the interpretation the students turned their gazes toward the professor at the same time he shot them a look. The students were at a loss. Chaehyŏng wondered if he would have to answer on behalf of his classmates. The silence grew heavy. He considered his classmates, met Yanling's eyes, and sighed inwardly. Why such a thorny question? He felt sorry for both the reporter and the students.

It was Yanling who finally answered. "I am very sorry. It is not that we do not understand your question. Rather we are lost for words because the site is so neglected. I am sure your question is based on your surprise. I am also sure our Chairman decided Beida students would be the best representatives to express the gratitude of our people to Mr. Snow. But over time we have allowed the site to fall into this ruined state. Students from other departments can be excused, but not those of us who study history. The spirit of history is based in the past, but by illuminating the past we can grasp the present and see into the shining future. We know this but we have failed to put it into practice. Our neglect shows in the state of this grave. I myself confess I come to this lake several times a week but I never think about Mr. Snow. I will make sure we learn from our embarrassment and look after the site. We thank you for your interest, and Mr. Snow, we hope you will forgive us."

She lowered her head and the other students followed suit. Chaehyŏng was loath to do so but went along, not wanting to draw attention to himself and be revealed to the news team as a Korean.

"Are you the student representative?" asked the correspondent.

"No," said Yanling.

"Then please have mercy on your humble interpreter and give me shorter sentences to work with. You talk like the Great Wall, no end in sight."

The correspondent's jocular words broke the ice. Yanling smiled bashfully, and the other students as well.

After the interpretation, the male reporter said, "We certainly understand. In terms of economic development you have accomplished in thirty years what the West took two hundred years to achieve. In this respect Korea is similar to China. In such a fast-changing world it is difficult for young people to keep looking back to the past, and so they can easily neglect it. It is just that we were shocked to see Mr. Snow's memorial in such wretched condition when the Chairman continues to be worshiped. We appreciate this opportunity to learn a slice of the history of present-day China. At the same time, we understand how you feel and do not wish to make you uncomfortable."

The professor looked down. "I am sorry. It is all my fault."

"Not at all, sir. Perhaps the site is taken for granted because it is so close by." The reporter shook hands with the professor.

"How many students, either Beida or countrywide, would you say know about Mr. Snow?" asked the female reporter. "Let me rephrase it: how many Beida students out of ten know about Mr. Snow, and how many out of ten know about Starbucks?"

More silence. "Be honest," said the professor. "And remember, you're not speaking just for yourself."

"Maybe ten out of ten for Starbucks and one out of ten for him?" one student ventured with an uneasy grin.

"Thank you," said the woman. "And now, if I could change the subject, what do you think of the US being the dominant superpower in the world?"

"I don't like their style," shot back a student. "It's too unilateral and violent."

"Wow, that was quick, thank you," said the woman. "Next—you have surprised the world by gaining G2 status. No one doubts you will soon be G1. What do you think will be *your* style in this dominant role?"

There was a pause. "It's a difficult question," said one of the female students. "Right now we think we should coexist on the basis of mutual interest and on an equal footing, unlike the American style. But we can't predict how our political leaders might deal with G1 status."

The male reporter regarded the students. "That's a well-thought-out answer, thank you. There's so much more we'd like to know about your economic miracle. For example, what percentage of your G2 status would you say is thanks to the Party, and what percentage is thanks to the people? We have heard that the Party claims one hundred percent credit. This might be a difficult question given the present political climate..."

Another gap in the conversation. Chaehyŏng was beginning to think the interview could last until midnight.

The woman smiled. "I realize that question could be answered differently depending on one's position and age group. And perhaps your silence itself is an answer. Shall we try another question? China is known as knockoff heaven. As young intellectuals, what do you think about that?"

The question brought an immediate response from one of the male students. "It's not a label we're proud of, but we're not ashamed if it either. It's inevitable in developing countries. We have a saying 'Many fakes become real.' We were late getting into the game, and imitation was never an issue, because we were eager to catch up with the technology of the advanced countries. In fact, we've transformed many of our techniques for imitation goods into technology for new products. And the more new products, the fewer fakes. We believe we'll soon shed the knockoff-heaven label."

"Thank you for that straightforward answer," said the male reporter. "You know, we wanted specifically to meet with history majors; you'll see why from our next question. Your professor mentioned that China and Korea are bound by a common destiny to remain cordial friends united by mutual interests. That's very impressive. Our question is, considering that China absorbed our ancient kingdom of Koguryŏ into Chinese history as part of its Northeast Asia Project, and considering the distorted history of that region has been taught in Chinese classrooms since 1993, will you not also teach that version of history when you become a history teacher? As you probably know, our people disagree with your government on this issue—we think it's wrong. What is your opinion?"

"Because it's a government issue," broke in the professor, "it's not for our students to say." His message was obvious: certain question were out of bounds.

"We understand. But as Koreans we had to ask. I will take that as an answer, professor."

A chill hung in the air. Yanling lowered her eyes and Chaehyŏng looked off into the distance.

For the next question the woman adopted a genial smile. "Conflicts large and small are bound to arise between neighboring countries. It takes diplomacy and open channels of communication to devise sensible solutions. This interview could be one such measure. I would like to clear the air a bit and ask your thoughts and opinions on Korea. Hallyu has spread throughout Asia and is now making waves in Africa. China is the country that set those waves in motion and we thank you the Chinese people especially for your interest in Korean dramas. So what are your thoughts about Korea? Good or bad."

"Koreans are smart and diligent," ventured one student.

"They are sincere and meticulous," said another.

"They have ethnic pride, public spirit, and strong unity," said a female student.

"Any bad points?" said the reporter with the same friendly smile.

"They're too impatient and they eat too fast."

"Too much of a do-or-die attitude; it can make them inflexible."

"They're too stuck-up." The students all smiled, as if they'd exhausted their inventory of Korea stereotypes.

The male reporter likewise adopted a softer expression. "We appreciate your honesty. Can we talk more about Hallyu? For example, why are Chinese so fond of Korean dramas?"

"We don't have such a variety of cozy family dramas," said a male student.

His friend added: "And many of the types of love conflicts, we don't get to see them in our programs. And those hot kissing scenes…"

"And the actors and actresses are all good-looking."

"And they're all so good at acting," said a female student. "It's not clumsy, and their crying scenes are something else. How come the guys can cry so well? It's amazing."

A student from the back of the group piped up. "It's fun to see what a good life you have—everybody lives well. We want to fix up our homes like yours, too."

Thanks to the Korean wave, the atmosphere had become more animated. "Don't fall for those good-looking actors and actresses," said the reporter. "Their good looks are artificial—they've had their noses and eyes fixed, even their eyebrows and teeth, and they get Botox shots. There's also a TV program about how that gets done."

"We know that," one of the Hallyu fans replied. "But they're all handsome and pretty to begin with, so maybe the surgery is just a touch-up?"

The reporter gave a hearty laugh, which proved infectious. "You're right."

"We thank you for your time," said his counterpart as she brushed back her long hair. "You've been very patient. Any last words about Korea?"

After a pause, one boy said, "Your Red Devils, they have the craziest fans. I saw them play when I was thirteen."

"Korea's so tiny—only fifty million people—but you have so many number-ones," said another student.

"My parents always say we have to watch out for you Koreans; it's scary how motivated you are. They always mention the gold campaign during the IMF crisis."

"You're so near and yet so far. We have a relationship that goes back thousands of years, historically, geographically, and in terms of trade volume, so we know we're close." The girl paused. "But your security depends so much on the US I'm wondering what your position will be when we get bigger and military tension erupts with America."

A student standing next to the reporters spoke up. "I see the true face of Korea through the Korean businessmen here. They all speak good Chinese and understand our history and culture. I don't think that's possible without genuine interest and affection—it's not just a money-making mentality. Westerners and Japanese are different. We all know they're interested in China as a way to generate profit, not as a place to share their feelings. In that sense, we understand you are our true friend. We're rooting for you to make the most money out of all those countries."

The correspondent concluded by thanking the students and promising them a copy of the resulting article.

Yanling and Chaehyŏng stayed behind. "I'm sorry," said Yanling. "I dragged you outside on a hot day, and all for nothing."

"Not at all. It was a golden opportunity to see what my fellow students think about Korea. You don't easily show your inner thoughts, you know."

"That business about the distorted history," she said in a subdued voice, holding his hand tight. "I was so embarrassed."

"You shouldn't be. I don't like your government's position, the whole world agrees it's screwy, but it has nothing to do with us. The world media and historians can ridicule the Chinese position all they want, but it won't influence our relationship. Please don't worry, Yanling. Our love is here to stay." He locked her hands in his grip.

"Oh, Chaehyŏng." Her eyes pooled with tears.

"Yanling!" He pulled her to him, his powerful embrace bringing her lips to his. In the thick shade the cicadas sang more dizzily, as if cheering them on.

Preparation for the Nanjing field trip consumed Chaehyŏng for the next three days. Normally a field trip concluded with a discussion after the students returned. But this time, to coincide with the seventy-fifth anniversary of the massacre at Nanjing, a seminar with Nanjing University students would take place after the visit to the War Memorial. All students were welcome to participate—there would be no designated presenters.

Chaehyŏng had decided to focus on Japan's disavowal of the massacre, comparing it to the Japanese disavowal of the Korean comfort women. In the case of the comfort women, Japan's demand for material evidence and other proof from the victims struck him as a hideous tactic designed to avoid complicity and apologies. The survivors, all of them grandmotherly women by now, had testified that they were kidnapped and forced into sexual servitude for the soldiers of imperial Japan. Graphic evidence indeed. But the Japanese government deemed it insufficient—there was no documentary evidence of coercion. As if the young women had in their possession an imperial certificate of kidnapping! There had to be documentation, thought Chaehyŏng, secreted away in the Japanese archives.

From here it was a short step to the Japanese revisionist stance that China had fabricated the Nanjing massacre, a claim that outraged the Chinese. All thoughts about the sultry Beijing summer were forgotten as Chaehyŏng plunged into the possible reasons for this monstrous claim originating with the Japanese politicians.

Arriving by night train at the Nanjing station, Chaehyŏng and the group were met by some twenty Nanda history majors and their professor, and all together they boarded a waiting bus.

"We welcome you to Nanjing," intoned the professor as the bus got under way. "We do not allow the Japanese press in our city. Other newspapers are welcome, of course. Nanjing citizens like to say they will donate ten *yuan* if we go to war with Taiwan, but all of their assets if we have a war with Japan. So you can imagine how we feel about the country. We are honored and grateful to share with you our wounds and suffering and to observe with you the seventy-fifth *datusha* remembrance. We will take you to your lodgings and then proceed directly to the War Memorial."

The anti-Japanese sentiment, the burning hatred, felt to Chaehyŏng like a cold knife thrust into his heart. One of the traits he found most shocking among the Chinese was their indifference to others. They could ignore the rape of a foreigner, a five-year-old run over by a car, an old man collapsed on the street, a shopkeeper chasing down a thief. And yet these citizens of a land that went berserk over money would offer up their life savings if war broke out with Japan?

He whispered to Yanling, "I don't think I need to visit the memorial."

Her large eyes grew wider. "Why not?"

"I've heard all I need to hear—what he said about people's assets going toward a war with Japan is proof enough for me that Japan slaughtered three hundred thousand people here."

"Very smart! Don't forget to mention that in the seminar."

"I wish you wouldn't be sarcastic." He reached for her hand.

"I'm not. I just want you to understand that group hatred and rage don't happen without a bone-deep communal experience. Think about the Jewish experience of the Holocaust and fanatical Zionism—do you suppose there's a connection? At the memorial you can relive the massacre, and *that's* the proof you need."

"All right…"

"You don't sound very excited. Don't you want to add that to your seminar talk?"

"I'm not much into theorizing."

"So humble. If you're not going to use my idea, then sell *your* idea to *me*."

"What do you mean?"

"You know—like when you have a lucky dream…"

"You're funny. All right, you can have it for free."

"No deal. Money has to change hands, otherwise it doesn't work."

"I didn't know you were so superstitious."

"Here, payment in full." Giggling, she handed him one *yuan*.

"Rich at last. Thank you, my highness!" Bowing, he accepted the money with both hands.

Depositing their belongings at the inn, they washed up, had breakfast, and got back onto the bus.

"All right, everyone," announced the professor. "We're headed for the memorial. This trip is for *you* to experience, and I won't say much. Please take it all in and then we'll share our thoughts at the seminar afterward."

The bus passed through the gate of the memorial and came to a stop before a vast lawn bearing only a gigantic ash-colored rock. No buildings were in the immediate vicinity. Everyone disembarked, no one speaking. Stiff with tension the students filed into the memorial, a tunnel whose walls bore glass cases displaying images of the three hundred thousand people massacred by shooting, *nippondo* decapitation, hanging, live burial, immolation, rape, and flaying—every manner of killing the human brain could devise.

"We are entering Wan Ren Keng, the pit of ten thousand corpses," the professor announced.

The tunnel sloped gently down, and with every step Chaehyŏng imagined walking into a hellhole of mass slaughter—this must have been the goal of the architects, the apparent lack of structure allowing viewers to be sucked into a ghastly, lifelike environment. The artistic and philosophical imagination reflected in this underground memorial gave him an appreciation of modern Chinese art.

The display started with Japan's merciless and undeterred advance with armored tanks. Then came the gruesome photos of slaughter. One showed several dozen Japanese soldiers looking down toward the bottom of a hill where other soldiers were bayoneting Chinese bound and variously crouched or lying on the ground. Behind them another human target was being dragged, followed by another soldier.

In another photo some two dozen soldiers stood at their leisure, hands in pockets or behind their backs, watching a small group of civilians with their hands tied behind their backs, one of them clothed in white, walking toward a ditch. Dirt was piled high on both sides, a shovel at the ready. A live burial was about to commence.

A hazy photo showed a kneeling man bent at the waist, neck grotesquely elongated. Above him a Japanese soldier with his sleeves rolled up was striking down with his *nippondo*, the shimmering blade appearing beneath the man's chin. The camera had captured the moment of separation of neck from body. A dozen Japanese soldiers looked on.

A bare-chested man with cropped hair was kneeling on the ground. Behind him stood a Japanese soldier in undershirt and vest, scowling at the victim, *nippondo* at the ready. Behind the soldier stood three of his comrades, mouths open in laughter, hands on their hips or behind their backs at parade rest. Chaehyŏng imagined the sword poised to strike to the rhythm of their laughter.

A severed head was suspended from a barbed-wire fence. The closed and sunken eyelids and the fleshless checks were covered with blood, and the mouth held a half-smoked cigarette. Surely the man's hands were tied. Who then had provided the cigarette? An altruistic soldier granting the wretched man's last wish? Or had the executioner framed the severed head and played nice-guy with the cigarette butt?

Two haughty soldiers stood proudly, hands resting on the hilts of their *nippon-do* as if the swords were canes. Next to the photo was a headline from a Japanese newspaper: "Mukai 106, Noda 105, Reign Triumphant in 100-Head-Chopping Contest."

Photos of hundreds of bodies strewn along the banks of the Yangzi.

A woman naked from the navel to her knees, where a soldier, posing with a heroic smile, had lowered her skirt. A trophy photo.

A woman with her skirt covering her face, underwear down to her knees, a stick poking out of her vagina. Chaehyŏng assumed she had been raped and killed.

Dozens of women, heads lowered, shoulders hunched, backs curled over, flanked by a pair of soldiers, each with a rifle over his shoulder. One woman, face ridden with fear, looked back at a teenage girl consumed with terror. Where were they going—to a "comfort station," to serve the soldiers at any hour of the day or night?

Who had taken all these photos? The question lingered in Chaehyŏng's mind. In 1937 a camera was as fancy as an automobile or an airplane. Photographers were a talented group who not only took photos but developed them. When Japan invaded Nanjing, Chiang Kai-shek's army had retreated with the wealthy in close company. The poor and the powerless were left behind. Finally Chaehyŏng spotted the answer on a small label by one of the photos: the pictures had been taken by Japanese soldiers, a record of their victory celebrations. The film was sent to a Japanese photo shop in Shanghai to be developed, and the Chinese working there secretly released the photos to the world.

A single photo changes the world. Chaehyŏng was continually reminded of this. These photos did not lie or offer excuses. They were proof, witness, and testimony all in one.

The emotional climax of the visit was a display of mud-encrusted skulls. Chaehyŏng bristled at the sight, confused, ashamed, and regretful. He thought about the claims voiced by Japanese prime ministers, the governor of Tokyo, and officials of similar stature—that China had fabricated the massacre—and imagined their words deflecting impotently from the glass encasing the skulls.

When the group emerged from their descent into this unplumbed historical hell their faces were hard, clenched teeth visible between tightened lips. The professor was the last to come into view. "Let no one doubt why we study history." He took a deep breath. "We will now have lunch. The seminar will begin at two."

The same professor delivered the opening remarks. "We designed this seminar without a specific format, to encourage a free and open exchange of sentiments and opinions, and to help you expand your awareness. You don't even have to think of it as a seminar. Please feel free to express your thoughts, and the more of you who participate the better. So let us begin."

"I'm sure all of you felt the same," said a student in a ringing voice and the earnest tone Chaehyŏng had come to associate with public speaking here. "During our tour I tried to suppress my boiling rage and my hatred. But for the first time in my life I lost my appetite. Two issues came to mind. First, such vivid evidence being treated as fabrication. And second, how do we respond to that ilk who make such claims? I have no answers. And that makes me even more angry; I feel helpless as a scarecrow. How can I get over this? Help me, please."

The room was a sea of dour, grim faces. The silence weighed heavy in the southern China heat, broken only by the whizzing of fans.

The Beida professor scanned the circle. "Your silence reflects your suffering and pain as students of history, as well as our people's indignation and torment. Perhaps it is through the language of silence that suffering and pain engrave themselves in our souls and conscience. As historians we must develop this basic capacity; we must be aware of this our basic task. Our discussion doesn't have to be theory-based, rationalized, or over-conceptualized. So whatever thoughts you have, please feel free to express them."

A second student looked about the group passionately before speaking. "Japan killed a total of 45 million people in the war, and among them 35 million were ethnic Chinese. In other words, the number of people Japan slaughtered equaled about half the population of Japan at that time. By comparison the number of Japanese who died is 2.1 million, and then there are the 170 to 200,000 A-bomb victims in Hiroshima and Nagasaki. Japan has repeatedly complained it is the first A-bomb victim in world history, and it does this to dilute and whitewash its brutal invasions. Adding to this, they make the wicked claim that the *datusha* is a fabrication. I have to wonder if they still think of us as dismissively as they did in 1937. And if so, how much longer can we be expected to bear that humiliation? What if we were to jeer at their claims of A-bomb victimization, like they ridicule our claims of massacre?"

A Nanda student gestured to another student. "I think you want to answer. Go ahead, speak up."

"It's nothing new, but I suggest that through insinuation we make them angry just like they've made us angry. I have two ideas. One is to keep reminding them that their invasion deserved consequences, and one of those consequences was the A-bomb. In other words, it served them right."

"Right on!" came a guttural cry, followed by a round of applause.

"And your second idea?"

"We tell them that dropping the A-bomb was the best thing the US did in the Pacific War. If not for that, Japan could have killed four to five times as many people."

"This is new to me, at least," said a Nanda student. "But I'm afraid such a statement would draw international criticism. Can you back up what you said?"

"Yes. According to my research, in February 1945, when it was clear that defeat was looming, Prime Minister Konoe advised Emperor Hirohito to begin negotiations for a peaceful surrender. But the emperor refused. He was still seeking a *tennozan*, one great victory. The commander-in-chief of General Defense Headquarters decided on one last operation to defend against the expected Allied landing—they would concentrate their forces at six possible landing sites in Japan and a seventh on Korea's Cheju Island, with orders to fight to the end. So seventy-five thousand troops of the imperial 58th Army were deployed on Cheju. The US forces landed on Okinawa, and during three months of fighting, twelve thousand American soldiers were killed, sixty-five thousand Japanese soldiers, and two hundred and twenty thousand civilians. We must pay special attention to the civilians. They were asked to die for the Emperor and not surrender to the US And so the civilians went on a rampage—parents killed their children, children killed their parents, and neighbors killed their neighbors. Otherwise the military would do it for them. When Okinawa fell, the 58th Army troops on Cheju repositioned themselves on the southwest coast of the island, expecting the US would attack there in preparation for landing on the main Japanese islands. Please pay attention to what I'm going to say, and remember that it is hypothetical. Cheju's population at the time was two hundred thousand. The rule was that you fight to the end. On the basis of what happened in Okinawa we can predict that about two hundred thousand more people would have been killed—fifty thousand soldiers and a hundred and fifty thousand civilians. And when the US landed on the main islands, and if they advanced on Tokyo Headquarters, there would have been many more casualties. So: if the A-bomb had not been dropped, the Emperor's stubbornness would have led to at least one million and perhaps two or three million additional casualties. We should not overlook this possibility."

"Excellent!"

"Dissertation quality!" Loud shouts came with applause.

"That's a good approach, very original," said the Nanda professor. "Exactly the kind of analysis I was hoping to reap from this session. I hope you develop it into a solid essay."

Yanling passed a note to Chaehyŏng: *Are you going next?*

Encouraged, he rose to the occasion. "Hello. My name is Chaehyŏng and I come from Korea. I would like to share a few observations with you. First, during our tour I found Japan's atrocities much worse than what I have read. I realized yet again that Japanese can be shameless and wicked, even when they are presented with all the evidence. I thought only Koreans suffered during their colonization by Japan, but I was shocked that you also experienced unfathomable suffering. And all day, I was impressed by the quantity of material in the exhibition—it tells me how perceptive and interested you are in preserving history.

"And now I would like to talk about my belief that Japan has withheld a sincere apology. I always wonder why Japan has not performed the kind of atonement Germany did, and why its officials often come out with ludicrous statements and claims. I have tried to locate the roots of this mentality, and I think I have found a clue. But first I must ask, are you familiar with the Imperial Rescript, signed by the Emperor on August 15, 1945?" Chaehyŏng surveyed the group; no response. Happy to be speaking on a potentially new topic, he continued. "The answer is implied in the Emperor's statement. May I read it for you? It should only take a few minutes—is that all right?"

"Sure," said the professor.

"Good idea," said one of the Nanda students.

"Thank you. So here it is." Chaehyŏng began to read:

TO OUR GOOD AND LOYAL SUBJECTS:

After pondering deeply the general trends of the world and the actual conditions obtaining in Our Empire today, We have decided to effect a settlement of the present situation by resorting to an extraordinary measure.

We have ordered Our Government to communicate to the Governments of the United States, Great Britain, China and the Soviet Union that Our Empire accepts the provisions of their Joint Declaration.

To strive for the common prosperity and happiness of all nations as well as the security and well-being of Our subjects is the solemn obligation which has been handed down by Our Imperial Ancestors and which lies close to Our heart.

Indeed, We declared war on America and Britain out of Our sincere desire to ensure Japan's self-preservation and the stabilization of East Asia, it being far from Our thought either to infringe upon the sovereignty of other nations or to embark upon territorial aggrandizement.

But now the war has lasted for nearly four years. Despite the best that has been done by everyone – the gallant fighting of the military and naval forces, the diligence and assiduity of Our servants of the State, and the devoted service of Our one hundred million people – the war situation has developed not necessarily to Japan's advantage, while the general trends of the world have all turned against her interest.

Moreover, the enemy has begun to employ a new and most cruel bomb, the power of which to do damage is, indeed, incalculable, taking the toll of many innocent lives. Should We continue to fight, not only would it result in an ultimate collapse and obliteration of the Japanese nation, but also it would lead to the total extinction of human civilization.

Such being the case, how are We to save the millions of Our subjects, or to atone Ourselves before the hallowed spirits of Our Imperial Ancestors? This is the reason why We have ordered the acceptance of the provisions of the Joint Declaration of the Powers.

We cannot but express the deepest sense of regret to Our Allied nations of East Asia, who have consistently cooperated with the Empire towards the emancipation of East Asia.

The thought of those officers and men as well as others who have fallen in the fields of battle, those who died at their posts of duty, or those who met with untimely death and all their bereaved families, pains Our heart night and day.

The welfare of the wounded and the war-sufferers, and of those who have lost their homes and livelihood, are the objects of Our profound solicitude.

The hardships and sufferings to which Our nation is to be subjected hereafter will be certainly great. We are keenly aware of the inmost feelings of all of you, Our subjects. However, it is according to the dictates of time and fate that We have resolved to pave the way for a grand peace for all the generations to come by enduring the unendurable and suffering what is unsufferable.

Having been able to safeguard and maintain the structure of the Imperial State, We are always with you, Our good and loyal subjects, relying upon your sincerity and integrity.

Beware most strictly of any outbursts of emotion which may engender needless complications, or any fraternal contention and strife which may create confusion, lead you astray and cause you to lose the confidence of the world.

Let the entire nation continue as one family from generation to generation, ever firm in its faith in the imperishability of its sacred land, and mindful of its heavy burden of responsibility, and of the long road before it.

Unite your total strength, to be devoted to construction for the future. Cultivate the ways of rectitude, foster nobility of spirit, and work with resolution—so that you may enhance the innate glory of the Imperial State and keep pace with the progress of the world.

The moment Chaehyŏng finished, a student pointed with his pen and snarled, "I didn't hear a single word of surrender!"

"That's right. You see the point."

Another student, red-faced with irritation, said in a trembling voice, "Could you re-read the section 'Our sincere desire to ensure Japan's self-preservation and the stabilization of East Asia'?"

"Sure." Chaehyŏng obliged the student.

"I can't believe he said, 'it being far from Our thought…to infringe upon the sovereignty of other nations.'" He banged the desk with his fist.

"'Or to embark upon territorial aggrandizement'?" said another student in exasperation. "How the hell could he say that?"

"I am glad you noticed those sections, they are the ones I want to talk about. I also want to consider a third point," said Chaehyŏng as he surveyed his audience.

"I think I found it," broke in another student. "There was no apology to the countries Japan victimized. Could you repeat what he said about the East Asian nations cooperating with the Empire?"

Chaehyŏng read the section a word at a time.

"What kind of crap is that? It wouldn't be enough if he bowed thousands of times for mercy. Instead he comes out with this f—sorry—blithering. It's the most unconscionable thing I've ever heard."

"Now I see," said another student. "I think I can understand why the politicians keep coming out with preposterous statements instead of a sincere apology—they're taking their lead from the Emperor, aren't they?"

"Yes," said Chaehyŏng. "In his Prescript the Emperor is establishing guidelines for his people. This is why I believe the Japanese politicians will not apologize but instead will continue with their outrageous claims about the *datusha* and the comfort women. So I suggest that as historical allies and comrades China and Korea must jointly make a vigorous response to Japan."

"Well done!" said the Beida professor. "I'm impressed."

"So you're from Korea," said the Nanda professor. "Well, your Chinese and your presentation are excellent, and I go for your suggestion wholeheartedly." With that he clapped. Everyone joined in, Yanling applauding the loudest as she gazed at him.

Not long after the field trip, Japan nationalized the islands they referred to as Senkaku, reigniting daily anti-Japanese demonstrations in Beijing. China responded by dispatching maritime surveillance vessels to the area, and the anti-Japanese rallies spread to the other metropolises and from there to smaller cities. The media maintained active coverage of the unrest, while the PSB watched from a distance. The rallies were not only spreading but heating up.

The rallies reached one hundred cities, rowdy protestors trampling the *hinomaru* flag and burning the Rising Sun flag as symbols of imperial Japanese aggression. The rallies always ended at a Japanese embassy or consulate with the demonstrators chanting, "Diaoyu belong to the PRC!" and "Shame on Japan's rash behavior!" and enjoying some exercise in the bargain, working their arms out lobbing bottled water and eggs at the buildings.

Stunned by the vehemence of the protests, Japanese businesses and shops closed down temporarily, as did shops specializing in Japanese goods.

Chaehyŏng, come!" said Yanling breathlessly as she rushed into his apartment.

From his seat at his computer he stared at her. "What's going on?"

"Don't you know? It's the eighty-first anniversary of National Humiliation Day." The Japanese invasion of parts of mainland China on September 18, 1931, known to history as the Manchurian Incident, was commemorated by the PRC as a day of national shame. "Our History Department is joining the rally. Let's go. Don't you remember, 'historical allies and comrades'?"

"Sure, I'm with you." He sprang up from his desk.

"You're a man of your word! I tell you what—if Japan menaces your Tokto, I'll be there demonstrating with you."

"Promise? All right, let's go!" Holding hands, they rushed outside. As they neared the Japanese embassy they saw that the huge crowd was growing, the street taken over by the demonstrators.

"Defend Diaoyu!"

"Boycott Japanese products!"

The chants were fierce and furious.

Yanling broke off chanting long enough to say, "When it comes to rallies, you're tops in the world, right?"

"How do you know?"

"Because your anti-regime demonstrations were the model for your Red Devils rally spirit."

"Is there anything you don't know?"

"Not if it has to do with my lover's country—pretty soon my husband's country."

"All right, cutie." Chaehyŏng pretended to pinch her cheek.

"There it is, the embassy." The building was surrounded by protesters.

"Diaoyu belongs to the PRC!"

"Hands off Diaoyu!"

As the chanting intensified, Chaehyŏng saw water bottles and eggs being launched. He looked ruefully at his empty hands.

"Here!" said Yanling with an impish smile. Out came eggs from her shoulder bag.

"You're something else." He gave her an ardent look and felt an egg being deposited in his palm. "A shame to waste them on—"

"Ha—so I got fake ones."

"Really?"

"Throw as many as you want."

"What would I ever do without you! All right, let's limber up the arm."

Approaching the embassy building, Chaehyŏng screamed until it hurt: "Diaoyu to the PRC, Tokto to Korea!" Then he let fly an egg.

Yanling joined in, her voice sharp and shrill. "Tokto to Korea! Diaoyu to the PRC!" And then it was her turn to fling an egg.

6. The Grand Betrayal

"You are a company president and you know nothing," said the investigator with a menacing look. "I'm supposed to believe that?"

Andy Park swallowed, which made him all the more thirsty. "I repeat—I am in charge of design and construction, not management. The companies in our Gold Groups operate somewhat independently. The only person who sees the whole picture is our chairwoman."

"I am familiar with the concept of division of labor, but no one would believe she was the only person who knew the extent of this affair. You aren't telling me the truth. We need to know when this plot began."

Park clutched the front of his company work jacket in frustration. "You can ask me all you want, but I know nothing. I feel betrayed by our chairwoman—she abandoned me at the construction site."

"That is a lie. We are familiar with this kind of act; we get it over and over from the guys we detain. So, I'll ask you once again. I suggest you tell me the truth while I still treat you like a gentleman. If you were not a US citizen," said the investigator, Park's passport dangling from his fingertips, "then by now you would—" He slammed the passport onto the desk.

Park flinched, his amiable face crinkling tearfully. "I am more angry with you than our chairwoman."

"What do you mean?" The investigator scowled at him.

"The PSB knows everything. So why did the PSB not know that our chairwoman was planning this bankruptcy, or that she was going into hiding? I did not plan any of it, but you are accusing me. That is why I am furious."

There was a crack in the inspector's equilibrium. He stared at Park with dubious, penetrating eyes. "When was the last time you saw her?"

"It was four months ago, in Xian."

"What was she doing there?"

"She asked me to expedite construction."

"Then she was already planning the bankruptcy. But you sensed nothing?"

"That is correct. Whatever company you work for, you will always hear the CEO asking you to speed up the project. Saving time means saving money. So I did not find her request unusual."

"All right. Let us suppose you were in the dark, as you say. Once this case is closed and you are released, if she reestablishes contact you'll rejoin her, correct?"

"Please spare me your insults," an indignant Park protested, staring at the investigator. "I am an architect, not a businessman, and I detest unethical moneymaking. It may be that because she knows this, she kept the affair a secret from me."

"Are you telling me you do not wish to make money?"

"Not at all, I value it highly. But I do not wish to be greedy; I want to make my money honestly. I want to do good work and make money for a good life. I value my designs and my architecture work more than money."

"Tell me what you know about your CEO."

"Well, I am very disappointed, but it is possible she could do such a thing."

"Please explain."

"She is super-smart and capable. Like all business people, she is ambitious. Ambitious enough to manufacture this affair. You must know the saying that businessmen should not have a conscience and they may downplay their methods as insignificant—misdemeanors at worst. Perhaps that was the thinking of our CEO."

"Even though you say you know nothing, do you understand how much damage has been done at the Xian site?"

"Yes, I do."

"And are you aware that the responsibility lies not only with your CEO but with you as company president?"

Park was speechless.

"Are you or are you not?"

"Yes, I am aware of that."

"All right. That's all for today." The investigator stretched and yawned.

Back in his cell, Park plopped down on the wooden floor and leaned his head back against the wall. He was physically tired but mentally exhausted. It still had not sunk in: she had planned this bankruptcy and run.

As he had said to the investigator, she seemed brave enough to have pulled it off. Charismatic, clever, and agile, she had so many faces. And now, somewhere, she was wearing the cunning face of a fox.

Where to start? Most shocking was the realization that she had concocted the bankruptcy and fled. Scarcely less surprising was the implication of her act: China no longer interested her; no prey was left to hunt. Why would wolf-sharp, deer-quick Wang Lingling come to this conclusion when all her underlings among the Gold Groups presidents contemplated another two decades or at least ten years of gold to dig in China? Most hurtful, she had ditched him in remote Xian, the inland construction site. How cold-blooded she was—like a lioness, she had thrown her cubs from a cliff top and would nurse only the ones that survived the fall. He was the first casualty. How many of her boys would be sucking her tit back in the US? And of course there were plenty more architects of his caliber to be had there. The final indignity was his own cluelessness. Perhaps the bankruptcy might be covered up as a fluke. Still, it must have been brewing for some time. Why didn't he catch on when she had come rushing over to Xian? An obtuse workaholic like him couldn't hope to survive in a jungle where you attacked your prey and flew off with it clenched between your teeth.

Park knew the concept of a planned insolvency but he'd never imagined he might be part of one. Crafty as she was, Wang would not have tried to single-handedly pull off the scheme of siphoning off project funding—the Gold Groups assets were too vast and complicated. For the last decade the Gold Groups had built skyscrapers here without a single failure. So, who else was involved?

Maybe Cooper, the number two, the most trusted man among senior management. Anyone else? He flipped through the Harvard-Berkeley photo album in his mind, but none of the dozen or so familiar faces stuck until he came to Thomas. He must have been the money connection—Thomas the stock trader in Hong Kong, which like Wall Street was awash in a sea of money. Any scheme involving the defrauding of creditors could be launched from there. So, the three musketeers were crossing the Pacific, the two men nestled in the bosom of the third, each sucking a tit, while the rest, himself included, had been thrown over the cliff. Who knew, maybe a couple of the others had been salvaged as well.

Park grimaced. Would he have wanted salvaging? What if she had offered him a seat in the ejection capsule, like she used to offer him dinner? He wanted to give her the benefit of the doubt and believe she was too rushed to have given him full consideration, but if she *had* asked, would he have been able to steer clear? Yes, he told himself, if he had known of her scheme. But at this point it was all conjecture. And he was naïve to even think, *What if...* It was wishful thinking that the menacing beast he now saw in her would have transformed into a house pet.

Where had her gluttonous ambition originated? He could forget for the time being the bank loan they had taken out to get the Xian project off the ground. The urgent matter now was the workers' next paycheck. And how was he to explain to them that they no longer had a job? Such thoughts made her conspiracy feel all the more merciless. That a woman of her elegance could appreciate agnosticism, artistic sensitivity, and religious tolerance and at the same time be so venomous. Did it all come down to money? Had the nefarious nature of business desensitized her?

Lingling—what will I do if I run into you? He wrapped his head in his hands and decided he never wanted to see her again.

His meal lay untouched. The food was gross, but he'd lost his appetite anyway.

Again the next morning he came face to face with his interrogator.

The man peered at him with nasty eyes. "Are you on a hunger strike?"

Park met his gaze. "No—I have no appetite."

"You should force yourself to eat. If you get sick and collapse, it's a big responsibility for us. I don't want that."

"All right, I will try to eat."

"I'll ask you two questions, and you will answer me honestly. Then you sign. Then we release you." Deliberately he spread open a document. "First question. Do you agree not to leave Beijing for one month?"

"Yes, I agree." Park had already decided to do whatever it took to get out of jail.

"Second question. Do you agree to report to us daily during that time?"

"Yes, I agree."

"All right. Here you sign and stamp."

"I'm sorry, I don't have a seal."

"No, of course not. Sign first and then just press here with your finger." He demonstrated pressing his index finger on the vermilion ink pad and then the document.

Park did as instructed, his first experience with finger-stamping.

"We will return you to your cell and you will wait there until we bring you out."

Park tried to eat his lunch—not for the sake of the interrogator but out of consideration for his family. He finished barely a third of it. The afternoon wore on interminably. To win their *manmandi* you have to learn *manmandi*. He wasn't here to earn merit points; he was being detained for an alleged corporate crime and should not expect to be released *quaiquai*.

Park tried his best to put down three more meals, and the following afternoon he was freed, five days after being brought from Xian here to Beijing. Those five days felt longer than his thirty-eight years of life. How could he ever have imagined being locked up in China? On the bright side, thanks to Wang, he'd had an exceptional five-day experience. He didn't know whether to laugh or cry. He felt forlorn and empty realizing his ties with her had been severed. The document he had signed was presumably meant to discourage any attempt on his part to contact her. She was not stupid. She had created a financial scandal and managed to slither away from the all-knowing PSB. The PSB's only option was to watch over him in case she surfaced.

"Sir, we had to close out your account. Your company card is not authorized. We are very sorry," said the familiar hotel receptionist.

Aha. "I understand. May I keep my room for one month using my own credit card?"

The receptionist bowed, more deferential now. "Thank you, sir. We will return your belongings for you."

Park kept to his room the following day—there was no one to see anyway. He wondered about the other presidents, scanning their numbers on his cell phone, but gave up on the idea of contacting them. He knew the PSB would not be derelict in their duty, and with their X-ray eyes everywhere trained on him, a phone call could turn into one more pretext to accuse him.

The next morning, and every day thereafter, he checked in with the PSB and filed a report of his activities of the previous day—he had rested at his hotel. On the eleventh day he was stunned to see on the front page of his English-edition newspaper: *$1 Billion Planned Insolvency Carried Out by* Ernai *of 10 High Officials!* The sensational headline put it all in perspective. Park closed his eyes and shuddered. Part of him wanted to pitch the paper into the trash, another part badgered him to read. Curiosity won out in the end.

As he surmised, she had used her beauty to broaden her connections with powerful officials, had used the resulting benefits to expand her business and maximize profits, and had schemed the insolvency as an exit strategy—all of it out of greed. And now she was on the run. Why should he be surprised?

The oldest tactic in a spy war was using a beautiful woman as bait. It was a potentially pernicious game, but if you used caution and vigilance it was foolproof. So why not use it in industrial wars, where the battlefield was an open business market requiring maneuverability sweetened with money?

Park did not believe everything he read. In China a story could be blown up or shrunk tenfold. In any event, this scandal would not be advantageous to the Party or the government. But whether the scandal involved ten billion *yuan* and a hundred high officials, the important thing was the public display.

The good news was that taking a story public usually meant the case was about to close. Perhaps his one-month house arrest would be shortened.

The next morning, he received a call.

"*Wei*," said the caller before switching to English. "This is Wan Yenchun!"

"Hello, Mr. Wan. Long time no see. Is it you, really?"

"Yes. You sound surprised." Wan, the Gold Groups president for public relations in China, sounded unconcerned.

"Excuse me? Aren't you shocked about what's happened?"

"Indeed I was—very shocked. But the investigation will soon be concluded and the story will be buried, and then you need worry no more. Here we have so many big scandals reported every day that people tend to forget quickly, and that is good."

How could he be so relaxed? Park wondered. "Didn't you get harassed?"

"Of course, I was investigated. Why don't we meet and talk about it?"

"Where—"

"I am at the coffee shop downstairs."

"Really? All right, I'll be right down."

Park dashed to the elevator. Now this was exciting! Sure enough, the investigation was drawing to a close—he would no longer be under PSB scrutiny. All the more reason he was eager to see Wan. Plus, it was stifling and lonely being shut up at the hotel with nothing to do but gaze at his navel and wonder what he should be doing. For example, should he have notified his wife? And whom to see first, her or his parents? All these unanswered questions had left him with frayed nerves.

From the elevator he rushed to the coffee shop.

"Andy Park!"

He froze at the sight of the two men waving to him. There beside Wan was Cooper!

"Andy—did I give you a jolt, good buddy?" said Cooper, offering his hand.

"I'll say. Cooper, I can't believe you're still here." As he took Cooper's hand a thought flashed through his mind. Cooper's insouciance had tipped him off.

Wan tittered. "What is so strange about that?"

Park said nothing. Cooper was supposed to be with Lingling—what was he doing here? Gazing at Wan, he felt his intuitions solidify.

"I guess you might think it is strange. But Cooper is the one who contacted the PSB when he saw through the scheme of Wang and Thomas. So, even though those two slipped out of Hong Kong without a scratch, Cooper received lenient treatment." Wan was beginning to sound like Cooper's mouthpiece.

Park stared at them both, lost for words. *You betrayed her, then.* He managed to stifle the words. Two more dots connected in the mystery.

"Anyway," said Wan, "yesterday's report is in the past. And so is Wang. We are devising a new business, a cram school for learning English. You know one of the ten richest men in the land runs such schools, right? We predict this business will be good for another two decades. If we expand nationwide, especially to the interior, two more tycoons will be born!"

Traitors! Park chewed on this word as he listened to Wan's effusive plans. The mystery came together at light speed. During his years at Harvard Park he must have read at least a hundred mysteries—they were a good stress reliever. He'd long since found himself mentally writing a mystery whenever he came across an intriguing incident. Nationwide? That meant they'd need a lot of dough. "Then the two of you have formed a partnership?" This was one of the last clues to the puzzle.

"No. The contract specifies that I will be in charge of public relations, and to start with I will do some of the instructing. I will receive thirty percent of the profits. You know, Cooper wants to expand to Korea too. Korea is even more rabid about English than China. So Andy, why not take over the Korea operation, with the same terms as me—what do you say?"

Cooper sat smugly, arms folded. Park imagined a puppet delivering this pitch. He pretended to consider the offer.

"I appreciate your thinking of me. But I have a job waiting for me back home. My father-in-law has a few businesses, and he asked me to take over his construction company," said Park, lying through his teeth. This being a mystery, it wouldn't suffer from one or two fictional elements.

Cooper let this sink in. "Too bad. Oh well, we tried. Shall we go?" His attitude was placid yet overweening. He reminded Park of a rich plantation owner.

Park watched the two men depart. Lingling's face kept overlapping with theirs, but the peacock feathers he was wont to imagine were dull and ruffled. There were still a few loose ends to his mystery.

Checking in at the PSB station, he wavered before deciding to report that he had met the two men. He would leave no opening for further misunderstandings or accusations. You couldn't take chances with the PSB bugs picking up conversations two kilometers away.

Every day was tedious. He had never realized how sickening it could feel to have to work at killing time. His thoughts inevitably led him to definitions of happiness. People often compared it to air—it wasn't visible to the eye, couldn't be taken in hand. As the wise man had said, when you are not unhappy is when you are happy. But that definition was too figurative and abstract. It took Park's current desperate experience to convince him that his happiness index was highest when he was insensible to the passage of time, when he was engaging in activities he loved.

To kill time, he read the English daily from the headlines to the ads. It wasn't enough. And every morning he checked in and studied the expressions on the PSB faces, which gave no inkling of his status. As if they would worry themselves on his account.

All right, fight *manmandi* with *manmandi*. Soothing himself with this thought, he filled his days digesting the newspaper and drinking up to a dozen cups of coffee. If he ventured thoughts about his future his mind tended to blank out, and not even the mysteries displayed in the corner of the hotel gift shop could tempt him.

Ten more days passed. And then another bombshell in the newspaper, but this one tucked far inside. Cooper and Wan were dead. Their car had gone into a lake on the outskirts of Beijing, apparently at high speed, and they had drowned. It was a bare-bones accident report, twice mentioning the pair were American and accompanied by thumb-sized photos, possibly from their passports, showing docile faces.

His stomach clenched with anxiety—would the PSB bring him in for questioning? But when he checked in the following day, not knowing what to expect, his reception was no different from usual.

The month came to an end. He could add a month of house arrest to his life experience list.

"This is my thirty-first day," he reported at the daily check-in. "May I leave tomorrow?"

"Where are you going?"

"To Seoul. My family is there now."

"All right. You may leave."

Toyotomi Araki took money from his wallet and dropped it on the counter. "This is it," he announced to the woman. "So long."

"What?" She snatched the bills. "Do you go back?"

"No."

"Then, is there an issue with our service?"

"Where have you been, woman? You're helpless. Didn't you read the paper yesterday? The government declared a crackdown on foot massage parlors, to clean up you-know-what—and it's going to last indefinitely."

She cackled. "I have been right here, manager Toyotomi. I am not the helpless one; you are the naïve one."

Why didn't these women ever cover their mouth when they giggled? But what could you expect of females who rode bicycles on the street, not giving a shit if their panties were showing?

"What do you mean?"

"You should know better; you are an old-timer. Do you really believe everything you read?"

"They swear this crackdown is different."

"That is why I like you *nihonjin*. You are fine, law-abiding citizens. But you seem to forget you are in China. The government says this and that, but it is all hot air, like the cawing of crows. Have you not heard the saying 'Government has policies; we have measures'?" She fixed Toyotomi with a gaze, then batted her eyelids playfully.

"Yes, I've heard it—it's a great saying. So are you telling me—"

"*Mochiron da yo!* Of course. We need to keep our VIPs safe and secure. We are already taking measures. You do not have to say *sayonara* yet." This time she gave him a saucy wink.

Toyotomi was drooling with curiosity. "Tell me, I have to know."

"We are working at night, after all our guests leave," she whispered conspiratorially. "Construction will be finished by tomorrow."

"What construction?" asked Toyotomi, muffling his voice.

"A tunnel, to send you to a different floor."

Toyotomi shook his head doubtfully. "Won't they find out?"

"My innocent Toyotomi-*san*! We take our measures, and the PSB takes it easy. Their body is government policy but their heart is our measures, and everything is peachy, *ne*? Otherwise, how can they end with five times as much spending money as their paycheck? Life is great, is it not?"

"It *sounds* great. It's wonderful you have wiggle room. And I love 'Government has policies, we have measures.' But I still have a concern." Toyotomi heaved a sigh, his shoulders drooping.

"Dear me, what could that be?" she said, equally theatrical.

"I'm so blessedly happy here, how can I go back and live in my bland Japan?"

"Please, *Toyotomi-san*, enough of the sighing! Do not worry, you will live with us forever!"

"I would love to. But I don't see how I could, I'm so nervous these days." Toyotomi, no longer the buffoon, wore a grave expression.

"What now?" she said, likewise serious.

"Didn't you see the rally a few days ago?"

She flinched. "Ah, yes, I did."

"Well, everybody was all excited, so I understand how they could be a bit extreme, but when I saw only Japanese cars getting set on fire, I realized I can't live here any longer, it's too scary." Toyotomi shuddered as if he were witnessing the scene firsthand.

"Toyotomi-*san*, do not be alarmed. You know they do not do that out of love of country. They are all poor; they have no money to buy a car. So they were venting their grievances and taking their revenge on those poor cars. Please do not over-think the situation." Outwardly she tried to soothe him while inwardly she was laughing. *Why set your jaw against us? If you continue to do that, not a single car of yours will be left.*

He nodded. "I guess you're right—about some of them at least." Then came a sly grin. "When did you say you're finished with your measure?"

"Tomorrow. You will be the first one," she said with a cloying smile. "We will give you special service."

"All right. I should have some fun as long as I'm here." And with a wave he left.

He was in the elevator when his cell phone rang.

"*Moshimoshi.* Ito Hideo *desu*! When is the get-together with Ishihara, tonight or tomorrow?"

"Don't tell me you have dementia already. It's the day *after* tomorrow, at seven."

"Ha ha. Don't try to fool me. Maybe my short-term memory is shot, but be-yond that I remember perfectly, and I know it's *not* the day after tomorrow. You're the one who's demented."

"All right, you win. It's tonight at seven."

"*Arigato.* I'll see you then. I might be a little late."

"Did something happen?"

"Yes, a little something. I'll tell you when I see you. Until then."

What now? Toyotomi stared at his cell phone screen as if it were a dead face. He tried to downplay the premonition. The ominous feelings had become fre-quent, and he blamed them on the stress and jitters from the television coverage of the rallies a few days before.

Heated demonstrations had ignited in all the major cities, drawing throngs of spirited protesters. He knew Koreans were consummate demonstrators, but the Chinese were catching up. He'd noticed Koreans were organized, disciplined, and slogan-based; they steered clear of arson and destruction, while the Chinese rallies were larger, disorganized to the point of chaos, and erupted in property damage, like the protests he had seen from the Middle East.

Toyotomi was irked by the failure of the PSB to quash the rally. They exer-cised more authority than American police, were more aggressive, and yet there they were, staged at the perimeter of the rally, looking on with their hands behind their backs. For a moment Toyotomi thought he was in London or Paris watching the Bobbies or the gendarmes making their leisurely rounds. *Thank god they were there, though.* How many more Japanese shops and restaurants would have been trashed, how many more Japanese vehicles would have been torched? And what if he had been there? He didn't want to think about it, apart from deciding he would no longer walk down the street even in broad daylight. The Chinese intolerance toward Japan was much more violent, a reaction he hadn't noticed a decade ago. As China's economic power grew, its people's attitude changed. The underlings were now the dominant power, and every suppressed emotion transformed into confidence. The explosive ethnic rage for revenge was powerful. Toyotomi shuddered. Deep down inside he would have been happy to stay here, but with each new day fueling his disgust with the growing anti-Japanese sentiment, he realized it was time to go home. He heaved yet another sigh. If only there were a kind ear to hear him out.

Where to buy a gift for Ishihara? He decided on a department store. If he wanted to bargain at the shops he would have to speak Chinese; English would not work, much less Japanese. At the department stores, the prices were fixed—no haggling necessary, though he recalled there was still one foreigner group in Shanghai—the Koreans of course—who would try to bargain at the department store.

Japanese were welcomed with fanfare at the retail shops because they paid full price, no questions asked, just as they did at home. They had no skill at haggling. Toyotomi preferred to interpret the fanfare not as an expression of love for Japanese customers but delight at the prospect of dealing with pushovers.

But the Koreans, they were something else. If a merchant called for an outlandish price, they would slash it 80 percent as a launch pad for bargaining. So why did the merchants prefer these bargain hunters? Toyotomi wanted no haggling, no talking, no wasting of time and energy—just paying the amount on the price-tag. What was to be gained from a pricing tug-of-war?

In Xiushuijie, the fake market heaven, he remembered a men's watch with an imitation-diamond-studded face priced at one thousand *yuan*. A Japanese shopper would bargain it down to seven hundred or eight hundred and leave the shop gleeful, but a Korean would get the same watch for two hundred or in rare cases one hundred. Or a dozen Koreans would gather, whether strangers or friends, and demand a group discount: "We'll each buy one at one hundred *yuan*." If the merchant said no, they would counter with "Then how about we each buy *two*, at one hundred?" Eventually the merchant would give in—*boli duomai*.

Strangers forming a bargain brigade? Never in Japan. It was a mystery to Toyotomi. What to call it—collective improvisation? Group power? Maybe collectivization was the best term. Whatever you called it, Koreans in the Chinese market used it effectively. Toyotomi knew that around Qingdao, Weihai, and Yantai, the nerve center of incoming ocean traffic, twenty-five thousand Korean businesses had built a manufacturing mecca, the seed of the Chinese economy miracle. On the aggressiveness index, Koreans were off the scale; the Americans and Japanese couldn't compare. With Korean enterprises forget it—once they felt comfortable, *kamikaze*! Get it done yesterday—that was their business mentality.

What about the Koreans working here? Dealing with stolid and picky Chinese customers, they countered with patience and relentless tenacity. Their reward? Expanded market share. Already passable in English, they quickly shifted gears and tackled Mandarin once in-country. With almost mechanical regularity, with devotion and passion, they worked. Their linguistic fluency beguiled the Chinese heart even before they launched their sales pitch; they saved their interpreters for the details. Winning hearts and opening wallets—killing two birds with one stone.

How were they able to learn the language so fast? They needed only a couple of years. Toyotomi had never recovered from the humiliation of hearing an American say how odd it was that Japanese were so quick in thinking and yet so abysmal in speaking.

He might as well face it—the Korean businessmen were devoted and tenacious; they would continue to expand and sink their roots. And they had another advantage—no lingering legacy of historical conflict and ethnic animosity with China.

Toyotomi goggled at the teacup display in the department store. It was inexhaustible, all the marvelous shapes and colors. There must have been as many different teacups as there were varieties of tea. Tea in China went back more than four thousand years; it permeated the venerable culture. Toyotomi selected the most expensive pair, the cups made of paper-thin white porcelain and bearing an image in blue of a man poling a small boat down a stream issuing from a large, mist-draped mountain. He had often wondered why teacups came in pairs. He had heard that tea was best drunk by yourself in meditation; next best was with a close friend, communicating silent words while you sipped. The more people you shared tea with, the less tasty it was. The scene on this pair of cups was perfect for tea combined with meditation. And the craftsmanship was exquisite. Was it any wonder European aristocrats back in the old days would purchase these delicate, thousand-year-old vessels at any price?

Toyotomi arrived at the bar first, then Ishihara.

"Hideo might be a bit late," said Toyotomi as he guided Ishihara to a private room. "But we can get a head start."

"Did something happen?" said Ishihara, forehead creased.

"I don't know. He said he'll tell us when he gets here. I just have a feeling."

"A feeling usually means something. Especially these days."

"Maybe. We'll see."

Their waiter arrived with beer and bowed at the waist. "Shall we bring the girls?"

"Not yet. There's one more in our party." Toyotomi handed him a hundred-*yuan* bill.

The waiter accepted it with both hands, head so low they thought he would bump it on the floor. "Thank you, sir. Thank you."

Toyotomi presented Ishihara with the gift. "On the occasion of your departure for home—lucky you. I didn't get tea because I can't tell what's real."

Sheepishly Ishihara took the box and began carefully to unwrap it. Placing one of the cups on his palm, he squinted at it. "It's marvelous. I've always wanted a set of these. You splurged. I'll cherish them and get good use out of them."

"It was the best I could think of; it symbolizes Chinese culture."

"Indeed. Their traditional crafts don't get any better than this. And the tradition is alive and well—only now it's a commercial product. The country amazes me."

"Sure. Where else could you find people who are so screwy yet serious, this combination of chaos and regimentation? A fake heaven with precious earthenware."

The two men were still discussing Chinese culture when Ito burst in breathlessly.

"Damn it all. Son of a bitch held me up thirty minutes. Sorry I'm late." He took off his suit jacket and threw it on the floor.

"What is it this time?" said Toyotomi, frowning.

"I can't believe it—this idiot is complaining about a hundred cans of paint, says the price went up and the color and quality went down."

"Well, did they?"

"Are you kidding? No, he's just trying to make trouble."

"You sure? It's not fallout from the rallies?"

"I'm sure that's what it is—they want to bad-mouth our products."

"So why not compromise on the price?"

"I tried and it doesn't work, and that's what drives me crazy. Our markets are going to tank, all on account of a few piece-of-shit islands. People can't even live there, for God's sake."

"You're right," said Ishihara. "Our cars are in big trouble too. No one wants to buy them; people are all afraid they'll get set on fire. And the US is pushing its chintzy little fuel-efficient models."

Ito heaved a sigh. "Shiro, you're a lucky dog, the envy of all the world."

"Lucky how?" said Toyotomi.

"I thought you were the smart guy," Ito answered. "But Shiro's bailing just when our markets are going to hell." He offered Ishihara his hand. "Congratulations! I just knew the Chink government would wake up someday. They stir up the people with their ethnic nationalism bullshit and herd them out onto the street for rallies while the PSB sit on their asses in the background and clap. All the world media are reporting corruption among the officials, and the people are getting sick of it. So they keep turning them in the opposite direction—direct them outward so they can practice the protest drill. Well, before long those same people will turn back and march on *them*. Remember, it was the farmers who toppled the dynasties. What a sick fucking feeling. Let's wash it away. *Kanpai*!"

The three men toasted.

7. True Love

The company social was beginning to wind down as a woozy Li Changchun eyed his dozen co-workers and gestured grandly for attention. "This is my last drink and my last cigarette for the next six months. My wife and I are starting a family. So I need all your help—starting tomorrow please keep your distance if you're smoking and don't offer me booze."

One of his coworkers laughed. "Poor guy—his long, sweet honeymoon's about to end."

"Don't worry. I'll keep you company when I smoke," another replied.

"Great! I save money not buying you drinks," someone shouted.

One of them applauded and the others joined in.

"Manager Chŏn, why is he saying that?" asked Kang Chŏnggyu, a young newcomer to the company.

"You know the one-child policy here," said Chŏn Taegwang. "He wants to get rid of all the impurities in his body before he and his wife make a baby, to make sure it comes out healthy. Make sense?"

"Very scientific and rational. When did that start?"

"Well…" Chŏn cocked his head. "I'm not sure. And I don't think we'll find it on Baidu," he said with a wan smile.

"Is there actually something you don't know?"

Chŏn smirked at the ludicrous remark. "What do you think I am, a walking encyclopedia? The more I know, the more I realize I don't know."

"That's not what I've heard, sir. I'm told the Chŏn Taegwang search engine is better than an encyclopedia and full of suave anecdotes."

"Kid, you amaze me. You're going to be promoted big time here. The great thing about bribes and flattery is they don't cost anything. So, my young pal with the honey tongue, let's take it to the limit and see what you got." Chŏn winked. His ever-so-amicable mug could blunt thorny words and pluck people's heartstrings.

"I'm sorry sir. You've taught me so much the last few days…I couldn't help it…."

"Don't take it personally. I just had to say something because you were coming on a bit strong. It doesn't reflect negatively on you. So come on, drink up!" He gave Kang a pat on the shoulder. "Look around you now and figure out your coworkers. Like they say, you get to know a man when you gamble together or go on a business trip. But a drinking party is even better—you see right through him. Business skill number one is sizing up your counterpart right away. Your body can be tipsy but not your mind—too many mistakes means failure."

Here was Chŏn in walking business encyclopedia mode. He'd been grappling with the notion of transitioning from a job to a vocation and had decided to take early retirement. He'd put in a request to leave at year's end. *Go for it!* Chisŏn had said. *I believe in you; you'll do good at whatever you set your heart on.* But he knew that deep down inside his good wife was nervous.

Meanwhile, the branch manager had been momentarily speechless. "I'm the one who should cut loose, but you beat me to it. You're a gutsy one, putting your experience to use before you end up hanging yourself out to dry. Good for you." Ever since, the manager had seemed the slightest bit dispirited.

All the other traders took parting shots at him:

"You scored and you're leaving me stranded!"

"Great move—otherwise they throw your ass out in the cold."

"What's next? Do we get a sneak preview?"

"You're aiming for one more big splash? Don't settle for sardines—you'll harpoon a whale if you're lucky, or at least hook a big fat mackerel!"

Headquarters had decided on his replacement, and in the meantime Chŏn had Kang to train. Which lightened his work load—instead of the usual hustle he could focus on the kid. As his final act of service he would pass on his knowhow and mold the kid into a good worker. He took the assignment to heart, eager to have a pupil who could benefit from the knowledge of his own blunders in this strange country, who could learn from him not to overreact to one's mistakes. In Kang he saw himself ten years ago.

"Two years ago we gave our staff *maotai* for Chunjie. You know it's the most popular spirit in the land, ever since people got it in their heads that Mao took it with his meals and lived a long life as a result. Well, with fame come fakes—everyone wants a piece of the action and you get five times as many bogus products as you do the genuine article. You have to be a high official to get a taste of the real thing. Which is why I thought it would make a great Chunjie gift. And so we proudly handed it out. Our Chinese staff were ecstatic—look what they could take back to their parents in the country. Well, what do you think happened? On the first day back from the long holiday, that guy Li comes marching in, fuming—we embarrassed him with fake *maotai*, we duped the staff. Apparently he took his bottle to a shop for resale and the owner took one look at it and gave him the boot. You see, you can resell if you pay a ten or fifteen percent 'restocking fee.' The point is, back home if an employee got suckered like that he'd never openly complain. Here they do complain, men *and* women. So don't ever try to hoodwink someone. Especially in the business world, the last thing you want to do is screw someone over—it earns you black marks for all time."

"So, the company got taken advantage of?"

"*I* got taken advantage of. The *maotai* was arranged my *guanxi*—he's a high official and he always bragged that what he drinks is the real thing."

"Are you telling me he was fooled too?"

"I'm still not sure. I just let it go."

"I don't understand."

"Several possibilities. First, maybe he's gullible and this happens all the time. Or maybe it was a one-time thing and his supplier cheated him. Third, maybe he decided to cheat me. Any way, if I start wagging my tongue, I could lose my precious *guanxi*, and all the business that comes with him. So I took the simple way out…I just let it go."

"I still don't understand. The third possibility—a person like him, in his high position, cheated on us…for profit?"

"Maybe. TIC, remember? And money trumps everything—regardless how high or low you are, whether you have face or not, whether you're titled or anonymous, man or woman, young or old."

"That's all I heard during the briefings back home. But where did this 'regardless' syndrome come from?"

"Two places. If you want to do business in this world, you have to learn from the Chinese—they've been at it for thousands of years. Just look at their acumen. They invented the abacus—'regardless' syndrome source number one—and when they had to upgrade it they knew what to do. It's a good example of accounting keeping up with business expansion and sales techniques. Which leads to syndrome source number two: the Chinese perfected the modern accounting system, through double-entry bookkeeping. That's why they were the number one economy in the world for almost two thousand years. That came to an end with Mao's Communist Revolution, but then Deng opened the floodgates. His reform policies were based on three slogans: it doesn't matter if the cat is white or black as long as it catches the rats; if you can get rich in the process, go right ahead; and if you're going to be rich, you might as well be rich and proud. Everybody went *Hurray!* and set out on the money crusade. From then on you could let go of your life but not your money. There was no shame in selling your body, but shame on you if you went out begging. Remember that woman on TV who said she'd rather cry in a BMW than smile on a bicycle? To get out of poverty we put in fourteen-hour days after the war and accomplished an economic miracle; here they got hooked on money and jumped into manufacturing. The later in life you get addicted, the stronger your attachment, and you can bet they'll keep craving the money drug another thirty years. And there are two hundred and fifty million potential addicts in the migrant workers, with another quarter million on the way. This is the future of China, and it's your future too." Chŏn emptied his drink.

Kang gazed at his mentor, fascinated by his knowledge and his volubility. How long would it take him to acquire that shrewdness?

"Are you familiar with the *Shiji* by Sima Qian?" asked Chŏn before popping a morsel into his mouth.

"Yes, I am."

"You'll recall he lived about two thousand years ago. In the *Shiji* he wrote that you will speak ill of he who is ten times wealthier than you, fear he who is a hundred times wealthier, labor for he who is a thousand times wealthier, and be enslaved by he who is ten thousand times wealthier. A sharp take on human psychology, wouldn't you say? He's the father of Chinese historiography, and his insights into people's mind are that keen. What that saying tells us is that two thousand years ago money exercised a powerful influence over the people and controlled their society. And it suggests that their economic system was capitalist even though the country was run like a fiefdom. In other words, China and money have a long and deep relationship."

"Ah, yes." Kang was still trying to keep Sima Qian's figures straight.

In the meantime, the party had broken into smaller groups nattering and laughing as they ate and drank, and by nine o'clock the social was over. How different from back home, thought Kang, where you had to binge drink, not splitting up into small groups, and you went to a second bar and even a third, all the way till midnight.

"I know our after-work drinking parties can be a problem, but here they're kind of different," Kang ventured.

"You mean no group building, no camaraderie?"

"Yes. Am I wrong?" said Kang with his perpetually befuddled look.

"No, it's natural that we see a difference. Here you have to keep it short. Get home after ten, you're in big trouble. The wife barks at you over the phone. 'Where are you? What are you doing? Get back here and take care of the baby!' The women here work outside the home too, and the men do all the housework. Excuses like, 'Oh, I went out to dinner with the guys at the office' get you nowhere. Keep your Chinese staff out after midnight? Forget it. They'll consider the dinner party as overtime and won't show up till the next afternoon, *and* they'll bill for the taxi they had to take home in the wee hours. We learned the hard way when we tried to do the after-work parties Korean style. Mock the local culture and how things work, you get screwed."

They took a taxi home. Drinking and driving was a no-no. You were locked up for two weeks if you got caught. The thousand-*yuan* gratuity didn't work. Some situations just didn't allow for bargaining.

"One more thing," said Chŏn the relentless teacher. "If we drink to one hundred and twenty percent of our capacity, then they drink to eighty percent. So they never get ugly. Unlike us—we often get ugly, we behave badly, sometimes a woman passes out on the street and gets assaulted. We can learn a lesson from the drinking culture here. It's an important part of doing business, but what you want is to get the other guy drunk and not you, right?"

"I'll remember that."

The next morning, he took Kang to the customs authority.

"This is the most important government body in the whole country. These officials determine whether we live or die, since we depend on imports and exports. You absolutely must get yourself a *guanxi* here. Otherwise you're on a street at night with no lights. You're in the desert with no water. I'll show you how it works. Look at all those officials doing their paperwork—half are men and half are women. Your Chinese is still ragged and you need some help with documents. So where do you go?" He stared at Kang.

Kang's face gradually hardened. The men or the women?

"I'll try one of the men."

"Why is that?" Chŏn made himself sound hard.

"Well, I'm kind of shy," Kang faltered. "I think I'd feel awkward going up to a woman I didn't know. Maybe it would be easier talking to a man."

"No wonder you're still single at age thirty-four."

"Excuse me?"

"You don't like women?"

"Sure I do."

"Are you afraid of them?"

"Not necessarily."

"You're kind of a shrinking violet?"

"Yeah…I guess so."

"No sisters?"

"Just a younger brother."

"I thought so."

"Yeah?"

"Did you get your spending money from Mom, or from Dad?"

"From my mother, of course."

"Who do you talk with when you need to talk about something?"

"My mother."

"Are you sure?"

Kang was silent.

"In this world of ours there is no man who doesn't like women, correct? Tell me, what's the inverse of that?"

"There's no woman who doesn't like men."

"There you go. Remember, if you have two magnets, north attracts south and repels north. So who do you think will give you and your wretched Mandarin a better response?"

Kang blinked, as if he'd been posed a physics problem.

"It's the woman who will try her best to help out the lost little boy. It's her motherly instinct. The man will laugh at you and your Chinese. When your Chinese gets better, *then* go to the man and he'll give you a big fat smile of surprise. But for now, stick with the woman. And that's practicum number one. Let's go."

Outside, Chŏn lit a cigarette. He exhaled with a big whoosh, like the men here. He thought back to this year's Chunjie, when he had returned to Korea with his family. One day he got stuck in traffic and tried to pull a U-turn.

His daughter in the back seat had called out, *Daddy, you can't do that, we're in Korea.* But it was too late. A patrolman blew his whistle and stopped the car.

Chŏn promptly presented his passport and business card and apologized. *I'm sorry, I thought for a moment I was back in Shanghai. I've been living too long in China.* The policeman asked what he did in China, and Chŏn told him.

Oh, you're a trader. You're doing good work for the country. We'll let it go this time. Drive carefully. And with a salute he returned the passport and business card. Chŏn bowed repeatedly in thanks.

His daughter was impressed: *Daddy, that's quick thinking.* His son had said,

Wow, Daddy, you're famous! Everyone here knows you. Leave it to his good wife to add, *What a softie—he should have given you a ticket!*

"Practicum number two is tonight—at the bar."

"A practicum at a bar?"

"Yes, a practicum in feeling a woman's tits in public."

Kang blushed and turned away.

"You didn't grow up with sisters, so you're shy and timid, you shrink back in the presence of women. You have to get rid of that fear and one way is to drink with your arm around a woman. Otherwise you'll never survive as a businessman and you'll never make manager."

"All right."

Watching Kang blink, Chŏn pictured him before a bare-breasted woman, unable to work up the nerve to touch. "You still have some time, so relax. In the meantime, we can go over to that teahouse."

It was a classic teahouse, the furnishings delicate and ornate, the interior steeped in the aromas of tea. This early in the day, there were no other patrons and the teahouse was placid except for the soft flow and reverberation of traditional music.

"Do you like tea?" Chŏn asked as he signaled a waitress in an elegant *qipao*.

"Not really…"

"Well, you better learn to like it. How can you deal with Chinese without any knowledge of tea? The Qin Emperor? Tang culture, Chinese temperament and customs, modern history and Mao. Reform and Deng. And don't say, 'Why should I?' Remember, you're here to make money. TIC—so do as the Chinese do. Pay attention to how she brews the tea and get used to it. If you're able to serve tea yourself, who knows, maybe your business will be slick."

Their *qipao*-clad server began brewing the tea, Kang dutifully looking on. Chŏn in turn watched Kang and had a leisurely smoke.

"You should start drinking tea daily, and before you know it you'll want to brew it yourself. It becomes part of your life. And along the way, get yourself a book about tea so you can learn its history and its health benefits. Your number one business weapon is fluent Chinese, remember? Number two is your general knowledge. You get that from books, so keep a few handy—on Chinese history, philosophy, poetry, pottery… I'll give you a list."

Having served the tea, the elegant server left.

Chŏn stubbed out his cigarette. "Another thing you'll learn is the differences between northern and southern China; you'll find them even in the culture of tea drinking. In the south every home and office has a tea brewing set, and drinking tea is an act of grace. In the north, people pop any old tea leaves into a cup and drink the tea like water. So you've got "fussy sippers" in the south and "barbaric slurpers" in the north. Either way, tea has a nice fragrance and taste, it helps get rid of bad breath, and it filters out carcinogens. It's one of the World Health

Organization's five most beneficial foods and beverages. Go on, try it."

"Thank you," said Kang, holding his cup with both hands. "Can you tell me more about dealing with male and female officials? It's not the same, right?"

"No, it shouldn't be the same. Even after you get proficient in Mandarin, pretend you're still struggling, at least during your first encounter with a woman. Then once you get to know her, treat her like the finest lady in the land. Open the door for her, let her go first into the elevator, pull out her chair at the restaurant. And make sure it's a fancy hotel restaurant that serves fine French wine. Give her designer goods for gifts, whether it's cosmetics, a purse, a muffler, hankies, whatever. All this and she'll feel wonderful. You gain her trust, she becomes your *guanxi*, you also get some business for her, and you get to expand your territory. Another benefit is her boss might tend to give her less of a hard time because she's a woman, and so the job gets done quicker." Chŏn had a sip of tea.

"Now if you're dealing with a guy, whether it's an official or your counterpart in business, language proficiency comes first. You show off and let him know you worked hard to get where you're at. Remember how your heart goes out to a white guy with good Korean—you want to do business with him out of awe and curiosity? Chinese men will react the same to you. But when you advertise your knowledge you have to start very carefully. Let's assume you're meeting for the first time with a senior director. So what do you do—do you start off gabbing at length about the supplier's history, public trust in the company, the superiority of the product, comparison analysis, and so forth? That's what a Western businessman would do. If you go on like that for half an hour, you might as well pack up and leave, because you flunked—you showed you were desperate and impatient. You talked too much because you lack confidence in the product, and he gets to doubting your character. He thinks you're a featherweight. TIC again. See? They look at *you* before they look at the product—*Is this man worth my trust? Is he knowledgeable? Is he a good guy?* Or do you come across as crafty and imprudent? They'll read your face and dissect you. Instead, you have *him* talk for the first forty minutes, and then you pounce. And don't forget to let slip that you're good in English, you studied in the US, and know your Chinese history, literature, and culture. Do that and I bet your success rate is over ninety percent. Can you do that?"

No way, Kang's eyes were telling him.

"Well, I can't think..." And in fact his head felt like a rat's warren and his mind was blank.

"Relax. We all start out not knowing much of anything. The problem with businessmen is that once they set a goal they have to attack, and they feel a sense of urgency. And with Koreans it's always hurry up, faster! And the faster you go the more you tend to gab. That can be fatal here. So you do the opposite, you fight *manmandi* with *manmandi*. Have you noticed how every high official's office comes with a display of Chinese nature scenes and porcelains? Or maybe the scenes are on the teacups. So you start off mentioning the cups, saying it's amazing that they fit such a magical scene on a delicate little cup, you add that when you were studying at Berkeley you went to an Asian art exhibition and were served tea in a cup like his and the Americans marveled at it and were so curious they asked you how it was made, and for the rest of your life you'll remember how you parlayed your meager knowledge into a brief explanation of the history of Chinese porcelains even though you were sweating like a pig. So what does that take, two or three minutes? And there you are, you've covered almost everything—study in the US, good Mandarin and better English, knowledge of Chinese history and culture. How do you think they'll respond?" The implication was obvious.

"So," continued Chŏn, "you've pushed two of their hot buttons. They love it that you studied in the US, with its dream education system. And they drool over your research on your host country's proud culture. So what's your next step? Instead of running off at the mouth, you ask questions: What's the difference between Master Gong and Master Meng? Why did Han Liubang decide to serve Master Gong's shrine? Do you consider Qin Shi Huangdi a wise emperor or a tyrant? Who are considered the sage-emperors? When did foot-binding start, and why? What was Chairman Mao's greatest achievement? Chairman Deng's greatest achievement? Think about what you gain. First, by asking these questions you allow your man to be the boss—you give him control of the conversation, you give him a sense of fulfillment and an opportunity to put his cultural knowledge to use. Number two, you're showing him you're not just a businessman with a narrow focus, you're brainy in other areas, including China and its culture. Third, by asking questions you're showing modesty and humility, and that's an absolute must. No time to discuss your product? Don't worry. Leave him the catalog 'for the time being,' tell him it has all the information, and thank him for his time— tell him you enjoyed the opportunity and you look forward to seeing him again. And out you go. So, if you were him, would you follow up or not?" He stared at Kang.

Kang jotted a note on his memo pad, looked up, and smiled. "Sure I would."

Chŏn noticed Kang had stopped fidgeting. This was a good sign. "Definitely. For me it never failed. Read those books I mentioned and you'll find all the questions you need."

"Yes, sir. I'll do that."

"Finally, remember that you're not doing business with products, you're doing business with people. Especially here in China, success or failure depends on how you manage your relationships. Assume you're on a journey to heaven with your counterpart. Make sure you remember his wife's birthday and their kid's birthday, and don't forget to give them presents on the holidays. They don't have to be substantial; the important thing is you didn't forget them, and they like that. Feeling you're being treated well feeds a man's *mianzi,* and we know how important *that* is. It's a matter of pride. When you establish mutual trust, they forget about your title, your position, your age, and they simply try to help you. The crucial thing is your attitude—you want to love them dearly. If you can do that, then things like pollution don't matter as much, and you can enjoy a one-*yuan* bowl of noodles from a street stall and block out the hawking and spitting."

Kang took a moment from his memo-pad scribbling to bow. "I'll remember."

The following Friday Chŏn paid a surprise visit to Ha Kyŏngman in Qingdao.

"Look what the tiger dragged in," Ha gently scolded when he met Chŏn at the factory gate." Why didn't you tell me you were coming?"

"I'm glad to see you too," said Chŏn, offering his hand. "But go easy on me, I'm a sensitive man. I need to pick your brain about careers—remember we talked about that? So how have you been, Mr. President?"

"Career? Don't tell me you quit?" said Ha as he shook hands.

"I gave notice for the end of the year. I'm already training my replacement."

"That's a gold-medal life move—congratulations!"

"See, you gave me the courage, so I took out the sword. Actually I was considering it for several years."

"So what did you decide?" asked Ha on their way to his office.

"Well, I have a few ideas, a lot of pressing thoughts, but not much in the way of startup funds, and that's why I'm here."

"Good. You came to the right place. The markets here are just getting off the ground. There are plenty of opportunities—1.4 billion of them!" Ha punctuated the figure by stamping his foot on the first of the steps leading up to his office.

"Thank you." And that was all Chŏn could say at the moment, touched as he was by Ha's heartfelt reminder. His reaction surprised him. After submitting the retirement paperwork, he'd been hit by a blast of anxiety—had he left himself out in the cold? He'd remembered the face of Kim Hyŏn'gon, now the POSCO branch manager in Xian, and Kim's outpouring of gratitude for Chŏn's visit—gratitude expressed not out of sadness but in jubilation after a long bout of loneliness and frustration.

Ha sat Chŏn on the sofa in his office and brewed tea for his visitor. "Let's hear your grand notions—how do you propose to become a company president?"

Accepting a cup of tea with both hands, Chŏn bowed in acknowledgment. "Like I said, I have a few ideas but they're kind of shaky. I thought maybe I could firm them up talking with someone who has more life experience under his belt. So here I am."

"*Aigu*, life experience? We're about the same on that score. But I've been in this business long enough that maybe I can tell you if something's feasible or not. So what do you have in mind?" After a here's-to-you gesture with his teacup, Ha had a sip.

"The first thing I thought of is long underwear. As many as a hundred million sets are sold during Chunjie, but it's a tight market and a newcomer would have a hell of a time opening a supply chain. But I came up with two ideas for getting in the door. One is to customize my product with that year's zodiac animal, stitched in gold on red fabric, and two is to price it high. That's what E-Land did here, and it was a big hit. And I'd go with the CJ home shopping channel—"

Ha slapped his knee. "All right—now I get it. But I see a potential problem. You succeed this year, but then everybody copies you next year, so it's not sustainable. Another problem I see is that the underwear will have an upbeat, luxurious look with the red background and gold thread, but hand stitching would cost you— your profit margin wouldn't be very big...." He shook his head.

"Those are excellent observations. First, I only thought of it as a one-time deal, just for Chunjie. As for the stitching, I'd use machines."

"In that case, why not? It looks good to me. But you're making tens or even hundreds of thousands of sets in a very short time—do you have the manpower?"

"Yes. My nephew has a pal whose uncle is a wizard and has a workshop. I was thinking I'd sign with him after I talked with you."

"Sounds good. But CJ home shopping will be a challenge too. Everybody wants to hop onto CJ just before Chunjie—how can you get a spot? It's like picking a star from the sky." Ha's mind was racing.

"Yes, I know. That's where Chairman Pak of CJ comes in—I was hoping he could help me with that."

"Well...I'm not sure—you know how people are..."

"I think it will be all right. Pak is a fine man, with a strong will and deep trust in people."

"Then sure, dive in. I'd give you a ninety-nine percent chance of success. If the Chinese can sell a hundred thousand sets, why can't you sell several hundred thousand—and it's a fancy item." Ha beamed at Chŏn. "A great man with a great idea."

"Thank you. I feel much better now. So it's full speed ahead." With a sigh of relief, Chŏn sampled his tea.

Ha rewarded him with a refill. "You said you had some other ideas?"

"A few, but they'll require more funding. One of them is a sure thing and it's long term, and no worries about counterfeits, but..." Chŏn smacked his lips in frustration.

"But?" said Ha, amiable and patient.

"Baby formula."

"Oh, that. Yes, you'll need money and you'll need a network. But as long as babies are being born, the market's there."

Chŏn could almost hear the wheels in Ha's mind lurch into motion again. "I wouldn't need that much startup money, and stores are certain to stock it, since every mother is a potential customer. My biggest regret is I don't have a model for an ad."

"I don't get it."

"You know, there's no guarantee of success with a product itself. You also need a good brand and an eye-grabbing ad. Here we have thirty million babies, but with all the fake-milk crises, parents don't trust the local products. But they give high marks to Korean-made formula. It's the best possible market condition. If I work with a Korean company under a contract that gets me OEM certification, I can get maximum use out of my startup funds. I've already decided on the brand name—Little Emperor and Little Princess. Now for the ad, there's a Korean actress who would grab every Chinese mom's heart and wring shrieks of delight out of her. She's the goddess who's responsible for the spread of Hallyu here—everybody knows her. You know she got married and recently had twins, right? A cute little boy and girl. I was thinking, a picture of her with a baby in each arm and the slogan *Nothing but the Best for My Little Emperor and Little Princess.*"

Ha slapped the armrest. "That's it!"

"But I can't get her to do it."

"Why not? She wants more money?"

"She said no way will she put her babies in an ad."

"That's too bad."

"So the bottom of that idea dropped out. Damn, I thought I was in heaven."

"Well, you gave it your best shot."

"But I'll trademark the name anyway. Maybe I'll have another chance; if not I can always sell it."

"I like the name Wang Zi Cheng Long—it's exactly what all parents want for their kids, to grow up big like a dragon. It's a perfect brand. Why not try one of the big Korean companies? Our formula makers need to expand here where there's a large market instead of fighting one another for a limited market share back home."

"I haven't given up. But what about the shortage of workers and the cost of labor? Aren't foreign companies and even some Chinese ones threatening to move to Vietnam and Cambodia?"

"I heard that too," said Ha, "problems with manpower and labor costs—had to happen sooner or later. Companies will go anywhere for cheap labor—Southeast Asia, India, Pakistan, Afghanistan. But if you move there you have a couple other obstacles—workmanship and productivity. Our companies here got settled quickly because Chinese workers can master the skills as fast as we can. Plus, we had ethnic Koreans who could act as interpreters—I'm sure we had some isolated problems but on the whole the Chinese made a huge contribution. The other issue is productivity. The problem used to be the socialist mentality. It took ten years to change over to capitalist intensity, and it's a known fact that Chinese productivity still lags behind ours by twenty percent. But in South Asia you'll run into both problems. It's a different climate both weather-wise and in terms of temperament. Those are two sinkholes I wouldn't want to fall in."

"You mean there's a tropical mindset?"

"You could say so. Temperamentally you get desensitized and physically you get sluggish. It's not something you can change through will and effort."

"I guess not. So, you're satisfied with the workforce here, but there's a shortage looming and a wage problem too, right?"

"I've got a trick up my sleeve," said Ha, stretching back with a Cheshire grin.

"A trade secret, you mean?"

"No, nothing that miraculous. It's something everybody knows about, a uniquely Chinese shortage. But the cause of the shortage implies the solution: it's not a shortage of people but a shortage of people who would rather not leave home to work. So what do we do? We're the ones who are thirsty. Do we sit on our butts and wait for someone to bring us water? No, we go to the water source. It's the same with labor—you go to the source, meaning deep in the back country. Go to the source—that's my motto."

"And nobody else thought of that?"

"You tell me. Anyway, you go to the farming villages and almost half the workforce are women. You find the village head, he's the guy with the power, and you hire him. So you have a group of women for your labor, you have a foreman in the village, all that's left is to bring in the unfinished product—wages aren't an issue."

"But how can you hire unskilled women for finish work on accessories?"

"There are various skill levels—delicate work like studding the tiny cubics, and simple labor like stringing the beads. It's the simple jobs we send to the village head—and he and the women do wonders!"

All Chŏn could do was nod. "Ah, now I see, Mr. President. This trick up your sleeve, it wasn't exactly the apple dropping on Newton's head."

"I'll tell you, there have been big changes in the last ten years, and the deeper I go inland, the greater they are. On my first recruiting trip all the villagers turned out at the local grade school. I needed thirty people and I got a crowd of two thousand. Their faces were telling me they would do any work I wanted them to—it reminded me of the 1960s back home. 'Good god!' I was thinking, but on the other hand I was so happy. My immediate challenge was to hire thirty people. How? Ask for resumes? No, no such thing. Written exam? No, not all of them could write. So I sifted out the people who could write their name and write 'Hail to the PRC.' If they weren't literate, they would have had difficulty understanding our training procedure. Today there are fifty million illiterates, so you can imagine how many there were ten years ago. Anyway, that cut the recruiting class by about half. Next I divided them into groups of ten and asked them to thread a needle. If they could do it in two or three seconds, they passed the eyesight and speed test—and those were the two musts. I felt like a king, picking and choosing. Now it feels like a dream."

"That's so far from the experience of me and the other trader stiffs."

"But coming up with a work force is something all manufacturers have to deal with. Which reminds me. I have an ethnic Korean in Manchuria who works for us, and he told me there are a lot of North Korean women working in Dandong, near the Amnok River. He said why not hire them—they're good workers and their wages are affordable."

Chŏn lurched forward. "Is that so?"

"I couldn't believe it either."

"So, China's using North Korean labor—because it's cheaper." Chŏn grimaced. "What can the North Koreans do? They're so desperate for paying work they don't care if their rice is cooked or not. You think I should hire them?"

"I wouldn't. Our relations with the North are bad enough as it is. No more tours to Kŭmgang Mountain, no civilian aid, the Kaesŏng Industrial Complex is barely breathing. The situation's too unstable, you might get stuck with some sort of political accusation. You know what they say—businessmen should stick to business."

"I guess so. The North-South thing is so damned complicated. We're the same blood and all…"

"I know; you want to do it out of the goodness of your heart." Chŏn frowned. "Damn, the guy was right. Several years ago this writer, what's-his-name, suggested the North and South should have ten more complexes like the one at Kaesŏng."

"When was he writing?"

"I think it was seven or eight years ago."

"I'd like to read it."

"I'm sure it's on the Internet."

"Do you think you could find it?"

"Sure." They got up from the sofa.

"Here it is," said Chŏn after a couple of minutes.

Their monthly wage is the equivalent of 56 dollars US. Even at 1200 wŏn to the dollar, that comes to only 67,200. But this is not a story of some poverty-stricken African nation thousands of kilometers distant. It's about the Kaesŏng Industrial Complex, forty kilometers north of Seoul, the first tangible evidence of the mutual trust that is necessary for the peaceful reunification of South and North. The two Koreas decided to set the wage for the workers from the North at that amount.

Fifty-six dollars a month? I couldn't believe it. Was it a misprint? Was it actually 560 dollars? I checked the newspapers—they all said 56 dollars. That made me all the more dubious. Fifty-six dollars, or 67,200 wŏn—half the cost of a dinner for a wealthy South Korean at a fancy hotel restaurant in Seoul, a price she would pay without a second thought. And that is the monthly wage for North Korean workers. I bet they don't keep the whole amount—it is a socialist society after all.

Then, how much of that wage does the worker actually keep? I felt my heart numb and then tear—it was a question I would never be able to answer. How could any South Korean feel easy knowing this? Those laborers who work for such a meager wage are none other than our blood in the North with whom we have lived for five thousand years. They are related to us: they speak the same language, they observe the same customs, they have the same looks. We were divided from them by ideology during a tumultuous period. During the recent Asian Games, we saw with our own eyes that it took only three days after the initial awkward rendezvous for the North Korean athletes and their comely cheerleaders to mingle with the citizens of the South like a family united by blood. The ideological wall built by the two sides over a fifty-year period crumbled helplessly among a people descended from the same bloodline. A young South Korean man shouted a marriage proposal and asked the name of a lovely young North Korean woman on the cheerleader tour bus. Bashful and smiling amiably, she wrote Suni on the window. If three hundred North Korean athletes invited by the South Korean government with citizens' tax money can be considered a tiny trickle of reconciliation and harmony, then the exchange of gentle feelings by those two young people who wished to become a couple is a broad river that leads us to a clear and obvious answer to the question of why we should reunify.

The competition among South Korean companies to establish themselves at the Kaesŏng Complex is severe—I imagine the odds of doing so at something like a thousand to one. We all know why—the profit they can expect when their labor costs are fifty-six dollars per worker per month.

A recent survey indicates that 85 percent of Korean companies plan to establish factories in China within two to three years. China is large and its wage structure varies. Shanghai's highly skilled technicians are known to be paid more than six hundred dollars a month—ten times the wage earned by our North Korean workers. But South Korean companies are undeterred and jostle for position in China. Wages are cheaper there than at home and the companies can expect a secure profit margin even if labor costs keep increasing.

Let's suppose the wage in China is five times that of North Korea. How many Chinese workers will fill all the new Korean factories? How much will they earn? The answer is, both amounts will be astronomical, and not just in the short term.

This prospect has gotten me daydreaming. What if all those companies set up plants in the North instead of China? Imagine the economic benefits. Employment opportunities in the North would skyrocket, and for the South Korean companies the savings in wages alone would bring five times more profit than those companies extract from China. Besides, we could communicate in the same language and double production. Our innate super-dexterity could maximize productivity. Even further, we could strengthen our unity as one people and at the same time sink deep roots for a renewal of mutual trust. Such will be the foundation of the wide road to reunification.

How best to attain this goal? I believe there is a simple solution. Build ten more industrial complexes like the one at Kaesŏng, perhaps five on the west coast and five on the east coast, for convenience of transportation on each side of the peninsula and with no disruption of the political system in the North. Such a project would help the North overcome its economic hardship and offer the South a springboard to the twenty-thousand-dollar benchmark in its GNP. And think of the savings in the cost of our reunification.

Is this only a fantasy? It was—until the June 15 Joint Declaration. The announcement by President Kim Taejung and National Defense Committee Chair Kim Jong Il changed the historical reality of the divided peninsula. It was a paradigm shift from a divided history of conflict and confrontation to a unifying history of harmony and cooperation. This historical paradigm shift cannot be reversed or opposed by any of us. It is one of the arts of politics that fantasy can be made reality. Making the impossible possible is a mark of political excellence.

The road to the June 15 Joint Declaration was treacherous. But now that road is open and the impossible is behind us. To realize the Declaration both sides must forge a mutual trust that is stronger than steel, whose roots are deeper than the ocean depths, a trust based on a mutual non-aggression treaty and the systematization of peaceful co-existence. That accomplished, the new Kaesŏng Industrial Complex could transform to ten or even twenty practically overnight.

Our President No Muhyŏn will soon be free of the shackles of impeachment. I suggest to Kim Jong Il, Chairman of the National Defense Committee, to convene North-South Korean Summit talks as the first task to welcome our President who is about to start a clean slate. There is no reason the two summits continue to sit on opposing horizons of history. Even our middle-schoolers know that the four powers that have encircled us since the war do not want us to reunify. The key to unlock this puzzle of history rests with we the people; it is we who can enable the two summits to exercise their historical responsibility.[2]

8. To Skin a Flea

"He ran off!" cried Sŏ over the phone. "He's gone!"

"Who's gone? What are you talking about?" said Chŏn.

"Shang—Shang Xinwen. He went to the US, or maybe it was Canada. He's gone!"

Chŏn pictured Sŏ in tears, trembling. "When?"

"I'm not sure. Maybe two or three days ago."

"But why the hysterics?"

"Well, he...he took all...my money..." The rest was lost in a moan.

Money? Something terrible must have happened. "What can you tell me?"

"I just...can't...explain it over the phone."

"All right, I'll come over." Chŏn ended the call. His head was spinning. What did it mean? Shang took Sŏ's money? All of it? How? A get-rich-quick scheme? And Shang had taken off—so maybe the divorce was the first step. So many high officials had disappeared overseas—but Shang? The man was a patriot, and ambitious.... Once again Chŏn found himself in a human jungle. You could see a foot into murky water but barely an inch into a murky mind. There was only one certainty—Shang was after money, so money had to be part of his exit plan. Chŏn shuddered.

"He said he could get me on a solid fiscal footing," said Sŏ in his office at the clinic. "And I bought it. I was thinking of my kids. He said he could get me twice the bank rate, he said he had a friend in construction, and then..." Sŏ broke into sobs.

"Aha." Chŏn waited for the doctor to compose himself. "Let me get this straight. Every month you took your half of the proceeds from the clinic," he said, recalling the terms of Sŏ's contract, "you subtracted for expenses, and you gave him the rest." He sighed. Sŏ had to be either naïve or stupid.

"Yes. Every month, without fail."

"Did he pay you the interest like he promised?" Chŏn couldn't resist smirking.

"No. He said he'd add it to the principle instead."

"*Aigu*—you offered meat to a tiger! Have you ever had an arrangement like that?"

"Only with the bank."

"You should have stuck with the banks then. This is hard to believe. And you never suspected anything?"

"No. I trusted him. Since you're so close to him..."

"But you could have let on to me."

"He told me not to tell anyone. He said if people found out they'd talk behind my back."

To Chŏn this sounded like an excuse. Sŏ must have wanted to keep it quiet too. The devil called money had tempted another human mind. And here he was letting Sŏ cry on his shoulder now that the deal had fallen apart. Shang had worked the doctor like a pair of chopsticks.

"But that's not the worst of it," said Sŏ, still trembling.

Chŏn scowled. "This is maddening. How could anything be worse than what you just told me?"

"I'm about to lose my job."

"What the hell! How can you lose your job?"

"The lease for the clinic was under his name and he took the deposit."

"So the Chinese doctor was involved too."

"He told me he was sorry; he'd promised Shang he'd keep it a secret. What could I say?"

"Shang planned the whole thing, a perfect scam! I just can't believe—"

"So it's a complete surprise to you too? You trusted that man...." Sŏ gazed at Chŏn with teary, resentful eyes whose message was clear: *Why did you introduce me to him in the first place?*

Finally, it all came together—Shang had conned him in order to swindle Sŏ. Well, now that he was here, he might as well accept the blame, thought Chŏn. Sŏ had worked as hard and doggedly as a migrant worker, hoping for a quick comeback after the debacle at home, and now he was penniless again, just like when he'd arrived. And add to his despair the blow of losing the clinic.

Swept by that despair, Chŏn was too numb to think of anything he could do for Sŏ just then. But he couldn't countenance Sŏ returning home with nothing to show for it.

"I'm very sorry, Doctor Sŏ. I've embarrassed myself. I know the situation seems impossibly tangled, but let's not give up. We'll find a way. You can't go home now; we both know that."

Sŏ slowly shook his head. "You're right, I couldn't face my family. They're expecting me to return with my pockets full of money."

Time to shift into salvage mode, Chŏn decided, irritating and burdensome though it felt. An image of his buddy Han Minu surfaced, as if to remind Chŏn that Han had introduced the two of them. What would Han think if he left Sŏ stranded? It would be like driving past a car with a flat tire and watching it get rear-ended.

"When's your last day here?"

"They said they'd give me another ten days."

"That's generous! All right, let's figure something out. How about if you go to work for someone?"

"Well … I'd have to think about that … but … I'm sorry. Would it be possible for me to enter into a partnership like before? This time I'll arm myself with a lawyer."

And suddenly the crybaby was replaced by a steely man. Chŏn couldn't remember the last time Sŏ had project such a virile image—the male survival instinct, last-ditch valor on behalf of family when you faced starvation or death.

"Yeah. With a lawyer you'll be safer for sure."

Back at his office, Chŏn tried in vain to get down to work. He attempted to erase Shang's flickering face from his mind but ultimately gave in to the mental tug of war. Shang Xinwen … Chŏn had become attached to the man, he couldn't deny it. Haughty yet caring, street-smart and knowledgeable, ambitious for success like any Beida graduate, and a great *guanxi* who had kept up their relationship and helped him immensely. His only character flaw? He craved money. But was it wrong to love money in a capitalist system? Was there anyone here who didn't like money? But Shang's love affair with it was different from that of a businessman. Businessmen wanted money so they could make more money, but Shang wanted it because he was ambitious for success. He had been relentless in his pursuit of money, and he spent that money generously in pursuit of success. When he was tipsy, he used to ask, "Can you guess where I'll be ten years from now?" Chŏn would say, "In the Politburo in Beijing." Shang would break out in a belly laugh and say, "What about you, then?" And Chŏn would answer, "A branch manager, if I am lucky. Or retired." "Retired?" Shang would bray. "You must come see me. You're too valuable to be put out to pasture. I'll find something to keep you out of trouble." To which Chŏn would reply, "I would like to record this. Ten years from now I bet you will play dumb." And Shang would say, "I'll call your bluff. Go ahead and record me." The two of them used to laugh their hearts out.

And now Shang was gone to the far side of the ocean. For what reason? Were his grandiose plans for success in Beijing only a smokescreen? Was he merely a shirt-sleeve moneybagger in the immigration jet stream to North America? Shang's desertion was only the tip of an iceberg. Chŏn had to find out what lay below the waterline. First in line was Chen Wei, the jilted ex—she might know something.

Her looks may have faded but the voice coming over his cell phone was ever so sweet and clear. "Ah, Chŏn *xiansheng*. What a coincidence. I've been thinking about you. Sure, I would love to see you."

"It must have been a shock," she said when they were settled in the coffee shop. "But I wasn't fooled. Shang is no better than his associates—they're all in the same league." She sampled her coffee.

"Then, you knew it was coming?"

"How did you learn so quickly, anyway?"

Very clever, thought Chŏn, taking in her mystifying smile and admiring her skill in evading the question.

"From Dr. Sŏ. He called me just now. It seems Shang has done him wrong—very wrong."

"He did?" Her gaze sharpened.

Chŏn immediately regretted the remark, but it was too late.

"He ruined him. To make a long story short, he defrauded the doctor out of his two years of savings. He has nothing left."

"That disgusting creature—he would eat a flea's liver if there was money in it. I'm not surprised. He ran off to the US with one of those *ernai* bitches he was lusting over. I'm sure he stuffed his suitcase with money. How about you, did he fleece you too?" Her bitterness toward the man who had betrayed her left Chŏn with a knife-blade chill.

"No. My company's job was to transfer business to him, so we were not affected."

"I see. But you worked with him a long time, you must be shocked. And you are dying to know why, am I right?"

Finally, thought Chŏn. "Yes. I do not understand why a person with such a bright future would do that."

"A bright future?" She snorted so loud she startled him. "To you he must have looked very capable, a man soon to climb the ladder of the Shanghai inner circle and from there travel the highway to Beijing and success. But it was all a show, and he loves to show off. I'm sure people believed him and were nice to him. But they didn't see him for who he actually is. You may have noticed that his speedy promotion was not because of his capability but because of my family's clout. My father is a core figure in Shanghai politics. Shang was on the fast track of advancement and it clouded his judgment. He convinced himself that his success was all his doing. And then he became addicted to *ernai* and requested a divorce. I was flabbergasted. It hurt my pride but I didn't waver, I gave him his divorce. And guess what? His life began to fall apart. Have you heard the saying *A stab wound can heal, but not a slander wound*? As long as I have to bear an open wound, he should too. The idiot learned too late that the life he picked will not be a peachy one. Who cares if he ran away with the bitch. But emptying the poor doctor's pockets? That's how low he is." Again she snorted.

Chŏn could almost taste the venom coursing through her. She was a typical southern beauty, soft of bone. Her beauty was fading now that she was in her fifties, but she was still impeccably feminine and sleek of body. This vast land with its 120-degree temperature differential must be home to a wildly diverse temperament differential as well, thought Chŏn. To think that this delicate, frail-looking lady could harbor such viciousness…It was true—a woman's icy craving for vengeance could leave a frost in midsummer. If life was a struggle to the end, then love was mortal combat.

"So, is the doctor going back home?" she said before finishing her coffee.

"No, he cannot. He does not have the nerve to face his family. I advised him to think he has purchased an expensive lesson that he can use to make a new start. And from now on I will make sure he has a lawyer to prevent further damage."

"He seems like a nice person and he's a highly skilled doctor. It's too bad that had to happen. Well, I must go now, I have a meeting…."

As Chŏn watched her disappear, Shang's face came to mind yet again and he tried to imagine how the man had felt as he shed his dreams, packed up, and fled his country. The Internet would have a field day with him. He would earn two distinctions—a *seguan*, a public official who kept mistresses, and a *taoguan*, a public official who siphoned public funds and absconded.

Chŏn had read of studies conducted by the government and the Central Bank reporting that as many as eighteen thousand government officials and businessmen had funneled the equivalent of 120 billion dollars abroad over two decades. He wondered how much more money had been bled in the past year. Shang must have made off with an enormous amount. As a customs supervisor he could have raided the till as easily as he drank tea. That China was prospering, undiminished, in spite of all the money leaks was a mystery to Chŏn. With 3.5 trillion dollars in foreign-exchange reserves, more than in any other country, the loss was as a drop of blood from a mosquito's leg. How many one-*yuan* bowls of noodles would 120 billion dollars buy? There were presently a hundred and thirty million people in the land who couldn't afford that bowl. Best to forget about the mysterious Shang and the tangle of questions he had left behind.

Two days later Chen Wei called. "The other doctor at the clinic told me everything," she said in a subdued and measured tone. "Shang did much wickedness."

"Yes, that is—"

"It seems you did not feel comfortable telling me the story the other day, so I decided to look into it. I was again very impressed with your dignity. Most people would have criticized and cursed him."

"You are too kind. I do not think I am dignified."

"As I remember, you are seeking a new partner for the doctor."

"Yes, ma'am." A light went on in Chŏn's mind.

"How about me?" She spoke more quickly. "He might not want to…"

Sure enough. Relief coursed through him. "Really? I don't see why not. If we involve a lawyer, he will feel more comfortable. And he knows I know you well."

"I am very happy to hear that." After a pause, she said, "Since I have you here, I should ask you a favor."

Chŏn imagined her smiling. "I am at your service, ma'am."

"Exactly. Since I'm no longer Shang's wife, don't you think I should no longer be called ma'am?"

"Ah yes, right you are. I just could not think…." But how else could he refer to her—*xiansheng*, president, something else?

"That's quite all right. You became used to calling me ma'am. Is there another term you would find suitable?"

"Well, I am trying to think…."

"Then, let's stick with Madam. Madam Chen. Does that sound safe to you?"

"Yes, it does." *Madam Chen.* He muttered it to himself. Why hadn't he thought of it?

"How soon could we sign a contract?"

"The sooner the better."

"Excellent. Please contact me when you're ready."

"I will ask my company's lawyer and try to set up an appointment for the day after tomorrow. And then I will call you."

"Thank you."

"Yes, ma'am—I mean, madam."

"It sounds nice, don't you think? Madam Chen—it makes me sound like somebody, and you won't have to think about Shang."

"Yes, Madam Chen."

Two days later Chŏn had a new seal made for Sŏ and went with him to see the lawyer and Madam Chen. After greetings all around the lawyer read the prepared contract.

"Is the contract agreeable to both parties?"

Both Chen and Sŏ answered yes.

"Then please stamp here," said the lawyer.

Chen produced her seal. Flustered, Sŏ turned to Chŏn.

Helpless! Chŏn lamented silently. He took from his pocket the seal he had made for Sŏ. "Here you are, Doctor."

Chen was surprised. "How is it that you have the doctor's seal?"

"Well, the good doctor only had a seal with Korean lettering. So I had this one made for his new business. It is my gift." Chŏn grinned at Sŏ.

Chen smiled radiantly. "Such a pretty red seal!"

"Yes," Chŏn chuckled. "Red jade for good luck."

Chen rose and offered Sŏ her hand. "Please forget about the past and look to the future. I am sure it will be better. I will take charge of public relations. All my friends are at an age where they want to lose their wrinkles."

Sheepishly Sŏ took her hand, "Thank you, I will do my best."

The meeting had taken no more than thirty minutes. Bidding Chen goodbye, the two men moved to a teahouse.

"Did you see her face when I took out the seal?" said Chŏn as he prepared the tea. "Want to know why she looked so surprised?"

"Why?" said Sŏ as he took the seal from his pocket.

"Here they say your seal should be kept as close to you as your balls. That's why."

"Excuse me?"

"Your balls are always with you, see? Never separate from you. That's why she was startled to see *I* had it."

"Is the seal that important?"

"You know we use a certified seal, but it's not as important as the personal seal used here—which, believe it or not, is more valuable than the person who uses it."

"How can that be?"

"Well, back home you need your certified seal for important documents, such as a mortgage certificate. Here you don't—you stamp it, everyone honors it."

"That's absurd. What if it's stolen? Could the thief use it to get a loan?"

"That's the point. You know we have a concentration of businesses in and around Qingdao. Many of those companies went belly up, and in a few cases it was because the owner entrusted his seal to the accountant, who used it to take out a massive loan and then flew. I'd say a seal rates higher than a person here."

"*Aigu,*" Sŏ mumbled. "China's so complicated. Why such a big deal over a little seal?"

"There's a history behind it. Before Qin Shi Huangdi, it was used only by the king and queen. But after him it came to symbolize the power of the emperor and empress, military might, the property of the wealthy, and the authenticity of the artist. I saw a fifteen-hundred-year-old painting stamped by forty-five different seals—a painting of a *horse*, for god's sake. That's how deep the custom goes. Don't lose it, otherwise the contract is null and void."

"Sure. I'll keep it as safe as my you-know-what." Sŏ blushed at his off-color remark and pocketed the seal. "Is her family really a political powerhouse in Shanghai?"

"I'm not sure, but I don't think she's bluffing."

"That's good to know. Then why don't you set up a general trading company after you retire?"

"Why would I want to do that?"

"Well, she could be your *guanxi*. You might be better off with her than Shang. I sense she trusts you and she seems to like you."

Chŏn nodded, but the notion had caught him unawares. It might work, though. "That's not a bad idea. It's quite feasible, actually. It's just never occurred to me. But I'd better tackle one thing at a time."

Sŏ smiled brightly.

Kang Chŏnggyu inched toward Chŏn's desk. "May I ask a question?"

"Anytime; that's what mentors are for," said Chŏn with a mischievous smile.

"Well, it's one of those history questions. China bulked up after the Tiananmen Square protest in 1989, and a year later the Soviet Union collapsed without any protests. I'm trying to figure that out, and I'm wondering if it's related to Deng's reforms." He swallowed nervously.

For effect Chŏn slammed shut the thick book he'd been reading. "Yes, absolutely!"

Kang startled.

"Why don't we go somewhere?" said Chŏn, straightening his desk and rising. "This will take some explaining and we need a suitable practicum site." And he led Kang off to a teahouse.

Chŏn gestured toward the tea set before them. "As they say, seeing is believing, and I'd add that believing is doing. Why don't you give it a try?"

With trembling hands Kang set to the task. Chŏn sat back and looked on, cigarette in hand, thinking the kid had a lot to learn about tea-making in addition to everything else. He began to put together an answer to Kang's question.

When Kang was done he tried to mimic a serving lady, but in his attempt at alacrity he came out looking all thumbs. "Would you like to try it? I hope it's…"

Chŏn broke off from his tutorial planning. "It's ready?" He had a sip. "Not bad for a first try. Next time put in more leaves, and only pour two thirds full. Think of the remaining third as a space to fill with your mind as you appreciate the tea."

Grateful for the gentle critique, Kang silently repeated the fill-your-mind mantra as he sipped.

Finally Chŏn launched in. "It's a crucial question—it tackles two big issues, the fall of communism and rise of China and the success of China's reforms. Let's go over the timeline. In 1978, eighteen farmers in Anhui Province held a secret meeting. They decided to divide up the farmland in their commune, pay the quota, and keep the rest of the harvest themselves. They were risking their lives—breaking up a commune and rejecting collective farming, breaking the socialist rules, that was high treason. Now tell me, can you guess how much they harvested that first year?"

Kang had been trying to keep up with Chŏn, and the question startled him. "Well…maybe the same, or twice as much?"

Chŏn shook his head slowly, spread the fingers of one hand, and stuck out his other thumb. "No. Six times as much. In one year they harvested as much as the commune did in the previous five years."

"I can't believe it!" said Kang, mouth agape.

"So, the same land with the same people farming it, but the new way brought a seismic shift. It was quite an awakening—the commune system was unproductive and ineffective, it left commune members with a lollygagging, pass-the-buck mentality. What better proof of the feverish desire for privatization? What better proof that people are basically capitalist rather than socialist beings? So, can you imagine what happened next?"

"It influenced the reform policies?" Kang ventured.

"Correct. Instead of admonishing the farmers the Anhui government tried the new method throughout the province. The comrades loved it—they came up with a whopping harvest. The central government heard about it and Chairman Deng spread the good news nationwide. Farmers paid twenty percent of their crop to the government and kept the rest. Imagine—the PRC used to import rice from South Asia, where there's triple-cropping, and now they export. The Party communiqué proclaimed that for the first time in history the comrades didn't starve."

"You mean the Party took credit?" asked Kang, incredulous.

"You know the audacity of politicians. Khrushchev once said politicians are the same all over—they promise to build bridges even where there are no rivers. During the first decade of the new farm system the increased yields propelled the reform policies. But the Soviets stuck to collective farming and their shortfalls got worse. Collective farming is like two guys doing a three-man job—the guy in front plows and the guy behind fills in the soil, but the guy in the middle who sows the seed is missing and the other guys don't take up the slack. That was the Soviet system—you only do what you're supposed to. Their state-run grocery stores were short on bread and milk, while the Chinese stores had plenty of sausage, bread, even cookies, candies, and shampoo. So the Soviets fell and the Chinese rose. It took twentieth-century communism to remind us that even in ancient times, feudal regimes couldn't survive if people were starving. Paradox though it was, Deng made socialism flourish. He hijacked the economic system —he had the eyes to see, the ears to listen, and the brains to think—and became a hero."

"Then, Mao was the hero of the political revolution?"

"Of course. He and Deng are the two-horse carriage of modern Chinese history."

"I think I'm starting to sort it all out." Kang looked down, wrestling with the next question. "The last time, you mentioned something about *qi* fighting. Could you explain it again? I'm having a hard time with the concept."

"Ah, *qi* fighting. It's so Chinese. I noticed last time out you can hold your booze.

That's a big plus—it means you have a strong constitution. Do you see where I'm going with this?"

"Not really…."

By now Chŏn realized that the lack of a neat explanation bothered his neophyte. "Let's suppose you're negotiating to supply two or three hundred thousand tons of steel to a tractor-trailer manufacturer. Everything goes swimmingly till you meet the president of the company for drinks. He fills a beer glass with *maotai* and says, drink three of these and you get the deal. *But*, it's not just three glasses for the president, you've got his two top men to drink to in addition—meaning three glasses for each of the three men. What do you do?"

Kang sucked in his breath and stiffened.

"It's all up to you. Nine glasses of that stuff in a row could kill you. So, which do you choose, your life or the deal?"

Kang was like a deer caught in headlights.

"All right, I'll tell you. There was a guy who was actually in this situation. 'Thank you,' he said. 'It is my pleasure—I will drink it like sweet juice. We have a tradition that for every drink you receive you offer a song in return. Instead, how about if I offer you a song for every three drinks? May I?' The three men were momentarily puzzled but then they clapped in agreement. So he downed the first three doses of poison and sang a popular Chinese song. Then three more glasses and another song. At this point he said he needed to relieve himself. The men said sure, but by then they were getting demoralized. In the toilet our man put his finger down his throat and threw up the first six drinks, and back out he went. The rest was easy. And that, my young friend, is *qi* fighting. China is home to *Romance of the Three Kingdoms* and *Water Margin*. All the leading characters in those stories are *qi* fighting. It's in their blood."

"Are you by any chance…the one…who—"

"Do you have to taste bean-paste and shit to figure out which is which?"

Kang's timorous eyes dropped like lead weights.

"And there's a guy who had to eat a live snake," said Chŏn. Might as well give the kid a real scare.

"While it was still alive?" Kang shook his head.

"You don't believe me? It was Mr. Kim, the branch manager of POSCO Xian. He was *qi* fighting for a contract for two hundred thousand tons of steel. The other guy said, 'If you eat a live snake I'll sign.' And out comes their waiter with a live snake. He chops off the head, skins and debones it, and serves it up still wiggling and coiling. So our Mr. Kim chugs a glass of *baijiu*, grabs the snake, and has it for a snack."

"Oh my…" Kang shut his eyes and moaned.

"That deal earned him a big bonus—he was able to last two hours doing you-know-what."

"Two hours?"

"Yes. You know, snakes do it for forty-eight hours. The one Mr. Kim ate was a male, and Mr. Kim inherited its stamina, see?"

"Is that actually true?"

"Ha—got you worked up, didn't I. We need to spice up your sense of humor. The quicker you are with a joke, the better. That's one of the basics of business."

9. Everyone Is Precious

Awhirl with people and abuzz with voices, Yonghegong, the former Palace of Peace and Harmony, was as crowded as Beijing's international airport or Jinjiang Railway Station. The temple was so named because it used to be the palace of the crown prince before it was converted to a monastery for Tibetan Buddhists.

Chaehyŏng already had a numbing headache navigating the swarm with Yanling, and now he began to feel nauseous. "The people, the noise, the chaos—I feel light-headed." He narrowly avoided colliding with a man who had turned back to curse at someone.

"Nice move!" said Yanling, giggling. "You're so athletic. Great form, too."

As always, he was taken with the prettiness of her gaze. But his annoyance got the better of him. "I have to put up with this shit and you're complimenting me? How can you be so laid-back?"

She gently took his hand and in a mellifluous tone said, "How many years have you been here, anyway? Isn't it time you got used to the crowds? Just chant, *ren tai duo, ren tai duo* as you pass them by. It helps, believe me."

"I know," said Chaehyŏng, scanning the crowd. "But hell, it's not even the weekend—what's the occasion anyway?"

"Either they're tourists or they've come to leave a prayer, like us."

"I guess. And there's probably a story behind each prayer. But why so many prayerful people in the capital of a socialist country? I don't get it."

"Blame it on the reform policy!"

"What do you mean?"

"Before the reforms we couldn't practice religion, so we came to places like this as sightseers, not to burn incense and make a wish. But after the reforms, the prohibition died off and now everybody comes here to pray for a better life. Add all the foreign tourists, and what do you expect?"

"Not peace and quiet, that's for sure. Another history lesson for me."

"A living history lesson. And you need to look up to your esteemed teacher."

He pretended to pinch her blushing cheek. "Honorable mentor, how kind of you to condescend to teach your humble servant!"

They soon arrived at the main hall, where they fell in with the mass of people.

"Why so quiet?" he whispered as he eyed the surroundings.

She put a finger to her lips and whispered back, "Why? They're praying, silly."

And in fact all were absorbed in prayer, armed with burning incense. Unlike back home, where the faithful offered up their prayers to the image of the Buddha in the center of the hall, here they adopted different postures and turned in several directions and bowed repeatedly, sticks of incense rising from their upheld arms. Surely the Buddha would attend to their wishes—they looked so ardent with the yellow and blue smoke streaming from the big sticks. Most held three, some as many as ten.

Adding to the acrid smoke that curtained the interior were hundreds of still-burning sticks stuffed into rectangular burners. An initiate appeared with a huge tin bowl and gathered the spent sticks, which he then deposited in a rectangular metal urn. In no time the burners had filled with a new forest of sticks.

She joined the line to buy incense, leaving him feeling guilty about adding to the air pollution. Why couldn't the sticks be smaller, like the skinny Korean ones? In comparison these were monstrous. The bigger the better?

"What are you thinking?" said Yanling when she returned, three sticks in each hand.

"About the pollution."

"Why are you thinking about pollution at a temple?"

"Because…look at that smoke. How much do you figure is produced every day by firecrackers and incense?"

"You have a point. But can't you forget it? It's one of your father-in-law's businesses, you know." She winked at him.

"Oh, right," he said, tapping his forehead as if he had forgotten this crucial piece of information. "See no evil, pass on by."

She giggled. "All right, let's go." She handed him his three sticks and led the way farther into the temple grounds. They passed building after building of well-wishers burning incense, and then she stopped. Before them stood Wanfuge, the Pavilion of Elysium. He had never seen a temple so grandiose and splendid.

"Believe it or not," said Yanling deliberately, "that statue of the Maitreya Buddha you see inside is twenty-six meters tall. It doesn't look that tall, does it? That's because it's sunken eight meters into the ground. It's also famous because it's carved from the trunk of a single white sandalwood tree brought from Tibet hundreds of years ago. The tall Buddha was meant to symbolize all the happiness that would come to the people of the future. The Buddha of the future and the myriad blessings of the future—fascinating, isn't it? That's why I had to come here before we see my dad to get his blessing for our marriage." She looked at him with a searching gaze.

"I know. To guard our future—"

"Our *happy* future," she corrected him. She led him to the incense stand and lit each of their sticks. Watching the bluish smoke, she spoke as if to herself, "At the front of the hall you bow three times straight ahead, three times to the left, and three times to the right. Then you kneel and do it all over again. We pray in every direction for protection against evil spirits and misfortune, and for a bright future."

Seeing her inviolable reverence, Chaehyŏng felt for the first time the necessity of praying for all that was precious in life, regardless of one's religion. Together in front of the hall they raised high their sticks of incense. He bowed first for the sake of their love, second for a smooth wedding, and third for their blessed future.

Prayers finished, they walked side by side to the burner and planted what remained of their sticks. They gazed at each other, her eyes becoming liquid. He wondered what prayer could have moved her to tears. He felt his heart throbbing, his own eyes pooling with moisture.

"I love you, Yanling." He pulled her close.

"And I love you, Chaehyŏng," she said, clutching him.

At the Guangzhou airport Yanling was met by her father's driver, who scurried up to bow and fetch her bag. "Welcome, miss. You must be tired."

As she clambered into the back seat of the Rolls-Royce she recalled her first ride in the cumbersome vehicle. She should have felt happy for her father; the limousine should have been grounds for celebration of his ever more prosperous business. Instead she felt unsettled—it was such an eyesore. He could have exhibited his wealth and *mianzi* with a more discreet-looking vehicle. She was well aware of his rustic limitations: subtlety was not his style, and he was ribald and garish in his tastes. But, recalling the axiom that it's useless to give advice to anyone older than forty, she held her tongue. Why bother? Her father was over fifty, a man with an inferiority complex about his education and a superiority complex about his success as a businessman. Put those two characteristics together and you had obstinacy personified.

And the house—the epitome of boorishness, excessive even by the standards of countrified exhibitionists with unbridled imaginations. Who would want to host a person there? She was terrified of what Chaehyŏng would say about the exorbitant Italian marble, the ostentatiousness of the ghost building add-on. He'd once observed, with the disclaimer that he was speaking as an outsider, that China seemed to have two major problems: the corruption of officials (which was a slap in the face to the masses) and the tyranny and hedonism of entrepreneurs (which was a kick in the backside to the workers). What if he had seen the Rolls Royce and the mansion? Yanling had worried.

Her mother had once responded to these concerns: "You think your father would listen to me and stop his antics? If he wants to build a thousand ghost houses who's going to prevent him? Chairman Mao? Qin Shi Huangdi? It's his own money he's spending." So much for the possibility of an ally. Her father was the king of his realm and there was no opposing him.

Such was the father who greeted her. "Oh, my pretty daughter! Come in. I've missed you so much!"

Her mother took Yanling's hand. "You must be pooped. Aren't you hungry? We'll have dinner ready in no time." Her smile had disappeared after she'd discovered her husband had had a son by an *ernai*. Would she go through with a divorce or continue to live with a husband-turned-stranger? She couldn't decide. One thing was for sure: her designer-goods shopping blitz with Yanling couldn't compensate for the humiliation she felt—there was no audience to which she could flaunt the fancy items.

At dinner Yanling tried to read her father's face, searching for an opening in which to insert Chaehyŏng. Her father's ideal son-in-law had to be a Beida grad and occupy a key Party post in the capital, the latter obviously disqualifying Chaehyŏng. Besides, he wasn't Chinese!

"TV time," her father announced when dinner was over. "I tell you, these new shows are a real kick." So saying, he belched and moved to the sofa.

Bingo! The Korean dramas, complete with Chinese subtitles, were showing up only days after their first appearance on the networks in Korea.

She was about to join her father on the sofa when she noticed him using the long nail of his little finger as a toothpick. "Dad, will you *please* stop doing that! I told you, there are so many germs."

He responded with another burp.

"Let him be," her mother snapped. "Don't you see, he's made it *big*—he can do whatever he wants. Why waste your breath!"

"Shut up and watch, girls, now that your bellies are full."

Yanling turned away, nauseated. Now he was now picking his ear. Long fingernails denoted wealth and status. You wouldn't see them on a person doing manual labor. Who needs toothpicks and Q-tips?

Two dozen deep breaths and one drama later, Yanling sat down next to her father.

"Dad, I'm going to marry as soon I graduate."

"What?" His head jerked toward her, his eyes bulging. "You have a guy?"

"Yes."

Struggling to contain his excitement, he squared himself and fixed her with his gaze. "A Beida graduate and a Party member, right?"

She met his gaze and spoke evenly. "A Beida graduate yes, a Party member no—he's a Hanguoren."

"What? You mean to marry one of those Korean minorities?"

She glared at him. "No, he's a Korean from Korea."

"What's the damn difference?" he bellowed. "You must be crazy. No way."

"Why not?"

"You, marrying a guy from one of our subject states? There'll be shit to pay!"

"What are you saying? Hanguo never belonged to us. It's an equal country."

"You're a history major and you don't know any better than that? They *served* us, they paid us tribute for thousands years. Don't you remember *The Jewel in the*

Palace? It's all there."

"Dad, that's not quite true. We *tried* to control Korea and Vietnam. Sure, they recognized us as a big country and paid tribute with specialty products, but that was just to keep on good terms. You keep saying 'tributary,' but all that means is bullying a small country to strip away its rights. Korea and Vietnam were too strong for us to colonize. They had their own armies, they kept up relations with other countries, and they were independent. But they're small and less populated, so their big neighbors thought they could get away with harassing them. We wanted to flaunt how big and powerful we were, so we kept using the term 'tributary.' It's an admission that we've been a bully. So please stop using that word!"

"Listen to little miss know-it-all! Sure, give your stupid dad a lecture since he never got to college. I didn't send you off to school to get so mouthy. If you feel the slightest bit indebted to your poor father, you'd marry yourself off to a Beida kid on the fast track for Party membership to help me with my business. Why does it have to be a vassal? A big-nose bum would be better than that. A son-in-law from a subject state—no way!"

"I *said* it's not a subject state!"

"And you're the only one who thinks that."

"Dad, I'm *not* the only one. Dr. Qi from The First Historical Archives said that 'tributary' can no longer be used in historiography. The Ryukyu Islands, Korea under the Chosŏn kingdom, and the neighboring countries maintained close relations with Qing and paid tribute, but essentially they remained independent—they were different from modern colonies."

"Stop lecturing. That's all academics. The bottom line is, it'll be the death of me if you marry this guy."

"Same here if I *don't* marry him."

"You're mental! How in heaven could you depend on a guy from a subject state for the rest of your life?"

"Now that you ask, this 'subject state' man won't ditch me like you did Mom—how could you humiliate her like that?"

"What? How dare you—that's fucked up."

"Oh? If I were mom, I would have killed myself. So what if I marry a fast-track Party member? What comes next, a bedroom full of *ernai*? And I end up like Mom?"

"Listen, you airhead! What makes you think this jerk is any different? How do you know his heart won't change ten or twenty years from now?"

"Dad, for your information, in Hanguo the government officials don't fool around with *ernai*. If they do they're sacked! And even if you're a billionaire, you don't put your *ernai* on display. The society won't accept it—just like in the West. Do you get it?"

Yanling's mother saw the opening and charged. "*Wa!* Hanguo is a paradise! Spirits in heaven, let me be reborn there—what use is money when your husband turns bad? Go for it, daughter. You can trust a man from a country like that!"

"Shut your mouths! You girls can gang up on me but I won't budge. I have status and *mianzi* to worry about. I can't take a guy from a subject state for a son-in-law. You'll have to kill me first."

Yanling saw him shudder, could hear his teeth grinding. Status and *mianzi*! A Chinese man's last bargaining chips. "Dad, don't waste your energy. We're going ahead with it. I wanted to tell you in person because I want your blessing—I'm pregnant, do you understand that?"

"What! You got knocked up?" He jumped from the sofa, his fist shooting into the air. "Get rid of it!" he bawled. "Tomorrow!"

"Dad, how can you say that? You like watching the officials drag women off for an abortion when they're seven months pregnant? We're the number one country in the world for abortions, did you know that? Sure, you've built yourself a nice business with the help of your thugs, and all you have to do is snap your fingers and my fetus is gone. The problem is, I won't live with that. I'm different from Mom. I'll kill myself—and have a nice long suicide note with all the juicy details sent to the media beforehand. So go ahead, drag me off to get poked and scraped!"

Her father threw himself back onto the sofa. "You witch. You're not my girl, you're worse than any thug of mine. Why did I ever raise you?"

"All right, here's the deal. I'm going to finish my graduation thesis, then introduce him to you. It's only proper that you receive a big bow from your future son-in-law." And then she rose from the sofa and was gone.

Her father was left writhing like a poisoned pig. "Gods in heaven…"

"Chaehyŏng," came the voice of Chŏn Taegwang over the phone. "Remember when you took your aunties to buy handbags?"

"Hello, Uncle. Yes, I do."

"Is that guy still in business?"

"I'm sure he is."

"A hundred percent sure?"

"I haven't seen him for a while, but I'm pretty sure. He loves the life here."

"Can you hook me up with him?"

"What for?"

"I need to ask him something."

"Oh? Now your company's in the knockoff business?"

"I'm glad to see your brain still works. No, I'm quitting."

"Why? Did you get into some kind of trouble?"

"No, it's my own decision."

"You mean it's voluntary?"

"Yes, voluntary, as in honorable retirement."

"How come? It's a tough world if you're looking for a job."

"Not even thirty but so cynical. Ha ha. I'm going into business on my own, and I can use this guy's help for my maiden voyage. So look him up and let me know ASAP."

"Uncle, I repeat, the only thing he knows is making fakes."

"I know. I'm not going into the knockoff business, so relax. I'll let you go now."
Half an hour later Chaehyŏng called Chŏn back. "Uncle, he's still there."

"Good. You feeling energetic enough to arrange a meeting? Sooner is better, tomorrow if possible."

"I'm very curious—your lips are sealed, but your legs are flying."

"Kid, you sound jittery. The quicker you set up the meeting the quicker you'll find out—all right?"

"*Aigu.* Quick-quick! You're the jittery one."

"Yes, I am. I need to nail this down."

"Got it. The good news is, he's not a busy man. I'll get to work on it and give you a ring. Tomorrow if possible, right?"

"As long as it's not in the morning—I have to fly up there, remember?"

"That much I know."

"You better, at your advanced age—all of twenty-five."

"Uncle, would you believe I'm losing sleep and wasting away?"

"I'm so sorry to hear that. Join the club, my dear nephew. Your poor uncle is terrified—he feels lonely and helpless trying to scratch out a future for himself."

"So why are you taking a voluntary out?"

"Dear boy, you're about to graduate and start riding the rough seas of life. So listen to me. The high-flying bird sees more, the early bird gets the worm, and a fearless sailor will ride huge waves to get to shore."

"I get the message. See you later, or hopefully sooner."

The next morning, when Chŏn emerged into the arrival hall of the Beijing airport, Chaehyŏng was waiting for him.

"Well, this is a surprise!"

"Shouldn't be," said Chaehyŏng nonchalantly as he reached for Chŏn's bag. "Can't have you arriving in the nation's capital without some sort of fanfare."

Relinquishing his bag, Chŏn tapped his nephew's shoulder. "You're just afraid I'd get lost."

"Sure. Shanghai bumpkins can do that." With that, Chaehyŏng stepped aside and a young woman popped into sight. "Uncle, I'd like you to meet Li Yanling. Yanling, this is my uncle."

Yanling bowed to Chŏn. "*Annyŏnghaseyo,* Uncle. I'm Li Yanling."

Chŏn's eyes grew wide and he glanced at Chaehyŏng, "The surprises never end! You speak Korean well." Chaehyŏng interpreted.

"Oh, not at all," said Yanling, lapsing into Mandarin. "I wanted to impress you, so I practiced all night." Her face, free of make-up, took on a tinge of red and she smiled bashfully.

Chŏn stuck out his hand, by now a knee-jerk reaction. "Nice to meet you. I'm Chŏn Taegwang."

Shyly she took his hand.

As they waited for a taxi, Chŏn teased out their relationship in his mind. Statistics indicated that two thirds of the girls nationwide had had sex by the time they graduated from high school, and women lived with an average of two or three partners before marriage. Add to this the fact that she had come out to greet him and had practiced her Korean to get more points. They were serious, he decided.

In the taxi, Yanling sat up front, with uncle and nephew in back.

"You aren't thinking about getting married, are you?"

"Wow, you're more perceptive than you look!"

"Listen, kid, marriage can be a license for trouble, more so than changing your major."

"Are you saying that because she's Chinese?"

"Wake up! Koreans are bone-deep one race, and you know it. We've got the DNA to prove it."

"That's so old-fashioned. This is the global age, not the stone age. Our generation couldn't care less."

Chŏn rested his head against the seatback cushion and closed his eyes. "Yes, the global age. All right, do what you want."

"Uncle, you can't turn your back on me. I'm all for your business, and I hope you're all for my well-being."

"Give and take, is that it? You'd make a good hustler."

"Not really. But wouldn't it be nice if uncle and nephew helped each other?"

"Uh-uh, I'm steering clear of this one. Remember how nasty it got last time? This is over my head, you know."

"Too bad. I don't really have a choice in the matter."

Chŏn lurched forward and spun to face his nephew. "What do you mean?"

"We're expecting."

"*Aigu.* What a mess!" Chŏn sank back.

Chaehyŏng turned away with a wry grin and silently congratulated Yanling. Her subterfuge was working perfectly.

The taxi pulled up in front of a hotel. Chaehyŏng had arranged the meeting for the coffee shop there.

Yanling bowed again to Chŏn. "It's wonderful to meet you. I'll see you again."

Chŏn eyed her with mixed feelings. "Sure, we'll meet again." Not bad, he thought as she walked off.

"What does she do?" Chŏn asked as they walked through the revolving door.

"She's a student."

"Same school?"

"Yes, and the same department."

So that's why you changed your major. Chŏn managed not to blurt this out. *Well, kid, you picked the right one.* He smiled acerbically.

They settled in at a table in the back corner. They were twenty minutes early.

"Uncle, I've been worrying about you," said Chaehyŏng warily. "You even showed up in my dreams."

"I'm scared too, I'll admit it," said Chŏn with a pensive grin. "But don't worry. The market here is a deep blue sea with enough fish to last us another thirty years."

"But where's your startup funding? You've got to have money to make money."

"That's right. There's something called a niche market—it's based on a concept and not just money. Arm myself with a few niche markets and I can go to war."

"Do they actually exist?"

"I've seen a few of them."

"Really? Care to explain?"

"It's Heaven's Plan. You'll see."

"Can't even confide in your dearest nephew?"

"Nope. It's top secret, can't afford leaks. I'm going to follow your example and save the big news for the end, when it has the most impact."

"Well—here they are." Chaehyŏng sprang up to greet Namgŭn and his uncle. Chŏn shot to his feet and bowed deeply to the other man. "Nice to meet you. I'm Chŏn Taegwang, Chaehyŏng's uncle."

"I'm Yi Samsu," said the other, offering his hand.

"You wanted to see me," said Yi after they'd ordered coffee.

"Ah yes," said Chŏn, straightening. "I'm retiring from my trading company at the end of the year and going into business on my own. For my maiden voyage I am in need of your esteemed assistance, sir."

Chaehyŏng was speechless. His uncle's expression was stern, the tone weighty. But he liked what he saw—a businessman able to transform himself in an instant.

"Well, I'm just a humble guy who makes fakes," Yi said dryly as he took his cup in hand. "I'm sure Chaehyŏng filled you in. I don't see where I could be of much assistance...."

Sitting next to his uncle, Namgŭn silently pounded his chest, his lips forming an inaudible *Oh no*. Chaehyŏng attempted to calm him with a look.

Chŏn reached into his briefcase, "Sir, would you mind having a look at this?" It was the top to a set of long underwear in Chinese red. "As you can see, sir, this is everyone's favorite Chunjie gift—a hundred million pairs a year are sold. What I would like to do is customize my product by stitching the animal of the year, here, in gold thread, and take out a trademark." He illustrated by placing a small sketch over the left chest of the garment. "Sir?" And after a deep bow, "Would you please do the machine stitching?"

"I see. It's a nice idea. What do you think?" Yi asked his nephew.

"That's cool," said Namgŭn. "It'll be a hit for sure."

Chaehyŏng was thinking the exact same thing. He felt a surge of relief.

But then Yi shook his head deliberately. "I wish we had met yesterday. An urgent order just came in, and I am pressed for time...."

Chŏn leaned forward, perplexed. "Excuse me?"

The two nephews regarded Yi in astonishment. Chaehyŏng nudged Namgŭn, who took the hint. Clutching his uncle's arm, he jiggled it gently. "Uncle, I really hope you can help Chaehyŏng's uncle. He's trying to start from scratch. And don't forget, Chaehyŏng saved you several times from you-know-where. Solidarity, you know."

Why did he have to mention that? Chaehyŏng lamented.

Yi took a coin purse from the inner pocket of his jacket. "Hey kid, I'm not joking. Don't get me worked up with this solidarity stuff."

"What's that?"

"It's a coin purse, can't you see?"

"What's the rush with a coin purse?"

"Stop yapping and listen. These things are selling like fried cakes, they're gone in a second. It's a French designer brand, made specially for the market here. The idea is, you give it as a gift with a hundred *yuan* inside, and you'll get rich. It's a hot item. And look at the name, *Lihua*, pear blossom, a symbol of wealth—I'm still trying to understand how that French bastard figured this out. So, am I supposed to sit on my butt and watch the money flying by? I have an order for several thousands of these things. Quick work for sweet catch." Yi was practically drooling.

"Hey, look at this," said Namgŭn. "The *lihua*, with a red base and a gold emblem —the Chinese will love it. Uncle, can I have this?"

"Idiot, that's my *sample*, it's what I work from." Yi pretended to knuckle his nephew's head.

With his eyes Chŏn signaled Chaehyŏng for the coin purse.

"Can I see?" Chaehyŏng took the purse from Namgŭn, briefly inspected it, then handed it to Chŏn.

Chŏn scanned the item and was stunned by the branding—the name, the flower, they were just as catchy as his concept for Little Emperor baby formula. A red Cartier coin purse with a hundred *yuan* inside was a favorite gift given by Korean businessmen here. *It's ingenious. Why didn't I think of that?* But the next moment he had changed his tack. *What the hell are you thinking? Get back in the groove. You're about to take your first step—don't ruin it!* With this thought he sprang to his feet. "Sir, I'll agree to any terms, any conditions you ask. All I want is a chance to try. Please, I beg you." As three slack-jawed faces gaped at him, Chŏn sank to the carpet and bowed.

"Oh no, I can't let you do this." Yi shot up, dithered a moment, then plopped himself down beside Chŏn. "All right, you win. I'll help you. I've been working those damn machines for forty years and I've taken all the shit I'm going to. You're the first man who's ever showed me respect—that means a lot." To make his point he helped Chŏn to his feet.

10. Love Is Heaven's Doing

Chisŏn was hit with emotion as she stepped out of the empty apartment. She would not be returning. Another sad goodbye to the spaces she and her family had occupied during their time in China, to the places she had touched with her own fingers.

The wives of the trading company men liked to say they bawled twice—once when they landed in China to face the language barrier, and again when they packed for home, reminiscing about all they had grown fond of, the comforts that had spoiled them. How true it was! She swallowed her burning tears. The affluence she had enjoyed—the affordable food, the cheap labor, even an *ayi*. She had shunned prepared food, not knowing what was genuine and what imitation, in favor of fresh produce, crab from the deepest and clearest of waters, pork still dripping from the butcher's block.

She recalled the tour of the market district that Chŏn had taken her on. "Westerners are always picking on China for being uncivilized and unsanitary, and unrefrigerated pork is the example they use. There they are, lecturing from the other side of the world, yet they don't have a clue that the pig is butchered and all the meat is sold the same day. There's nothing left to refrigerate, unless they want to make some of it into braised pork belly. So don't believe everything you read."

"Braised pork belly—that was the Chairman's favorite, wasn't it?"

"That's my smart wife!"

"Let's see if you're smart enough to be my husband. How many pigs get consumed here in a day?"

"Seven hundred thousand."

"You know-it-all, I hate you. Can't you play dumb once in a while?"

"Oops. Sorry."

One of many nice memories.

The Korean wives in the complex were constantly telling her how lucky she was—her capable husband would make a killing, it was only a matter of time, and then Chisŏn's rags-to-riches saga would be complete. As much as she trusted in Chŏn's prudence, she felt snarled in anxiety. With only sketchy startup funds he was walking on thin ice. He hadn't been sleeping well since requesting his early out.

They had had to vacate two months before the retirement date, so the apartment could be cleaned and fixed up for Chŏn's successor. Two months was actually an improvement over ten years ago, when the work would have taken four-plus months—as opposed to one month back home. Everything here tended to drag on—classic *manmandi*. Their broken-down toilet had taken a blessed week to fix. The plumber's skill was suspect, and then there was his irresponsibility, his indifference, and his repertoire of excuses—a family gathering, a hospital visit to an injured friend, an entire day shopping for parts. Each day the finishing touch was "Right away, sir." The most annoying part was having to use the neighbors' toilets for a week. "I'm terribly sorry. But I'm so grateful you live next to us …"

"Don't worry, it's not a problem. We might have to ask the same favor someday." The other wives had taken her in with a welcoming smile.

And now that too was a memory. She felt like they were being evicted. How frustrating it must be when a husband reached full retirement age. Thinking these thoughts, she took the elevator down. The children were already in the car, while Chŏn was having a smoke. He opened the door for her—now there was a surprise!

"Here are the keys," she said.

"I guess I'm really retired now!" With an awkward grin he regarded the keys.

She nodded. In the back seat the children kept mum. They too sensed the anxiety and worry emanating from their dad's decision to start all over. They had been quiet ever since he made the announcement, and tinges of anxiety had appeared on their faces as the process of transferring to a school back home set into motion. A new school could be so intimidating. She wished she could spare them the pain.

Staying here, they would have needed a new place to live. But the cost of housing in Shanghai and Beijing was exorbitant, especially with their cash-in-hand earmarked for Chŏn's startup funds. Which made the offer from Chisŏn's father all the more welcome.

"Just send her and the kids back home," he had said to Chŏn over the phone. "We'll take care of them till you're launched. We have enough space, so don't worry."

As Chŏn started for the airport, he turned on the radio, hoping for some cheery music. It was so quiet Chŏn imagined for a moment he was alone in the car.

At the airport Chisŏn handed the children their passports and boarding passes and ushered them toward their father. They walked up to him, one on each side, and each took an arm. As Chŏn bent down first to his daughter, his son drew closer. They both whispered in his ear.

"Daddy, we love you! Go get 'em!"

"You bet I will!" was all he could say before he choked up.

"No skipping meals, honey. And watch your drinking!" Chisŏn felt tears pooling in her eyes.

Holding her hands, Chŏn bit down on his lip. "I know. It won't take long."

She turned away just as the tears started spilling.

Chŏn stared at the closed door through which his family had been sucked. *I'd do anything for you kids. Just be patient. Daddy's going to make out good!*

"You really are leaving!" said the admin head, morose with envy, as he eyed the apartment keys Chŏn had just handed him.

"We'll see what happens," said Chŏn with appropriate gravity.

"Well, you've been on the frontlines all this time, and now you've got a foothold in your new venture. I'm just a paper pusher, can't even dream about an early out, just stuck here till retirement age. Pity."

"I wish I had the answers," said Chŏn, turning away from the dispirited man.

At his office he turned to find Kang hard on his heels.

"Glad I caught you, sir. Can I ask you something?"

"Better adjourn to the teahouse," said Chŏn with a smirk, at the same time delighted not to be cooped up. And in the sponge-like Kang he had a tailor-made receptacle. It was if he existed solely for Kang and his ravenous curiosity.

At the teahouse, Kang was at ease brewing the tea under Chŏn's watchful eye. Waiting for the Longjing tea to infuse, Kang said, "Sir, I liked your story about *qi* fighting. So what should I do when someone gives me a hard time here, especially the officials? Back home we have the same problem, right? Do I suck it up or do I get down on my knees and beg?"

"Remember what I said last time? If it's a guy, you have to wait till you're comfortable with the language. And male or female, you have to know what you're talking about."

"Yes, I remember."

"Public officials are the same everywhere. They're not bad people, but they're a byproduct of authoritarianism and bureaucracy, which makes them lazy-ass, snooty, know-it-all, say-no bullies and power-mongers. The best-case scenario is to oil all wheels. The other option is to find the guy's Achilles heel and go man to man, *qi* fighting, 'kill him and I live.' The downside to that is you may have lost a relationship. You might be surprised, though—a breakthrough is always possible. Once you go for it, make sure you bite hard and you have a just cause. Speak up, say what you have to say as loud as you can. Your oratory will grab everybody's attention and a senior official will come running to make a fix. And there you are."

"But then my first opportunity to make a relationship is ruined—"

"That's giving up too easily—not what a pro like you does. Instead, try this: You've won the first round, so the next day you go look for the guy and when you find him, of course he's hostile, but he's not up on his high horse. So you tell him you're sorry for what happened yesterday and you buy him a drink and show him your big heart—the guy he chastised and rebuffed is going to schmooze with him, imagine that. So you buy him the most expensive dish and the best booze. It's a golden chance, so don't blow it. If you want to go whole hog, you add a designer gift—a money purse or a muffler and slip a gift certificate inside. By then the two of you are buddy-buddy. As the saying goes, a fight makes a friendship stronger."

"A man needs guts for that," said Kang, draining his cup of tea.

"Not really. Always remember the golden rule of business: Stick to your guns and don't be afraid of rejection. You just keep pounding till the steel gets soft. And always remember: the strong is no match for the skilled, the skilled is no match for the young, and the young is no match for the diehard. And we businessmen are diehards—keep that in mind."

Kang couldn't keep still. Jaw cupped in his palm, he tried to process the advice.

"But what good does all of that do if I run up against someone who's corrupt?"

"Corruption—that's where the Party is most vulnerable. The Party hates the word 'corruption' second only to the word 'democratization.' The elites here like to indulge in two what-ifs. First, what if Mao's son had survived the Korean War? Second, what if Deng were still alive? Remember what I said last time about the fall of the Soviet Union—the lazy, pass-the buck mentality? I should also have mentioned the brazen corruption among the ruling elite. The wives divvied up the treasures from the families of the czars, chartered an airplane, and went on shopping sprees in Paris and Rome while the comrades were lining up for eggs in the frigid Siberian cold. But the new China is different—there's a healthy manufacturing sector, and the people are more diligent. Still, the corruption is alarming. It's inevitable in a one-party dictatorship—you know, absolute power corrupts absolutely—but maybe if Deng were still around, it wouldn't be so bad. Hell, corruption brews even in a democracy. If I was a public servant here I'd want to flex my muscles too."

Chŏn poured Kang some more tea. "There's a delicate issue of perception here. The West is jittery about China's expanding economic power, so it focuses on the corruption and predicts public unrest, which in turn will affect the regime's prospects for survival. But remember, that's the narrow view of an outsider. After you've been here a year you'll learn the inside story, namely that the Chinese are surprisingly forgiving and trusting of the Party and the officials. You hate the tyranny and you criticize it, and yet you give the Party officials the benefit of the doubt. This is a complexity that Westerners and even Koreans don't get. Look at it this way: You happen to run into a classmate of yours, an honor student, ten years in the future and he still looks great. Well, all of these Party officials were once honor students, they got to where they are through fierce competition, and the average Wang gives them credit for that. At the same time, he feels small in the presence of their absolute power. No wonder he worships Mao like a god. He'll always remember the land reform, one of the mightiest achievements of the new China—especially if his family was among the eighty-five percent of the farmers who were tenant farmers. And who opened the gate to heaven for reform in general? The Party—and that's why he trusts it.

"Another problem lies with the government itself. Beijing hears the buzz, it's no dummy. It can look in the mirror and see the corruption. So why don't you clean up the mess, says the West. Well, in order to mobilize the colossal Party, Beijing would need absolute loyalty from every cell. So instead the government tries to ignore the corrupt mice, and that's one of the reasons an authoritarian power structure has lasted for thousands of years here. Now do you see why they're laid-back? Do you see the Great Wall crumbling around you?" And with that Chŏn helped himself to several gulps of tea.

"Do you agree with all that?"

"Not necessarily. I like to keep up with what's going on here, but I'm not sure the government made the right decision about the mice. You know Korean civil servants are compared to a steel rice bowl, because they're set for life. Well, the Chinese use the same expression for their civil servants."

Kang had a faraway look in his eyes, nodding. Running his thumb around the rim of his teacup he said, "I didn't know Mao's son died in the war. You're asking what if he'd lived? Do you think the political situation would have been different?"

"It's an intriguing question. Everyone speculates but no one talks about it publicly. Ask the intellectuals and they'll tell you 'he'—meaning Mao Anying, the son—would have been the successor. Just like in North Korea, there would have been a further succession, and no reform would have happened."

"*Aigu*, that's a scary thought. You might be right." Kang had a sip of tea. "About that word 'democratization.' I know Beijing hates it, but Westerners love it."

"It's a standard item on the Western media menu. Koreans are curious too about the prospects for democracy here. It's another case of differences in perspective. The West has two measures for judging whether a country's advanced—economic power and democracy. Under Western eyes, one-party rule is unacceptable and uncivilized; democracy needs to take root. China doesn't stomach such criticism and it never lets down its guard over its system. The way it crushed the Tiananmen Square protests in 1989 showed it won't tolerate Western intervention." Chŏn furrowed his brow.

"The problem is that the Western countries judge other countries by their own standards, and the people here don't necessarily accept those standards. The Western scenario is that the stronger a people's democratic awareness, the easier it is for them to mobilize and fight for democracy when corruption and tyranny worsen, the rich-poor divide deepens, and the poor and the migrant workers get more vocal. But it's sleep- talking, all of it. Why? To the Chinese, the present situation is heaven. A decade ago they were pedaling bicycles, now they can buy a car. So, it's hallelujah to the Party.

"The new China gives its people the freedom to own private property, to choose a job, to move to most cities, to marry whomever they want, to have hobbies, to travel, and to study abroad. Why complain? If something is wrong, just be patient and it will get better. That's what they believe. Elections? Forget it! Democracy? Far off. Sure, you hear a few peeps out of the 1.4 billion here, but they carry about as much weight as foam on a wave. The dissidents are so far ahead of everyone else they can't be effective, and the rest of the people are too far behind."

"I guess I shouldn't believe everything I read in the Western media," said Kang. "Say, do you remember that man a few years ago who said that feeding one-plus billion people on its own was the Party's biggest contribution to the world? Doesn't it sound kind of weird?"

"How so?" said Chŏn with a knowing smile as he took his cup of tea.

"I feel he was patting himself and the Party on their collective shoulder. But how did the people take it?"

"Precisely! The Party boasted it was the only political entity in Chinese history to feed the masses, and it did this even as the Eastern Bloc and the fatherly Soviet Union were collapsing. This boast captured the people's hearts. But there were two holes in the argument. Number one, material abundance was the result of the masses' capitalist labor; the Party's only accomplishment was to collect taxes. What a bluff! You think global citizens are going to buy into such arrogance? When the Party can feed *all* the hungry people in the world, *then* they can pat themselves on their shoulder. The second hole in their argument is that it sounds like the Party is doing the people a *favor* by feeding them—when actually that's the Party's *responsibility*."

"Why do the people listen to this rigmarole?"

"Goebbels, the Nazi propaganda minister, said that if you tell a lie that's big enough and you keep repeating it, people start believing it. And that's what happened here. Parents drill it into their kids from a very young age that the bird that sticks its neck out gets shot, and that you can do anything you want as long as you don't rub the Party the wrong way. They've seen with their own eyes what happens when you challenge or disobey—starting with the Great Leap Forward, the Cultural Revolution, the Tiananmen protests, and the Falun Gong roundup. And they learned that silence is golden."

"So to the people the Party is a benevolent god and a fearsome devil."

"Yes. It's a Janus."

A few moments of companionable silence passed as Kang digested this strange taste of his new environment.

"You know," he said, "I've been debating whether to ask you—"

"Just ask. I told you I'm open to anything. You don't have much time left to put up with me, and I might be hard to pin down later on, you know."

"All right, then. This might be indelicate, but—why is their sex life so messy? Did the reforms have something to do with it?"

"I wonder about that too, but I haven't found an answer. But judging from some of the sayings I've heard here, it probably has something to do with a man's tendency to regard women as his personal property." Chŏn checked his watch and rose. "Anyhow, looks like our time's up—I have an appointment."

Kang stayed behind, watching as Chŏn disappeared from sight. What dream would prompt Chŏn to want to traverse the sharp ridge of the wall of skyscrapers in this jungle of aspiration? There was something lonely about that vanishing image, but it was admirable, the man was doing it all on his own. That took a lot of nerve, a ton of courage. Would Kang be able to do that ten years from now? Would he be able to scale the skyscrapers rising above this tangle of human avarice? Kang found himself praying Chŏn would be a Tarzan in this jungle.

As Chŏn was leaving the teahouse he called Chaehyŏng. "How's work going with Namgŭn's uncle?"

"Everything's on schedule."

"Excellent!"

"So you don't need to call him. I'm checking in with him every day."

"Every day?"

"Yes."

"With your schoolwork and all? How come?"

"Well, I just feel like it."

"Hey, I don't want you feeling obligated."

"No, nothing like that. Just being there and seeing how it's done is fascinating, really. Namgǔn's uncle is a whiz. And he's doing it all for us, so I feel grateful."

"What! He's doing the stitching himself?"

"Yes. He was feeling the time crunch, so he jumped right in. And he's like a magician. You wouldn't believe it. The young ladies are quick but they can't keep up with him. You ought to see the buzz when he joins them."

"I owe him big time!"

"And guess what—Namgǔn's been showing up. He helps move stuff around, things like that. It would be nice if you say something the next time you see him."

"For sure. Many thanks."

"One more thing. Because time is so tight, his uncle brought three helpers over from Korea. I don't know how he figures to handle the paperwork, but I thought you might want to know."

"All right. I'll take care of it."

"I'm about to head there now. I've got to go."

"I'm impressed, Chaehyǒng—you've really grown up."

"Don't say that. It makes me uncomfortable ..."

"I know, saying thanks to the people you're closest to sounds awkward. But thank you anyway. You'd make a pretty damn good employee. You could join me, you know—I'd fit you right in."

"Oooh, that's laying it on thick. Seriously, Uncle, don't forget your special assignment."

"Right, you and your love life! Won't forget. I've got to go. Bye."

"All right. See you later."

A few days later Chǒn was invited to dinner by Chen Wei. "Are you available?" Her voice was amiable as ever, if anything a touch warmer.

Chǒn laughed at himself—what a lonely guy he must be to react like that. "I sure am."

"It's on me."

"But I am the man."

"How gentlemanly! Thank you, anyway. But when we meet you will know why I wish to treat you."

"All right, you win." And he was relieved when she mentioned the place— Cloud 9, a fancy hotel sky lounge. Lately he'd been feeling constrained about his spending. He who spends the least becomes the richest—he could almost feel that adage growing inside him like a tumor. What a change of thinking from his time as a nine-to-fiver.

"I understand you're starting your own business," said Chen as soon as the wine was served. "Congratulations!" she said, beaming serenely as she raised her wine glass.

"Thank you. But who told you?"

After a sip of wine, she answered Chŏn's question. "Dr. Sŏ."

"Dr. Sŏ?"

"I saw him a few days ago. He asked me to do you a big favor."

"Me?"

"Yes! He made two suggestions. Either I become your *guanxi* like Shang used to be, or I form a partnership with you like I have with Dr. Sŏ, so you can get off to a good start. He said he worries about you in bed at night. What a sweetheart he is."

It must have taken all his courage, coming from such a shy man. Chŏn felt heartened as he refilled her glass.

"I would have asked to be partners with you anyway. I've never forgotten how you helped my brother, and you proved to be dependable with Shang. But now my only son is in the US with Shang and I have nothing else to do. That's why I entered into business with the doctor. *Guanxi* or partnership, I'm fine with either—you decide."

"Thank you, madam. I have just started a small project, something that feels like a safe bet. Please give me a little time until I complete it. I feel as if the sky is opening with your offer. *Hen ganxie.*" He bowed deeply. Shanghai was one of the four pillars of political clout in the land—if he could have her as a connection, the way ahead would be paved with gold.

"Well, then, *ganbei!*"

"*Ganbei!*" The clink of their glasses produced a jovial ring.

Chŏn crossed off another day on the calendar. Three days until the end of the year. He had already cleaned out his desk, and his mind was elsewhere—his physical self was all that remained with the company.

Kang came up to him. "I would love to treat you to lunch."

"Great. As long as we don't argue about who pays." Pocketing his cell phone, Chŏn rose from his bare desk.

"I've been wondering," said Kang in the elevator, "what's the reasoning behind the Northeast Project?"

The man seemed determined to pump his mentor for every China topic possible before the two parted. Obligingly, off went Chŏn on another spiel. "They're digging their own grave. You'll notice that as the economy gets stronger here, there's a meteoric rise in talk of the 'China threat' and the 'China crisis.' But China knows how to claim power—it's all about history. China's more concerned with rewriting history through the Northeast Project than it is about the disputes over the Xisha and Spratly islands. And not just recent history—why not go for our Koguryŏ as well? Toynbee said Koguryŏ was one of the three indigenous states of Korea, Fairbank and Reischauer said it was the first, and *The Times* joked that for *China* to claim Korguryŏ would make as much sense as Germany claiming King *Arthur's Camelot*. I just wish the current leadership had an ounce of Deng's qualities. He had a good sense of perspective. He made some crucial observations. Someone asked him about income disparity he told them to look back no more than a hundred years—meaning China should be humble to the world. But his successors don't seem to get it."

The lecture continued as they walked out onto the street and into the restaurant. Goggling at Chŏn, Kang imagined an audio tape, one among hundreds, unspooling in the man's cranium. He thought carefully about what he'd ask next, in what little time he had left. "Sir, do you believe China will overtake America?" he asked as they were ordering.

"Definitely," said Chŏn with a nod.

"Any estimates as to when?"

"Read for yourself. The economists, the scholars, the IMF are saying 2016; others predict 2020. So you can average that."

"Soon, then. But it's not like the US will just stand by."

"China has some advantages, one of which, obviously, is its population."

"Population in what sense?"

The waitress brought their meals.

"In the sense that the Chinese labor force, one hundred million strong, is undercutting a US manufacturing empire that's been building up over a century. It took the global financial crisis of a few years back for the US to realize this, and they tried to lure their manufacturers back home with special tax breaks. That'll ease their unemployment rate, but it's not going to revive their manufacturing sector, is it? China's labor costs are one fifth America's, which means the US competitive edge is gone for good. What do you think Steve Jobs said when the President asked over dinner if iPhone production work could come home? No, he said, those jobs weren't coming back. A product here needs a sudden redesign? No problem, a foreman can round up thousands of workers by midnight. In America, forget it, you couldn't rouse a single worker. The US lacks that kind of flexibility."

"Understood."

"One more thing the US can't beat—" Chŏn seemed invigorated at the chance to unfurl his panoramic perspective for such a willing audience "—there's a reserve force of two or three hundred million, all of it cheap labor."

Kang cocked his head. "That I don't understand."

"Right now the farm population stands at six hundred and fifty million. But with the government continuing to mechanize farm work, almost half of those farmers will move to manufacturing jobs in the cities. Can you guess who predicted this, half a century ago?"

"Who?"

"Mao."

"What did he say?"

"He said more population means more power—it's the third of his famous sayings."

"It's amazing how perceptive he was!"

"Yes; he was a real tiger. But, there's still one way the US might win."

"What's that?"

"So many Latin Americans are risking capture or death to cross the border into the US. Why not let two hundred million of them in, give them green cards, and add them to the workforce? Hell, even if they overrun the country, it shouldn't be a bad thing. And they deserve it—most of them descended from aboriginals, you know; it's one of the big circles of history." The wry grin on Chŏn's lips made him look like the victor in a debate.

Kang chewed thoughtfully. "When China is crowned G1, what happens to us?"

"Do you remember who our export partners are?"

"Yes, roughly. China's way ahead, they get about twenty-five percent, followed by the European Union, the US, and then Japan."

"Not bad. But China's going to grow to thirty percent, maybe more. So we have an economic adjustment to make, but also a political adjustment, and the question is, do our lawmakers have the brains for that." Chŏn tutted.

"My concern," said Kang, "is if they're so belligerent now, what happen when they unseat the US? Can you believe they've got their eyes on our Iŏ Island now?"

"That's why the whole world has *their* eyes on Beijing—what's its next move going to be? Maybe the government should listen to that hundred-and-six-year-old linguist Zhou Youguang—he said China mustn't be the center of the world but rather a member of the world." Chŏn had one last spoonful of soup and took a deep breath, looking out the window. "A treat from a junior colleague can give you heartburn, but I enjoyed the meal. Till we meet again…thank you." Chŏn wiped his mouth.

"Till we meet when?" Kang was flummoxed.

"Today's my last day. And I have some things to square away."

"It is?" Kang looked down in dismay.

It was Chunjie, the Spring Festival, a fifteen-day holiday, and the airport was more crowded than ever. How could the country afford to go off production for that long? Well, back when there were no expressways, if a man working in Xinjiang in the northwest wanted to go home to Harbin in the northeast, he'd have to spend two weeks on the road, leaving him only one day with his family. But the highways had reduced that travel time by ten days. If the profit-pursuing owners were to band together and flex their muscles, more powerful now with the reforms, they could have shortened the holiday layoff, but the burgeoning sales figures during the festival appeased them.

Yanling and Chaehyŏng were navigating the throng.

"Are you coming down with *ren tai duo* fever again?" said Yanling.

"No," chuckled Chaehyŏng. "I always get excited on holidays."

"I'm glad we're not taking the train—can you imagine the exodus? And all the ticket scalpers? They're everywhere, even at the lines in front of the clinics. I'm glad they don't deal in airplane tickets—I guess we can thank airport security for that."

"It blew me away when I heard about the scalpers at the clinics."

"Waiting a couple of hours in line to get a ticket you can sell for fifty *yuan* beats collecting bottles all day in all kinds of weather for a profit of ten or twenty *yuan*."

"Doesn't surprise me now that I know about selling fetuses over the Internet here. People certainly find creative ways to make a profit. But what about the PSB—don't they go after scalpers?"

"By the time the PSB arrive, the scalpers are long gone. Do you need to spend the rest of your life here to figure that out?"

"Land of my lovely wife, thou art too much." He placed a hand to his forehead in mock dismay, drawing a giggle from Yanling.

They boarded and found their seats.

"I just read that Air China carries more traffic than Singapore or Lufthansa—amazing," said Chaehyŏng as he secured his seatbelt.

"What's so shocking about that? Did you also read about the casinos? They do more business than Las Vegas."

"My god, the country is number one in everything—trademark registrations, sales of Haier products, two hundred thousand demonstrations a year, two hundred and fifty thousand suicides. Good and bad—what a mix."

"How can you remember all those details? I guess that's what makes you a good China historian. Still, I don't know how you can you focus on your studies with all these changes taking place around you. I can see you're overwhelmed already."

The beverage cart appeared, trundled along by a smiling flight attendant. They asked for coffee.

Chaehyŏng sipped his beverage and craned his head to look out the window. "Yanling, you know the seventy million overseas Chinese—they're in a hundred and seventy different countries, right?—they're supposed to have something like forty billion dollars in assets. Do you think they'll have more influence when you're G1?"

"The *overseas* Chinese—well, that's a question of economy *and* history. It's hard to tell. Let's not think about *your* dissertation topic, and instead talk about *our* future. I bet you're bringing up these heavy-duty social issues because of my father." She patted his knee. "Don't worry about him; just be yourself. My father is wild, but he's uncomplicated and he likes having fun. Think of our visit as a treat for him." She locked her arm in his. "If I see you having difficulty, it'll get me down too."

Outside the Guangzhou airport they hailed a cab. She was loath to rely on her father's driver—what would Chaehyŏng think?

"My dad is a lucky upstart, a 'prince of the reform.' And like every other prince, he wants to show off. And that's his problem—he overdoes it. I'm always begging him not to act like a country boor. I'm scared about how you'll take him."

He caressed her soft hand. "You haven't told me this, but I sensed your family was affluent. If your father wants to show off, let him. A politician wants to flaunt his power, a businessman likes to flash his money. It's only natural. Try to understand him. Anyway, you're more important to me than your father."

She passed a hand across his chest. "Thank you, for understanding. You have a great heart." And just like that her concerns about showing him the ghost building evaporated. "We're almost there. Remember, don't be nervous. Just think about me, all right?"

She clutched his hand as they climbed out of the taxi. He nodded and gave her hand a squeeze.

But as soon as they passed through the gate he could feel himself smoldering. He had never seen such a grand and resplendent residence. It was obscene how rich her family must be! But instead of rejecting or distancing himself from her, he felt a welter of emotion. Now he understood her caveat. *Just think about me.* He tried to do just that.

"Mom, we're here!" called Yanling as she skipped inside.

"Finally! Come on in, Yanling," came her mother's voice, audibly exuberant. "Oh, look, you're even taller and more handsome than in the photo. No wonder she fell for you."

From farther within the father slowly emerged.

"*Nimen hao.*" Chaehyŏng introduced himself and bowed at a 90-degree angle.

Li Wanshing kept his hands clasped behind him. *Not bad-looking.* And yet he couldn't rid himself of the thought that an upstart kid from a subject state had designs on his daughter.

"Let's go in and sit," said Yanling's mother. beaming as she ushered them inside. "You're handsome enough to be an actor," she said to Chaehyŏng. "Please, make yourself comfortable."

But Chaehyŏng remained standing, posture erect, on the large, colorful carpet. Hands clasped before him, he announced, "First I would like to offer you a Korean-style bow. Please allow me."

"*Shenma?*" barked Li, who had plopped himself down on the sofa. "Korean style? A big low bow is the best in China too, so I'll take it." So saying, he lowered himself from the sofa onto the carpet.

Yanling quickly positioned her mother next to him.

Recalling the efficacy of Chŏn's deep bow to Namgŭn's uncle, Chaehyŏng knelt and bowed low to the floor.

"Well, your family taught you well." With a pleased expression, Li rose and returned to the sofa.

Yanling's eyes met Chaehyŏng's with a look of silent applause.

"Chaehyŏng, you have gifts for Mom and Dad," she reminded him.

"That's right!" Producing two red boxes from their luggage, he offered one to each parent.

"Open it, Mom."

"Oh my!" her mother exclaimed. "What is *this*?"

Li's face brightened. "Hey, this is amazing!"

Yanling peered eagerly at the contents, which Chaehyŏng had kept a surprise. "That's so cool!"

Each parent displayed a set of red long-underwear. To the left of the chest a tiger was embroidered in gold, and below it the two best-loved characters in all the land, 壽 for longevity and 福 for blessings.

Chaehyŏng recalled Namgŭn's uncle's suggestion. *You said they're both fifty-two? Then how about a roaring tiger for him and a gentle one for her.*

Holding the underwear close to her chest, Yanling's mother said to her husband, "Honey, I give him an A-plus. How about you?"

Feeling the underwear, Li chuckled exuberantly. "My dear, what makes you happy makes me happy."

Endnotes

The poem on p. 195 is reprinted from *Poems* by Mao Zedong [translators uniden-tified] (n.p.: Open Source Socialist Publishing, 2008), p. 25. "This work is free to use and distribute under a creative commons license, but must remain in this form in this edition." https://socialistpublishing.files.wordpress.com/2010/05/maopoems-newsetting.pdf

The Imperial Rescript reprinted on pp. 333-34 was translated by Hirakawa Tadaichi and appears courtesy of Wikipedia: https://en.wikipedia.org/wiki/Gyokuon-hōsō.

The article reprinted on pp. 361-362 was written by author Cho Chŏngnae and first published in the *Sŏul shinmun*, a Seoul daily, on May 10, 2004.

Glossary

aigo/aigu/haigo: (Korean) Exclamation of frustration, dismay, and/or surprise.

airen: (Mandarin) Term of endearment—"sweetheart."

L'Angleterre: (French) England.

Annyŏnghaseyo: (Korean) Polite greeting—"hello," "good morning/afternoon/evening," "are you well?"

arigato: (Japanese) Expression of gratitude—"thank you."

ayi: (Mandarin) Literally, "auntie"; form of address from a woman to an older woman.

Baidu: Chinese search engine.

baijiu: (Mandarin) Literally, "white alcohol"; a distilled Chinese spirit.

baka: (Japanese) Idiot.

bao, baozi: (Mandarin) Baked good of yeasty bread filled with meat and/or vegetables.

baofahu: (Mandarin) A person with "new money" who comes from an obscure or lower-class backgrounds; a parvenu.

bâtard: (French) Bastard.

boli duomai: (Mandarin) Strategy of making a small profit on numerous sales of an item in order to secure a large overall return.

bonjour: (French) Greeting; literally, "Good day."

Bu shi Riben guizi, shi Hanguoren: (Chinese) Literally, "I am not a Japanese devil, I am Korean"; "Riben guizi" is one of the pejorative images and epithets deriving from Japan's World War II occupation of China.

bunpai: (Japanese) Bribe money, payoff.

Cao Cao: Chancellor of the Eastern Han dynasty; one of the central characters of the Chinese historical novel Romance of the Three Kingdoms.

ce qui sera sera: (French) "What will be, will be."

c'est dommage: (French) "Too bad."

c'est fou: (French) "That's crazy."

chaebŏl: (Korean) A large business conglomerate, typically family-owned.

ch'emyŏn: (Korean) "Face," similar to the Chinese concept of mianzi

Les Chines: (French) The Chinese people.

Chōsenjin: (Japanese) Pejorative term for Korean person(s).

Chunjie: (Mandarin) Literally "spring festival," the Lunar New Year.

cintāmani: Wish-fulfilling jewel in Hindu and Buddhist traditions, akin to Western alchemy's philosopher's stone.

datusha: (Mandarin) "Rape"; generally used in reference to the Japanese massacre of residents of the Chinese city of Nanjing.

deng deng deng: (Mandarin) "Etc., etc., etc."

desu: (Japanese) Grammatical filler used to link subjects and predicates, often corresponding to English "to be."

Dui ya, shi shi shi: (Mandarin) Emphatic agreement—"exactly," "definitely," "yes."

duo shao: (Mandarin) "How much (is it)?"

ernai: (Mandarin) Mistress(es), esp. of powerful officials.

fantastique: (French) Fantastic.

faring hau: (Mandarin) Also known as baling hou; the generation born after the family-planning laws of the 1980s went into effect.

ganbei: (Mandarin) Expression used for a toast—"cheers."

guanxi: (Mandarin) Literally, "relationship"; used to designate a personal connection with an influential figure.

hai: (Mandarin) Adverb of addition—"more," "still," "yet."

Hallyu: (Korean) Literally, "Korean Wave"; used to describe the recent global surge in popularity of Korean culture.

hangŭl: the South Korean name for the Korean alphabet (known in North

Korea as chosŏn'gŭl/chosŏn muntcha).

Hanguo: (Mandarin) Korea.

heihaizi: (Mandarin) Children who go unregistered because of the one-child policy.

hen ganxie: (Mandarin) An expression of deep gratitude: "I'm very grateful," "thank you so much."

hinomaru: (Japanese) Literally, "circle of the sun"; refers to the Japanese flag, especially the version with red rays extending from the central red circle, used during various conflicts before World War II, often to assert Japan's imperial power.

hongbao: (Mandarin) A red envelope filled with a traditional money gift.

huaqiao: (Mandarin) Overseas Chinese nationals.

incroyable: (French) Unbelievable, incredible.

kalbi: Korean dish of barbecued beef short ribs.

kamikaze: (Japanese) Literally, "divine wind"; usually refers to a pilot or airplane during World War II assigned to make a suicidal crash attack.

kanpai: (Japanese) Casual expression used while toasting—"cheers."

koshitsu: (Japanese) A private room.

kwangye: (Korean) Connections, backing, relationship; similar to the Chinese concept of guanxi.

lao pengyou: (Mandarin) Literally, "old friend"; address of trust and affection.

lao po bing: (Cantonese) Literally, "old lady cake" or "wife cake"; a traditional flaky Cantonese pastry with a sweet filing and a five-spice powder.

laoshang: (Mandarin) A trustworthy (Korean) trader.

lihua: (Mandarin) Pear blossoms, though similar in pronunciation to lifa, "money blossoms."

mademoiselle: (French) Form of address for a young woman—"miss."

mais oui, mais-certainment: (French) Expression of agreement or confirmation—"but yes," "but of course," "certainly."

Maotai: Top-shelf, brand-name Chinese baiju.

manjū: (Japanese) A Japanese confection, usually with a soft shell of rice powder, flour, and buckwheat surrounding a red bean paste filling.

manmandi: (Mandarin) "Take it slow," "slow and easy."

mao: (Mandarin) Unit of currency throughout the greater China region (including Taiwan and Macao) worth one-tenth of a yuan; also known as a jiao or hou.

mei guanxi: (Mandarin) Phrase of dismissal—"it's okay," "it's nothing," "it doesn't matter."

merci bien: (French) Expression of gratitude—"thank you very much."

merde: (French) shit; as in English, refers vulgarly to the material and serves as an exclamation.

merveilleux: (French) Marvelous.

mianzi: (Mandarin) "Face," as in "saving face"; concept of pride and dignity as personal and social worth.

misin: (Japanese) Sewing machine.

mochiron da yo: (Japanese) Expression of confirmation—"of course."

monsieur: (French) Respectful form of address for a man; analogous to "sir."

moshi moshi: (Japanese) Greeting typically used on the phone—"hello."

ne: (Japanese) "Right?" "isn't that so?"

Nihongo: (Japanese) Japanese language.

Nihonjin: (Japanese) Japanese people.

nimen hao: (Mandarin) Polite greeting to more than one person (for greeting a single person, ni hao)—"hello," "welcome," "how are you?"

Nippondo: (Japanese) Where capitalized and Romanized: "the [military] way of Japan;" where lowercase and italicized: the traditional Japanese sword used in such a martial art.

oppa: (Korean) Form of address from a female to an older brother or an older, unrelated male.

oyabun: (Japanese) Boss, head, or chief, especially when referring to Yakuza.

pardonnez-mois: (French) Polite apology or request for attention—"pardon me."

pibimbap: (Korean) Also known as bibimbap; literally, "hash rice," a Korean dish of steamed rice covered with sautéed and seasoned vegetables, chili paste, soy sauce, and fermented soybean paste, often with meat and a fried egg on top.

punbae: (Korean) Literally, "allotment," "distribution"—bribe money; payoff.

qi: (Mandarin) Literally "breath," "air," or "life force"; an element in living things and an underlying principle in Chinese medicine and martial arts.

qiguanyan: (Mandarin) Henpecked male.

qipao: (Mandarin) Chinese dress with high collar and slit sides in the lower half.

kuai kuai: (Mandarin) Literally, "quickly"; a scrambling, hurry-hurry approach.

ren tai duo: (Mandarin) Literally "too many people"; an expression used to express exasperation and/or explain problems related to overpopulation.

renminfu: (Mandarin) Gray Chinese "Mao suits" popular after the Cultural Revolution.

ri: (Korean) Traditional unit of measurement taken from the Han dynasty li; often expressed as "ten ri"—an hour's walk.

sacrebleu: (French) An antiquated exclamation and mild expletive.

samil: (Korean) Literally, "three-one"; often refers to the March 1, 1919 independence movement, now celebrated in Korea as a holiday.

sancai: (Mandarin) Literally "three colors"; a form of pottery glazing popular during the Tang dynasty usually utilizing brown, green, and cream.

sayonara: (Japanese) An expression of farewell—"goodbye."

seguan: (Mandarin) "Horny officials"—bureaucrats with many ernai.

seppuku: (Japanese) Ritual suicide by disembowelment, usually by falling on one's nippondo or plunging it through one's stomach.

shenma: (Mandarin) question word—"what?"

shijo: (Korean) also spelled sijo; a traditional Korean lyric form with three lines, usually of fourteen to sixteen syllables each; shijo were originally sung, but now are enjoyed primarily as poetry.

shengxiao: (Mandarin) Twelve-year Chinese zodiac; each year is associated with an animal (rat, ox, tiger, rabbit, dragon, snake, horse, goat, monkey, rooster, dog, or pig) which carries perceived personality types for those born during the year.

t'aekwŏndo: Korean martial art formed in the mid-twentieth-century by fusing karate with indigenous Korean fighting forms.

Tangren: (Mandarin) Literally, "people of Tang," used by overseas Chinese to refer to themselves

Tangren jiye: (Mandarin) Literally, "avenues of the Tang people," the name overseas Chinese gave their communities.

taoguan: (Mandarin) A public official who absconds with public funds.

tennozan: (Japanese) A decisive stand. The phrase comes from the Battle of Mt. Tenno in 1582, a decisive battle for Toyotomi Hideyoshi.

totsugeki: (Japanese) Literally, "fight," or "assault"; used in Japan as a battle cry—"charge!"

très belle: (French) "Very beautiful."

tudi tai da: (Mandarin) "The land is too big"; phrase used to express exasperation and/or explain problems related to the country's unwieldy size.

voici: (French) Expression of indication—"look here."

wa: (Mandarin) Exclamation of surprise; "wow."

waiguoren: (Mandarin) Foreigners.

wei: (Mandarin) In this context, "hey," or "hello."

Weibo: colloquial name for Sina Weibo, a Chinese social media website; one of the most popular sites in the nation, it hosts microblogging for users.

wŏn: Korean currency.

Wuliangye: Top-shelf, brand-name Chinese baiju.

siansheng: (Mandarin) Extremely respectful form of address to a man—"sir."

xiao pin fu xiaoso jiang: (Mandarin) proverb meaning "people scoff at you if you're poor, but not if you're a prostitute."

yuan: general term for Chinese money; the basic unit of the official currency, renminbi.

CHIN MUSIC
P R E S S